THE
BACKWOODS
BRIDES
TRILOGY

THE *BACKWOODS BRIDES*

TRILOGY

Three Stories of Redemption and
Romance in the Old South

MARCIA GRUVER

BARBOUR
PUBLISHING

Raider's Heart ©2011 by Marcia Gruver
Bandit's Hope © 2011 by Marcia Gruver
Hunter's Prize © 2012 by Marcia Gruver

Print ISBN 978-1-63058-148-0

eBook Editions:
Adobe Digital Edition (.epub) 978-1-63058-512-9
Kindle and MobiPocket Edition (.prc) 978-1-63058-513-6

All scripture quotations are taken from the King James Version of the Bible.

This book is a work of fiction. Names, characters, places, and incidents are either products of the author's imagination or used fictitiously, except characters based on historical people. Any similarity to actual people, organizations, and/or events is purely coincidental.

Published by Barbour Books, an imprint of Barbour Publishing, Inc., P.O. Box 719, Uhrichsville, OH 44683, www.barbourbooks.com

Our mission is to publish and distribute inspirational products offering exceptional value and biblical encouragement to the masses.

 Member of the
Evangelical Christian
Publishers Association

Printed in the United States of America.

RAIDER'S HEART

DEDICATION/ACKNOWLEDGMENTS

To Lisa Ludwig, for your giving heart, helping hands, and eagle eyes. This one is yours, babe.

MY HEARTFELT THANKS TO:

My husband, Lee, who bears the weight of author deadlines on strong and willing shoulders.

My daughter Tracy Jones, a collaborator and plot consultant, in both writing and real life.

Janelle and Rodney Mowery, my experts on all matters related to seedtime and harvest.

Aaron McCarver, my copy editor at Barbour Publishing. Aaron, you make me shine!

Pembroke, North Carolina (Scuffletown), and the Lumbee Tribe of North Carolina for the fascinating story of their folk hero, Henry Berry Lowry.

Doug Hansen, president of Hansen Wheel & Wagon in Letcher, South Dakota, and Hugh Shelton of Texas Wagon Works in Gonzales, Texas, who kept the wagons rolling.

Author disclaimer: No chickens were harmed in the writing of this novel.

A bruised reed shall he not break,
and smoking flax shall he not quench,
till he send forth judgment unto victory.
MATTHEW 12:20 KJV

A bruised reed—A convinced sinner: one that is bruised with the weight of sin.

Smoking flax—One that has the least good desire, the faintest spark of grace.

Till he send forth judgment unto victory—That is, till he make righteousness completely victorious over all its enemies.

—Wesley's Notes on the Bible

PROLOGUE

Fayetteville, North Carolina, 1852

Silas McRae crashed through the moonlit cornfield and burst out the other side panting like a hounded deer. Free of the noisy stalks, he lit out at full speed then tripped and kissed the bottom of an irrigation canal. Cursing his foolhardy decision to return to Fayetteville in the first place, he lifted his mud-smeared face and took stock of the situation.

Not one soul of his band of misfits lurked across the wide expanse of newly mowed grounds, and no one hunkered along the tree line past the nearby manor. They'd cut out on him when the heat turned up. As simple as that.

A surge of warmth crept up his neck at the thought of the skirmish he'd just dodged. Every lead slug exploding from the end of a scattergun had missed him cold. Every indignant hand on the scruff of his neck had fallen away as he ran.

By thunder! He loved the thrill of the chase. The bulging knapsack of loot under his arm only topped the cake.

His roaming gaze eagerly swept the stately main house, and he closed his eyes for fear their sudden twinkle might be spotted from afar. It appeared his night of plunder wasn't done. What treasure lay behind those gilded walls? Beckoning. . .

As stealthy as a panther, Silas crept toward the siren's call. With any luck, he'd have a king's portion to lay at Odie's feet on his return. His lovely wife would be most proud.

He angled across the courtyard to the back side of the house and came to the first window. Squinting in disbelief, he watched the curtains gently sway. With a sense of destiny, he raised the sash higher and peered inside. Cocking his head, his trained ears strained for the slightest noise.

Nothing.

Smiling, he swung his lithe body over the sash and soundlessly touched the floor. When his eyes adjusted to the meager light, he gasped.

Trinkets and charms of every description lined the top of the polished dresser. On one side a solid brass bell, a fine kerosene lantern on the other. In the center, a delicate silver tray held an infant's brush and comb along with matching vessels of various shapes and sizes. Fanciful folderal, his for the taking.

He placed the lantern near the window to snatch up as he slipped out. But first. . .

Stuffing a crocheted doily into the mouth of the bell to silence the clapper, he opened his sack to add it and the silver pieces to his collection. Rubbing his hands together, he took inventory of the dusky room to see what might be next.

A glint of reflected moonlight caught his eye from across the room. He tiptoed toward it, amazed that the shimmer seemed suspended in midair. Closer inspection revealed an item displayed on a glass-topped table.

A chill shot up his spine. Had he stumbled across Aladdin's magic cave?

The curious low-slung lamp had a long spout and ornate handle—fashioned of gold, if he knew his business. Breathless, he hefted it to test the weight and smiled.

Worth a fortune!

Rustling in the corner spun Silas toward the sound. More startled by what he saw than what he heard, he crept close for a better look. Heart racing, he parted the mosquito net draped around the crib and gazed at the unforeseen windfall.

A baby sat up in bed, propped by legs so fat they creased in impossible places. A white nightdress tucked under one side of its bum made it difficult for the little mite to stay upright. Struggling to keep its balance, the child stared at him with round, questioning eyes.

Laying aside the lamp, Silas's hands inched forward, stopping when sudden creases feathered the delicate brow and the rosebud mouth puckered to cry.

Odie's words flew at him like darts from the shadowed corners. *"Promise me! Swear on your life you won't steal a babe and leave its mother with empty arms—not even for me."*

He straightened and patted the pudgy leg. "S'alright, snippet. Don't aim to hurt you none."

With practiced hands, he eased the child down on the mattress, tucking the cover into the folds of its chubby neck. The delicate threads of the blanket were so fine, they snagged on the tips of his calloused fingers. "There you are, little one," he cooed. "All snug in your bed."

The baby blinked up with wary eyes.

Silas chuckled. "Don't fret, now. Go on to sleep. Tomorrow's another day."

He carefully swept up the nearby bounty and bundled it into a spare knapsack. Satisfied, he nodded. "Your husband's a man of his word, Odell McRae. What I take from this room will leave no empty arms behind."

Crossing to the door, he cast one last glance at the sleeping baby in the cradle and nodded. "That's right, good wife. A man of his word."

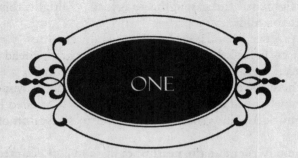

ONE

Fayetteville, North Carolina, December 1871

Dawsey gasped and ducked behind the broad trunk of a live oak, her lovely mood snuffed like a hearth doused with dishwater.

Aunt Lavinia had charged onto the columned porch and stood peering down the tree-lined street, shading her eyes with both hands. "It's no good, child," she shrilled. "I've seen you."

So much for pride in a timely escape.

Dawsey hid her bundle behind her back and searched her mind for a fitting Psalm.

"Because he hath set his love upon me, therefore will I deliver him."

Whispering a prayer for strength, she stepped out onto the path. "Morning, Aunt Livvy."

Scowling, her old aunt scurried to meet her. "Dawsey Elizabeth Wilkes! Were you hiding from me?"

No sense denying. It would be a lie. Dawsey swallowed hard and fessed up. "Forgive me, dear. Not hiding from *you*, really, more from what you're about to say."

"Then I'll have it over and done. Did you keep your appointment with the dressmaker?"

Dawsey hung her head. "Not exactly."

Aunt Livvy caught her chin and raised it. "Kindly explain."

"I reached the door this time, Auntie. Touched the knob before a basket on display in the general store caught my eye." She pulled the package from behind her, attempting a winsome smile. "Sweet potatoes.

For the Christmas meal. Once I saw them, I forgot everything else. Father adores them sugared, and you know how he loves my holiday bread."

Aunt Livvy groaned and sought the heavens. "What is this fixation with the kitchen? Winney's a perfectly capable cook, dear."

"Yes, but I—"

"Young lady, I've tried to be patient, but sweet potato bread is hardly more important than your coming-out party."

This time Dawsey groaned. Inwardly, of course. "I respect your opinion, Auntie, but in this case, I can't agree." She softened her tone. "Father seems to love my special dishes, and I'm eager to offer him every comfort."

Aunt Livvy drew a breath, her lips moving as she counted on the exhale. She made it to number five before frowning and stamping her foot. "Your stubbornness in this matter is outright indecent. Your refusal to cooperate has positioned this family soundly beyond the pale. This is Fayetteville, North Carolina, Dawsey! General Sherman burned our buildings to the ground, but not our spirits. You must conform or be blacklisted." She tilted her head. "Don't you wish to marry well?"

Dawsey took her arm and started for the house. She dared not voice the thoughts swirling in her head. The truth was, after surviving the ravages of war, few citizens of the Old South concerned themselves with coming-out parties. Marrying well seemed the last thing on their minds, especially Dawsey's. Only the elders held fast to fading traditions. Sadly, no matter how stubbornly they clung, the old ways bore the stench of death and begged a decent burial.

Sadder still, stubbornness oozed from every pore of her well-meaning aunt. Lavinia believed Dawsey's standing as the only daughter of a wealthy planter would suffer crisis should she stay her meddling hand.

Despite Aunt Livvy's zeal, more pressing matters consumed Dawsey's heart. Her father's depression had worsened, if such a thing was possible. Curiously, her aunt seemed too busy to notice her only brother losing his mind.

When they reached the front porch, Dawsey found the courage to answer. "To be honest, Auntie, marriage hasn't entered my mind. I'd be perfectly happy to stay in this house forever, cooking for Father and tending his needs. Is he in his room?"

As always, when Dawsey mentioned him, her aunt grew flustered.

She sputtered and waved behind her. "In the den, I think."

"Is he alert today?"

Aunt Livvy promptly changed the subject. "Take those silly tubers to the root cellar or they won't be edible by Christmas. Then freshen up and meet me right here." She poked Dawsey's shoulder with her finger. "Don't keep me waiting. I only hope the seamstress will work us in after you've missed two appointments in a row."

As she spoke, the gangly boy who tended the grounds ambled up the walkway behind them. Barely out of knee pants, the lad made a vague impression of grimy overalls, tattered coat, tousled red hair, and a willful cowlick.

Aunt Livvy wiggled her fingers in his direction. "Yes, you're late. Don't waste my time apologizing. Get out back and weed the roses. We'll address your habitual tardiness when it's time to settle up."

Without a word or a missed step, the poor boy—Tiller, if Dawsey remembered his name correctly—lowered his head and crossed the lawn in a sulk.

When he disappeared, Aunt Livvy spun on her heels and entered the foyer still muttering under her breath.

Dawsey followed her inside. Dawdling at the coatrack, she waited until her aunt reached the top landing then placed her bundle on the hall table and crossed to her father's den. Sweet potatoes and dressmakers could wait.

Dreading what awaited her on the other side, Dawsey held her breath and pushed open the door. She strained to see her father in the dimly lit room, but the horrid smell reached her first. A mixed odor of stale cigars, musty wool, spoiled food, and unwashed body assailed her nostrils. Suppressing a retch, she briefly wished to step outside and slam the door against the foul smell and her heartrending pain.

Father coughed, the sound a damp rattle, and concern propelled her inside.

"What's this I hear? Are you ill?"

He jerked as if he'd been dozing then lifted shaggy brows, his gaze bleary. He grunted but didn't speak.

Dawsey felt his brow. Clammy, but blessedly cool.

Smoke saturated the oppressive air, providing an excuse for her watery eyes. The real reasons for her tears—dried egg on his tattered sweater, three days' growth of whiskers, and his vacant stare—she'd never allow him to know.

She lifted the pitcher and poured a shallow bowl of water. Dipping a rag, she wiped the sleep from his eyes and a spot of drool from his bristled chin. He didn't shrink from the cold cloth.

Squatting, she sought his face. "Are you hungry? It's nearly noon."

Eyes straight ahead, he responded with a cough.

"If you keep that up, I'll have to call the doctor."

This earned her a twitch in his cheek.

Laying aside the cloth, Dawsey sat next to her father, wondering how much deeper he could sink before losing his way back, how much further he could slip before she lost him forever.

The dark paneling and deep mahogany furnishings, meant to create a rich, impressive space, thrust the dismal room into shadow. A swirling beam of sunlight, the only bright spot in the room, pierced the gloom like a beacon of hope. Dawsey gazed at it, grateful for any hope she was offered.

She closed her eyes and leaned against his chair, longing for something she'd never known. Whatever force pulled her father into darkness by degrees had been tugging him away her whole life. There were stories about the brilliant man Colonel Gerrard Wilkes had once been, and Dawsey loved to hear them. She'd caught glimpses of that man in her early years but had never known him whole.

The door behind her opened with a flourish, drawing a rush of cold air from under the sash. Her aunt hovered on the threshold as if she couldn't bear to step inside. "I might've known."

Dawsey hustled to her feet. "I was just coming."

"Don't tell lies, dear. I know you forgot." She held up the package. "About these potatoes as well."

"I'm sorry, Auntie."

Aunt Livvy glanced at her brother and a grimace twisted her face. "I'll have Levi draw him a bath. Finish up here and meet me out front by the carriage."

"Yes, ma'am."

The door closed as briskly as it had opened.

Approaching the window, Dawsey shook her head and pushed down the familiar wave of sadness. She raised the sash higher, reached for the peculiar golden lamp on the sill, and came face-to-freckled-face with the boy, Tiller, kneeling in the flowerbed. Their eyes locked briefly before Dawsey snatched the lamp inside and lowered the pane.

She knew her efforts were wasted. The next time she entered the den, the window would be open, the lamp outside on the ledge. The pointless ritual had gone on for years.

Crossing the room, she placed the gaudy bauble in its proper place on the glass-topped table, resisting the urge to rub it and summon the genie.

It would take a grander wish than a genie could grant to help her understand what was happening to her father. . .and a God-sized miracle to save him. Fortunately, Dawsey believed in God-sized miracles.

Casting a hopeful peek over her shoulder, she slipped into the hall and closed the door.

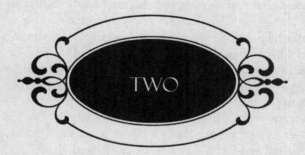

TWO

Robeson County, North Carolina, December 4, 1871

Hooper McRae watched his hero's back until the low-lying mist and dense tangle at the edge of Bear Swamp swallowed him in silence. He wouldn't see Henry Berry again until Henry Berry summoned him and only on Henry's terms.

There wasn't another man Hooper respected more, not even his own father. Silas McRae gave his utmost in the fight for justice and was a notable man in his own right, but not equal to the likes of Henry Berry Lowry.

But then, who was?

Hooper turned his horse and headed through the quagmire to rejoin his brother Duncan and their weary band. Ears attuned to every sound, he picked his way along the same route he'd come.

The men of Robeson County took their first toddling steps in three inches of mud and knew every inch of the swamp by heart. Those unfamiliar with the area soon found themselves in trouble trying to navigate the marshy lowlands.

Many lost their lives in the maze of identical cypress. The mirrored trunks, jutting from the shallow pools that stretched for miles, tricked the mind and stifled a man's sense of direction. With no distinct markers, befuddled men rode in circles for days, never arriving where they were bound.

Outliers claimed Scuffletown hovered atop the water like a straddle-legged spider, its flooded roads and waterlogged houses floating free.

To Hooper and others like him, it was home, and he couldn't wait to get there.

He came to the clearing and found his men where he'd left them. Slump-shouldered and dozing, they seemed ready to topple from their horses, his bleary-eyed brother the worst offender.

Disgusted, Hooper shook his head. "Snap to, you sorry lot! I could've been Sheriff McMillan slipping up to cart you off to jail."

Duncan yawned and pushed back his soaking wet hair. "We've been riding all night in the rain. I'd welcome a cell in Lumberton with a dry cot to stretch out on."

Hooper snorted. "They'd stretch out your neck for you is all."

The memory of Henry Berry's proud back strolling fearlessly out of sight clashed with the sight of Duncan slouched in the saddle, a hollow-eyed, bedraggled mess. A sniveling ninny with no stomach for righteous vengeance, his brother suffered in comparison with Henry.

For that matter, their sister Ellie was a braver soul than Duncan. The little spitfire had more gumption asleep than Duncan did wide awake.

As if he'd read Hooper's mind, Duncan looked up and squared his shoulders. "What did Henry say?"

Hooper glanced away. "He said to hold our ground tonight. Go home and guard the folks. He sent word to the militia to stay out of Scuffletown business or suffer the consequences."

"And after tonight?"

The exhausted band of men crowded close to hear the answer.

"Henry promised to send word."

Wyatt, second in command to Hooper, whooped as loudly as he dared with the dogs on their heels. "That means we sleep in our own beds tonight?"

Wyatt's brother Nathan grinned. "And belly up to our mama's table?"

The rough-and-tumble brothers beamed so foolishly, Hooper might've smiled, too, if he remembered how. He nodded at the other two boys instead. "Jason and Richard will bunk at your house tonight. Until we get the all clear, it's not safe for them in Moss Neck."

Wyatt raised his brows. "Suppose Henry can't hold 'em off? Will we have to leave again?"

Hooper took up his reins. "We do whatever Henry says."

Duncan made a sound in his throat. "*You* will. I'm tired of lying out in this godforsaken swamp. I'm bound for Scuffletown, and once I cross the Lumber River, that's it for me. If I make it home in one piece this time, I won't be leaving again"—he squinted at Hooper—"no matter what Henry says."

A sour taste in his mouth, Hooper spat. "Suit yourself. If I were you, I'd steer clear of turkey blinds and watch the brush for the flash of arms."

"They're not looking for us, Hooper."

Richard, the youngest of their group, pulled a folded paper, tattered and well creased, from his breast pocket. "Sure they are, Duncan. It says so right here."

The boy's cousin, Jason, groaned and shook his head. "You're still carrying that around?"

Interested, Hooper nodded at Rich. "What have you there?"

"Old news," Jason grumbled. "Not worth your time, Hoop. It's an article the *Wilmington Star* ran a year ago."

"What does it say?"

Jason's face reddened. "It's nothing. The way Rich makes over it you'd think his own name graced the headline. He's read it so often the words have all run together."

Ignoring Jason, Hooper lifted his chin. "Read it to me."

Richard grinned. "Yes, sir." Clearing his throat, he pulled the paper close to his face and read in a halting voice:

"October 15, 1870—If we were the. . .c–citizens, we should feel pretty well. . .satisfied that there is no law there and would favor Lynch law, ex–ter–extermination, tomahawking, anything else that would prove. . .effective in putting to death Henry Berry Lowry and his band of outlaws."

Wyatt tilted his head. "Didn't you hear, Duncan? They're gathering hunting parties to capture or kill us for the reward. The Conservative legislature in Robeson County offered two thousand dollars for the delivery, dead or alive, of Henry Berry, and one thousand dollars each for his men."

Nathan gave a hearty laugh. "Henry answered by offering one thousand dollars for the county commissioner's head. Ain't that a hoot?"

Duncan scowled. "If you think a nickel of that reward is pinned on our heads, you're fooling yourselves. They're after Henry's real gang, men like Steve and Tom Lowry, Boss Strong, and George Applewhite."

Jason squinted. "There ain't no truth to that, is there Hoop?"

Cutting Hooper off, Duncan raised his voice. "You may wish it to be different, but no one even knows we're helping the resistance. Half the time, Henry forgets who we are." He swiveled to Hooper. "You're lucky he didn't step out of that thicket back there and slit your throat."

Hooper whirled his horse to cut in front of Duncan. "Thunderation, man! What's your problem?"

Duncan met his charge with blazing eyes. "Hunger's my problem. Exhaustion, too. Living in swamps and doing without is my problem. Looting houses and bushwhacking men in their beds, and for what? To aid Henry and his men?" He tucked his chin and his tone softened. "Now that you mention it, my problem might be Henry Lowry himself." His anguished eyes sought Hooper. "What are we doing this for, brother?"

"How can you ask? You know why."

"Do I? All this stealing and killing ain't done the just cause a lick of good."

"You've killed no one, Duncan," Hooper said. "None of us gathered here have taken a life. We steal food and goods to distribute to Scuffletown's poor. But know this. . .if called upon to take a life in defense of my family, I wouldn't hesitate no more than Henry did."

Stillness settled over the men.

Duncan's eyes on him never flinched. "You didn't need to tell me, Hooper. There's bloodlust in your eyes."

"Is passion wrong, brother? You don't find our people worth fighting for?"

"Our people, yes. I'm not convinced they're the source of your passion. . .or your first concern."

Hooper tightened his grip on the reins, the sting of the leather a welcome distraction from his rage. "Tell me my first concern, since you know me so well."

"I fear you're using Henry's uprising as an outlet for your anger. An excuse to strike at the wind."

"What does that mean?"

"It means stealing from the Macks' fine houses helps you forget we're half-breeds scratching a living off the bank of the Lumber. It means burying your fist in a pasty-white Confederate helps you forget we'll never be counted as equals while there's a drop of Indian blood in our veins—even if our name is McRae."

Hooper lunged. His arm thrown around Duncan's neck took them both from their saddles and landed them with a splash in the musty-smelling water of Bear Swamp. As they rolled in four inches of swirling green slime, Hooper fought the urge to hold his brother's head beneath the surface until the traitor breathed his last.

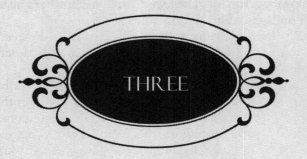

THREE

Ellie McRae perched like a wren at her papa's feet, basking in his cheery voice and warm smiles. The yarn he spun lifted her from the dirt floor of their two-room shanty and carried her to a faraway mansion whose walls bulged with treasure like a tow sack stuffed with corn.

She'd heard the story many times but never tired of listening. Each time she slapped her leg and howled at the part where he plowed through a cornfield and landed facedown in a ditch. She patted his hand and felt his pain when he claimed his carelessness robbed the family of the chance for a better life.

"Had I been in my right mind, I'd never have left that lamp behind. Blasted thing was worth a king's ransom." He held his head and moaned, and Ellie mourned with him.

"Was the magic lantern pretty, Pa?"

He stared over her head, a sparkle in his glazed eyes. "Prettiest thing I've ever seen." His head swung to Ma. "Besides you, Odie."

Mama turned from the hearth. "You've worn the shine off that tale, Silas McRae. The children all know it by heart." She sighed. "Like I've told you too many times, if you keep looking back at that golden lamp, you'll wind up going nowhere."

Pa lifted mournful eyes. "You're right, Odie, my love. No good comes of dwelling on bad fortune."

"Then why do you persist in brooding on it?"

He winked at her. "It gives me something to do, woman."

Mama came from behind and gathered Ellie's hair off her neck with cool fingers. "It's a marvel you can hold up your head, child, with the weight of these curls down your back. The good Lord didn't short you none on hair, did He?"

Never passing a chance to tease, Papa grinned, his eyes still moist from his recollections of the past. "Reckon you got befuddled and stood in the hair line more than once, Ellie?"

Mama chuckled. "I think you've hit on the answer, husband. That's why her locks can't decide on a color. Fresh out of bed in the morning, they look as brown as a coffee bean." She tugged on the horse's tail she'd fashioned. "Let the light hit just right and we have us our redhead."

Ellie craned her head to smile, and Mama leaned to kiss her forehead. She let go of Ellie's hair and lifted her coat from its wooden peg.

Cut from cypress knees and staggered in a crooked line along the front wall, there was one bumpy knob for each member of the family.

Papa's hook was the highest, though he wasn't the tallest. The boys' slots, empty far too often to suit Ellie, were about the same height, though Hooper stood a head taller than his brother.

Ellie measured close to Duncan's height, but her peg fell below the men's, right alongside her short little mama's.

Sliding her arms in the sleeves of her coat, Mama frowned. "There are chores to be done before the noon meal, Silas. Do you have plans in that direction?"

Ellie watched her fasten the row of buttons. "Where you going, Ma?"

Ma leaned to peer out of the cabin's only window, bobbing to see past the oily smears on the pane and the split logs stacked on the porch. "Nowhere yet"—she stifled a smile—"but I want to be ready when the boys ride up."

Ellie swung around. "They're coming?"

She nodded. "I feel it in my bones."

Never one to doubt her mama's bones, Ellie sprang off the floor and dashed to open the door. "*Wahoo!* From which direction?"

Recovered from his slump, Papa grinned and cocked his head. "I doubt she's privy to the details, honey." He blinked and swiveled in his chair. "Are you, Odie?"

She ignored him. "Ellie, shut the door. There's enough winter inside these walls without you inviting more."

Ellie grabbed her shotgun, reached for her coat, and stepped out on the rickety porch. The menfolk had thrown it together in a single day, stripping the bald cypress and cutting the jagged planks themselves, and it showed. She counted the creaky boards to the steps, skirted the soggy mess around the rain barrel, and perched on a stump to wait.

She loved big-hearted, childlike Mama and cheerful, blundering Pa, but after weeks alone with them in the cabin, she craved a dose of Duncan's booming laughter and Hooper's flashing eyes.

Watching the woods for any sign of her brothers, she let her mind wander to the reason they'd fled. Two weeks ago, word of the latest rampage by the Guard had ricocheted through the trees, bouncing off every cabin in Scuffletown and sending their men scrambling for the swamps.

Papa, bent on keeping their names off enemy lips, hustled the boys from the house before they'd properly dressed, with orders to hide out until the danger passed.

Ellie begged to ride with them. Knowing she had a keener eye, sharper ears, and a straighter aim than any man, Papa said she could go, but Ma's word carried in the end.

She laid her shotgun aside and watched him pick his way past the bog holes on his way to join her. Scuffletown was a muck swamp. Living within its borders meant wet socks and spattered britches, sodden cuffs, and muddy boots. Papa trudged up sporting the lot, his gaze sweeping the trees. "Ellie, my girl. . .you reckon your mama's on target?"

Ellie brushed off the stump beside her. "She seldom calls it wrong."

He sat with a groan then leaned close and lowered his voice, the spark of a smile in his eyes. "Don't let on I told you, but it's no hunch she's going by. A message came in the night from Henry's wife. Henry's sending them home today."

She spun and gripped his knees. "They're coming for sure then?"

He shot her a crooked grin and winked. "Don't be so hasty, Puddin'."

She jabbed his leg with a raised knuckle. "Stop that and answer."

He howled, part pain, part glee, and caught her hand before she delivered another blow. "If you're bent on pounding it out of me, I'd say it's only a matter of time." He rubbed his hands together. "It'll be good to see those two huddled around the table again."

By the light in his darting eyes, Ellie guessed what he was thinking. "You mean Hooper."

Pa's head swung around, his weathered forehead creased. "Duncan as well. I miss them both."

She met his shifty stare. "I know you love Duncan." Ducking her head, she thumped a loose piece of bark from the stump. "But Hooper's special."

Pa sniffed. "There's no man his equal."

Ellie cut her eyes to him. "Duncan doesn't seem to mind."

"No, and that's part of what makes him special in his own right." He slung his arm around her neck. "Remember the story of Jacob and Esau?"

"Yes, sir. From the Bible."

He shifted on the stump. "Old Isaac favored Esau for his rugged ways and his skill in bringing meat to the table." He held out his open palm as if Esau perched there. "Jacob was the quieter sort." He raised the other hand to hold Jacob. "He liked to hang about the house, so his mama liked him best."

Gripped by the story, Ellie wagged her head. "Like our boys. Brothers, but different in every way."

Papa "lowered" the biblical twins. "In our story, Hooper is my Esau and Duncan is Ma's Jacob. I suppose it's my nature to get on better with rugged men." Raising his brow, he shook his finger in her face. "It don't mean I hold less affection for Duncan. Don't you go thinking otherwise."

They sat in silence for a spell before he cleared his throat and spit off the side of his stump. "There's another likeness in our stories, Ellie. The Almighty knew His business about Jacob and Esau from the start. He saw both men's hearts, saw the greed in Esau, the potential in Jacob. Hence, the good Lord favored Jacob."

He worked his jaw as if dreading to come to the point. "If you were to weigh Hooper's heart against Duncan's"—he paused, ripping up a shallow root with the toe of his boot—"I'm not sure Hooper would come out on top."

Stunned, Ellie glared at his shaggy sideburns. "I don't know why you'd say such a thing."

He shifted his gaze to hers and lifted his hands in surrender. "Don't fault me for speaking my mind. You know how I love that boy. You just accused me of loving him too much." He drew a ragged breath. "But there's a dark side to him, Ellie."

She set her jaw. "You're wrong, Pa. Hooper pretends to be hard, but inside he's pulled taffy."

Pa widened his eyes. "You've never watched him on a raid. Or seen his hands tighten around an enemy's throat."

"Hooper believes in what we're fighting for, that's all. There's a fire inside that he struggles to harness, but he'll turn it to good. I just know it."

Papa patted her knee. "I hope you're right, honey. If not, we're bound to lose him."

A whistle trilled from the trees along the marsh to the east. An outlier would mistake it for the call of a winter bird, but Papa hauled to his feet. "They're here!"

Ellie shoved two fingers in her mouth and blew an answering blast before Papa could pucker.

Six men on horses parted the curtain of brush and struck out across the shallows.

Her heart soared to see Hooper and Duncan in the lead, but the sight of Wyatt Carter riding alongside them poured honey on the biscuit. As they approached, her brothers' drawn, sober faces afflicted with cuts and bruises dampened her pleasure. She bolted off the stump and hurried toward them. "What on earth happened?"

Papa followed her to Hooper's side and stared up at his battered son. "Did you boys meet up with an ambush?"

At his words, the men grew restless. Turning away, Wyatt fiddled with his saddlebag. Nathan quickly dismounted. Richard suffered a sudden coughing fit, and Jason wiped his nose on his sleeve.

Like Ellie, Papa was nobody's fool and noticed their silly grins. He glared around the circle of waterlogged men. "What the devil's going on here?"

Duncan snorted and jerked his thumb at Hooper. "The only ambush I met came at the end of his fist."

Pa's attention jumped to Hooper. "Is that so?"

Avoiding his searching gaze, Hooper dismounted and gathered his reins. "I showed him mercy," he growled, his eyes blazing beneath pitch-dark strands of hair. "The penalty for treason is death." His back stiff as a plank, he moved to lead his horse past them.

Papa clutched his arm. "There ain't enough enemies hiding in these woods to suit you, son?"

A bit of the swelling left Hooper's chest. His jaw clenched but he didn't speak.

"Whatever this latest squabble is over, you'll set it to the back of the hearth for now," Pa said. "I don't have time to stand between you."

He paused to watch Mama hurry down the steps. "The truth is," he continued, his tone grave, "I've an unsettling problem of my own, and I need your help."

Hooper studied his anxious face, one brow drawn to a peak. He finally nodded, his throat working with unspoken questions.

Lifting his steely gaze to Duncan, Papa scowled. "That goes for you, too."

Duncan nodded grimly and dismounted.

Ellie crowded between them. "Help with what, Pa?" She gave her brothers a worried look. "He's mentioned nothing to me."

Pa took the reins from Hooper. "It'll keep for now. Go greet your mama, boys. She missed you something fierce."

He slipped his arm around Ellie's shoulders and squeezed. "Wipe the worry off your face, Puddin'. We'll meet around the table tonight and talk it through. You'll know everything then."

He turned with a smile. "Meanwhile, let's go sample some fine rabbit stew. This poor woman has danced with the hearth all morning."

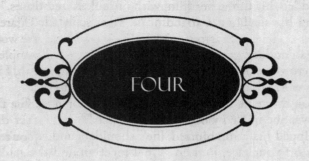

FOUR

Dawsey balanced on the dressmaker's pedestal, watching the gaunt widow pin the endless hem of her gown. The poor woman's knobby fingers moved so swiftly over the bright blue fabric, one might never know how grievously she ached when the cold weather stiffened her joints.

Yet Dawsey knew. With her skill in the healing arts, she wound up privy to the sufferings of most of Fayetteville's old and infirm.

"Stand straight, niece!" Aunt Livvy barked. "Lest we be here all day."

Mrs. Gilchrist's thin shoulders jerked, and she frowned at Aunt Livvy from the floor. "For heaven's sake, Lavinia Wilkes, I nearly rammed this needle through her legs. Hush now, or it won't be the girl's fault if this hem takes all day. You have me shaking like meal in a sifter."

Ignoring her rebuke, Aunt Livvy fingered the strap of the gown. "This is good work, Mary Gilchrist. The fabric beneath hardly shows. It's as if these delicate ribbons are holding up the dress." She ran her hand along Dawsey's side. "The full skirt and fitted bodice are very flattering on you, dear. Your waist looks as thin as a wisp." Staring at Dawsey in the faded looking glass, sadness doused Aunt Livvy's smile. "Ah, but you're so like your mother, dear. It's like gazing at Margaret through time."

The words pierced a tender spot in Dawsey's heart. She clasped her hands and beamed at her image. "Am I really?"

"It's true, dear," Mrs. Gilchrist said, pinching the straight pins from her mouth. "You bear her delicate frame, with the same lithe body and narrow hips. Except you're taller. A tiny little thing, she was."

Dawsey blinked down at the seamstress. "You fitted my mother?"

Mrs. Gilchrist lifted her chin and nodded. "Many times."

Aunt Livvy touched a strand of Dawsey's hair. "Margaret had the same tangled mane—chestnut colored like yours—and she wore it loose and flowing, same as you. You inherited her milky complexion and freckled nose, too." She looked closer. "In the same pattern, I believe."

Dawsey laughed. "Nonsense. How could that be?"

Hiding a grin, Aunt Livvy busied herself with the blue flowers on Dawsey's shoulder. "It's possible, isn't it? As for the other details, my memory is certain." She blinked away the brightness. "You're a replica of Margaret Wilkes."

Stepping off the pedestal, Dawsey stared harder at her reflection, trying desperately to see her mother. "Oh, Auntie, I wish I could remember."

Mrs. Gilchrist struggled to her feet, dusting her hands on her skirt. Hugging Dawsey from behind, she pressed her wrinkled cheek against her face. "You don't need to remember, dear. She's standing right in front of you."

The door opened and sunlight flooded the room, ushered in by Flora, Mrs. Gilchrist's daughter. She stopped short at the sight of Aunt Livvy and Dawsey then recovered from her displeasure enough to greet them with a frown. "Afternoon, ladies. Your appointment has run past the noon hour again, I see."

"Mind your manners, Flora," her mother said.

The girl carried a small bowl, balanced on a plate and covered with a dishcloth. Shoving aside scattered bolts and scraps of fabric with her elbow, she placed the food on a nearby workbench and turned with her hands on her hips. "If you won't come for dinner, then dinner must come to you." Concern flashed in her eyes. "Really, Mama, you must take better care of yourself."

Aunt Livvy patted Dawsey's shoulder. "Flora's right, of course. Let's get you out of this dress and into your own things. We've imposed enough on Mrs. Gilchrist's good nature."

Flora's manners grudgingly returned. "Forgive me, Miss Lavinia. Mama's aching joints have her down more than she lets on—especially the pain in her back. If she pushes herself, she'll wind up bound to the bed."

Alarmed, Dawsey spun and put her arm around Mrs. Gilchrist's waist. "You never mentioned your back. If that's the case, the blue cohosh I brought you won't do. You need windflower tonic and mountain laurel for sudden onset of misery. Does the pain move from one joint to another? Or travel down the body?"

Wide eyed, Mrs. Gilchrist nodded. "A little of both."

"Hot baths will work wonders then. Soak yourself once in the morning and again at night."

Flora rolled her eyes. "She could be shed of her affliction once and for all if she'd follow Grammy's advice."

"Oh?" Dawsey turned. "Please share. I'm always seeking new cures."

Flora smiled and stood a bit taller. "Of course, Dawsey. You take a dead cat to the woods. Stand near a hollow stump that still has some life in it. Twirl the cat overhead three times then toss him to the south. Walk away to the north and don't dare look back." She winked for emphasis. "Grammy swears by it."

Mrs. Gilchrist waved her off. "I'll have you know I tried that silly old cure. All I got for my trouble was a stiff shoulder and a second glance at my supper." She gathered Dawsey close. "But this dear lamb's advice brings relief every time."

She cocked her brow at Aunt Livvy. "You've a treasure stored in this one, Lavinia. I hope you realize her worth."

Beaming, Aunt Livvy crossed her arms at her chest. "I do indeed."

Cheeks aflame, Dawsey excused herself and scurried to the dressing room. Their praise embarrassed her and felt undeserved, considering the urge to help bubbled from within like a wellspring.

Before the door had closed behind them or Mrs. Gilchrist turned the sign, Dawsey knew the questions clawing at her insides were bound to come out and upset Aunt Lavinia.

They summoned the carriage, and Levi urged the mare past the rows of houses and shops, and then over the Cool Spring bridge. Rounding a curve, they made the turn toward home.

Breathless, dreading Aunt Livvy's reaction, Dawsey lost the battle with her tongue. "Tell me about the day Mother died."

The warmth and goodwill of the day swirled away like a mist, replaced by Dawsey's tight chest and Aunt Livvy's thin lips. "Again, Dawsey? The story won't change by the telling. I've grown tired of repeating myself."

"Please? It helps to hear the details, what few there are."

Aunt Livvy sighed. "Your mother was ill. Frail. She couldn't fight anymore. It's as simple as that."

Dawsey nodded. "Her heart, then?"

Her aunt paused. "In a manner of speaking. It seemed she lost the will to go on."

As always, the cruel words pierced Dawsey. She wrung her hands. "I simply can't understand what that means, Auntie. She had Father and me to live for. How could a mother, a new mother at that, lose the will to live?"

The haunted look in Aunt Livvy's eyes spoke of matters too deep, too far away for Dawsey to fathom. "I wish I could say, dear. It's an unanswered question for me as well."

"And you'd tell me if she really died. . .in childbirth?"

Aunt Livvy spun to face her. "I'll answer that question one last time, to put it to rest for good. *No*, dear. Birthing weakened Margaret, there's no doubt, but you were six months old when she passed." She gripped Dawsey's hands. "I'd never lie to you about a thing like that."

Years of frustration welled in Dawsey's chest. "Then why won't anyone talk about her death? Why do the locals in Fayetteville point and whisper, change the subject if her name comes up?"

"Calm down, dear. You're upsetting yourself."

"You're not telling me everything, and I know it. Why are there no photos on display of me as an infant and none tucked away in boxes? No baby clothes or mementos of my birth?"

She clenched her fists and pounded on her knees. "It's as if Father wants to forget I was ever born!"

Aunt Livvy turned on the seat and gripped her wrists. "Stop it, now. You'll do yourself harm."

Past caring about her welfare, Dawsey pulled away from Aunt Livvy and hid her face in her hands. "The most important question of all," she wailed, "what terrible secret about her death has driven poor Father insane?"

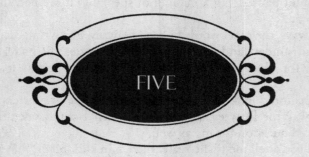

FIVE

Most meals in the McRae house passed in a blur of flying elbows and reaching fingers. The boys shared the appetites and manners of feral hogs, with Papa no better. To fill her stomach, Ellie had to stay poised and nimble, ready to grab a stray biscuit or overlooked chicken wing.

Tonight was different. No one would recognize the family seated around the table, their elbows grounded, fingers stilled.

Her brothers loaded bread on their plates and ladled rabbit stew in their bowls quietly, taking their share and passing the dishes. Ellie supposed an outlier would mistake their hushed tones and careful bites for manners instead of dread of what Papa had to say. McRae family meetings were seldom good news.

The thought of sharing a meal with Wyatt had pleased Ellie, but he and the boys were too anxious for their own hearths to accept Papa's offer of a meager bowl of stew. They'd ridden out of the yard a half hour ago, headed for home.

Though she called it to no one's attention, Mama held back from the table again, prepared to go without to see her family fed. Most nights, she'd go hungry if Ellie didn't smuggle her a few bites.

She started to clear their plates, but Pa raised a staying hand. "Leave it, Odell. Sit yourself down."

Settling into her chair, she watched him. For the first time, Ellie noticed her eyes were steady and calm. Whatever Papa was about to spring on his children, his wife already knew.

He peered at them, beginning with Mama and sweeping to look at each of them in turn. "Family. . ."

Ellie's breath caught in her throat. She clenched her fists in her lap.

"There's another place about to be set at this table and another sleeping mat spread before the hearth." He held up a hand in answer to their frowning faces. "Don't matter if we like it or not. We're about to have another mouth to feed."

Startled by the thought, Ellie's gaze shifted to Ma, and the question flew out of her mouth. "A new baby?"

Mama squirmed and blushed.

"Don't talk foolish!" Papa boomed.

He held up a folded paper. "A few days ago, this letter came from your aunt Effie in Fayetteville. It says she can't care for that boy of hers since my brother's passing." He glanced heavenward and crossed himself. "God rest him."

Ellie gaped. She had an aunt? A cousin? A now-departed uncle that Pa had never mentioned?

A thousand questions burned in her chest. She opened her mouth to ask them, but Mama motioned for him to continue.

"Effie's asked us to take in my nephew, so we will." He slammed the letter on the table with a grand flourish, as if pronouncing a sacred decree.

Duncan stood. "In a two-room cabin? Tell her no. It's hard times everywhere. Aunt Effie can care for him as good as we can."

Ellie's head swung around. Duncan knew about Aunt Effie?

Papa pointed his fork. "Hush up and sit. Effie's penniless. Besides, she claims Reddick's a handful. Gone wild as a buck and won't mind her."

Hooper put down his knife. "That's what a hickory switch is for."

Ellie's gaze swiveled to Hooper. He knew as well.

"Hard to spank a boy standing three heads taller than you," Pa said. "First she'd have to catch him."

Duncan grinned. "That never stopped you." He sobered. "Hooper's right. The boy just needs a good thrashing."

Papa shoved his plate aside. "I didn't call this meeting to ask permission. We're taking Reddick McRae into our house and that's final. I need you boys to go fetch him for me."

Duncan and Hooper shared a look, their brows arched to the rafters.

Hooper cocked his head. "You made us swear an oath never to go

33

into Fayetteville. You said—"

"I know what I said." Papa gave a curt nod. "Just like I know what I'm saying now. You'll go to Fayetteville, and this is how you'll do it—you're to ride straight there and straight back, never veering from your path. Tell no one you're coming and no one you've gone. You'll see nary a soul, save Effie and her boy, and they'll know I've sent you when they lay eyes on you. Not before." He raised a warning finger. "Enter town after nightfall. Leave before first light." Sniffing sharply, he glared. "The most important thing to remember is this—tell no one you're a McRae from Scuffletown. Let neither fact pass your lips." He leaned to squint into each of their faces. "Have I made myself clear or will you be needin' a do-over?"

Mama cleared her throat. She didn't often utter her opinion at a family meeting, so every eye looked her way. Whatever she had on her mind, it must be important.

Biting her lip, Ellie waited.

"For too many years, we've kept you children out of Fayetteville. We raised you without benefit of family ties, your own blood relations." She gave Ellie a somber look. "I spoke of them often to Hooper and Duncan when they were young in the hope that if we ever returned, the family wouldn't seem like strangers." She sighed. "Over time, I let them fade to distant memories." A faraway look darkened her eyes. "The McRaes and Presleys are good stock with kind and generous hearts." She wiped a falling tear with the corner of her apron. "Especially my own dear parents." She glanced at Papa. "I don't even know if they survived the war, and if so, how they're faring."

"Don't do this, Odie." Papa moved to rise from the table.

She waved for him to sit. "Our children deserve to know their kin, Silas."

Duncan pushed back his chair and knelt at her side, caressing her hands. "Then why, Ma? Why have you warned us away from them all these years?"

Staring into his eyes, she drew a deep breath. "Because—"

"Odell!"

She shot Papa a weighty glance. "*Because* son. . .we had to." She patted Duncan's shoulder. "Take a seat, and let me have my say. I can't tell you the whole story, but you're about to learn more than you've ever known." Papa stirred and she lifted her hand. "It's all right, Silas. It's the only way."

He shook his head, but she swallowed and continued. "I met your pa in Lumberton while I was visiting distant kin. He followed me to Fayetteville where we started our lives together among my friends and family. Before long, he moved me seven miles south to Hope Mills and built me a fine house." She smiled with her eyes. "We were so happy there."

After a long pause, Hooper lifted his head in her direction. "Go on, Ma."

She tightened her lips. "Something happened that changed everything. On a trip into Fayetteville, poor judgment landed your pa in a pitiful stink."

Ellie's eyes flew wide. Now Pa would stomp and bellow for sure.

Shoulders bowed, he sat with his chin nearly grazing the table.

Unable to trust her own eyes or ears, Ellie shook herself and forced her attention back to what Mama was saying.

"I can't tell you what the trouble was, so don't ask." She sighed, a lost look in her eyes. "But the stench of it drove us from Hope Mills in the dead of night. Papa's folks had passed on by then, and his brother had followed him to Fayetteville, but our ties with the Lumbee Indians were still strong. We fled to Scuffletown, where the Lowrys swore to hide and protect us. They've kept their word all these years, especially dear Henry."

Hooper blew out a breath. "How did Aunt Effie's letter find us?"

Papa squirmed. "I felt someone in the family should know our whereabouts, for emergency's sake. So I got word to Uncle Sol."

"Against my counsel," Mama said, her face hard. "I knew it would be a mistake, and look where it got us. Now Effie knows. Who's next?"

Papa's jaw tensed. "I suppose Sol told her on his deathbed. Otherwise, he'd never have given me up."

Mama drew her chair closer to the boys, her voice so low Ellie strained to hear. "There's a powerful man in Fayetteville, one we've grievously wronged. If you make one misstep while you're there, you'll bring his wrath down on our heads." She shuddered. "His vengeance will be fierce, and there are no more places to hide. Even the Lowry gang won't save us from our due."

Ellie copied her shudder. "Who is this terrible man?"

Papa bolted to his feet. "That's enough. This meeting is over." Back in charge, he rested both hands on the table and barked orders at Hooper and Duncan. "There's an hour left of daylight, at best, so let's make good use of it. I patched the busted wheel, but the hitch needs fixing, so get to it."

Duncan blinked. "We're taking the rig?"

"Yes, in case the lad has no horse. Pack light; he'll want to bring his belongings. Besides, you won't need much. This will be a mighty short visit." He pushed back his chair. "Find your bunks early tonight. I want you on the road by daybreak. With a rest stop or two, that puts you outside of Fayetteville just before dark."

Ellie steeled her spine. "Can I go, too?"

Papa's gaze jerked her way. "Out of the question."

Mama stood and began stacking their plates. "It's too dangerous, Ellie."

"My brothers will protect me. I'd dearly love to see Fayetteville. . . and meet my family."

On the way to the door, Papa stopped and slid his arm around her neck. "Let it be, Puddin'. There's a better chance of you leaping off the barn and winging your way to Boston."

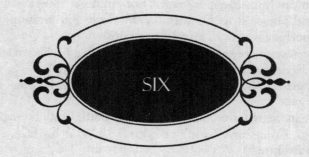

SIX

Hooper pulled the pin and dropped the hitch, scrambling to catch it before it hit the ground. If he busted the evener, there'd be a price to pay, and he didn't relish a glimpse of Papa's temper. He'd set himself at odds with enough family members for one day.

The relative in question ambled into the barn, absently rubbing his battered face. The angry black and blue reminders of their scuffle stirred Hooper's regret until Duncan's eyes flashed a threat. "You stay on your side of the barn, and I'll stay on mine," he growled. "Maybe I'll let you walk out of here in one piece."

A surging band tightened around Hooper's head and blood pulsed a war cry in his neck. "If you'll check your likeness in a mirror, you might guard your words more carefully. It would be a challenge to find a spot I haven't pummeled to mush, but I don't mind trying."

Duncan's hand fluttered to his cheek before he clenched his fist and glared. "All the gals that trail you through town would turn aside today." A head shorter, he swelled his chest and lifted his chin to smirk. "They wouldn't find you quite so tempting with that pretty brown eye swelled shut."

Hooper cocked one brow. "I'm in no mood for reckless games. Can you really afford to try me?"

A step closer brought them toe-to-toe. "I can if you can."

Familiar aching fire lit the roiling pit of Hooper's stomach. The last clutching grasp on his unwelcome temper slipped as he glimpsed the challenge in Duncan's eyes. Balling his fist, he drew back to swing.

Papa's arm shot between them and caught Hooper's taut knuckles midair. "By crick, that's enough!" With his other hand, he tugged Duncan away from Hooper's rage. "Son, in most things you show fair good sense," he said to Duncan. "Why don't you know pulling your brother's trigger is akin to kissing a rattler?"

Struggling to control himself, Hooper took a backward step. "Put it down to ignorance, Pa. The boy don't seem to learn."

Papa glared. "No need to throw fuel on the fire, Hooper. I'll handle this."

Duncan pulled free, still poised for battle and bouncing like a restless fox. "You think I can't take him? Look at his face. I split that pretty lip for him."

Pa gripped his shoulder. "You caught him off guard, that's all. Got in a lucky punch. Have the sense to know it won't happen again." He sighed. "Persist in this foolishness, Duncan, and you'll find yourself hurt."

Clutching both of their sleeves, he dragged them to a bench along the wall and shoved them down. "We're going to have this finished here and now. I'm depending on you boys to ride to Fayetteville, but you won't leave the yard until you've buried the hatchet." He jutted his chin. "And not in each other's skulls."

Hooper snorted.

Duncan crossed his arms and swiveled on the seat, turning a frosty back to Hooper. "If you send us to Fayetteville together, only one of us will make it home."

Squelching a grin, Pa cleared his throat. "I hate to hear you say that, son. We'll miss you around here."

Duncan bolted forward on the bench. "What?"

Resting his hands on his hips, Pa gazed thoughtfully toward the ceiling. "It won't be the same around the breakfast table, that's for sure. We've gotten used to seeing your face."

If Hooper laughed, he'd undo Pa's efforts to smooth Duncan's feathers. He held his breath, squirming from the urge to bust loose and pound his knee. He didn't have long to wait.

"Pa!" Duncan's howl rattled the rafters. "You slippery old coot."

Shaking with glee, Papa shoved Duncan over and squeezed between them on the seat. When the laughter died, he slid his arms around both their shoulders and gave them a shake. "I won't have you two pounding on each other, you hear? Even with the chance it might knock some sense into you, it's flat wrong." He turned to Hooper, deep sadness in his eyes. "You're brothers." He switched his gaze to Duncan. "You'll always be brothers." Pushing off the bench, he stiffened his jaw and took a warrior's stance. "If you two come to blows again, I'll ask the both of you to leave. It won't matter who throws the first punch." He swallowed, his throat working hard. "So do me a favor, don't let it happen again."

Hooper bit his bottom lip. "Yes, sir. You have my word."

Duncan nodded. "Mine, too."

"Now you're talking." He offered them both a hand up. "How about giving an old codger a peaceful night's sleep? Shake on it like men."

Feeling foolish, Hooper made the first move.

Smiling shyly, Duncan took his hand and squeezed.

Meeting his brother's eyes with effort, Hooper returned his smile.

With a shout, Papa wrapped them in his arms like a charging grizzly. "There's the sons I raised. I knew I could count on you." He pounded on their backs with strength Hooper didn't know he had.

"I'll leave you boys to your work now. It's getting late. Finish up here and go to bed. I want you well along the road before the rooster crows."

Dawsey tossed aside the smothering weight of her comforter and flipped to her back. With her head propped on her arms, she could see past the mahogany footboard to the darkening window.

How odd to spend the day lolling beneath the covers when she wasn't sick. Yet "Shuck down and climb into bed" were Aunt Livvy's strict orders.

Dawsey's sigh produced a little hitch, the aftereffects of all her crying. She crossed her ankles and frowned at the high ceiling. Embarrassing hysterics had gained her no ground in the quest for truth. She'd wound up hoarse and puffy eyed but no wiser. It seemed profoundly unjust.

Her thoughts drifted to her father. By now, they'd trundled him off to his room, too—like a lad sent to bed without his supper.

Each evening, he'd start out in his four-poster bed, lying "meek-as-you-please" with the sheets drawn up to his chin. Each morning they found him in his study, dozing in a chair or standing with his nose pressed to the glass, staring out at the golden lamp.

She sighed. Always the lamp, glinting in the first muted rays of sunlight on the windowsill, a futile offering to his personal god of suffering.

Squinting at the ceiling, Dawsey riffled through the catalog of psalms she kept in her mind.

"Thou shalt increase my greatness, and comfort me on every side."

She let the ancient words sink in.

"Let, I pray thee, thy merciful kindness be for my comfort, according to thy word unto thy servant."

She touched her chin. So God's merciful kindness, which she found in abundant measure in His Word, was sufficient for her comfort?

Before she could settle on the right scripture to apply to her pain, the door opened with a squeal of hinges. "I heard you stirring, so I brought your supper."

Dawsey sat up and plumped the pillows at her back while her aunt slid the bed tray into position.

Despite the rousing *clink* and *rattle*, Aunt Livvy managed to unburden herself of her offering without sloshing a single drop from the delicate teacup. She stood and appraised the overflowing tray with a satisfied smile. "There now. Eat all of that, and you'll feel better."

Dawsey lifted the silver dome. "If I eat all of this, we'll need a wheelbarrow to cart me out."

Beaming, Aunt Livvy pointed. "Look under the saucer. It's your favorite."

Dawsey peeked beneath the china saucer, turned upside down over a steaming bowl of soup. The rich aroma of potatoes, onions, and butter swirled out on a puff of steam. "Umm. I love Winney's potato soup."

Aunt Livvy nodded. "Her spice cake, too. There's a slice for you under the napkin."

Cutting her eyes to her aunt, Dawsey cleared her throat. "Have I slept for three weeks? It's not Christmas, is it?"

Her smile too bright, Aunt Livvy perched on the side of the bed. "What do you mean, child? I don't need a special occasion to pamper my only niece."

Dawsey watched her closely. Furrowed brows and anxious, darting eyes gave her away. The thief caught red-handed. Moving the tray aside, she picked up her aunt's trembling hand. "I won't eat a bite until you tell me what this is about."

Aunt Livvy bit her lip and lowered her head.

Dawsey leaned to see her face. "You're keeping something from me, aren't you?" She waved at the tray. "All of this is because you feel guilty."

"Oh Dawsey." Aunt Livvy wadded her hands into fists and pressed them to her eyes. "I wish I could say something to make you feel better."

"Why can't you?"

"It's a secret, dear. And not mine to tell." She squirmed, twisting her skirt into knots. "I gave your father my word a long time ago."

Dawsey swung her legs over the side of the bed and gripped her aunt's trembling shoulders. "You must tell me, Auntie. So I'll know what to do for him."

Shifting her weight, Aunt Livvy turned her face to the wall and moaned. "I can't go back on my word. Please don't ask me."

Dawsey stared in disbelief. "Pain and grief are eating into Father's soul—destroying him—and you won't let me do one thing to help?"

Aunt Livvy lifted tortured eyes. "That's what you think? That heartache is killing him?" Dazed, she shook her head. "No dear. Neither pain nor grief has taken your father away from us." She paused, her eyes heavy with sadness. "It's hatred he battles, Dawsey. Pure, raw hatred has festered inside my brother for the last nineteen years of his life."

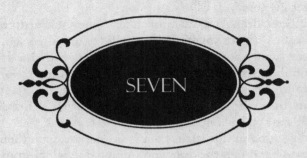

SEVEN

Ellie shivered on the porch in the gray dawn, watching Old Abe Lincoln, Pa's gelding, pull the buckboard up the lane. Her brothers didn't glance back or spare a wave, but why should they? They didn't know she hunkered there, pining to ride along.

"Where's your shawl, baby?"

The cool hand on Ellie's back startled her more than the sudden voice in her ear. She clutched her fists to her chest to settle her leaping heart. "You scared me silly, Mama."

"Guilty conscience?"

She snorted. "A body would need to live a little to have one of those. You and Papa don't give me the chance to be guilty of much."

Mama's chuckle hurled a white puff of mist in the air. "Be grateful. A sore conscience is hard to bear."

Ellie bent to read her face in the meager light. "Why do you carry the load for something Papa did? Your hands are clean."

She stepped forward and gripped the rail. "I allowed what he did to stand. Insisted on it, after a little time had passed."

"How could you have changed it?"

"I should've pressed him to go back to Fayetteville and turn himself in, made him do whatever it took to make it right."

Her head lowered so far, Ellie strained to hear.

"But I couldn't. Right or wrong, some things can't be undone."

The pain in her voice pierced Ellie's heart. "Was it so awful, Mama?

What he—what the two of you did?"

In a rush of emotion, Ma spun and gathered her close. "I wish I could tell you no, but I won't lie. What we done was plain awful."

Eager to comfort, Ellie slung her arms around her. "Hush now. Don't think about it if it makes you sad. It's a shame to be in such a state with the day not yet started."

Mama lifted her head and gazed over Ellie's shoulder. "It has started, I'm afraid. The sun's already over the horizon. In fact it's—"

She stiffened and pushed Ellie behind her just as Papa stepped onto the porch, his Winchester in the crook of his arm. "What do you want, mister?"

Scolding herself for letting the strange man catch them off guard, Ellie reached through the door and lifted her shotgun from the rack.

The uninvited visitor straightened in his saddle and cautiously lifted his hat. "Morning folks. There's no call for all that firepower. I come in peace."

Papa edged closer. "Slipping up so quietlike could get a man shot. Matter of fact, my trigger finger's twitching pretty bad." He jutted his chin. "What are you doing on our property?"

The dapper stranger smiled, slow and toothy.

Ellie stole a glance at his hands. "Might've known," she whispered to herself. "Never trust a man with back-bending thumbs."

"I have a message"—he leaned forward and lowered his voice, as if he and Pa shared a secret—"from Henry."

Pa never flinched. "Don't know any Henry. You got the wrong house."

Her pa was no fool. Henry always signaled first and never sent a grown man to their door. A messenger from Henry would be a woman carrying a tin cup, asking to borrow coffee beans. Or an Indian girl with a basket of corn on her head. Not a preening dandy reeking of foul play.

The man looked left then right, a smirk on his face. "The wrong house, huh?" He pushed back his hat with his thumb. "Well, I might consider that suggestion if there were rows of houses to choose from." His mocking smile widened. "But there aren't that many around, are there?"

Pa held his gun steady and didn't answer.

"So you claim you don't know Henry Lowry?" The dandy snickered. "You insult my intelligence, Mr. McRae." He craned his neck to peer through the door.

Papa took aim.

"Whoa there." He held up his hands. "I mean you no trouble. Just need a word with your boy, Hooper." He cleared his throat. "Unless you deny him, too."

Ellie's skin crawled and her mouth filled with sand.

Mama trembled beside her.

The Confederates had paid no attention to her brothers—seemed ignorant of their part in the resistance—until now.

The intruder didn't know Silas McRae well enough to hear the tension in his voice. Ellie heard, despite Pa's unruffled manner. He chuckled. "Best friends with Henry Lowry and acquainted with Hooper McRae, too? You get around some, don't you, mister? Considering those two don't wade the same ponds."

A hearty laugh exploded from the man. Wiping his eyes with his crooked thumb and forefinger, he gave Pa an amused grin. "Mr. McRae, I like you. Tell you what, let's get properly introduced." His saddle groaned as he leaned and stuck out his hand. "The name's—"

Pa advanced two more steps, cutting him off. "Not interested. I'll ask you to move on now. Give my regards to Sheriff McMillan."

The corner of his mouth twitched. "McMillan? The sheriff has no part in this."

"Mister, when you lie down with devils, you get up smelling of brimstone."

"Beg your pardon?"

"Won't do no good to beg. You'll get no pardon from me."

The mocking smile returned. "I'm offended, sir."

"You're offended?" Papa tilted his head. "You've got me standing on a drafty porch without my flannel drawers, and I think the wife's biscuits are burning. My daughter's teeth are clattering, but she won't lay down that shotgun and fetch her wrap until you head that filly's nose off my land."

Gathering his reins, the rascal sniffed. "In that case, I reckon I'll be on my way. It's plain I'm not wanted here."

Papa nodded. "You wore the welcome off your visit with the first lie you told. Now git."

Laughing, he tipped his hat, wheeled his horse, and trotted away.

Staring after him, Mama pushed down the barrel of Ellie's gun. "Cocky devil."

Dancing with impatience, Ellie waited until the stranger gained some distance then fumbled for her coat on the hook inside the door.

Mama frowned. "Where are you going, girl?"

"I have to warn the boys."

Papa clutched her arm. "Let them get to Fayetteville. They'll be safe there."

"That stranger may go after them," Ellie said, her voice shaking.

"If he knew where they were, he wouldn't have wasted time coming here."

Worry lined Mama's face. "Unless he came to throw us off while his men set up an ambush."

Papa flinched and his eyes widened. "You're out-thinking me this morning, wife. These woods could be crawling with snakes just like him."

"That's it." Ellie leaped off the porch. "I'm going to find my brothers."

Pa shouted her name.

Blowing an impatient breath, she turned. "Let me go. Time's wasting."

"Not so fast," he said, rubbing his chin. "The way I see it, we have two problems. We've got to make sure the boys are all right, and we need to get word to Henry."

Worrying his bottom lip with his teeth, he met her eyes. "I'm afraid you'll have to do both, Ellie. You're the only one who can slip through unnoticed."

She moved again, but he held up his hand to stay her. "Hear me out, girl. First, scout the situation with Hooper and Duncan. If they're in trouble, you'll know what to do. Once you're certain they're safe, slip away without them knowing you were there. If they suspect something's wrong, they'll turn back and ride into danger."

She nodded.

"Be careful," Mama called, wringing her hands.

Papa reached to comfort her, his burning gaze still on Ellie. "If all is well with the boys, hustle out to Henry's place and tell him what happened here today. Maybe he can shed light on what we're dealing with." He cast an angry scowl up the lane. "And who."

He barely finished talking before Ellie spun and bolted for the barn. She rode so hard her formerly chattering teeth rattled. She'd ridden Toby so often through the marshy woods, the young gelding seemed to know the way by heart. Rounding hawthorn brush and leaping quicksand bogs with hardly a nudge from the reins, he made quick work of catching up to the wagon carrying her brothers.

Ellie winced at how easy it was to find them. Old Abe Lincoln's unmistakable *clop*, along with the *creak* and *rattle* of the wagon, echoed so loudly through the trees the boys might as well have been shouting and pounding drums.

Eyes alert to any movement, ears attuned to every sound, she rode a few yards ahead and slipped off her horse. Ducking between thick poplar trunks and woody vines, she belly-crawled the last few feet, in time to watch the rig rattle past.

Hooper held the reins, eyes fixed on the road ahead. Duncan sang a quiet ditty, one foot propped on the front rail, the other keeping time with his song. He leaned to speak to Hooper, his words lost in all the noise, but Hooper's laughter boomed, rousing a nearby covey of quail.

She longed to leap from cover and chase them down, slap her hand over his mouth to quiet him. Remembering Pa's stern warning, she held her ground. She followed in the brush for close to a mile, watching the foggy tree line for movement and scanning the road for turkey blinds. A hastily constructed blind could mean an ambush at best. At worst, a stealthy shot between the eyes.

Knowing she'd taken far too long from her other task, Ellie hunkered in the bushes and watched the buckboard shrink to a wobbly speck in the distance. Papa said if all was well, she should hustle to Henry's house. Thankfully, all seemed well.

She found her horse where she'd left him and swung into the saddle. Leaning to pat his neck, she whispered in his ear. "If you get me to the Lowrys' as fast as you got me here, I'll steal you a nice juicy apple."

Toby must've understood. He wound his way along much the same track he'd come, only this time tighter and faster. Ellie reined him away from the trail home with its promise of pilfered apples and urged him into the dank, murky mists of Bear Swamp.

Long past the point where most folks dared to go, the track grew so muddy and dense, Toby's clumsy gait slowed her down. She tied him to an island of Doghobble shrub and continued toward Henry and Rhoda's cabin on foot.

She couldn't remember a single instance when she'd made it to the front door unchallenged. This time was no different. The soft *crunch* of leaves said she had company.

The dim figure of a man appeared in the corner of her right eye, and she froze midstep. Heart pounding, she waited. By the time he reached her, gun drawn, three others had sidled up behind him.

"She's all right," a soft voice called from the shadows. "Take that gun out of her face."

Warmth washed over Ellie at the sight of Boss Strongambling toward her. Boss, Rhoda Lowry's younger brother and Henry's second-in-command sported lighter skin and shorter hair than most Scuffletown men, not counting Duncan. In the sunlight, his dark waves had an auburn cast like the hair of his sideburns and the soft curling tuffs around his lip. Sweet faced and quiet, Boss could turn mean at the nod of Henry's head.

She released her breath. "Hello there."

"Ellie McRae." He flashed a gentle smile and hugged her neck. "How are things up your way?"

"Not good. I need to see Henry."

His brows crowded together. "Trouble?"

She nodded.

"Henry's up at the cabin. Follow me." Barely out of his teens, but a better man than most, he pushed past his men and led her through the twisted brush to Henry's weathered shanty.

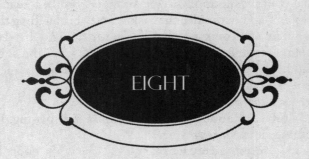

EIGHT

Dawsey's heart leaped in her chest.

The boy, Tiller, stood beneath the window of Father's den with the gold lantern in his hands. Staring with rounded eyes, he held it above his head, turning it this way and that to catch the light.

She jabbed his shoulder. "Put it back!"

Tiller jumped as if she'd popped him with a dishrag. The lantern flew into the air, but he caught it before it hit the ground, juggling a bit to regain control. Scrambling to the ledge, he replaced the lamp, working with shaking fingers to restore its balance.

"Just what do you think you're doing?"

He turned, his bottom lip protruding and his arms harmlessly crossed. "I didn't hurt it none. Wanted to see it up close, is all."

Breathing hard, she pushed past to stand between him and the window. "Did you have a good look? Because it will be your last." She pointed over his shoulder. "You may take your leave. And don't bother coming back."

Fury darkened his face. "Suits me fine, since I planned on quitting today anyway." He shoved out his hand. "You owe me three dollars."

"Three whole dollars? For what?"

He hitched up his pants and scowled. "A sore back and a passel of blisters."

Dawsey gave him a sideways look. "My aunt's not here at the moment. Come around later, and she'll decide your wages for you then."

His bottom jaw jutted to the side. "Uh-uh." Stubbornly shaking his head, his hand shot out farther. "I need it now."

She jammed her fists on her hips. "Why do you need it so soon?"

"To buy food for me and Ma. We ain't got nothing to eat."

Dawsey twisted her mouth and squinted. "Are you telling the truth?" He squinted right back and nodded.

"And your father?"

"Dead."

She winced.

"Last May," he said. "Consumption."

"I'm awfully sorry." She sighed, sympathy and regret tugging at her heart. "All right, meet me out front in five minutes."

She turned on her heel and started for the back door. Thinking better of her trusting nature, she stalked back and snatched the lamp. Trying to look as fierce as possible, she leaned close to his face. "If anything ever happens to this lantern, I'll know you're the culprit. You understand that, don't you?"

He smirked and ducked his head.

Dawsey gripped the front of his collar and forced his chin up. "I'll find you, wherever you are. I'll sic the dogs on you. Am I clear?"

The cocky swagger disappeared. He swallowed hard and nodded. "What use would I have for the dusty old thing?"

"Don't bother trying to figure it out." She thumped his ear. "Just keep your hands off."

He clutched his reddening ear and howled. Pulling away from her, he rounded the house, still mumbling under his breath.

Fishing the jangling key ring from her bodice, she made her way to the back door. On the stoop, she slipped the key into the lock and entered the hall. Smiling in anticipation, she hurried into the brightly lit kitchen. Winney's stove smelled of bread and cast a warm glow over the cheeriest room in the house.

Dawsey fought the urge to roll up her sleeves and bake something. No matter the dish, elbow-deep in mixing, stirring, or kneading were the only times she felt at peace.

Winney grinned over her shoulder. "Saw them pretty sweet potatoes in the larder. I told Levi we ain't to touch 'em. They must be for Christmas dinner." She turned, smiling. "What you aiming on making, missy? Sure do hope it's your special bread."

Returning her smile, Dawsey winked. "How'd you guess?"

Winney cackled, her dark cheeks round with glee. "It's the colonel's favorite, that's how."

Dawsey lifted the towel draped over a row of bread pans and poked her finger into one. The soft dough sank in, leaving a small dent in the loaf. "Speaking of bread, we can't possibly eat this much. Why do you make so many?"

Winney clutched the front of her apron. "My old mama taught me to bake, Miss Dawsey. She cooked for her masta's family all her life. Six boys amongst his brood, and they was always hungry." She hung her head. "I tried cuttin' the recipe in half, but that don't always turn out right."

Dawsey motioned at the loaves. "So where does all of this wind up?"

Winney brightened. "Oh, I puts it to real good use. I bake some hot and fresh for supper then slice a loaf for breakfast next day. I toast extra and keep a mess for crumbs to coat my fried chicken." She touched her bottom lip. "Oh, and I shred a loaf for baking." She grinned. "Where you reckon all that bread pudding you like comes from?"

Dawsey crossed to pat her shoulder. "I'd call that thrifty thinking." She motioned at the pans. "But that still won't make use of all this."

"Well. . ." Winney ducked her head again. "The rest I wrap up and send off to Widow Douglas." She blinked. "And Widow Gilchrist."

Stunned, Dawsey studied her glowing face. "You do that, Winney?"

Winney squirmed, one of her plain leather shoes turning inward. "Yes'm, I do. I sure hope you don't mind."

"Mind?" Dawsey leaned to hug her. "On the contrary. It's a lovely gesture."

Levi opened the door into the front hall. "Miss Dawsey, there's a boy dancing a jig on the porch. Never saw the like for fidgeting. He say he's waiting for money."

"Oh my goodness, Winney. Your kitchen has cast a spell and robbed me of my senses." She lifted her chin at Levi. "Tell him I'll be along shortly."

Levi held the door, and she scurried through.

Dashing to Father's den, she stopped outside and knocked. No answer came, as she expected. He never answered.

She entered, surprised to find no sign of him, and hustled to his desk. Reaching inside the shadowy hutch, she opened the bottom drawer where Aunt Livvy kept the household funds. If the cashbox was locked, Tiller would have to wait until morning. Dawsey didn't have a key.

Lifting out the small silver box, she tried the lid. It stuck a bit at first then popped open. Lucky for Tiller.

Dawsey counted out three dollars' worth of coins and dropped them into her pocket. She reached to close the lid when a curiosity caught her eye and stopped her cold. Bending closer, she peered inside the box.

The tip of a yellowed slip of paper peeked out from what appeared to be a false bottom. She pinched and tugged, pulling out the wrinkled square.

Two ragged edges and two straight meant that someone had torn the snippet from the top corner of a writing tablet. In the center, smudged but legible, a single word was written.

On closer inspection, she realized the writer hadn't merely scrawled the word but dug it into the paper with great force, as if spelling it out in a fit of passion.

In a rage perhaps?

She turned it over and stared at the inked word, bled through, upside down and backward.

McRae.

Was it a name?

She jumped and clutched the paper to her chest as the door squealed open behind her. "Levi! Please knock next time."

"Sorry missy. Didn't mean to spook you." He hooked his thumb behind him. "Only that boy outside's in a frightful hurry about somethin' and he's gettin' mighty antsy."

Her heart still pounding, Dawsey's charitable mood slipped. "Well, he can be patient if he wants his money."

Levi frowned. "He don't seem to have much patience. No manners either, and that's a fact."

The sympathy she'd felt for Tiller returned in a rush. "I suppose he's afraid I won't pay, and he needs his wages awfully bad. Go tell him I'll be right along."

Levi turned to go, but Dawsey lifted her finger. "Have Winney wrap a few loaves of bread to send with him, along with a jar of blackberry jam. Tell her to add the boy's mother to her list. She's the Widow—"

She lifted her brows. "Goodness, I don't know his family name."

Levi nodded vigorously, looking pleased to be of service. "Well, I do. It's McRae."

Dawsey's fingers closed around the slip of paper in her hand. "What did you say?"

"I said McRae." Still grinning, he backed out of the door. "His name be Tiller McRae."

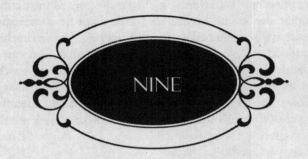

NINE

There were no fellow travelers along the quiet stretch of road for Hooper to tip a hat to or bid a good day. Most Scuffletown folks avoided a wagon ride to Lumberton by hopping the train into Moss Neck every Saturday to lay in supplies for the week. A shame really, since the trip was so pleasant.

They wouldn't see Lumberton proper. Duncan snickered and called it a needless precaution, but Hooper planned to slip past without showing themselves. With a sigh of satisfaction, he leaned against the seat and propped the heel of his boot on the dash.

Beside him, Duncan gazed into the distance, grinning like a dolt.

The silly smile was catching, tickling the corners of Hooper's mouth. He nudged his brother from his thoughts. "What's so funny?"

Duncan's grin widened. "Just thinking about our rear guard. What you reckon Ellie was up to, skulking about in the brush?"

Hooper chuckled. "There's an easy answer. She sorely wanted to join us, so she tagged along as far as possible without setting off Pa's temper."

"You think she followed us the whole way?"

"Sure she did. Ellie could tail us clear to Fayetteville and never be spotted. She's a fine tracker." He jutted his chin. "I taught her myself."

"Ha!" This time Duncan nudged him. "Except we did spot her."

Hooper frowned. "She got careless this time. Left in such a hurry, she assumed we weren't watching our backs. I'll have to teach her to be more careful."

Duncan gazed toward Chicken Road, an ugly scowl replacing his smile. "Then teach her to be less like you before she gets her head shot off."

Familiar irritation crowded Hooper's throat. "That's senseless talk. Learning to survive in the swamp will keep her head where it belongs."

Duncan faced him and blew out a breath. "Ellie watches your every move, Hooper. I fear she'll follow your reckless path to an early grave."

Frustration from years of constant tugging with Duncan swelled Hooper's chest. "Ellie and the rest have no problem with who I am. Why do you have to be different?" He leaned toward Duncan and raised one brow. "But then, you always were the odd duck, right, brother?"

Duncan stilled and shrank in the seat.

Hooper felt bad for goading him, but the boy stuck out like a chokecherry on a cornstalk.

Shorter than Hooper, he had a wide, stocky build where Pa and Hooper were narrow at the hips and broad shouldered. He sported pale gray eyes under busy brows, and his hair tended toward light brown. Unlike the warm, toasted skin of the other McRae men, Duncan's legs were pale where the sun never shined.

The outside trappings were only half the story. Inside, he was nothing like a McRae. Duncan marked these differences and they bothered him something fierce.

Guilt settled over Hooper's heart. "What I mean to say is you're the sensible one in the family. Without you around to corral me, Pa, and Ellie, I suppose Ma would pack up and leave home." He patted Duncan's rigid back. "Speaking of Ellie, don't worry. With Henry and Boss watching the swamp, we left her in capable hands."

Ma always said men were like candy. Past the crackle and crunch, most had mushy, sweet insides. Some were taffy and needed a bit of stretching to turn out right. Others were toffee, nice but a bit hard to manage. She warned Ellie to cut a wide swath around the pralines, dainties that fell apart under pressure, and the brittles, nutty with sharp edges.

Henry Berry Lowry was a chocolate buckeye kiss. Soft enough to yield, but never dainty. Firm, yet far from brittle, Henry was the finest, bravest, most handsome man Scuffletown had ever turned out.

Ellie watched him from under her lashes as they drew near the cabin. He sat on the lopsided porch, a king in woolen overalls and a faded beehive hat.

She took care not to watch too closely because Rhoda, his Scottish-Indian queen, perched at his side. She caught Ellie's eye and nodded.

Henry stirred and dipped his head.

Boss urged her forward then slipped away to resume his watch.

Henry's legend was far reaching. Brave men quivered like pork jelly in his presence. As he leaned forward, gracing her with a sunny smile, fear was the last thing on her mind. "What brings you?" A man of sparse words, his voice oozed like melted wax—despite his straight back and tense shoulders. Even surrounded by his army, letting his guard down for a second could cost him his life.

"A stranger came around this morning asking for Hooper." Saying the words aloud bumped her heart into motion. "Claimed he had a message from you."

Interest flickered in Henry's eyes. "Militia?"

"Not sure. Papa has him lumped with Sheriff McMillan, but he hopes you know something different." She shifted her weight to the other foot and glanced toward home as if she saw it through the trees. "The sneaky devil slipped up on us."

"He come alone?"

She nodded.

Henry arched his brow. "Don't mean he was. Did he mention Duncan?"

She shook her head.

Henry gnawed on his cheek. "Silas worried?"

"Pa has sorely dreaded this day," she said. "Once they link a man's name with the resistance, he don't last long in Robeson County. Up to now, they've been so careful, but I'm afraid their lives may never be the same." Why was she chattering like a rousted squirrel? Unclenching her fists, she drew a breath, embarrassed when her nostrils flared.

"Hooper got away then?" Henry asked.

"He wasn't home."

Frowning, he leaned to study her face. "I sent them there."

"They came, all right." She shuffled her feet. "But a family matter called them away."

Nodding thoughtfully, Henry picked up a river birch twig and ran it sideways through his lips.

Rhoda uncrossed her legs and stood. "You must be cold. I'll fetch some scuppernong wine."

Ellie's breath caught in her throat. "Umm...thank you, ma'am, but—"

"Ellie's folks don't allow strong drink, honey. Brew a pot of sassafras tea." His eyes, always tender when they lit on his wife, tracked Rhoda to the door. She stepped through the shadowed entry and disappeared.

Ellie thought back to July when the Guard captured Rhoda and held her hostage in the Lumberton Jail. The Wilmington *Morning Star* printed the warning that Robeson County had "aroused the lion."

They were right.

Henry, who never breathed an idle threat, sent word to the county commissioners to release Rhoda or he would capture their women and carry them off to the swamp. He added that they wouldn't be so eager to return.

Rhoda was on the next train home.

Henry stirred, drawing Ellie from her ponderings. She glanced up and he motioned.

"Come. Sit."

She closed the gap and settled on the edge of the steps. Rhoda's black cat peeked from beneath the porch then glided in and out through her legs, mewing softly.

"The woods may not be safe just now." Henry grinned. "Even for you."

Ellie glowed from his praise.

"We'll have our tea then Boss will see you home. Before nightfall, your pa will know who came sniffing around your place."

Relief flooded her limbs. "Thank you, Henry. For this and for being so good to my family."

He gazed over her head, his eyes bright with pain. "They've made it a crime for a man to take up arms in defense of his own." Grief sagged his cheeks, smudging charcoal circles under his dark lashes and etching deep grooves between his brows. "I'll be tried and sent to the gallows for what they claim as a right."

An ache swelled Ellie's heart, and she choked back a sob.

Henry ran his hands over his handsome face from forehead to chin, blotting out the ugliness of sorrow in one fell swipe. His eyes softened, and a smile rounded his cheeks. "I suppose if they catch me, I'll meet the hangman without benefit of a trial."

Ellie lifted her chin. "They won't catch you."

His gaze swung her way so fast she sucked air. Wiggly hairs danced on her arms, but she resisted the need to squirm and watched him.

His hand slid to the gun belt slung over his shoulder, determination churning his blue gray eyes. "You're right about that, little girl. They never will."

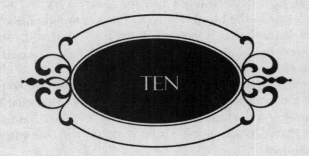

TEN

Dawsey argued with herself on the way to the door, Tiller's three dollars clutched in her hand. What good would it do to ask the boy about the slip of paper? The chance that he or his mother had something to do with the scribbled name in Father's cashbox seemed ludicrously slim.

Still. . . Coincidence or not, there were a few things to clear up, and Tiller McRae could be the very one to ask.

Dawsey spied him through the front window, slouched against the porch rail with one foot cocked behind him on the slats. Muttering to himself and impatiently tugging the brim of his hat, he held the wrapped loaves Winney had given him under one arm.

Drawing a deep breath, Dawsey opened the door.

At the sight of her, his hand jerked to his thumped ear. Then he straightened and wiped his nose with the back of his hand. "About time, if you don't mind my saying."

She drew up to full height and squared her shoulders. "As a matter of fact, I do mind. That's no way to speak to your elders."

Easy, Dawsey. You need to gain his favor.

She relaxed and smoothed her skirt. "However, I do apologize for keeping you so long."

Ignoring her apology, his customary frown deepened. "You don't look like no elder to me."

Dawsey huffed. "Then look again. I happen to be the mistress of this household."

Aunt Livvy's face loomed, pulling her down a notch. "Well, practically. Besides, anyone older than you is your elder. I certainly qualify."

He jutted his chin. "How old are you?"

She wiggled a warning finger. "You must never inquire of a lady's age."

Tiller shrugged and stuck out a grimy palm. "Suit yourself. I'll take that money off your hands now."

Dawsey drew the jingling coins out of his reach. "Not so fast." She summoned a winsome smile. "I thought we'd have a nice chat first."

Suspicion darkened his eyes. "Chats are for grannies at tea parties. I know you ain't that long in the tooth." He scowled. "Are you planning to pay me or not?"

She extended her open hand. "Certainly."

"That's more like it. I've wasted too much time here already." He scooped up his wages and spun to go.

Dawsey latched onto his arm. "Of course you have. What with you being the man of the house now. Your mother must be as proud as a peacock. I suppose she counts on you for everything."

His tense body eased. Shifting the bread to his other arm, he tucked the thumb of his free hand around his suspenders. "That she does, ma'am, that she does."

"And you shoulder the burden alone? With no family to call on?"

A thoughtful look crossed his face. "Well there's Ma's brother, Uncle William, for all the good he does. He can't tell corn from oats." He tapped his temple. "Soft in the head. Come back from the war that way. Old codger slumps in a corner all day, whittling Union soldiers and catching them afire."

"Oh Tiller, I'm so sorry to hear it."

He shrugged and grinned. "Don't be sorry. Uncle Willy don't realize the state he's in."

"So you're the only McRaes left in Fayetteville?"

His bare nod and tight lips wouldn't do. Dawsey needed to draw out more information, but she'd fare better pulling teeth.

"Have you always lived here in town?"

Another nod.

She hid her clenched fists behind her back. "Where does your family hail from?"

He squinted. "Don't know what you're asking."

"McRae. It sounds Gaelic. Are your ancestors Scottish?"

He pulled away. "Say, what's all this? I've never worked harder for a measly few dollars."

"Whatever do you mean?"

"Why are you drilling me?"

"I'm sorry. I didn't mean to pry. I'm concerned about your mother's welfare, that's all. With her shortage of help, she's quite lucky to have you."

The suspicion in his eyes dimmed, and his chest swelled like a turkey's. "You speak the truth, ma'am. Can't see how she'll manage without me."

Dawsey cocked her head. "Are you going somewhere?"

"Reckon I am."

Her mind soared to the poor Widow McRae, left alone and destitute. She patted the boy's thin shoulder. "Well, don't you fret. We'll look after her while you're gone."

He grinned, spreading the freckles on his cheeks. "That's mighty Christian of you, ma'am."

"And you can forget what I said earlier about not coming back to work. Your job will be waiting when you return."

He stuck out his bottom lip. "Won't be returning. I'm leaving town for good."

Dawsey's brows shot to the vaulted eaves. "How can you leave for good? Your mother needs you."

"Too bad she don't have sense enough to know it."

Reams of information lurked in the pain shining from his eyes. Dawsey longed to draw him out, but she didn't have the time.

"Who'll be left to care for her?"

His scowl darkened. "She wanted shed of me, didn't she? I reckon she'll have to fend for herself."

Dawsey rested gentle fingers along his jaw. "Where are you going?"

He pulled away. "To live with my uncle Silas."

Her heartbeat quickened. "Would that be Silas McRae?"

"How'd you know?"

"Only a guess. Where does this uncle live?"

He scratched his head. "Come to think on it, I never heard nobody say."

"You're going to stay with family, but you're not even sure where they live?"

"Don't know and don't care, as long as I can get out of here." He gazed around with flashing eyes and tugged on his baggy trousers. "Yes, sir. I'm on the way to better things than Fayetteville, North Carolina. Can't wait to see what's around the bend." Despite the false posturing, fear lurked on the edge of his broad smile.

"When do you leave?" she asked softly.

He shrugged. "They'll be fetching me soon. That's all I need to know."

"Your uncle Silas said this?"

"Nah. He never answered Ma's letter."

"Then how do you know they'll come?"

He jutted his lips and nodded. "They'll be here. Ma says Uncle Silas won't dare rile her with all he has at stake."

Dawsey's stomach tensed. "What did she mean?"

"Who knows?" He sniffed. "Old folks' ways are too knotty for me to cipher."

She opened her mouth to question him further, but Aunt Livvy's carriage rattled up the lane, stopping in front of the house. Levi scurried down from the driver's seat to open the door, but he was too slow. Aunt Livvy stood outside the carriage smoothing her skirts before his feet ever hit the ground.

"There you are, Dawsey," she said. "You saved me the breath to call you. Help me with these porcelain dishes, dear. I don't dare trust Levi. Such delicate pieces require a woman's careful touch."

Dawsey hurried forward. "Certainly Auntie."

Aunt Livvy unpinned her hat and tossed it on the seat. "Bring that insufferable contraption, too, will you?" She glared at the tall, feathered cap. "I can't imagine what the milliner lines his hats with these days. The silly thing makes my head sweat in the dead of winter." She started up the walk, wiggling her finger at Tiller. "Stand there, boy. I'll bring your wages."

Dawsey gathered the bundles and closed the carriage door. "It's all right, dear. I've paid him."

Aunt Livvy cocked one brow. "Oh?" Pulling on the fingers of her gloves, she continued for the house. "Very well. Did you mark a dollar off the ledger?"

Tiller hustled off the porch and down the brick path, but Dawsey moved in front of him, blocking his way with the packages. "One dollar, Auntie? Not three?"

Aunt Livvy chuckled over her shoulder. "What fool would shell out three dollars for weeded flower beds?"

Stopping short, she slowly turned. "Dawsey, you didn't."

Dawsey's gaze flashed to Tiller. "Why, you deceitful little—"

He bolted, knocking Aunt Livvy's packages from Dawsey's grasping hands. The delicate chinaware landed at her feet with the *crash* of broken glass. As the scoundrel ran, he lost his hold on the wrapped loaves. The bread fell, rolling end over end across the yard. Weaving side to side, he snatched them up at a dead run then streaked across the lane.

Dawsey watched until he ducked into the woods and disappeared.

"Go after him, Levi," Aunt Livvy shrieked.

Levi hitched up his britches and poised to sprint.

Dawsey caught his arm and hauled him around. "Leave him be."

Her aunt stalked to where they stood. "What are you saying?"

"Let it go, Auntie. What can you do to that wretched boy any worse than what fate has dealt him?"

"I'll take back the two dollars he stole." She waved her arms in a frantic circle over the broken dishes. "I'll make him pay for this damage."

Dawsey shook her head. "You'll squeeze precious few pennies from him, dear. He simply doesn't have it. Anything you manage to get will only pluck food from a poor widow's mouth." Taking her arm, Dawsey gently led her toward the house. "Let's forget about him, shall we? They need that two dollars worse than we do, so let them have it."

She glanced in the direction the boy had gone and sighed. "After today, young Tiller McRae's shenanigans will be someone else's problem."

Basking in the glow of Henry's company, and especially his flattering remark, Ellie allowed Boss and his men to shepherd her home. The family liked to brag on Ellie's knack for vanishing in plain sight, but knowing Henry took note of her skill swelled her heart to bursting.

Yes, Henry had called her "little girl," an offensive term another man would swiftly regret, but his tone was free of teasing or haughty airs. The warmth in his voice and the fire of shared passion turned the simple words to sweet gum sap, binding their wounded hearts.

Ellie smiled to herself in the darkness. Wyatt Carter had once called her "little girl," but she hadn't minded then either. The fire in his eyes when he said it had little to do with the zeal of a shared cause.

Henry Lowry was a chocolate buckeye kiss, but he was Rhoda's kiss. Ellie knew Wyatt was destined to be hers. No man quickened her heartbeat or dried her throat the way he did. The music in his voice was livelier than the strumming of Pa's banjo, and the way he spoke her name was as close to a man's caress as she had yet to know. She spent hours pondering the challenge shining from Wyatt's dark-eyed glances.

Boss whipped his horse into a thicket. "This way."

The hoarse whisper pulled Ellie from her guilty thoughts in time to rein Toby sharply into the scrub behind Boss and the others. The warmth of Henry's confidence in her faded to a scalding vat of dishonor. Angry with herself for mooning when she should be watching, Ellie scoured her surroundings for a glimpse at what had forced them deeper into the swamp. Though she heard rather than saw them, it didn't take long to find out.

A band of riders passed behind them on the road, doing a pitiful job of keeping quiet. Six, maybe eight horses, if she counted the hoofbeats right. She'd bet her last dollar the cocky man who came asking about Hooper rode with them.

Boss reined up and motioned at two of his men. They split off to tail the riders, careful to keep a healthy portion of trees between themselves and the strangers. Without a backward glance, Boss skillfully led Ellie and the rest away from the intruders. None spoke a word until they reached the edge of her yard and heard Pa's answering whistle.

They broke through the trees, and he hurried to meet them, flashing a welcoming grin. "Look what the hound dragged in."

Boss laughed and swung his leg over the saddle. "I admit I'm as gaunt as a gnawed bone, Silas, but I hope you ain't calling Ellie a dog. She's way too pretty for that."

Turning away to hide her blush, Ellie slid to the ground. "He knows better, Boss. I'd skin his wrinkled ears."

The men laughed uproariously, worsening Ellie's embarrassment. Thankfully, they turned their attention to more serious matters.

Boss laid a sympathetic hand on Papa's arm. "I hear they're sniffing around after Hooper."

A shadow crossed Papa's face. "I knew this day had to come. Thought I'd be ready." He raised sad eyes to Boss. "I thought wrong."

"You reckon your uninvited guest was sent out here by the sheriff?"

Pa snorted. "I did right at first. Now, I'd put my money on bounty hunters."

Frowning, Boss spat on the ground. "Vultures. Lining their pockets with the flesh of innocent men." He looked up with a light in his eyes.

"Don't worry, Silas. The situation's bad but not hopeless. Hoop will have to leave home to stay alive, but he will stay alive."

Ellie touched his arm. "Where will he go?"

"He can join us at the cabin. Henry's told him a dozen times he's welcome to hide out with us in Bear Swamp."

Papa grimaced. "The most dangerous place in Scuffletown is at Henry's side. At the same time, it's the safest. Don't make sense, does it?"

Boss laughed softly and gave Pa's shoulder a shake. "Henry would lay down his life to keep Hooper out of harm's way." He motioned toward his men. "Any one of us would."

Tears moistened Papa's eyes. "I reckon I know that."

Ellie dreaded asking but had to know. "What about Duncan?"

Pa's sorrowful look broke her heart.

"Duncan won't leave, honey. No matter how dire the risk, he'll dig in his heels here at home."

Tugging on his bottom lip, Boss stared toward town. "Silas, they'll come and blast him right out the front door."

"Boss,"—a grim look aged Papa's haggard face—"I'm afraid they'll have to."

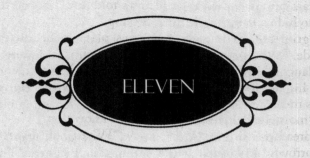

ELEVEN

Under cover of darkness, slipping into Fayetteville unseen was a simple task. Even the silvery slip of a moon lent a hand, casting meager beams to light their path. Hooper kept to the back roads, skirting the town square and more crowded streets, until they crossed the bridge over Cool Spring near the old mill.

Past the graveyard, as gloomy and misty as he remembered as a child, Hooper turned the buckboard down the narrow lane to Uncle Sol's place. As pleased as the plodding horse must be to see the outline of the barn in the distance, Hooper was more grateful to see flickering lights behind the thin curtains.

He felt a stab of sadness when he realized Uncle Sol wouldn't be greeting them with his rousing laughter and booming voice. The house and all its memories now belonged to Aunt Effie—a woman he couldn't recall, no matter how he tried—and her wayward seed, their scalawag cousin, Reddick McRae.

Hooper grinned at the thought of his troublesome relation, the sole reason for their unscheduled journey. He figured a spell wallowing in Scuffletown's mud and trouble would smooth young Reddick's ruffled feathers.

From what Hooper could make out in the dusky moonlight, the ramshackle dwelling had fallen into serious disrepair. It appeared the roof buckled in places. The windows sagged. A felled tree blocked the broken brick path, and no one had bothered to cut it away.

Pa had taught them to always park the rig facing the way out so they'd be ready for a quick getaway should the need arise. Hooper made a sweeping circle in Aunt Effie's front yard and set the brake. Leaning over, he shook Duncan awake.

He came up sputtering with ready fists.

Laughing, Hooper punched his arm. "Keep it down, you dolt. You'll get us shot." Watching the house for movement, he lowered his stiff body to the ground.

Grumbling his displeasure, Duncan eased down on the other side. He joined Hooper at the tailgate, blinking to focus his bleary eyes. "Hasn't changed much, has it?"

Hooper gaped at him. "Are you still asleep? Look again. The place is falling down." He gazed at the entrance and sighed. "The biggest change is the worst, I'm afraid. We won't find Uncle Sol behind that door." He glanced at Duncan. "Do you remember Aunt Effie at all?"

"I think she was sort of loud."

A piercing scream from inside the house brought them up off the ground. A startled look passed between them before they hurdled the downed tree and lit out for the porch.

Hooper teetered on his toes, one hand on the knob, the other poised to knock, when a string of angry curses poured from within the house. Foul threats and ugly promises scorched his ears, aimed at a poor soul named Tiller.

Blushing at the bad language, especially distasteful in a woman's voice, Hooper raised his brows. "It appears she's gotten louder. What do we do?"

Duncan shrugged.

Gritting his teeth, Hooper pounded hard enough to be heard over the ruckus.

Without a break in her rant, the woman's screaming voice approached the door. ". . .then I'll split your lousy skull with my broom and won't bother to mop up the mess, you wretched. . ." The door jerked open with a boisterous *rattle*. "What the devil do you want?"

Hooper caught the vague impression of large bare feet, wide hips, and a tall wispy bun atop a broad, sloping forehead. The face below the glaring eyes was mottled and red.

"Don't stand there with your tongue in your mouth," she shrilled. "I asked you a question."

Duncan took a backward step.

Hooper jerked off his hat, wishing it was big enough to hide behind. Clutching it tightly in his fists, he cleared his throat and tried to answer. "Ma'am, we—"

"How dare you knock at a decent widow's house at this hour." She squinted. "You'd best have a stinking good reason."

Not sure she'd find their reason good, stinking or otherwise, Hooper retreated to join Duncan.

Jerking her head to the side, she fixed them with bulging eyes. "Wait a minute. You boys are McRaes, ain't you?"

Hooper cleared his throat. "Yes ma'am, we. . .um, Aunt Effie?"

"Took you long enough. I'm ready to string up your no-account cousin." She spun on her heel and left them on the porch, as if rattling hinges was an invitation to enter.

Hooper shot Duncan a knowing glance. "Uncle Sol didn't die. He escaped."

Duncan poked him in the side. "Lower your voice or we'll join him."

Pointing past the entrance, Hooper grunted. "Look's like we turned up just in time to help that poor fellow make a getaway."

Every ounce of Scottish blood still residing in the McRaes had found its way into the skinny, freckled body lurking in a corner across the room, his face the image of Uncle Sol.

Elbowing his way closer, Duncan stared. "That's Reddick?"

"Has to be."

"Then who's Tiller?"

"Not sure." Hooper grinned. "I'm just glad it's not me."

Aunt Effie swept past in a huff. "Why are you still outside? Get in here. You're letting in the cold."

Flinching, Hooper stepped cautiously past the threshold, a reluctant Duncan in tow.

Aunt Effie had disappeared, likely to the kitchen, given the rattle of pots and pans coming from the other room.

The slender lad in the corner stood, wiping his hands on his pants. "Are you two my cousins?"

Hooper nodded. "That's right. You Reddick?"

The boy hitched up his sagging britches. "Name's Tiller."

"No it ain't!" Aunt Effie bawled from the other room. "It's Reddick, like you said."

Reddick's back straightened and he scowled. "I won't answer to it."

Stepping closer, Hooper offered his hand. "Nice to know you, Tiller."

Duncan winked at him. "Tiller, huh? What sort of name is that?"

Aunt Effie appeared in the doorway, drying a plate with her grimy apron. "It ain't no name at all. Folks call him that on account of he's right good with the soil." She sneered at her son. "This silly thing took a shine to it."

Hooper shot him a sympathetic look. "How old are you, son?"

"Sixteen."

His mama cackled. "No he ain't."

Red faced, he whirled on her so fast he nearly dropped his drawers. "Almost, and you know it."

"You're barely fifteen." She sneered then grinned at Hooper. "Don't believe him. His birthday's in May."

Hooper squeezed Tiller's shoulder. "Five more months, huh? You're better than halfway there." He beamed at the upturned freckled face. "I reckon that counts."

The deep lines between the boy's brows relaxed, and the hint of a smile lit his eyes. He opened his mouth to speak, but whatever he was about to say was lost when his mama caught his arm and propelled him toward the kitchen.

"Get in there and finish those dishes. Then go pack your things. You don't want to keep your cousins waiting."

Color drained from Duncan's face. With a smattering of freckles, his complexion would match Tiller's. He lifted a faltering hand. "Ah. . . Aunt Effie? I mean, well, we've just ridden an awfully long way. We're hungry and—"

Her bug-eyed glare closed his mouth. "Leave it to Silas McRae." Each syllable rose in pitch until McRae came out a sharp bellow. "He's supposed to take Tiller off my hands. Has he sent me two more mouths to feed instead?" Fuming, she flapped her dish towel. "I don't have food enough for my own empty stomach. Nor for Tiller's. How can I be expected to fill yours?"

Duncan gulped like a catfish but made no sound.

Hooper pushed him aside. "Don't fret, ma'am. We're not here to eat." Ignoring the added shock on Duncan's face, he flashed a winsome smile. "All we need is shelter for our horse, and a few oats if you can spare them."

Aunt Effie brightened. "I can provide you with that much, but you'll have to share the barn with your animal." She took in her surroundings with a scornful glance and a backhanded wave. "As you see, extra room is as scarce as bread." Again, she whirled without another word and left the room.

Duncan grabbed Hooper's arm. "What are you doing? We've ridden all day. I'm tired. And *hungry!*"

Hooper chuckled. "What are you complaining about? I got you a nice pile of hay for a bed. And a portion of oats, if the horse is willing to share."

"I don't think this is funny," Duncan fumed. "Now I see why Pa sent us instead of coming himself."

"Stop moaning." Hooper jerked his thumb toward the kitchen. "Just be glad you're not that poor lad. Can you imagine the misery his life has been? The sooner we get him free of this dung pit, the better."

Duncan flicked his hand, his shoulders rounded in defeat. "Have it your way. . .as usual." He cut his eyes toward the kitchen. "Besides, I'm not all that eager to eat from those filthy dishes. I'd sooner stick my muzzle in Old Abe's feed sack."

Grinning, Hooper patted his back. "We'll rest a few hours in the barn then get on the road. I'll drive first then we can relieve each other on the way." He patted the pack tied around his waist. "I still have a piece of jerky. Maybe some hardtack in the rig. With any luck, we'll be home in time for breakfast."

"No need to fret about food," Tiller said. "I'll fetch you some after Ma goes to bed."

Hooper's gaze bounced to where he slouched near the kitchen door. "Don't let your ma hear you say that or you'll be in trouble."

The lad straightened and pulled his pants higher. "She's out back with the hogs." He sneered. "Feeding them leftover grub she could've fed you."

A sudden grin lit his boyish face. "You fellows like bread? Fresh baked and spread with jam? I have all you could eat stashed in my room." He nodded, eager to strike a deal. "If you let me bunk with you in the barn, I'll share."

Duncan rubbed his hands together. "Sounds like a bargain to me." He paused. "I don't suppose you have a slice of cheese to go with it?"

Tiller snorted. "You funning me? We ain't had nothing as tasty as cheese since Pa died."

Duncan's brows lifted. "You've had a hard time of it then?"

The boy poked out his lips and nodded.

Hooper beckoned him closer. Laying a hand on his neck, he peered into his eyes. "Are you sure you don't want to leave some of that bread here for your ma to eat?"

He stiffened and backed away. "You can't tell her. If she knows I have food, she'll skin me good then feed every crumb to the hogs." His desperate gaze bounced from Hooper to Duncan. "I'm telling you, we won't see a bite."

Duncan cocked his head, his top lip pulled up in disgust. "She'd do that?"

Tiller's nostrils flared. "Get that look off your face, mister," he warned. "Ma wasn't always like this." He swiped the back of his hand over his shining eyes. "She used to be nice. When I was little, she held me on her lap and stuff." Embarrassed, he tugged on the waistband of his trousers. "When Pa died, times got hard and she changed."

Hooper unbuttoned his suspenders from the waistband of his pants. Gathering them in his hand, he started toward Tiller.

The boy ducked and flinched, his hands thrown up like a shield. "No don't," he cried. "I didn't mean to sass."

Hooper froze. With a sharp pang in his heart, he patted Tiller's arm. "Stand up, son. I'm not going to hit you."

He stood, fear and distrust shining from his eyes.

Slowly, gently, Hooper slipped the suspenders over his shoulders and fastened them to his pants. "There, now. No more losing your drawers."

He took Tiller's shoulders and sought his frightened eyes. "You listen to me. I give you my word that no one will strike you again if I'm around to stop it, not with suspenders or anything else. Do you understand?"

His eyes round with surprise, Tiller nodded.

Hooper patted his back. "Good man." His stomach growling, he hooked his arm around the boy's neck. "What do you say we head to the barn and feast on jam and bread?"

He twisted to grin at Duncan. "I think we'll leave the oats for you and the horse."

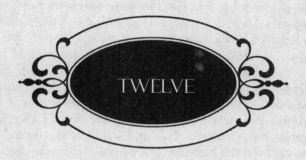

TWELVE

Dawsey opened the oven door with her dish towel and bent to slide in the popovers. Before they made it safely in, her father bellowed her name from somewhere inside the house. She leaped, sending the gem pan one direction, the popovers another.

"For goodness' sake," Aunt Livvy said from inside the larder. "I do wish he'd stop that."

Her head appeared around the pantry door. "Are you all right, Dawsey? I heard a ruckus."

Before Dawsey could answer, she gaped at the mounds of dough scattered over the floor. "What a shame. So sorry, dear."

Father howled again, and Levi stuck his head inside, panic lining his face. "Colonel Wilkes crowing for you, Miss Dawsey."

"We're well aware of it, Levi. We can hear for ourselves." Aunt Livvy motioned with her chin. "Go and settle him down, please."

Levi backed away then popped in once more. "How, Miss Livvy?"

"Tell him Dawsey will be along soon." She covered her ears when Father cried out for the third time. "Tell him anything you wish, as long as you silence him. Now go."

Dawsey bent to scoop up the ruined dough with her dish towel. Aunt Livvy picked up the muffin tin and tossed it on the counter with a clatter. "I truly loathe this brutish conduct. I much prefer his silence."

Dawsey swallowed her irritation. Aunt Livvy could be quite insensitive at times. Struggling to keep her voice even, she untied her apron and placed it near the sink. "What do you suppose has gotten into him? I'd become used to his sullenness, but this. . ."

Aunt Livvy walked to the window. Dawsey recognized the angle of her shoulders and set of her jaw. Her aunt had something to say. She turned and met Dawsey's watchful eyes. "It's not the first time your father has behaved badly. Even as a child, he was gloomy and pouting." She frowned. "When he wasn't being stubborn and willful."

Anger shot through Dawsey. She bit her bottom lip. "That can't be true. People recall my father as a kind and generous man, a brilliant leader, and a doting husband. I've heard wonderful stories."

"Of course you have. All of them true." Aunt Livvy leaned her weight against the back of a chair and stared at the floor. "Your dear mother brought out the best side of Gerrard. When she died, I lost my brother to bitterness." Her bosom rose and fell with a sigh. "Then that wretched war came along to finish him off."

Aunt Livvy crossed to Dawsey and took her hands. "Forgive me, dear. I shouldn't unburden myself to you. Especially when you carry your own dreadful load. I suppose I've lost patience with the stranger in the den. I miss the man he used to be."

Dawsey's shoulders sagged. "What happened to him, Auntie? Other men lose their wives. . .go to war without losing themselves."

The wall Aunt Livvy used to protect her brother's past rattled into place. Eyes veiled, she waved a dismissive hand and crossed to the pantry. "Your father has suffered many losses, dear, crushing blows every one. But the truth is Gerrard lost himself when he lost his faith."

Dawsey let the truth she'd suspected settle over her heart. Despite her own sorrow, the love of God filled her with peace and hope. Her father seemed devoid of either emotion. Surely, if he had yielded his burdens, they wouldn't have affected him so deeply.

Sadness swept over her. "Then we must help him find his way back to faith. If I knew his terrible secret, then I could—"

Both heads turned as Levi pushed open the kitchen door. "Someone here to see you, Miss Dawsey."

"At this hour?" She frowned. "Who is it?"

"Flora, that's who. Miss Gilchrist's girl. She say her mama down in the back. Sufferin' something fierce." He rolled his eyes to Dawsey. "She needs you to come along right away."

"Poor Mrs. Gilchrist. Levi, fetch my medicine bag and bring the carriage around."

He left to do her bidding, but Aunt Livvy snatched her sleeve as she passed. "You can't go, honey. Not with your father like this. You're the only one who can quiet him." She tightened her grip. "He'll be calling for you all through the night, Dawsey, and I simply couldn't bear it."

"But Auntie. Mrs. Gilchrist. . ."

"I'll go tend to Mary myself. I know just what to do. I've watched you enough times to learn."

Dawsey rubbed her temples. "Oh my. Are you sure?"

"Quite sure. Stay here with your father. If I can't ease Mary's suffering, I'll come straight home and relieve you."

Before Dawsey could open her mouth in protest, Levi hurried in with her medicine bag. "Miss Dawsey, the colonel tuning up to squawk again, and I got no more tricks to hush him."

She shot her aunt a helpless glance. Without a word, Aunt Livvy swiped the bag from Levi's hand and hustled out the door.

Tiller droned like a pestered hive.

The boy had yammered throughout their meal of crusty bread and slathered jam, through Duncan's lengthy nap, and during the three hours of swapping memories and family gossip. He didn't seem inclined to wind down anytime soon, so Hooper decided Duncan should have a turn.

He spread his coat on the floor of the barn then reached for an armload of hay. Rolling the coat tightly around it created a fair pillow. Shoving his hat down over his eyes, he lay back to rest.

The hat wasn't enough to shut out the flickering lantern, so he turned over and buried his face in the straw pillow. Sadly, nothing could shut out Tiller.

"Why do you call that old mule Abe Lincoln?"

Duncan feigned an offended gasp. "Why, that's a horse, boy. Don't let him hear you say different. We call him Abe Lincoln on account of he's faithful and dependable." He laughed deep in his throat. "And ugly as mud."

Hooper grinned to himself when Duncan and Tiller howled.

"But he does lean a tad toward crazy at times," Duncan said. "We don't spend a lot of time within reach of his teeth."

"Our Uncle Willy's crazy, too," Tiller informed Duncan. "Matter of fact, he's just as batty as a loon. The old coot sits in a corner all day playing with toy soldiers."

Duncan grunted. "Is that a fact?"

"Gospel truth. But come to think on it, he's Ma's brother, not Pa's. I reckon that means he's no relation to you boys." He whistled. "Lucky for you." The little fellow heaved a deep sigh. "No, sir. When it comes to family, me and Ma are in short supply. We're the last of the McRaes in Fayetteville. And now, I—"

Duncan cleared his throat. "Mark your place in that story, little cousin, and toss me another hunk of that bread."

"It's *good*, ain't it?" Tiller's laugh echoed in the barn. "I told you so."

Paper rustled behind Hooper.

"And look here. She gave me three whole loaves."

"It's good, all right," Duncan agreed. "Some of the best I've ever tasted." He paused. "Pass me that blackberry jam while you're at it."

"You know, it's funny," Tiller said, his voice strained from reaching. "The lady who gave me this food has crazy kinfolk, too."

"You don't say?" Duncan mumbled, his mouth obviously full.

"I ain't lying. It's Miss Wilkes's pa, but she calls him "Faawtha." He tittered like a girl. "Only he's worse off. At least Uncle Willy plays with something fun like toy soldiers." His laugh rang so loud, Hooper jumped. "That poor codger stares all day at Aladdin's magic lamp."

Hooper sat up so fast he left his hat in the straw. "What'd he say?"

Duncan had thrown his sandwich aside and come up on his knees in front of Tiller, gripping his skinny arms. "You heard right. He said magic lamp." He gave Tiller a shake. "Didn't you, boy?"

Tiller had paled as white as sugar and his eyes bulged with fear. "Y–Yes. . .m—magic lamp."

"Have you seen it?"

Tiller's frightened eyes hopped back and forth. "Did I say something wrong?"

"Just answer the question."

"Lots of times!"

"Then you can describe it."

"S–Sure I can. It's shaped funny. Has a long skinny spout and a sissy handle. It looks to be made of solid gold, but it ain't, of course."

"How do you know?"

"Well, it cain't be, can it? They leave the fool thing sittin' on a windowsill."

Duncan released Tiller and sat back on his heels. "It's Pa's lamp, ain't it?"

Hooper swallowed hard. "Has to be."

Free of their frightening questions, Tiller scooted to the corner, watching them.

Swiping his hand over his mouth, Duncan stared at the barn wall, his eyes glazed over. "But that would be crazy, wouldn't it? After all these years?"

"You heard the boy. Aladdin's lamp. That's what Pa always called it."

A grin split Duncan's dazed face. "I'd give my right arm to see that blasted thing."

Hooper chuckled. "Wouldn't that be something?"

Tiller scrambled toward them on hands and knees. "That's easy. I can take you."

Both their heads swung around to stare at him. Excitement surged in Hooper's chest. "You know where it is right now?"

The boy's chest swelled importantly. "I know exactly where. Sitting in the window of the biggest house in Fayetteville."

Hooper's eyes met Duncan's over Tiller's head. "More proof. Pa said the same about the house he raided."

"I do yard work for the family," Tiller continued. "At least I did before she ran me off"—he grinned and nodded for emphasis—"for touching the lamp."

Hooper shot to his feet. "What are we waiting for?"

"Are you serious?" Duncan scrambled off the floor. "We can't, Hoop. You know what Pa said."

"This is different," Hooper said. "It's all he's talked about for years. He'd understand." He chuckled. "If he was here, he'd be the first man in the wagon." He walked to pick up his hat. "The horse is rested. No sense lying about in this barn. We'll see the magic lantern then head for home."

"I don't know. . . ." Duncan scratched his head. "You've had no sleep at all, and we still have a long ride ahead."

"I'm too excited to sleep. You've snoozed a bit, and like I said before, we'll take turns at the reins."

"What's your plan? It's the middle of the night. We can't just sashay up to the door."

"We won't have to. The boy said they leave the lamp in a window." He nudged Tiller. "You know which window, right?"

Tiller nodded.

"There, you see? We'll just take a look, and then we'll go. They won't even know we were there." He clapped his hands and rubbed them together. "What a story we'll have to tell Pa."

Frowning, Tiller tucked his thumbs in his new suspenders. "Say, what's all this about anyway?"

Hooper tugged his ear. "Gather your things while we hitch up Old Abe. On the way I'll delight you with the tale of young Silas McRae and his magic lantern." He chuckled. "I think you'll find his adventure far more exciting than Aladdin's."

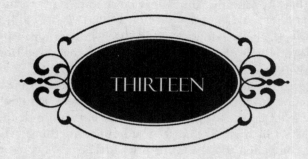

THIRTEEN

There are moments when I see the rush of the Indians, hear their war-whoops and terrific yells, and witness the massacre of my parents. . . .

Dawsey frowned and skipped ahead.

The little girl whom I before mentioned, beginning to cry, was immediately dispatched with the blow of a tomahawk from one of the warriors. . . .

She shuddered and laid the book aside. *Memoirs of a Captivity among the Indians of North America* turned out to be a poor choice of reading material while seated alone in Father's den in the dead of night.

How horrid to watch the murder of your parents, the pillage of your home. Then to be bound against your will and carted off to a strange place? Another shudder took her, mostly from the terrible thought but partly because of the draft blowing in under the window.

Dawsey had given up on sleep hours ago. Father had never been more restless, and she wondered what new evils plagued him. Each time she dozed off in her room, he called her name. Each time she ran to meet his needs, he seemed only to want her company.

She hadn't talked to him or held his hand. She'd just brewed more chamomile tea and perched at the edge of a chair by his bed until he slept again. The last time he drifted off, this time more soundly, she'd slipped downstairs to his study to wait for Aunt Livvy.

Sighing, Dawsey glanced at the eight-day clock as it chimed the eleventh hour. Apparently, Aunt Livvy decided to stay overnight at the Gilchrists'.

Crossing to the window, she parted the heavy drapes and peered out. By the dim light of the backyard torch, the shadowed front wheels of the carriage were visible inside the shed.

Her gaze jumped to Winney and Levi's quarters. If Aunt Livvy had left instructions to return and fetch her, Levi would be nodding at his kitchen table until time to go, but no lanterns burned inside their house.

Poor Mrs. Gilchrist! She must be suffering something awful if Aunt Livvy felt compelled to stay. Guilt pricked Dawsey's conscience. She shouldn't have let her aunt outsmart her when sweet Mary Gilchrist needed her help. What Dawsey had done for Father, Aunt Livvy could've managed quite well.

Drowsiness pulled at her heavy lids. Jumping awake, she rubbed her eyes and contemplated another cup of tea. Thinking better of it, she snuggled into the soft fabric of the sofa and pulled a blanket over her lap.

Staring idly at the wall, she counted the plaster mounds covering the holes left by four tenpenny nails. According to Aunt Livvy, the nails once held a small quilt stitched in fanciful, prancing lambs. She insisted Father's den had once been the nursery, though Dawsey found the news impossible to fathom. If so, hidden nail holes were the only evidence that the dark, gloomy room had ever housed an infant.

A brisk wind howled beneath the window, driving her to tighten her dressing gown and hurry to pull down the sash. Huffing her frustration, she shoved it up again and pulled the golden lamp inside the house. In no mood for anything related to her father's suffering, she tossed it on the floor behind her.

The lamp was nowhere in sight when Dawsey turned to head up to her bedroom, so she assumed it slid beneath the corner table. *A fitting place for the irksome thing!* No doubt, she'd be on her knees fishing it out the next morning, but it could stay where it was for the night.

Hooper pulled the rig off the road about a hundred yards from the dim glow of lights in the distance. There was little chance of anyone passing by so late at night, but just in case, he drove a ways behind the trees before he stopped the wagon.

Laughing like loons, the three of them scurried to the ground and ran into the woods. The moon overhead shone just enough to keep them from slamming into each other or plowing into a tree. They didn't stop running until they came upon a towering wall of shriveled cornstalks standing between them and the house.

Duncan clutched Hooper's sleeve. "Do you realize where we are?"

Laughter bubbled up Hooper's throat. "This is Pa's cornfield. . . which means there's a ditch we need to dodge on the other side." He peered at Duncan in the moonlight, wide grins on both their faces. "I think we should go find out, brother."

Duncan tipped his head at the stalks. "Let's go!"

Tiller at their heels, they barreled into the field.

With a brisk wind whipping past his ears, Hooper bounded like a two-legged deer. Shoving aside withered leaves and jumping broken stalks, he relived his pa's adventure. For all he knew, Silas McRae had trod the same ground, breathed the same air. He could almost hear the braying dogs and the roar of a shotgun behind him.

His heart swelled to bursting when they reached the far edge of the corn and hit their bellies. Scouring the ground, disappointment welled in his chest. "Where is it? Where's the ditch?"

Gasping for breath, Tiller crawled up between them. "Don't remember seeing no ditch around here. I reckon there ain't one."

Hooper strained to see Duncan's face in the meager light. "Were we wrong? This isn't the right cornfield?"

Duncan gnawed his bottom lip. "It's been years, Hoop. They could've filled the trench in by now." He sniffed. "It could still be the right house."

"Right or wrong,"—Tiller piped up, pointing his finger at the line of rear windows—"there's a lamp sittin' right over there. That much I know for sure."

Grinning again, Hooper nodded. "Good enough for me."

Bent low and skulking like thieves, they broke through the stalks and scurried for the back side of the house. Tiller crouched under the first window and pointed overhead.

Hooper bobbed up to look then dropped down again. "Not there."

Throwing caution aside, Tiller rose and felt along the ledge. "Huh?" he whispered. "It's supposed to be here."

"Well, it's not," Duncan hissed.

"It's sitting just inside then." Tiller strained to see past the darkened windowpane. "The lady takes it in sometimes. I've seen her."

Duncan fell back on the ground. "That's it then. Let's get out of here before this boy gets us shot."

Hooper joined Tiller at the glass. "I'd risk the mean end of a pistol to see that lamp." Without thinking it through, he worked his fingertips under the sill and the window squeaked open a crack. Excitement churning his stomach, his eyes searched Tiller's. "Little cousin. . .is there a gold lamp inside this room?"

Tiller slapped one hand over his heart. "I swear on my life."

Duncan scrambled to his feet. "Hoop, are you crazy? This ain't Scuffletown, and these folks ain't Macks. If you break in here, it's not to feed the poor and hungry. It's just plain wrong."

Hooper grabbed his collar and jerked him to the ground. "Lower your voice. We're not going to steal from them, Duncan. We'll take a look and then climb out the way we came—empty handed."

Duncan wagged his head. "No, sir. I want no part of it."

Hooper stood. "Then sit there. I'm not passing up this chance."

He looked left and right then slowly raised the window. Tiller squirmed anxiously beside him, but Hooper held up his hand. "Stay with Duncan."

He scrunched up his face. "Aw!"

"Be quiet, and do like I say."

Hooper strained to pull himself up to the ledge, but it was too high. He nudged Duncan's foot with the toe of his boot. "If you give me a leg up, I'll show you the lamp when I find it."

Grumbling under his breath, Duncan made a sling with his hands and hoisted him up to the sill.

Hooper went through headfirst, catching himself with his hands and rolling silently to the floor. Kneeling, he felt around on the ledge, then under it, but found nothing. "It's not here."

Tiller poked his head inside. "Sure it is." He pointed. "Look on that table yonder."

Hooper groped his way across the room, wincing and covering his mouth when he stubbed his toe on a chair. Shaking off the pain, he felt his way to the table, where his searching fingers found only a fringed lamp and a large book. He turned to grumble but choked on his words.

The shadowy outline of a pleasing apparition hovered near the window facing Tiller, a breeze billowing her nightdress and lifting long strands of her hair.

Stunned, Hooper rubbed his eyes and looked again. His disbelief vanished when the dreamlike figure doubled her fists and shrieked with all her might, "Tiller McRae!"

A *thud* shook the ceiling. Footsteps echoed overhead, then a man's voice bellowed from the top of the stairs.

Snatching a blanket from the couch, he threw it over the woman's head and lifted her struggling body. Racing to the window, he threw one leg over the sill. "Here! Take this!"

Duncan hurriedly reached for the bundle. "What is it?"

The man roared behind Hooper. With no time for his brother's questions, he tossed her at them and jumped.

They caught her, grunting under the weight. She wiggled, and Tiller screamed and let go. Duncan cursed and dropped her.

Struggling on the ground, she screeched and clawed at the blanket twisted around her head.

Before she could escape, Hooper snatched her up and slung her over his shoulder.

"Rrrrun!"

They bolted for the cornfield, Hooper going as fast as he could manage carrying the extra weight. With anguished bellows echoing from the window behind them, they crashed headlong into the merciless stalks.

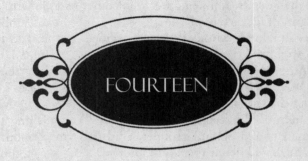

FOURTEEN

Dawsey fought to breathe.

The suffocating blanket flattened her nose, and the man's shoulder pounded her stomach each time his running feet hit the ground, forcing air from her lungs in little gasps.

Short of oxygen.

Arms pinned cruelly to her sides.

Swift feet carrying her into the night.

Dawsey violently sucked a breath of air and exhaled on a scream.

The man beneath her jolted and lost his stride. He stumbled, and she prayed he'd fall. Recovering his footing, he swatted her hard on the behind. "Hush! You'll send us sprawling."

Indignant, Dawsey flailed her feet, hoping to knock him down, but he was too strong for her. The effort only increased her need to breathe. Gasping, panting in terror, she cried out to God for deliverance as white dots swirled past her eyes.

She vaguely sensed being carelessly tossed and rolling into a lifeless heap. Hands pulled her, twisted her, jerked on her arms as disjointed voices floated overhead.

"Are you mad, Hooper? What the devil are we doing?"

"Hooper! Why'd you take her?"

"Be still, both of you. What choice did I have? She called Tiller's name."

The frantic quarrel faded as the white dots sped up and swirled her away to darkness. She dreamed of tomahawks, baby quilts, and fields of rotted corn. Of Mrs. Gilchrist hunched over a stump, twirling a yowling cat.

Dawsey's eyes flew open, and she gasped for breath. Blinking against a wall of blackness, her heart pounded as she remembered. She smelled the musty scent of cornhusks on the blanket, and the heavy wool blocked her sight. Mercifully, someone had folded the cover away from her mouth. Terrified, but thanking God to be alive, she hungrily gulped the air.

She lay very still, desperate to get her bearings. Feeling every bump and shift beneath her, hearing creaky wheels and rustling grass, she figured out that she lay bundled in the bed of a jostling wagon. Stunned, she realized they'd tied her hands behind her back. Struggling against her bonds, she tried to sit up. Without her arms to brace her, she fell hard on her shoulder with an anguished cry.

"She's awake!" Tiller shouted. He sounded close, maybe seated right behind her.

"I told you she wasn't dead," a strange voice called. "Give her a drink from the flask."

Tiller scrambled about in the wagon bed then scooted around in front of her. "Here you go, Miss Wilkes. Some water for you."

She turned her head. "If you touch me, I'll scream."

Silence followed, then Tiller's desperate plea over her head. "What do I do? She says she'll scream if I touch her."

"Let her. We're too far out for anyone to hear."

"I don't want her to scream."

"Then leave her be. If she gets thirsty enough, she'll ask for water."

Tiller shifted and sighed, making little mournful sounds in his throat. He leaned so close she felt his breath on her face. "I'm real sorry, Miss Wilkes," he whispered. "Please tell me you're all right." He heaved another sigh. "If I'd known they'd take you, I'd never have showed them your house. I swear it."

Tiller brought them! She might've known. The boy had been nothing but trouble. "Just go away."

"No," he whimpered. "I won't."

"Then make yourself useful. Help me sit up."

He scurried behind her and lifted her by her shoulders.

"Now cover my legs."

He dutifully tugged her nightdress down over her exposed calves.

"Will you untie my hands, please?"

A squirming pause. "Hey, fellows. She wants her hands untied."

"Sorry, ma'am. I can't do that," a clipped voice replied. Obviously the leader.

"Aw, come on," Tiller said. "What would it hurt?"

"I don't like it either, but we have no choice."

Irritation spiked through Dawsey. "At least take this ridiculous blanket off my head." In the pause that followed, she dared to hope he might be considering her request.

"Hand me a knife, brother."

Hope turned to choking fear when he swept close and tugged at her. He cut off most of the cover, fashioning a heavy blindfold of sorts, then moved away again.

Braver with some distance between them, she lifted her chin. "Oh please. . .can't you take it off? I can't see a thing."

"Miss, that's sort of the point. If you need food or water, we'll be happy to oblige, but we can't untie you or uncover your eyes. Don't ask again."

Her heart sank. What a horrible human being. Yet what other sort of being would seize her from her home and hold her against her will?

Though she couldn't see him, she twisted her head his direction. "Mr. McRae?"

Saying the name aloud reminded her of the yellowed slip in the cashbox—this man's name viciously ground into the paper. Remembering made her even more afraid. "May I ask why you're doing this to me?" Her heart hammered while she waited for him to answer.

After a tense silence, he cleared his throat. "What makes you call me by that name?"

"You are a McRae, aren't you? Tiller's uncle Silas, come to fetch him?"

Tiller laughed. "Nah, he ain't my uncle. He's my—"

"Hush, boy!" the stranger growled. "Come away from her. Haven't you done enough damage?"

Tiller's boots scraped against the rough boards as he scooted to the front of the wagon.

Determination surged through Dawsey. "Won't you answer my question, Mr. McRae? What are you planning to do with me?"

The harsh answer she expected didn't come. Instead, defeat laced his words. "Just lie back and rest a bit, miss. There's a long stretch of road ahead."

Exhausted, Dawsey longed to lie down, but with her hands tied, she couldn't manage by herself. She gritted her teeth. She'd sooner perish than ask for help.

"There you see, brother?" The low hiss, floating to her on the brisk night air, jolted her alert and struck fresh terror in her heart. "Whatever happens, that woman can never return to Fayetteville."

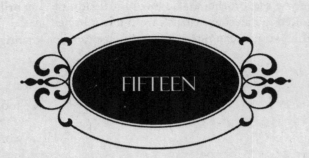

FIFTEEN

Ellie opened her eyes and blinked at the cypress slat inches from her nose. She gingerly felt her face. No bumps or soreness this time. Relieved, she stretched and rolled off the bed.

Mama claimed Ellie wrestled gators in her sleep. Waking up with scraped arms and busted lips from thrashing against the wall made her tend to agree.

When she turned thirteen, Papa announced that a budding flower needed a private space to grow. So he built her a bedroom, set off from the main house, on the last available patch of high ground. Ellie spent most of her time inside with the family, taking her meals and playing table games with the boys, but she loved her time alone to daydream. And to moon over Wyatt Carter.

She washed her face and dressed then peered outside her little bedroom door. Light flickered in the window of the big house, and smoke streamed from the chimney. Mama would soon have breakfast on the table.

Sailing off the highest step to the ground, she trudged through the mud to the cabin, pulling up short at the corner.

Wyatt himself leaned on the porch talking to Pa.

Ellie crouched behind a patch of dead weeds to watch.

Wearing no shirt or shoes, despite the cold December morning, Papa stood with his back to Ellie, rubbing his tousled head. "You're up and about early, boy."

Wyatt nodded. "Hope I didn't disturb you folks. I have business that won't keep."

Pa sniffed. "The missus has breakfast about ready." Thankfully, he slid into his dangling suspenders before he lost his droopy britches. "I'll go tell her to lay a place for you."

Wyatt had lost the smile that usually graced his downright pretty face. "Don't need food, sir. Just conversation."

Papa scratched where he shouldn't in public.

Embarrassed, Ellie squirmed.

"The boys ain't here this morning. I expect them later today."

"Mr. Silas, it's you I've come to see."

The side of Pa's jaw worked, chewing on Wyatt's words. "Son, I won't pretend I don't know why. You're here about my Ellie."

Wyatt flushed but held his gaze. "I'm keen to court her."

The hoot that surged inside exploded past Ellie's lips in an unexpected squeal. She ducked and covered her mouth, hoping they hadn't heard.

Papa had the nerve to chuckle. "Are you right sure you're the man to skin that bobcat?"

Wyatt squared his shoulders. "Reckon I am."

"You may as well know we've spoiled her putrid."

Wyatt nodded firmly. "Yes, sir."

"Ellie ain't prone to girly pursuits. She'd sooner skin a rabbit than fry one."

"I know that, too."

"She can't sew a lick."

"Don't care."

"She's a mite shiftless, too." Pa pointed over his shoulder with his thumb. "Here it is pushing seven o'clock, and she's still out there piled in bed. The girl's used to having her way."

Anger fired through Ellie. With Pa doing the peddling, she'd rot on the shelf.

Wyatt shook his head. "I don't mind bending to Ellie's whims a bit... right at first."

This brought her to her feet. *Right at first?*

Shifting around, her pa leaned beside Wyatt, staring as if taking his measure. "You might be good for my little girl, Wyatt Carter. You're bound to do a better job than her ma and me did. The little scalawag has us bound around her finger."

Wyatt grinned for the first time. "A mighty cute little finger, too."

Papa's chin shot up and he glared down his nose. "Say again?"

Hanging his head, Wyatt cleared his throat. "Sorry, sir."

Easing his harsh stare, Papa folded his arms. "Well, then, my answer is yes. You can court my Ellie." He pounded Wyatt on the back. "Now, if that's all you've got. . .my eggs are cackling for me."

In a blinding flash of teeth, Wyatt found his smile again. He watched Pa amble inside then turned to go. Catching sight of Ellie skulking beside the house, his eyes softened and his smile turned tender and sweet.

Ellie grinned and ducked her head, her cheeks ablaze. When she raised her eyes, the cocky rogue winked and gave her a jaunty wave. She wiggled her fingers—her cute little fingers—and Wyatt turned away whistling, his thumbs hooked around his suspenders. She watched until he slipped past the trees and disappeared.

Spinning on her heels, she dashed up the steps to her room. Breakfast could wait. Ellie needed time alone, to leap and twirl, to fall across her bed and moon.

She wasn't Papa's budding flower anymore. Beneath the light in Wyatt's eyes, she'd blossomed into a fully grown woman.

Hooper moaned with relief when Duncan turned down the lane toward home. He had cocked back against the seat and dozed through the last long stretch of road then paid for his folly with painful cricks in his neck.

He longed to be home yet dreaded getting there. His mind couldn't conjure the conniption they'd face when Papa laid eyes on the woman.

What he'd done seemed the only way in the black haze of night. By the light of a new day, he wasn't so sure.

They'd driven straight through, switching up drivers when needed and taking regular short breaks for Abe Lincoln. Wracked with guilt, Hooper longed to untie the girl's hands, but he didn't dare give into her pleas. Not after her last stunt.

Hog-tied and blinded, she'd thrown herself from the wagon into an overgrown field. After twenty minutes of beating the brush, they'd finally found her. Thankfully, she didn't break her neck.

The blindfold seemed to bother her most of all, but Hooper wanted no chance she'd recognize her surroundings or sort out the direction they were traveling. Ellie could chart a path by the moon and stars, but then Ellie wasn't like most girls.

Tiller hovered by her side the whole way, talking her ear off and giving her sips from the canteen and bites of jam and bread. He finally gave in to sleep, but not until his self-appointed charge drifted off.

Glancing over his shoulder at the huddled bodies, shame cut through Hooper like buckshot. He should probably fear his mama more than Pa, once she saw the poor girl in her nightdress.

Duncan pulled up to the house with Hooper still rehearsing what he'd say to them both.

Tiller sat up rubbing his eyes. "Where are we?"

Easing his aching body to the sodden ground he loved, Hooper limped to the tailgate. "You're home, little cousin."

Tiller gazed around with an ugly scowl. "I'm too tired for teasing. What is this place?"

Hooper saw the ramshackle cabin with its dirty windows, rickety porch, and waterlogged yard through Tiller's eyes and grinned. "You'll have time to get used to it. Don't worry, it's cozy inside."

Duncan hobbled to join them. With arched brows, he pointed at their reluctant visitor, her thin nightdress hugging her back so closely Hooper could count the bones of her spine. "What do we do with her?"

"We show her to Pa. He'll decide."

The door burst open behind them, and Pa blustered out with a welcoming shout. Hooper cringed. "Here he is now. Hold tight to your backside."

Duncan turned with both hands in the air. "I had nothing to do with this, Pa."

Hooper shot him a glare.

Papa's stride slowed, and his broad smile wilted. "Nothing to do with what, son?"

Mama hurried onto the porch, drying her hands on her skirt. "Welcome home, boys!"

"Not so fast with that welcome, Odie," Pa called over his shoulder. "These two have been up to something again." He pushed between them and stilled, his hand tightening on the tailgate. Murder in his eyes, he spun, his low growl chilling Hooper's blood. "There'd best be a blasted good explanation for this one."

Hearing the rage in his voice, Mama grabbed the handrail and made her way to the ground, her eyes huge cisterns of dread. "For heaven's sake Silas, what's wrong?" She scurried over to squeeze in amongst them, and a hush fell over the yard. Lifting her head, she searched Hooper's face, her unspoken question searing his heart.

"Ma, it's not what you think."

Pa slammed down the tailgate. "It don't matter what we think. Get that poor girl out of there."

With a sigh, Hooper nodded at Tiller. "Help her to sit up."

Leaping into action, he lifted the woman from behind. She sat hunched over with her chin buried in her chest, a forlorn captive in a dark blue headdress. "I won't climb down," she whispered. "Not until all of you turn your heads."

Pa handed Tiller his knife. "Cut her loose and come away from her."

Tiller freed her hands then scrambled out of the wagon.

"All right," Pa said. "Turn around, all of you."

Hooper cleared his throat. "I don't know, Pa. She's pretty slippery."

"Turn your heads!" he roared.

They spun like dancers on cue.

"Just tell us when you're ready, ma'am," Papa called over his shoulder in a far more civilized tone.

They waited.

Hooper began to fidget. "Pa?"

There wasn't a sound behind them.

Pa glanced nervously at Hooper. "You ready, miss?"

No answer.

Hooper whirled. The blue headdress lay on the ground at their feet.

"Yonder she goes!" Tiller cried, pointing.

Hooper sprinted to where she'd slipped in the mud, too weak to run far. He caught her around the waist from behind and spun her about. "See? I told you she was slippery."

As he carried her, kicking and squealing, Pa stared like a man possessed, and a strangled sob tore from Mama's throat.

Her eyes wide pools of fear, she backed away, nearly tripping on the bottom step. "Get it out of here!" she screamed. "Hooper, turn it loose. It's a changeling."

Dumbfounded, he watched his ma scramble onto the porch while he fought to keep his grasp on the squirming body in his arms.

"Let her go!" Mama shrieked. "She's a witch."

Ellie's bobbing head rounded the corner of the house, catching

Hooper's eye. She walked with a merry step, and a big smile lit her face.

Tiller turned at her footsteps, his jaw going slack. "M–Miss Wilkes?" he said to Ellie, rubbing his startled eyes. Then his head whipped around to stare at the woman in Hooper's arms. "Take me home this minute," he whined. "This place is cursed."

Moaning, Mama rushed down the steps to head off Ellie before she reached the wagon.

Dazed from all the commotion, Hooper carried the struggling woman to the wagon and plopped her down. She raised defiant eyes, and his blood drained to his feet.

The girl glaring at him with dreadful hatred was his sister, Ellie. A certainty made impossible by the fact that Ellie stood five feet away, clutched in her mama's arms.

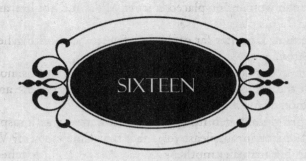

SIXTEEN

Dawsey's abductor—her bitter enemy—released her and backed away.

Circles of fire burned her wrists, and her arms tingled. The dim morning light tortured her eyes after hours swaddled in a thick wool blanket. The scraped knees she earned by jumping from the wagon stung like salted wounds. And if these indignities weren't enough, she sat on display for a half dozen strangers in nothing but a torn cotton nightdress.

Yet none of these atrocities were foremost on her mind. She was too busy memorizing every shadow, curve, and line of her captor's face.

She'd never hated another person, never wished a man dead, but with every ounce of burning fury in the pit of her stomach, she wished violent harm to this one.

Squinting through streaming eyes, she sneered and lifted her chin. "Stop gaping at me. It's your fault I look a fright."

He drew farther away, his mouth ajar.

Among the odd mix of people, shuffling feet drew her eye. A stocky man took two steps closer, his eyes bulging like a bullfrog's. "Brother? Do you see what I see?"

Her captor gulped and nodded. "She's hexing us."

Tiller shoved between them, his voice high and shrill. "Who, Miss Wilkes? She ain't hexing nobody." He wiggled his finger at a tousle-haired girl dressed in trousers and boots. "That one's the witch."

The older woman, her pale face streaked with tears, clung to the boyish girl. "Take it away from here, Silas. It's a doppelgänger. An omen of death."

The man beside her placed a steadying hand on her arm. "Now, Odie..."

"I mean it. Take her far off before she finishes casting her spell on our daughter."

He gave her a shake. "Calm down, Odell. There's no witchery afoot." He glared at the two young men. "All we have here are a couple of sons who've been where they weren't supposed to go."

The girl pulled free from the woman's desperate grasp. "Stop it, Mama. Will somebody please tell me what going on here? Who's that in the rig?" Ignoring her mother's frantic pleas, she approached Dawsey. Two feet away, she stopped cold and gasped.

Dawsey's gaze swung to the stranger's face, a mirrored reflection of her own horror.

They jumped away from each other.

Dawsey drew in her legs and crab-crawled to the front of the wagon, the words *changeling* and *doppelgänger* tearing through her mind. Scared speechless, she huddled in the corner and watched the frightening image of herself shivering in her mother's arms.

The man called Silas—Tiller's uncle?—clutched his head. "This is my fault, every last bit. Oh blast it, what have I done?"

He pulled the crying girl from her mother and held her to his chest. "I'm sorry, Puddin'. Don't be scared. That girl's no threat to you. No threat at all."

"How can you be sure, Pa?" her captor asked.

"Oh I'm sure." He took a deep breath, his nostrils flaring. "Because the truth is"—he cast a fearful glance around the circle of anxious faces—"the little gal in that wagon is Ellie's own sister."

All eyes swung to Dawsey then back to the open-mouthed girl.

The man's wife spun to face him. "What are you saying, Silas McRae?"

He squared his shoulders. "I'm saying I left no empty arms in Fayetteville, just like I promised."

The woman stared at Dawsey but directed her dire words at him. "Husband, what have you done?"

"I told you I left a sister behind."

"A sister! You never said she was Ellie's twin."

"But don't you see?" His eyes begged understanding. "That's what made it right. Why should they have two little girls and we have none?" He nodded as if to justify himself. "Take one, leave one. It's fair."

Glaring, his wife shook an accusing finger. "Now our boys have taken the other." She gathered double handfuls of her hair atop her head and pulled. "It's a curse come back to haunt us. Our just desserts for what we've done."

The stocky young man clutched the old one's sleeve, his head cocked like a befuddled hound's. "Wait a minute, Pa. Are you saying Ellie's not really our sister?"

The girl cried out and tore free of her father's arms. Sobbing pitifully, she bolted around the corner of the house.

Stricken, he reached a trembling hand. "Wait, Ellie, I can explain."

Dawsey's captor scowled. "Let her be, Pa. There's nothing you can say to her now."

The mother lifted the hem of her dress and rushed after her daughter.

Dawsey watched, no longer concerned about her own welfare. Her heart had followed the fleeing girl.

Turning, she found her adversary watching her, his eyes troubled behind fallen strands of pitch-dark hair. She scrambled for the remnant of the blue blanket and tugged it up to her chin.

Blushing, he lowered his gaze. "What do we do with her, Pa?"

"Pa" lifted dazed eyes. "Lock her in the shed then meet me around the table. There's some reckoning due—and it's judgment day."

Ellie flung her body across the bed where a lifetime ago she'd mooned over the promise of courting Wyatt. Now that childish girl didn't exist.

She gazed at the rough-hewn wall that she often wrestled in her sleep. If not the scrapes and bruises, at least the details of her struggle always faded with the dream. Never in her waking hours had she felt so battered and spent.

Mama opened the door without knocking. "Baby, it's me."

Ellie buried her head in the pillow. "Go away."

"Not until we talk."

"Don't want to."

Mama pushed her over and sat down beside her. "Then listen." Ellie's broken heart ached at the light touch on her shoulder, the cool hand of the woman who'd been "Mama" her whole life.

She eased away. "I want to know everything. Don't leave nothing out."

"Very well." Mama's answer seemed to rise from a deep well of sadness, and her weight shifted to the edge of the bed. "Lord knows, you deserve that much."

Ellie's heart sank. Where was the outrage? The shocked denial? "So it's true?"

A ragged sigh. "Yes, honey. It's true."

Her answer tossed Ellie's life in the air like a scattered deck. Breathless, she waited for the cards to fall. "So the powerful man in Fayetteville, the one who's looking for you and Pa. . .he chased you here because of me?"

"That's right."

"You let me call him a terrible man."

"I know," Mama said. "We shouldn't have done that."

She touched Ellie's arm. "Do you remember asking why I share the load for Papa's sin?"

Ellie tried to answer, but she couldn't form the word. She turned over and sat up, searching her mama's tortured eyes.

"I told you that I allowed what he did to stand." Her voice grew husky. "It's because I couldn't bear to let you go, Ellie. You filled a need in me." The barest smile touched her lips. "You were the cutest little thing. . .with your apple dumpling cheeks and tiny spit curls." Her smile deepened. "And such a good child." She tilted her head at Ellie. "You still are." She bent to dab her eyes on her skirt. "And now you know the truth." Her voice broke and she wiped her nose on her hem. "Papa and I had nothing to do with your goodness."

Ellie wanted to shake her, to cover her mouth and blot out the terrible words. Instead, her shaking fingers closed over Mama's hand, the only comfort she could manage.

Mama lifted sad eyes. "I'm so sorry, baby."

"Can you. . ." Ellie's chin dropped. "Can you tell me why?"

The mattress sagged, as if Mama's burden of guilt weighed her down. "I'll do my best to explain, but you might find it hard to understand since you've never ached for a child of your own." Pulling one knee on the bed, she scooted closer. "You see, your papa carries an uncommon passion for me, Ellie. The need to keep me happy wrestles inside him. He's toiled for nothing less since the day we met."

Ellie watched her. "You weren't happy?"

Mama looked at the floor. "I needed babies." She drew a deep, shaky breath. "Always have. As a girl, I dreamed of walls bulging with rowdy children."

"You had the two boys."

She nodded. "I wanted me a girl." A tear fell on her folded leg. "Your pa couldn't accept our plight. He blamed himself for my grief." With a trembling hand, she caressed Ellie's cheek. "I longed for a daughter, so he brought me one."

Ellie sat quietly, trying to make sense of her story. It seemed ruthless at the core. They wanted something, so they took it. Told those hurt by their actions to go hang themselves. People like her real parents, whoever they were. And the girl in the wagon. People like Ellie herself. "Is that all, then?" She didn't intend the harshness in her voice.

Mama blinked then raised her brows. "There's one other thing." She stood and held up her finger. "Wait here." Shuffling to the door, she pulled it closed behind her.

Ellie tried hard to think, worked her mind to sort out all she'd heard, but seething anger blocked her thoughts.

Returning with a somber look on her face, Mama sat down in front of Ellie with a delicate wisp of cloth in her hands.

Ellie stared at the tiny white dress. "Mine?"

Mama bit her lip and nodded.

Ellie took the soft fabric and ran her fingertips over the tiny crocheted flowers. Cross-stitched letters on the hem spelled out a name, the threads puckered and faded with time.

Sounding out the letters, she glanced up. "You're mistaken. This dress wasn't mine."

Tears welled in Mama's eyes.

Shaking her head, Ellie squinted at the stitching again. "This says D—Dilsey Elaine Wilkes." She peered into Mama's sorrowful eyes, and the truth pierced her heart.

"That's me." Her lips felt numb. "So even my name is a lie?"

Mama gripped her hands, still clutching the dress. "Of course not. We took Ellie from Elaine, your middle name."

"But my given name is Dilsey." The strange word sounded hollow in her ears.

"Yes, but we couldn't call you that. It was too risky. You understand, don't you?"

Ellie watched her.

"People were looking for you, baby. And Dilsey is so. . .unusual. We couldn't make it easier for them to find you."

"Them?" Ellie nodded. "My parents you mean."

Scowling, Mama squeezed her fingers. "Ellie McRae, Pa and me are your parents. That hasn't changed a whit."

She pulled her hands free. "So they looked for me?"

Mama cleared her throat. "Well he did, but the woman—" Her gaze flickered and she lowered her voice. "We heard the woman died before your first birthday."

Ellie crawled to the comfort of her pillow. "Please go. I've heard all I care to."

After a time, Mama's weight lifted from the bumpy mattress. Eight steps later, she closed the door behind her.

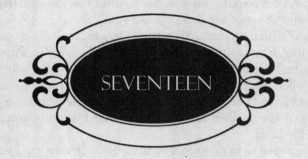

SEVENTEEN

Dawsey cowered in the dirt beneath a low shelf in the shed, too broken to care about spider webs or darting creatures. Whether due to a lumber shortage or sheer laziness, the uneven floor stopped at the row of shelves, two feet shy of the wall. Sitting on the floorboards would be warmer, but fear kept her huddled in the corner.

The cotton gown wasn't enough between her and the cold ground, so she crawled out of her den long enough to grab the folded blanket and stack of clothes they'd tossed through the door. She fumbled into the flannel shirt and tattered trousers then pulled the cover around her shoulders.

The clothing smelled of lye soap, and the old quilt felt stiff and scratchy from hanging too long on the line. Still, they comforted her greatly and warmed her frigid bones.

The shouting in the house had gone on for what seemed like hours. After one last bellow and a slammed door, all had gone silent.

Dawsey leaned her head against the wall and stared at the beam of light coming through the slats they'd nailed over the entrance. The shed had a single window, also covered in planks, lined up like the bars on a cell.

Of one thing she was certain—if they kept her too long in the confines of the tiny space, she'd go mad. For now, two spellbinding matters held her mind captive. First, she must escape and find her way home to Aunt Livvy and Father. Second—no matter how she tried, she couldn't shake the thought of it—she had a sister.

A sister!

The knowledge brought sense to her life in a rush. How could her father display baby pictures when two faces smiled from the photos? How could he keep infant things about when there had been two pairs of booties, twin hair bows, and identical dresses? Somewhere along the way, Father had decided he didn't want Dawsey to know. Most likely to shield her from the grief. What power and influence he wielded over his friends and neighbors, as well as Aunt Livvy. They'd kept his secret for nineteen years.

McRae.

The bitterly scratched name in the cashbox.

Father had known or suspected who broke in and stole her sister. He must have searched for years before giving up. No wonder his mind couldn't cope. Especially after losing his wife.

Her stomach lurched.

Aunt Livvy said Mother lost the will to live, an explanation Dawsey had never understood until now. Knowing she was sick, frail, and bereft of a child made all the pieces fit.

Such a twisted fate! Dawsey had uncovered the greatest mystery of her life, only to face a more frightening question.

Why had the kidnappers returned for her? What had they hoped to gain? Clearly, her sister knew nothing, so it wasn't for her sake. Even the older folks were surprised to see her.

Why would the two young men come to Fayetteville and drag her away to such a godforsaken place?

Approaching footsteps jolted Dawsey's heart. Had they come to do away with her?

Tears sprang to her eyes as shadows lurked outside the door. The wood planks cracked and splintered, and light burst inside the shed. Wincing, she shrank deeper into the dim cranny.

"Thou art my hiding place; thou shalt preserve me from trouble."

A figure loomed, outlined by the bright sunlight.

"Thou art my hiding place and my shield."

Pitiful cries escaped her throat. Blackness threatened as her heaving lungs struggled to keep up with her heartbeat.

Her kidnapper ducked under the low door, both palms raised. "Whoa there. We mean you no harm. Just thought you might be hungry."

The ordinary words sounded odd to her terrified mind. His slow, easy manner didn't fit her expectation of a cruel executioner. She struggled to control her fear.

From under the shelf, Dawsey watched the sinister man.

Wispy strands of black hair hung in his face, and whiskers shadowed his chin. His eyes appeared sunken in the low light, his cheeks hollow.

The crazy mother followed him inside. Her eyes were red and swollen like she'd been crying, and she wore a pinched frown as though she were in pain. Ducking her head, she stared at Dawsey as she passed.

Dawsey lifted her chin in defiance.

The woman looked startled then dropped her gaze, busying herself with balancing a laden tray on a squatty three-legged stool. After one more glance, she spun for the door in tears.

The concern in the man's eyes as he watched her go surprised Dawsey and gave her courage.

"Mr. McRae," she called from under the shelf, "you must take me home right away. My poor father has withstood enough loss at the hands of your family. There's no telling what my disappearance will do to him."

Ignoring her request, he bent to lift a cloth off a steaming bowl. "There's soup here and a slab of venison roast. Corn bread, too." He took a square and offered it to her. "With butter and wild berry jam."

Dawsey's hand snaked out and dashed the food to the floor. Frightened by what she'd done, she shrank from his reaction.

He merely sighed and pointed behind him. "Water in the canteen over there."

"I want to go home."

Crossing his arms, he gazed at something over her head. "If there's anything else you need, best tell me now. You won't see anyone for a while."

She leaned so her face would be in the light. "Please Mr. McRae, won't you please let me go?" Tears sprang to her eyes, and hope hastened her words. "There's no need to take me back to Fayetteville. If you'll just point me in the right direction, I'll make my own way. I'll—"

Spinning on his heel, he took two long strides to the door. "I'm sorry," he said over his shoulder. Without another word, he nailed the wood planks into place and then he was gone.

Dawsey moaned with frustration and withdrew as far into the

corner as the splintered wall allowed. A shiver took her body, but not from the cold. Pressing her head against her knees, her fists closed around handfuls of dirt.

The idea came like a whisper, taking form as she gouged holes in the soil. Flipping over, Dawsey ran her hands along the wall. Her probing fingers followed the boards deep into the soft ground until she found the splintered bottom. Excited, her thoughts grew bold.

The uncouth brutes had forgotten this bare patch of floor when they'd pitched her inside like rubbish. Or they underestimated her.

Dusting her hands, she darted to the tray and devoured the hot bowl of soup. Wrapping the venison to take with her, she spread jelly on a thick square of corn bread and shoved it in her mouth. She ate to fill her aching stomach, but more importantly, she ate to keep her strength up. Strength she'd need when the sun went down.

Dawsey would see Fayetteville again. She would escape these lunatics and find her way home to Aunt Livvy and Father. She would live to see his face when he learned she'd found his missing daughter at last.

Hooper's best sweet talk hadn't convinced Ellie to come to supper. Neither had Mama's tears. When he told her Pa had called an after-supper meeting to decide the fate of Miss Wilkes, Ellie said she didn't give a fig what happened. Yet there she stood on the threshold with the door banging against the wall, daring them with her eyes to say a word.

Mama said more than one, just not directly to her. "Move down, Tiller, if you don't mind. That's Ellie's seat."

Tiller scooted, staring so hard at Ellie that his skinny body slipped between the chairs and hit the floor. Blushing, he scrambled up and sat, his gaze still fixed on her.

Ellie ignored him, sitting tall as she took the platter of roast from Mama's hands and shoveled some into her dish.

Beneath the table, Hooper reached across and tapped Tiller's ankle with his boot. Tiller jerked around, and Hooper frowned and shook his head.

The boy got busy filling his plate.

Except for the scrape of forks and an occasional quiet cough, they finished the meal in silence.

Papa wiped his mouth and laid aside his napkin. "We have three matters to ponder tonight, so let's get at it."

With a rustle and scrape of chairs, the family shifted around to face him.

"First off, we haven't properly welcomed young Reddick"—at Tiller's scowl he cleared his throat—"young Tiller, I mean, to the family."

He nodded toward the boy. "I regret that you turned up in the midst of a whirlwind, but we're mighty glad to see you." Dabbing the corner of his eye with his napkin, he sniffed. "You're the spitting image of my brother, son. Did you know that?"

Tiller bit back a smile and lowered his head while all but Ellie mumbled a welcome.

Pa blew his nose then sat forward in his chair. "Next on the list, we have the question of Hooper's and Duncan's safety."

A grim look crossed his face. "Henry checked out the scoundrel who came sniffing around for Hooper. Sheriff McMillan turned a pack of no-account bounty hunters and trumped-up deputies loose in the swamps." He sneered. "The cowards are too scared to go after Henry, so they've set their sights on some of our local boys. They're all greedy and trigger-happy men, so these are perilous times in Scuffletown."

Fear shone from Mama's eyes. "How can we protect them, Silas?"

Duncan reached for her hand. "Don't fret, Ma. Nothing will come of it."

Papa frowned. "We won't be making light of this, son. Your mama's got every reason to worry." He shoved aside his plate. "We'll make no proud or stupid mistakes. Mistakes will get you boys killed."

His anxious gaze swung to Hooper. "You're both headed into the swamp to stay with Henry."

Hooper shot Duncan a startled look. "But Pa, we—"

Pa's hand shot up. "Henry swore to protect you. That's banked money in my book, and a sight more than I can promise." He banged his fist on the table. "It's settled. We'll hear no more on the subject."

The legs of Duncan's chair squalled as he jumped to his feet. "I'm not going, and you can bank on that. I won't be run out of my own house."

Hooper sprang up beside him. "Duncan's right. I say we hold our ground. We're not youngsters anymore. We can protect ourselves."

A threatening hush stilled the room. Papa stood with a loud *crack* from his bad knee. Bracing his meaty hands on the table, he leaned with an angry stare. "You'd place our womenfolk in peril before you'd abide by my wishes?" He dipped his chin for emphasis. "Because that's what it amounts to. As long as they get their reward, those dogs don't care who gets in their way."

Not so sure now, Hooper glanced toward his ma.

She leaped up and stood between her sons. "They'd best care if I get in their way, old man. I'm a McRae, too, and I can still aim a shotgun. These boys stay right here with me."

Outmatched, Pa's head drooped. "That's it then. I've done all I can." He plopped down on his chair with a weary sigh. "Sit, you reckless knotheads. We have one more pressing quandary."

Clearing his throat, he glanced at Ellie. "Puddin', you may not want to stay for this part."

Her face paled. "Why?"

"It might be best if you didn't, that's all."

Color rushed to her cheeks, washing away her pallor. "Since when am I not welcome at a McRae family meeting?"

"It's not that, honey. It's just. . .well, the matter at hand is sort of delicate."

Tears sparked her eyes, and she clutched her napkin with white-knuckled fingers. "You're going to talk about that girl, and I have a right to hear." A tear spilled from one corner and slid down her cheek. "She shows up, and all of a sudden I'm not welcome?"

Pa's jaw went slack. "Now Ellie—"

She bounced up so fast, her chair clattered to the floor. "Go on and have your *family* meeting."

Her mournful cry pained Hooper's stomach.

Mama clutched Ellie's arm, but she pulled free and bolted. Opening the door with a *crash*, she glared from the threshold, her eyes menacing slits. "Listen up, you blasted McRaes. Ellie McRae is dead and gone thanks to you, and I'll never answer to her name again. If my name is Dilsey Wilkes, then by thunder you'll call me Dilsey Wilkes."

Mama reached a trembling hand. "Now Ellie."

She shook her head so hard her hair flew out at the sides. "I'm Dilsey!" Throwing her napkin across the room, she sailed into the night without closing the door behind her.

Silence hung like pork in a smokehouse. A soft sob from Ma as she whirled to her room broke the stillness like a hammer on glass.

Pa hung his head. "Well boys, have a seat. I reckon it's down to us to decide the fate of that poor little gal in the shed."

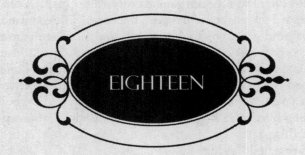

EIGHTEEN

Dawsey dreamed of little girls in white dresses. Two happy little sprites, glowing and giggly, wearing identical blue sashes and feathered hats. Knee-length pantalets peeked from beneath their hems, pulled on over black leather shoes.

The two frolicked. Skipped rope. Played chase in a green meadow. They laughed over cups of make-believe tea and ate pretend biscuits. They held hands, smiling into each other's faces, and saw their own.

She sat up gasping. Shivering. Every inch of her body ached.

With nightfall, the cold earth beneath her had turned to ice. The December chill seeped into her bruised muscles and battered joints. Moaning, teeth chattering, she rolled onto the rough plank floor.

A muffled cry came from the window over the door. The girl, Ellie, stood outside, staring through the slats.

Dawsey guessed she'd been peering inside, searching the candlelit shed for her, never expecting her to spin out of nowhere.

Their eyes met and held, and the dream returned. Dawsey sought to reconcile the blissful little twins with the pitiful wretch on the floor and the wild-eyed wraith at the door.

Then Ellie was gone.

Dawsey shook her head to clear it, thinking she must still be dreaming.

She tugged the blanket around her shoulders and prayed for strength and courage to carry her through the coming task. Comforting herself with thoughts of her warm bed in Fayetteville, she crawled under the shelf and set to work.

The topsoil came away easily until she reached the frigid, hard-packed dirt beneath. Dawsey dug until her fingernails ached from clawing.

The longing for her bed became an aching desire to see her father's face, and the thought of him grieved her to tears. She clenched her teeth and scrubbed them away with a grimy palm, which only ground stinging, gritty dirt into her eyes.

Setting her jaw, she went at her digging with renewed vigor. Tears may wet her cheeks, but no matter what happened, she wouldn't cry.

It seemed hours before she sat back on her haunches and surveyed the gap she'd made. Satisfied that it appeared large enough, she tried to wriggle through. After several grunting attempts to squeeze past the boards, she sat up with bloody scratches on her cheeks and went at the stubborn hole again.

On the second try, she slid through with no problem—no problem soap and a hot soak wouldn't cure. Greeted by a gust of cold air, she fumbled behind her and pulled the blanket through to wrap around her shoulders.

Both a blessing and a curse, the vast moon sitting atop the trees swallowed most of the sky and lit the yard as bright as daylight. She'd have to lie low at first to avoid being seen, but once she cleared the yard, the moon would light her way. She needed rest, but the urgency to flee tightened her chest. She pushed off the ground, poised to run.

"Hold up there miss." The deep, rasping growl stopped her cold.

Dawsey didn't need to spin around. She knew his dreadful voice. In a burst of strength, she shot across the soggy yard.

Splashing footsteps approached from behind, jogging her heart. "Don't make me chase you."

Shedding the blanket, Dawsey sped up.

He closed the distance.

She screamed as strong arms encircled her waist. Flailing blindly, she dug in with heels and fists.

"Be still."

"Take your hands off me."

"I can't do that."

"Oh please. Haven't you hurt me enough?"

His sigh stirred her hair. "Likely so, but right now I'm saving your life."

Helpless against his strength, she fell limp.

Leaning to retrieve the discarded blanket, he carried her to a rise and sat her on her bottom.

She scowled up at him from the ground.

Handing her the cover, he tilted his head toward the woods. "Ten steps past those trees would've landed you in a quicksand bog."

He leaned to pick up a shotgun and Dawsey stiffened.

"If you were lucky enough to miss the bog, you'd like even less what came next. Scores of critters roam the marsh at night searching for their supper."

She sneered. "I should think scores of critters feasting on my flesh would serve your purpose well, Mr. McRae."

The horrible man squatted beside her. "You'll have me looking over my shoulder for my pa. Call me Hooper."

Tiller's voice rang in her head. *Hooper! Why'd you take her?*

Sliding away from him, she snorted. "I'll do no such thing. I despise you."

He shrugged. "Suit yourself. I suppose you call all of your enemies mister."

Dawsey bit her lip and raked him with her eyes. "Have you enjoyed sitting here watching me dig for hours?" She held up bruised and blistered hands. "If you'd made your presence known, you might've saved me from this."

Before she could react, he laid down the shotgun and took her hand, studying it in the moonlight. "You need salve on this."

"Stop that!" She jerked free and scooted farther away.

He motioned with his finger. "On that cheek, too. You're bleeding."

She reached for her face but otherwise ignored him.

Hooper sat on the grass and wrapped his arms around his knees. "If it makes you feel better, I didn't sit here and watch you dig. You were worming your way under when I showed up." He grunted. "And lucky for you I did. You'd be gator bait by now."

Anger roiled in Dawsey's gut. "Suppose I believed you, which I don't, why were you skulking about?" She dipped her head at the shotgun. "And with that thing, no less?" She shot him a distasteful look. "I hardly think such measures are necessary to subdue me. As you've proven numerous times, I'm no match for your brutish strength."

The horrid Hooper reached behind him and slid the gun onto his knees. "What, this?" He had the impudence to laugh. "I assure you, this has nothing to do with corralling you." Raising his head, he scanned the distant tree line with a curious mix of sadness and determination. "Like I said, there are all sorts of critters lurking in these woods." He patted the barrel. "Old Bessie here evens the odds."

Dawsey's head throbbed worse than her cheek. She'd used up all her nastiness and scorn trying to get a rise out of him. . .to no avail. Fed up with pretense, she spun on the ground to confront him. "I have the right to know how you plan to dispose of me." She waved toward the swamp. "If not the alligators, then what?"

Hooper tilted his head. "Dispose of you?"

"I heard what you whispered to your friend. You'll never allow me to return to Fayetteville." Her eyes bulging with dread, she paused to swallow. "We both know there's only one way to stop me from finding my way home."

He nodded, watching her. "Yes ma'am, I reckon so."

Heart pounding, Dawsey tried to read his expression. When he casually leaned to pull a blade of grass and poke it in his mouth, she lost control. Leaping to her feet, she stood over him with her hands on her hips. "If you're going to kill me, I'd just as soon have it over." She pointed behind her at the shed. "It's positively cruel to lock me in there alone to await my fate."

Throwing the grass aside, he jumped up and grabbed her arms. "Wait a minute. Kill you?" He narrowed his eyes. "That's crazy talk. Nobody wants to hurt you."

She gaped at him, fighting for the strength to pull away. "But you said—"

"What I said, I spoke in haste. Pa reminded me of the same thing. There's only one way to keep you from running away, and we never once considered it."

"Then. . .what?"

His gaze flickered over her face. "Pa said when the trouble in Fayetteville dies down, me and Duncan will take you home."

His words released a flood of gratitude in her heart. A pardon granted to the condemned.

"Oh thank you. Thank you so much." Relieved tears spilled onto her cheeks, and she drew her first easy breath. "How long?"

Smiling down at her, Hooper tilted his head in thought. "A couple of months ought to do it. Four at the most."

Stunned, she backed away. "Four months?"

"It'll take at least that long for the stink to fade. Otherwise it won't be safe." He spoke calmly, as though he expected her to find his explanation remotely reasonable.

Aghast, Dawsey stared. "You can't be serious. You see, my father is quite ill. Mentally frail, I'm afraid." She took a step closer. "He'll think I'm never coming home. His poor mind won't be able to cope."

Hooper lifted his hands to his sides. "It's the best we can do."

Something inside Dawsey shattered. Rushing him, she pounded his chest.

An immovable wall, he held his ground and gripped her arms. "Whoa there. Settle down."

Her fists still clenched, she moaned. "I don't understand why you took me in the first place. What do you want with me?"

"Miss, if you'd stayed in your room last night, you wouldn't be here now."

She opened startled eyes. "If you'd stayed out of my house, I wouldn't be here."

His jaw tightened. "Believe me, it's a mistake I regret."

She lowered one brow. "If you didn't come for me, why *were* you in my house?"

He released her arms. "It's a long story that has nothing to do with you."

"If it has nothing to do with me then release me."

"I'd love to oblige you, but I can't."

"That's a ridiculous answer," she said, thrusting her chin. "My father needs me. Why won't you let me go to him?"

Looming over her face, his eyes begged understanding. "Because I love my pa, too. Turning you loose will put him in harm's way. I won't do that."

She stared vacantly. "Your father should pay his due for hurting so many people. My father is the victim here."

Anger flashed on his face. He bent to snatch the shotgun off the ground. "It's time for you to go inside. You want to squeeze under again or try the door this time?"

She eyed the gun nervously. "You're not throwing me back in that horrible shed?"

"Just for tonight."

"But it's cold." She lifted one shoulder, reluctant to beg compassion from him but too desperate to keep still. "And overrun with creeping things."

"I'll board up this hole and bring you extra blankets. The creeping things won't be a bother. They're more afraid of you." He stilled. "Except for snakes. Watch out for them. They'll crawl right into your bedroll."

Cringing, she glanced over her shoulder at the warm lights flickering inside the house. "There's no place else?"

"After Ma breaks the news to Ellie that you're taking her room, you'll sleep out there from now on."

Her breath caught. "You mean I–I'll be rooming with her?"

Hooper chuckled. "I don't see that happening. You'll have her room to yourself." He motioned with the gun. "Enough talk. Go ahead now."

Dawsey crawled beneath the wall and peeked out. "Your boards can't keep me inside, you know." She smirked. "I got out once. I can do it again."

He scowled. "If you lack the sense to fear these swamps, then fear me." He patted the gun over his shoulder. "I'll be keeping watch tonight."

Shame chafed Hooper like a woolen shirt. Each time the girl's eyes lit on his scattergun, they sparked with fear. His troubled stomach already ached from the dreadful wrong he'd dealt her. Having the frail, delicate woman afraid of him didn't hardly sit right.

Still, better that she fear him and stay put than perish in Bear Swamp's belly.

He smiled picturing her thin shoulders wiggling from under the shed but flinched recalling her battered cheek and blistered hands. She fought the ground until it yielded and almost made good her escape. How could a woman with so much pluck seem so fragile?

He picked up the hammer and nails then grabbed a sturdy cut of lumber left over from boarding up the door. Kneeling beside the hole she'd dug, he wedged the wood into the ground.

"Miss. . . ?" He struggled to remember her name. *What had Tiller called her?*

A pale face appeared at the gap. "Wilkes. Miss Dawsey Wilkes. You see, I have a name. I'm a human being, endowed by my Creator with unalienable rights. Rights you've selfishly trod asunder."

He groaned. "Just shove some of that dirt around the plank, will you?"

Gaping at him, she stilled. "You want my help to entrap me? Sir, I think not."

He couldn't see her in the daylight without thinking of Ellie. The glow cast by the full moon and her fancy words almost made him forget that she was Ellie's twin. He blew out a puff of air. "Fine. Have it your way."

He dropped to his belly to peer inside the shed.

Miss Wilkes didn't retreat.

"Move aside, please."

She set her lips and shook her head.

If Ellie acted so pigheaded, he would scoop a handful of dirt on her. With Miss Wilkes, he dare not.

She had spunk, but not the same kind as his sister. With Ellie a man got spit and sass, a knot on the head with a broomstick. He could punch her in the arm and laugh when it raised a lump. When this girl hit him, he'd clutched her arms for fear she'd hurt herself.

"Miss Wilkes, if you don't let me get at that dirt, I'll have to pry open the door."

She tilted her head. "That sounds like a fine idea."

Seething, he moved to push off the ground then froze and sprawled again. "You're going to crawl out, aren't you?"

She raised her brows.

Hooper threw down his hammer. "Blast it!"

He stretched his arm past her to scoop dirt in the hole.

She rose to her knees and hauled armloads out of his reach.

Beat at his own game, Hooper sat up and scratched his head. Maybe a handful rubbed in her hair wasn't such a bad idea.

Jerking the board loose, he stood and tossed it aside. "Miss Wilkes, come out here, please."

She peeked through the slats. "Why?"

"Just do like I said."

Disappearing again, she called in a timid voice, "Not while you're angry."

He gulped fresh air and worked to control his tone. "I'm not angry. Now come out."

Her face appeared, watchful eyes staring at him before she slithered into the open and stood up brushing her hands. "Where are you taking me?"

He gripped her arm and pulled her along beside him. "Where do you think? We'll have to tell Ellie ourselves. Her room is the only place left to put you."

With surprising strength, she jerked her arm free. "Don't touch me."

Hooper exhaled through pinched lips and nudged her with the butt of his gun. "See to it you walk a straight line, and I won't have to."

NINETEEN

Smiling through tears, Ellie covered her mouth and hunkered deeper into the brush. She didn't think anything could be funny on the most dismal night of her life, but laughter bubbled in her throat, threatening to give her away.

Not many folks got the best of Hooper McRae. Ellie was pleased she had the chance to watch.

Sobering, she gazed after them. It had been impossible to squelch the thoughts scurrying through her mind since the morning. She'd replayed her first sight of the girl countless times, though in the memory she had no features, as if Ellie's mind refused to share her likeness.

It was easy to watch her in the moonlight with her face muddled by long hair and shadows. A bit trickier facing her in the shed. Startled, Ellie had bolted. Now if only she could stay away.

Wondering where Hooper was taking her, Ellie tailed them, surprised when they stopped in front of her room. She peeked around the corner and watched.

Hooper knocked as if afraid someone might actually answer. "Ellie?" he called in hardly more than a whisper. "You in there?"

Pa rounded the main house and lumbered toward them. "What are you scalawags up to?"

Hooper spun on his heel, dragging his prisoner with him.

Pa laughed. "Didn't mean to startle you, son. I was looking for my Ellie."

He slunk toward the strange girl, his hat in his hand. "I'm sure glad Hooper found you, baby. I need to talk to you."

Hooper tucked the girl behind him. "Hold on, Pa. This ain't Ellie."

Pa looked like Hooper had dashed him with the rain barrel. He mumbled under his breath then frowned at Hooper. "What's she doing out of the shed?"

"The shed won't hold her. She dug out under the wall. If I hadn't showed up to stop her, she'd be gone."

Pa tapped his leg with the brim of his hat. "Well, I'll be..." He peered closer. "You sure are a ringer for our Ellie. Especially dressed in her clothes." He dropped the hat on his head. "What do we call you, missy?"

The girl stood with a stiff back toward Pa, her eyes cast down. Only Ellie could see her biting back tears. Setting her jaw, she turned and spoke to Pa in an uppity manner. "My name is Dawsey Elizabeth Wilkes. Miss Wilkes, to you."

"Dawsey Elizabeth," Ellie whispered to herself. The stitching on the infant gown swirled past her eyes. *And Dilsey Elaine.*

The girl—Dawsey—took a bold step forward. "Mr. McRae, you must release me. My father has suffered much over the injustice you've dealt him. I fear he won't survive another blow."

Pa pouted his lips, the first sign of irritation. "You're some kind of fancy talker, ain't you?"

She squared her shoulders. "I demand to know why you brought me here. Wasn't stealing one daughter enough for you?"

"A little sassy, too." He shook his head. "I take it back. You're nothing like my Ellie."

Ellie bolted from her hiding place. "Stop it, Papa! She's nothing like me because she ain't me." She folded her arms over her chest. "And I'm not your Ellie. I've told you what to call me."

She shot a warning glare at Hooper. "Don't take my stand for weakness. I don't care a thing about her, but she's right. You two have wronged her family, and I'm ashamed of you."

Wilting like spinach in hot fat, Papa hung his head. "Baby, I know what I done was dreadful bad. But I swear to make it right."

Ellie's stubborn head persisted in turning toward Dawsey. With each stolen glance, she met Dawsey's darting eyes.

Ellie pointed at her. "How do you reckon to make this right, Pa?"

He squirmed like a naughty youngster. "I aim to take her back to Fayetteville. Just as soon as it's safe."

One finger beside her nose, Ellie pretended to ponder his answer. "That plan just might work." Hands going to her hips, she shifted her angry gaze at him. "If her pa lives that long." She patted her chest. "What about me? How will you make *me* right again?"

A frustrated exhale puffing his checks, Papa turned to Hooper. "Put Miss Wilkes inside and guard the door. I'll help you rig a latch when I'm done talking to Ellie."

Ellie raised a threatening brow. "Paaa. . ."

"When I'm done talking to your hardheaded sister."

He clutched Ellie's arm and hauled her toward the house. Over her shoulder, her gaze locked with Dawsey's until they turned the corner.

"Where are you taking me?"

"You're coming inside with your ma and me. It's time we chewed the fat."

When he pulled her onto the porch, she caught sight of Ma through the window, hunched over the table with her head in her hands.

Ellie's heart stirred with pity.

Mama only sinned by loving Ellie too much. Who could fault her for that?

Ellie's conscience tugged. *The Wilkes family, that's who.*

As they gathered around the table, Ellie pondered the fact that the folks with the odd name were her real family. The people she called "Ma" and "Pa" were meant to be strangers. Yet the two dear faces gazing at her with loving eyes were hardly strangers. She loved them fiercely.

Her heart throbbed as Mama shyly touched her hand. "Can you ever forgive us?"

Ellie's "yes" came out on a sob. She lowered her face to her hands and cried like a foolish child.

Papa stood behind her, kneading her shoulders. "We never meant to see you hurt by what we done, Ellie." His voice quavered. "You weren't supposed to find out."

She sat up and clutched her ears. "I didn't want to know. Not ever."

Mama stretched her arms across the table and pulled Ellie's hands down. "Your pa and me, we lost sight of one thing. The Good Book says nothing's covered that won't be revealed, nothing hid that won't be known." She shook her head. "I wish we'd paid more heed."

Ellie wiped her eyes with her palms. "I just need to know why."

Mama handed her a dish towel, and she blew her nose. "I already told you why, honey." Her gaze flickered to Pa. "You see, we—"

"I'll answer for myself, Odell," Pa broke in. "This whole tangle is my doing."

He came around and sat beside Ellie at the table. "I didn't plan to take you out of your crib that night." He pointed over her head. "The girl out there had the same pluck then that she has now, sitting up in bed watching me, daring me to touch her."

His mouth softened. "But you? Well, you were another story."

Papa stared into the past and chuckled. "Laying there beside your sister, jerking and twitching in your sleep just the way you do now." He grinned. "Smiling one second, frowning the next. You were the cutest little thing."

He laid his hand over Ellie's. "I gazed at you and saw you in Mama's empty arms, as content as a fat pup. I forgot the reason I crawled in the window. Forgot the sack of loot. I even forgot the gold lantern."

Her jaw dropped. "You left the magic lamp because of me?"

Rubbing his forehead, he nodded firmly. "Given the chance, I'd do it again. I didn't have another sensible thought until I carted you in the house and eased you in Mama's arms."

Mama sighed. "And I couldn't think straight once I saw you. I touched your chubby face, and you opened your big, button eyes and smiled." She held up her hands. "And that was that."

Pa's gaze jumped from Mama to Ellie. "From that moment, we knew we'd give up everything for you. We left home, family, and common sense behind in Hope Mills and fled to Scuffletown."

Mama squeezed her hand. "And I've never regretted one loss." She lowered her head. "Until I saw we broke your heart."

Ellie slapped her palm on the table. "What you done was wrong. I need to hear you say it."

Papa hung his head. "I'm starting to see just how off the beam it was."

"It was dead wrong," Mama cried. "It's haunted us for years."

Ellie bolted from the chair and rushed to her side.

Papa hurried around to wrap them in his arms. "I know you asked us to call you Dilsey, but you'll still answer to Puddin', won't you?"

Biting her lip, Ellie nodded.

He smiled through his tears. "We'll call you whatever pleases you, Puddin'"—he sniffled—"but some things don't change. Until I draw my last ragged breath, you'll still be my Ellie."

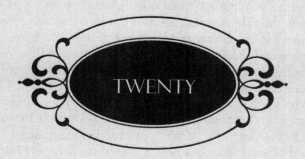

TWENTY

Dawsey curled into a tight ball of misery. By her count, it was Wednesday morning. A full week had passed since her capture. It seemed she'd spent each minute plotting her escape and praying for her father.

Every Wednesday afternoon, Aunt Livvy and her tittering cronies gathered in the parlor for a ferocious game of whist, Levi swept the fireplaces, and Winney baked bread. Dawsey pined to see Winney bustling about the stove, longed to tease her and poke holes in her dough. Her heart ached to see them all, and she wondered how they fared without her.

Ellie's bedroom was better than the shed, but not by much. A little roomier at least, with a small, corner fireplace to warm one's toes. Gazing at her surroundings in the first morning light, Dawsey decided it had less character than the drafty shed. There she at least had the possibility of escape. Here, there'd be no digging out, and Hooper had boarded up the only window.

She flopped to her back and tried to shake the oppressive cloud of despair. *"My voice shalt thou hear in the morning, O Lord; in the morning will I direct my prayer unto thee, and will look up."*

"Good morning, God," she whispered, staring past the low ceiling toward heaven. "Hear my prayer and deliver me."

Her gaze shifted to the door. Over the last week, a curious parade of kidnappers had filed into the tiny room bringing food, water, a basin for washing up, and clean clothes.

Dawsey dreaded Mrs. McRae's visits. She was a pleasant-looking woman, lovely in fact, with a kind face and soft brown eyes, but she always wore a meddling stare and usually left in tears.

Duncan, the elder brother, always came along to make sure Dawsey didn't escape. He brought with him sweet smiles and heartening words and never crossed the threshold without his mother. If he came alone, he'd rap softly on the door and wait for permission to open. Then he'd pass his offering over the doorstep and leave. At times, he lingered on the steps to chat awhile—long talks she'd come to enjoy. Duncan seemed genuinely repentant for his family's indecent behavior.

Unlike Hooper, who lacked his brother's attention to proper manners. He barely knocked before lifting the bar and bursting into the room, oblivious to her scowling irritation. Hooper had no qualms about entering without a proper chaperone and never stayed longer than necessary.

Mr. McRae hadn't shown his face, and Dawsey was glad. Neither had Tiller, and she couldn't help wondering why.

Once, Ellie came. She stood in the entrance staring into Dawsey's eyes for long seconds, neither of them blinking. When she opened her mouth to speak, no words came. Before Dawsey could stop her, she backed out of the door and barred it behind her.

At the thought of her sister, Dawsey rolled off the bed and sat on the edge of the mattress.

Her given name was Dilsey. Duncan complained about how hard it was to remember, and how angry she became when he forgot. Insisting they use her rightful name said a great deal about the girl's mindset.

Dawsey and Dilsey. How clever Mother had been.

The thought gave Dawsey pause. The pain of never knowing the one who gave her life wasn't hers to bear alone. Dilsey was a living link between Dawsey and her mother and joint heir to Dawsey's loss—whether she realized it or not.

Life had cheated them, especially Dilsey. Instead of growing up side by side, sharing laughter, love, and secrets, Dilsey had been forced to live in muddy squalor while Dawsey enjoyed the comforts of their father's house.

Dawsey slipped from her borrowed nightshirt into Mrs. McRae's housedress, embarrassed at how much ankle showed below the hem. The tiny woman's frocks were inches too short, but Dawsey preferred them to Dilsey's coarse shirts and scruffy britches.

Hooper had belly-laughed when she'd asked for one of Dilsey's dresses. Dawsey took it to mean such a thing couldn't possibly exist.

A polite rap on the door signaled a visitor. Lonely for conversation, Dawsey prayed for Duncan. She hurriedly tied the yellow sash behind her back and called the all clear.

After enduring the scrape of the heavy beam lifting from its hooks, followed by the *squeal* of rusty hinges, Duncan's wide grin was her reward. More pleased than she should be to entertain a McRae, Dawsey gave him a shy smile. "What's this you've brought me?"

His lowered the plate for her to see. "Eggs, grits, and ham. The ham is a gift from our raiding Lowrys. Ma found it on our doorstep this morning and fried a few slices. I hope you like it"—he grinned and offered the food—"just not too much. The rest she's saving to roast for lunch."

The smell of crisp ham wafted from the plate to Dawsey's eager nose. Steaming grits swam with butter and the edge of a fluffy biscuit ran yellow with busted yolk. She blushed when her stomach moaned with anticipation.

Her blush deepened when she spotted Mrs. McRae crossing the yard behind Duncan. Dawsey knew the purpose of her mission and hoped she knew to show discretion in front of her son.

She huffed up the steps puffing wispy clouds of mist into the cold morning air. "What are you about, son? I told you to wait till we got back from the outhouse."

Dawsey shrank to fit the dress. So much for discretion.

Duncan tipped his hat and backed away, turning on the bottom step and loping for the house.

Laying her breakfast aside, annoyed that it would be cold when she returned, Dawsey wrapped the musty shawl around her shoulders and followed Mrs. McRae out the door.

The first time the woman took Dawsey to the crude little building with the carved-out crescent moon, her heartbeat quickened at the prospect of escape. She'd combed the woods, charting her getaway, until her gaze landed on Hooper, perched on a distant stump.

Dawsey's heart sank seeing him there to make sure she didn't run, and she kicked herself for letting him outsmart her. She cut her eyes and gave him a sullen look.

He bent to pluck a twig from the ground, pretending not to notice.

As Mrs. McRae led her back along the path to her prison, her sister's voice rang out through the wooded hollow. Eagerly searching, Dawsey spotted her through the tangle of trees. She had joined Hooper, sprawling on the stump facing him, her back to Dawsey.

As they passed, Hooper laughed at something Dilsey said, his voice a low rumble.

Dilsey stood to ruffle his hair then bent to kiss his cheek.

Dawsey's mind jumped to the book in Father's den, the frightening account of the boy abducted by Indians. Hadn't the same fate befallen her and Dilsey? They'd been bound and carried from their homes by a ruthless and arrogant tribe—Dilsey while tiny, innocent, and too weak to resist.

Watching them, Dawsey's jealous heart squeezed her chest. It grieved her to see Dilsey teasing and caressing the savage enemies who took her.

Determination surged. The blasted McRaes had duped, hoodwinked, and swindled Dilsey out of her God-appointed destiny. Dawsey would beat them at their own game and steal her sister back.

Furthermore, she knew exactly how to do it. When Dawsey set her mind to something, she could be quite persuasive.

Fighting a smile, Hooper watched over Ellie's shoulder as Miss Wilkes passed. She hopped and dodged the mudholes with the nimble feet of a woman born in Scuffletown. As they started up the rise to the house, she stiffened and raised her chin, as if she'd settled the answer to a pressing matter.

Shrugging, Hooper allowed his attention to return to Ellie, as he should, since her words had her pixie face twisted and troubled.

"I can't say why I'm so drawn to her when I honestly wish she didn't exist."

Hooper gave her a tight smile. "I wouldn't fret over it, Ellie. It's only natural for you to be curious." Remembering, he slapped his leg. "Sorry, honey. It's hard to think of you as anything but Ellie."

She waved him off. "It's hard for me, too. Why should I expect more from all of you?"

Ellie propped her elbows on her knees and gripped both sides of her head. "The truth is I'm not Dilsey *or* Ellie." She raised teary eyes.

"I don't know who I am anymore."

Hooper scooted closer and took her hands. "What do you mean? Nothing about you has changed. You're still my little sister."

She pulled her hands free and wrapped her arms around his neck. "That's the thing, Hooper. I'm not at all. I never was."

Hooper's heart lurched when his rough-and-tumble sister laid her head on his shoulder for the first time in her life.

Ellie sniffed. "Dawsey's so different from me, and such a lady. I look at her and think, 'Is that what my life should've been?'"

Burrowing deeper in his neck, she started to cry. "Why'd you bring her here?"

His pain turned to guilt. "I wish I had it to do over, honey. Everything happened so fast that my mind was a muddle. When I heard Miss Wilkes call Tiller's name, I lost my head. I thought I was protecting Pa. I just didn't know, Ellie. I didn't know." He wrapped his arms around her and let her cry out her grief.

When she slowed to a sniffle, he set her up, wiping her tears and brushing the hair from her eyes. "I think I know what you have to do. It won't be easy, mind you, but you have to talk to Miss Wilkes. It's bound to help you sort things out." He ducked his head and caught her eye. "Might even help you find our Ellie again."

She searched his face. "Are you sure it's the right thing?"

He nodded. "I reckon I need to have a talk with her myself. It's time I followed my heart and apologized for what I've done to her." He jutted his chin at the trail. "But you first. Your time with her is more important."

Big eyed, Ellie stared. "Now?"

"Can't think of a reason to put it off. Now go."

She stood on shaky legs, staring up the trail and rubbing trembling hands on her britches.

He swatted her leg. "Have I ever steered you wrong?"

Ellie bit her lip and shook her head.

With a last desperate glance over her shoulder, she made her way up the path.

Watching her go, Hooper's hands began to sweat. Had he offered bad advice?

At best, she would come back with a clear head. If their chat turned sour, Ellie could wind up more confused than ever.

Leaning to snatch up another twig, he groaned at his own stupidity.

Dawsey was Ellie's twin, for heaven's sake. He'd heard of strong bonds forming between twins. What if his hasty advice cost them Ellie's loyalty?

Regretting his folly, he threw the twig on the ground. Worse, suppose it cost them Ellie?

TWENTY-ONE

Dawsey sat on the bed with her hands in her lap, gazing at the dismal furnishings in Dilsey's room. She wondered again how the girl slept in such dingy, meager surroundings.

The quilt on the bed was clean but tattered and gray, the single window bare of curtains. There'd been no effort to decorate the walls with photos, pictures, or plaques. The only thing adorned with the slightest woman's touch was a pretty cane basket in the corner, painted white and trimmed with lace.

Dawsey wrinkled her nose. It overflowed with muddy clothes. She laid back on the musty-smelling bed, missing her room at home, the model of feminine decor.

All at once, she longed to see Tiller's familiar freckled face. The boy was her closest link to home, the only person for miles she felt she knew. He'd been so attentive during the horrid wagon trip, so worried Dawsey would blame him. Of course, she had until Duncan told her why Tiller brought them to her window that night.

Father's ridiculous magic lamp, that golden burden and bane of her existence, had brought her untold grief for years. Now its shadow had crossed many other lives and landed Dawsey in her present dilemma.

A tapping, so light she almost missed it, set her upright. It sounded different from any knock she'd heard before. Might it actually be Tiller?

Bolting from the bed, she hurried to stand in front of the door. "Come in," she called, her heart pounding.

The bar lifted and dropped. The hinges squealed. She stepped back as the door swung toward her, and. . .

Hooper stood on the top step, his impossibly black hair slicked back, his hat in hand.

Dawsey slumped with disappointment. "What do you want?" She hoped she sounded rude enough.

On closer inspection, she realized he'd changed into a clean shirt and scrubbed his face until his nose shined. Sleep had erased the dark circles from under his eyes, and a fresh shave had lifted the sinister hollows of his cheeks into pleasing, smooth valleys.

Her once-over reached his eyes. He smiled and lifted his brows.

Embarrassed, she glanced away.

Instead of strolling in without an invitation, his usual behavior, he tilted his head and looked behind her. "Is—" He looked again. "Am I interrupting?"

Dawsey gaped at him. "What on earth might you be interrupting? A garden party? My sewing circle, perhaps?" She walked to the window, feeling foolish when there was nothing to look at but crisscrossed boards.

Behind her, the door soundly closed.

She turned and pointed. "I'll thank you to leave that open."

He glanced over his shoulder. "I'll open it. After I've had my say."

"You can talk with the door open."

"If you don't mind, I have a private matter to discuss." He frowned. "Where did Ellie go?"

She blinked. "If you mean my sister, Dilsey, I wouldn't know." Curious now, she watched him. "Why?"

Hooper stared at the floor, scratching his temple. With a shake of his dark head, he seemed to dismiss the topic of Dilsey. "Never mind. I'll find her later. Right now, I need to see you."

Dawsey crossed her arms. "I'm standing right in front of you."

Usually so frustratingly self-assured, the man seemed jittery. What mischief might he be pondering?

He motioned her toward the bed. "Sit down, would you? I need room to pace."

Aghast, Dawsey looked over her shoulder at the lumpy mattress. "I will not. It would be highly improper, especially with the door closed."

Fidgeting in the narrow space, Hooper waved his hand. "Fine, just listen."

He strode past her a few more times before he spoke. "I've been doing a lot of thinking over the past few days, and I have something to say to you." He cleared his throat. "Miss Wilkes, I've broken into houses to steal money and goods. I've ambushed men, threatening some so fiercely they fled the state. I've rebelled against sworn officials and stirred the passions of local folks to do the same."

He flicked his wrist. "I'm guilty of many things I'd rather not mention"—he whirled to face her—"but I lay down in peace each night because every deed was against a sworn enemy, to further a just and honest cause."

With two strides, he closed the distance between them. "Lately, I'm not sleeping so well. I know I've grievously wronged you, an innocent woman who didn't deserve it." He took a deep breath. "So I've come to ask your forgiveness."

Stunned, Dawsey backed up and plopped on the bed.

Hooper squatted in front of her, pleading with sincere brown eyes. "I hope you can find it in your heart to forgive me."

Ellie shouldered Pa's Winchester and kicked her way through the canebrake, eyes and ears trained for the rattlers that used the switch cane stands for cover. Eager to join Tiller and Duncan's hunt and even more eager to run from Hooper's harebrained idea, she'd left the trail and cut across the dense underbrush.

She whistled when she caught sight of Tiller's light red hair bobbing over a young grove of hickory. Duncan whistled back as she broke past the trees to the trail.

Ever mindful of Papa's warning, she scanned the edge of the clearing for lurking bounty hunters. Satisfied they were alone, she hustled to join the boys.

Duncan grinned. "I should've known you'd be on our tails. Can't keep you home once you catch wind of a hunt."

She laughed, and it warmed her insides. "Reckon not."

Tiller, who could finally look at her without frowning and scratching his head, smiled as brightly as Duncan. "Did you bring us something to eat?"

Ellie nudged him and pointed at Duncan's forty-four caliber Henry. "You've got that backwards, don't you? You two are supposed to bring me something to eat."

He chuckled but rubbed his stomach. "I sure could use a bite. I'm as hollow as a gourd."

Duncan tucked in his chin. "After the breakfast you put away?" He rested his arm around Tiller's shoulders. "Four eggs and six biscuits should last you past suppertime."

Tiller's eyes glazed over. "That sounds mighty fine. I could go for seconds." He feigned pouring from a ladle. "With another big dollop of grits."

Tightening his arm around Tiller's neck, Duncan pulled him along the trail. "Hush, boy. You'll have us turning back to the kitchen."

Ellie leaped for them, catching the backs of their shirts and pulling them into the brush. They tumbled over each other in a tangle of arms and legs, with Tiller landing hard on his bottom.

Red faced, he shoved Ellie off his lap. "Hey! What are you—"

Duncan jumped him, slamming a hand over his mouth.

Tiller stared at him with wide, frightened eyes.

Pulling his freckled face closer, Duncan frowned and shushed him with a finger pressed to his lips.

Tiller nodded, so Duncan took his hand away.

Ellie rolled to her belly and carefully parted the brush.

Duncan crawled up beside her. "Where?" he whispered.

She nodded in the direction she stared.

"Can't see them."

She elbowed him. "Just wait."

Tiller scrambled up the other side, his head bobbing to see.

Might as well wave a red flag, Ellie thought, shoving his bright head lower. She stiffened and pointed. "There."

The forelegs of three horses appeared briefly though a break in the scrub, along the back side of a far stand of trees.

Duncan followed them with the barrel of his Henry.

Tiller's thin body trembled beside Ellie as they passed out of sight. "Who were they?"

"Trouble," Duncan answered. "Looked like patrolling Guard to me." He rolled over on his back. "At least they're headed away from the house."

The rustle of wilted cane jolted Ellie's heart. She spun and raised Pa's gun.

Duncan whirled to his knees, his rifle aimed at the brush.

A familiar chuckle dropped her heart to its proper place but sped up the pounding tenfold.

Wyatt.

Somehow, in a haze of pain, she'd forgotten he existed. Hadn't years passed since he'd asked permission to court her?

That girl who twirled about her room had been a giddy child, free of heartrending calamity. Searing truth had doused her joy and ended foolish daydreams. What could she offer Wyatt Carter? He wanted Ellie McRae, not Dilsey Elaine Wilkes.

Wyatt crawled out of the canebrake grinning like a fool.

Duncan lowered his gun. "That's a good way to air out your gizzard."

Still laughing, he scuttled over the high grass and swung up beside them. "The Guard?"

Duncan nodded. "Had to be. They were riding high and proud. Bounty hunters creep about like egg-sucking dogs."

Wyatt's gaze slid to Ellie, and he smiled their secret smile.

She looked at him and felt nothing. Her heartbeat slowing to normal, she rolled over to scan the far trees.

Duncan sighed. "I suppose that marks the end of our hunt. Can't venture a half mile off the place these days without running into bad business. We'd best lay low for a spell."

Tiller sat up and crossed his legs. "Fine by me. It's bound to be lunchtime."

"We need to warn Henry," Ellie said over her shoulder.

Wyatt snorted. "It's more likely that Henry has already warned your folks. Not much happens in this swamp that he's not the first to know."

Ellie remembered the man who'd come searching for Hooper. "Not always." She pushed to her feet and brushed off her behind. "It's safe to move on now. They're gone."

Her glance flickered to Wyatt.

He watched her with a troubled frown. "You feeling all right, Ellie?"

Tiller's head jerked around. "I wouldn't call her that if I was you."

Duncan cleared his throat. "She don't go by Ellie no more, Wyatt. Best to call her Dilsey."

A frown spread over Wyatt's forehead. "Who?"

"Dil–sey," Tiller offered from the ground.

Fuming, Ellie brushed past them and started up the trail. "Don't call me nothing. How about that?"

Furious with the lot of them but not sure why, she ran ahead, feeling their eyes on her back. She reached the place where her shortcut hit the trail and ducked out of sight. Tears seared her eyes, making her madder than ever. Brushing them away with the backs of her hands, she picked up her pace.

Why hadn't she listened to Hooper? The only thing left was to see Dawsey Wilkes.

Talking to her would either heal Ellie's heart or worsen her pain, but it was a chance she'd have to take.

To go on shunning her was madness.

TWENTY-TWO

Realizing he'd dropped to one knee in front of Miss Wilkes, Hooper shot to his feet. He hadn't come to beg, after all, and he sure wasn't proposing. He had asked the pouting woman sitting on the bed to forgive him. The rest was up to her.

She sniffed delicately and cocked her head to the side. "Mr. McRae, are you serious?"

He grinned and held up his finger. "Not so polite. We're enemies, remember?"

She cleared her throat and tried again. "Hooper. . .as a rule, I'm a very tolerant person." She gazed around the room. "But in these circumstances, a mere apology will not do."

"A mere apology? You don't believe I'm sorry?"

One brow cocked scornfully, she shifted on the bed. "That I'm still trying to decide. But don't you see? No matter how sincere you are, it doesn't lessen the damage you've caused."

Hooper rested one hand on his hip. "Such as?"

Anger flashed in her eyes. "Such as my father, for one. Your coming to me spouting so much flummery won't relieve his suffering. Or lesson the threat to his health."

He squinted. "So much what?"

"Flummery," she repeated. "Flattery. Empty talk."

Hooper glared. "That's what you call my apology? Empty talk?"

Lifting her chin, she challenged him with her eyes. "Are you prepared to unbar the door? To take me home, perhaps?"

Swallowing hard, he backed off his anger. "It's not that I wouldn't like to."

"But you won't."

"I can't. Not yet, anyway."

She snorted and crossed her arms. "Flummery."

Warmth crept up Hooper's neck. He reached to loosen his collar. "You're hardly being fair. You're asking me to trade my father's safety for yours."

She drew herself up proudly. "My father is a fine Southern gentleman. A decent, law-abiding man."

Hooper seethed. "Unlike mine? Miss Wilkes, my pa makes no secret of his shameful past. He was a bandit and a scoundrel in his youth, but that was a long time ago. Now he spends his days helping our people carve out a life under the harsh rule of an unjust government. I think that more than makes up for his past crimes."

She shook her head. "You'll pardon me if I don't agree, at least concerning his most notable and heinous offense."

Hooper turned his back, struggling to control his temper. His apology wasn't going so well. He needed to find a way to start over.

Behind him, Miss Wilkes released her breath in a rush. "If you don't mind my saying, even the just and honest cause you speak of sounds like criminal behavior to me."

He spun on his heels and stared.

She leaned away from him but kept right on talking. "A moment ago, you confessed to stealing, ambushing, and rebelling against sworn officials. I've never heard of a just cause that required such reprehensible conduct."

"Then you've never been oppressed."

They glared, pecking with their eyes like a pair of rival roosters.

"Miss Wilkes, my people are Indians without a tribe, proud folks forced to live like poor men. They branded us 'free people of color' and pulled us into a war that had nothing to do with us, using us for free labor and a place to lay blame."

"Hooper, the war's over."

"Not where I live. Some days I wonder if it will ever end." A dull ache slammed Hooper's chest, and his nose flared. Shame surged through him when his eyes watered. He blinked furiously, but a tear spilled onto his cheek. "Every day a mother's son disappears in Bear

Swamp. She knows she won't see him again, unless he bobs up before the gators get him. Elderly women, left without husbands or sons to provide for them, are starving. Still, they're the lucky ones. The young girls are beaten and used." He wiped his eyes with his sleeve. "If I don't help them, who will?" He steeled his voice. "I'll die to keep Ma and Ellie from such a fate."

"I had no idea," Dawsey said, compassion softening the stubborn set of her jaw. "It appears it's my turn to apologize."

Hooper waved her off. "You don't have to say you're sorry for something you don't understand." He sighed. "Just be thankful you'll never have to." Settling his battered slouch hat on his head, he hooked his thumb. "I'll be leaving now. I've wasted enough of your time."

"You haven't."

"You were right to say mere words aren't enough. I wish I could give you what you want. Only it's out of my hands. But I do aim to prove my apology was more than empty talk."

"How will you do that?"

He shrugged. "I still need to work that part out." Saluting, he started out the door.

"Wait, please."

He paused.

"Why do you insist I call you Hooper, yet you still call me Miss Wilkes?"

Hooper nudged his hat off his forehead. "First off, you haven't given me permission to call you nothing else." He grinned. "And second, I don't consider you my enemy."

Dawsey leaned against the door, her mind whirling. Seething fury warred in her heart with a newfound respect for Hooper McRae. He deserved to suffer for what he'd put her family through, but the sight of his flooded eyes and swollen nose had touched her heart.

She'd never met a man with such passion. Of course, the only men in her life were meek and docile Levi, and a weak, useless father who'd given up on life.

Dawsey slapped her hand over her mouth, and tears filled her eyes. Shocked at her own conduct, she whispered a prayer for forgiveness. It wasn't like her to be hateful. She needed to draw closer to God in her current distress, not struggle with sins of the flesh.

Hurried feet pounded up the steps, jolting her away from the entrance. It seemed like time for lunch, so she expected Mrs. McRae and Duncan. Only why would they be running?

The door clattered open, and Tiller stood on the threshold, watching her with a hopeful expression. He held out his arms, as if he meant to block her escape. "Please don't try to run off, Miss Wilkes, else you'll land me in terrible trouble." He glanced over his shoulder. "I ain't supposed to be here."

In a rush of excitement, Dawsey tasted freedom. Tiller couldn't hold her and probably couldn't catch her, though he'd squeal like a pig when she ran. If Hooper was inside the house, she had a chance.

She took two determined steps, her heart pounding. Two more, and she reached the doorsill with Tiller's arms around her waist and the sweet smell of liberty in her nostrils.

Dilsey sailed around the corner of the house like a girl on a mission. Barreling toward them, she glanced up and nearly tripped over her feet coming to a stop. She stared at Tiller, a mixed hash of emotions on her face—surprise, irritation, and then longing—before she bolted down the trail toward the outhouse.

Tiller tightened his grip and dragged Dawsey inside. Sticking his head out for one last look, he shut the door and plastered his body against it. "What'd you go and do that for?"

Gnawing her cheek, she watched the floor.

"Promise you won't try it again?"

She nodded, and he pried his hands from the knob.

"Are you all right, Miss Wilkes? I've been so worried, I can't even eat."

Fondness pricked her heart. Smiling, she wound a lock of his hair around her finger then pushed it from his eyes. "That's awfully sweet of you."

He flashed an angelic smile.

"But you needn't fret so." She gazed around the room. "Though I'd much rather be home, they're taking good care of me."

"They feeding you and stuff?"

She smiled down at him. "Yes they are. In fact, I expect Mrs. McRae any minute with the noon meal."

His face lit up. "You'll like it, too. She cooked the best roasted ham I ever tasted." He gave a hearty nod. "Savory greens, too, seasoned with pork fat. If you drop your corn bread in to sop up the juice, it makes for some mighty fine eating." He paused to belch. "Repeats on you, though."

Dawsey narrowed her eyes.

Catching himself in his own lie, Tiller held up his hands. "Don't go giving me evil looks. I choked down enough to keep my strength up, that's all."

He burped again and glanced at the floor. "I really have been powerful worried about you."

Laughing, Dawsey pulled him close and kissed his cheek. "I'm sure you have. You were very kind to me in the wagon."

He blushed and brushed off her kiss. "If I'd known what Hooper was about to do, I swear I'd never have brought him to your house."

She patted his shoulder. "You couldn't have known, because Hooper himself didn't know." She paused, excitement building. "Can you tell me something, for my own peace of mind? How did Hooper know the lamp existed?"

"That's easy. You see, Uncle Silas—"

"Tiller McRae!" Mrs. McRae stood just inside with a tray balanced in one hand.

Duncan peered from behind her, a huge grin on his face. "Caught in the chicken coop, huh?" He swatted at Tiller as he ran past. "Git, boy!"

Tiller yelped and scurried down the steps.

Dawsey steeled her spine. The time had come to begin working her plan. As long as she acted angry and eager to escape, the McRaes would watch her too closely.

She smiled brightly at Mrs. McRae. "Thank you so much, ma'am. Whatever you have under that cloth smells divine."

A startled frown creased her brow. "W–Why, thank you, honey."

Dawsey lifted the dish towel. "Oh my, it looks even better. You're a wonderful cook, you know." She rolled her eyes. "Breakfast was delicious."

Blushing now, Mrs. McRae tittered. "I'm real glad you liked it."

"Do you keep a recipe box, Mrs. McRae? Because I'd love to riffle through it."

She waved her hand. "Please, call me Odell." Her bottom lip protruded. "There's no box, I'm afraid." She tapped her temple. "I keep my recipes right up here."

Dawsey took the tray and placed it on the bed. "What a shame. I'm quite the cook, too, if I say so myself." She hooked her arm through

Odell's and walked her toward the entrance. "Have you ever made sweet potato bread?"

Her eyes widened. "No, but I tasted some years ago in Hope Mills. It was delicious."

"You must let me teach you to make your own."

Flashing a doubtful glance at Duncan, Odell began to stammer. "W–Well, I d–don't know. Silas, he. . ."

Winking at Dawsey, Duncan slid his arm around his mother's shoulders. "I think it'll be just fine, Ma. I'll stay right there in the kitchen with you two. You know. . .just in case?"

His mother cut her eyes to him. "Are you sure?"

He nodded, his expression solemn.

Odell smiled and clasped her hands. "All right, then. I'll send for you this afternoon."

Dawsey squeezed her fingers. "Wonderful. I'm looking forward to cooking with you. I may even jot down some of your secrets."

Odell chuckled until she reached the bottom step. "That'll be just fine, honey. I'm pleased to share."

Grinning, Duncan paused on the threshold. "You're as smart as you are pretty."

He closed and latched the door, and the jolly tune he whistled as he crossed the yard made Dawsey smile. "You're fairly wise, yourself, Duncan McRae."

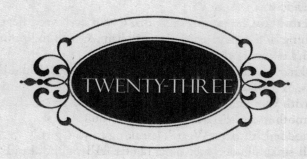

TWENTY-THREE

Ellie huffed and fumed for a quarter mile before she doubled back and started for the house.

Blast that hollow-legged Tiller for gobbling three times more grub in half the time as anyone else at the table. When he excused himself, still chewing a mouthful of corn bread, Ellie had no inkling where he aimed to go or she'd have found a way to beat him to the bedroom.

Of course, that meant getting past Mama without cleaning her plate, a next to impossible trick. If the stubborn little woman had ever taken no for an answer, Ellie would've skipped the noon meal outright. Instead, she wolfed down food she hadn't the slightest interest in eating then hurried out back to find Tiller had gotten the jump on her.

By thunder! Before the day was out, she'd find a way to talk to Dawsey without a passel of prying eyes.

She trudged into the yard with her mind settled on her favorite stump and a quiet think. Too late, she noticed Pa and Wyatt perched at the edge of the porch like roosting hens, cackling as if they'd both laid an egg.

"Here she comes," Papa hollered. He had the bothersome habit of announcing her like she was Mary, Queen of Scots.

Pretending not to hear, Ellie veered toward the shed.

"Hey, gal, scoot yourself over here," he called.

Snared. Shoulders drooping, she slumped their way.

Pa greeted her with a big smile. "Where you been, Puddin'? This is your second walk since breakfast. Before long, you'll wear out your boot leather."

Troubled by Wyatt's presence, she crossed her arms and sat tight lipped on the other side of Pa.

Hooper's horse, stretching his neck to nip at a weed near the rain barrel, stood saddled and tied to the rail. Ellie longed to know why, but she wouldn't ask since she didn't care to speak.

Wyatt leaned into sight at the corner of her eye. "Where'd you run off to so quick after vittles?"

She gritted her teeth and took a sudden interest in the bank of dark clouds forming in the distance.

Pa cleared his throat. "Wyatt's speaking to you, girl."

"Nowhere at all," she said quickly, staring straight ahead. "Just felt like a stroll."

His hazy figure seemed to fidget. "I'd sure like to take a stroll sometime."

She flicked her wrist. "It's a big swamp. What's holding you?"

Wyatt's laugh sounded strained. "I meant with you."

She felt the urge to push off the porch and run headlong into quicksand. Instead, she gripped the splintered cypress and swallowed her rising tears. Grinding holes in the dank soil with the toe of her boot, she shrugged. "I may go again someday."

Two sets of eyes bored into her so hard she felt lashes tickle her skin. If Hooper hadn't stepped out of the door, she'd be darting for the swamp.

"Where's Ma and Duncan?"

Pa peeled his stare from Ellie and lifted his chin. "Right there in the cabin, last I saw."

Hooper grabbed the rail and lowered his lanky body to the ground. Squeezing between Ellie and the post, he sat down on the porch. "Well, they're gone now."

Pa grunted. "Must've slipped out while me and Wyatt were in the barn." He pointed beyond the shed. "Might be in the chicken yard"—he grinned—"wringing and plucking for supper."

Hooper rested his arm around Ellie's shoulders and gave her a little shake. "Where've you been all morning?"

She read the gentle question in his eyes. "I've been sorting out some things."

He nodded, his lips pressed together. "Did you get them sorted?"

She smiled shyly. "I reckon so."

Wyatt, with the dunderheaded reasoning and poor timing of most men, picked that moment to scoot around in front of her, offering his hand. "Come along, Ellie. Your pa won't mind if we take a little walk." He grinned stupidly. "Ain't that right, Silas?"

Her pa—curse his wrinkled hide—flashed as many teeth and little sense as Wyatt. "You two go on and spend a little time together. Just be careful, and don't go too far."

Wyatt stuck his hand out a bit farther, their secret look shining from his sick-cow eyes.

It was the last blow Ellie's busted heart could bear.

Ellie stiffened beside Hooper, and he knew trouble would follow. Wailing, she sprang to her feet, nearly shoving Wyatt to the ground, and tore out past the shed, most likely headed for the chicken yard and Mama's comforting arms.

Wyatt spun on his heels, but Hooper clutched his arm. "Let her go."

The rattled boy pulled free. "I need to go after her, Hoop. You saw what she was like."

Hooper grabbed the back of his collar and pulled him around. "Not just yet. Ellie needs to simmer for a spell."

The worry on Wyatt's face boiled over into fury. "I want to know what's happening here."

He whirled from staring after Ellie to pin Pa and Hooper with an angry glare. "First, Duncan tells me to call her by a different name. Now she's acting like a different girl." He stomped his foot like a pouting child. "I want answers, and I want them now. What happened to my Ellie?"

Hooper watched his ears for puffs of smoke. "Wyatt, calm down."

Fire in his eyes, Wyatt's chin jutted. "I'll kill any man that hurt her."

Still seated, Pa raised his hand. "Since you'd have to start with me, let's hold off on that killing talk." He gazed at the spot where Ellie disappeared. "At any rate, the ache in my old heart may do the job for you."

Wyatt's mouth parted. "What do you mean? You hurt Ellie?"

Standing with a chorus of creaky joints, Pa patted him on the shoulder. "Let's finish my work in the barn while I tell you the whole story." He brandished a finger. "I warn you, it's a right fanciful tale."

Hooper touched his arm. "Before you go, there's something I need to say."

Pa arched his brows. "Sounds serious."

Tightening his mouth, Hooper nodded. "You're going to think so."

"What is it, son?"

After a deep breath, he took the leap. "I'm going to ride out and see Henry, ask him to send Boss with me to Fayetteville."

Pa's head shot forward, one ear toward Hooper, as if he couldn't believe what he'd heard. "You what?"

"I want to get word to Dawsey's folks that she's in one piece." He shifted his jaw. "It's the least I can do."

"Dawsey?" Wyatt took a step closer. "Is that the name Duncan told me to call Ellie?"

Pa pushed him out of the way. "No, it ain't. Stand there and be quiet while I sort out my lunatic son."

Hooper held up his hand. "I know it sounds crazy, but I have a plan. Boss Strong's as slippery as Ellie. He could get in and out faster than you can spit, and no one in Fayetteville would ever tie him to us."

Pa swung his arm, brushing the idea aside. "It's foolishness, Hooper. If you're going to take the risk anyway, load the girl in the wagon and haul her home, set her out on the edge of town and be done with her."

Hooper braced his hands on his hips. "Don't think I haven't considered it." He hooked his thumb in the direction of the shed. "It's not that simple now. We made a mess we still have to clean up. Is that the Ellie you want to live with from now on?"

Pa's eyes widened. "No, sir."

"All right then. Send me and Boss to Fayetteville."

Pa stared at the ground for a long time then shook his head. "Can't do it, Hooper. The last thing we need is a tie between Fayetteville and the Lowry gang." He raised determined eyes. "Son, if just my hide was at stake, I'd say go. If you bring a firestorm on our house, your ma and Ellie will burn with the rest of us." He spat across the yard. "It's a bad idea."

Hooper's steely gaze challenged him. "I won't be responsible for bringing harm to Dawsey's pa."

Gnawing his bottom lip, Papa studied him. "That feisty little gal cast a spell on you?"

Hooper scowled but didn't answer.

After a bit, Pa blew out his breath. "Whatever happens to Mr. Wilkes is on my head, like it's been from the start." He rested a hand on Hooper's shoulder. "Rest easy, son. None of this is your fault." His usual smile in place, he dipped his head at Hooper's horse. "Unsaddle that nag and you can help us in the barn." He turned to Wyatt. "How skilled are you at shoveling manure?"

Wyatt scrunched his face. "It don't take much thought. Why?"

Pa took his arm and herded him up the muddy path. "You can show me what you mean while I tell you my story."

Still uneasy, Hooper took the horse's reins and followed.

TWENTY-FOUR

Ellie sat with her back propped against a black gum tree, moisture from the cold ground seeping through her britches to her skin. Papa had steered her wrong. The chicken yard was empty, unless she counted clucking hens, skinny pullets, and one strutting rooster.

She wiped her nose on her sleeve but left the persistent tears to drip. She didn't remember crying so hard her whole life and couldn't seem to dry up.

When she ran toward the coop, bawling for Ma, the chickens had scattered to the four corners. Now that she'd settled to hiccups and sniffles, a curious hen ventured forward, her head bobbing as she planted one spindly leg in front of the other. She reached the fence and stood craning her long neck toward Ellie, muttering softly in bird-talk as if asking if she was all right.

Ellie smiled through her tears, thinking it downright sad that chickens didn't have a face. All eyes and beaks with no lips or cheeks, they had good reason to be mad at their Creator.

As a child, Ellie sat at Mama's feet and listened to her read the scriptures. Her favorite mentioned God's thoughts toward them of peace and an expected end.

Ellie had long since given up on the God of Mama's Bible, certain He'd turned His back on Scuffletown. Had He planned the awful thing that happened or just allowed it?

Either way, He'd hardly kept His word about an expected end, which meant her case against Him rivaled that of the chickens. The only thing left was to learn what sort of life she'd been born to live. Maybe then she could survive the one fate had handed her.

"Don't fret about me, little speckled hen." She pushed off the ground and swiped at the muddy circle on her backside. "I reckon I know what I have to do."

She hurried to the shed and peeked around the corner. No one sat on the porch, and Hooper's horse was gone. Muted laughter drifted to her from inside the barn.

Lying low, she scurried to the house and sidled along the wall to the rear. Busting past the corner, she ran toward her room. Halfway there, she slowed to a walk, the hair on her neck crawling. Near the bottom step, she came to a full stop, gaping at the open door.

With slow, cautious strides, she made her way to the threshold. Holding on to the frame, she leaned to peer inside, sure of what she'd find.

Dawsey was gone.

Spinning, Ellie hurled herself off the porch and landed with a *thump* on the uneven ground. Turning her ankle, she limped a few steps then dashed for the house. Taking no time for the front stoop, she threw her legs over the side rail and hit the door so hard with the palm of her hand, it slammed against the wall, rattling the front window. "She's gone, Ma! Dawsey got away. She—"

Three sets of eyes gawked at her. Duncan from the table where he held a knife and a knotty potato. Mama from the counter, sifting flour into a wide metal bowl. Dawsey, with a dishcloth in her hand and Mama's apron tied around her waist, blinked at her from the sink.

Ellie blinked right back. "W–What's going on here?"

Ma beamed. "Dawsey's teaching us to make sweet potato bread."

Sweet potato bread? Ellie fought the urge to rail, to storm at Duncan and rake potatoes to the floor, to dash the bowl from Mama's hands.

The only one without a simpering smile was Dawsey. She lifted an apron toward Ellie. "Would you like to help?"

"I don't cook." The witless answer fell from her mouth. Blushing, she ambled to the hearth to stir the fire. She longed to flee their staring eyes but refused to run again.

Duncan went back to peeling, Mama shook her sifter, and the kitchen sounds took up again.

Ellie sat on the stool near the fireplace, feigning interest in the flames. Hefting a split log from the box, she balanced it cut side up on the burning stack.

A wood beetle slipped from a narrow crack and scurried over the flat surface, desperate to find a way out of his fix. Wavering heat drove him from the back side, black smoke from the front. Ellie offered him the poker to escape, but it frightened him. He bailed off the edge and soared into the flames, meeting his fate with a *pop* and *sizzle*.

Look before you leap!

In a frantic effort to save himself, the bug took a death-leap off the wrong side of indecision. Ellie worried she was about to do the same, but going up in flames would be better than her frenzied dash around the truth.

She stood so fast, the legs of the stool squealed against the floor.

The three unlikely bakers stilled, watching her.

Wiping moist hands on her britches, she nodded at Dawsey. "I need to talk to you."

The girl across the room, so like her yet utterly different, nodded back. "All right."

Ellie started for the door. "Alone."

"Go on, honey," Mama said softly to Dawsey. "This batter will keep."

Ellie took the steps on stilted legs. A cool afternoon breeze blew up and chilled the beaded sweat above her lips. Turning the corner, she made her way to her bedroom with Dawsey dogging her heels.

Duncan followed at a distance, his heavy footsteps swishing in the grass.

At the entrance, Ellie stepped aside and let Dawsey go first. She motioned to Duncan. "Lock this door. Don't let anyone in or out until I say."

He nodded. The bar slid into place with a jarring clatter.

Ellie swallowed hard and turned. No sense dancing around, her feet were too tired from running. "I want to know everything. Don't leave nothing out."

In her innocence, she'd asked for the same on the night Dawsey came then stumbled under Mama's unburdening. This time she sensed the weight she'd asked to bear. Her back pressed to the door, she steeled herself and motioned to Dawsey. "Go on."

"What do you want to know?" Dawsey whispered.

Ellie tipped her chin. "What are they like? You know. . ." She bit her bottom lip. "The Wilkeses."

Dawsey flinched. She settled on the bed, arranging her skirt around her legs, and patted the quilt. "Come sit down, please."

Fists clenched, Ellie perched at the edge of the mattress, as far from Dawsey as she could get without falling off the end. Heart pounding, she waited.

"I'll tell you everything," Dawsey said. "But first. . ." She reached a trembling hand toward Ellie's face. "Do you mind?"

Ellie shook her head.

Dawsey scooted closer, a look of wonder on her face. Brushing the hair off Ellie's forehead, her roving eyes traced her features while her fingertips lightly touched her chin then smoothed her cheek. She tweaked both their noses at once and giggled.

Fighting a smile, Ellie brushed her away.

Dawsey caught her hand, measuring Ellie's palm against her own. Lacing their fingers, she closed her hand, and Ellie did, too.

Staring at their matching fists, crazy, cleansing mirth bubbled up Ellie's throat. Pulling free, she covered her mouth and howled until she wept. Without warning, the riotous tears became aching sobs that threatened to burst her heart.

Dawsey, her own wild laughter silenced, gathered Ellie in her arms and rocked her. "There's only Father, Dilsey. Our mother died. . .shortly after you disappeared."

Ellie stiffened against her shoulder. "Yes, Mama told me. Do you remember her at all?"

"Nothing. I was far too young when it happened." Dawsey set Ellie up and smoothed her hair. "Father raised me the best he could, with the help of an only sister." She smiled. "You'll like Aunt Lavinia. Aunt Livvy, I call her. She's stern but only on the surface. At heart, she's fluffy meringue."

Ellie had spent hours picturing the woman who birthed her, giving her kind eyes and a handsome face. It grieved her to think she'd never feel her touch or hear her voice. "I can't help wondering how she looked."

Dawsey hummed thoughtfully. "That much is possible. Simply look in the mirror." She laughed softly. "Or at me. Aunt Livvy says we're her image."

Trying to imagine, Ellie stared at Dawsey's face. Sudden sympathy pricked her heart. "It must've been hard growing up without her."

Dawsey nodded.

"Our father never remarried?"

Dawsey studied her freshly scrubbed nails.

Embarrassed, Ellie slid hers beneath her legs.

"I'm afraid not," Dawsey finally said. "Your disappearance, followed so closely by Mother's death, changed him, and not for the better. He grew quite distant over the years, leaving the burden of raising me to Aunt Livvy."

Ellie frowned. "Why would he do such a thing when you'd already lost your ma?"

Their eyes met. "I believe he blamed himself."

"For what?"

"For not finding you in time to strengthen and encourage Mother. She was frail and ill, but they say she lost the will to live." Dawsey sighed. "At last, I understand why."

"At last?" Stunned, Ellie watched her face. "You didn't know about me?"

Dawsey shook her head. "They hid the truth behind a shroud of secrecy. I knew something was terribly wrong but had no idea you existed."

Ellie leaned to grip her forehead. "You must despise my family. They've caused yours such dreadful heartache."

Dawsey touched her shoulder. "Don't you see, Dilsey? My family *is* your family. The same blood runs in our veins. You're a Wilkes, not a McRae. You belong with us."

Ellie slid from under Dawsey's hand and stood. "Mind your tongue. I am so a McRae."

Standing with her, Dawsey clutched her arm. "But you're not. By an act of cruel fate, Silas lifted you from our crib instead of me. A different role of the dice, and I would be living in this mudhole and you with our father in Fayetteville."

Ellie furiously shook her head. "You're wrong. Papa chose me."

Gazing fondly, Dawsey stroked her cheek. "Now that we've met, I almost wish it had been me so you'd be spared this life of hardship."

Ellie pushed her hand away. "That's what you think? That I'd trade lives with you?" She stamped her foot. "I don't live in a fine house or wear fancy clothes, but unlike you, I have two parents who love me."

Dawsey winced and fresh tears filled her eyes.

Ellie stormed to the door and pounded with her fists. "Duncan, unlock this blasted thing."

The door rattled open, and Duncan gaped at her. "You look like death. What happened?"

Ignoring him, she pushed past, stopping fast on the bottom step.

Wyatt leaned against the back of the house, a determined glint in his eyes.

Dawsey followed her out and clutched her wrist. "I didn't mean to hurt you, but whatever happens now, we're sisters, Dilsey. We have to stick together."

Moments before, Dawsey's hands exploring Ellie's face had filled her with joy. Now the grasping fingers seared her flesh.

She yearned for Ma's soothing strokes to blot out Dawsey's hateful touch, Pa's familiar yarns to dim her words. As usual, Hooper was right. A talk with Dawsey had settled her mind at last.

She squirmed free and lifted her chin. "I'm not your sister, Miss Wilkes." Her jaw set, she bounded to the ground and glared. "And don't call me Dilsey no more. I'm Ellie."

Dawsey stared after Ellie until Duncan moved in front of her, blocking her view.

He took her shoulders and gently guided her over the threshold and closed the door. "Are you all right?"

She nodded vacantly.

"What stung Ellie?"

Dawsey pressed her palm to her forehead. "I'm afraid I did. How could I have been so stupid?"

"It can't be that bad. What did you do?"

She met his laughing gaze. "I said she wasn't a McRae."

His laughter died. "That's bad. You can steal Ellie's horse, kick her dog, but don't ever say she's not a McRae."

Dawsey nodded. "I just learned that lesson firsthand." She searched his eyes. "Will she ever forgive me?"

Duncan lightly touched her arm. "Don't worry about Ellie. She'll come around as long as you don't make the same mistake twice."

She bit her tongue.

No matter how stubborn the McRae mind-set, they couldn't alter the facts, but it would do no good to argue the point with Duncan. There was wisdom in biding her time.

He glanced over his shoulder then pulled her away from the door. "There's something I'm itching to tell you."

Intrigued, she sat on the bed and felt only a brief pang of impropriety when he sat down beside her. "Goodness, what now?"

He smiled. "I had me a little talk with Wyatt just now."

She frowned. "The man outside?"

"He's Ellie's beau."

Her mind reeled at the news. "Ellie has a suitor?"

He shrugged. "Well, she did. Wyatt's still sweet on her, but she has no use for him lately."

"I see," Dawsey said. Only she didn't.

Duncan took off his hat and mangled it. "Dawsey, I'm trying to tell you something important."

She patted his hand. "I'm sorry. Go on."

He wiggled around to face her. "So Wyatt wanders up looking for Ellie, and he commences to talking. Seems Hooper came up with the idea to ride into Fayetteville, to get word to your pa that you're all right."

Remembering Hooper's promise to prove himself, Dawsey's breath caught in her throat. "He did?"

Duncan nodded. "Yes, but he let Pa throw cold water on his plans."

Her heart sank with a thud. "Then why bother telling me?"

Looking like a cat in a canary cage, he winked. "Because I'm going instead."

She gasped. "To see my father?"

He chuckled. "I won't exactly knock on his door, but I'll find a way to leave him a message. I've muddled it over in my mind, and I don't see how such a kindness could hurt."

"And your father?"

"He told Hooper not to go." He grinned. "Never said a word to me."

She sat back and stared. "You'd ride all the way to Fayetteville for my sake? Why, that would be wonderful."

Duncan dropped his hat on his head. "That's exactly what I aim to do."

She scooted closer and clutched his hands. "Oh, Duncan! Can you go before Christmas?"

He frowned. "That's a bit soon, but before the first of the year for certain." He squeezed her fingers and stood. "When you hear I've left for a couple of days, you'll know where I've gone."

Filled with gratitude, she walked him to the door. "I don't know how I'll ever repay you."

He chucked her under the chin. "No charge for my services, ma'am. Just keep it under your hat or it won't work."

Thrilled, she leaned to kiss his cheek. "You've made me so happy."

Beyond his broad shoulder, Hooper strolled across the yard, his troubled eyes fixed on them. Warming to her toes, she pulled away from Duncan and stepped inside.

Long after the door slammed shut and the bar rattled into place, she stood with a wobbly smile on her face. Tears sprang to her eyes as waves of relief flooded her shaky limbs.

Could she trust Duncan to keep his word? The very man who'd helped to kidnap her?

Something told her she could, and the bands on her heart loosened.

Father wouldn't receive the good news for Christmas, but soon after, his anxious mind would be put to rest. After that, despite Dilsey's reaction to the truth, Dawsey would find a way to take her home.

TWENTY-FIVE

Ghostly mists swirled in the faint yellow glow of the lantern, adding a touch of magic to Silas McRae's long-winded tale. Like most of his stories, the latest centered around Henry Berry Lowry, his mysterious tribe's only hope. Hero to the downtrodden Indian, scourge to the Scottish farmers scornfully dubbed "the Macks" by their sworn enemies, Henry sounded one part champion and two parts whimsical figure.

Dawsey couldn't wait to hear more.

Tightly wrapped in his own story, Silas peered closer at the spellbound listeners gathered around his chair on the front porch. "Henry's bulletproof, you know. They've wanted him dead for years and not one day closer to killing him."

Silas's fervor drew Tiller to his knees. With his hair rumpled to spikes in front and his bulging eyes aglow, he tipped so close to Silas they almost bumped noses. "You're funning us, ain't you Uncle Si? Henry Berry's just a man, after all. Flesh and blood, like the rest of us."

Silas cocked his head, his eyes gone to narrow slits. "You're sure about that, are you?"

Tiller's throat bobbed like a mole in a hole. "What are you gettin' at?"

"I'll tell you by thunder," Silas crowed. "You've heard of giants, ain't you? Like Goliath of old?"

Tiller swallowed again and nodded. "He's that fellow from the Bible."

144

Bug-eyed, Silas nodded. "I'm saying there be giants among us today, Henry Lowry the biggest one of all."

Tiller cocked his head. "Uncle Si, King David felled Goliath with a little old slingshot."

Silas slapped his leg. "Son, I'm glad you brought that up." He squinted at the sky. "The truth is, Henry is more of a giant in the way David was—able to take down his biggest foes with little more than his bare hands."

With every day that passed among the McRaes, Dawsey felt less like a captive and more like a visiting friend. Since that fateful day a week ago, when she'd mixed sweet potato bread with Odell, Dawsey spent most of her time puttering in the kitchen or huddled around the table with the family. Each evening they gathered for one of Silas's stories before Duncan walked her to the little room and locked her inside for the night.

Dilsey still danced a wide circle around her, refusing to look up or answer when Dawsey called her name.

Despite constant brooding over her sister, she had come to enjoy Duncan's company, and she blessed sweet-faced Odell for surrendering her hearth and allowing Dawsey to cook to her heart's content. Odell taught her to fry rabbits, stew venison, and roast a wild boar, foods Dawsey seldom saw back home.

Hooper sat across from her beside Duncan, silent as usual. On frequent raids with Henry, he had ducked in and out over the last few days. One day he'd be a brooding presence at the table, the next his chair sat empty.

Dawsey pretended to get along with him as well, but in the deep places of her heart, she found it hard to forgive him for taking her out of Fayetteville against her will.

Silas still avoided her eyes when they spoke. At breakfast that morning, he'd offered her the last golden biscuit with a soft smile on his face. Far from an apology, but Dawsey sensed his repentant heart. She told herself that being kind to Silas furthered her plan of escape, but the inscrutable truth was she found him hard to resist.

Returning her thoughts to the story, she leaned toward him. "How has Henry avoided capture for so long?"

Silas winked. "He's smart, missy. Bold as a bull and slick as a slug. He once dressed like a Confederate and hopped the train, shared lunch with the soldiers and listened while they told tales about the fugitive they were hunting." His eyes twinkled and he grinned. "That fugitive was Henry himself."

Dawsey laughed along with the rest of the family. "He sounds fascinating. And brave."

"Henry has to be brave with all he's up against."

"What started the uprising, Mr. McRae?"

Silas scratched his bearded chin and gazed into the past. "During the war, the Confederates started rounding up men to build Fort Fisher." His jaw tightened. "A fate that turned into a death sentence."

Dawsey's father spoke often of the effort at Fort Fisher, but he'd never mentioned forced labor. "Go on."

"After watching their brothers starve, drown, or die of the fever, our people hid out in the swamps to steer clear of the Home Guard, the devils appointed to round up the work crews. A rogue conscription officer rounded up and killed two of Henry's cousins, so Henry and his men killed the officer. They struck back by executing Henry's father and elder brother. That grave mistake began a war between Henry and the Macks that's lasted all these years."

Odell stood, dusting the back of her dress. "You've told enough stories for one night, old man. It's getting late." She hugged herself and gathered her shawl under her chin. "Besides, it's cold out here. I need to get inside by the fire and warm my feet."

Despite her striking beauty, only slightly beginning to fade, Odell McRae seemed naturally innocent and childlike, with a tender, loving heart. Swaying playfully in front of Silas in the moonlight, she looked like a teasing girl.

The effects of her spell shone from his adoring eyes, and he grinned at his timeless wife. "Are you trying to say it's time for me to hush?"

Her smile meant just for him, she shook her head. "I'm not trying to say it, I did."

Tiller spun her direction. "Not yet, Auntie. I want to hear more stories about Henry."

Silas offered his hand and Odell pulled him to his feet. "Your uncle has a dishpan to empty and a fire to bank."

Silas groaned. "Now, Odie, that's the reason I keep these boys around. It's too costly to feed them otherwise."

They all laughed merrily, except Hooper, who seemed preoccupied with his thoughts.

Dawsey yawned, hiding it with the back of her hand. She glanced at

Duncan, hoping he'd be ready to take her to her room.

Instead, Hooper jumped up and held out his arm. "I'll walk you, Dawsey, so Duncan can help Pa with those chores."

The look on Duncan's face made his displeasure clear, but Hooper gave him no chance to object. He quickly led Dawsey away from the family and around the side of the house.

Near the bottom step, he paused and cleared his throat. "Do you mind if we sit a spell before you go in? There's something I need to tell you."

Dawsey patted his arm. "Be a gentleman and let me jump ahead of you. I have something pressing to share."

He took her hand and helped her to sit. "What I have to say is important, too."

"Me first," she insisted. "It won't take long."

He smiled and dipped his head. "Go on then."

"Your father's story opened my eyes, Hooper. I'm afraid I've held a narrow view of the war. North against South—very cut and dried in my mind. I never considered the impact on those who chose to remain neutral." She raised her head and sought his eyes. "You must be honored to know Henry."

Hooper nodded, a frown teasing his brows. "Henry's a fine man, but don't be misled. He's done some ruthless things." He sighed. "Some folks call him a cold-blooded murderer."

"What do you think?"

Hooper tensed. "I don't hold with all of his deeds, but I know his heart. They pushed until he pushed back, and. . .well. . .Henry pushes hard."

She glanced at him in the moonlight, her mouth twisting. "So do you—when you think you have the right."

The foolish man preened, taking her angry words for a compliment. He jutted his chin. "None of us struck first, but my people won't accept sprawling in the dirt."

Dawsey tilted her head to study his dark eyes and hair. "Just who are your people, Hooper? With a name like McRae, I would expect your loyalties to lie with the Scots, and yet you don't resemble them in the least."

A flush darkened his face in the moonlight. "My grandpa was a Scottish immigrant. He settled here on the Lumber River and married an Indian girl." He smiled. "Grandpa never held with the ways of his people. He'd say, 'Don't mind the Mc before my name. I ain't no lousy Mack.'"

Hooper studied his hands, flicking his thumbnails together. "Sometimes I feel I'm the only McRae left to bear the weight. Pa's getting on in years, and Duncan... Let's just say Duncan doesn't share our passion."

"You don't have to bear your burdens alone, you know." The words fell unbidden from Dawsey's lips. Already out on a limb, she decided to flap her wings. "There are strong arms waiting to lift the weight off your shoulders."

He stilled. "And whose would they be?"

She held up her finger. "Wait." Closing her eyes, she strained for the words. "Oh, yes, I've got it now. 'Some trust in chariots, and some in horses: but we will remember the name of the Lord our God.'"

He folded his arms and leaned against the door. "What was that?"

"Comfort for the downtrodden."

He squinted at her.

"A scripture, Hooper."

He laughed. "I may be a backwoods heathen, Miss Wilkes, but I recognize Bible words. I meant that I don't see how scriptures can help."

"Then you haven't spent much time reading them."

He shrugged. "Not as much as you, I suppose. Ma reads to us sometimes."

"She does?"

"Well, she used to, when we were young. It's the only book she owns. In fact," he said, "I've patterned my life after two of the Psalms."

She shifted toward him on the step. "Really? I dearly love the Psalms. Please quote them for me."

He swelled his chest. " 'Defend the poor and fatherless: do justice to the afflicted and needy.'"

She clasped her hands. "One of my favorites."

" 'Deliver the poor and needy,'" he said, clearly waiting for her reaction. "Rid them out of the hand of the wicked.'"

She tightened her lips. "I fear you've taken the verses out of context, Hooper. David is calling on the Lord for deliverance. The Creator is our champion. It's His place to avenge."

She took a deep breath. " 'O God, to whom vengeance belongeth, shew thyself.'"

Hooper snorted. "It wouldn't do for God to show Himself around here unless He's a Mack. The Scots show little patience for outliers."

Dawsey tensed. "Please don't make light of spiritual matters."

A sheepish look crossed his face. "You sound like our ma."

Pouting, she straightened her skirts. "If so, your ma gives wise counsel."

Hooper grinned. "I didn't mean to offend you." His teasing mood turned solemn. "My people are penniless, hungry, and scared they'll be cast into irons. They need a real reason to hope. If God could end this war, His help would be most welcome." He lifted one shoulder. "Since He doesn't seem inclined to lend a hand, I'll do what I must to relieve them."

Dawsey huffed impatiently. "I know your desire is to render aid, but the scripture says, 'Happy is he. . .whose hope is in the Lord his God.' It doesn't say, 'Whose hope is in Hooper McRae.'"

He stood, gaping at her. "There's no talking to you about this." Spinning on his heels, he clenched his fists and stalked away.

Shame crept up Dawsey's neck. Her advice was spiritually sound and every scripture true, but she'd been harsh with Hooper, needling him on purpose. Worse, she'd thoroughly enjoyed seeing him squirm.

Watching him round the corner of the house, Dawsey wondered if she should call him back. The urge to run after him and apologize took her three steps across the yard before the truth enveloped her in a wave of excited disbelief.

She smiled at the irony. The blundering man who'd brought her to a godforsaken swamp had just unwittingly released her.

With utmost quiet and lightning in her steps, Dawsey whirled and hurried inside her room. She threw on layers of clothes then picked up a chunk of leftover bread from a plate on the bedside table, wrapping it in a white embroidered napkin. Her fingers itched to take the lantern, but she couldn't risk the light giving her away. Instead, she snatched several matches, shoving them in the pocket of Dilsey's trousers.

Pausing at the door, she stared toward the darkened house, thoughts of her sister tugging her heart. "I'll come back for you, Dilsey," she whispered. "I promise."

The shadowy outline of the shed became the needle for Dawsey's compass. The cavernous bog lurked directly in front of the loathsome building, waiting to swallow her whole. To get her bearings, she checked the position of the moon then lit out for the trees.

She knew where she was and where she was going. Forgetting to lock her in Dilsey's room wasn't Hooper's first mistake of the night. He'd let it slip that his people were Lumbee Indians, living along the Lumber River—which meant she must be near Lumberton in Robeson County.

Her heart a throbbing lump in her throat, she hunched lower and darted into the woods, kicking a tangle of thorny vines off her foot as she ran. The stand of trees broke sooner than she expected and she paused, but only briefly, before wading into ankle-deep water.

Tasting freedom, Dawsey's determination surged. It would take more than quicksand, alligators, and the Lowry gang to keep her a prisoner of Hooper McRae for another minute.

If she had to crawl from there to Fayetteville, no one could keep her from going home.

Hooper stretched out on his bedroll in front of the fire, Dawsey's offense like burning embers in his throat. For reasons he couldn't comprehend, he longed for her to understand about the injustice forced upon the Lumbee people. Stranger still, he craved her approval.

He'd explained his feelings to her the best he knew how to no avail. With a haughty air and a sassy mouth filled with Bible words, she'd taken him by the ear like a naughty child.

Turning over, he kicked his covers so hard his toes shot out and hit the woodbox with a clatter.

Across the room, Ellie sat up and stared with bleary eyes. "Hooper? What on earth?"

"Pipe down, you two," Duncan growled over his shoulder. "I'm trying to sleep."

Hooper mumbled an apology and pulled the blanket up to his chin, his mind consumed with Dawsey. The ill-mannered girl hadn't given him a chance to speak his mind, to tell her he at least tried to send word to her pa.

He wished he'd never heard about Papa's golden lamp and regretted the day he'd ever set eyes on Dawsey Wilkes. He saw only one way to rid his family of the blight he'd brought down on them. He'd have to find a way to take her home.

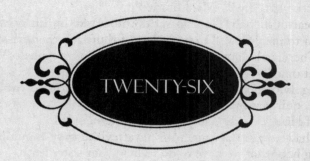

TWENTY-SIX

Hooper awoke to the bitter smell of burned bacon. Groggy and confused, he buried his nose in his quilt and tried to go back to sleep.

Papa nudged him none too gently with the toe of his boot. "Up there, boy."

"Cut it out, Pa. I'm awake." He rolled onto his side and blinked sleepy eyes toward the hearth.

Ma stood beside Ellie, guiding her hand over the skillet.

The soft murmur of their voices almost lulled him back to sleep.

"Like this, sugar. Slosh the fat real careful-like over the yolks. Make sure they're floating free before you try to turn them or you'll bust the yellow. Nothing makes a man madder than sopping a biscuit in a hard-cooked egg."

Duncan groaned and turned over on his mat. "You've got it wrong, Ma. Nothing makes me madder than burned bacon. What'd she do, turn it to embers?"

Mama angled toward Duncan with her hand on her hip. "Hush, or you'll find them on your plate while the rest of us enjoy Ellie's do-overs."

Duncan laughed and sprang to his feet, crossing to the steaming basin to slosh water on his face. Spinning, he shook his wet hands toward Tiller, asleep in the corner.

The boy yowled and sat up swinging his fists.

With a grunt, Papa returned to his place at the head of the table. "Careful with them do-overs, Ellie. Good bacon's hard to come by."

Mama swung the metal arm holding her teakettle into place over the fire. "There may be more mistakes before Ellie learns, but there won't be any wasted food, Silas. I'll eat it myself."

Ellie scowled. "I will, Ma. I burned it."

Pulling out a chair, Duncan sat down to pull on his boots. "That sounds fair to me. Just so I never have to eat the stinking mess."

Tiller sat up rubbing his eyes. "I'll eat it," he mumbled. "What are we talking about?"

Duncan ruffled his hair. "No-account bacon, boy. Can't you smell it?"

"It's not all that bad," Ellie said.

He laughed. "Worse. I know ruined when I smell it."

Ma blew a strand of hair from her eyes and gave him a blistering look. "We'll do what we have to do to help your sister learn."

"Don't worry, Ma," Hooper said. "I can get you more bacon."

Duncan laughed. "I reckon you can, straight off the hook in a Rebel smokehouse." He glanced up from folding the cuff of his shirt. "Or will you crawl into Sheriff McMillan's kitchen window and lift it from the breakfast table?"

"That's enough, Duncan," Pa growled.

Ma expertly flipped two eggs onto a plate with a biscuit and held it toward Duncan. "Set this on the table then fetch Dawsey. It's late. She must be starved."

Snatching the plate from her hand, Duncan slid it in front of Papa then hustled for the door.

Ellie's head jerked up. "She's not going to help us cook, is she?"

Ma's brows arched, but she bit back whatever she thought to say. "We're about done anyway."

Ellie shot her a satisfied smile. She shoved the spatula under one of the eggs, frowning when it came up smeared yellow.

Mama bumped her with a hip. "That can be mine, honey. I like 'em hard-cooked and stuck between slices of bread." She gave her a heartening nod. "You know, like a sandwich."

Grinning, Hooper stretched then pushed off the floor. He rolled his mat and placed it against the wall. Steeling his resolve, he glanced toward the table. "There's something we need settled first thing this morning, Pa. It's about Dawsey."

Pa's eyes widened over the top of his coffee. He finished taking a sip and lowered his mug. "Before we belly up to breakfast? You ain't even washed your face."

Hooper hitched up his pants. "This won't keep. I think it's time we took Dawsey home."

Pa frowned and leaned back in his chair. He opened his mouth to speak, but the door blasted open with a *crash*.

Hooper spun and Tiller dove under the table.

Duncan tripped over the threshold and stumbled inside gasping for breath. "Pa!" he managed before he doubled over, panting for air.

Upsetting his coffee, Papa bolted from the table and ran to his side.

Hooper and Ellie reached the rack at the same time, readying their guns. Ellie sidled to the window, carefully peering out while Hooper's gaze jumped from the door to his winded brother.

"What is it, son?" Pa shouted.

"Sh—She's gone." Duncan glanced at Ellie. "Really gone this time." He held on to his knees and took several ragged breaths before he continued. "The door's wide open. I checked everywhere—the outhouse, the chicken yard—everywhere. She's nowhere to be found."

Bewilderment wrinkled Pa's brow. "How can that be?"

Duncan straightened and pointed an accusing finger. "He didn't bolt the door."

All eyes swung to Hooper. The room spun as he wracked his mind, desperate to remember. He'd walked her back. Sat with her on the porch. They'd quarreled.

He gripped his forehead. "It's my fault. I left her standing by the steps."

Ellie drew in sharply. "What were you thinking?"

Tiller crawled from under the table, freckles jumping off his chalky face. "We have to find her."

Hugging herself, Ma stared over their heads. "That poor girl, wandering through the swamp all night." She gasped. "Oh Silas! She might've stumbled into the bog."

Rage flashed in Papa's eyes. "If anything happens to her, it's on your head, son."

Hooper nodded. "None of you could blame me more than I blame myself."

Ellie stared with glazed eyes, gripping her gun with white fingers. For the first time in her life, she seemed small and unsure of herself.

He took a step toward her. "I'm sorry, honey."

She flinched and shook her head. "Just find her."

He squeezed her shoulder. "You have my word."

Duncan snorted. "You may find pieces. She's gator bait by now."

Tiller balled his fists and scowled. "No, she ain't."

Pa punched Duncan's arm. "Hush that kind of talk, and go with your brother to search. Dawsey has eight or nine hours on you, at least."

Ellie lifted her coat off the peg. "I'm going, too."

"Me, too," Tiller said, starting for the door.

Pa pulled him up by the collar. "No, sir. You'll stay right here with us."

"Aw, Uncle Si."

"Scoot," Pa said, and Tiller slunk away to sulk at the table.

Ma caught Ellie's sleeve. "Wait just a minute." Hovering near the table, she dumped biscuits and bacon into a napkin and tied it into a bundle. "Take this. You'll be hungry later."

Pressing it into Ellie's hands, she gripped and held them. "It's enough for Dawsey, too."

Ellie took the food and spun for the door. Duncan followed her out.

Grabbing his coat, Hooper paused on the threshold. "I'm sorry, Pa."

He tipped his chin toward the woods. "Just find her, son."

"When I do, I'm taking her home where she belongs."

Pa's jaw tensed. He glanced at Tiller then lowered his voice. "Let's hope it's not in a pine box."

Dawsey dragged herself clear of the crisscrossed branches only to have an identical wall of brambles spring up in front of her face. She moaned but not aloud. The last thing she wanted was to give away her position in the brush. Not out of fear of the McRaes; she'd give her dowry to see one of their familiar faces. She hid from whatever had stalked her all night in pitch darkness, the frightening noises only lessening as the light of dawn pierced the thick canopy.

She ran her tongue over her dry, cracked lips. Water surrounded her, so murky and covered in scum she feared trying a sip, despite her burning thirst. A rumble deep in her stomach made her long for the chunk of bread she'd shoved in her pocket, but she'd lost it somehow during the night.

Fighting her way through the dense vegetation took every ounce of her strength. Desperate for sleep, she released her breath on a sigh and lay down to rest her head on her arms.

Jerking awake, she swatted a slimy, clinging lizard from her hand. The creature wriggled beneath a layer of flattened grass, his horrid tail the last part to slither out of sight. Near tears, Dawsey pushed to her scraped, stinging knees and forced her head and shoulders forward into the brush. After crawling through the woods all night, help should be just a little farther. She had to keep moving.

She prayed, straining her eyes for a glimpse of a road, a campfire, or a cabin. She stared so hard, her eyeballs stung. Reaching to wipe away her frightened tears, she stilled with a gasp.

Just ahead, a white cloth hung, snagged by a thorny branch. The blue embroidery around the edges stood out like a lighthouse beacon. Shaking her head and denying furiously under her breath, her aching heart knew the truth from ten feet away. She scrambled for the muddy napkin she'd carried with her from Dilsey's room.

The bread was gone, every crumb. Animals and insects had eaten her breakfast while she circled in the dark like a blundering fool.

She wiped her eyes and raised her trembling chin. Suddenly, her confinement didn't seem so bad. The locking bar clattering into place became the sound of security in her feverish mind.

If she knew the way to the McRaes' cabin, she'd scramble there as fast as she could and lock the door herself, but every way she turned, the same thick-trunked cypress towered overhead. The same branches hung with mossy gray beards. Most upsetting of all, the same three inches of foul-smelling water covered the ground as far as she could see.

Forcing herself to stand, she peered around, desperate to get her bearings. Across a shallow pond was a slight rise covered by a field of tall yellow cane. If she could make it to the other side without plunging into quicksand, and if the rise was dry, she'd hollow out a place in the cane to rest.

After a little sleep, she could decide what she had to do next.

For the first time, Ellie's actions felt driven by her heart instead of good sense. Reason said, "Move slowly, listen closely, read the ground for signs." Her burning heart cried, "Run! Beat the brush. Shout Dawsey's name until your throat aches."

Hooper rode alongside, his horse's easy gait a balm to Ellie's jangled nerves. Duncan had branched to the left in front of the house. She and Hooper would ride together until they passed the bog then split off, Ellie to the right and Hooper down the middle.

Feeling his gaze swing her way, she glanced up. "I'm scared, and I don't mind saying it."

He gave her a tight smile. "Dawsey's tough and ornery. If anyone can last the night in a swamp, she can."

Ellie's eyes grew round. "She's as stubborn as a deep root, but she's hardly tough. Dawsey's downright girly, Hooper. She cooks and sweeps up and darns socks." She wiggled her finger at the gloomy clutch of trees. "What could she know about lasting ten minutes out there?"

Hooper shifted toward her in the saddle. "Settle down, honey. She's not you, and that's a fact, but she's sturdier than she looks."

Ellie sighed, the sound closer to a strangled sob. "I hope you're right, because her life depends on it."

He didn't seek to reassure her. If Hooper declared Dawsey as good as dead, it couldn't have scared Ellie more than his brooding silence. Dread seeped into her gut when they reached the outer rim of the bog.

Hooper lifted and settled his hat. "I'll search in a line straight to the Lowrys' cabin. If I reach there without finding her, I'll ask for their help."

"Good." She stared past him toward the woods. "I'll take all the help we can get."

"Be careful," he said. "Watch out for McMillan and his paid assassins. They're as thick as ticks in these woods."

"If that's so, then maybe they'll find Dawsey." She caught his eye. "You be careful, too, you hear?"

He winked and gave her a crooked smile then spurred his horse up the middle of the swamp.

Ellie rode on, forcing herself to pay attention to her tracking. In the summer, she'd watch for crushed or bent blades of grass, the greening of broken twigs, or leaves flipped to their dark bellies. In the heart of winter, with no sap flowing, she'd have to scour the ground.

Hooper's bass fiddle voice throbbed in her head.

Deep toe marks in short steps means a man bears a heavy load. If widely spaced, he's running. Water in a fresh footprint stays muddy for about an hour. In time, the water seeps away, and the outline of the print fades a bit. Turned-over rocks look dark and wet with yellow green patches on the other side.

Remembering the next part, she shuddered.

Stains spilled on the leaves and underbrush may be blood—red when fresh, brown with the passage of time. Low-lying drops are usually from minor wounds. High splatter is more serious. Low or high, a lot of blood spells trouble.

Blood was the last thing Ellie wanted to find. Squinting against the thought, she shook her head. No, a lifeless body would be far worse.

She longed to give up the hunt, to whirl her horse toward home and seek the comfort of Mama's arms. Dawsey's guileless eyes, pleading for forgiveness, kept Ellie's nose to the ground, searching for signs of her sister.

The breath caught in her throat. Just ahead, streaks of mud painted the dry grass a speckled brown. Not the miry muck they saw by the house—this was the soupy, light-brown sludge near the pond. A little farther, she found a rounded, knee-sized hole pressed into a line of deer tracks left before sunrise.

Her heart thundered in her chest as the facts lined up in her head. The soupy sludge and recent knee print told her Dawsey had gone deep into the swamp then circled back. An hour ago, maybe less, she'd come within half a mile of the house. Dawsey was lost and crawling in circles.

Ellie nudged Toby's side with her boot and hurried him through the brush until she reached the edge of a shallow pond. Instead of marking the end of the trail, the widening streak of rippled water quickened her breath. Dawsey's crossing had painted a muddy arrow from one reedy bank to the other.

She rode across, her gaze locked on the other side, searching for the next sign pointing to her sister. It came far sooner than she expected.

Beyond the lapping water, a tunnel opened into a stand of bent and broken cane. She pushed Toby into a gallop and closed the distance in the space of three heartbeats. In even less time, she was on her knees peering into the shadowy den. Fear shot up her throat, and she bit back the cry that sprang to her lips.

Dawsey sat against the back of the wallow sobbing piteously, both hands clutching her leg. She had shed her boot and torn strips from the leg of her britches to tie above and below the white-rimmed, oozing bite.

Not a rattler!

Sensing her there, Dawsey's head jerked up.

"Oh Dilsey, thank God." Her sobs became a whimper, and she stretched out her hand. "Help me?"

Ellie whirled away from the cane and hurled herself on Toby's back, turning him before her backside touched the saddle. She drove him across the pond, slinging water in her wake as Dawsey's hollow cries echoed through the swamp.

TWENTY-SEVEN

Dawsey slowly counted backward from ten, drawing deep breaths between each number. She had to settle her frantic heartbeat and hold very still to keep from spreading the venom.

Her head hurt and her mouth filled with moisture, the way it did before her stomach emptied. Weakness drained her strength, and her insides trembled.

She scoured her mind for a snakebite remedy. She'd read of cutting the wound and applying salt and gunpowder, but she didn't have a knife or either ingredient. Frightened, she realized she'd already done all she could remember from her books on the healing arts.

Seeking just as hard for a psalm, she could only come up with, *"He made a pit, and digged it, and is fallen into the ditch which he made."*

What had she been thinking? Hooper warned her repeatedly with terrible stories of wandering men found dead in the swamp. With insufferable arrogance, she'd counted herself stronger and smarter than all of them. Now, her reckless determination to get home had landed her in a desperate fix.

The thought of Hooper strangely saddened her and pricked her heart a bit like a touch of homesickness. Confused, she brushed away the silly notion.

"Please, God? I'm not ready," she whispered, gazing toward heaven. She'd left too much unsaid, too much undone. If she died miles from home, Father would never know. He'd go to his grave haunted by the mysterious disappearance of both of his daughters.

Feeling quite unladylike, Dawsey leaned over and spit to rid her mouth of a foul taste. Overwhelming drowsiness jolted her with fear. Unsure if the venom caused it or simply fatigue, she refused to give in to her whirling head.

Wasn't it pointless to sit and wait for rescue? What help could she expect after Dilsey had come and gone? If her own flesh and blood had abandoned her, what hope did she have?

Her bottom lip began to quiver. She knew her thoughtless words had angered Dilsey. Still, hadn't the impossible happened? Without a second glance, her sister had ridden away and left Dawsey to die in a backwoods swamp.

Henry Berry shifted his weight to one foot and jutted his chin at the marsh. "How long?"

Hooper gnawed the inside of his cheek. "Ten hours. Maybe more."

Twisting his mouth to the side, Henry shook his head. "It don't sound good, Hooper."

"You're right, but I'd lay a wager we'll find her breathing."

Plucking a long grass straw from beside the lopsided porch, Henry placed it between his teeth. "What makes you think so? She's not a Lumbee woman."

"She's powerful strong-willed, that's why. Not in the same way as Ellie. This one's thickheaded strong. Too stubborn to let the swamp win."

Boss Strong grinned. "We'd best find her quick then and spare some hapless gator."

Henry motioned with his head.

Boss hustled to where the rest of the men slouched around a firepot in wooden chairs. He reached them, barking orders at their upturned faces.

Eager to help, they unfurled their lanky bodies and quickly found their feet.

Beside Hooper, Henry tensed. He gave a sharp whistle and raised one long arm overhead, his slender finger pointing at the woods.

Snapping to attention, Boss whirled and scanned the staggered trees. One hand on his gun, the other shading his eyes, he glanced over his shoulder. "It's Ellie."

Hooper's head whipped around. "She must've found Dawsey."

Ellie wove through the trees like a shot, ducking low branches and launching off sugarberry trunks. Skirting Boss and Henry's men, she ran full out for the porch.

Hooper caught her at the bottom step and spun her to a halt.

She struggled against him, her breath coming in panting gasps, her eyes wild with fear. "Let go. I need Rhoda."

Hooper's stomach lurched. "Dawsey's hurt?"

"Snakebite." Ellie spat the distasteful word.

"Moccasin?"

"Maybe rattler."

Hooper groaned.

Ellie's gaze jumped to Henry. "Please get Rhoda. There's not much time."

Henry reached the door in three long strides, speaking in a voice too low to hear. When he turned, Rhoda followed him out, her medicine bag in her hand.

Hooper followed Ellie to where they'd tied their mounts. They were barely in the saddle before Henry, Rhoda, and Boss rode out of the shadowy brush.

"Follow me," Ellie called and laid her heels to Toby's side.

They rode single file behind her, first Hooper and Henry, followed closely by Rhoda, then Boss, their rear guard. The riders knew the land, so they swiftly covered the distance to the pond.

The horses splashed across, parting the scum and sending snakes slithering to the bank. Hooper pulled up and dismounted then passed Ellie, already running for the hole in the canebrake. She caught up and slid into the opening beside him, a moan escaping her lips.

Dawsey lay just inside, staring up at them with glassy eyes.

"Don't move, honey," Hooper said. "We're here now."

Delirium must have settled in Dawsey's fevered mind. Hooper's stern face swirled above, promptly joined by Dilsey's, her familiar brows crowded in concern. Dawsey opened her mouth to apologize for not heeding Hooper's warning, but he and Dilsey faded to the background while two stately angels hovered into view.

The male, the most glorious being Dawsey had ever seen, leaned over to look at her, his gray blue eyes softly smiling. The sun glinted off his long black hair and graceful goatee, and his nearness stifled her shallow breath. A dark crescent scar under his left eye was the only blight on his beauty. When he summoned the other angel, his rich voice floated through Dawsey's thick haze like a pleasant song.

The woman, small and straight with a billowing halo of hair, hurried forward and knelt at Dawsey's side, touching her throbbing leg with cool hands.

Dilsey scrambled up to squat beside her head. Their eyes met, and Dilsey reached hesitant fingers to smooth her hair. The unexpected gesture pierced Dawsey's heart with unspeakable grief, and tears muddled her sight.

The beautiful woman produced a leather pouch and riffled through the contents. Pulling out packets and vials, she barked orders at the men to gather roots and wild herbs. Dawsey knew some of the plants she called for, but most of the names she'd never heard before.

They jumped to her bidding while she fashioned a splint with sticks and strips of cloth. When the healing herbs came, she crushed them and mixed them with powders from her bag. She tied the poultice to Dawsey's aching calf then bound up the splint. Finally, she duckwalked to Dawsey's side and raised her head, tipping a bitter liquid into her mouth.

Dawsey sputtered and coughed but choked it down.

When the woman stood and nodded, Dilsey moved aside and Hooper swept in and gently lifted Dawsey. He carried her from the stand of cane, cradled in his arms.

Too weak to resist, too limp to sit upright, she lay against him, her cheek pressed to his chest.

The night he'd taken her from the window returned in a rush. Hooper had been anything but gentle, roughly tossing her over his shoulder like a sack of feed then swatting her on the behind. She found it hard to believe the same man held her now, his careful hands a fond caress.

"Keep her warm," the healer said, running along behind them to the horses.

Hooper passed Dawsey to the mysterious man long enough to strip off his shirt and wrap it around her shoulders. In one quick motion, he mounted his horse and waited while the man lifted her to the saddle.

Dawsey groaned when her dangling leg shot fire past her knee.

"I know it hurts," Hooper crooned in her ear. "We have to keep the wound below your heart."

Dilsey sprang onto her horse. "I'll ride ahead and tell Ma to ready a bed."

"I'll go, too," the healer said.

Reining sharply, Hooper pulled in behind them. He rode carefully, she suspected to keep from jostling her, so before long the others passed out of sight.

They picked their way slowly through the swamp. Holding tightly around her waist, Hooper dodged low limbs and dripping moss and swatted vines out of her face. Weak and dizzy, she lurched forward, her chin grazing her chest. Hooper wrapped his long fingers around her forehead and drew her head back to nestle against his shoulder. She rested next to the searing warmth of his bare skin, feeling safe for the first time in weeks.

Floating high and free like a dandelion seed, she stretched to press her face into the hollow of his neck. Nuzzling close, she breathed the earthy smell of him and felt his thudding heart against her back. He tipped his head, and her searching lips found the corner of his mouth.

When his trembling hand came up to smooth her hair, it broke the spell. Embarrassed, she shrank away and closed her eyes.

The next time she opened them, she lay on Hooper's mat in front of the fireplace, with Odell's worried face hovering overhead. She didn't stay awake for long but drifted dreamily until she couldn't tell which parts of her blurred memories were real.

Several times the woman who had bound her leg—Dawsey heard them call her Rhoda—braced her up with one arm and trickled more of the foul-tasting tonic between her lips.

Dilsey flitted close by, and Hooper seemed never to leave her side.

Once, she awoke to the sound of hushed voices. Turning her head, she found Dilsey and Odell hovering near the sink, Duncan, Tiller, and Silas clustered around the table. The window was a dark square on the wall, and Rhoda was nowhere in sight.

Someone touched her hand, and her head lolled to the side. Hooper sat cross-legged beside her mat, his shy fingers caressing hers beneath the quilt. She gazed up at him, and his dark eyes softened, a look of surprised wonder in their depths.

Joy welled inside of her as the fog in her head chased his face into shadows. She closed her eyes, hoping her smile reached her lips in time.

TWENTY-EIGHT

Dawsey's snakebite had come to her fairly. At least the serpent played a gentleman's game and shook a warning rattle. Dawsey had quietly lifted her head and struck a blow to Hooper's heart with the barest touch of her lips.

He hadn't forgotten the harsh words she'd said to him on the night she fled. In fact, his newfound affection made her lack of sympathy all the harder to bear. But the swell of feelings he felt for her left no room in his heart for anger.

He'd just have to sway her, convince her to understand—a challenge that kept him staring at the ceiling in Ellie's room half the night, where he and Duncan would sleep until Dawsey was well again.

The day had dawned clear and dry, and now the sun shone high overhead. Hooper should've been riding a raid with Henry or tracking bounty hunters. Instead, he hunched beside Pa on the porch, working a deer hide to make it soft enough to drape around Dawsey's shoulders.

Papa sat beside him with a carving knife, whittling a cypress knee into a trinket for Ma. "These stiff old hands need greasing," he said. "I hope I get your ma's present done in time. Only three days left till Christmas."

Hooper raised his head. "Only three? It don't seem possible."

Twisting his mouth, Pa grunted. "Christmas has a way of sneaking up on a feller. I should've remembered that before I chose cypress. It's a hard wood to cut." He leaned to peer at the hide. "That's turning out real nice. Who's it for? Ellie?"

Warmth flooded Hooper's neck. "Um…no, sir. This one's for Dawsey."

Understanding flickered too quickly in Papa's eyes. "Dawsey, huh?"

Hooper nodded and went back to his work. "What do you think of her, Pa?"

Pa's hands stilled, and he stared past the shed. "A brush with death brings your true nature to the surface." He hooked his thumb toward the house. "That little gal has a pure heart."

"But she tricked us all into trusting her, and then she ran."

"She used what she could to try and get herself home." He shrugged. "Wouldn't you do the same in her place?"

Hooper gnawed his bottom lip and nodded. "I suppose so."

Blinking back tears, Papa shook off his thoughtful stare. "I don't deserve it, but both girls seem inclined to forgive an old fool his worst mistake."

Hooper sought his eyes. "You've done all you could to make it up to them."

Wincing, he stopped whittling and flexed his fingers. "It will never be enough. I often wonder if God Himself could set my sins to right."

They sat together in silence until Papa turned his head and gazed toward the barn. "I haven't seen Tiller all morning. Where'd that rascal sneak off to?"

Unease pricked Hooper's stomach. "He rode off with Nathan Carter and two of his cousins. They've taken quite a shine to Tiller."

Pa lowered one brow. "Which cousins?"

"Jason and Richard."

"Ain't those three boys a little rowdy?"

Hooper shrugged. "No worse than most, but I worry about their lust for adventure. They're not afraid to try anything, as long as there's a loose dollar or a good time to be had."

Pa nudged him. "Look yonder."

Ellie cut out of the woods holding two rabbits by their hind legs, her shotgun slung over her shoulder.

"On the outside, those girls are like two wrens on a rail," Pa said. "Under the skin they're as mismatched as you and Duncan."

Hooper studied his words. He remembered thinking the same, that Ellie and Dawsey looked just alike. Now when he gazed at Dawsey, he never thought of his sister. Ellie was indeed a perky little wren. Dawsey was more of a redbird.

Pulling Hooper from his thoughts, Papa chuckled and pointed at Duncan, creeping up behind Ellie. "Watch this."

Ellie spun, but she was too late. Duncan snatched the rabbits from her hand and ran for the porch.

Holding them aloft, he taunted her. "Thanks, Ellie. These will make a fine rabbit stew for Dawsey. She'll be grateful I'm such a good hunter." With a sinister laugh, he sailed around the house with Ellie's kill.

Her face a mottled red, she tore out after him, screeching like a hag.

The way his brother spoke of Dawsey, as if he held certain rights to her, pounded drums in Hooper's temples. It vexed him something fierce when Duncan hung around her sickbed, spouting jokes and singing foolish songs, but he'd almost forgiven him the first time Dawsey smiled.

She'd grown stronger through the night as Rhoda's drawing poultice pulled the venom from her leg. This morning, Mama warmed her three more cups of Rhoda's healing soup. Dawsey had bravely downed the last dregs before lunch, her face puckered to a point.

Too weak to sit up for long, she rested on his mat in front of the hearth.

Hooper's spine tingled with pleasure at the thought of sitting beside Dawsey, holding her delicate hand. With one tender smile, she had answered the burning question in his heart.

Rhoda said she'd been lucky. . .or blessed. By the close, shallow marks he left, the snake had been small and hadn't looked on Dawsey as a meal. Meaning only to defend himself, he left very little venom in her leg.

Hooper thanked God for sparing her life.

A whistle shrilled across the backyard. Papa whistled back and Wyatt rode out of the brush. He trotted close and dismounted. With an answering salute aimed at Pa, he sat on the bottom step.

"Ain't seen you in a while," Papa said. "What sort of courting you call that?"

Wyatt snorted. "Last time I came around, Ellie wouldn't even talk to me."

Papa cut two curling slivers of wood before he glanced up. "Ellie's been going through a baffling time, but she seems to be coming around." He nodded. "I reckon you'll find her a little more agreeable soon."

"I reckon I'd better." Wyatt's jaw clenched. "This time I won't leave until she talks to me."

Pa blew a puckered breath. "I admire your determination, son, but I'd tread more careful if I was you. You don't want to spook her again."

Leaning against the rail, Wyatt swung his feet up on the wide step and crossed his ankles. "You got any advice for me, sir? On what I should say or do?"

Pa hooked his thumbs in his suspenders. "Since you're asking, I know a thing or two that might help." He peered at Wyatt's earnest face. "First off, go easy on the mush. Sweet talk's like salt. You can add some later, if need be, but if you pour out too much, you can't sift it out again."

Big eyed, Wyatt nodded.

Pa aimed his pointer finger. "Ellie's too spirited to be led around by the nose. Keep a gentle hand on the reins if you want to break her. Before you know it, she'll be eating right out of your hand."

Two skinned and gutted rabbits slammed on the porch so hard they bounced. Wyatt leaped like he'd been stuck, and Papa shouted an indecent word.

Ellie stood behind them glaring, her hands on her hips. "I ain't no blasted workhorse."

Wyatt jumped to his feet. "Ellie—"

"I'll tell you another thing, Wyatt Carter. I happen to like a little salt."

A slow grin lit his face.

She took his arm and pulled him up beside her. "The next time you need advice on romancing a woman, you'd be wise to start with me."

They disappeared around the corner, and Pa slapped his leg. "Now, don't that take the bacon?"

Hooper stood up laughing. "Better stick to whittling, Pa, and leave courting to the young folks."

Duncan ambled around the opposite corner, smiling and rubbing his shoulder. "That's a mean little gal you raised, Pa. She nearly twisted my arm clean off." He swiped at Hooper, just to be ornery, and ducked inside the house.

Rolling the hide under one arm, Hooper leaned and gathered the rabbits. "I'll take these fine plump hares to Ma."

Leaving poor Pa still shaking his head, he opened the door to the cabin. The sound of Dawsey's feeble laughter strummed his heartstrings—until the sight of Duncan by her side twanged in his head like a busted banjo.

His brother appeared entirely too content sidled up next to Dawsey.

She glanced up at Hooper but quickly lowered her gaze.

Duncan beamed like a drunken man. "Afternoon, little brother. Come see how much better Dawsey feels." He stroked her hand. "All she needed was a good dose of my humor."

Dawsey turned the warmth of her smile on Duncan, leaving Hooper in the cold. " 'A merry heart doeth good like a medicine.' The Good Book says so."

Squeezing her fingers, Duncan gulped her down with his eyes. "See there? I told you."

Hooper's stomach curdled. He couldn't deny what he'd long suspected. Duncan was sweet on his girl.

He balled his fists. Duncan could peddle his goods elsewhere. Dawsey Wilkes made her choice when she kissed him.

"Before long, she'll need Pa to cut her a walking stick," Hooper said, despising the strain in his voice.

Dawsey's chin came up. "Nonsense. I could get up and walk right now."

Mama turned from the hearth. "You only think you can. Rhoda's rattleweed tea makes you feel you could turn cartwheels."

"Rattleweed tea?"

"Rhoda brews cohosh with elderberry wine to make a pain tonic."

Dawsey gasped and pushed up on her elbow. "Wine? You mean strong spirits?"

Ma poked out her bottom lip. "Not too strong."

Shock then fury flashed in Dawsey's eyes. "That won't do! Alcohol has never once passed my lips."

Duncan grinned. "It has now."

She sputtered like a doused fire. "Well, I'll thank you all to make sure it doesn't happen again."

"It wasn't enough to corrupt you, honey," Ma said. "Just a little to ease your pain and help you sleep."

"I don't care. I won't take another drop."

The urge to protect her surged in Hooper. He squatted beside her and lifted her chin. "It won't happen again, Dawsey. I'll make sure of it."

She gazed at him, surprise widening her big eyes. For mere seconds, something else flickered there. Tiny lines creased the smooth skin above her nose, as if her mind fought to remember something important.

Ducking her head to free her chin, she whispered a hoarse, "Thank you," then eased her head against the pillow.

Mama leaned to pull up her covers. "Go away, you two. You've tuckered her out."

"Me?" Duncan squawked like a scolded girl. "I had her laughing. You're the one who spilled the news about the liquor."

Papa cleared his throat from the doorway. "Mind your ma, son. And watch how you speak to her." He crossed the room and held out his hand.

Grumbling, Duncan allowed Pa to pull him off the floor and herd him to the table.

Hooper squatted near the hearth and placed another log on Dawsey's fire. He could handle not talking to her for a spell, as long as he could stay close—and especially if it meant Duncan would leave her be.

TWENTY-NINE

Drowsiness hovered, but Dawsey fought sleep. Before she allowed herself to rest, she had to sort out her muddled thoughts.

Uncertainty plagued her about Hooper. One man had stalked away from her after their spat; a completely different man had taken his place.

Gazing into her eyes and caressing her chin were not Hooper's usual behavior.

A compelling force drew Dawsey, pulling her thoughts, her eyes, her longing heart to him, in a way it hadn't before he'd rescued her in the cane.

She'd found his coal tar eyes and laughing mouth attractive from the beginning. But he was her captor! Entertaining silly notions about him was unthinkable.

Until now.

Dawsey didn't need to look past her feet to the hearth. Every nerve in her body felt him stooping there. She didn't need to peek beneath her lashes to know he watched her. His longing looks burned her flesh.

What had the rattlesnake done to them? Was there a primitive charm in the venom? An irresistible potion they were powerless against?

The sputtering fire pulled his attention.

Breathless, Dawsey studied his face, her eager eyes tracing his handsome nose, the strong line of his jaw—until pretend sleep turned the trick on her and she began to drift off.

Powerless to resist him? She smiled dreamily. *So be it.*

Stirring, she warmed with shame at her scandalous thoughts. No matter what, she'd stand firm against Hooper McRae, her reckless abductor. He'd kidnapped her body and invaded her mind, but he wouldn't win her heart, no matter how he tried.

More importantly, she'd never let him know how close he came.

A brisk wind rattled the bare limbs overhead, the haunting clatter like sparring antlers.

The breeze, mild for three days shy of Christmas, lifted and stirred Ellie's hair, tickling her cheeks with long strands. She gripped her knees and leaned forward on the stump. "You're going to marry me, Wyatt Carter."

Grinning, Wyatt scooted to the edge of his seat. "You have it backwards, don't you, gal? It's my job to ask that question."

Ellie cocked her head and pretended not to hear. "Yes, sir. You'll marry me and be my chocolate buckeye kiss."

Wyatt laughed and grabbed her hands. "If that means I'll be your sweetie, it's fine by me." His eyes twinkled. "I'd sure like to have a kiss before you reel me in."

She tilted her chin. "Pa would knot your skull for such talk"—she smiled and batted her lashes like she'd seen Mama do—"but I don't mind."

His fingers crawled up and gripped her wrists. Pulling her toward him, he closed his eyes. They met in the middle of the two stumps, suspended on bended knees. His face closed in and Ellie retreated an inch then swooned to meet his puckered lips.

The jangling branches overhead swept her up in a quick-rising cyclone. Wyatt's gentle kiss was the only steady point in the world spinning about her. Her trembling legs weakened, so she tried to sit, missing the stump by a foot.

Wyatt caught her in time and eased her to the weathered seat, his laughing mouth releasing her too soon. Chuckling, he held her face between his hands. "You almost sat in the mud."

She grinned. "If you ever drop me in the mud, you're going in with me." They laughed together with only inches of space between them.

He kissed her nose. "It was just the way I dreamed it."

A picture came of Wyatt sprawled across his bed, mooning over her. "You dream about us, too?"

He nodded soberly. "Every night."

She reached for his hands. "Tell me what you see."

He blushed. "You mean when it's not about kissing?"

Giggling like a girl in pantalets, she nodded.

Wyatt backed up to his stump. "I see us sitting at opposite ends of the table, with a whole slew of little Carters lined up between us."

She gaped. "A slew?"

"At least."

She lifted one finger. "All boys then. I don't know enough things to teach a girl."

His eyes softened, and he stood to smooth her hair. "Don't fret, honey. Your ma can teach our daughters. Mine will pitch in, too."

She narrowed her eyes. "Only if they want to learn."

"That's right, sugar." He pulled her head to his chest. "Only if they want to."

The sound of sloshing feet sprang them apart with the force of a trap.

Nathan, Wyatt's brother, and their cousins, Jason and Richard, stood ten feet away with rifles slung over their shoulders.

"Look here! We caught them spooning. Kiss her again, Wyatt, so we can watch."

Fisting his hands, Wyatt spun toward Nathan.

Ellie caught his arm and held on.

"Nate, that's enough." Jason scowled and shoved Nathan in the chest.

Tiller crept out of the brush, his face darting between a grin and a grimace.

Ellie motioned him over, and the scowl won out.

He sauntered toward them, his thumbs hooked in his suspenders.

Ellie rose to meet him. "Why are you slipping up on people?"

His face flushed crimson. "We didn't go to slip up. I swear."

She swatted his arm. "Do it again, and you'll answer to me." She glared at the others. "That goes for the lot of you."

They mumbled and shuffled their feet.

"Where have you been all morning?" she asked Tiller.

"Nowhere special. Hunting with the boys."

Glancing around, she raised her brows. "Didn't bag much, I see."

More muttering and uneasy glances.

Gnawing her bottom lip, Ellie studied each guilty face. She shot Wyatt a glance.

His clear blue eyes studied the boys, settling on his brother. "Nathan, if Henry catches you boys stealing to line your pockets, he'll grind every nickel out of your hides."

Nathan glared. "Who told you?"

"No one had to," Wyatt said. "You're that bad at hiding the truth."

Ellie spun on Tiller. "If Pa hears you're taking needless risks, he'll run you clear out of Scuffletown. Do you want to go back to your ma?"

His mouth fanned like a fish's gills. The fear on his face said more than his silence.

Nathan's mouth twisted, and his eyes flashed in defiance. "You're starting to sound like an old woman, Ellie." His gaze jumped to Wyatt. "In fact, so are you."

Wyatt swooped on him and took him by the scruff. "Let's go see Pa. Maybe his strap will convince you to change your thinking."

With the memory of Wyatt's first kiss still fresh on her lips, Ellie watched him cross the yard and disappear into the brush. He didn't even say good-bye.

Angry with the boys, feeling scorned by Wyatt, she stood over Tiller and planted her finger between his eyes. "What about you? Do you care to explain your shenanigans to Pa?"

Tiller's eyes rounded to full moons. He shrank onto the stool, shaking his head.

Ellie poked him hard on the forehead and he yowled.

"See to it that you mind your steps, so he'll never have to know."

He gulped and nodded.

Grumbling, Ellie spun on her heel and stalked toward the house.

"You ain't near as nice as Miss Wilkes," Tiller called in a sullen voice.

"No, I ain't," she flung over her shoulder. "A fact you'll do well to remember."

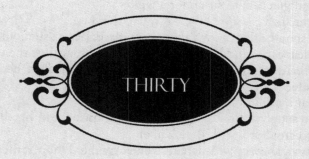

THIRTY

Dawsey flipped to her back in her four-poster bed, pulling the soft quilt under her chin. She blinked sleepily, stretching her toes toward the crackling warmth. She must ask Aunt Livvy to praise Levi for his diligence. He'd banked a hearty fire in her room that had burned through the night.

Rustling skirts meant Winney or Aunt Livvy had come to wake her for breakfast. Dazed by sleep, she peered up at the dim figure hovering over her bed.

"You awake, sugar?"

Dawsey's heart jolted, startled by a voice she couldn't place. She squinted and rubbed her eyes. Bright delusions of fresh bedding, sunny windows, and frilly curtains darkened into a lumpy mat on a plank floor in a dim, cluttered cabin. Her peace and contentment swept up the chimney with the dancing blaze.

"It's suppertime, honey," Odell said. "You've slept the day away."

Leaning closer, she grinned. "You must be plain tuckered if the smell of my fried chicken didn't rouse you. You slept so still and sound, I considered holding a mirror to your nose."

Duncan chuckled behind them. "Dead folk don't snore, Ma."

Tiller laughed wildly.

Odell twisted around to scowl at them. "Hush up, boys."

Dawsey rubbed her face with both hands, trying to chase the cobwebs from her head. "Did I really snore?"

173

Dilsey came and squatted beside Odell. "Don't listen to Duncan. He's a simpleton. Are you feeling better?"

Warmed by her concern, Dawsey nodded. "I think so."

"Would you care to sit up for a while?"

"I'd love to."

With the stealth of a cat, Hooper appeared. Before she could protest, he had his arms around her, lifting her up to lean against the wall.

For the first time, Dawsey realized someone had washed her and dressed her in a clean nightshirt.

"Adjust her pillow," he said.

Dilsey scurried to slip the lumpy cushion behind her back then covered her modestly with the blanket.

Blushing, Dawsey whispered, "Thank you," to Hooper; then, fearing the state of her breath, placed her hand over her mouth.

He dipped his head and smiled sweetly, his tenderness further jumbling Dawsey's mind. "I'll go fix you a plate."

Duncan rose halfway out of his chair, both hands stretched across the serving dishes. "I've got it, Hooper."

Hooper took the dish and ladle from his hands. "That's all right, brother. I can manage."

Swiping the plate again, Duncan loaded on a drumstick and a biscuit. "See, I have it. Now hand me the ladle."

Crossing behind him, Hooper relieved his brother of the job again, flipping his offering onto the table. "Dawsey likes light meat best and prefers crispy edges on her biscuits." He made the proper adjustments then dipped the ladle in a nearby bowl of corn.

Duncan snatched up his own food and dashed around his chair, headed for Dawsey. "Here you are, darlin', take mine."

Dawsey jumped a foot when Hooper dropped the heaping plate with a *crash* and charged after Duncan.

Before he reached him, Silas dropped his fork and stood up with a roar. "Freeze!" he bellowed.

They did just that, Hooper mid-dash with murder in his eyes and Duncan crouched to flee.

Fury singed a dark path from Silas to where they stood. "You boys ain't dogs and Dawsey's not a bone."

Tiller giggled, ending on a snort when Silas glared his way.

Dawsey hid her red-hot face with the cover.

"Duncan McRae, march over here and sit. Bring your supper with you, if you plan to get any."

His angry gaze swung to Hooper. "Clean up the mess you made of my table and make quick work of it."

Hoarse from shouting, he cleared his throat. "Dawsey's sister will fetch her supper. Left up to you two, we'll be sweeping her vittles from the corners."

Dilsey delivered the tempting plate with a rueful smile and the family settled down to eat in silence.

After a steady diet of broth and tonic, Odell's fried chicken delighted Dawsey's senses. The smell set her mouth to watering, and she couldn't wait to sink her teeth into the crispy brown coating. She swooned over the first bite, which soon became her last since she finished the chicken before touching anything else.

Casting a furtive glance at the serving dish, she felt certain of the answer before she looked. There wouldn't likely be an extra piece. Food was hard to come by for the family. Without Odell's skill in stretching flour into biscuits and quick breads, they'd all leave the kitchen hungry.

It felt good to sit up and eat solid food, but the longer she sat, the worse her leg throbbed. Rhoda's spirited tonic had gradually worn off, leaving unexpected pain behind. She laid aside her dish and glanced toward the others.

Hooper's gaze met hers across the room. She tried to look away, but the concern in his eyes held her. "Would you like to rest now, Dawsey?"

She sighed. "I suppose I should, but I'm not ready. It's nice to be able to see all of you. It's a bit lonely over here by myself."

He pushed back his chair and came to squat beside her. Taking her hand, he placed a golden fried wing in her palm.

Dawsey's heart swelled. He'd given her his food, and it might have been treasure. She smiled at him through damp lashes.

Hooper tugged at his bottom lip with his teeth, a pleasing motion that flipped her middle. "Rest now so you'll feel up to watching Ma and Ellie tomorrow."

She swallowed the lump in her throat. "Watching them?"

Odell clasped her hands. "We're going to decorate the hearth for Christmas. You can help if you'd like."

Dawsey's eyes widened. "Will you be trimming a tree?"

Hooper gave his head a little shake. "I've heard rich folks do, but we never have."

Dawsey gasped. "Never?" She couldn't believe her ears. Aunt Livvy's lavish trees were the centerpieces of every Wilkes Christmas. She couldn't imagine the season without one. "Then you must." She gripped his hand, forgetting her painful leg in her excitement. "I'll help. We can string garlands of pearls and silk roses then group brightly colored birds and candles on each limb." She could see Aunt Livvy's lively tree in her mind. "Oh, I can't wait. It will be wonderful."

The room had stilled.

The excitement building in Dawsey's chest deflated as her gaze bounced to each somber face. "Oh my. . .have I said something wrong?"

Odell shrugged. "Not wrong, exactly. It's just that we don't have all those"—she waved her hand about—"pearls and roses and birds." Her brows lifted hopefully. "I suppose the boys could shoot us a passel of winter birds to string up." She tilted her head. "But won't they start to stink?"

Embarrassed, Dawsey cringed. How could she be so thoughtless?

"We don't need pearls and birds," she said. "They're too gaudy, really. We'll link paper chains and hang apples instead. I'll bake cookie stars and make bows from the ribbons in your sewing box. The tree will be just as beautiful. Better, in fact, with handmade decorations."

Hooper took her shoulders and guided her down to the mat. Plumping the pillow beneath her head, he gave her a stern look. "You won't be doing anything until you get some rest." She winced, and he lifted one brow. "Are you sure you won't take a swig of Rhoda's tonic?"

She firmly shook her head.

"Ornery woman," he mumbled then went back to his supper.

Dawsey watched the fire, thinking of Levi and Winney, Aunt Livvy and Father, wondering if they would celebrate Christmas without her. She pictured her sweet potatoes, bought to make holiday bread to cheer her father, shriveling in a bin in the basement.

Tiller's strident voice pulled her from her lonesome thoughts. She craned her neck to see what had upset him.

"You can't mean it, Uncle Silas. They're the only friends I've got in this sinkhole."

In her dreamy daze, Dawsey hadn't heard what Silas told the boy. She could tell by Tiller's angry scowl and mottled face that he didn't like it one bit.

Silas leaned over his plate, matching Tiller's glare. "Defy me, and see how much I mean it."

Tiller turned a hateful look on Dilsey. "You told."

Still chewing, Dilsey's head shot up. "I never told him nothing." She wiped her mouth on her napkin, her outrage turned to sudden amusement. "But I reckon you just did."

Silas struck the table, rattling the utensils. "Now you're hiding things from me?"

Tiller jumped and stiffened.

Softening his voice, Silas touched his arm. "I'm trying to save you from yourself, nephew. The blunders you make as a youth can chase you into old age. Don't make a mess of your life while you're still damp behind the ears."

The boy jutted his chin. "I ain't no blasted baby."

"You're four years shy of Richard Carter, and he's the youngest. You've got no business hanging about with those older boys."

Tiller huffed. "They ain't so bad."

"They're young bucks full of mischief." Silas raised a warning finger. "Mischief can turn sour under the right conditions. I don't want you with them when it happens."

Tiller shoved away from the table but didn't get far before Silas grabbed his wrist.

"Rein your horses." He tugged, and Tiller plopped in his chair. "I mean you no grief, son, but these are troubled times in a dangerous land. We'd hate to see anything happen to you."

Tiller's slight body heaved with rage. Staring straight ahead, he released his white-rimmed mouth enough to speak. "Can I be excused?"

With a ragged sigh, Silas released his hand. "You might as well."

Stiff armed, fists clenched, he stormed for the door, tears glistening in his eyes.

Dawsey held out her hand as he passed. "Tiller?"

He didn't slow down or spare her a glance. Reaching the door, he slung it open then slammed it behind him.

"*Whooee!*" Duncan hooted, reaching for a biscuit. "Now we know why Aunt Effie wanted shed of him."

"Button up, boy," Silas said, pushing away his plate. "If being a pain in the rear was ample reason, we'd be shed of you by now."

Hooper coughed, choking on his food and his laughter.

"Let me help you, brother." Grinning, Duncan rounded his father's place to pound on Hooper's back.

Laughing harder, Hooper leaped up and shoved him, then slid an arm around his neck and tugged him close.

Dilsey ran around and squeezed between them, kissing both of their cheeks while Odell and Silas looked on with wide, beaming faces.

Dawsey watched in awe. She'd never known such warmth, never experienced such free expressions of love.

For all of their faults, the McRaes were a family. They taunted and teased, sparred and cried, but in the end, they sought each other for comfort.

In a make-believe game, Dawsey pretended to trade places. She saw herself as Dilsey, surrounded by affection, and saw Dilsey in Fayetteville, with a stern maiden aunt and self-absorbed father.

An ache hit her chest, so sudden and fierce it took her breath. Two babes lay in a crib that night, one lucky and one ill fated. The lines had blurred on which was which.

Guilt stabbed her heart, but she couldn't push away the truth. Covering her ears to block out the McRaes' merry voices, Dawsey rolled to the wall and shed bitter tears on her pillow.

THIRTY-ONE

Shivers roused Hooper from a sound sleep. Angry with his shiftless brother, his mouth tightened with irritation. Pa told Duncan to lay a fire in the hearth before bedtime, which meant the freezing cabin was his fault. Ma and Pa would be even colder stuck off in their room.

Groggy, he rolled off his mat to throw a log on the dwindling coals—and tumbled from Ellie's bed to the unforgiving floor.

Feeling foolish, he groaned and bit back a curse. Duncan, asleep on his mat on the other side of their sister's room, grumbled in his sleep and turned over.

Hooper sighed and pushed off the floor. He'd forgotten Ma had banished them to Ellie's room so she could keep Dawsey close enough to tend. It seemed his family played games in the night, swapping beds more often than they changed their underwear. Was it any wonder he awoke confused?

Yawning, he placed a log on the grate for Duncan then pulled on his trousers and washed his face. Grabbing his coat from the doorknob, he stepped outside. Since he was up early, he'd tend the horses for Pa, feed the chickens for Ma, and save them the trouble.

At the thought of his own chores, his stomach moaned in protest. He supposed his list of daily tasks could wait until after breakfast.

Early or not, Old Abe and the other horses seemed sorely glad to see him, and the hens and roosters didn't squawk none, not about the early breakfast, at least.

By the time Hooper loped up the path from the henhouse, Pa stood shivering on the porch, shading his eyes against the rising sun. "What are you doing up and about so early, son?"

Hooper grinned. "If you'd ever slept on Ellie's short bed, you wouldn't have to ask. Besides, neither of us thought to bank a fire." He rubbed his arms at the memory. "That little room gets colder than it does outside."

Pa sniffed. "That's right chilly, then, because it's freezing out here." He nodded toward the barn. "I'll grab my coat. I reckon the old man is eager for his oats."

"No, sir. I fed him for you," Hooper said, smiling. "The chickens, too."

"Well, I'll be." Pa pounded on Hooper's back as he mounted the steps. "You're a mighty fine lad. My aching joints salute you." His eyes twinkled. "Since we're handing out surprises, I've got a nice one for you." Clutching Hooper's sleeve, he herded him through the door.

Hooper paused then nudged him and winked. "Yours is by far the better gift."

The kitchen glowed with light from the flickering lanterns, the blazing hearth, and the bright smiles of three busy women.

Ma stood over a yellow bowl, beating eggs. Ellie hovered beside the table, cutting biscuits with a tin can.

Dawsey, Pa's big surprise, sat beside Ellie, folding scraps of paper into tiny linking chains. She glanced up and beamed, putting all other sources of light to shame. "Good morning."

He took a few steps closer. "Same to you. You must be feeling better."

She nodded, the pretty coil of hair on top of her head dancing. "Oh, yes, I'm much improved." Picking up the carved stick beside her chair, she shrugged. "I still need this to get around, but at the rate I'm healing, I'll soon be running."

Ellie glanced up from her dough. "Please, Dawsey. . .can't you find a better word? Running put you in that fix."

"It's a true Christmas miracle," Ma said from the hearth. "She's been better since we first mentioned decorating the cabin."

Dawsey held up the long paper chain. "See? It's nearly finished. Next we'll dip it in beet juice for color and hang it to dry."

Hooper's glowing praise died on his lips. He crossed angrily to the table and picked up the chain, rolling it around in his hands. "What is this?" He turned to Ma. "You gave her newspaper?"

Wide eyed at his tone, Ma put down the ladle and wiped her

hands on her apron. "Well. . .yes, but they're old newspapers, son." Her surprised look turned to worry. "Did I do something wrong?"

Hooper strode to her and motioned for Pa to join them. "What were you thinking, Ma?" he demanded in a low voice. "If she'd thought to read any of it, she'd know exactly where we are."

Ma pressed her fingers to her mouth. "Oh Hooper, I wasn't thinking."

He squeezed her shoulders. "You have to be more careful."

Pa put both hands on his hips and released a shaky breath. "It's all right, baby. What's done is done."

Behind them, Dawsey cleared her throat. "What's done was done before I ever laid eyes on the *Robesonian*."

Ma gasped and Papa groaned.

Hooper spun to face her. "What are you saying?"

"I'm saying"—she fairly simpered—"I've known for days that I'm in Robeson County, somewhere along the Lumber River. Most likely near Lumberton, considering that's where your paper is printed."

Hooper's nostrils flared. Stalking to her, he lifted her to her feet by her arms. "Who told you? Was it Tiller? I'll wring his skinny neck."

"Stop it, Hooper," Ellie cried. "Don't you dare hurt her."

Fear flashed across Dawsey's face, but her chin jutted in defiance. "Turn me loose this instant."

Hooper struggled to control himself, his breath coming in gasping pants. "Not until you tell me what fool put my family in danger."

Her long lashes swept down, and the corners of her mouth twitched.

He gave her a little shake. "You find this funny?"

"I'm afraid I do."

Bewildered, Hooper stared. What was she up to?

Tilting her head back, she raised her face to him. "You asked which fool?" She batted her eyes. "Why, it was you, Hooper. You told me yourself."

The surging blood at his temples turned to ice. "Me?" Cursing himself for croaking like a frog, he laughed harshly to cover his discomfort. "That's pure nonsense. I'd die before I'd tell you."

She laughed. "Oh but you did. You said your Scottish grandfather married an Indian girl and settled on the Lumber River."

As she spoke, he heard his own voice repeating the words in his head. He'd felt so free with Dawsey that night, so safe to speak his heart. Denial was pointless. Unbridled passion had gotten the best of him again.

Silence rang in the rafters. Tiller, asleep in the corner throughout the tempest, sat up scratching his head. "Why's it so quiet in here?"

Hooper's hold on Dawsey loosened. He caught her before she fell and lowered her into the chair while they sparred with flashing eyes. Resting his fingers on his hips, he blew out a shaky breath. "Well done, Miss Wilkes. You outsmarted me."

The smile disappeared and her brows crowded together.

"Women have snookered men since time began," Hooper sneered. "Never thought I'd be stupid enough to fall for a female's tricks."

Her mouth parted slightly. "What do you mean?"

"Was the kiss part of your plan?" He spun and slapped his leg. "What a muttonhead. Of course it was."

"Kiss?" The shouted question came from four directions at once. Mama, Papa, Ellie, and Tiller all gaped at them.

Hooper waved an accusing finger. "She kissed me. On the neck first then on the lips."

Dawsey groped for her walking stick and shot out of her chair. "I did not!"

Her shrill voice rang in Hooper's ears. "You're going to deny it?" He marched over to her again. "I suppose we never held hands under the covers."

Mama gasped. "For pity's sake, son. Not in front of Tiller."

Grinning, Tiller pushed off his mat and loped across the room. "It's all right, Aunt Odie. I've seen my share of sparking. Just yesterday, Wyatt and Ellie—"

He squealed as Ellie latched onto the back of his neck. "It's past time for you to hush, cousin."

Papa's eyeballs looked ready to pop. "Any more talk of holding hands and kissing, and I'll be fetching my shotgun to plan a wedding."

Outraged and disgusted, Hooper brushed the wretched paper chain to the floor. "She's used every swindle she knows against this family. I'd rather have a backside full of lead than marry this wily trickster."

Dawsey's face paled. "I don't remember proposing marriage to you." She looked ready to spit. "I'd sooner perish."

Papa crowded between them, a peculiar sadness lining his face. "That's enough, now. There's no need slicing each other to pieces." He laid his hands on Dawsey's shoulders. "My jig is up. It's time to take you home, and I know you're ready." He ducked his head. "I'd like to ask a favor first, though I know I don't deserve it."

She watched him with wary eyes, casting several hurt glances at Hooper. "Go on."

Papa went down on one knee in front of her. "If I promise to deliver you myself and confess my guilt to your Pa, will you give me one last Christmas with my family?"

Tears sprang to Mama's eyes. "No Silas. He'll turn you in. . .if he don't kill you."

Ellie draped herself around him. "Papa, don't—"

Hooper clutched his arm. "That's crazy talk. They'll never let you leave Fayetteville."

"Now, family, I've been thinking about this for a while." He shook his head sadly. "The past catches up to us all, whether here or in the hereafter. I'd just as soon have it over with now. I'm closer to the grave than I was yesterday. When I go, I'd like to go down at peace with God."

Dawsey's head drooped. "I don't know, Silas. You're asking to celebrate Christmas with your family, a gift my father will do without."

Papa sighed. "I suppose I am, honey. I'll understand if you say no."

She gazed around the room, tears shining in her eyes. "I suppose a few more days won't make a difference."

Papa beamed at each of them in turn then blinked tearfully at Dawsey. "I'll be forever grateful."

She held up one finger. "Not yet. I want to strike a bargain."

He cocked his head. "Name your price. Nothing's too precious to trade for more time with these dear ones."

"I have your solemn word?"

Hooper touched his shoulder. "Be careful. She's tricky."

Dawsey cast him an angry look.

Pa shrugged off Hooper's hand. "Throw in Hogmanay and you have my word."

She frowned.

"New Year's Day," Ma provided.

Dawsey returned her piercing stare to Pa. "Then we have an agreement. You'll have your Christmas celebration. New Year's, too. I'll even do what I can to keep Father from naming you to the sheriff. . . ." A determined glint in her eyes, her gaze jumped to Ellie. "As long as she returns to Fayetteville with me."

Hooper's stomach lurched as bedlam erupted in the cabin.

Dawsey met Hooper's glare, his eyes twin kettles of rage, across his father's shoulder. She held up her hand. "I don't mean for good. Just long enough to meet my father."

"It's too risky," Hooper growled. "Once he has her, he won't let her go."

Dawsey shook her head. "No one will hold her there. I'll see to it."

"I don't believe you."

She glared. "After all I've been through at the hands of your family, do you really think I'd make a prisoner of my sister?"

He blushed and turned away.

"Suppose I say no," a small voice asked.

Dawsey swung toward her sister. "I won't force you."

Silas brightened. "And the bargain?"

Casting a wistful look at Dilsey, her shoulders fell. "If she won't go, I'll remove the condition. You'll have your time with the family, and I'll still try to sway my father."

Hooper grinned. "That's it then. Ellie won't—"

"I'll need time to think about it."

Hooper spun toward Dilsey. "No, honey, you can't."

She touched his arm. "This is my decision."

Dawsey gave her a sweet smile. "You have until after New Year's Day to decide. I pray you'll say yes."

Tiller moaned and clutched his stomach. "If everything's settled, can we have a little less talk and a little more bacon?"

Odell and Dilsey moped toward the kitchen, salvaging breakfast while Dawsey cleared her Christmas project to make room at the table. Bending to pick up the folded links of newspaper, she felt a little sad that the merry little streamer meant to bring joy had stirred so much trouble.

Hooper shot her a dark look then went out mumbling that he'd lost his appetite.

Dawsey stared at the door, feeling sick.

Over the last few days, the hateful man who'd whisked her out of a window became a sweet-faced charmer. Had the scoundrel returned or never left?

She stared at the hands Hooper said he'd held, touched the mouth he claimed had kissed him. Her lips seemed to burn with a memory of their own. Had she done such a shameless thing?

Her gaze slid to the mat by the fire. His mat, filled with the musky scent of him.

One thing she remembered clearly. As the haze of Rhoda's tonic faded from her mind, Dawsey had watched Hooper near the hearth, irresistibly drawn to him.

Had he told the truth?

With her eyes closed, she could almost feel her lips nuzzling his. Shivering, she yanked her lids open to the sight of Duncan's looming grin.

She leaped and he hooted with glee. "Mornin', Dawsey. Dreaming about me again?"

Blushing, she glanced away.

"Nice to see you up and about. Did I startle you?"

"Leave her be," Silas growled from the head of the table. "Did you figure to sleep all day?"

Duncan whirled to sit next to him. "I gave it a good try, but the sun came pestering me through the boards on Ellie's window."

Odell shoveled a rack of bacon onto a platter and set it between him and Silas. Duncan snatched one, juggling and blowing on the crispy strip before shoving it into his mouth.

Tiller, who had gaped at Dawsey from the time Hooper said she kissed him, picked that moment to display the tactlessness of youth. "You missed the whole thing, Duncan. We had us a big old ruckus while you slept."

Silas lifted his bushy brows high over the rim of his cup. "Hush, boy."

The warning came too late.

"I missed a ruckus?" Duncan stared around the table then over his shoulder at Odell and Dilsey. "What sort? Was it bounty hunters?"

Dawsey's cheeks warmed. They must've colored, too, since Duncan's wandering stare landed squarely on her face.

"Nothing like that," Tiller said, flaunting the tactlessness of males in general. "Dawsey kissed Hooper."

Silas slammed down his cup. "Say another word, and you'll be doing chores on an empty stomach." His eyes rose to his wife, scurrying toward him from the hearth. "Can't you manage your household, woman? Is a peaceful table too much to ask?"

She smoothed his hair. "Breakfast is ready now, darlin'. It's hard for a boy to talk with food in his mouth."

Duncan scowled at Dawsey, an angry fire building behind his eyes.

Odell nudged his chair with her hip, so hard he scooted, and pressed a fluffy biscuit to his lips. "Ain't that right, son?"

He tugged his gaze from Dawsey and took a dutiful bite. "Yes, Ma," he mumbled with bulging cheeks.

"Here." She tossed one at Tiller. "I reckon your yap needs filling the most."

Dawsey was grateful to see his mouth busy with something besides her business.

Shaking her head, Odell took her place at the table. "I swear, Tiller McRae, with you around, the *Robesonian* may as well close their doors."

THIRTY-TWO

Hooper hoed the last six inches of the trench and watched the muddy water rush past his plowed rows then downhill to the stream where it belonged. He loved Scuffletown, but more for its sturdy, hard-wearing people than its soggy-bottomed land.

The rivers, creeks, and streams seemed determined to reclaim every inch of ground. In the dry season, the waters crouched, gurgling quietly, waiting for the rain. With very little invitation, they pounced from their banks, gobbling up crops, animals, and hapless people, sweeping them away without a trace.

Hooper spent so much time routing water from the fields, he had little time for anything else. On that particular morning, he welcomed the backbreaking work. It gave him a good excuse to pound on the ground with a stick.

Dawsey's taunting face flashed through his mind. With a furious grunt, he laid his shoulders into attacking the next furrow.

She'd denied their kiss. The idea made his head spin more than her dizzying lips. The kiss he'd replayed in his mind a thousand times—surer with each recalling that he'd lost his heart forever—Dawsey wouldn't even admit.

There was no one to blame but himself. The girl had spun her web then languished on the sticky strands, waiting to lure him in. Like a witless fool, he'd blundered willingly into her net.

He could accept his defeat, even admire her skill, but he'd never allow her to take down his family. If he had to lock them in the shed, he'd fight against Pa and Ellie going to Fayetteville.

He'd get rid of Dawsey if it meant tossing her over his shoulder again and carrying her all the way home.

One at a time, the McRaes filed out of the cabin—Silas to his chores, Odell to pull beets for their dye, and Dilsey with a hunting rifle slung over her shoulder.

Duncan waved off his father's invitation to the barn with a vague promise to be right along.

Tiller stood near the fire, running the last biscuit along the bottom of a skillet.

"What are you doing, boy?" Duncan growled. "Rubbing a hole in the iron?"

Tiller shot him a guilty glance. "I'm sopping the rest of this bacon grease for Aunt Odie. Makes the pan easier to clean."

He shoved the soggy bread in his mouth, and Duncan shuddered. "That bottomless stomach must be made of solid lead. Don't you have chores to do?"

Tiller wandered to the scrambled egg pan, to peel the papery slivers from the sides and nibble them. "Not right now."

Duncan cleared his throat. "I think you're mistaken. In fact, Pa's calling you now."

The boy tilted his ear. "I don't hear nothin'."

Duncan cocked his head, listening. "Wait, that ain't Pa. It's Saint Peter." He made a threatening move. "You'll be answering, if you don't scat."

With a shout, Tiller bounded for the door, stretching his arm to snatch his coat off a peg.

Laughing, Duncan sat across from Dawsey. "I guess that takes care of him." He sobered. "Now we can talk in peace."

Dawsey studied her hands, folded on the table. "What do you want to talk about?" Foolish question. She already knew.

Duncan closed his fingers over hers. "I want to know more about the uproar you and Hooper caused."

Dawsey glanced at his earnest face. She had to tell him something. Careful to avoid any mention of a kiss, she told him what had happened before breakfast.

She reached the part about the bargain she'd struck with Silas, and he withdrew the warmth of his hands. "Pa can't go with you, Dawsey. You know that, don't you? He'll spend the rest of his life behind bars." He blew out an anxious breath. "They might even hang him."

She pulled her rejected hands to her lap. "I didn't ask him to go. That part came from him, and he's very adamant. I only want the chance to show my father that Dilsey's alive."

Worry creased his brow. "Can't you just tell him?"

"It wouldn't be the same." How could she explain that she needed a miracle, one only Dilsey could provide? "Besides, he deserves the chance to see for himself."

"He'll want her back for good."

She nodded. "I'm certain of it, but he won't try to force her."

Duncan stared thoughtfully over her head. "What does all this have to do with Hooper?"

She lowered her lashes. "He feels the way you do, that neither of them should go." She shrugged in the midst of her half truth. "So he raised a bit of a. . .well, a ruckus."

Duncan quirked his mouth. "And you kissed him?"

She slapped the table. "No! At least I don't think so." She blushed. "I don't remember."

"Really?" He bit one side of his lip. "Poor old Hoop."

"Stop that. It's not his fault."

He leaned to cup her chin. "If you kissed me, you'd remember."

She swatted his hand. "Not with a snoot full of Rhoda's tonic."

Understanding dawned in his eyes. He laughed and straightened. "Fair enough."

A pang struck Dawsey's heart. "I'm beginning to regret my bargain. It would be wonderful to make it home in time for Christmas."

Duncan's gray eyes shone with an idea. "We could outfox the old man and put an end to the whole thing."

"How?"

He slammed his hand on the table. "I'll take you to Fayetteville myself. If we leave now, you'll be home in time for supper."

Her head whirled at the thought of walking through the high arched doorway, strolling past Winney's fragrant kitchen and into Father's den. "I'd dearly love to go."

He stood. "I'll hitch the wagon."

She caught his arm. "It's out of the question. I won't leave without

Dilsey, and she'll only agree to go if she thinks she's helping your father."

He gave her a solemn nod. "Then I'll do what I've already promised. I'll go to Fayetteville and get a message to your pa. At least he'll have the promise of your return to get him through."

She tilted her head. "You'd do that?"

He dropped to the chair and took her hand. "I would."

"But why?"

"For you, Dawsey," he said. "I'd do anything for you."

The door slammed, rattling the windowpane.

Dawsey leaped, but no higher than Duncan.

Hooper stood snarling at them. "Well, this is sweet. What has she suckered you into, brother? Hacking off your right arm? I see she's already cut the legs out from under you."

His harsh tone chilled Dawsey's spine. She stared in shock as he sauntered toward them, his dark scowl raising the hairs on her arms.

Duncan glared at his brother. "You can't talk about Dawsey like that."

"I need to speak to you, Miss Wilkes. In private."

Duncan held his ground. "You'll have to say it in front of me, because I'm not going anywhere."

Hooper opened his mouth, his chest like a swollen rain barrel. The shout he suppressed seemed to pain him. He winced and started over. "I need you to git, brother, so I can have a little chat with Dawsey before the house fills up again."

Duncan looked at her. "It's up to you."

Hooper leaned close to his face. "Duncan. . ."

His forehead arched in a plea, Duncan persisted, "You don't want to talk to him, do you, honey?"

Dawsey crossed her arms. "No, I don't." Breathing in sharply, she exhaled through her nose. "I'm afraid I must, at least one more time." She glowered at Hooper. "To defend my honor."

Launching himself from the table, Duncan stormed to the door. "I'll be right outside."

The second he left, Hooper swung into his chair, waving a threatening finger. "You won't take my pa to Fayetteville."

She closed her eyes. "Hooper, you're behaving like a lunatic."

"I won't allow him to go."

"The trip to Fayetteville was your father's idea. You were standing right here when he said so." She let her head fall back. "I'm tired of denying things I haven't done."

He smirked. "Just not the things you have?"

The room stilled. Every sound grew louder. The fire spit and crackled in the hearth. The wind whistled outside the cabin.

Hooper's labored breath rasped and a pulse pounded in her ears. She straightened and gazed at him. Unruly strands of hair hung in his eyes, dancing each time he blinked. Shadowy whiskers colored the soft skin of his cheeks, and zeal burned from his warm brown eyes. He'd never looked more handsome.

"Did I kiss you, Hooper?"

He flinched. "You know you did."

"Do I?" She struggled for words to explain. "Strong drink and dizzying herbs had never passed my lips before that day. The two together are quite potent, it seems."

His chin came up. "Rhoda's tonic?"

She nodded grimly.

Lost in thought, he studied the tabletop. The angry frown melted slowly as he blinked away his doubt. "You really don't remember."

Her cheeks warmed. "There's a foggy sense of *something* happening between us." She tilted her chin. "A pleasant memory, but it's only a vague shadow in the back of my mind."

He crossed his arms on the table and rested his forehead. "I said terrible things to you," he confessed to the crook of his arm. "Accused you in front of my folks."

"Yes, you did." On this score, she wouldn't go easy. "You humiliated me and brought my honor into question."

He sat up and squared his shoulders. "I'm sorry Dawsey, though an apology won't be enough. How can I make it up to you?"

"Will you tell your parents the truth? I don't want them thinking the worst."

He nodded. "Anything else?"

She ducked her head. "Will you accept my apology?"

"Yours?"

"Your accusations weren't far from the mark. I did use trickery and wiles against your family in order to escape. I purposely sought to gain your trust so you wouldn't watch me so closely." She struggled to hold back her tears. "Along the way, I began to care very much for you McRaes." She laughed. "As addlepated as that sounds."

Hooper whistled through his teeth. "I don't suppose there's a fitting

Psalm for that one." He grinned. "Am I the only one you kissed?"

They laughed together, and he shyly reached for her hand. "Please help me keep my pa at home where he belongs. Ma would be lost without him."

"I think his mind is made up to go." She squeezed his fingers. "It may be possible to convince my father not to bring charges though. I promise to try."

Hooper stood, pulling her into a gentle hug. "I couldn't ask for more."

THIRTY-THREE

Pleased with the number of whole pieces Papa had pried from the stubborn shells, Ellie took his full bowl of black walnuts and handed him an empty. "Keep going. You're doing a fine job."

Focused on Duncan, he took the bowl with fumbling fingers. "You going somewhere, son?"

Duncan stood beside Ellie's horse with a saddlebag over his shoulder. "Yes, sir. For just a day or so."

"Where to?"

"I. . .well, I'm not sure yet. Not exactly."

Pa leaned in his rickety chair and set the bowl on the porch. "Who's going with you?"

Something big had wiggled up Duncan's craw. It took several minutes of coughing to clear it out.

"The details are still sketchy." His eyes jumped to Dawsey. "A friend's in trouble and I offered to help. That's all I know right now."

Bent over a pail of beet juice, stirring handmade ornaments with Mama, Dawsey seemed as fidgety as Ellie's squirming brother. No doubt about it, they were up to something.

Mama stood with her hand on her hip. "Do you have to go now? Tomorrow's Christmas Eve. We're going to decorate Dawsey's tree."

Duncan grinned and patted the horse's neck. "Don't worry. Ellie loaned me Toby. He'll have me back with time to spare."

Mama scowled. "Suppose you don't make it?"

"Then I'll be home in time for presents, but only if you stop asking questions and let me get down the road."

Still smiling, he settled the bag on Toby's back and fastened it down with leather straps. With a jaunty salute, he reined the horse toward the lane.

Shading her eyes with her hand, Dawsey stared after Duncan with a tender smile on her face.

The breath caught in Ellie's throat. *She's sweet on him!* What else could her moony-eyed glances mean?

Hooper swung around the house and flung his body over the rail, landing with a *thud* next to Dawsey. She leaped and squeaked like a mouse. Mama screamed and clutched her heart. Papa laughed so hard his belly shook.

Grinning, Hooper slid his arms around Mama's waist. "May I have this dance?"

She poked him with her elbow. "You scared the soup out of me."

He kissed her cheek and let her go. "Guilty conscience?"

"Oh, you." She swatted him. "My sore conscience has nothing to do with it."

Hooper waltzed around Dawsey, jabbing her in the side as he passed. She yelped and sloshed him with her dye. He spun to dip one finger and touched the tip of her nose.

"Oh, Hooper!" She dropped the stirring stick and covered her face with both hands. "My nose will be red for days."

"You'll make a fetching ornament. We'll let you top the tree."

Batting her lashes like a silly schoolgirl, Dawsey blushed and looked away.

Ellie felt like scratching her head. Was Dawsey sweet on both of her brothers?

Papa fetched his bowl of walnuts and started peeling again.

Love shone from Mama's eyes. "You'll get an extra slice of brown sugar pie for your trouble, Silas."

"I'd best get an extra pie." Raising his head, he gazed toward the barn. "Anybody seen Tiller?"

Hooper snatched two fat walnuts and squeezed them together with a loud *crack*. "Not since breakfast. Maybe he's with your other son"—he smirked—"the homely one."

Papa jabbed a thumb, stained brown with nut sap, in the direction Duncan had gone. "No, the smart one just rode off, and he didn't have Tiller with him."

Hooper chewed his pilfered walnut and stared down the lane. "Where'd he go?"

Pa shrugged. "Can't say." He laughed. "And neither could he. The boy didn't seem to know where he was headed or with who."

Frowning, Hooper hooked his arm around a post. "That could be risky, Pa. Outright dangerous. Why'd you let him go?"

A concerned frown wrinkled Papa's nose. "I figure he's off with Henry or Boss. Maybe the Carter boy."

Hooper scratched the side of his head. "It's not like him to go off without saying a word to me, but he's grown enough to take care of himself, I reckon."

Mama laid aside her half-red stirring stick and wiped her brow. "Don't fret, Hooper. He promised to be home tomorrow evening. Christmas morning at the latest."

Deep in thought, Hooper nodded. "All right then."

Papa shifted his bulk in the chair. "It's Tiller who has me vexed." He gazed toward the swamp with a puckered scowl. "He's not roaming out there alone, no matter what he claims. The lad has deliberately disobeyed me by linking arms with young Nathan."

He looked ever his shoulder at Ellie. "For the Carters' sake, I hope Nathan matures with half of Wyatt's sense."

She nodded. "He will. Wyatt will see to it."

In better spirits again, Hooper rubbed his hands together and looked at Dawsey. "Are we still going for that ride?"

"I'd very much like to," she said.

"Then it's settled. We'll leave right after lunch, so eat hearty."

"Wait a blasted minute," Papa said, raising his hand. "Where do you think you're taking her?"

"Along Drowning Creek to search for holly."

"And greenery," Dawsey added.

"Bring me some possumhaw boughs," Ellie said. "The red berries are ever so pretty."

Pa slumped in his chair. "Did I die, and you lot forgot to bury me? I'm the last to know everything around here."

Ignoring his sulk, Mama peered at Dawsey's eyes. "Are you sure you're strong enough?"

"Oh yes, ma'am," Dawsey assured her. "Stronger every day."

"Besides," Hooper said, "we're taking the wagon."

Rising with a groan, Pa handed his basket to Ellie. "I'm more concerned about a chaperone."

Holding one finger aloft, Hooper cleared his throat. "All tended. We're taking the pest."

"Tiller?" Papa snorted. "What sort of chaperone is he?"

Mama leaned to pat his arm. "The very best kind. He's so afraid to miss them sparking, he won't take his eyes off for a minute."

They all laughed, except for Pa. "No telling where he is. You'd best hope he comes home in time."

Ellie grinned. "He'll be here before Ma sets the table. Tiller won't miss a meal."

Hooper ducked his head at Dawsey. "Speaking of Tiller's appetite, you'd better pack a biscuit or two. If hunger sets in, he'll squawk the whole time we're gone."

Crossing the porch, he took her arm. "Why don't you go inside and rest until we leave?"

He led her to the door with Mama fussing behind them. "He's right, Dawsey. It's an hour yet before the noon meal. I'll help you lie down."

They slipped inside the dim cabin and shut the door. Papa held his shushing finger to his lips and scooped out a handful of walnuts. Tossing his head back, he poured them into his mouth. "Picker's profit," he explained, his eyes twinkling.

Ellie hugged him around the waist. "There went a slice of your pie."

Still chewing, he shook his head. "Tastes more like Duncan's slice."

Giggling like naughty children, they followed the others inside.

THIRTY-FOUR

Ellie knelt beside the chicken fence, holding the picket still while her mama wired it into place. Without the plank, the fence had a snaggletoothed grin. Now it smiled in gratitude.

Giving the wire one last twist, Mama stood up, dusting her hands. "Blasted greedy 'coons. They eat more than Tiller. You wouldn't think they could squeeze those fat bellies through such a slim opening."

Ellie laughed. "That's what busts the wood."

Mama swatted the empty air. "I'll bust them, if they don't stay out of my feed."

Ellie shouldered her shotgun and Mama gathered the tools. On the way to the house, she listed the chores she expected Ellie to do before Christmas.

Ellie moaned. "Why on earth do you insist on sweeping the yard? It don't make sense."

"Don't mock things you don't understand," Mama warned. "All the best families in Fayetteville sweep their yards every Saturday. Once more if company's coming."

Baffled at her logic, Ellie took in their surroundings. "This ain't Fayetteville, we never have company, and what little yard we have is mostly underwater."

Mama scowled. "The part that's dry is getting swept." She poked Ellie's nose. "By you."

"Where's Papa? He can sweep."

"He won't. He calls it women's work. Besides, he's taking a nap."

Ellie whined. "Can't I wait for Dawsey? She should help. This fancy Christmas was her idea."

They reached the steps, and Mama swiveled on her heels. "Dawsey will be helping me in the kitchen."

"Why can't I? All the jobs you gave me, the men could do."

"And so can you." Mama shot her a rueful look. "I need Dawsey in the kitchen, honey. She's a wonderful cook."

Ellie followed Ma onto the porch. "And I'm not? You said my last biscuits turned out better than yours."

Her eyes softened. "It's true. You're getting much better, but Christmas is a special occasion."

Ellie opened her mouth to demand she explain, but Mama's hand shot up. "Did you hear something?" Tilting her ear toward the house, she searched Ellie's face.

Swallowing hard, Ellie nodded. The cold fear in Mama's gaze slithered under her skin. "Don't be scared. It's just Papa rattling firewood."

Ma's eyes were as big as wagon wheels. "It's not your pa," she hissed, "unless he has ten feet."

"Hooper?"

"Gone with Dawsey to fetch holly."

Ellie raised the shotgun. "Stay here."

She eased the door open a crack, wincing when the hinges creaked. Placing one eye to the narrow slit, Ellie's heart shot past her throat.

Long shadows, visible through the open door to Papa's room, danced a curious waltz on his wall. She held her breath and pushed inside then crept across the floor, past the hearth and the table, past the counter, to the door of her parents' room.

She had little time to decide her next move. Papa's yelp of pain fired heat to her chest and life to her hands and feet. With a war cry, she burst inside the room.

Two men held her pa against the wall, one with his hands around his throat, squeezing with a white-knuckled grip. The other was the bounty hunter who'd come looking for Hooper.

"Turn him loose," Ellie bawled, blinking away angry tears.

The one choking the life out of Papa wore a badge. He turned, his cruel face twisted with spite. "Well, look here. It's a little gal." He leaned close to Papa's ear. "Is this pretty little thing your daughter, Silas McRae?"

Ellie's gaze jumped from his pale fingers to Papa's bug-eyed plea for help. "I said turn him loose!" she screamed.

Mama plucked the gun from Ellie's hands. The look on her face was one Ellie had never seen before—one she hoped she'd never see again.

Her soulless stare had the same effect on the bounty hunter. He backed away from Pa, his hands held high. His pitiless friend tensed, loosened his grip enough for Pa to suck air in a rattling gasp. Then his shoulders relaxed and he leered. "Go ahead. Pull that trigger, ma'am. You'll scatter lead over half this wall and cut Silas down with me."

Mama cocked one brow and raised the barrel. "Just as well. I can't abide the old fool."

Mucky swampland and scum-covered ponds were all Dawsey had seen in Scuffletown, the place she'd lived for endless weeks. As the wagon rolled toward the river, a different side of the North Carolina countryside danced past.

His eyes glowing, Hooper leaned to point out a black-water stream that flowed in and out of sight around twisted bends. Moldy mushrooms jutted from thick loblolly pine trunks like fairy stairwells wending to tiny houses in the branches.

Ellie had loaned Dawsey a pair of slacks for the occasion and a woolen shirt that made her uncomfortably hot in the sunlight. With Tiller tugging on the sleeves, she pulled off her borrowed coat and rested it over her lap. "Much better. Thank you."

He smiled and ducked his head. "Sure thing, Miss Wilkes."

She turned on the seat. "Please, call me Dawsey. Everyone else does."

Grinning, he picked at his cuff. "I'll try. Course I might slip a time or two, since I ain't never called you nothing else."

She patted his hand. "If you forget, I'll remind you."

Hooper reined Old Abe near the riverbank and turned with a smile. "This is it. The place I told you about."

He'd stopped in a clearing too small to call a meadow but with all of the same charm. Surrounded by towering pine and wide oak, a quaint trail led across the browning grass. Holly trees, bright with berries, grew in clustered groves around the rim.

Dawsey stared in awe. "It's lovely."

"I knew you'd like it."

She crossed her arms to keep from clasping her hands and squealing. "I simply love it, Hooper."

Scrambling to the ground, he hustled to her side and helped her down.

She stood with her hands on her hips, surveying the clearing. "I don't know where to start. There are so many."

With one hand on her shoulder, he leaned close and pointed. "Plenty of evergreens, too."

Tiller pulled a long, thick-handled knife from the wagon bed. "Want me to start cutting?"

Sucking in his stomach to dodge the blade, Hooper relieved him of his weapon. "Don't be waving that thing about, boy." He ruffled Tiller's hair then grabbed the back of his neck. "It's best to let a man do the cutting."

"Can't." Tiller sniffed. "Duncan ain't here."

Hooper swatted at him, but Tiller was too fast. He tore across the field with Hooper on his heels.

Halfway across, Hooper doubled back for Dawsey. Bowing, he offered his arm. "May I?"

Feeling like a debutante, she curtseyed. "Sir, you may."

For the next half hour, they cut bushels of holly branches, picking only the reddest berries to stack inside the wagon.

On their way up the path for the last time, Tiller groaned. "I've never seen so many cuttings. What are you planning to do? Cover the walls?"

Dawsey tweaked his ear. "Yes, I am. Inside and out."

He squinted up at her. "Why?"

"Because holly trees are very important at Christmastime," she said. "Do you know what they signify?"

"Huh?"

"Signify," she repeated slowly. "It means suggest or be a sign of."

Gnawing his bottom lip, Tiller nodded. "So what do they s–signify?"

"Very good." She patted his back. "Well, the thorny leaves"—she plucked one off to show him the tiny curved spikes—"suggest the crown of thorns on Christ's head."

Hooper took it from her hand. "They do?"

"Yes, and the red berries bring to mind drops of His priceless blood."

Making a face, Tiller took the leaf from Hooper. "Why is His blood so priceless?"

Dawsey tilted her head. "I can best answer your question with my favorite carol." Drawing a quick breath, she began to sing:

"Cedar and pine now cheerily twine:
Crown every scene with evergreen:
Now is the reign of darkness o'er:
Jesus is king for evermore!
Boughs of the holly this day adorn:
Sharp are the leaves as crowns of thorn:
See, in the berries all blood red,
Blood that, for us, this babe shall shed."

Silence filled the woods around them, as though nature had hushed to listen.

Hooper seemed stunned. "That was beautiful, Dawsey."

"He's right, Miss Wi—I mean, Dawsey. You sounded real pretty. What does it mean?"

"It means that Jesus shed His blood, so we might live. This makes the blood precious indeed."

He frowned. "A babe shed his blood?"

She smoothed his hair. "No, but a babe born to that very purpose."

"Oh." His interest fading as fast as it had sparked, Tiller punched Hooper's arm. "Race you to the rig."

Dawsey longed to finish the story, both for the boy and for Hooper, who seemed to be listening carefully. Sadly, the mood was broken.

They reached the wagon and she placed her sticky evergreen branch atop the rest.

Tiller tossed in his holly. "Can we go now? After all that work, I'm powerful hungry."

Hooper handed his branch to Dawsey. "We expected you to say that."

He stretched to reach under the seat and pulled out a bundle tied with string. "How about one of your aunt Odie's biscuits?"

Tiller hunched over the food and sniffed. "My nose tells me there's more than plain old biscuits in there." He lifted the edge of the towel and smiled. "I knew it. Bacon."

Dawsey spread a blanket while Hooper pulled out a jug of sweet cider. They sat under the clear blue sky and finished Odell's simple fare in no time at all, especially with Tiller's help.

Dawsey hugged herself and shivered.

Watching her, Hooper wiped his mouth. "Are you cold?"

"A little. There's a hint of a chill in the air."

He pushed off the ground. "I'll fetch Ellie's coat for you."

Tiller lay back on the blanket and wrapped himself with the corner. "It's 'cause we worked up a sweat."

Back with the coat, Hooper bumped him with his foot. "Mind your manners."

He gaped. "What'd I do?"

"You're not supposed to mention things like sweat in front of a lady."

"Why not?" He rose up on his elbow. "Ma says she can sweat like a washerwoman."

Hooper cringed.

Caught off guard, Dawsey laughed, spewing biscuit crumbs. Horrified, she clutched her mouth, the laugher dying in her throat—until Hooper doubled over, howling.

"I told you." Tiller cackled, his high-pitched voice echoing through the trees. "There ain't nothing special about a woman. They burp and spit just like we do."

Hooper sat up wiping his eyes. Sobered, he swung toward Dawsey with tears of glee caught in his lashes. "You're dead wrong, cousin." He pressed so close, his breath warmed Dawsey's cheek. "Some women are very special."

Tiller pulled a face. "Aw, there you go spooning. Just when we was starting to have fun."

Dawsey whirled. "There is no spooning happening here, young man. Don't you go telling stories to Silas."

Hooper stood, pulling Tiller up by his collar. "Come on, you. Get this blanket folded and in the wagon. It's time to get Dawsey home."

Shading her eyes, she turned her face up to him. "We can't go yet. We forgot Dilsey's boughs. She made a special request."

Hooper's hands went to his hips. "She did, at that." Turning, he searched the edge of the clearing with darting eyes. "I think I saw a possumhaw tree a little past those pines."

He loped to the wagon and pulled the knife from the bed. "Let's go, Tiller. I'll let you cut this time, if you promise to come back with both legs."

They shuffled away, jostling against each other as they trudged up the beaten trail.

Dawsey stood, shaking the embarrassing crumbs from the blanket and folding it small enough to tuck under the seat. Smiling to herself, she stared at the wagon bed, mounded high with deep red berries over a bed of cedar green. The lovely sight seemed so Christmassy, it brought happy tears to her eyes.

Recalling the beautiful story she'd shared about the holly, Dawsey closed her eyes and basked in God's love amid the quiet calm of the clearing. Despite her recent trials, she'd never felt such peace.

On the way home, she realized Hooper had left her alone in the clearing with a horse and wagon, the perfect opportunity to escape, but it hadn't occurred to her to do so. Frowning, she searched her heart for the reason.

Pushing aside the outrageous idea that it had anything to do with Hooper, she told herself she didn't run because she couldn't leave Dilsey behind.

THIRTY-FIVE

Mama motioned to Ellie, crouched behind her. "Stand back, honey, and plug your ears."

Fear pooled in the hateful man's dark eyes. He heaved Papa on the bed and bolted, barely clearing the room before the blast of the gun rang Ellie's ears like a gong.

Mama whirled on his friend who seemed to have wet his pants. "I think you were just leaving."

Nodding, he slid along the wall until he reached the opening then shot through with Mama on his heels. He sailed through the cabin, knocking over chairs in his haste, and bolted from the house.

She slammed and barred the door behind him then whirled to gape at Ellie. They stared at each other in silence until Papa groaned from the bedroom. Heaving great gulping sobs, Mama ran past Ellie to kneel beside him on the bed. "Oh Silas! Please tell me you're all right."

Papa clutched her hand, reaching a clumsy finger to wipe her tears. He tried to speak but only managed to croak, so he nodded instead.

Mama stretched out beside him, gently caressing his hair.

Smiling through her tears, Ellie slipped out and closed the door. She knew in her head that the men weren't likely to return, not without more hired guns. Still, she set up a watch near the window, alert for any movement, while her heart willed Hooper to hurry home.

Mama appeared, rattling her pots.

Ellie abandoned her post to throw another log on the hearth then sat down in front of the fire. "Chicken soup?"

Mama nodded.

No matter the ailment, in her mind, chicken soup was the cure. Ellie couldn't figure how steaming broth might ease a near strangling, but if it promised a cure for jangled nerves, she'd gladly sip a cup.

Mama finished her healing brew and sat beside Papa's bed, blowing the heat off bites and spooning them into his swollen mouth.

He tried to speak, but Mama hushed him. "Rest, darlin'. Let the warm soup loosen your throat before you try to talk."

This nugget of wisdom shed light on Mama's claim. Ellie resolved to try a bit of soup on the pesky lump in her own throat.

Waving away the cure, Pa stared at Ellie, his eyes troubled.

She settled on the other side of the bed and took his hand. "I know, Papa. You're worried about Hooper."

His head bounced up and down.

"Do you want me to ride out and find him?"

He nodded faster.

Mama stood, sloshing soup on the mattress. "She'll do no such thing."

"But Ma—"

"Forget it, Ellie." She bore down on Papa. "There are lunatics in those swamps, Silas. One of them almost killed you. I won't risk my only daughter, not even for our son."

Concerned for Hooper, Ellie girded herself for battle. Before she decided her best line of attack, three loud raps on the door, followed by persistent hammering, threatened to loosen the hinges.

Papa swung off the bed, reaching for Ellie's gun. The fresh terror shining from his eyes tore at Ellie's heart. With his wife and daughter behind him, he crept toward the rowdy noise.

As she passed the gun rack, Ellie lifted a loaded rifle with shaky hands.

The door shuddered under a fresh wave of pounding.

"Who's there?" Ellie called, dread thick as porridge in her throat. Mama gripped her arm and yanked her two feet away.

"Open up this instant."

Ellie squealed. Her fear lifted and comfort took its place as she hurriedly lifted the bar.

Hooper stormed inside with an angry scowl. "Who locked this blasted thing?"

Mama burst into tears. "Oh Hooper."

His startled gaze swung to Pa and shock paled his features. "Thunderation! What happened here?"

Shouldering his gun, he hurried to Papa and touched his battered face. "Who did this?"

Trembling, Ellie pulled Dawsey and Tiller past the threshold and slammed the bar home. "They're still out there somewhere. Mama got a shot off, but it didn't slow them down."

"Bounty hunters?"

"One of them. The other wore a cheap star on his vest."

Chest heaving, Papa groped the empty space behind him. Dawsey dashed for his chair and they lowered him down.

"Let me catch my breath, son," he begged in a raspy croak. "Then I'll tell you what we need to do."

They had him seated near the window beneath the last rays of the setting sun. The eggplant-colored marks seemed to glow, lining his swollen neck like a hand still gripping his throat.

Wincing, Hooper touched them then smoothed Papa's grizzled head with an unsteady hand. "We both know what I have to do. For now, you need to rest."

Watching Hooper, Ellie shivered. She'd seen him this way before, with black rage simmering beneath a quiet voice and calm manner.

He motioned to Tiller. Between them, they herded Papa on shuffling feet to his bed. Ma flitted around him, pulling the covers to his chin and tucking him in on both sides.

Lying still, he gazed fretfully at Hooper. "Wait for Duncan."

Hooper's jaw formed a grim line, and he wouldn't meet Pa's searching eyes. "Some things won't wait."

One of Papa's long feet stuck from under the quilt, the dingy toenails like talons. Hooper patted his foot then moved for the door.

"Son?"

He turned.

"Don't go alone. Fetch Henry or Boss to go with you."

The glint of unshed tears in his eyes, Hooper nodded.

Ellie followed him to the gun rack. "I'm going."

Dawsey gasped and covered her mouth.

Shoving a long-barreled handgun into his waistband, Hooper shook his head. "Don't be daft."

"It'll be dark soon. I'll hide out in the brush and pick them off. You know I'm the best shot in this family."

"No."

"But it makes no sense not to take me. I can cover for you."

She'd gone too far. He whirled and gripped her arms, his face twisted into a stranger's ugly mask. "If you leave this cabin, you'll have a price to pay."

Shrinking away from him, she nodded.

Tiller jostled close. "Can I go?"

Hooper lifted his Spencer from the rack. "I need you to look after the women."

Drawing the false veil of calm around him again, he crossed to Dawsey standing near the door and cupped her face in his palm.

In that moment, Ellie knew Hooper loved her.

The way Dawsey gazed at him left no doubt which brother she preferred. "You will be careful." Her quiet words were not a request.

Hooper patted her cheek and nodded. "I'm always careful."

Before the heavy door closed behind him, Ellie dashed to sling it wide. "You'd best do like Papa said, Hooper McRae! Take Henry. . .or Boss. Don't you dare go alone!"

Dawsey's hand touched Ellie's shoulder and she spun. In a tearful daze, she stumbled headlong into her sister's comforting arms.

THIRTY-SIX

Dawsey tugged Hooper's blanket closer and willed his knock to sound. Stretched out on his mat, she'd tossed like a landed trout through the night, sleeping in drips and dabs. Dilsey's rest appeared even more fitful, so Dawsey welcomed the soft, steady breaths coming from her direction.

The hushed whispers that carried to her long into the night drifted out to her now from Silas and Odell's room, and she wondered if they'd slept at all.

The cabin seemed to yearn for any sign of Hooper. Only Tiller, with a youth's blind trust in fate, slept from the instant his tangled red hair hit the pillow. Cutting holly branches must've worn him to a frazzle.

Dawsey rolled off the mat, wincing when she put weight on her injured leg. She'd done too much the day before but wouldn't trade her day in the holly grove for two strong limbs.

With an absent rub, she put the pain aside and lifted Dilsey's shotgun from beside her on the floor. Tiptoeing past her sister, she eased the bar from its hooks, turned the knob, and tugged on the door.

"Dawsey?"

She spun, her hand clutching her heart. "Goodness, you startled me."

Dilsey sat up on her mat, her brows drawn in suspicion. She pointed at the shotgun. "Where do you think you're going with that?"

"Out back. I was afraid to go alone, but I didn't want to wake you."

Dilsey stood and crossed to her. "You'd best let me have the gun.

You don't even know how to shoot."

She gladly handed it over. "Maybe not, but I'm a pretty fair bluff."

Leaning on the wall, Dilsey struggled into her boots. She straightened and nodded at Dawsey's bare feet. "Were you going like that?"

She shrugged. "I was trying to be quiet."

Shaking her head, Dilsey held Dawsey's boots while she slid them on. Easing the door open a crack, she peeked out.

Dawsey pressed closer. "What are we looking for?"

"Anything out of place. You get a feel for it after a while." She pointed to the porch. "Look there. Ma shot that rascal after all."

Dark splotches, trampled in some places, led from the door to the ground. Dawsey frowned. "What is that?"

"Blood." Dilsey backed away from the door and pointed. "See, there's some in here, too. In all the commotion, we didn't notice."

Dawsey looked under her feet and shuddered. Rusty-brown footprints led through the door then scattered over the wood floor. Prints she, Hooper, and Tiller had tracked inside last night.

Dilsey stepped outside and she hurried after her.

"There's a lot," Dilsey said, worry creasing her forehead. "Ma may've killed him."

Her eyes flickered, and she gripped Dawsey's shoulders. "If the sheriff comes for her, we'll say I did it. You'll back me up, won't you?"

"No!" The word shot from Dawsey's mouth. "I—I mean, then they'll take you, won't they? I can't see anything happen to you."

Dilsey gave her a shake. "Ma shot a lawman. Some cruel drunk sworn in at the last minute, but that won't matter in Robeson County. If he's dead, they'll come for her."

"We'll pray it won't come to that."

Her trembling lips rimmed in white, Dilsey gazed toward the swamp. "Don't bother. Prayers uttered in Scuffletown never reach heaven. God forgot us a long time ago."

Shame coursed through Dawsey. Whatever warmth she'd missed in Father's absent parenting, thankfully, Aunt Livvy had honored Mother's wish to pass along her abiding faith in God. Affection had its merit, but assurance of God's protective love was a priceless gift.

Sudden longing filled her heart to see Dilsey with the same assurance. She took her hand. "You're wrong, Dilsey. God hasn't forgotten. He cares about you very much."

Dilsey flinched. "About you, maybe."

Drawing her sister to the rail, she pulled her close. "God calls Himself our refuge and fortress. Does that sound like an uncaring God?"

Dilsey shrugged.

"Have you ever watched a hen defending her brood?"

"We have a chicken yard, silly. Lots of times."

"In the same way, God promised to deliver us from the snare of the fowler, to tuck us under His wing and cover us with His feathers."

She had offered the perfect example. Hope shone from Dilsey's eyes. "He said that?"

Dawsey nodded and squeezed her arm. "Yes, so trust Him. He'll take care of you if you let Him. The same scripture says, 'Only with thine eyes shalt thou behold and see the reward of the wicked.'"

Dilsey tensed. Tugging free, she started down the steps. "That's our problem in Scuffletown. Sometimes it's hard to tell the wicked from the just."

She turned at the bottom step, grief etched in her face. "If you need to go to the outhouse, then come on."

Blinking back tears, Dawsey hurried to catch up.

They spoke very little on the way down the trail and back. Dawsey mentioned the warm day. Dilsey nodded and said it wouldn't last. A curtain had dropped, shutting them off from each other, as if the comforting whispers and gentle hugs of the night before had never happened.

They rounded the house, and Dilsey spun toward the porch, raising the barrel of her shotgun. "Pa, for heaven's sake, I nearly shot you."

He poured out a steaming pan of water and set to whisking with Odell's yard broom, slinging gory splatter. "I have to clean this mess before your ma sees it. She thinks that varmint got away."

Dilsey rushed up the steps and took the broom. "You're making a mess. Beside, you're not supposed to be out of bed. Go inside and keep Ma busy. I'll clean this up."

"She's still resting, bless her. Didn't sleep a wink all night with fretting over Hooper."

Dawsey took Silas's arm to steady him. "Shouldn't Hooper be here by now?"

He glanced at her with red-rimmed eyes. "He won't come home until he finishes what he left here to do."

At the door, he looked back at Dilsey. "Make sure you get it all. Your ma don't need more fear added to her plate."

"Yes, Pa."

"I know it won't be easy, but I'd be beholden to you girls if you'd conduct yourselves today like nothing's wrong." He lifted his chin toward the wagon. "Go on with your plans for sprucing up the house. It'll take her mind off things."

Hooper had unhitched Old Abe before he left, but the load of colorful boughs still sat in front of the house. For Dawsey, all the joy had gone out of decorating for Christmas. By the look of her, Dilsey felt even less inclined, but she bit her lip and nodded. "Yes, sir. We'll do it."

Dawsey tugged on Silas's arm. "Let's go inside. I'll fix you a nice breakfast."

"Did somebody say breakfast?" Tiller stood on the threshold rubbing sleepy eyes. Bare from the waist up, a lone suspender held up his britches.

Silas hustled forward, his bulk driving Tiller inside. "You heard right. Dawsey's offered to cook for us." Staring at the soiled planks at his feet, concern wrinkled his shaggy brows. "After she mops, that is. You boys have tracked in mud."

A willing conspirator, Dawsey whirled for a damp rag—and nearly tripped over Odell standing behind her.

Wearing a white cotton dressing gown, she stood with her shoulders back, her head high. Her serenity and strength brought to mind an angelic queen. For a moment, Dawsey forgot she was short.

On the porch, Dilsey stilled with the broom in hand and stared through the open door at her mother.

Odell glanced at her then back to Silas. "Did you really think I wouldn't notice blood stains on my own floor?"

"Now, Odie," Silas soothed, his eyes bulging. "Go back to bed, darlin'. I'll bring you some breakfast in a bit."

A smile tugged the corners of her mouth. Gliding to him on bare feet, she pinched his face and kissed him. "I saw how bad I shot him, Silas. The lead tore holes in his shirt."

Tears welled, her brave front slipping. "They'll come for me today."

Silas drew her to his chest. "They'll haul you out over my dead body."

Dilsey slung the broom and ran inside, her arms enveloping her mother. "Over mine, too."

"And mine," Dawsey vowed, stretching to hug them all.

Tiller slammed and locked the door. "I have a better idea. Don't let 'em in."

Amused by the wisdom of his simple plan, Dawsey bit her lip to keep from smiling.

Showing less restraint, Odell's shoulders shook with laughter. "Oh, Tiller, if only that would work. I'm afraid nothing will keep the sheriff out." She sobered. "What I won't do is cower inside my own house like I done something wrong. We'll do just like you said, Silas. We'll adorn this house and trim Dawsey's tree the way we planned."

Her trembling fingers smoothed Dilsey's hair, patted Dawsey's cheek, then clung to Silas's hand. "I just pray when the morning comes, I'm still alive to see it."

Weaving endless holly wreaths and tying sprigs to pine bough garlands had stained Ellie's hands a merry red. She had to admit, the decorations and the young Virginia pine they'd hauled from the woods gave the cabin an enchanted feel.

Dawsey had mixed dough and shaped it into cookie stars to hang on the tree, along with a long string of pinecones. She raided Mama's button box, sewing the most colorful onto scraps of cloth, and folded them into ornaments. After that, she tied fabric strips into bows of many shapes and sizes and hung them, too.

Between her and Mama, they'd turned bowls of sticky batter into cakes and cookies and rolled flaky crusts for the brown sugar pies.

Shortly after lunch, Rhoda came bearing gifts. Surrounded by Henry's men, she stayed long enough to see that her patient was well and to pass Mama a gunnysack filled with precious sugar, butter, salt, and two dressed ducks. Mama repaid her in eggs and warm smiles.

Once she left, more wonderful smells than before floated outside from the kitchen.

Ellie perched on the edge of the steps, staring toward the distant tree line. If a horse poked his nose from the brush, it could be good news or bad. With both her brothers due any minute, she hoped for the good and strained her ears for a whistle.

The day had dawned warm, but a brisk wind and a bank of clouds from the north had chased the warmth toward the coastline.

Pa sat in his chair flicking finishing pieces from the angel he whittled for Ma's Christmas present.

Ellie shivered and glanced his way. "You want me to fetch your coat?"

He grunted. "Not yet. I'm enjoying the breeze after sweating all night."

"Don't catch a chill," she warned over her shoulder then went back to scanning the trees.

His chair groaned as he leaned back, propping his boot on the rail next to Ellie. "I'm glad to see it cooling off. Fanning yourself while eating Christmas dinner just don't feel right."

"I could use a fan right now," Dawsey said behind them. "This cool hasn't reached the kitchen."

Ellie squinted up at her. "Come out and rest a spell. You look plain tuckered."

Pa twisted around to see. "She's red in the face, Ellie. Take her out to sit in the yard so the wind can cool her down."

Ellie stood. "I will, but fetch our coats off the pegs, Dawsey. From the look of that sky, you won't be hot for long."

They skirted the rain barrel and hopped puddles on the way to the shade tree, not that they needed shade with the black sky closing in. Ellie perched on her favorite stump, leaving Pa's for Dawsey.

"You're right," Dawsey said. "It is cold out here."

Ellie stood. "Let me help you with your coat."

Slipping her arm into the sleeve, Dawsey glanced at her. "May I ask a question? One that's burned in my heart for days?"

Ellie shrugged and sat down. "I suppose you'd better. A burning heart sounds a mite uncomfortable."

Smiling, Dawsey's lashes swept her cheeks. Head down, she picked at a speck of dried flour on the leg of her pants. Dawsey had taken a shine to Ellie's trousers. Since she washed them often and hung them to dry, Ellie didn't mind. Pulling clean britches off the line was easier than digging through her laundry basket for the cleanest pair.

Clasping her hands in her lap, Dawsey drew a deep breath. "Are you glad we found each other?" Her doe eyes begged Ellie to say yes.

Longing to please her, Ellie managed a sweet smile. "I'm glad you're my sister." A sprinkle of sugar on the tongue took the bite out of castor oil. "But I wish the whole thing had never happened."

Dawsey cocked her head. "Which thing? Silas taking you, or you knowing about it?"

Biting her lip, Ellie met her eyes. "If I had my way, you'd never have come. I wouldn't be wondering what my real folks were like, and I'd still feel comfortable hearing my own name."

The swirling dark clouds overhead couldn't match the distress on Dawsey's face. "You'd rather we'd gone to our graves never knowing each other?"

Ellie nodded. "That would've been fine by me."

Dawsey turned aside, pretending a sudden interest in a knobby root. Her shoulders rose and fell in deep sighs that seemed to catch in her chest.

A strange ache swelled inside Ellie. She swiveled toward the girl fate had tossed in her lap. "Are you all right, Dawsey?"

She sniffed and pulled farther away.

Ellie caught her arm. "I'm sorry. I don't mean to sound cold." She paused and swallowed. It wasn't in her nature to seek pity. "It's just been so hard since you came."

Dawsey turned, her face damp with tears. "You've grieved for a few weeks. I've suffered for years."

Ellie gaped. "You? How have you suffered?"

Standing, Dawsey loomed over her. "Don't you see? You never really left our house. You were there, every hour, every minute of the day, sucking the life from us. I just didn't know who to blame until now." She whirled to stalk toward the house.

Ellie lit out after her. Clutching her sleeve, she tugged her around. "What are you saying?"

Dawsey's face was livid. "Your disappearance stole my family's chance for happiness. I didn't have a funny, carefree father like Silas. I lived with a man consumed by rage."

"None of that was my fault."

Dawsey jerked away. "I never had a mother because your absence killed her."

The scathing words pelted Ellie like buckshot. She stumbled away from their sting and ran toward the woods.

Dawsey caught up with her, snagging her around the waist. "Please wait. I'm sorry." She dragged Ellie to a halt and threw both arms around her neck. "Forgive me. I didn't mean what I said. You must know I didn't. I was hurt and lashed out."

Before Ellie could react, a whistle sounded from the swamp.

Dawsey raised her head, her eyes searching Ellie's face. "Duncan or Hooper?"

Papa blew a sharp blast, and Duncan rode into sight.

Trotting closer, he grinned, his arm raised in greeting.

Dawsey sucked in a breath, and Ellie's heart stopped as a man slipped out of the brush behind Duncan, pointing a long-barreled pistol at his back.

Ellie's frozen feet sprang to life and she ran, remembering too late that she wasn't armed.

A shrill cry rose from Dawsey as she sprinted alongside.

With a shout, Hooper shot out of the opposite clutch of trees, waving a rifle.

The stranger turned too late and met the barrel of the Spencer with his jaw. He fell like a stone, his pistol firing to the sky.

Duncan's horse reared, unseating him.

The strangled scream that ripped from Dawsey's throat rocked the clearing, echoing through the swamp. Arms waving, she overtook Ellie and dashed toward the men.

Duncan sat up, smiling. "It's all right, honey. He didn't shoot me."

She passed him in a blur then sailed past Hooper. Shrieking like a woman possessed, she streaked to the fallen man and threw herself on the ground.

White faced, Hooper stalked to her and pulled her to her feet. "What are you doing? Get away from that stinking bounty hunter."

Struggling against him, Dawsey pulled free and fell on the limp and bleeding man. "He's no bounty hunter, Hooper." Sobbing, she raised stricken eyes. "You just killed my father."

THIRTY-SEVEN

Hooper gazed wistfully at Dawsey's Christmas tree. The cookie streamers, button ornaments, and colorful garlands brought a false cheer to the cabin. The wreaths, red with holly, reminded him of her hopeful tale of Christ's birth. Meant to bring joy, the sight of them worsened the ache in his chest.

Pa slumped before the hearth, staring into the fire. "It don't feel like Christmas Eve, does it?"

Hooper sighed. "No, sir, it sure don't." He laid a comforting hand on Pa's shoulder. "Why don't you get some rest?"

Ignoring the idea, he leaned in his chair and gripped his head. "This whole thing is my fault."

Hooper squatted beside him. "I don't see how you can think so. I'm the one who bashed in Mr. Wilkes's head."

Papa moaned. "I'm responsible, son, not you. Taking Ellie started a fire behind me, and the flames have chased me ever since." He sat up and slapped the arm of his chair. "I pray the man's all right, but by thunder, I won't let him take her away."

Ellie got up from the table and crouched at his feet. "I'm a grown woman now. No one can make me leave Scuffletown." She snorted. "I dare them to try."

"I dare them, too," Mama said, passing a tray filled with mugs of warm milk. She glanced around the cabin. "Where's Tiller?"

"He took off awhile ago," Hooper said. "Didn't say where he was headed."

Papa grunted. "He's spending too much time with those older boys. I can't shake the feeling they're up to no good."

"I'd trust those feelings if I were you." Ellie's troubled eyes said more than her words.

"I'm failing Effie," Pa said. "If I can't get a handle on Tiller, he may be better off back in Fayetteville."

Remembering Aunt Effie's shrill voice railing at Tiller, Hooper blew out a breath and stood. "I don't think so, Pa. Most anything would be better for him than that."

The door opened and Hooper turned with a start.

Dawsey slipped in quietly with downcast eyes, her red, swollen lids visible even with the evening shadows. "Rhoda needs a pan of hot water and something to use for bandages."

Mama rushed to see to her request, and Ellie ran to Dawsey. "How is he?"

Dawsey drew a deep breath. "He's still out, but Rhoda's sure he'll be fine."

Hooper stood, moving a few steps closer. "That's good news, honey."

"Thank you."

He tried not to wring his hands like a fretful woman. "I hope you know I feel awful about what happened."

"I'm sure you do."

A shock jolted Hooper. She wouldn't meet his gaze.

Mama rushed around him with a washtub. "Stay inside and eat something, Dawsey. I'll take this out to Rhoda."

"And the cloths?"

She lifted her arm, draped with cotton rags. "Right here."

Dawsey fidgeted with her nails. "I really should get back to him."

"You will. . .after Ellie dishes you a bite of supper. We'll call you if he wakes up."

Dawsey opened her mouth to argue, but she was already out the door.

Fearing for his mama's safety, Hooper glanced after her. "Shouldn't we—"

Dawsey spun with brimstone eyes. "Duncan's guarding him, if that's what concerns you. Really, Hooper, there's little to fear now that you've cracked his skull and taken his pistol."

His stomach lurched. "I meant no harm. I just—"

"I understand perfectly. You're protecting your own. It's what you do." She pointed toward Ellie's bedroom. "He's a tired old man. He'll pose no more threat to you."

Ellie fixed a plate and set it on the table for Dawsey.

Without looking up, Dawsey politely thanked her.

Something had happened between them. They pecked and strutted around each other like wary hens.

Papa looked up from the fire. "You never told us what happened, son. Did you find those men?"

Bile filled his mouth and he cleared his throat. "It's tended."

"What became of them?"

Hooper pulled in his lips then blew them out with a frustrated breath. "Pa, don't ask. Ma's safe now. That's all you need to know."

Dawsey met Ellie's gaze across the table. Both heads swung toward Hooper, but they kept their silence.

"I have a more important question." He crossed to them and pulled out a chair. Softening his tone, he sought Dawsey's eyes. "I don't mean to raise a touchy subject, but how did your pa find us?"

She paused midbite to lift one brow then finished chewing before she answered. "I would think it's obvious."

Hooper raised his chin. "Not to me."

"He followed Duncan from Fayetteville."

Speechless for once, Papa swiveled in his chair.

Ellie lowered her mug and stared.

Drumming softly on the tabletop, Hooper allowed the answer to settle in his head. "Duncan went to Fayetteville?"

She nodded.

"And you knew he was going?"

"He did so as a kindness to me. He decided if I could go out of my way for his father, he would do the same for mine."

"That's my brother," Hooper crowed in a loud voice, "noble to the core." He gritted his teeth to control his surging anger. "So Duncan traveled to Fayetteville against Pa's counsel then let a tired old man like Mr. Wilkes—forgive me, Dawsey, you said it yourself—tail him unnoticed for forty miles?"

She pushed her plate aside. "That's Colonel Wilkes to you. My father began his career as a scout with the 26th North Carolina Regiment."

He pursed his lips. "Is that a fact?"

"It is."

Spinning in his chair, he slapped the table hard. "That's it, Pa! We should send that faithless traitor packing."

"Which faithless traitor?" The lamb to the slaughter, Duncan stood on the threshold holding Ma's empty water pail.

With a roar, Hooper charged. The last thing he heard before slamming into Duncan's chest was the *crash* of the pail hitting the floor and Papa's anguished cry.

THIRTY-EIGHT

An old man lived inside the moon. He walked beside a little dog carrying a bundle of thorn-twigs. As a boy, Hooper would stare out the window with one eye shut and trace the ragged figure with his finger. Some nights, when the moon perched low and full, he still saw him.

He couldn't remember who told him the fanciful story. Likely Pa, with his lively sense of humor and love of a far-fetched tale.

Hooper led his horse from the barn and swung into the saddle. Lifting his anguished face to the sky, he searched the faint yellow surface. Sure as snuff, the man still hung there, smiling down while he trod his endless path. He seemed the last friend Hooper's vile temper had left him.

Mad at himself, he swiped his damp face with his sleeve. No sense bawling. Papa had given fair warning of the cost of another fight with his brother, a warning that escaped him until Pa loomed over their sprawling bodies, ordering Hooper to leave.

Duncan's memory had served him better. He hadn't lifted a finger in his own defense but only covered his face and rolled—an act Hooper mistook for cowardice until he realized Duncan would wake up in his own bed on Christmas morn.

His stomach lurched at the memory of his fist connecting with Duncan's gut and the grunt of pain as the wind left him in a rush. He winced, recalling the shuddering *thud* against his palms as his Spencer connected with Colonel Wilkes's skull.

Staring at the hands curled around his horse's reins, he wished they weren't capable of such awful things.

Mama's gentle voice echoed in his head, reading the words of Jesus from her Bible. " 'And if thy right hand offend thee, cut it off, and cast it from thee.' "

Hooper's right hand was his worst offender, bowing too often to the whims of his rage.

He looked over his shoulder for one last glimpse of the house. The single window glowed red from the festive decorations inside, lit by the flickering fire.

Two days ago, he sat on the porch working a hide as soft as butter, imagining the family around a Christmas tree, laughing and sharing gifts.

He patted the bulge in his saddlebag, the hide meant for Dawsey, and a bullfrog swelled in his throat. Gritting his teeth, he gathered the reins and turned the horse.

Running footsteps spun him around, reaching for his pistol.

"Hooper, wait."

He released his breath and drew his hand from the gun at his waistband. "That was foolish, Ellie. It's dangerous to sneak up on me." The truth of his words rained more shame on his head.

She ran to him, gripping the saddle horn with one hand and the leg of his britches with the other. "I can't bear to see you go. Come inside and talk to Pa. If you apologize, he'll change his mind."

"I did apologize. To him and to Duncan." He glanced longingly at the house. "It's no good, honey. His mind is set. He won't go back on his word."

"Blast his word! It's Christmas Eve."

He patted her hand. "Try to make tomorrow nice for Ma and Dawsey. They worked so hard."

Ellie clung to him, stubbornly shaking her head. "Christmas won't be nice for any of us without you. We may as well tear down the holly and toss the presents in the bog."

"You'll do no such thing. In fact, I have more gifts for under that tree. Will you tend to it for me?"

"Yes, but—"

"Get them from your room. I wrapped them in newspaper and stuck them under your bed." He reached for the saddlebag. "Except for Dawsey's." He reached inside and handed the hide down to her. "Will you make sure this gets wrapped and placed under the tree?"

Ellie watched him with tearful eyes. "Where will you go?"

He shrugged. "Henry's, where else? At least for now."

"Can I come see you there?"

He shook his head. "Too dangerous. Maybe after Sheriff McMillan cools down." With a sad smile, he saluted. "Merry Christmas, Ellie. Take care of things around here."

"Hooper?" Her pout had disappeared. "What happened to those men?"

A shudder tore through him, and he glanced away. "Trust me on this, little sister. You don't want to know."

Before she could ask more big-eyed questions, he dug his heels into his horse's side and trotted from the yard.

Dawsey sat in Dilsey's room, watching the slow rise and fall of her father's chest. She struggled to focus on prayers for his recovery, but praying for anyone else came hard after watching what happened to Hooper.

When he came to himself, his face had gone slack with shock. Realizing what he'd done, he stood up, wiping his hands on his britches as if trying to remove his guilt. When Silas raised a stern finger and roared at him to go, he'd marched to the door like a soldier accepting his fate. A soldier with tears glistening in his eyes.

Hooper's rash, impulsive nature had finally gotten the best of him. The frightened girl cowering in a shed the night she arrived longed to be glad for his comeuppance, but the woman who'd come to love every line of his dear face wouldn't allow it.

Her heart aching, Dawsey glanced at her father, mumbling in his sleep. Love Hooper or not, the violent side of him scared her witless. He'd almost killed her father and, by his own near admission, had tracked down and murdered two men in the swamp.

Perhaps such acts were necessary to survive in Scuffletown. For Dawsey, accustomed to the genteel behavior of life in Fayetteville, such rampant brutality was unacceptable. She shuddered. What more might he be capable of to protect his way of life?

The door burst open, startling her out of her gloomy thoughts.

Dilsey stood just inside, a stunned look on her face. "Oh," she said. "I'm sorry. I—for a minute, I forgot he was in here."

Her eyes widened as they lit on Father. She yanked them away and backed up two steps. "Where's Duncan?"

"Inside the house."

She nodded. "Dawsey, would you mind?" She waved toward the bed. "There are some bundles under there, and I need them."

Dawsey walked to meet her. "Don't you want to see him?"

She shook her head and retreated farther.

"He's your father, Dilsey. The man who gave you life."

Leaning, she looked past Dawsey. "He's still asleep?"

Dawsey took her hand. "Yes, he is. So he can't possibly bite you." She gave a little tug. "Come along."

The frightened girl let Dawsey lead her a little closer before she stiffened. "I'm sorry, I can't." She swallowed hard. "I just can't." Her eyes pleaded with Dawsey. "Will you gather the packages from under my bed and bring them inside to the tree? I gave Hooper my word." With that, she bolted, slamming the door behind her.

Dawsey spun, wondering if the sharp noise had disturbed Father. Truthfully, she wished he had stirred, but he lay as still as death.

Frustrated with herself for letting Dilsey escape, she ran outside to call her and nearly tripped over her sitting on the steps. Dawsey eased down beside her and hugged her close. "Taking a look won't be disloyal to Silas. It's perfectly normal to be curious."

Her sister shivered. "I'm afraid."

"There's nothing to fear, I promise. He won't even know you're there." On impulse, Dawsey stood. "I'm going inside for a while. I feel the urge for a cookie and a nice glass of milk. Please don't leave him alone."

Dilsey stretched out her hand. "No, wait."

Dawsey crossed the yard with a determined step. "I won't be long." She peeked over her shoulder as she rounded the house.

Dilsey stood with one hand on the doorknob. Pulling her shoulders back, she disappeared inside.

Smiling, Dawsey decided to take time for a slice of pie, too.

Ellie leaned her head against the door, staring at the peculiar man on the bed. How would she cross the yawning space between where she stood and the truth?

Shadowed memories of her childhood filled her mind like rushing water.

223

Cradled in Pa's lap on the porch, the rocker gently swaying, his shining eyes caressing her.

Balanced atop the porch rail, Papa shoving sweet melon in her mouth, laughing when she spit the seeds across the yard.

Tin cans set along an overturned tree so Ellie could practice her aim, Pa crowing with pride each time she hit one.

On his belly, half drowned in the bog, fishing her out with a stick. Rocking in his lap when he pulled her free, both crying and covered in mud.

Ellie didn't need to see the man who'd given her life. The only one who mattered was the man she'd give her life for.

Turning to go, she paused when Dawsey's father moaned and began to cough. The cough turned to hoarse hacking then desperate gasps.

Ellie sailed across the room, terrified when his bulging eyes opened and fixed on her. She longed to run and fetch Dawsey, but there was no time. If she left, he'd choke to death. Yanking him by the arm, she pulled him up and pounded on his back.

Red in the face, he brayed furiously for several minutes then fell against the pillows, groaning and clutching his head. "What the devil hit me?" His watery eyes wandered the room and then jerked to her face. "Dawsey! Merciful heavens, I've found you."

Stricken, all Ellie could think to do was tell the poor man the truth. "I'm not Dawsey, sir. I'm the other one. I'm Dilsey."

Dawsey pushed the door open, juggling two mugs and a plate of sugar cookies. Joy warmed her soul at the sight of Dilsey hunched over the bed.

"Lay back and hush, old man. Dawsey will have my hide."

"Stop talking nonsense, young lady, and get out of the way. I'm taking you home."

The mugs hit the floor with a *crash*. Dilsey and Father were wrestling!

"Calm down, Father. I'm here." She rushed to his bedside and crowded in beside Dilsey. Too late, she realized the sight of them standing together might be too much for him.

His head whipped to Dawsey then Dilsey. His mouth was a yawning cavern, his eyes blazing pools of doubt. He stared from one to the other, gulping for air.

Dawsey sat down, smoothing his hair. "Don't be frightened, dear. It's all right."

"I'm seeing things, Dawsey," he cried. "Hearing them, too. Apparitions. Ghostly beings that aren't really there." His eyes pleaded with her for the right answer. "Am I sleeping?"

She laughed. "There are no apparitions, Father, and you're wide awake. What you're seeing is real." Catching her sister's reluctant arm, she pulled her close. "It's our own dear Dilsey, come back to us at last."

Slowly, carefully, he reached a shaky hand and touched Dilsey's face. With the other, he groped for Dawsey's fingers.

His tremulous smile melted into a mask of grief. With a mournful bellow of long-denied pain, he covered his face and sobbed.

THIRTY-NINE

Dawsey awoke to the sound of quiet knocking. She longed to return to her dream, where she and Hooper strolled in the holly tree clearing. The gloom surrounding Hooper had lifted; the doubt in her heart had vanished. She trusted him again and felt no fear. No anger shone from his eyes.

The rapping came again, chasing her dream to the shadows. Throwing back the quilt, she hurried to the door before the noise disturbed her father.

Duncan stood outside, with his hat in his hand. He'd dressed in what looked like his Sunday best and wiped his boots to a shine. "Merry Christmas."

Dawsey couldn't help but smile at his freshly scrubbed face. "Merry Christmas to you." Fighting a yawn, she rubbed her sleepy eyes. "What time is it?"

He lifted his brows. "Early, I'm afraid. How's your father?"

She glanced over her shoulder. "Still sleeping."

"I'm sorry to disturb you. Ma sent me. She's been darting around the kitchen since well before dawn, rustling in cabinets and rattling pans. Something about roasted ducks."

Dawsey frowned. "She wants to go ahead with dinner?"

He smiled. "She insists. Stockings, gifts under the tree, noggins of spiced posset, the whole holly-berried shebang."

"Noggins of posset?"

He feigned alarm. "Stay away from those. Hot sweetened milk curdled with wine." He gave her a knowing look. "Rhoda's scuppernong wine."

"I appreciate the warning." She frowned. "I'm a bit surprised at your mother, to be honest. I mean, with Hooper gone and everything."

"Hooper's the reason for all the fuss. How else can she make Pa squirm? The bigger shindig she throws, the worse he'll feel about Hooper missing out." He chuckled. "If she works things just right, Pa will be blubbering and ordering me out to fetch him."

Hope stirred in Dawsey's heart. She remembered the murdered men in the swamp and pushed it down. "You're not terribly angry with him?" She wrinkled her nose. "I fear I would be, in your shoes."

Duncan waved his hand. "Nah. I'm used to his blustering." He winked. "Gives me the chance to punch him back every now and then." He pointed over his shoulder. "Do I tell Ma you're coming?"

She paused. "Goodness, I'm not sure. I long to help, but my father was so frightened and confused last night. If he wakes and finds me gone. . ."

"When you're ready, I'll sit with your pa. I promise to fetch you the minute he stirs."

Tenderness surged for the good-hearted man. "Thank you, Duncan. You're a very special person."

He backed away, turning his hat in his hands. "So are you, Dawsey." His eyes softened. "So are you."

For privacy, Dawsey hung a sheet in front of Father's bed. She hurried to wash and dress, shuffling around the room as quietly as possible so she wouldn't wake him. Then she lifted the makeshift curtain to peek inside. He was fast asleep.

Still afraid for him, she checked his chest for movement. It rose and fell with each steady breath. Satisfied, she let the sheet fall into place. Bounding down the steps, still pinning her hair, she hurried for Odell's kitchen.

Her jaw dropped when she stepped inside the cabin. Odell had hung even more decorations than before. She'd strung more pinecones—these dabbed with flour paste to look like snow—and tied candles to the branches of the tree, placing some in a staggered row along the mantel. They'd pulled in the last of the cherry red possumhaw boughs and arranged them in brilliant clusters.

"Merry Christmas!" A chorus of voices cried.

"What do you think?" Odell called from the hearth.

Dawsey beamed. "It's lovely." She gazed in awe at the bulging sacks on the counter. "Where on earth did you get all that food?"

"Isn't it wonderful?" Odell asked. "It's a Christmas miracle. Every time I look, there's another sack on the porch."

"Henry?"

She nodded slyly.

"Don't fret about your pa. I'll keep a close watch on him," Duncan said, touching her hand lightly as he swept past.

Dilsey, wearing more flour than was mixed in her rolled-out crust, watched Dawsey from the table. "How is he?"

"Exhausted." She grimaced. "We gave him quite a shock, but he finally settled down sometime before morning."

Odell glanced up from stirring her pot. "Before morning? Then you're tuckered, too, child. Go back to your mat for a few hours."

Dawsey waved her hand. "Honestly, I'm fine." She reached for an apron and tied it around her waist. "I'd feel positively left out if I slept through all the fun."

Tiller snorted from the corner. "Fun? I'd rather have a tooth yanked." He sat on the floor peeling nuts, surrounded by bits of shell.

Dawsey leaned to inspect his bowl. "Pecans?"

Odell grinned. "Henry sent them. We'll put them in the sweet buns." She winked and nodded. "Hooper's favorite."

Silas hunched over in his chair with downcast eyes and deep furrows in his brow. He held a stray button, tumbling it absently between his fingers. It hadn't escaped Dawsey's notice that his voice wasn't part of her Christmas greeting.

She squatted in front of him. "How are you this morning?"

He averted his eyes. "Not worth the asking."

Odell lifted her simmering stew from the hook over the fire and hustled it to the counter. "Don't mind him. He's danced his jig, and now he's not keen to pay the fiddler."

His head jerked up. "It's not the waltz you're thinking, woman." His sorrowful gaze swung to Dawsey. "The debt I can't pay is to your pa." He groped for her hands. "Your forgiveness was a powerful blessing and a testament to your good nature. I ain't expecting the same from him."

She squeezed his fingers. "I'm afraid you're right. I doubt he'll be very forgiving."

He straightened. "Still, I have to ask."

She nodded. "Let's wait until he's stronger, shall we?"

"Whatever you say, darlin'."

Dilsey, her eyes flashing, banged the table with the rolling pin. "What about Hooper? He asked forgiveness, and you shunned him."

More hurt than anger sparked Silas's eyes. "It ain't the same. I wronged folks who were strangers." His eyes flicked to Dawsey. "At least at the time." He balled his fist and slammed the arm of his chair. "Hooper strikes out at his own flesh and blood."

Dilsey's hand went to her hip, dusting flour over her clothes. "Hooper protects his own in the only way he knows. Duncan had no business riding to Fayetteville after you said no." She lifted her chin. "Truth be told, Hooper was standing up for you."

Silas leaped to his feet. "With brutality and hatred toward his brother? The boy's fuse is too short," he shouted. "I won't have it in my house."

Odell's hands stilled over her mixing bowl. "Good thing I don't feel the same. Look at you, bellowing and blustering about, punishing our son for what he learned at your knee."

Silas plopped in his chair, shrinking from her words.

"What Hooper did was wrong," she continued. "But tossing our son out of the house on a cold Christmas Eve ain't right, neither. Hooper needs love and guidance to change." She pointed toward the swamp. "He won't find much out there."

Dawsey crossed her arms and huddled near the fire, praying the argument would swing in Hooper's favor. She didn't get the chance to find out.

Father's loud, frantic rant swept through the door on Duncan's heels. Wide eyed, he pointed. "He's calling for you, Dawsey." He glanced at Dilsey. "For both of you."

Dilsey's flashing eyes melted into fear. "I won't go." Her head whipped back and forth. "Last night was enough for me."

Odell laid aside her ladle. In one quick motion, she untied Dilsey's apron and placed a dishrag in her hands. "Wash up and go with Dawsey. Can't you hear the pain in that poor man's voice?"

Silas stood. "Wait, Odie. Are you sure?"

Her firm gaze bounced to him. "He's in no shape to spirit her off. If he tries, I believe Ellie could stop him." She sobered. "You want a chance to tell that man we're sorry?"

He nodded.

"It starts right here." She gave Dilsey a little shove. "Go on, honey."

Sulking like a child, Dilsey toddled to Dawsey and clung to her. "You won't leave me alone with him, will you?"

Dawsey hugged her arm. "I promise." She smoothed a flour-crusted curl from her sister's face. "There's really nothing to fear. He sounds gruff, but he's just afraid."

Dilsey inhaled sharply through her nose. "All right, then. Let's get it over with."

Arm in arm, they trudged around the house, Dilsey growing stiffer with every step.

Dawsey had to admit Father's hoarse cries raised the hairs on her arms. She could imagine how they affected her poor sister.

They reached the steps with Aunt Livvy's words about him echoing in Dawsey's head.

Even as a child, he was gloomy and pouting. . .when he wasn't being stubborn and willful."

Dilsey trembled beside her as they opened the door, so frightened she seemed to be holding her breath.

The reunion Dawsey had dreamed of between Father and his long-lost daughter seemed doomed by his awful tirade.

Without planning her actions, she left Dilsey at the door and stalked to the bed. Clutching the makeshift curtain in both hands, she ripped it down in one fierce jerk. "I believe that's quite enough caterwauling, if you don't mind."

Pressed against his pillow, both hands clenched at his sides, he looked like the willful child Aunt Livvy remembered. Shocked into silence, mouth still wide from shouting, he stared at Dawsey as if he'd never seen her before.

She supposed, in all the years they'd spent together, he never had.

His eyes blazed and his mouth worked furiously, but nothing came out.

"That's better. Now we can hear ourselves think." She settled on the bed beside him and motioned Dilsey closer.

As she approached, Father's head swung toward her with a hoarse gasp. "I feared I'd dreamed you."

Dilsey shrugged. "No, sir, I reckon you didn't."

Blinking against sudden tears, he swallowed several times and attempted a smile. "I'd given up on ever seeing you again." He seemed mesmerized, studying his daughters with an awestruck gaze. "You're just the same. . .but different. Just like when you were babes." He stared over their heads into the past. "Other people couldn't tell you one from the other, but your mother and I could from the start." His face seemed to crumble. "Forgive me, Margaret. I failed you."

Dawsey clutched his arm. "You haven't."

His head wagged up and down. "She made me promise to never stop looking. She knew our baby was alive."

He lifted swimming eyes to Dilsey. "I failed you, too, child. Please forgive me."

She moved a rigid step closer. "Oh no, sir. You ain't failed me at all, Colonel Wilkes. Shucks, I'm real glad about all that happened."

Dawsey waved a warning finger—too late.

"Otherwise I'd never have wound up a McRae." Smiling, she shook her head. "And that wouldn't do."

Father's mournful look turned to stone. His head spun to Dawsey. "What did she say?"

"Never mind, dear." She shot up and pulled the extra pillow from behind him. "Lie back and rest. You've had a great shock."

Ignoring her, he sat up straighter and groped his head. "What hit me, Dawsey? Surely I have injuries to the brain. I thought she said she was a McRae."

Dilsey beamed. "My brother, Hooper, gave you that awful bump with the butt of his gun." She tilted her head. "But he's real sorry."

"Your b–brother?"

"And don't fret about hearing things, Colonel. I said McRae, all right." She smiled and almost curtsied. "That's my name. Ellie McRae."

Father bolted upright and roared, struggling to climb off the bed. "I'll kill them all!"

Dawsey clutched his flailing wrists. "Run, Dilsey. Send Duncan."

Her eyes impossibly round, she stumbled away. "What did I say?"

"Just go! And don't come back."

She didn't need to say it twice. Dilsey whirled on her heels and bolted. The bar slammed into place from the outside, locking Dawsey inside with her frenzied father.

She'd once wished for a genie to bring the gloomy, sullen man to life again. *Be careful what you wish for, Dawsey.*

She never expected the God-sized miracle she prayed for would show up as a backwoods version of herself.

FORTY

Hooper laid aside the ax and gathered the pile of kindling he'd split for Henry's woodbox. Proud people, his folks had taught him that a man should pay his own way in the world. By the look of the bounty steadily mounting on Rhoda's kitchen counters, he'd soon have a debt to cancel for a nice Christmas dinner.

He rolled the logs in the box with a clatter and stuck his head through the door. "Where does Henry keep the chicken feed?"

Rhoda waved him in. "Henry's already tended those squawking birds. Come sit a spell. I've got fresh coffee brewing."

Hooper hid a grimace. Rhoda's coffee was as strong and dark as she was but not as pretty. Oil swam in the thick cup she'd handed him when he awoke. Three hours later his ears still rang. He held up his hand. "I'll pass, thank you." He rubbed his stomach. "My belly don't appreciate good swamp coffee."

She flashed a smile. "You wanted to say swamp mud."

He grinned.

"Suit yourself, but come inside and jaw for a spell. I don't get much company out this way. Lord knows, Henry don't do enough talking."

Hooper ducked his head, his eyes combing the yard for Henry. As appealing as Rhoda was, Hooper never heard it said that her husband was the jealous sort. One thing was certain—he didn't aim to be the man to test him. "Bring your coffee out here to the porch."

"It's too chilly. Besides, I can't leave my pies."

He gulped. "It's not so bad. Slip on a shawl or something. I'll remind you about the pies."

Cold fingers the size of corncobs clamped on Hooper's neck. Their strength, helped along by his fright, lifted him from the ground.

"You'd best watch out," an ominous voice mumbled.

Hooper's body tensed, and the swamp mud he drank threatened to spew.

The hand released him and he spun.

"Is Rhoda coaxing you into her lair?" Henry's tight smile, the same as a rousing laugh for him, eased Hooper's racing heart.

"Good morning, Henry. Much obliged for the scare."

Giggling, Rhoda pointed at him from the door.

He hung his head and shot her a sheepish grin.

"Now will you come inside and stop acting foolish."

Agreeing with her estimation, he followed Henry over the threshold.

Hooper lounged at their simple table, listening to Rhoda talk, a need she seldom got to vent, living with quiet and stoic Henry. His silence was the price the Queen of Scuffletown paid for her title—along with never knowing when she would be digging her husband's grave.

The two had welcomed him to their hearth and home without a single question. Henry opened the door wide at his knock, and Rhoda sought every way to make him feel comfortable.

He'd stretched out in front of their fire all night, his head pining for home and his heart longing for Dawsey.

"My pa threw me out." The words fell from his mouth and bounced off the rafters.

Rhoda stopped talking somewhere between her winded tirade against Sheriff McMillan and her mama's gingerbread recipe. Sadness darkened her lovely face. "I figured as much, with you not keen to talk about it."

Henry looked up from weaving a leather strap. "Silas will change his mind."

"Not this time."

"What'd you do?" Rhoda asked.

Henry's head whipped around. "Rhoda."

"It's all right," Hooper said. "I don't mind saying what a fool I am."

Rhoda stretched across the table with an eager look on her face. "Go on then."

"I have a quick temper." He lifted his eyes to the man who never made a move he didn't plan. "I don't suppose you know what that means."

Henry pointed at his wife. "I've learned from watching her."

Rhoda slapped his finger aside. "Don't mistake a woman's sass for temper." Her eyes swung to Hooper. "There's nothing so terrifying as a man given to rage."

"You're not helping," Henry said, his brow cocked.

Hooper held up his hand. "Let her speak."

Rhoda snatched his fingers and drew him across the table, her pretty eyes casting a spell. "People rest within their safe borders," she said quietly. "Like us, here in the hideout. We know how far from the house we can go without worrying about getting shot."

He nodded.

"When you fly off in a fury without warning, your stakes are always moving. Folk get lost around you so they're always dodging lead." She sat back watching him. "Do you understand?"

Somehow he did. Picturing Papa's grieved face drove her point deep. "I never could make out why my anger bothered my pa so much. I think I know now. It kept him at the ready."

Rhoda pushed up from the table. "Knowing how you've gone astray is the first mile on the road to change."

He sighed. "I sure wish that road could get me home in time for Christmas."

She set a thick slice of apple pie in front of him then ruined it with a mug of her coffee. "You are home for Christmas, as far as we're concerned. Ain't that right, Henry?"

Hooper supposed an offer like that might be worth a rotted-out belly. Smiling, he forced a sip. "Thank you kindly."

"That's not true."

Hooper's head swung with Rhoda's toward Henry's quiet decree.

She blushed to her collar. "What a mean thing to say. Hooper's welcome here for as long as he likes."

Henry shook his head. "There's nothing here for him. The only place a man should be on Christmas Day is beside his own hearth, surrounded by his folks." As if spent from talking and fresh out of words, Henry winked and picked up his fork.

Hooper swallowed his mouthful of pie and stared. It was the most he'd heard him say in one breath.

Wiping her brow, Dawsey sat on the porch of the main house to rest, feeling she'd lived three days since breakfast. She longed to push her father out of Dilsey's room and lock herself away from the madness. Instead, she and Duncan had shoved him inside and bolted the door.

It broke her heart to do such a thing, but she couldn't allow him to stumble around with a wounded head trying to kill the McRaes. By the look on his face as the door swung shut, she wondered if he'd ever forgive her.

"Can I sit with you?"

Dawsey looked over her shoulder and nodded.

Dilsey took the three steps to the ground and settled between her and the rail. "Is your pa all right?"

Weary with strife, even more weary with Dilsey, she gave her a sullen glance. "He's your pa, too, you know."

Instead of a backlash of denial, Dilsey surprised her. "I reckon I should be more careful with my words." She nudged Dawsey. "But so should you. I can allow that the colonel is my father, but I only have one pa."

Dawsey gently bumped heads with her. "Point taken."

Instead of drawing away, Dilsey rested against her shoulder. "What happened back there? What set him off?"

Lifting her sister's hand, she laced fingers with her. "You have to look at things from his perspective. For nineteen years, you've been the kidnapped daughter he needed to save from a villainous man named McRae. To hear you've become one of them was too much for him to bear."

Her eyes widened. "He knew it was Pa all along?"

Dawsey shrugged. "I don't think he knew exactly, but he had somehow traced your disappearance to that name."

Little wrinkles marred Dilsey's brow as she stared toward the trees. "Ma said they fled Hope Mills in the dead of night. Maybe he got wind of it."

"If he did," Dawsey said, "it would certainly arouse his suspicion."

Dilsey nodded. "It would mine."

"Of course, then he couldn't find them. It had to be very frustrating, as well as heart wrenching, considering he was racing to bring you home in time to save our mother."

"He was?"

"Well, in his mind, at least. I'm not convinced it would've made any difference in the end. She was very weak and frail."

Dilsey's shoulders slumped. "Then I prance in there and brag about my name." She slapped her forehead. "I have mush for brains."

Laughing, Dawsey hugged her close. "Don't be silly. You didn't know." She gave her a sideways look. "Rocks, perhaps?"

Dilsey jabbed her with an elbow. They shared a laugh before she grew silent again. "Do you think he'll ever forgive me?"

"I was just wondering the same about me"—Dawsey grimaced—"considering I helped lock him up. As for you, there's nothing to forgive. None of this is your fault, Dilsey."

Smiling, Dilsey accepted her pardon. "I have another question." She pouted her mouth. "Will you ever stop calling me Dilsey?"

Grinning, Dawsey shook her head. "Not likely. It rolls so nicely off the tongue."

Dilsey punched her arm. "Oh you!"

"Besides"—she swallowed the lump in her throat—"I picture our mother selecting our names with great care. You don't really mind, do you?"

Dilsey's arm slid around her shoulders. "I reckon not."

Behind them, Duncan cleared his throat. "Your pa will be fine, Dawsey. Once he settles down."

She bounced to her feet, brushing dirt off her britches. "I don't know if he'll ever be fine again, but there's nothing I can do if he won't let me."

Duncan held the door as she passed into the house. "Don't worry," he said. "We'll take him a heaping plate of roast duck and Indian dumplings. A fine meal should mellow him some."

She paused. "I know what a duck is, but what's the other thing you mentioned?"

Odell glanced up from her mixing bowl. "The Indian dumplings? You'll know soon enough. I need you to mix them for me."

She took the apron from Odell and gathered ingredients as she called them out.

"You'll need a pint of milk and four eggs, a salt-spoon of salt, flour to dust your hands, and a pot of boiling water." She jerked her chin toward the fire. "I've already started the water heating for you." She pointed to the shelf over the counter. "Once you beat the milk and eggs, fetch that sack of meal and measure out enough to make a stiff dough.

Flour your hands and roll it into balls about the size of goose eggs. Flatten them with a rolling pin, tie them into those cloths yonder, and simmer until they're done."

Dawsey cracked eggs in the bowl. "That sounds easy enough."

"Watch them close. They'll go to pieces if you leave them too long in the pot."

"Yes, ma'am."

Odell answered the question running through Dawsey's mind. "They're good alongside meat or afterwards with molasses and butter."

Duncan slid into a seat at the table. "I'll leave the Indian dumplings for all of you, to make sure your stomachs get nice and full."

Dawsey cast him a sweet smile. "That's very thoughtful."

"Don't flatter him," Dilsey said. "That's a sugarcoated trick. He means to fill us too full to eat brown sugar pie."

Duncan smacked his lips and rubbed his middle. "With toasted black walnuts."

Odell threw an apple.

It glanced off his head, and he howled with laughter.

"Go make yourself useful to that cantankerous old man in the barn. He's determined to do both his and Hooper's chores all by himself."

Duncan bounded for the door, stopping to toss the apple in a slow arc to his mother. "We should oblige him. It might make him change his mind."

Odell shook her head and pointed at her paste of flour and butter. "This should make him change his mind. Silas knows how Hooper loves my apple potpie." She raised a brilliant smile. "He'll think of Hooper the minute it hits the table. If that don't do the trick, I'll soften his tough hide with my Tipsy Parson cake."

Duncan slipped out with a rumbling laugh.

Odell raised a brow at Dilsey, seated at the table with her head idly propped, drumming her fingers. "Ellie McRae? It's Christmas Day, not your birthday. March over and stir these onions."

FORTY-ONE

The table was set, the rolls browned, and the last fragrant pie squeezed onto the counter. Dawsey gazed at the bountiful spread, arms linked with Odell and Dilsey. "No one will leave this table hungry."

Odell laughed. "If they do, it's their own fault."

She patted Dilsey's back. "Go tell your pa and Duncan to wash up. Christmas dinner is ready."

She sprang for the door.

"See if you can find Tiller," Odell called. "He's been missing since morning."

Dilsey poked her head back inside. "That rascal's hiding from all the extra chores. You did him in with those pecans."

Odell sniffed. "We'll see how he feels about pecans while he's shoving a bun down his throat."

"One bun? Not a chance." Dilsey grinned and disappeared.

Odell handed Dawsey a broad plate. "Load this up for your pa, honey. I'll have Duncan take it out back."

She shook her head. "I'll take it myself. I'd like to eat my meal with him, if you don't mind."

Odell's eyes softened. "I think it's a fine idea." She paused and squinted. "Don't go by yourself, if your pa's still feisty. He might get loose and wind up lost in the swamp."

She sighed. "I suppose you're right. I'll wait for Duncan."

While Dawsey waited, she lovingly filled the plate with a sample of each dish. When nothing else would fit, she covered it with a dishcloth and laid it aside to serve herself.

Duncan breezed in drying his hands, and his mother him asked him to walk with Dawsey.

"Sure thing," he said. "Let me carry one of those plates for you, Dawsey." He raised the cloth. "You're planning to eat all of this?"

Odell laughed. "Don't listen to him. You won't be here to watch, so he'll eat three times that much."

It felt wrong to be laughing, teasing, marching across the backyard laden by a feast, with Father lost and broken inside Dilsey's bedroom. "I'm a little scared," she confessed outside the door.

"Don't be. I'll go in with you."

"That's not a good idea." She touched his arm. "Wait for me, though? At least until I give the all clear."

He smiled. "I won't leave this step."

Expecting a war whoop and a hurtling body, Dawsey braced herself and sucked in a breath as the bar lifted. Her legs tensed.

Nothing.

Duncan raised questioning brows.

She shrugged.

Dread trickled down her back as they stepped inside the dim, hushed room.

Father lay on his back with one arm resting on his forehead. He stared intently at the ceiling and didn't acknowledge their presence.

She took the food from Duncan and nodded.

He retreated to the steps to wait.

The brooding figure on the bed reminded her of the father she'd left behind in Fayetteville. His mouth was set in a grim pout and defeat lined his face.

Dawsey approached with caution. "I've brought your lunch."

Hoping he'd forgotten, she decided to forego any mention of Christmas. "You've missed two meals at least. You must be starved."

He rolled his tongue in a slow arc across his bottom lip. "If it's all the same to you, I'm a trifle more interested in a drink."

"You've had no water?" She whirled to check the pitcher by the bed. Gone.

"I don't understand. I filled it myself."

She searched the floor and found the handle next to her feet and shards of pottery in a heap between the table and the bed. "I'm so sorry.

I had no idea. It must've been broken in the struggle."

She hurried to ask Duncan to bring a new pitcher. While she waited, she wet his lips with a dish towel dipped in applesauce.

Duncan returned, striding boldly into the room.

Father's hate-filled eyes tracked him across the floor.

"Can I bring you anything else, sir?" Duncan asked.

"Yes. My pistol."

He chuckled. "That might be bad for my health, Colonel." Smiling, he nodded at the covered plate. "Enjoy your meal." With a wink for Dawsey, he strolled out whistling.

Father crossed his arms in a huff. "Who is that insufferable whelp?" He glared. "A McRae, no doubt?"

Ignoring the question, Dawsey gave him a drink then removed the dishcloth and held the food under his nose. "Look what I've brought you. Roast duck, gravy, and all the trimmings." She held up a thick slice of sweet potato bread. "Look. I even made your favorite."

His hungry gaze roamed the plate before suspicion clouded his eyes. "Do you mean to say you've been cooking with them? Standing shoulder to shoulder with our enemy?"

Her spirits drooped. "It's not what it seems."

"What then?" He shoved the plate away. "Dawsey, I find all this quite confusing."

"Of course you do, but—"

"When those men took you, I knew in my gut they were the same scoundrels who took your sister. The knowledge frightened me, stirred me from the dark abyss where I'd fallen. I had purpose again, to find you since I failed in finding Dilsey."

"You seem much more alert. I'm very grateful."

He waved his hand. "Then why do you have me questioning my sanity again? We should be on our way home to Lavinia. Instead, my own daughter has me locked in a makeshift prison while she bakes bread with her captors." His outburst ended with a hoarse shout.

Wincing, Dawsey gripped her forehead. "I know it's difficult for you to understand."

"Difficult?" The strain of his voice brought him up off his pillow. "No, daughter, impossible."

"I can explain." She wiped sweat from her top lip. "You see, I've been here for weeks, living among them and learning their ways."

He gaped. "In that short time you've forgotten who you are?"

"They've been very kind to me."

"Kind?" His eyes bulged.

"Yes. They saved my life. I was snakebit, and—"

"They've bewitched you. Your sister, too." He pointed an accusing finger. "That man took Dilsey from her crib."

"It was a long time ago. He made a mistake." The ridiculous words sounded hollow and trite. Why couldn't she find the right ones?

Tears pooled in Father's eyes. "Then the vipers came for you." He shifted his gaze to the wall. "And you've crawled into the pit with them."

"No, I—"

"Just go."

Dawsey clutched her chest. "Please give me a second to collect my thoughts. I know I can make you understand." She licked her dry lips. "I made a deal with Silas. He promised to take me home right after Christmas. It was the only way I could bring Dilsey."

He held up his hand. "I said go—back to your blasted McRaes." He flicked her away like a bothersome pest. "I imagine they're holding Christmas dinner for you."

Dawsey stumbled away, shaking her head. Bursting into tears she fled, nearly falling over Duncan outside the door.

He pulled her to his chest with one strong arm and locked the door with the other. Leading her toward the house, he tucked her closer. "It's all right, honey. He'll feel better soon, and you can take him home." He smiled down at her. "Away from us blasted McRaes."

She lifted soggy lashes. "You heard?"

Duncan shrugged. "You gave me the best seat in the house."

Guilt lay heavy on her chest. Why *did* she feel more comfortable, more at ease with the McRaes than with her own father?

Perhaps his accusation held merit. The enchanting McRaes had woven a spell on her mind from the first, a hex that grew stronger and more deceptive each day, wooing her until she couldn't tell right from wrong.

If so, Hooper possessed the most beguiling spirit, since his charms held sway over her heart.

"Don't you worry about what your father said. No one could understand how things fell unless they'd walked it out in your shoes."

Staring into Duncan's sincere gray eyes, watching the set of his handsome jaw, she wondered why quarrelsome, hotheaded Hooper had invaded her thoughts and not his good-natured, dependable brother.

Had her heart made the wrong choice?

"Honestly, Duncan, I don't understand it myself. How can I expect my father to?"

He gave her shoulders a squeeze. "Put it out of your mind for now. Let's enjoy Christmas, since it will be our last. I expect you'll be going home soon."

The thought saddened her, adding to her guilt. "I don't know if I can contribute much cheer. I'm terribly worried about him."

He cupped her face. "That won't do. I'm afraid Ma's happiness depends on us having the time of our lives." He winked. "It's all part of her big plan to bring Hooper home."

She smiled.

"Besides"—he peered at her from the corner of his eye—"I get the feeling you've spent too many holidays worrying about your pa."

She shrugged. "I don't think I know how to stop."

"Come inside with me, and I'll show you." Tugging her arm, he led her up the steps.

Dawsey couldn't help but feel better as they entered the festive cabin.

Odell turned from the hearth. "At last, here's Duncan." She lifted her brows. "And Dawsey, too?"

Dawsey nodded and took a seat.

"That just leaves Tiller, wherever he is." She cast a pitiful glance at Silas. "Of course Hooper's chair will be empty."

Silas grumbled in his wife's direction, but Dawsey saw through his blustering. She caught the look of disappointment when she and Duncan came in, and he still watched the entrance closely.

Dilsey glanced up from buttering rolls. "Should I go find Tiller?"

Her father waved his fork. "He'll turn up when his bloodhound nose catches wind of this grub. If not, it's his fault. He's supposed to stay close to home."

He gave Dilsey a teasing look. "Where's Wyatt, Puddin'? I figured he'd be at our table this year."

She blushed. "He's coming this afternoon. Says he has a special gift for me."

Dawsey shared a knowing glance with Odell. Earlier, they'd held a whispered conversation about Wyatt's intentions over a roiling kettle of dumplings.

Bowls, platters, and pitchers made the circuit until everyone filled their plates and cups to overflowing. Dawsey stared at the wonderful bounty with a ball of lead in her stomach. How could she eat and pretend to enjoy her food? Every nerve in her body jangled, every thought hovered over her father in Dilsey's room. She prayed he'd settled down to eat before his food got cold.

Silas slightly bowed in her direction, yanking her from her brooding. "Dawsey, we're pleased as peacocks to have you with us for this occasion."

She clutched her napkin in her lap. "Thank you, Silas."

"Would you honor me by asking a blessing over our meal?"

Dawsey squirmed like a netted fish and blinked up at him. How could she give thanks without a single thread of gratitude in her heart? Silas had asked her to converse with God when they weren't on speaking terms. In the muddle of confusion and pain, in the turn her life had taken, she'd somehow left God by the wayside. She couldn't even dredge up a fitting psalm for the occasion. Sweat beaded her top lip, and her breath quickened. "Silas, I—"

Dilsey pushed to her feet. "Pa, I want to say the blessing."

Every head swung her way.

Silas frowned. "That's nice, Puddin', but I've already asked Dawsey." He leaned and lowered his voice. "She's our guest."

Dilsey lifted her chin. "She won't mind." She glanced at Dawsey. "Will you?"

Dawsey recognized a lifeline when it landed in her hands. Her sister, convinced her prayers never reached heaven, had offered one in Dawsey's stead to save her.

Silas's wizened eyes watched them. "Dawsey?"

She flashed a grateful smile at Dilsey. "I won't mind a bit."

Dilsey folded her hands and bowed her head. Cracking one lid, she wiggled her finger. "Well, go on everybody, close your eyes."

Dawsey quickly obliged and the room stilled.

"Well God," Dilsey said, "I reckon You're surprised to hear from me after all this time. In case You don't remember, I'm the one who pestered You for a pony till You brung me Toby. That was a long time ago, but I ain't forgot Your kindness."

She cleared her throat. "About this meal. . .it's a fine spread, one we wouldn't have without land to farm and the strong backs of Pa and my brothers, so I'm grateful." With a sigh of resignation she continued. "I don't know if You can accept our thanks for these fine ducks and the other pilfered things. If not, at least bless Henry for his kindness in sharing and send an angel to keep him safe. Scuffletown needs him."

She drew a ragged breath. "And, Sir, I've never once thanked You for my folks, so I'm thanking You now. Please don't be mad at Ma and Pa for what they done. They were young and foolish and didn't mean no harm."

She paused for so long, Dawsey stole a peek.

Her eyes were squeezed shut, and tears rolled down her cheeks. "I know I claimed I wasn't," she said, "but I'm powerful glad You gave me a sister."

Dawsey bit her trembling lip.

"I saved the last part for Hooper." Her shoulders jerked with choking sobs. "Please bring him home where he belongs." She dropped into her chair and hid her face in the crook of her arm, her "amen" a muffled cry against the table.

Odell stood and rushed to Dilsey, smoothing her hair and cooing in her ear.

Silas pushed away his mounded plate. "Odell, cover this food and keep it warm." He turned to Duncan who had already leaped to his feet. "Son?"

"I'm on my way." He hustled to his peg and pulled on his coat. "You reckon he's at Henry's?"

"Where else would he go?" Silas stood. "Wait, I'm coming."

The sound of approaching riders stilled the scene like one of the pictures in Father's books. Dawsey didn't know to be afraid until she read fear on their faces.

Odell stared at her husband, her mouth ajar. "Silas?"

He pointed at Duncan as footsteps hit the porch.

Lifting a shotgun from the rack, Duncan whirled and aimed it at the opening door.

Hooper stood on the threshold, Henry Lowry looming at his back. Men on horseback filled the yard, evidently Henry's escort.

With a tight smile, Hooper held up his hands. "Don't shoot until I've had my say, brother."

Grinning, Duncan dropped the barrel and leaned the gun against the wall.

The room seemed to heave a relieved sigh, and butterflies tumbled in Dawsey's stomach.

Dilsey spun around the table and threw herself at Hooper.

Henry's bulk, as he squeezed past them, jostled Hooper and Dilsey further into the room.

Dawsey stared, struck again by the uncommon good looks of the big man and intimidated by the arsenal he wore.

Two ammo belts crisscrossed his chest, and two more rode his hips. He wore a holster strapped to his side and the handle of another pistol peeked out from his waistband. He carried a rifle in one hand, another slung across his back by a shoulder strap.

"Merry Christmas, folks." He slid off his hat and nodded at Odell, but it was clear who he'd come to see. "Silas?"

Silas pumped his hand. "Merry Christmas, Henry."

Odell crept around the table with her hands clasped. "We were about to sit for the holiday meal, Henry. We'd be pleased to have you join us."

He declined with a smile. "I come to plead for Hooper."

Short in stature, Silas craned his neck at Henry. "What do you mean?"

Henry motioned at the table, the festive walls, the cheery fire, and the mantel, red with holly. He paused at the tree, staring with glowing eyes and a determined nod. "He belongs here." He pointed at Dilsey, still clinging to Hooper's shirt. "With his family."

"You're right about that." Beaming, Silas jerked his thumb at Duncan. "We were just on our way to fetch him."

Hooper's head came up and his eyes shone. "You were?"

Silas clutched his sleeve. "We're going to help you get a handle on that temper, son. We'll work at it together until we beat it."

Odell hugged Hooper and got Dilsey in the bargain. "You won't be asked to leave home again, no matter what."

Silas shook a warning finger. "But I may lock you in the shed next time."

Henry gave Silas's shoulder a firm pat. Angling past the clustered family, he strolled across the porch to the yard and mounted a large horse. He disappeared from sight as the wave of men closed in around him.

Hooper eased his mother and sister aside and crossed to Duncan.

Smiling, Duncan met him with his hand out.

Hooper gripped it and pulled him close for a hug. "I'm sorry, brother. I give you my word, I'll never raise a hand to you again."

FORTY-TWO

Ellie led Hooper to his place at the table. Handing him a napkin, she waited while their mama filled his plate then set it down in front of him with a merry chuckle. "There," she cried. "Now it's Christmas."

Smiling, he winked at her and tucked the square of cloth around his collar. "I was just thinking the same." He gazed at each of their faces, lingering a bit on Dawsey. "There's no place I'd rather be than seated at this table."

He tilted his head at Tiller's chair. "Where's the boy?"

Papa scowled. "Someplace he shouldn't be, I'm sure. We'll wait on him like one hog waits on another." He cut into his roasted duck and gave Ma a crinkled grin. "This meal is fit for a sovereign, Odie."

Comparing them to pigs proved more truthful than Pa intended. When Ellie leaned back, two plate loads and a slice of pie later, the table looked like a herd of swine had rooted down the middle.

Pa held his stomach and groaned. "I'm not sure if that was a blessing or a curse, family."

A dreamy look on her face, Ma wiped her mouth and smiled. "An uncommon blessing for me."

Pain tugged Ellie's heart. Mama didn't often get the chance to eat her fill.

Duncan wrinkled his nose. "Why doesn't the food look good anymore?"

Reaching around him, Dawsey stacked his empty plate on the rest.

"It's to protect you from yourself."

Mama laughed and patted Pa's rounded stomach. "I can boil up some sassafras tea. It'll ease your bloat."

He shook his head. "No thank you, darlin'. I couldn't truck it in sideways. There's not a smidgen of room left."

Ellie leaped up clapping her hands. "Time to open presents."

Pa moaned. "Not yet, honey. Let's give our duck time to settle." He belched. "See? Mine's still quacking."

"You won't have to do a thing." She kissed his cheek and hurried to sit cross-legged on the floor by the tree. "I'll pass them out."

Hooper turned his chair around to watch. "Looks like you're outnumbered, Pa."

Mama cast a worried glance at the door. "We should wait for Tiller. He should be here by now. He's missing Christmas."

"You're right, darlin'," Pa said. "It's not like him to miss a meal."

Ellie slumped, frustrated with her harebrained cousin.

"He should be here and not out gallivanting," Duncan said. "I say we go ahead without him."

Hooper winked at Ellie. "Let's get started, at least. If he's not here soon, I'll go find him."

Ma bit her lip. "All right. I suppose so."

Ellie whooped and gathered an armload of presents. She picked through, reading the names. "There you go, Pa, and here's one for you, Duncan." She smiled at Hooper. "I think this one's yours." Tilting her head, she grinned at Ma. "Papa made this himself. You're going to love it."

When she'd handed out everything under the tree, stacking Tiller's near the hearth, she carried the last two bundles to Dawsey. With a grateful smile at her mama, Ellie slid the first neatly wrapped package into Dawsey's hands. "Careful, it's very old and fragile."

Stunned, Dawsey gently turned it over in her hands. "Goodness, what could it be?"

"You'll see. I didn't make yours or anything, but I think you'll like it."

Placing the second package in Dawsey's lap, she gave her a knowing wink. "Hooper worked on this for weeks."

Chattering like excited children, they took turns opening their gifts.

Duncan pulled on the sweater Ma had knitted, colored gray like his eyes, and pranced around the room to hearty laughs and teasing.

Grinning, Pa clutched a new hat from Hooper to his chest.

Ma shrieked with joy when she pulled back the paper on the angel

Pa had whittled, holding up her prize for them to see.

With little else to work with, Dawsey had strung buttons into colorful necklaces for Ma and Ellie and made candy for the men. Her chocolate buckeye kisses for Hooper brought a secret smile to Ellie's lips.

Dawsey opened Hooper's first. She squealed with pleasure and ran her hand along the deer hide then draped it around her shoulders. "Thank you, Hooper. It's lovely."

His face shone brighter than the candles on the tree.

Ellie bounced up from her place on the floor. "Now mine."

Flashing a nervous smile, Dawsey picked up the bundle and untied the string. Frowning slightly, she didn't seem to understand until she held up the dress and read Dilsey's name along the hem.

"I'm sure you had one just like it, with your name and everything." She shrugged. "I thought you might like a tie to our past."

Dawsey laid aside the garment and gathered Ellie in her arms. She cried so hard, Ellie began to wonder if she'd done the wrong thing.

"Oh, Dilsey, it's the most precious gift I've ever received. I'll treasure it always."

Ellie heaved a relieved sigh and pretended to wipe sweat from her forehead.

Dawsey laughed, and the others joined her.

A thin cry, like that of a bleating lamb, faded with the end of their laughter.

Ellie looked around the table. "What was that?"

Duncan shrugged. "I didn't hear it."

She held up her hand. "Be still for a second."

Tiller's shrill voice, calling for Pa, echoed in the distance.

Duncan chuckled. "That, I heard."

Papa straightened in his chair. "Brace yourselves, folks. Yonder comes Tiller, and he sounds hungry."

Closer to the porch, Tiller shrilled Pa's name in a choked voice.

Hooper whipped around. "That's not hungry. That's scared." He sprang from his chair at the same time Tiller blasted through the door.

The window exploded into the room. Hooper dove and rolled Tiller to the floor. Covering the boy's slender body with his own, he kicked the door shut with a *crash*.

"Down!" Pa shouted, pulling Mama and Ellie to their knees.

Duncan caught Dawsey around the waist and spun her beneath the table as a storm of gunfire cut across the back wall of the cabin.

The room leaped to life in a dizzy, bouncing spray of wood chips, shredded holly, and shattered dishes. One blast toppled Dawsey's tree, sending cookie stars flying in crumbled pieces.

"Led them straight down on us," Pa roared, his angry gaze on Tiller.

Dawsey pulled away from Duncan and gathered Ellie to her with grasping hands, breathing Bible words in her ear. " 'He that dwelleth in the secret place of the most High—' "

Ellie lunged. She had to get to the gun rack.

" '—shall abide under the shadow of the Almighty.' "

Dawsey held her and Duncan shouted, "No!"

" 'I will say of the Lord, he is my refuge and my fortress' "—

Ellie fell against Dawsey again as a fresh volley ripped through the air.

—"my God; in him will I trust.' "

Pa belly-crawled to Hooper. "We're doomed, son. Do something."

No Pa! Ellie's heart cried. *You'll get him killed.*

" 'Surely he shall deliver thee from the snare of the fowler, and from the noisome pestilence. He shall cover thee with his feathers. . .' "

Hush Dawsey.

" 'A thousand shall fall at thy side, and ten thousand at thy right hand; but it shall not come nigh thee.' "

"Wait." Hooper held up his hand. "Do you hear that?" Blessed hope oozed from his voice.

Ellie strained to hear. The gunfire hadn't stopped, just moved away from the house. Angry, threatening voices faded to the distance.

The battle had turned. The ambushers had been ambushed.

"We're saved!" Duncan shouted.

Dumbfounded, Ellie turned to stare at Dawsey.

Dawsey smiled through her tears, as if they shared a secret. She tucked Ellie's hair behind her ear. " 'Only with thine eyes shalt thou behold and see the reward of the wicked.' "

They heard familiar voices, and the door flew open. Henry and Boss stood on the porch, guardian angels with weapons drawn.

Henry stepped inside. "Everyone all right?"

Ellie rushed the gun rack.

Hooper beat her there. "Who are they, Henry? They followed Tiller to the house."

Henry's eyes turned black with a mixture of sadness and rage. "The Guard." He nodded at Tiller. "Young pups walked into a trap."

Boss looked mad enough to spit. "They've been raiding for profit, Silas. Pedaling their goods in town." He glared at Tiller. "Hit the wrong house this time. Scared the dickens out of a county official's wife."

Pa glared. "Who told you this?"

Boss pointed behind him. "We've got the Carter boys outside, quivering in their britches. Wyatt threatened the truth out of his brother. He was on his way here to tell you himself when he ran into us. I sent him home to tell his pa instead."

Ellie's heart lurched. Everything she and Wyatt feared had happened. She should've told Pa the truth instead of tossing gutless hints.

She gazed around at their shattered celebration. The candy Dawsey spent so much time making for the boys lay scattered over the floor. A bullet had blazed a hole through Papa's new hat. Ma's angel lay at her feet with a broken wing.

Filled with dread, Ellie's eyes jumped to the table where Dawsey had placed the little dress. It was gone.

She hurriedly searched the floor around the chairs. Nothing.

Frantic, she kicked through the rubble that had been their cozy Christmas. Against the back wall, she saw what she'd dreaded. With a gasp, she ran to the riddled paper, holding it up with an anguished cry.

Dawsey caught her arm from behind. "Looking for this?"

Ellie stared as she smiled and held up the dress.

"Oh, Dawsey, I thought it was lost."

"I couldn't bear the thought, so I pulled it under the table with us."

Weak with relief, she melted into Dawsey's hug.

"Ellie?" Scowling, Hooper motioned with his head.

Henry, Boss, and Papa were watching her, too.

Flushed with embarrassment, she hurried to join them. Had she gone soft, fussing over a baby's frock while her family needed her? She raised her chin and steeled her back. "Yes, Hooper?"

"It's not safe for you women with us here. We're going with Henry."

Ellie's throat tightened. "All of you?"

He nodded.

"Pa, too?"

"If you want him to stay alive."

Dawsey pushed past her. "What are you saying? You're leaving us here alone?"

His eyes softened. "Those men are no threat unless you have a price on your head." He touched her shoulder. "They won't waste time coming here once they get wind that we're gone."

"And they will get wind of it," Boss said. "We'll make sure of it."

Hooper's hand lingered on Dawsey's neck. "Don't fret. You're as safe with Ellie as you'd be with me."

Ellie's chest swelled with pride, and her plea to ride with the men died in her throat. What was she thinking? Of course she'd stay behind to mind Ma and Dawsey and keep them safe. Her hand tightened on her shotgun. "I'll take care of them, Hooper."

He nodded and ruffled her hair. "We'll stack wood and nails on the porch. Board these windows as soon as you can."

She nodded.

Ma flitted like a bee, tying bundles of clothes together for them. She found a basket of cookies, untouched by the ruckus, and poured them inside Rhoda's gunnysack. Wrapping a brown sugar pie, she slid it in, too. At the last minute, she tucked in the Tipsy Parson cake.

Smiling grimly, she handed the sack to Pa. "You may need this."

Going red in the face each time he glanced at Tiller, Pa finally caved in to his rage and caught him by the scruff of the neck. "If we live through this, Tiller McRae, you'll be on the fastest train to Fayetteville."

Wincing, he cowered away.

The men filed out, watchful, determined looks on their faces as they scoured the distant trees. Duncan, waiting outside, had already saddled the horses.

Ellie stared from the shattered window as they mounted up, watching until the last horse rode out of sight. *Please Dawsey's God, look out for them.*

Dawsey stood next to her, her nose too close to the broken glass. "Keep them, God," she breathed. "Bear them to safety in the hollow of Your hand."

Ma lifted her broom from the corner and started sweeping. "Might as well get started on this mess. It should take me all night."

Dawsey turned. "Don't fret, Odell. I'll pitch in as soon as I help board the window."

True to her word, Dawsey held the rough planks in place while Ellie nailed, leaving a space between the last two for the barrel of Ellie's gun.

Taking the broom from Ma's hand, Dawsey patted her back. "I'll finish this. Why don't you go see to the food? Hopefully we can save most of it."

Ellie picked up Pa's new hat, now trampled as well as shot through.

"What can I do to help?"

Ma pointed. "You can hold tight to that shotgun and keep your eyes pinned to the yard."

Ellie sat on a low stool and stared through the crack in the boards until her eyes watered and her back ached.

A crash spun her around.

Dawsey had gone rigid, the broom slipped from her hand.

"Heavens," Ma cried from the counter. "That scared me blue."

Ellie frowned. "What is it, Dawsey?"

She raised stunned eyes. "My father." Tearing off her apron, she hurried for the door. "What's wrong with me? I completely forgot him."

"Wait. Don't go out there, honey."

She struggled with the locking bar. "I have to, Odell. He must be terrified."

"I'm sure he's fine," Ma assured her. "Otherwise he'd be calling for you."

"With all that gunfire? He's probably too frightened to make a sound." Dawsey paused, a look of horror in her eyes. "Unless he did start shouting and—" She wrenched the door open, looking over her shoulder at Ellie. "Is there anything I can use for a weapon?"

The men had emptied the gun rack. Even Hooper's long blade was gone.

"Take the shotgun."

Shaking her head, Dawsey started outside. "I won't leave you defenseless."

Ellie clutched her arm. "I'll go with you."

"No, you won't. Stay here and guard your mother."

Odell ran toward her with the broom. "Here, honey. Take this."

"Ma, what good will that do?"

She lifted one shoulder. "She could hit someone over the head with it."

Ellie begged with her eyes. "Don't go, Dawsey."

Dawsey squeezed her hand. "Wait here. I'll be fine." With a wary glance toward the trees, she darted off the porch and disappeared around the corner of the house, waving the broom handle.

Ellie stamped her foot and locked the door.

Ma finished clearing the food, swept the floor, then set to work scrubbing what dishes escaped the ambush.

Ellie glanced up. "You must be tuckered. Wait for Dawsey to help you."

Hunched over a pan of water, she shrugged her shoulders. "I may as well keep my hands busy. It keeps me from thinking."

Ellie knew what she meant. In her fevered mind, she'd tracked the men safely to Henry's house a dozen times. "Why don't you sit and rest? We can talk a bit to take our mind off things."

Ma poured herself a spiced posset and dragged a chair up beside Ellie. "What's keeping Dawsey? Shouldn't she be here by now?"

Ellie stared through the crack at the long shadows across the yard. "I was just thinking the same." Reluctant to raise the subject, she smoothed her mama's hand. "It'll be dark soon and too dangerous for Dawsey to go outside." She winced. "Should we bring the colonel in here with us for the night?"

Ma choked a little then swallowed her sip of spiced milk. "Is it safe?"

Ellie drew a deep breath. "I suppose we could tie him up." She ducked her head. "Or hold a gun on him."

"Oh Ellie."

They sat quietly for a spell.

Ma shot her a hangdog look. "The truth is I dread facing the man."

"Then we'll leave him right where he is."

Ma waved her off. "We'll do no such thing. As soon as Dawsey comes, we'll tell her our plan. I'm sure it will rest her mind."

Ellie peered through the opening again. "Something doesn't feel right." She shot a worried look over her shoulder. "She should be back by now."

Ma sat forward, clutching her cup. "Go out and check on them, honey."

"I can't leave you alone."

"You certainly can. I'll lock the door."

Ellie stood, kicking the stool from behind her. "Are you sure?"

"Positive. Now go."

Waiting to hear Ma slide the bar into place, Ellie climbed over the rail and hurried down the side of the cabin. Painfully alert, she scanned every bush and tree, watching for movement.

She slowed at the back corner to scour the trail leading down to the outhouse. Seeing nothing out of place, she sped up, tripping over something on the ground.

Ellie rolled to her back, waving the barrel of her gun at an unseen enemy. Feeling foolish, she stood, glancing to see what had sent her sprawling.

Prickly hairs tingled on her neck, and her feet turned to stone. The broom lay on the ground, spookily out of place.

She spun toward her room, sickened to confirm what she feared.

The bar still rested on its braces, locking the door from the outside. Dawsey had never made it to the colonel.

FORTY-THREE

Eyes and ears alert, Hooper weaved through the brush, a soldier in a silent army of ghosts.

Henry's men, skilled at easing soundlessly through the swamp, rode in a protective circle around him as the fenland pulled them in and the swamp tuned up for its nightly chorus.

A quick clash with the Guard led to an ugly skirmish that left Hooper with bells in his head and Duncan a bloody ear where a bullet grazed him—a minor wound that he would moan about for weeks.

Hooper prayed they'd run their foes clear back to Lumberton. He didn't relish another scuffle.

Boss led them along the small, hidden paths between dry spots, the route a well-kept secret known only to Henry's trusted circle of friends. They'd spend the next few nights at Henry's hideout, the last place Hooper expected to see again so soon. His heart ached with gratitude for the Lowrys, but the idea of leaving home had tasted of bitter swill.

Gritting his teeth at the memory of the smashed decorations and ruined tree, the broken dishes and the wide swath of ripped-up wallboards, he wondered if home would ever feel the same.

Anxious thoughts drifted to Dawsey. He regretted leaving the women alone with night approaching, but he trusted Ellie with his life. He knew she'd give hers to protect them.

Pa moaned behind him. "Is that a light I see?" His question was more of a grateful announcement.

Hooper looked over his shoulder. "Are your knees bothering you again?"

Soft laughter rumbled. "I'd use a stronger word to express it, but yes, they hurt. I'm not as young as I used to be." He grunted. "Paining me or not, I'm going down on these knees as soon as I get off this horse."

Duncan chuckled. "To thank God you're alive?"

"No, son." Pa's voice matched the mournful sigh of the wind. "To beg safety for my gals."

The men ushered Henry to his door then fanned out and merged with the swamp to keep watch.

Guilt tickled Hooper's conscience as he swung off his horse. They'd sleep safely that night. Could he hope the same for Ma and the girls? Weary of second-guessing himself, he caught hold of Pa's saddle. "Did we make a mistake, leaving them behind?"

Pa settled stiffly to the ground before he answered. "I've been wondering the same, but it's too late to fix it now. We'll send someone in the morning to fetch them."

Hooper nudged his hat aside and scratched his dampened head. "Should we wait that long?"

Rhoda appeared at the door. Backlit by lantern light, every line of her body showed beneath her thin nightdress.

Hooper yanked his gaze to the ground.

"What's wrong, Henry?" she called. "I feel a spirit of unrest over the earth."

"You're causing most of it," Henry growled. "Get inside and cover up."

"Don't know about the whole earth, Rhoda," Boss called as she ducked from sight. "Most of Scuffletown is a bit uneasy tonight."

Rhoda returned wrapped in a quilt. She shaded her eyes against the light pouring out behind her and searched the yard, her head bobbing. "Who you got out there? Do I see Silas McRae?"

Pa chuckled. "Evening, Rhoda."

"Merry Christmas, Silas. Don't stand out there in the damp. Come on in."

Papa hobbled toward her.

"I see my warning came too late." Rhoda rushed to take his arm and she and Henry helped him up the steps. "Don't fret. I have just the remedy for those stiff knees."

Duncan touched Hooper's arm. "We going back for the women?"

With a sigh, Hooper stared at the ground. "I don't know. My head tells me Ellie can handle things. My heart yearns to mount a fresh horse and race home."

Duncan idly ground the toe of his boot in the dirt. "Would Dawsey have anything to do with what your heart wants?"

Hooper's head jerked up. "What sort of question is that?"

He lifted both hands. "Just curious. You've followed her around like a nursing pup." Before Hooper could answer, Duncan gave a harsh laugh. "I must be mistaken, though. That would be awfully strange considering she's the image of our sister."

Hooper tensed. "Those two are nothing alike, and you know it."

"Nothing alike?" Duncan snorted. "Brother, they're exactly the same."

Struggling with his newfound control, Hooper handed off the reins and shoved past him. "I don't have time for this. You and Tiller bed down the horses while I sort out what to do."

Seething inside, he sprang up the steps.

"Hooper?" Duncan's eerie voice stopped him cold.

"Now what?"

"Tiller's gone."

Hooper's hand slid off the doorknob. "What do you mean?"

"Do you see him anywhere? The boy's not here."

Hooper cleared the porch in one leap. "Did he ride off with Boss and the others?"

"No," Duncan said. "That much I'm sure of."

"When was the last time you saw him?"

Duncan rubbed his chin and stared, his color in the dusky light a sickly pale. "He was there during the scuffle with the Guard."

Hooper gripped his shoulder. "Are you sure?"

"Yes." He brushed the hand away. "I saw him myself."

"Tiller wouldn't wander off alone in all that gunfire." Sickness surged in Hooper's stomach. "That means the Guard has him."

Another dreadful possibility kicked him in the teeth. He clutched Duncan's arms. "You don't think he was hit?"

Fear sparked in Duncan's eyes. "What are we waiting for? Tiller could be lying out there with a bullet in him." He waved toward the house. "Get Henry. Have him round up his men."

Pacing now, Hooper shook his head. "We won't pull Henry from his house again tonight." He spun in the direction Boss Strong had gone. "Saddle three fresh horses and fetch some lanterns," he called over his shoulder. "I'm going for Boss. He'll help us search."

"Hoop?"

He turned.

"What will we tell Pa?"

"The truth, I reckon. Unless you have a better idea."

Cursing under his breath, Duncan struck out for the barn.

At Ellie's whistle, Mama nearly ripped the door from its hinges. "For corn's sake! What took you? I was worried sick."

"I'm dreadful sorry, Ma. I was searching the woods for Dawsey."

"What?"

Ellie's jaw ached from gritting her teeth. "She's gone."

"She can't be," Ma whispered. She shook her head as if she could make Ellie's words not so. "Where would she go?"

Ellie stood near the gun rack, filling a drawstring bag with shells. "The Guard took her. One of them ambushed her behind the house. She never had a chance."

Ma sucked in a breath. "Oh, Ellie, how do you know?"

"I tracked them as far as I dared. Two sets of prints, one of them Dawsey's. The other a fairly big man."

"What are we going to do?"

"What else, Ma? I'm going after Hooper."

Mama untied her apron. "You mean *we're* going. If I stay here alone, I'll be next."

Ellie started to argue, to tell her she'd be safer locked inside the cabin. One look at the fear in her eyes changed her mind. "Are you sure, Ma? They took all the horses."

She cast an anxious glance toward the barn. "Even the colonel's?"

"Tiller rode him."

She nodded thoughtfully. "I see."

Ellie touched her arm. "This won't be an easy trip. It'll take hours to get there on foot, and we can't leave until it's good and dark."

Clenching her jaw, Ma flicked her hand. "What of it? I've run these woods for years. I could find Henry's house with my eyes closed."

Beaming with pride, Ellie hugged her.

They paced and planned, Ellie keeping watch through the slats, until night settled firmly over the yard. Gathering her courage, she glanced up. "It's time. You don't want to change your mind?"

"I'm going," Ma said.

Ellie had to ask. "Are you sure you can keep up?"

Ma drew back, insulted. "Can you keep up with me?"

If their present troubles weren't so dire, Ellie would slap her knee and howl at the challenge shining from her mama's bright eyes. She slung her shotgun over her shoulder. "I fear you may get the chance to prove yourself. Fetch a canteen and let's go."

Ma spun and hurried for the water.

Ellie carefully opened the door, scanning the yard as far as she could see in the moonlight. She shuddered, partly for Ma's sake, when she imagined stepping past the rim of trees lurking in ominous shadows. She longed for daylight, but they needed the cover of night.

"I'm ready." Ma appeared at Ellie's elbow, startling her from her thoughts. She'd dressed herself in work boots and Pa's long-sleeved shirt. She pressed floppy hats on both their heads and wrapped scarves around their necks.

Ellie narrowed her eyes and took one last look before they slipped on their coats and stepped out on the porch.

Ten feet from the house, Mama stopped and tugged at her. "What about the colonel?"

Groaning, Ellie tapped her forehead with her knuckles. "He completely slipped my mind."

"Should we take him with us?"

Ellie thought for a minute then shook her head. "Too risky."

Mama pursed her lips. "After all that gunfire, he's bound to be beside himself. Can't we at least tell him we're going?"

"And you'll explain to him why Dawsey's missing?"

She wagged her head. "Not for money."

"Let's go then. We'll be back before morning. He'll be fine until then."

Gripping each other's hands, they darted across the yard and slipped into the yawning darkness.

FORTY-FOUR

There was no convincing their pa to stay behind once he learned Tiller was missing. While Rhoda wrapped a poultice on his knees to help him bear the ride, Papa gripped his head and moaned over the last words he'd said to him. "Blast this too-quick tongue in my head. If anything happens to the boy, I'll never get the chance to tell him I didn't mean what I said." His sorrowful eyes jumped to Hooper. "I wouldn't send him to Fayetteville, no more than I meant for you to leave home."

Hooper gripped his shoulder. He could understand Pa's regret. Not so long ago, he'd sat under a full moon mourning his own rash deeds. "No sense in fretting too soon. When the shooting started, Tiller likely ran home to hide behind Mama's skirts." He tried to smile. "After all, he was hungry, and home is where he can fill his stomach."

Rhoda stood up from wrapping Pa's leg. "Hooper's right. A boy that age has a bottomless belly and two hollow legs." She glanced at her brother, slouched against the wall. "Remember, Boss? You used to clean out the larder back home."

Henry sat forward at the table. "He does a fair job of it now."

She touched his arm. "You should go with them, Henry. I'd expect as much if it was Boss."

Hooper shook his head. "He offered, Rhoda. With all the trouble stirring tonight, it's best if he gets some rest. We may need him worse tomorrow."

She nodded and handed him a filled waterskin. "Be careful," she whispered. "My spirit is heavy."

He nodded grimly, wishing she'd kept the news to herself.

Duncan paced outside near the horses. "What took so long? Let's go." His gaze jumped to Papa easing off the steps and his jaw tightened. "He has no business going, and you know it."

Hooper raised his brow. "Go ahead and tell him. He won't listen to me."

They mounted their horses, and Boss led them back through the swamp the way they'd come.

They rode in silence, Hooper's anxious thoughts mingling with the night sounds. Tiller was a willful handful, no doubt, but he had a good heart. Hooper hoped no harm had come to the spirited lad.

The search party, made up of Hooper, Duncan, Pa, Boss, and three volunteers from Henry's gang, spread out over the site where they'd fallen upon the ambushing Guard. Knowing the risk they took was great, they combed the brush and called Tiller's name, shining lanterns in dark thickets and shadowed places.

At least an hour passed with no sign of him, and Hooper's spirit grew heavy.

Boss sidled up to him, breathing hard. "He's not here."

Hooper nodded. "Then he's at home, like I said."

Their eyes met, and Boss tried to hide his doubt. "Sure thing, Hoop. He's rocking by the fire right now, nursing a hearty slice of your mama's pie."

They both knew he lied.

Pa rode up panting. "What are you doing lolling about when we haven't yet found him?"

Lifting his hat, Hooper wiped the sweat off his brow. "It's no use, Pa."

He bristled. "What do you mean? That's my nephew we're looking for."

Hooper rolled his neck to ease the kinks. "I'm not done looking for him, just done searching here." He softened his voice. "We'll retrace our steps to the house. If he's not there, at least we'll feel better after checking on the women."

Pa leaned his head to gaze at the starry sky. "All right, son. It'll be a treat to lay these old eyes on my Odie again."

"Then turn and look, old man. I'm right behind you."

261

Hooper whipped around to stare as Ma and Ellie appeared in the circle of light.

"By crick," Pa bellowed. "It's really them." He slid from the saddle and hobbled to wrap them in his arms. "How did two little women manage to slip up on seven wary men?"

Ma lifted her chin. "We're Lumbee gals, that's how."

In the low light, Ellie squinted up at Duncan, who still had bloodstains running from his ear. "Gracious, what happened?"

His hand groped his head. "Had a run-in with the Guard. They thought I'd look better with one hat catcher, but I outsmarted them and ducked."

Ma sucked in a breath. "Oh, Duncan."

Pa glanced past them. "Is Tiller with you?"

Her eyes roamed his face. "He's supposed to be with you."

Hooper's eager gaze sought for Dawsey but didn't find her. Had Ellie left her and the colonel alone? Scowling, he dismounted. "What are you doing here? I left you to guard the house."

Ellie pulled herself from Papa's smothering grip. "We were on our way to Henry's cabin to get you." Frowning, she turned in a little half circle, gazing at each of the men. "Does this have something to do with Tiller?"

Fear niggling at his gut, Hooper turned her around. "I asked first. Where are Dawsey and the colonel?"

She bit her bottom lip and tears sprang to her eyes. "I failed you. You put your trust in me, and I let you down."

Dread seized him. He fought the urge to shake the rest out of her. "It can't be that bad, honey. Go on, tell me what happened."

Her chin wobbled out of control. "They took Dawsey."

Hooper's hands bore down on her shoulders, his fingers biting her flesh. "Who took her?"

"The Guard." Ellie winced but stood her ground. "They snatched Dawsey right out of our yard."

They raced for the house in darkness. Ellie clung to Duncan on Toby. Ma rode behind Pa on Old Abe.

"If they have Dawsey, they likely have young Tiller, too. Don't you reckon, Hooper?" Pa had asked. The hope shining from his eyes told how scared he was of being wrong.

When Ellie heard Tiller had gone missing, her heart filled with despair—until she remembered Dawsey's God.

He had granted safety for the men, even protecting them through a skirmish with the Guard. Though He likely granted Dawsey's fancy prayer and not her own, it filled Ellie with hope that He seemed to hear at all. Enough hope to dare pose two more requests.

"Please God," she whispered into the wind at her face, "bring Dawsey home. I should've mentioned my cousin by name before, since he's so much extra trouble. I'm fixing my blunder now by asking you to keep Tiller safe."

Duncan squeezed her hand, and she blushed to think he heard.

Ellie ached to start the search for Dawsey. Every muscle strained toward home, so the ride seemed to take longer than their grueling walk. Relieved tears stung her eyes when they reined up in front of the porch.

Hooper dismounted and strode her way. "Is the colonel still out back?"

Her stomach lurched and she nodded. She dreaded telling Dawsey's father that she was gone. "I expect he needs water by now." She swung from behind Duncan. "Hand me a lamp. I'll take him the flask and break the news to him."

Papa caught her by the arm. "I'll go."

She sought his face in the dim light. "You, Pa?"

He firmed his jaw. "Can you think of anyone who deserves the dreadful task more?"

"We'll all go," Hooper announced. "The colonel may've heard a struggle or voices, something to help us find Dawsey."

Ellie led them to the back of the house by lantern light. The broom still lay where she'd left it, the evidence of her stupidity. She kicked it out of the way. "They got her right here."

Hooper nodded. "Did they leave up the trail?"

She shook her head and pointed to the evergreen scrub to the left of her room. "They cut out through there."

Reaching the steps, Hooper paused and cocked his head. "Two sets of prints? You're sure?"

She nodded, fear setting in. What thoughts haunted him behind his darting eyes?

"We'd best pray the colonel heard something, then. Dawsey

would've raised a ruckus struggling against one man." He paused, his face stricken. "Unless she couldn't." He yanked the bar loose and took Ellie's lantern. Holding it high overhead, he shoved the door open and pushed into the room. "Colonel Wilkes? Sir?"

Ellie crowded in behind him with the others close behind. When she reached Hooper's side in the shadowy room, he stood with one hand on his hip, gazing at the emptiness. "That shrewd old dog." He spun to face them. "The Guard didn't snatch Dawsey. Her pa did."

Hooper didn't know whether to be relieved or more afraid. The Guard at least had some experience in the swamp. Dawsey could be in serious danger traipsing about with a dizzy old man.

"Her pa?" Ellie stared dumbly at the empty bed. "How can that be? What about the locked door?" She wiggled her finger behind them. "The broom beside the house?"

Duncan laughed. "Pretty smart thinking, really. The colonel set the whole thing up to throw us off for as long as possible." He shot Ellie a teasing glance. "I reckon he never expected his tricks to buy him a four-hour head start."

Ellie scowled and looked away.

Hooper blew a ragged breath. "If you ask me, his idea was dim-witted. They have to trek for miles out of here on foot. Treacherous miles in the dark. I can't believe the old man would try such a thing."

"I can," Ellie said. "Don't forget, he was an army scout."

Duncan nodded. "The old coot tailed me all the way here from Fayetteville."

"On horseback," Hooper reminded him.

Boss leaned against the doorsill. "He didn't carry the girl away from here. Would she go willingly?"

Sadness tugged at Hooper. Was Dawsey still that eager to get away from them? He shrugged. "I suppose she must have." He glanced at Ellie. "Why would she brave the swamp a second time after what happened to her?"

"Because Dawsey—"

"She wouldn't have," Pa said, interrupting Ellie. "Not after I promised I'd take her home."

"Did she believe you?" Boss asked.

Ellie nodded. "She—"

"I think she did," Hooper said.

"I'd stake my life on it," Pa said.

Ellie stamped her foot. "If you'd all hush and listen, I'll tell you what happened."

Their attention swung to Ellie, staring back in bug-eyed frustration.

Hooper nudged her. "Go on then. Tell us."

She took a deep breath. "Dawsey went to protect the colonel. Knowing her, she refused to go, but if he struck out on his own, she'd follow. Who knows better than Dawsey how treacherous the swamp can be?"

Mama pulled her close and patted her back. "That's exactly what happened. Dawsey has a tender heart toward her pa."

Hooper pushed past them. "Either way, she's in danger. We can talk about it all day or go find her." He paused at the door. "Ellie, trim a lamp. I'll need you riding up front."

She touched her throat. "You want me?"

"Is there a better tracker in this room?"

She looked at him from under her lashes. "I wasn't sure you'd ever trust me again."

He pulled her close and kissed her cheek. "I never stopped."

Boss, his lanky body still draped against the door, caught Hooper's arm. "How much head start do they have?"

Hooper searched Ellie's face in the lantern glow.

She scratched her brow. "The sun had just set when she left the cabin. I'd say they have four or five hours on us."

Boss uncrossed his ankles and stood upright. "It's an old man and a woman, stumbling through unfamiliar terrain in the dark. They're making roughly a mile an hour, if they're lucky. We can double or triple that distance." He gripped Hooper's shoulder. "But only by daylight with fresh men and horses."

Hooper frowned. "Are you suggesting we wait?"

"Those poor animals are spent," Boss said. "My men need food. I'm asking an hour, two at the most."

"The colonel and Dawsey could be on the train in Moss Neck by then."

"Maybe." Boss quirked his lips. "If they're traveling in a straight line, which I doubt."

"A couple of hours?" Hooper shook his head. "The trail will get cold."

Grinning, Boss lifted his chin. "With Scuffletown's two best trackers on it?" He shrugged and cocked his head. "We'll help you, Hoop. Whichever way you decide."

Pa touched Hooper's back. "Boss has a good argument, son. I'm long past tuckered, and this knee of mine could use the rest."

Ma took his arm. "Who said you're going anywhere, Silas McRae?"

He jabbed his chest. "I said. Tiller's out there somewhere, too. I don't aim to rest until I find him."

Hooper's heart sank. The thought that Dawsey might be with Tiller had eased his troubled mind a bit. If she was with the colonel instead, that left the boy to face the Guard alone.

He patted Papa's shoulder. "Don't fret, we'll find them both and bring them home."

Ellie clutched Hooper's sleeve. "You're not thinking of waiting, are you? I think we should go now." Her searching gaze begged him to agree.

Pulling free of her tight hold, he wrapped his arm around her shoulder. "We're going to go along with Boss's plan this time. Go help Ma fix food for the men."

Panic blazed in her eyes. "But, Hooper—"

He leaned to whisper in her ear. "If you don't trust Boss, then trust me. Dawsey will be fine, I promise."

Mama herded Ellie and Pa out the door. "Let's go, you two. After traipsing across Robeson County, I could eat a bite myself."

Hooper offered Boss his hand. "I want to thank you again for helping my family."

He smiled and lowered his head. "Anytime, Hooper. You'd do the same for us."

"I didn't just lie to my sister, did I?"

Boss fixed him with a steady gaze. "The swamp comes with no guarantees."

Hooper tightened his grip. "Right now, I'd settle for half a chance."

FORTY-FIVE

In the hours since the sky turned black as pitch, Dawsey had tried her best to lure her father in a gradual circle. Unfortunately, he wasn't easy to sway from his course. She wondered if he knew his way any better than she did. For all Dawsey knew, they could be miles away from Scuffletown or stumbling right past the McRaes' little shack. She longed to part the brush and see the cheery lights of the cabin in the distance, prayed to spot the darting points of searchlights.

Where could they be, the unlikely band of bandits who'd wormed their way into her heart and somehow become her family? Surely they were looking for her by now.

Lead thudded to the bottom of her stomach as she faced the truth. Her father stopped every few yards to cover their tracks, so it was possible the McRaes wouldn't find her.

"Keep up Dawsey, or we'll never get there. We've lost too much time already."

Father's voice floated back to her from somewhere up ahead. With a shudder, she hurried to catch up. It wouldn't do to be separated from him and find herself alone in the dark.

They carried a lantern, but he hadn't allowed her to use it in case the McRaes were behind them. Instead, they picked their way along by the bright moon overhead.

She trudged up behind him and tugged on his shirt. "Never get where? You can't possibly know where we are."

"Of course I do." He pointed. "Moss Neck is a couple of miles that way."

Her heart lurched. He really did seem to know which direction they traveled, as if he followed a built-in compass.

What had happened to her father? A month ago, he hardly knew who he was, much less where.

"And if we really are close to Moss Neck? What then?"

"What do you think? We'll contact the nearest officials and have that band of ruffians arrested."

Clutching his arm, Dawsey dug in her heels and pulled him to a stop. "Arrested?"

He shifted the strap of his canteen to the other shoulder. "Of course, dear. First, the elder McRae for taking my sweet Dilsey from her crib. Then the heartless cur who stole into my house and kidnapped you."

Aghast, she stared. "You can't mean it, Father."

He glanced at the starry sky then set off again. "I've never meant anything more."

Dawsey scurried behind him with her heart in her throat. "But I've explained everything, don't you remember? The McRaes made a mistake." She picked up the pace. "An absolutely horrid mistake, but they're sorry."

Father stopped so fast she plowed into his back. He spun with his hands in the air, his simpering smile frightening in the moonlight. "Oh I see. They're *sorry*. Thank you, dear, for clearing things up." He clutched his chest. "I feel so much better about them now."

Struck dumb, she gaped.

"Do you hear yourself? Defending your abductors?" He crossed to cup her chin in his hand. "What have they done to you?"

She closed her eyes and wagged her head. "I know how it sounds."

He grunted. "I'm not sure you do."

Dawsey wracked her mind. No matter what they'd done in the past, she couldn't allow her father to turn in the McRaes. Especially Hooper.

Wrapping his arm around her waist, Father pulled her along beside him. "Come, Dawsey. We grow closer to help with every footfall."

She tugged away from him. "I'm sorry, Father. I can't go another step without rest."

He struggled to hide his irritation. "I know the trek is grueling, dear, but we rested not twenty minutes ago."

"But I'm starving and limp with thirst." She let her shoulders sag. "And my leg hurts."

All of her excuses were true. Dawsey was tired and hungry, and her calf ached in the spot where the rattler had "kissed" her, as Duncan teasingly called her warning bite.

Wincing, Father gingerly groped behind his hat. "What a sorry lot we are. I fear my head hurts something fierce." He heaved a defeated sigh. "Very well. I suppose a short rest won't hurt."

He led her to a stump and spread his coat. Dawsey insisted he light the lamp and check the ground for snakes before she agreed to sit. He reluctantly complied then set the lantern away from them.

Easing down beside her, he handed over the canteen then pulled a bundle of food from his knapsack. Dawsey recognized Odell's dishcloth, filled to overflowing with sweet potato bread, Indian dumplings, and pecan-crusted buns.

She watched him, struck again at his shrewdness. "You planned this all along, didn't you?"

He kept his head down, his eyes on rationing their bounty.

"You thought of everything, the food, the water." She held up the flask and shook it. "The pitcher didn't get broken in the scuffle, did it? You were hiding the fact that you'd emptied it inside here."

"One of us had to think rationally," he said quietly.

Her mind went to the night she'd clawed the cold ground for hours and dug her way out of the shed. She'd been willing to risk her life to escape the McRaes and return to her father.

Whatever dizzy circumstances had changed Dawsey's mind, her father believed he was saving his daughters, and she respected his efforts tremendously. Somehow, she had to change his mind, too.

She longed to rest her head against his shoulder the way she'd watched Dilsey do with Silas. Not sure how Father would react, she leaned against the stump instead, chewing thoughtfully on a bun. "What if I told you Dilsey is gloriously happy?"

He laughed scornfully. "In that mud-soaked hovel?"

Trying to make light of her pain, Dawsey laughed, too. "Scandalous, isn't it? I was quite surprised to find that love could thrive in such an environment." She swallowed hard. "Even more surprised to see love so freely expressed."

She glanced at the side of his face. "The truth is the McRaes love Dilsey very much. Furthermore, she loves them. You won't change that, no matter how many charges you level against Silas and Hooper."

He tilted his head. "Turning in those monsters is how we get our little girl back."

She clutched his arm. "You're wrong. She'll be distraught. The McRaes are the only family Dilsey's ever known. If you hurt them, we'll lose her for good."

With a determined sigh, he patted her face. "You have to allow me to handle this. I know what's best for my girls."

Gazing around at the brush, he handed her a dumpling. "Finish eating, dear, then lie back and enjoy your rest. We can't dawdle here for long, so make the best of it."

Ellie slid off her horse and carefully scoured the ground. They'd lost the trail again, and Dawsey's life depended on finding it. Down on her knees, Ellie studied every patch of dirt, every shriveled leaf with a practiced eye.

The colonel turned out to be quite a match for her and Hooper. Over the past few hours, they'd tracked him in bits and pieces between home and Moss Neck, their search running hot and then cold.

They'd finally split up. Boss and his men searched toward Lumberton. Papa and Duncan made their way along the river. She prayed they were having more luck.

Hooper stood. "None of this feels right. I think we're off the mark."

Ellie stood, slapping her gloves against her leg. "I told you we shouldn't wait, Hooper. Why did you listen to Boss?"

He stared at the awakening sky. "Those few hours didn't make a difference. Time's not our problem. It's that wily old man."

Ellie bent her back to stretch out the kinks. "We've been all over this ground, from here to Moss Neck. They must've slipped into town." She glanced up. "If so, they're on the morning train."

Hooper's eyes looked hollowed out, his mouth white with strain. "Unless the colonel hangs around to see us arrested." He gripped his head. "I think I'd prefer that to Dawsey leaving."

"I'd prefer her leaving to being lost." Ellie moaned. "We have to make sure she's not out here somewhere."

"Don't worry," he said. "I won't stop searching until I know for sure."

"Wait a second." She brushed past Hooper and walked a few feet beyond him. In the first light, her skillful eye spotted an area that didn't look quite right. To anyone else it would appear to be a low spot, a shady hole. Ellie skirted the bed of scattered pine straws, a few of them flipped to their damp sides. "Over here, Hooper. They passed through here."

He came and squeezed her shoulder. "Good job, honey. Let's go."

They left their horses and continued on foot. Ellie quickly found a partial footprint then a patch of broken twigs.

"He's getting tired," Hooper said. "And careless."

They'd gone a quarter mile before Pa and Duncan slipped up quietly from behind. Pa placed a finger to his lips and pointed with a tilt of his head. "Trouble yon way," he whispered.

Ducking low, Hooper watched Sheriff McMillan and three deputies riding toward them in the distance. At the same instant, a flash of color caught his eye through the brush.

Dawsey awoke with a start, amazed to find they'd fallen sound asleep.

Her father leaned against her, snoring softly, looking more like the broken man she'd left in Fayetteville. His chin had gray bristles and his silver hair stood on end, aging him ten years in the morning light.

Watching him sleep, she ached for him. At the same time, she rejoiced over more time to reason with him.

Thankful they'd made it through the night, she yawned and stretched—until a rush of noise and motion bore down on them, nearly jolting Dawsey's heart from her chest.

The clearing erupted with loud, angry voices and pounding hooves. Cringing in fear, she huddled protectively around her startled father as strange men swooped down to encircle them.

A scowling man on horseback swung alongside and glared down at her. "Ellie McRae!" His eyes burned with sadistic pleasure, like those of a cat pouncing on a mouse. "You need to tell me where your menfolk are hiding."

Stunned, Dawsey stared up at the strange man who thought she was Ellie.

She glanced at her gasping, wild-eyed father. *Please forgive me for what I'm about to do.*

Hooper clutched Ellie's sleeve and ran, dodging young trees and leaping over bushes. They slowed near the clearing and slid down on their bellies. He motioned for her to stay put and be quiet, praying for once she would listen.

Crawling close to the ground, he reached the last patch of heavy cover and carefully parted the brush. What he saw was far worse than he'd imagined.

He reached for his gun then cursed himself for a fool. He'd left it on his horse. A rogue band of outlaws, he could outsmart. A bounty hunter or two, he could overtake. Sheriff McMillan and his gang of sworn men meant a trip to the gallows, a threat he might risk for Dawsey's sake. . .if not for Ellie.

He gritted his teeth. This was Dawsey's chance, and no doubt, she'd take it. One word against him and he'd be on the way to Lumberton Jail—no less than a hotheaded firebrand deserved—and she'd be on her way home to Fayetteville.

Desperation squeezed his insides. Once they took her, he'd never see her again. Gritting his teeth, he waited.

The sheriff sat tall in the saddle, towering over Dawsey to frighten her. In case that didn't work, he had a gun pointed straight at her head. "We know Hooper's here somewhere, Ellie. Go on and call him out."

Started, Hooper realized the sheriff's mistake. With Dawsey dressed in Ellie's clothes, he could see how easily a man might mix them.

"Be sensible, gal," the sheriff wheedled. "It'll go easier if you cooperate. If not, I can't promise to protect your ma and pa."

Dawsey unfolded from the ground and faced McMillan dead-on.

Hooper tensed. Now she would set him straight.

"Ain't seen my witless brother in a month." She propped both hands on her hips. "If you lay a hand on my folks, you'll have half the county down on your head."

Hooper's stomach jerked like Old Abe had kicked him.

"What's she doing?" Ellie whispered at his side.

He jumped then shushed her.

Colonel Wilkes found his wits and his feet. "Sheriff, you're just the man I need to see." His deep voice boomed in the clearing. "I seek justice in a matter of foul play"—he draped his arm around Dawsey's shoulder—"and protection for my daughter."

Hooper held his breath.

McMillan's puzzled gaze swung around to the colonel. "Who are you, sir?"

Dawsey pulled free and patted his back. "Don't mind him, he's. . ." She raised her brows and touched her temple. "You know."

The colonel's eyes widened. "What are you saying, Dawsey?"

The sheriff looked him over. "Who is this man?" He glanced at Dawsey. "What are the two of you doing way out here?"

Dawsey's father stood at attention. "My name is Colonel Gerrard Wilkes, from Fayetteville. This young lady is Dawsey Elizabeth, my daughter. We're fleeing our captors, the McRaes. The scoundrels ambushed me two days ago." He pointed at Dawsey. "They've held her prisoner for weeks."

McMillan scowled. "What's going on here, Ellie?"

She jumped in front of the colonel. "Sorry, Sheriff. This here is Ma's brother, come from South Carolina for Christmas. He got away from us, and I've been tracking him all night." She shook her head. "I'm afraid he's having one of his dizzy spells."

"Dizzy spells?" her father asked.

"There, there, Uncle Jerry." Dawsey leaned toward the deputies, speaking in a loud whisper. "Injured in the war, you know."

They nodded in sympathy.

"Look here, Dawsey—" the colonel blustered.

"See?" She pointed. "He don't even know my name."

Red in the face, the colonel charged the sheriff. "Sir, I demand that you help us. The McRaes must be arrested at once and brought to justice."

McMillan's horse danced nervously and the sheriff turned his gun. "Stand back, you dotty old fool."

Dawsey clutched the back of her pa's shirt and held on. "Please don't hurt him. He don't know what he's saying."

McMillan gazed around their camp with a sneer. "You expect me to believe you're out here all alone?"

Her shoulders squared. "Why not? You ever heard of me backing down from anything?"

One of the riders laughed. The rest shook their heads.

"Besides," Dawsey continued in a voice closer to Ellie's than Ellie's. "It's a free country, ain't that right?"

One of the deputies pushed back his hat and leered. "Suppose we take you with us? Hold you until Hooper turns himself in?"

Without a trace of visible fear, she swayed her hips toward him. "Suppose Hooper sends Henry and his men to fetch me?"

The man eased back in the saddle. The others cast nervous glances. Hooper could've whittled their fear with Pa's carving knife.

A challenge in her eyes, Dawsey hooked her arm in the colonel's and pulled him toward his coat lying on the ground. Speechless, he let her slide his arms in the sleeves then took the canteen and wadded dish towel she shoved at him. "If you boys will excuse me, I need to get Uncle Jerry on home. Ma's powerful worried about him."

The sheriff nudged up the brim of his hat. "I'll eventually find Hooper and your trouble-making little cousin." He flicked his first two fingers at her. "You tell him that, you hear?"

Pulling the defeated old man by the arm, Dawsey stumbled toward the woods.

"Ellie?" McMillan called, his eyes narrowed with suspicion.

She turned.

"You're going the wrong way."

Cool as springtime, she smiled and pointed. "I reckon I know that. I left my horse over yonder."

The milling men watched her in silence, until she slipped into an oak grove and disappeared.

"She's leaving," Ellie hissed.

Hooper slapped his hand over her mouth and held it there while the posse's last horse faded with a swish of its tail into the far side of the clearing. Pulling her face around, he stared into her wild eyes. "When I take my hand away, you don't talk. Just listen. Is that clear?"

She nodded.

He let go of her mouth, pressing a finger against her lips one last time for safe measure. "We'll circle around and cut her off," he whispered.

She nodded.

Tugging her sleeve, Hooper sprang off the ground.

They ran as fast as they could and still move with stealth. Passing the thicket where they'd left Pa and Duncan, they found them gone.

His heart lifted when he spotted them standing with Dawsey in the brush. The sight of Duncan's arms around her pierced his heart, but not as much as her red nose and wet cheeks.

The colonel had sunk to the ground, staring straight ahead. Pa squatted next to him, concern lining his face.

As he reached Dawsey, Hooper softly called her name.

She turned and melted against him, furiously wiping her tears. "Oh, Hooper, I was so frightened."

Chest heaving, his arms slid around her. "Then why, Dawsey? You could've told them everything and been on your way home. Why did you face down those men?"

"I had to." She lifted swollen eyes. "I wasn't afraid for me."

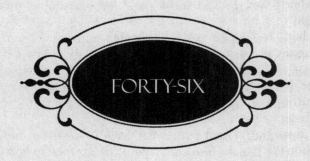

FORTY-SIX

Dawsey stared through the bars on Dilsey's window, watching her and Silas warming in a bright patch of sunlight. They sat as straight as posts and as solemn as death on a bench seat next to the corncrib. She watched their lips, trying to read them, but couldn't make out a single word. By their somber expressions, she gathered Tiller had yet to come home.

"Every day a mother's son disappears in Bear Swamp."

Hooper's words floated up from her memory. Hearing him speak of such things had broken her heart at the time. Witnessing the loss firsthand brought terrible pain.

Silas had grasped his knees and mourned when he learned Tiller wasn't with Dawsey. "Oh, Lord, let the Guard have him, and not the gators," he'd wailed.

A sick look on his face, Hooper assured him that Tiller would turn up by morning.

Dawsey glanced at the sky. By the position of the sun, she'd slept right through morning with no sign of poor Tiller.

Her father, hunkered behind Dilsey on the way to the cabin the night before, had ranted at Dawsey about her betrayal most of the way. Too tired to try to appease him, she'd let him vent his rage.

Before he would step one foot inside Dilsey's room, Dawsey had to swear on her mother's grave to go home with him as soon as possible. He vowed never to sleep another night under a McRae roof and had

275

kept his word by raving like a lunatic all night. By dawn, he finally succumbed to exhaustion and curled on Dawsey's mat where he still lay.

The door creaked open, streaming afternoon sunlight on the mud-tracked floor. Odell peeked inside holding a steaming tray. "You're awake, I see."

Taking the welcome food, Dawsey glanced toward her father. "I'd like for him to rest as long as possible." She didn't bother confessing that his welfare wasn't her only concern. She dreaded reliving his fury.

"Sorry, child." Odell ducked her head and grimaced. "Is he all right?"

Dawsey sighed. "As well as can be expected, but he's very angry with me."

"I can imagine." Odell patted her back. "Don't fret, honey. He'll come around. We'll make him understand." She turned to go but paused on the doorstep. "Will you tell us when he wakes up? Silas is so anxious to talk to him he's jumping right out of his skin." Her eyes softened. "He wants to apologize." She made a face. "Again."

For all the good it will do him, Dawsey thought. She smiled. "Of course, I'll call you."

Odell ducked back in. "Are you sure you want this door unlocked?"

"I promised him," Dawsey said. "Besides, he's not going anywhere." She cautiously approached the mat on the floor and leaned to see her father's face, cringing when he stiffened.

"I'm awake," he growled at the wall. "No one could sleep through all that mindless chatter."

Dawsey perched on the edge of the bed, her hands folded. "I plan to keep my word, Father. Just as soon as you're strong enough, Duncan will take us home."

He grunted.

"Do you think you'll ever forgive me?"

He lay so still and quiet, her heart raced with fear. Was it possible he wouldn't?

She refused to accept it. "Father, I—"

"Your mother took her own life, Dawsey."

The room swirled as his words sunk in, hateful words hurled in anger.

In her mind, she leaped to her feet, denial on her lips, but her shaky legs wouldn't hold her. "You're lying."

Father turned over and sat up, running his hands through his tousled hair. "Am I?" He waved his hand. "She didn't take too many pills or shoot herself. That would be too vulgar. She knew deliberate suicide was wrong, might cancel her ticket to heaven."

"Then she didn't—"

"She let nature do the dirty deed for her." He released a bitter laugh. "All it took was neglecting her medicine, not following the doctor's orders."

Tears flowed down his cheeks. "Margaret claimed she didn't believe in suicide. She swore she'd never do such a thing, but she lied." He clutched his forehead, his lips trembling. "Your mother simply sat down and died, Dawsey. She may as well have placed a gun to her head."

She longed to comfort him. Instead, she wrung her useless hands and let him cry out his heartbreak. When he quieted and raised his head, she whispered, "Why?"

The peaceful release on his face disappeared. He pointed toward the door. "Your beloved McRaes. There's your reason."

"Mother decided to die because Silas took Dilsey?"

"Yes." He glared at her from the floor until a shadow crossed his face. Glancing away, he repeated the answer with more force. "Yes, because they took our baby."

Dawsey watched him closely. "There's something you're not telling me."

His bottom jaw worked while he tried to hold on to his anger. Dawsey waited until he lifted sad eyes. "Your mother lived with terrible pain, arthritis in her joints. The disease led to other things—fevers, lung infections, weak blood." He sighed. "She suffered greatly, mostly because she couldn't care for her girls."

Deeply troubled, Dawsey stood and crossed to the window. "I had no idea."

Odell had joined her family outside, lightening the mood past the window.

"Your mother wouldn't want you to know," Father said. "She was determined to withstand all of it for your sakes."

The contrast between the carefree teasing outside the room and the tragedy unfolding inside tore at Dawsey's heart. She felt suspended between two worlds, two separate realities.

"When Silas McRae took Dilsey, the stress was too much. Your mother gave up the fight." Father's voice hardened. "What sort of person is capable of such a thing?"

Dawsey turned and reached out her hand. "Come here, please."

Father frowned. "What?"

"Come over here. I want to show you something."

Grumbling, he struggled to his feet and joined her at the window. Outside, Odell stood behind Dilsey, smoothing her long curls into a horse's tail with loving hands. Pulling her head back, she leaned to plant a kiss on her forehead.

Silas said something and Dilsey whirled, wide mouthed with laughter, to punch his arm.

Grabbing her hand, he tugged her onto his lap. Dilsey wrapped him in a tight hug, kissing both his cheeks, then rested her head on his shoulder.

Dawsey pointed. "That sort of person, I suppose."

He stared, his darting eyes taking in the loving scene.

"You have every right to be angry that Silas took Dilsey from her crib that night." She clenched her fists. "I'm angry, too, but it happened, and we have to be grateful her life turned out so well. It could've been far worse."

Father glanced her way. "You mean if they'd been harsh and cruel?"

Fighting tears, Dawsey shook her head. "If she'd been the one left behind." She spun away from the window and sailed out the door, running straight into Duncan's waiting arms.

Rounding the shed with a headless chicken in each hand, Hooper stopped so fast his boot heels plowed twin rows.

Duncan stood at the bottom of Ellie's steps, holding Dawsey against his chest.

Stunned, Hooper watched his conniving brother lead her gently away. He hurried closer to watch where they were going.

Halfway along the path, Duncan pulled aside a low branch and they ducked into the woods.

Blistering, bottomless fury rose inside his chest. Duncan had tried to shame him for loving Dawsey, as if his feelings were dishonorable, when all the time he had plans of his own.

"You squeeze those birds any tighter, they'll squawk."

Loosening his grip, Hooper glanced down at the dangling necks and exhaled some of his rage. "I'd pay to see that trick."

Mama waltzed closer and touched his arm. "You're flushed. What's ailing you, son?"

He handed her the chickens. "Better get these plucked."

Careful of the claws on the gnarled toes, she gathered their legs into one hand and pulled at his sleeve with the other. "Walk with me?"

Hooper dutifully fell into step beside her.

Ma seemed to smile at a private joke. "Back there, you looked ready to do some plucking yourself. Whose feathers are you gunning for?"

"I wouldn't stop at feathers," he said. "I'd go ahead and skin him, too."

"What did Duncan do now?"

He waved her question aside. "Can I ask you something, Ma?"

They reached the tub of hot water and she dunked the hapless chickens. "Ask me anything you want. I'll decide if I want to answer."

His face warmed. "Do you reckon it would seem, I don't know. . . indecent for Duncan and me to court Dawsey?"

Ma pulled in her lips then released them. "One thing's certain, both at once would be highly improper."

"All right, then." He rested his hands on his hips. "Would it be wrong for me to court Dawsey?"

She gazed at him, the picture of innocence. "What do you think?"

He jutted his chin. "Is that your way of saying yes?"

"Dawsey's a wonderful person." Yanking a handful of feathers, she tossed them behind her. "So is your sister."

Hooper's heart sank at the comparison.

"They're a lot alike—both loyal, honest, and hardworking."

Sighing, he held up his hand. "I see where you're going."

"Do you?" She laid aside the first bird and fished for the second. "I said alike, Hooper, but not the same girl."

Ma stood, shaking water from her hands. "It's all right to choose a mate who reminds you of a loved one, a person who bears traits you admire in, say, a mother or a sister." She shrugged. "I reckon we all do it. Your papa has always reminded me of my own dear pa. They have the same kind eyes and tender ways."

It was true, though he'd never noticed until she said so.

"Besides," she added grinning. "In most things those two girls are like night and day."

A weight lifted from around Hooper's heart. Avoiding her hands, covered with stink, he leaned to kiss her cheek. "Excuse me, ma'am, but I've got a rooster to pluck."

She caught his sleeve. "You don't need to fret over Duncan's flashy feathers. I've seen how Dawsey looks at you." Her smiling face turned grim. "It's that tough old bird in Ellie's room who might pose a problem. Even with your winsome ways, how will you ever sway the colonel?"

Ellie knocked at the door of her bedroom and waited to hear the colonel's muffled reply. Peeking inside, she found him slumped at the edge of the bed, his hands clasped in front of him. "Can we come in?"

Hope sparked in his eyes. "Is Dawsey with you?"

She shook her head. "Just me and Pa."

His body swiveled to the wall. "I don't want to see him."

Ellie motioned for Papa to wait. Moving soundlessly across the floor, she knelt in front of the colonel. "He's really keen to apologize. I wish you'd heard him out last night."

The colonel sniffed like he smelled something bad. "I have no interest in his apology."

Ellie sighed. "I can see you're awful mad, sir. I don't reckon a single soul could blame you." She fell back and sat on her heels. "I know his words won't bring back the chance to raise me like you done Dawsey."

"A job I failed miserably."

She tilted her head. "Huh?"

"Never mind." Swatting his words, he turned his head to watch her. "Go on."

"I was trying to say that I got powerful mad, too, when I heard."

He scooted closer. "You did?"

"Why, sure. Until Dawsey, I had nothing but two stinking brothers. What are they good for when you get right down to it, except teaching you how to hunt and track."

She paused for a breath. "Don't get me wrong, I love Hooper and Duncan an awful lot, but they ain't worth spit at girl stuff."

The colonel smiled. "I don't suppose they are."

"I always wanted a sister." She stared dreamily at the ceiling. "Not many folks can brag about having a twin, so I figure I got cheated out of a lot of years of boasting."

He perked up. "Are you saying you wish Silas had left you with us?"

She gasped and held up her hands. "Oh no, sir. I could never wish for a thing like that."

He scowled. "What then? Do you wish he'd taken Dawsey, too?"

She settled to her behind and crossed her legs. "How could I ask you to part with Dawsey? She belonged with you just like I belong here."

"That's not true," he said with a long face. "You belonged with us."

Ellie shrugged. "Once you bust a watermelon, you can't put it back the way it was, but it's still awful sweet."

He huffed. "A stolen melon may be sweet, but it deprived the rightful owner." He shook his finger. "You were meant to bring pleasure to the Wilkes family, not the McRaes."

"Now, Colonel, don't go twisting my words." She cocked her head. "You wouldn't drop a melon on purpose, would you? You'd place it on the table and cut it nice."

He nodded.

"What Pa done left us without pretty slices." She raised her brows. "Do we throw the whole thing away or take pleasure in the scattered pieces?"

Tears flooded Ellie's eyes, and she swiped them away. "Don't you see? I don't count it an accident that we all came together at last. I thank Dawsey's God every day for helping me find her." Sniffing, she wiped her nose on her sleeve. "And for giving me the chance to know you." She ducked her head. "If you don't mind, that is."

The colonel lowered himself to the floor and stretched his trembling hands to her. "Come here, child."

She scooted close and laid her head against his shoulder while he rocked her.

"I have a lot of this sort of thing to make up for." His sigh seemed to rise from the depths of his soul. "Not just with you, I'm afraid. I've been sinfully negligent at showing Dawsey how precious she is to me."

"Dawsey loves you."

He rubbed her back. "I suppose she does." Ducking to look at her, he made a face. "I can assure you I don't deserve it."

Heart pounding, Ellie sat up and gripped his arms. "Please don't put my pa in jail, Colonel Wilkes. I can't tell you how much we need him."

He went stiff and his jaw tightened.

Ellie's pleading eyes held his gaze. "What he did happened a long time ago. He ain't the same man he was then." She pressed closer to study his angry, darting eyes. "No more than you are."

His rigid chin relaxed. Staring over her head, he chewed the side of his mustache.

She waited as long as she could then waved her hand over his face. "Are you all right, Colonel?"

He blinked, his gaze wandering to hers. "Help an old man off the floor, will you?"

She stood and pulled him to his feet.

The colonel straightened his shirt and smoothed his silver hair. "I'm not sure I'll ever be ready to hear the man's apology." He patted her shoulder. "For your sake, I'll hold off on any charges."

Squealing, she wheeled for the door.

"Dilsey?"

She turned.

"Is there any chance you'll come home with us to Fayetteville? I can't make up for the years you lost, but I'll spend the rest of my days trying."

"Scuffletown is my home, sir. It's part of me." She shrugged. "If I was younger, things might be different, but. . .you understand, don't you?"

The corners of his mouth drooped, and the hopeful light left his eyes. "Of course, dear. I suppose I'm still trying to patch that melon."

"You'll come for my wedding, won't you?"

He leaned back, a stunned haze in his eyes. "You're getting married?"

She nodded.

"Do you love him?"

Her cheeks warmed. "I reckon I do."

The colonel rubbed his temples with the tips of his fingers. "Ah, Dilsey, I've missed out on so much." He sighed. "Might I hope that you'll visit on occasion? I'm sure your aunt Lavinia would love to meet you."

Ellie's heart fluttered. Seeing firsthand the life she might've had was an option she hadn't considered. "I think I'd like that very much."

She turned to go, but he held up his hand. "Tell Dawsey we're leaving first thing in the morning."

Her shoulders slumped. "So soon?"

"It's long past time." He smiled. "I have years of heartache to mend."

FORTY-SEVEN

Dawsey wiped her eyes on Duncan's handkerchief. "We'd best get back to the house now. They'll be looking for us." She touched his hand. "Thank you for listening to me whine. It seems you're always rescuing me."

Embarrassed to admit her jealous self-pity, she'd never mentioned why she was crying. Being a gentleman, he hadn't asked.

"Anytime you need a shoulder, honey, I'm your man." He gazed at her boldly, and the intimacy in his look brought a rush of warmth to Dawsey's cheeks.

"Thank you, Duncan. That's very kind of you." She presented her face for inspection. "Is my nose red?"

He grinned. "Like a holly berry."

Surprising herself, she laughed. "Oh you." Dawsey peered at him from under damp lashes.

Though Duncan was seldom serious about anything, no one could cheer her heart like him. From her first frightened day locked in Dilsey's room, the sweet, gentle man had been a comfort.

She wondered again why she felt so irresistibly drawn to Hooper when he made her feel the opposite of comfortable and safe, especially when she imagined what he'd done to those men in the swamp.

"Are you lost, brother?"

Her shudder leaped into startled dread at Hooper's voice.

He stood just inside the little clearing, his white-fisted hands gripping his suspenders and a cocky smile on his face. "You're a little turned around, I guess." He pointed over his shoulder. "The cabin's that way." Without an invitation, he sauntered closer. "Not that I blame you. I suppose Dawsey's smile has you blinded, but don't let her dimples muddle your mind. Pa would pitch a right fit if he caught you two spooning in the woods."

Dawsey shot to her feet. "How dare you?"

His anxious gaze flickered her way, but his anger with Duncan won out. "But then, you couldn't be spooning, could you, brother? Not when Dawsey reminds you so much of Ellie."

Duncan stood, his stance defiant. "All right, I admit it. She's nothing like Ellie. Dawsey makes a man want to shield her from all the evil in the world."

Hooper sneered. "You can start by protecting her from yourself."

Thrusting out his chin, Duncan poked Hooper's chest with his knuckle. "I aim to court her."

"Court her?" Hooper snorted. "I aim to marry her."

Dawsey gasped. "Stop it, both of you." Whirling, she ran for the trail.

Hooper caught up with her and spun her around. "Don't go, honey. We need to talk."

She ducked her head. "There's nothing to talk about."

"I meant what I said back there," Hooper said, twirling her away as Duncan snatched at her.

Duncan danced and bobbed, trying to see her better. "I want to marry you, too, Dawsey. I'm fairly certain of it."

Eyes veiled with passion, Hooper lifted her chin and pressed his lips to the corner of her mouth. "Say you'll be my wife, Dawsey," he whispered, just a warm breath away. "I love you with all of my heart."

Love for him surged in her chest, nudging her closer. She longed to say yes while her mind scrambled for strength to resist him. *Deliver me, O Lord, from the evil man: preserve me from the violent man.*"

As if sensing he couldn't compete with the strong feelings passing between them, Duncan hung back gaping in disbelief.

Dawsey's deliverance came in the form of footsteps, running up the trail behind them. She turned her head to watch Dilsey sail past, slowing when she caught sight of them.

She veered and hurried their way, her brows drawn into a frown. "Ma said I might find you down here." A puzzled look crossed her face. "What's wrong? You all look like you're choking on something."

Pulling free from Hooper's grip, Dawsey shook her head. "We're fine. Is something wrong at the house?"

She nodded. "Mama just noticed that Tiller's things are gone."

Hooper walked to meet her. "Everything?"

"His clothes, shoes, and Mama's gunnysack to put them in." She jerked her head toward the house. "She wants us there when she tells Pa."

Hooper nodded grimly. "We'll come right now."

Her eyes lit up and she clutched his sleeve. "There's good news, too. The colonel said he won't bring charges against Pa."

Duncan let out a *whoop* that echoed in the treetops.

Hooper beamed and hugged her close. "Are you sure?"

"He told me himself."

A jostling brother on each side, Dilsey started up the rise.

Duncan paused to cast a sheepish glance at Dawsey. She lowered her eyes, so he loped on without her.

Hooper, his mind firmly on the trouble at the house, wrapped his arm around Dilsey and never looked back. A little offended after his heartfelt proposal, Dawsey followed in a sulk.

She caught up with them near the porch, and Dilsey turned with a troubled frown. "I almost forgot. The colonel said to tell you it's time to go. His mind is set to leave in the morning."

Hooper stopped walking so fast he nearly toppled his sister. He caught Dawsey's arm and studied her face, his eyes full of questions.

With her heart on fire, she pulled away and angled past him, up the steps.

The family crowded around the table while Ellie broke her happy news. "The colonel practically promised me. He meant it, too. I could tell."

Dawsey smiled at her. "If Father said he wouldn't bring charges, he meant it."

Papa had grateful tears in his eyes. "I'm indebted to the colonel for his kindness, though I know I don't deserve it." His chest rose and fell. "I just wish he'd let me apologize."

Ellie's heart ached for him. "Maybe someday, Pa."

Mama stood in the corner, wringing a dish towel nearly to shreds. At Hooper's nod, she stepped forward and cleared her throat. "I don't mean to spoil the happy news, Silas, but I brought us together for a different reason."

One look at her face brought him to his feet. "What is it, wife?"

She waved him away. "Sit down. I can't talk with you hanging on me."

Pa sat, but he squared his chair around and didn't take his eyes off her.

Fidgeting with the ragged edges of the towel, she smiled, but it looked painful. "It's good news and bad, darlin'. Which do you want first?"

He cocked his brow. "I'm surprised at you for asking. I favor good over bad any day."

"Tiller's not lost in the swamp," she blurted.

Papa took a minute to soak up her words. Braying like a mule, he reared back and clapped his hands so sharply it rang Ellie's ears. "This is a fine day, Odie McRae." He beamed toward Ellie. "First the colonel grants me a pardon, and now I get my boy back. Where is the scalawag? We need to go bring him home."

Her throat working furiously, Ma's pleading gaze sought Hooper.

He stepped forward and touched Pa's shoulder. "That's the bad news. Tiller's gone. He left us."

Papa's eyelids fluttered. "Say again?"

"Gone, sir. Likely for good. He took all his things."

Braver now, Mama supplied more details. "He even took his Christmas presents. Packed everything in a gunnysack. Stole some food, too."

"That little rodent," Duncan said. "He had it planned all along."

Pa's face sagged with the sadness Ellie had dreaded. "It's my fault. I told him I meant to send him back to his ma."

Duncan whistled. "Tiller would do most anything to keep that from happening."

Mama swatted him with her dish towel. "You ain't helping."

Hooper squatted in front of Pa's chair. "Don't let it burden you so. You had no way of knowing."

Pa raised haunted eyes. "Still, I shouldn't have told him something I didn't mean."

Ellie jumped at a knock on the door.

"Are we expecting company?" Hooper asked, standing and reaching for the gun at his waist.

Duncan leaned to peek through the boarded window. "It's all right. It's Boss"—he looked again—"and Wyatt."

Ellie's heart took a breathtaking leap. She hadn't seen Wyatt for days—her face warmed—not since they'd kissed.

Duncan swung the door open on Boss's lanky body, slouched against the side post. "Afternoon, folks."

Wyatt's head ducked in, his eyes sweeping the room for Ellie. When he found her, his broad smile said he'd missed her.

She tried to say the same with her answering grin.

"I've brought some good news and bad," Boss said in his relaxed drawl.

Duncan chuckled. "Seems to be the day for it."

"The good first," Ellie called, watching Papa. "We could use some just now."

Mama took off her apron. "Where are your manners, children? Invite them inside first."

Beaming like a simpleton, Duncan bowed and waved them in.

Wyatt didn't wait for a second invitation. He scooted past Boss and worked his way around the room to stand by Ellie. Hidden behind their legs, his groping fingers found her hand and held on. He leaned to whisper, his breath warm in her ear, "I've got a special surprise for you."

"Later," she murmured, fighting a grin.

Boss took off his hat. "Miss Wilkes," he said to Dawsey, "I was glad to hear they found you in one piece."

"Thank you," she said. "It felt good to be found."

Ellie squirmed with impatience. "What's your news, Boss?"

Mama shot her a frown. "Mind your manners, girl."

Boss laughed and winked at Ellie. "All right then, the good first." His merry gaze swung to her parents. "Folks, I think you've seen the last of your troubles with the sheriff."

Papa leaned forward in his chair. "How's that, son?"

"Because Henry. . ." Boss stared at the floor by Papa's feet, his long fingers fumbling with his hatband. "Let's just say Henry *borrowed* the sheriff's wife overnight. Sent her home with a stern message about what fine fellows the McRaes are." He glanced up. "From what I hear, McMillan will give your boys a wide berth from now on."

Duncan broke the stillness with a rousing howl.

The family cheered and passed grateful hugs all around, a happy uproar that Wyatt used to his benefit. He pulled Ellie close and planted a thrilling kiss on her neck then stood back as blameless as a lamb.

Dawsey's mouth stood ajar. "That poor woman. She must've been frightened out of her wits."

His eyes shining with happy tears, Hooper patted her back. "Don't worry. They didn't lock her in a shed." He smiled. "The only frightening thing inside Henry's house is Rhoda's coffee."

The men hooted, Boss, the loudest of all.

Dawsey scowled. "Still, it doesn't seem right."

Papa tilted his head up at her with a thoughtful look. "You're dead-on, honey, and this family won't waste the turn of fortune that came at her expense." He shook his finger in Hooper's face. "From now on, we'll show our thanks to the sheriff's wife by staying out of trouble. Is that clear?"

Hooper nodded. "Yes, sir. I'll do my best."

Papa pinned Boss with wary eyes. "Let's get on with the bad news. I'd like to get it behind me so I can celebrate."

The weight of a serious matter smoothed the jolly lines on Boss's face. He cleared his throat. "It's about Tiller."

A hush fell over the room. Ellie wished just once that the news could stop at good.

"What now?" Hooper asked.

Boss nodded at Wyatt. "You want to tell them?"

Wyatt looked grim. "My brother's gone, too, Mr. Silas. Packed up his things and took off for the Natchez Trace. I reckon Nathan took Tiller and the other boys with him."

Papa stood on shaky legs and crossed the room. "How do you know that's where they're headed?"

Wyatt's fingers slipped away from Ellie's hand. "They heard about the looting along the Trace, and the brainless whelps figured on making a quick fortune. It's all they've talked about for weeks." He shrugged. "I chalked it up to bold talk. Never expected them to try it."

Pa seemed so wobbly, Ellie and Wyatt led him back to his chair and eased him down.

Ellie's heart caught when Wyatt hung his head. "I'm dreadful sorry, sir."

"Don't be," Pa said. "You're not to blame for my foolhardy nephew. Or for your reckless brother. You tried hard to turn him around." He slapped his leg. "Blast it! I dared to hope I might set Tiller on the straight and narrow. Instead he chose a violent path to destruction."

"That's right," Hooper said. "Tiller made his choice. There's nothing we can do about it now."

"Yes, there is," Dawsey cut in, wiping her eyes. "We can pray every day that he'll realize his mistake and come home."

FORTY-EIGHT

Ma's distress over Papa wearied Hooper to watch. She hovered around him most of the day, concern etched deep in her face. During supper, she stayed so busy pouring water in his cup and dishing ladles filled with seconds on his plate, she hardly took a bite herself. Tuckered out from fretting over him all day, she insisted they turn in early.

After she ushered him into their room and shut the door, Hooper took his coffee and went outside to watch the sunset.

Dawsey looked up from where she sat on the edge of the porch then lowered her gaze to her fidgety hands. Most likely for the colonel's sake, she'd traded Ellie's britches for one of Mama's too-short dresses, so she tugged on the skirt, trying in vain to cover her bare ankles.

Hiding a grin, he swung down beside her. "It's too quiet tonight. Where is everybody?"

She wouldn't meet his eyes. "Duncan's in the barn, I think, preparing the wagon for tomorrow. Dilsey and Wyatt took a walk. My father turned in early to rest up for our trip." She finally looked at him. "He suggested I do the same."

Hooper cocked his head. "You're not tired?"

"A little." Her gazed wandered the yard, from the shed and chicken coop on the right to the grove of sugar maples on the left, their trunks black with last spring's oozing sap. "I'm trying to take it all in. It's the last time I'll see this yard."

"It doesn't have to be."

She jerked her head to the side, her fingers gripping the porch so hard her knuckles turned white.

Blast it, Hooper. Slow down. "Say, that reminds me." He rummaged in the drawstring pouch at his waist and fished out a branch, clusters of holly berries still clinging to their stems. He handed it over. "This one somehow escaped Ma's broom." He smiled. "I thought you might like to have it, to remember our picnic in the grove."

His heart soared when she ducked her head and smiled. "We had a lovely day."

Hooper swallowed hard and reached for her hand.

She tensed but didn't draw away.

"I'll never forget your song about holly trees and the babe born to die. The story it told will set a man to thinking. I'd like to hear more someday."

Her head jerked up. "Would you really?"

Heat spread up his neck, but he nodded.

Dawsey studied him, a puzzled look in her eyes. "You're two men at once, Hooper McRae. Did you know that?"

He grinned and shook his head.

"One of you is charming and tender, like you were that day." She took a deep breath. "Like you are now."

He tucked his chin. "And the other?"

"The other is harsh and cruel, and too frightening to be around."

The bitter edge to her voice brought his head up. "That's how you see me?"

She squared around to face him. "You have to control your passions, Hooper. It's not wrong to defend your people, but it is wrong to lose yourself in the process."

"I disagree, Dawsey. Some things are important enough to die for."

She stood, her eyes flashing fire. "And to kill for?"

Why was she so angry? Hooper squinted up at her, his head spinning. "If it came to that."

Bright red blotches appearing on her cheeks, she shook her finger in his face. "There, you see? That's why I can never marry you." Though the end of Mama's dress fell far shy of the ground, Dawsey lifted the hem and sailed around the side of the house.

Hooper rested his arms on his knees and glared across the yard. It seemed whichever way he turned, she wound up mad at him. He wracked his mind to understand where he'd gone wrong.

Beginning to think the problem lay with Dawsey's temper and not his own, he picked up the holly branch she'd flung to the porch and twirled it between his fingers. She believed in a babe born to die for those He loved, yet Hooper's willingness to do the same angered her. The hardheaded woman made no sense, and he'd run short of time to sort her out. At dawn, she would climb aboard a rig bound for Fayetteville—unless he found a way to stop her.

Dread crowded his throat. Even worse, she'd sit next to Duncan the whole way. With Hooper's recent turn of luck, his simpering brother could return home engaged to the woman he loved.

He dashed the twig to the ground and pushed off the porch. Dawsey Wilkes said she could never marry him, but he knew different. Whatever it took, he'd make sure she saw things his way.

Dawsey charged around the back corner of the cabin, her eyes welling. Dilsey sat on the bottom step of her room, her upturned face glowing with pent-up bliss.

The news her sister waited to share could be only one thing, and Dawsey wouldn't spoil it. Her throat tight with pain, she blinked back her tears and smiled. "Goodness, you look like a child at Christmas." She laughed. "A bit late for Yuletide glee, aren't you? Or awfully early."

A tiny frown crept over Dilsey's forehead, marring her look of perfect joy. "You look like you're ready to cry. Is something wrong?"

Dawsey smoothed her skirt and sat, forcing a big smile to her face. "Of course not. I gazed too long at the setting sun perhaps." She clutched her sister's hands. "Now, tell me what's made you so happy."

Before Dilsey could answer, Dawsey drew back with a surprised little cry and gaped at her finger. "Oh honey, what's this?"

Dilsey's happy grin transformed her. "Wyatt gave me a betrothal ring."

"So I see."

"He rode clear to Charlotte to have it made special."

"Ah." Dawsey nodded. "That's why we haven't seen him around."

Dilsey held up her hand to admire the gold band. "It's a poesy ring. That means there's something written inside."

"Yes, I know. What does it say?"

"Just my name and some pretty words." She blushed and squirmed.

"It says, 'Ellie.' I hope you don't mind. That's the only thing Wyatt knows to call me."

Dawsey scooted closer. "Of course I don't mind." She cupped Dilsey's chin. "In fact, I've been meaning to start calling you Ellie myself—since you prefer it."

Dilsey's long lashes, the matched set to Dawsey's own, swept her cheeks. "I wouldn't prefer it one bit." She glanced up shyly. "Not coming from you."

"Are you sure?"

Dilsey bit her lip and nodded.

Dawsey laughed. "All right then. Dilsey it is."

"If we have that settled, can I ask a favor?"

"Of course," Dawsey said.

She wiggled the ring off. "Will you keep this safe for me?"

Dawsey took it from between her fingers. "You're taking it off?"

"Wyatt hasn't asked Papa for my hand yet. He meant to on Christmas, before those men shot up the place."

Dawsey grinned. "He's not good at keeping a secret, is he?"

Laughter bubbled out from Dilsey. "It was burning a hole in his pocket." She sobered and closed her hand over Dawsey's fist. "I wouldn't trust another soul with this ring."

Warmth stole over Dawsey's heart. "That means the world to me." She tilted her head. "You do remember I'm leaving tomorrow?"

She nodded. "Wyatt's planning to ask Pa right after breakfast. I'll put it on once he says yes."

"You're awfully sure he will."

"Pa likes Wyatt as much as I do." She giggled. "Well, almost."

Pushing down a wave of jealousy, Dawsey bit back a sigh. Even if she could allow herself to be with someone as dangerous and explosive as Hooper, her father would sooner die than give his blessing.

Dilsey wrapped both arms around her neck. "I wish you wouldn't leave. I'll miss you something fierce."

Smoothing her hair, Dawsey's grateful heart whispered thanks to God for the gift of a sister. "I'll miss you, too, terribly, but we'll see each other often."

Dilsey sat up. "Will you come for my wedding? And bring the colonel?"

"I wouldn't miss your wedding for anything. I'm sure Father will feel the same." She offered a wry smile. "As long as he doesn't have to speak to your father."

Developing a sudden interest in the tattered hole in her britches, Dilsey bent to pick at the fraying threads stretched across her knee. "You don't have to go at all, if you don't want to."

Angling her head to watch her sister's face, Dawsey frowned. "Of course I do."

Still pulling at strings, she wagged her head. "Not if you and Hooper—"

Dawsey's hand came up. "I don't want to talk about him."

Dilsey scowled. "Why not?"

"He terrifies me."

"Dawsey Wilkes! Hooper would never lay a hand on you."

"That's not what scares me." Feeling helpless, she decided to trust her sister. "None of this is easy for me. I've fallen in love with Hooper. Leaving him is breaking my heart."

Dilsey clutched her hands. "Then don't go. Hooper can't hide how he feels about you. I've seen it all over his face."

The tears Dawsey had denied earlier welled again. "We both know what Hooper did to those men in the swamp. Every time I look at his hands, I'll remember." Her stomach quivered and she felt sick. "I can't live with him, knowing what he's capable of."

Dilsey withdrew. "We don't know what happened out there."

"What he said left little doubt." Dawsey pressed her fingers to her temples. "He practically confessed it again just now."

Glaring, Dilsey stood up ramrod straight. "If Hooper did something bad, it was to protect our ma. It's the way things are in Scuffletown. We got no choice."

Dawsey rose, too. "Well, it's savagery, and it's not how things are done in Fayetteville."

Red in the face, Dilsey stalked toward the house. At the corner, she spun on her heels and came back. "Then why did the colonel come here looking for blood? If we hadn't locked him up, my pa would be just as dead as those men in the swamp."

Dawsey's mouth fell open. She sputtered, struggling for something to say.

Dilsey jutted her hip. "You want to be careful casting judgment. In the same fix, you might be just as capable as Hooper." She thrust out her hand. "Give me my ring."

Words wouldn't come to Dawsey's defense. She dropped the gold band in Dilsey's outstretched palm and watched her flounce away.

Hooper caught Ellie's arm as she swept by the porch. "Slow down, squirt. Are your britches on fire?"

She fell against him, trembling. "Oh, Hooper."

Alarm shot through him. "What happened?"

"It's Dawsey." She clenched her fist and brought it down on his chest. "She makes me so mad."

He led her to the steps and sat her down. "What happened? I just saw you two hugging and laughing."

"You watched us?"

"For a minute. I was waiting to talk to her, but"—he lifted Ellie's chin with his finger—"I saw you waving that ring around and decided my business could wait."

She held it up for him to see. "Don't tell Pa. Wyatt hasn't asked him yet."

Smiling, he placed his finger to his lips. "Our secret. Now tell me why we're mad at Dawsey?"

"You're mad at her, too?"

He tightened his lips. "Some days I could strangle her."

Ellie's eyes widened, and she peered behind them. "Whatever you do, don't let Dawsey hear you say such a thing."

Hooper drew back frowning. "I didn't mean it, honey. Dawsey knows I'd never hurt her."

"I'm not so sure." Pain flashed in her eyes. "She called us savages, Hooper."

He stared, unable to accept it.

"It's true. She don't understand our Scuffletown ways, and she never will."

"Savages?" The word sounded ugly. "Are you sure?"

Tears streaked Ellie's cheeks. She swiped her nose and nodded.

Hooper kicked at a clod of dirt. "I asked her to marry me." He gave a bitter laugh. "Practically begged her. That makes me a fool if she feels that way about me."

"That's the crazy part. Dawsey loves you. She told me herself. The trouble is she's too stubborn and narrow minded to give in to it. She claims she's afraid of you."

The words Dawsey flung at him rang in his ears. She'd called him harsh, cruel, and frightening.

Ellie fell against him, sobbing in little broken cries. "Let her go back to her fancy life in Fayetteville. She'd never fit in here anyway."

He'd never seen Ellie so hurt. He tightened his arm around her, ready to fight the world for her sake. "That's right, honey." His chest ached, but he forced out the words. "We'll let Dawsey go back where she belongs."

FORTY-NINE

Go ahead, Father. I'll be right along."

"Don't dawdle. We've a long ride ahead." He stiffened beside her then leaned to drop a quick kiss on her cheek. "There," he said, blushing, then hustled out the door.

Surprised, but pleased to the core, Dawsey stared after him, smiling.

She walked to the bed and ran her fingers over the freshly washed and folded stack of clothes loaned to her by Dilsey, while images swirled of her many days spent inside the rustic little room.

In the early days, Odell's chatty visits and Duncan's long talks provided lifelines.

Hooper's bungled apology, one she'd never officially accepted, had forced her to see him in a different light, at least for a time. Her heart ached to go back to those innocent days, before she learned the truth about him.

The most precious recollection was the day Dilsey barged in demanding to know about the life she'd missed. They'd stared at each other in wonder, giggling like children.

Cringing, she sensed God's displeasure. She'd allowed strife to mar the miracle of their reunion, and now she didn't know how to fix things.

Dawsey looked around one last time. She'd come to Scuffletown with nothing more than a ripped blue blanket and a tattered gown. She would leave in a borrowed dress. There was nothing left to take except her memories. Shrugging her empty hands, she crossed to the door and took the steps to the waiting wagon.

She rounded the house, and Duncan smiled at her from the driver's seat. "Morning, Dawsey." His brows drew together. "I hope you feel rested for the trip."

She'd hardly slept at all, and looked it, by his concerned remark. "I'm sure I'll be fine."

"Ma and Pa thought it best to stay inside." He dipped his chin. "For the colonel's sake. They said to tell you good-bye for them."

"Of course." Disappointed, she glanced toward the house. A figure ducked into the shadows beside the window. Somehow, she knew it was Odell.

Duncan held up a bulging dishcloth. "She packed a breakfast for us."

Dawsey nodded and forced a smile. Her traitor heart searched for Hooper but found Dilsey, strolling across the yard leading Father's horse.

"Why thank you, dear," he called as she grew near. "I nearly forgot him."

Dilsey tied the gelding near the tailgate then hurried around to wind both arms around his neck. "I'll miss you, Colonel."

Even Father's stoic demeanor couldn't withstand the force of a Dilsey hug. His stern face melted with surprised pleasure then heart-wrenching pain. "Come see us soon?" His deep voice wavered. "Won't you?"

She backed away and nodded. "I promise. Good-bye, sir."

The lump in Dawsey's throat grew unbearable. "Dilsey, come here, please. I need to speak to you."

With trembling chin and clenched fists, her sister looked up for the barest second before she spun and bolted.

"Dilsey!" She raised the hem of her skirt to run after her, but Hooper appeared from behind the shed and drew her out of sight.

Blinded by tears, she allowed Father to help her into the wagon.

Patting her hand so hard it stung, he tried to comfort her. "There now, don't fret. The poor little thing couldn't bear to say good-bye is all."

She didn't bother to correct him.

Gazing around the familiar, waterlogged yard, achingly empty without the bright-eyed, laughing McRaes, Dawsey fell back against the seat. "Take me home, please, Duncan. Get us there as fast as you possibly can."

He flicked the reins and Old Abe Lincoln surged forward. The wagon shuddered into motion, each turn of the wheels taking her that much farther from Dilsey and Hooper.

Hooper and Ellie reached the cabin just as Ma and Pa stepped out onto the porch. Shading his eyes against the early sunlight, Hooper watched the swaying wagon reach the end of the lane and turn onto the dirt road.

Every nerve in his body strained to leap on Toby's back and cut them off, to pull Dawsey down from her seat beside Duncan and beg on bended knee for her to stay.

"There she goes," Pa said in a hollow voice, his declaration searing Hooper's heart. "It seems a lifetime ago that she came."

Mama sighed. "Because of her, our lives will never be the same." Her arm slipped around Ellie's waist. "Especially yours, honey. I know you'll miss her."

Before Ellie spun off in a fit of tears, Hooper caught the back of her neck, kneading with gentle fingers. "We'll all miss Dawsey, but some things can't be helped." He tugged Ellie loose from Mama and held her close. "I reckon we'll get past the pain somehow."

Ma shot him a sideways look. "I'd come to hope she might stay in Scuffletown for good."

He shook his head. "It wouldn't have worked out. Dawsey's better off where she's going."

Papa idly drummed his fingers on the rail. "They could at least have stayed through Hogmanay like Dawsey promised. It's only four days away."

"Don't be an old fool, Silas. Your bargain with Dawsey ended the second the colonel arrived. I'm sure she'd rather celebrate the dawn of a new year with her own family."

"And her own kind," Ellie whispered, drawing worried looks from both their folks.

Before they could ply her with questions, a sudden motion in the yard drew their eyes. Hooper tensed, but thankfully, he didn't draw his gun. A young girl, barely ten years old, ran barefoot out of the sugar maple grove and came to stand by the bottom step.

Hooper recognized her, but not by name or face. She could easily belong to any family along the Lumber River. The girl's badge of loyalty was her high cheekbones and straight black hair.

"Mornin'," she called in a clear voice. "All is well?"

Papa smiled and nodded. "All is well, honey."

She darted back to the trees, returning with Henry's wife at her heels.

Weariness marked Rhoda's shuffle, but her eyes darted warily along the far trees until she reached them. Mama hurried inside for an extra chair, but Rhoda waved it aside and stood at the edge of the porch. "I can't stay, Odell. I've come to see Hooper, but I reckon you've all earned the right to hear."

Hooper stepped up and gripped the rail. "Has something happened?"

"Not yet," she said, her eyes veiled. "We don't want you taken by surprise when it does."

Poor Papa groped for his chair and sat. "Go on. Tell us."

Rhoda raised her proud head. "Henry's going away. He's leaving Scuffletown."

Hooper's mouth sagged. With a quick glance, he counted more flycatchers open for business. "What do you mean? For good?"

She nodded. "He's weary. What started as a fight for justice became a bloodbath with no end in sight. The balance between right and wrong shifted on us. We have no peace, day or night."

Rhoda stared over the treetops. "Henry feels, with him gone, things will settle down in Scuffletown. As long as Sheriff McMillan and the Guard are after him, the swamp will run red with bloodshed."

"And you?" Mama asked. "You'll go with him, of course."

She bit her lip. "It's better if I stay. Give Henry his fresh start."

"But honey—"

Rhoda shook her head. "I walked into my marriage with wide-open eyes. I knew what I'd gotten myself into." She sighed. "What's best for Henry is the way it will be." Her haunted eyes turned to Hooper. "I've delivered Henry's message. What I say next comes from me."

He took the steps to the ground. "I'd be proud to hear it."

She touched his arm. "Lay it down, Hooper. You've done all you could for our people without your soul turning black. If Henry's right, things will settle down once he goes." Nodding around at the circle of watchful eyes, she challenged them. "No more fighting and stealing. Do your best to be a good neighbor. Share what you have with those in need. Let's take care of our own." Tears spilled onto her cheek. "Otherwise, I'll lose Henry for nothing."

Hooper gave her a solemn nod.

She smiled through her tears and returned it. With an overhead wave, she led the girl to the grove and slipped from sight.

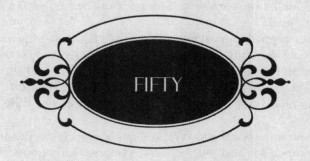

FIFTY

It had been two weeks, two days, and enough tears to fill the rain barrel since Dawsey rode out of their lives for good. As long as Ellie was awake, the insufferable pain and loneliness stayed with her. Each morning when her eyes opened, she probed her heart for tender spots, praying her grief had lessened. She decided God had hitched a ride with Dawsey, because the hurt stayed the same.

Duncan returned, spouting whimsical stories of the big house in Fayetteville with its immense rooms and towering gables. "The bed was three foot high," he boasted, "with scented sheets and down quilts as soft as a bed of feathers."

"A down quilt *is* a bed of feathers, son," Pa had teased.

When he began to speak in hushed tones about holding the magic lantern, Ellie covered her ears and ran for the shed. Hooper found her there, with Duncan in tow, and pinched the braggart's ear until he begged forgiveness and swore to say no more.

Ellie wasn't used to carrying grief tucked inside. Even Mama's boundless joy in planning her wedding couldn't reach through Ellie's sorrow to help her feel again.

With a heavy heart, she dressed and trudged to the house to help Ma with breakfast. The dark belly of the sky matched her mood but didn't bode well for the swollen creeks and rivers, overfed by yesterday's sheets of rain. Needed or not, they'd see a storm before the eggs were good and scrambled.

Just as predictable, Mama hovered near the counter cutting biscuits, and Papa sat at the table with a cup of coffee.

"Mornin', sunshine."

Mama fired him a warning glance.

"Well, a man can hope, can't he? I miss my Ellie. She's the only hope of sunshine we'll have today."

Mama popped him with a mixing spoon.

He howled and rubbed his arm. With a scowl in her direction, he pushed out the chair next to him. "Come sit by me, Puddin'. Let's you and me come up with some games to play. I reckon we'll be rained in for a spell."

He'd barely finished speaking before the bloated clouds burst with a crash of thunder. The rain battered the boarded window so hard, it sounded like pounded drums.

A war cry sounded from the yard. Seconds later, Hooper and Duncan skidded across the porch and fell through the door laughing.

"By thunder!" Duncan cried. "It's a downpour."

Mama rushed to them with dish towels.

Hooper took one, but Duncan dodged and flicked water in her face.

Mama squealed and chased him in circles. "Come here, you batty boy. You're mussing my floor."

A grin tugged Ellie's lips at their larking about, and she longed to join in. The sight of Hooper, smiling for the first time since Dawsey left, swelled her heart.

"Get over here, boys," Papa called. "You're just in time to help me find a game."

Hooper sat across from him with a somber face. "We'll be playing bob the bounty hunter, if that storm floods the yard."

Pa's cup stopped halfway to his mouth. "What do you mean, son?"

Hooper took a sip of the coffee Ma poured him. "If his body surfaces, he could float right up to the house."

Ellie gaped. "Hooper! How can you joke about such a thing?"

He frowned at her over his cup. "I'm not joking."

Duncan swung into his chair and leaned across the table. "They're in the bog?"

Hooper nodded. "One of them."

Ellie's mouth turned to soot. She forced her tongue from the roof of her mouth. "Where'd you put the other one?"

He glanced at her casually then lifted the dish towel and pilfered a slice of bacon. "I didn't put him anywhere."

Gracious, Hooper! You boast of murder then eat with the same mouth? Her hands clenched in her lap and her stomach felt queasy. Had Dawsey been right all along?

With a quick glace at Ma, standing at the hearth, she lowered her voice. "So you only killed one of them?"

She'd wasted her whisper. Mama's ears were too good. Her skillet hit the floor with a *crash*, and she spun toward the table. "Hooper?"

He lifted his gaze from the spilled eggs and stared back at her. "Yes, ma'am?"

Her eyes and nose turning red, she came toward him, wiping her hands on her apron. "I won't have my hide safe at your expense. Please tell me you didn't kill those men."

He calmly sat back in his chair. "I didn't kill those men."

Ellie barely heard him. "What did you think, Ma? They just decided they wouldn't come back?"

Mama studied the floor with darting eyes. "I just figured Henry took care of them or one of his men." She swiped her mouth with the back of her hand. "Dear Lord, anyone but Hooper."

Hooper stood up so fast, his chair crashed to the floor. "I didn't kill those men!" A deafening peal of thunder put a period on his denial. Lightning flashed, throwing flickering light on their startled faces.

In the silence that followed, bacon sizzled and spilled drops of egg sputtered in the fireplace. Ellie smelled the biscuits burning.

Hooper picked up the chair and plopped it down at the table. "They're dead, but I didn't kill them. No one did."

Ma sagged into her place beside Ellie. "Then how?"

His hand went to his hip and he shook his head. "Like I said, one stumbled into the bog."

Ellie flinched. "You didn't try to save him?"

"I wasn't there. I tracked his footsteps to the quicksand, and none came out the other side. That and his hat floating nearby were enough clues to his fate."

"And the other man?" Ma asked.

He sat down across from her again. "Gators. They smelled the blood and closed in on him. I'd guess he was at the water's edge, washing his wounds."

She moaned. "You're certain?"

Grimacing, he pushed away the plate of bacon. "I had the misfortune to stumble onto their picnic."

Mama stared at her open palms. "I killed him, then. I may as well have baited him and tossed him in the pond."

Hooper leaned to gather her hands. "He met a bad end, but it's not your fault. Those men came out here looking for trouble. They found it with no help from you."

Ellie slung her arm around Ma's shoulders. "Picture his hands tightening on Papa's neck. You had no choice but to pull that trigger."

She shook her head, a hollow look in her eyes. "It's not so, Ellie. He let go of your pa and ran. I shot him out of pure blind rage, and I'll answer to God for my sin."

Papa gripped her wrist. "Don't you mourn over this, Odell McRae. If I'd held the gun, I'd have blasted him myself."

Duncan nodded. "He's right. Any one of us would've done the same."

"If you want to unburden to the Almighty, go ahead," Papa said. "After that, we'll talk no more about it." He released her and gave her a tender smile. "Now go tend my breakfast before it turns to coal."

Ellie watched her go then poured her fury out on Hooper. "All this time I thought you killed them. How could you make me think such a thing?"

He tilted his head. "How could you think it?"

She hit the table with her fist. "Pa asked you what happened to those men, and you said—"

"I said not to ask, because their deaths were gruesome. You chose to think the worst."

She ducked her head.

"Ellie, I might engage someone in a fair fight if he wronged one of you, but I'd never hunt down a defenseless man. You should know that."

Relief flooding her limbs, she ran around the table and wrapped her arms around his neck. "I'm so sorry. It haunted me to think you could do such a thing, even for Ma."

Standing, he returned her hug. "How about showing a little more trust in me?"

She lowered her chin. "I'm not the only one who believed it. Even Dawsey—" She slapped her hand over her mouth. "Oh, Hooper."

He pushed her to arm's length. "What about Dawsey?"

"She thinks you ambushed those men and killed them."

Pain flashed in his eyes. "That's why she's afraid of me?"

Ellie nodded. "I think so."

His hands fell away. "How could she think me so ruthless?" He bit his bottom lip, his throat working. "But then, you all believed it, too."

With a knot forming in the pit of her stomach, Ellie clutched his sleeves. "It was a mix-up, that's all. We thought you confessed. Even then, I found it hard to believe."

"Dawsey didn't." He blinked back his tears. "With the way I've behaved, it's no wonder all of you thought the worst."

The cabin went silent as Hooper stood staring at his feet. With a ragged sigh, he hooked his arm around Ellie's neck. "If it takes the last ounce of my strength, I'm going to win this family's faith in me again."

Papa beamed, and Duncan leaped up to pat Hooper's back. The women crowded around, smothering him with kisses.

"But first"—he drew back and rubbed his chin—"Ellie, I need to borrow Toby. He's young and strong. He'll make good time."

Ellie danced an eager jig. "But I want to go with you. Take Duncan's horse. He's nearly as fast."

Pa looked back and forth between them. "Where are you going, son?"

"I have to go see Dawsey and set things right."

Duncan squirmed. "You can't, Hooper. The colonel said I was welcome anytime, but he wants nothing to do with you and Pa."

"I'll deal with that problem when I get there."

"He'll shoot you on sight."

Hooper pushed up his sleeves. "It's a risk I'll have to take."

"Well, you can't take my horse."

Papa glared. "Why not?"

Duncan slapped the table. "It ain't right," he shouted and wheeled away from them in a sulk.

Papa followed him to the hearth and slid one arm around his shoulders. "I know you fancy Dawsey. If you're honest with yourself, you'll admit you don't love her the way your brother does."

Duncan shrugged his arm off. "Who says I don't?"

"I know my boys," Pa persisted. "It may be winter outside, but in here"—he patted Duncan's chest—"there's a touch of spring fever." He turned Duncan to face him. "Are you prepared to marry Dawsey Wilkes? Give her a home and a passel of babies?"

Duncan dropped his gaze.

"That's what I figured." Pa patted his shoulder. "Unless I need eyeglasses, Dawsey loves Hooper, too. There's not much you can do to change her feelings, so why don't you step out of their way and wish them well?"

Duncan stole a shamefaced glance at Hooper. "Go on and take my horse. He's faster than your old nag."

"Thanks." Hooper grinned. "I'll take good care of him."

Mama worried her dishcloth. "You'll wait until it stops raining, won't you, children?"

Hooper crossed to the window. "It's not going to stop anytime soon, and I can't wait." He glanced over his shoulder at Ellie. "Bring a change of clothes. We're going to get wet."

Papa banged his empty cup. "Nobody's leaving this cabin just yet. I hereby call a McRae family meeting to order." His piercing gaze locked on Hooper. "There's some important business we need to discuss with you, son."

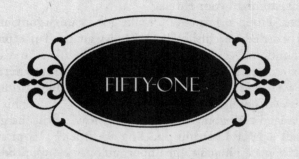

FIFTY-ONE

Fayetteville, North Carolina, January 1872

Dawsey carried a tray holding two cups of chamomile tea into the parlor. Handing one to Aunt Livvy, she kicked off her slippers and curled her legs beneath her in the chair. The rain, relentless throughout the day, still fell against the windows with a comforting murmur. "Do you think it will ever let up, Auntie?"

Her aunt's red-tinged cheeks glowed in the lantern light. "Let it flood if it wants to, dear. Nothing could douse my joy. Each time these old eyes see you again, I praise God afresh." The eyes in question shone with tears. "I had feared you were lost to us forever."

Dawsey swallowed her sip of tea. "I'm sorry you experienced such a trying time. However, I did send word that the McRaes promised to bring me home."

Aunt Livvy's expressive brows dipped and her china rattled as she laid aside her cup. "My milk curdles every time I hear that dreadful name. Lord knows, your father cursed it in blasphemous rants for days." She took a quick breath. "I'm telling you, he turned into a madman."

Dawsey leaned toward her nodding. "When I saw him ride up, sitting tall and sure in the saddle, I couldn't believe my eyes. He'd been so befuddled when I left."

Aunt Livvy swept her hand. "Like the raising of Lazarus. When those awful boys took you, fear and grief drove your father beyond his limits. The more desperate he grew to find you, the stronger and clearer he became—almost like the old Gerrard again."

She sat back, remembering. "The fog lifted from his eyes, replaced by a glint of purpose. Each dawn he saddled his horse and searched for you long into the night."

Dawsey groaned. "Poor Father."

"One morning, a girl no older than twelve appeared on our doorstep. The poor thing was sickly and dirty like one of those pitiful little wretches along the river." She huffed scornfully. "I'm sure it's where he found her, that. . .that. . ." Her finger danced. "Was his name Duncan?"

Dawsey nodded.

Aunt Livvy drew herself up and sniffed. "Whatever his name, he sorely underestimated your father. Gerrard simply paid the girl double to betray her deceitful benefactor. When he left the front stoop with her, we didn't see him again until he returned with you." Smiling, she lifted her cup. "A happy trade that was, I might add."

Gazing at the flickering fire, Dawsey sighed. "I suppose she led him straight to poor Duncan."

Sputtering tea, Aunt Livvy slid her wavering saucer to safe ground again. Coughing, she held her napkin to her mouth and stared.

"I'm sorry, Auntie, but he was on a mission of mercy on my behalf. Duncan McRae is a very nice man."

Her aunt's hand shot up, still clutching the lacy cloth. "Please, dear, I can't bear to hear you say such things. How your father allowed him to sit at our table was more than I could fathom." She shifted in the chair. "Let's change the subject, shall we?"

Dawsey lifted her chin. "As you like." If the very mention of the McRae name upset her, Dawsey didn't dare voice her true feelings.

She missed pausing at the door of the cabin to soak up the laughter echoing from inside, missed Duncan's teasing banter and Odell's childlike ways. She longed to slip into a pair of Dilsey's britches and sit in the swirling mists, immersed in one of Silas's charming tales.

Her heart ached for every second spent with Dilsey and mourned every second lost, but her traitorous thoughts turned most often to Hooper, no matter how hard she fought to resist.

She'd told him he frightened her. The pain and confusion on his dear face when she said it had become a constant companion.

Her emotions tempted her to put her fear aside and allow love for him to overtake her doubts. No matter how difficult, she had to stand fast in her resolve. If she allowed herself to dwell on his proposal, on his passionate plea and warm breath on her lips, she'd be undone.

Father appeared at the door with a big smile. "Is this a private hen party?"

Aunt Livvy glowed with pleasure. "We'll allow one old rooster, dear. Come in and pull up a seat." She curled her long fingers around the arms of her chair and pulled to her feet. "Visit with Dawsey while I go brew a fresh pot."

She'd hardly risen before a loud knock sounded at the front door. Her startled gaze jumped to Father. "At this hour?" She glanced at Dawsey. "Hide in the pantry. It could only mean trouble."

Dawsey laughed, but her stomach tightened. "Auntie, I'll do no such thing."

"Calm down you two," Father ordered. His wary glance toward the hall belied his steady tone.

Her eyes wellsprings of alarm, Aunt Livvy clutched at the air with both hands, as if to draw Father to her. "Don't go, Gerrard. Let Levi answer."

"Don't be silly, Lavinia. Levi and Winney have retired for the night. Besides, I'm perfectly capable of answering my own door."

The rapping grew louder and more persistent as they followed Father, skulking like thieves, into the foyer. One hand on his back, Dawsey drew a quick breath. "This is silly. It doesn't have to be trouble, does it? Perhaps Mrs. Gilchrist is down in her back again."

Aunt Livvy gripped Dawsey's hands, her anxious gaze fixed on the knob. "Not this time. I have a sense of foreboding."

The women clung together as Dawsey's father swung open the door.

"You," he growled, clenching his fists. "How dare you come here?"

His gaze jumped to the pitiful wretch next to Hooper, and he let out an agonized cry.

The specter of Dilsey leaned in the hollow of Hooper's arm, her lips blue and her hair streaming in rivulets. Drenched to the skin, her meager garments clung to her shivering body.

"Merciful heavens," Aunt Livvy croaked, gaping from Dilsey to Dawsey.

Dawsey hurried forward. "Hooper, for goodness' sake, bring her in."

As he gently handed off his sister, Dawsey felt his hands trembling.

She pointed toward the parlor. "Go sit by the fire. Once we get her settled, I'll bring you some dry clothes."

Between Dawsey and her father, they got Dilsey upstairs to

Dawsey's room. He hovered outside while she and Aunt Livvy changed the soaking waif into a dry dressing gown and slid her between the sheets.

Aunt Livvy peeked out. "Go and fetch Winney, Gerrard. Have her prepare hot tea and broth." She ducked out again. "And hurry!"

Dawsey leaned to plump the pillows. Her sister's grasping fingers closed around her hand. "I—I'll be all right now," she chattered. "P–Please go see to Hooper."

Dawsey shook her head. "I won't leave you."

Frantic hands threw back the covers. "Then I'll do it myself."

They caught her and eased her shoulders down.

"Very well," Dawsey said. "If you're sure you're all right, I'll take him some dry things then come right back."

Aunt Livvy frowned but nodded her approval.

Dawsey hustled down the hall to her father's room, emerging with clothing and a warm woolen sweater. Stopping for a towel in the hall closet, she bolted down the stairs.

Hooper hovered in a tight ball before the fire, as if unwilling to soil the parlor rug. He whirled when she rushed in, worry etched in his forehead. "Is she all right?"

"She's dry and beginning to warm. We can only pray she doesn't become ill." She handed him the towel. "What were you thinking to bring her out in a storm? Or yourself for that matter?"

His eyes flickered with guilt. "It wasn't a storm when we left. I thought it would pass."

She took the cloth from his hands. "You might've caught your death. What on earth are you doing here?"

He stood like a shearing lamb and let her roughly dry his hair. Of their own accord, her hands drew him closer until he nearly toppled into her, gripping her arms to stay upright. "Dawsey, I had to come." His piercing brown eyes studied her from under wet stands of hair. "I had to see you."

She stared up at him, her staunch resistance melting. "I've missed you."

"Deliver me, O Lord, from the evil man."

"I'm not as bad as you think."

Had she spoken her prayer aloud?

"I'm a man of strong convictions. I'll admit they've had the best of me lately, but I didn't ambush those men in the swamp."

She blinked at him. "You didn't?"

Gentle fingers lifted her chin. "No, honey. They were already dead when I found them."

"But I thought—"

"You thought wrong."

Confused, she rubbed her forehead and tried to think. "You as much as admitted it. You said your mother didn't have to worry because the problem was tended."

He squeezed her arms. "Think hard. Did I once say I stalked those men and killed them?"

Dazed, she shook her head.

"I'd never say so, because I didn't. I left home intending to put the fear of God in them and drive them from Scuffletown for good. The swamp exacted a much higher price."

"And the heavens shall declare his righteousness: for God is judge himself."

She had haughtily spouted scripture at Hooper. Now one of her beloved Psalms brought swift conviction. "Can you forgive me for misjudging you? Especially without all the facts?"

Hooper smoothed her hair. "Yes, because I earned your distrust." His eyes glowing, he cupped her face with both hands. "I love you, Dawsey. If you'll give me a chance, I'll prove I can control my foul temper. You don't have to marry me until you're sure."

She bit her lip. "What about the raiding with Henry?"

"Over and done. We're going to find a better way."

She leaned into his wet embrace. "Then I don't have to wait. I'm sure now."

His hand slid up her neck to tilt her face. "You'll marry me?"

She rose on her tiptoes and kissed him. "Yes. As soon as possible."

"Dawsey Elizabeth!" Father's bellow ricocheted off the four corners and rattled the chandelier.

Dawsey and Hooper leaped apart.

"Oh, Lord, be merciful," Winney moaned. She paused long enough to peek around the doorframe with owl eyes then streaked past.

Thoughts of murder danced on Father's face as he strode into the room. "What is this madness?"

Hooper faced him. "It's not madness, sir. I've come to ask permission to marry Dawsey."

Father sucked an indignant breath. "You what?" His cheeks seemed to pulse beneath their purple hue. "I'll die first."

Dawsey felt pride in Hooper's control. With a sincere smile, he tilted his head. "I hope not, Colonel, but if we have to wait that long, I'm willing."

A raging bull, Father charged.

Dawsey screamed, but Hooper sidestepped, catching the back of his shirt before he lunged headfirst into the fireplace.

"Father, that's enough."

Three sets of astonished eyes swung to Dilsey, leaning on the threshold in Dawsey's dressing gown. Aunt Livvy's arm around her slender waist helped her to stand.

Forgetting Hooper, Father pulled free and straightened, smoothing his hair into place with a shaky hand. "What did you call me?"

Dilsey limped toward them. "That's who you are, I reckon." She sat, motioning him to do the same. "I'm calling a Wilkes family meeting to order." She glanced at Dawsey. "I think my sister has something she'd like to say."

Weak with gratitude, Dawsey moved to stand behind her chair. "Yes, I believe I do."

Father glared at Hooper. "Not until I've tossed this ruffian outside on his ear."

"If Hooper goes, I go," Dilsey said, scooting to the edge of the cushion.

Dawsey drew herself up. "And so do I."

Father's throat worked furiously. "Don't be silly, Dawsey. Where would you go?"

"Ma and Pa will be happy to take her in," Dilsey said. "They miss her something awful."

With a fond glance at the top of her sister's head, Dawsey's fingers tightened on the upholstery. "You're outnumbered, Father. You may as well sit down and hear me out."

Aunt Livvy stretched to full height. "You heard your daughters, Gerrard. Dawsey has something to tell you. Now sit."

He stared. "Lavinia? What's come over you?"

With a tender look at Dilsey, she smiled. "We've had us a little talk upstairs. Dilsey's an insightful girl."

Over the next few minutes, Father sat like he'd been told, sipping Winney's broth and bravely taking his medicine. He barely sputtered when Dawsey informed him that she longed to have his blessing, but she'd marry Hooper without it.

"I love you very much and always have," she reminded him. "Even when you didn't offer the same devotion. Now I'd like for you to accept the man I'm going to marry." She shifted her attention to Aunt Livvy. "The same goes for you. Hooper did a terrible thing when he took me that night, but if he hadn't we'd never have found Dilsey."

Aunt Livvy nodded. "Yes, I can see that. Perhaps it was meant to be."

Dawsey tended to agree. Her fanciful mind wanted to believe the impish McRaes held some magic charm to make them irresistible. Her heart knew that God had mended the broken pieces and woven His will through all of their lives.

Still unaware of divine intervention, Father hung his head. "Yes, we found her, but now I'm losing you both. Dilsey's marrying a Scuffletown man, and now Dawsey will go live there, too."

Hooper took a hesitant step. "Not necessarily, sir. There's more news I haven't yet shared with Dawsey."

Turning, he stroked her cheek. "My folks own one hundred acres in Hope Mills. They abandoned it years ago when they fled to Scuffletown." His fingers traced her neck to her shoulder. "It's not what you're used to, and the house will need some work, but they've offered it to us."

Her arms went around his neck. "It sounds wonderful."

Aunt Livvy brightened. "Hope Mills is only seven miles away."

Father slapped his knees and stood. "An old soldier knows when to retreat." His eyes still veiled, he held out his hand to Hooper. "I surrender, son. I have no choice but to offer my blessing."

Beaming, Hooper pumped his hand. "I promise you won't regret it, Colonel."

Crossing to Dilsey, Father reached for her hand. "Will you allow me one request?"

She tilted her head. "I'd need to hear it first."

"Fair enough," he said, chuckling. "Will you bring your young man to Fayetteville and let me throw you and Dawsey a proper wedding?"

Always up for a party, Aunt Livvy squealed. "We can plan a double ceremony. I'll throw a grand celebration...Fayetteville-style."

In the clamor that followed, Dilsey stared holes through the floor.

Dawsey held up her hand. "Be quiet, everyone. I think it's my sister's turn to speak."

Dilsey lifted grateful eyes then sighed. "It's not that I don't appreciate it, Father. It's a wonderful offer, but I'm afraid I have to say no. My ma has a shindig all arranged. She's fretted over it for weeks." She smiled. "This one is Scuffletown-style, which I think will be more to my liking."

She gave Aunt Livvy a shy glance. "I'd be proud if you both would come."

Father and Aunt Livvy shared a look. Then with tears in her eyes, she took Dilsey's hand. "Of course we'll come to your wedding, honey."

"We wouldn't miss it for the world," Father said. His head came up suddenly, the spark of an idea dawning in his eyes. "Don't move a muscle, little lady. I have something for you."

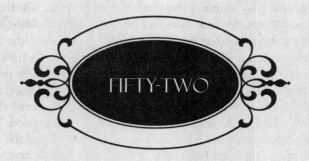

FIFTY-TWO

The colonel spun away so fast Ellie jumped. She stared after him as he sailed from the room, moving quicker than she thought possible. She questioned Dawsey with her eyes, but her sister only shrugged.

He returned as fast as lightning and stepped into the room smiling, a treasure cradled in his hands.

Behind her, Hooper gasped.

The magic lamp was the most fetching thing Ellie had ever seen. Golden fingers of fire leaped on its sides, reflected from the hearth, no doubt, but they lured her with a spellbinding dance. She longed to hold it, yearned to touch the flickering light.

No wonder Papa had grieved for so many years.

The colonel handed her the gold lantern then wiggled his fingers at it. "You may keep it, dear. A wedding gift."

Ellie's breath caught. "Oh no, sir." She leaned and held out his offering—but not too far. "I couldn't keep something as fine as this. Pa claims it's worth a fortune."

"And he's right," the colonel said, a distant look in his eyes. "When I found it in your crib, I realized Silas had laid aside his plunder and took you instead. For years, I held out hope that he would someday return for it and thereby lead me to where he'd taken you." He shook his head. "In my befuddled state, I began to believe I could lure him into offering an exchange."

Dawsey touched his shoulder. "So you placed the bait in the window every night and waited."

Rubbing his face with both hands, he nodded. "Delusions of a silly old fool," he mumbled between his fingers.

"Not necessarily," Aunt Livvy said, nudging him. "Both of your daughters are here in this room, and it's because of that bauble, if I heard the story straight. I'd say that means you netted your fish in the end."

He stared at her until the truth sank in. "I believe you have a point, Lavinia." Smiling, he swept his hand at Ellie. "Consider it my gift to you, dear. Sell it with my blessing, and put the money to good use."

Dawsey crossed to Ellie and closed her hands around the lamp. "Please take it. I'd love to see the blasted thing do some good."

Hefting her prize, Ellie felt like an unworthy trade for the splendid piece. She smiled through her tears. "There are a lot of memories tied up in this lantern. I hope I can bear to part with it." She lifted her eyes to the colonel. "I won't agree without telling you my intentions. If I sell it, I'd like to use most of what it's worth to give me and Wyatt a good start"—she paused—"but I'll use the rest to help the widows and orphans in Scuffletown."

The colonel settled into his chair with a satisfied nod. "Even better."

Laughing merrily, Hooper crouched beside her. "Wait till Pa sees you with that thing. I suppose he can die happy now."

Ellie grinned. "All those years ago, he thought he traded me for the magic lantern. Won't he be surprised to learn he left it for me instead?"

Dawsey knelt beside Hooper. "But, honey, it was your inheritance all along."

Ellie's grin slowly died and her stomach tightened. "That's true. It wasn't a trade. Pa had no right to either one, did he?"

Biting her lip, Dawsey shook her head.

Tears burned Ellie's eyes. "Will you ask your God to forgive my pa for all the hurt he's caused?"

Hooper gripped her wrist. "Only Pa can ask God for pardon, Ellie. Just like we both have to ask Him for our own, but Pa's been talking an awful lot about forgiveness lately, so it's on his mind."

Dawsey patted her knee. "Maybe you need to call a McRae family meeting about God's mercy when you get home."

Frowning, Ellie swiveled her head to Dawsey. "What Pa did was extra bad. Will God be able to forgive him?"

She smiled. "I have a psalm to answer that question. Would you like to hear it?"

"I'd like it very much."

"All right, it goes like this: 'If thou, Lord, shouldest mark iniquities, O Lord, who shall stand? But there is forgiveness with thee. . . .'"

Ellie frowned. "Is that a yes?"

Laughing, Dawsey stretched to kiss her cheek. "Not just a yes, sister dear. A resounding yes."

Dawsey nodded at the lamp, tucked in Dilsey's lap. "It's good that you've come into possession of that portion of your birthright, but there's more laid up for you, Dilsey."

She tilted her head. "What more could I ask than what you've already given me?"

Dawsey gathered her hands. "God's promises are an inheritance more enduring and a treasure far more valuable than anything this world affords. That's the legacy left to us by our mother. I hope you'll allow me to share with you the riches she wanted us to have."

"I reckon I'm willing," Dilsey said. "But how?"

"We can start by teaching you the Psalms."

"I'll help," Aunt Livvy said, sniffing.

Dilsey smiled. "Ma used to read them to us, so that'll give me a head start. We can teach Hooper, too."

The colonel cleared his throat. "Girls, I wouldn't mind sitting in on those lessons myself. It's been too many years since I opened a Bible."

Aunt Livvy leaned her head against his shoulder, fishing her handkerchief from her waistband. "I think that's a fine idea, Gerrard. An absolutely fine idea." Wiping her eyes, she held out her hand to Dilsey. "But first, we need to adjourn this meeting and get you upstairs into bed."

Dawsey took Hooper's arm. "And you may come with me. I'll show you where to get a hot bath and a change of clothes."

With a slight tug on her sleeve, he held his ground until the others had filed from the room.

When the last of their footsteps reached the top of the stairs, she gave him a questioning look. "What are you up to, Hooper? Are you trying to catch lung fever?"

Laughing, he spun her around. "Nonsense, I'm practically dry." He touched her nose. "We still have one matter left to settle, Miss Wilkes.

I figure today's as good a time as any."

She wiggled her finger. "Not so formal, Mr. McRae. Now, what is your pressing business?"

Sobering, he wrapped his arms around her waist. "You never accepted my apology."

"Apology?"

A slight frown creased his brow. "For dragging you out of a window, hauling you off to Scuffletown against your will."

Touching her chin, she pretended to ponder. "That was quite a ruthless thing to do."

Shame crossed his face. "I'm not proud of it."

"However, I realized something tonight," she said, "with all the talk of trading Dilsey."

He cocked his head. "Go on."

"In a way, I got traded, too. You came here to see the lantern, but you got me instead."

A roguish grin lit his handsome face. "Is it too late to change my mind?"

She squealed and swatted him then whirled for the door.

Laughing, he caught her before she got away. Pulling her so close she felt his heartbeat, his dark eyes pierced her soul. "That would be a foolish exchange, now wouldn't it, Dawsey? With my fondest wish already granted, I have no need for Aladdin's lamp."

EPILOGUE

Robeson County, North Carolina, February 1872

Silas leaned against the new windowpane watching Ellie and Duncan play a muddy game of chase. Hooper stretched across the top step, trying his hand at whittling and laughing at their tricks.

The long-awaited return of his children from Fayetteville hadn't come soon enough for Silas. They'd stayed with the Wilkes family while Dawsey nursed Ellie back to health and Hooper prepared the old home place for his bride-to-be.

Ellie's wedding would commence on schedule, despite the recent news of Henry's death. Boss came early one morning, shifting his eyes and shuffling his feet, to tell them Henry blew his face off while drawing a load from his shotgun. Silas never believed it for a minute.

Rhoda's casual style of mourning was the first clue that he was right. Rumors of a cloaked woman, seen scurrying toward the hideout late at night, confirmed his suspicions—Henry Lowry had staged his demise. Further proof was her heartfelt insistence to forego her husband's mourning period and proceed with Ellie's nuptials.

Henry had simply gone away, as Rhoda foretold. She said herself that Henry didn't want the McRaes taken by surprise at the news of his departure.

Ellie's upcoming wedding would give Silas the chance to see young Dawsey again and hopefully make amends with her pa. Following his children's lead, he'd hauled his many sins to the foot of the cross where they belonged and hoped to unburden himself to Colonel Wilkes, as well.

"What are you mooning at, husband?" The warmth of Odell's shoulder against his arm drew him from his hopeful thoughts.

Silas chuckled. "Watching our fine brood of children and thinking how blessed I am." He put his arm around her and hugged her close. "They're all handsome rascals like me. Don't you agree?"

She nudged him with her pointy little elbow. "That ain't a bit funny." Her wary eyes darted over his face. "The boys must never know, Silas. We learned firsthand how much trouble the truth can bring."

"It's not trouble that concerns me, love. That much I deserve, but it would do no good to tell them now. There's little hope they'd ever find their families."

"Hush, we *are* their family," she scolded.

He smiled. "I once feared we'd wind up childless in our waning years, with no one to tend our needs, but it's a fine bunch we wound up with, Odie."

She cut her eyes at him, her hard look meant to shame him. "At what cost to their parents?"

"Wife, I'm convinced I saved those boys from harsh and loveless lives." He pointed past the tattered drapes at their laughing brood. "Would you turn back the clock now?"

Pulling in her bottom lip, she followed his finger with her eyes then shook her head. "I couldn't part with a single one."

Silas glanced at Hooper, so handsome that some folks called him pretty, just not to his face. With his black hair and blacker eyes, he never once doubted where he belonged and would never guess he'd been lifted from a passing Gypsy wagon.

His gaze moved to good-natured Duncan, spinning Ellie around the yard. Short and stocky, lighter skinned than all the rest, his eldest son suspected what the others never questioned.

"Look at me," he'd cry. "Show me another Lumbee as fair as me."

"It's the Scot come out in you, boy!" Silas would lie. "Look at young Tiller. He got a double dose."

"But Pa," he protested, and rightly so. "My eyes are so different from yours and Ma's. They're clear and gray like a wolf's."

What could he tell the lad? *Son, I plucked you from a basket beneath a spreading oak while your ma pounded laundry on a riverbank?* The poor widow had a passel of mouths to feed and likely never noticed he was gone.

Ellie shoved Duncan aside and raced for the porch. Jumping

Hooper's prone body, she hit the door like a sudden gust of wind. "She's here! Dawsey's come for my wedding." Her excited face glowed. "The colonel and Aunt Livvy, too."

Silas stepped outside with Odell on his heels and shaded his eyes. Hooper loped like a spirited deer toward the fancy carriage jostling down the lane.

"Well, this is it, Odie, my love. Another chance to ask Colonel Wilkes to forgive me."

Ellie wrapped her arms around his waist and squeezed. "Suppose he won't?"

"Then I'll bide my time and try again. Maybe at Hooper's wedding."

She lifted her pretty face. "What if he chooses to never forgive you?"

Without waiting for his answer, she beamed like a sunray and sailed off the top step. Dawsey's carriage had arrived.

Silas watched the colonel climb stiffly from his coach. He smoothed his long coat and ran one hand across his silver hair. Smiling fondly at the girls, who stood laughing and clinging to each other, his gaze lifted past them to the porch. The smile faded, but he didn't flinch.

A good sign.

"Well?" Odie asked quietly behind him. "What if?"

Silas glanced over his shoulder. "For both our sakes, I pray he won't make that decision." He cocked his head. "If he does, I can't blame him, but I'll go to my grave trying to persuade him. Any reckoning due after that will be between the colonel and God."

He lifted his hand in greeting and crossed to meet the Wilkes family coming up the steps. "Don't stand there gawking, Odie McRae. Put some coffee on the fire. Ellie's folks have come to call."

CHEROKEE INDIAN SWEET POTATO BREAD

1 quart cornmeal
1 teaspoon soda
3 cups diced sweet potatoes
12 corn husks

Mix cornmeal, soda, and potatoes with enough boiling water to make a stiff dough. Knead well to make firm bread. Wash cornhusks and scald them in hot water. Put dough on large end of blade and be sure all sides are covered with blade and tie end of blade in a loop. Drop bread in boiling water. Boil 45 minutes.

From the Museum of the Cherokee Indian in Cherokee, North Carolina

INDIAN DUMPLINGS

1 pint milk
4 eggs
¼ teaspoon salt
Sifted Indian meal
Flour

Take a pint of milk, and four eggs well beaten. Stir them together, and add a salt-spoon (¼ teaspoon) of salt. Then mix in as much sifted Indian meal as will make a stiff dough. Flour your hands; divide the dough into equal portions, and make it into balls about the size of a goose egg. Flatten each with the rolling pin, tie them in cloths, and put them into a pot of boiling water. They will boil in a short time. Take care not to let them go to pieces by keeping them too long in the pot.

Serve them up hot, and eat them with corned pork or with bacon. Or you may eat them with molasses and butter after the meat is removed.

If to be eaten without meat, you may mix in the dough a quarter of a pound of finely chopped suet.

From the book *Directions for Cookery* by Eliza Leslie

BANDIT'S HOPE

Dedication/Acknowledgments

I dedicate this book with love to George Edward Breshears Sr.
I miss you, Daddy.

My Heartfelt Thanks To

My husband, Lee, for your desire to see me soar.

For what shall it profit a man,
if he shall gain the whole world, and lose his own soul?
MARK 8:36

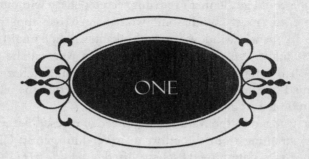

ONE

Pearl River, on the Natchez Trace, June 1, 1882

Mariah Bell reached the bottom landing, stumbling under the weight of the most precious cross she'd ever had to bear. Balancing her father's lifeless body as best she could, she reeled across the kitchen to the door she'd propped wide with her boots, a yawning gateway to the backyard and the early morning darkness.

A breeze laden with the smell of magnolias met her at the stoop. The fragrant gust wrapped around her face, and her labored breaths sucked in the scent of the blooms. Mixed with the odor of Father's pipe tobacco and the vile stench of his illness, the cloying wind threatened to turn her stomach.

Searching blindly with her toes, she found the top step then allowed the drag of her load to shift her forward and over the threshold. Heart pounding, her panting gasps a roar in her ears, Mariah tottered briefly at the edge of the second step.

Exhausted, she surrendered to the pull of the earth, and her trembling legs staggered wildly to the ground. When her bare feet touched the cold, wet grass, she glanced over her shoulder at the shaded windows of Bell's Inn and whispered a grateful prayer.

If one curious lodger peered out and caught her struggling along the hallway, knees bent beneath her unlikely burden, she'd be undone. With her clumsy gait and heavy tread, not to mention the squeaky step at the bottom of the stairs, it amazed her they hadn't.

"Just a little farther," Mariah whispered, a catch in her throat. "Almost there."

If she could get Father's remains secreted away without Mrs. Viola Ashmore, the most meddlesome woman in Mississippi, pressing her nose to an upstairs window, the unthinkable scheme might work.

Last night, the widow Ashmore—Miss Vee, as she liked to be called—had returned from her sister's down in Natchez. Her arrival threatened to ruin everything, and Mariah regretted the hasty decision to summon her home.

She trudged to the waiting wagon bed and eased Father down, her muscles straining from the effort to lower him gently. Clutching his nightshirt with determined fists, she lifted him aside to raise the tailgate.

Three months ago, toting him ten feet would've been impossible to imagine, despite her work-honed arms and sturdy Choctaw ancestry. Squinting in the moonlight at the dear face of the man who gave her life, his once burly frame reduced to a frail skeleton by the wasting disease, she bit off a cry of pain.

Not now, she ordered herself, choking on scalding tears. There'd be ample time for mourning once she hid the body. Covering up his disappearance would be another matter entirely.

From the time she'd leaned over Father's sickbed the night before to find him still and cold, she'd known exactly what to do. She sat at his bedside until the parlor clock struck three times, long past the hour when even the restless Miss Vee had doused her lamp.

Slipping inside the barn, she'd hitched Sheki to the wagon and loaded a shovel before pulling around to the door. The hard part, the dreaded part, had been carrying Father through the house. It took all the strength she could muster, of both body and soul, but somehow she'd managed.

Mariah reached over the tailgate and smoothed his hair. "Forgive me, *Aki*," she whispered. "It's the only way." Straightening, she wiped her eyes and steeled her trembling chin. She'd come this far, and she'd see it through.

Stealthy as a cat, she eased the back door shut, leaning inside at the last minute to snag her boots. Struggling, almost tripping, she pulled them on then crept to the rig.

The side springs moaned when Mariah climbed aboard. Wincing, she settled carefully onto the seat and lifted the reins, clucking her tongue at her little paint pony. Sheki eased forward, any noise from his hooves or the creaking wheels muffled by thick green tufts of damp summer grass.

Fearing a chance meeting with an approaching rider, Mariah avoided the road and crossed the backyard. She held her breath until the horse cleared the lawn and reached the bank of the river.

Sheki picked his way in the meager light, trudging down the yellow, sandy slope alongside the Pearl and into the welcoming shadows of a woody trail. Before the indigo brush and towering birch swallowed them whole, Mariah cast one last glance over her shoulder at the murky outline of the inn.

Just one more storm to brave. Searching the starlit sky with streaming eyes, she pleaded with God not to leave her to face it alone.

Mariah let the horse's nose guide them until they'd gone a fair piece upriver. Unable to bear the darkness another second, especially with her unsettling cargo, she lit the lantern and hung it from a post beside the foot brake.

Soon a swarm of flitting bugs joined the somber procession, dancing wildly around the swaying light. In a strange way, she welcomed their company.

They reached the high bluff overlooking the bend in the river before she allowed Sheki to slow his gait. Pulling up to the broad trunk of an oak, she tugged on the reins and brought her makeshift funeral bier to a halt next to her mother's grave.

In the scanty glow of the lamp, she squinted to read the inscription, though she knew every word by heart: ONNAT MINTI BELL, WIFE OF JOHN, MOTHER OF MARIAH. "The morning light" was a fitting name for her mother. Daylight had gone from Mariah's life the day she died.

Lifting the shovel from the wagon, she glanced at the sky. Dawn would wait for no man, not even the beloved proprietor of Bell's Inn. Drawing a shaky breath, she set to work digging a deep hole beside Mother's humble resting place.

Once she laid him in the ground, swaddled in a soft quilt and facing east as he'd requested, Mariah had a moment's hesitation. It felt wrong to be the only mourner for a man like John Coffee Bell. He deserved better.

Biting her lip so hard she tasted blood, she snatched the shovel. Careful to look away while the dirt rained down on her father, she quickly covered him before she changed her mind.

Hiding the site as best she could, she scattered rocks and dead leaves over the patchwork of grass she'd carefully pieced together over the busted clods. Her efforts might fool the casual eye, but it would take a heavy rain to settle the earth and root the grass again. Many days could pass before her secret was safe.

Unable to walk away and leave the spot unmarked, she hefted a sun-bleached stone and carried it to the grave. Sinking to her knees with an anguished cry, she bowed and placed a tender kiss on the strand of painted beads around her neck, a precious treasure placed there by her mother.

"I'll keep the promise, Mama. I swear on my life." What Father hadn't managed, for all his good intentions, Mariah was destined to finish. Pulling off the wooden beads, she gave them one last squeeze before tucking them beneath his unlikely tombstone.

Against the night sky, the oak tree stretched welcoming arms around her parents' graves. Ancient mourning songs crowded Mariah's throat as she draped her shawl around her head with trembling fingers. Clutching her stomach, she doubled over and wailed her lonesome grief in time with the oak's moaning boughs.

Reddick "Tiller" McRae stiffened and leaned forward in the saddle. Plodding hooves and the steady creak of wagon wheels echoed through the pine and hardwood forest, stirring his heartbeat. From his perch high above the Natchez Trace, his darting gaze watched to see who rounded the bend.

As the rig pulled into view, Tiller rolled the kinks from his neck and dried his palms on the legs of his britches. Some things never got easier.

Ducking beneath a sagging branch, he spurred his horse and rode downslope to the muddy, sunken road. Gritting his teeth, he forced a twinkle to his eyes and a winsome smile to his lips, two tricks he'd gotten plenty good at.

The white-haired old coot, slumped in the seat of the cargo wagon, shot upright and went for his gun faster than a greased thunderbolt, training it at Tiller's pounding heart. "Hold up there, stranger," he growled through shriveled gums. "State your business, and make it quick."

Both hands to the sky, Tiller widened his grin. "Relax, old-timer. I'm as harmless as a snaggletooth viper. Unarmed to boot." Both statements true enough on the surface.

The man's tongue flicked out to swipe his bottom lip, and his jaw shifted to the side. "You take me for a fool, don't you, boy? Nobody rides the Devil's Backbone unarmed." His eyes narrowed, and his gaze tracked up the rise to the shadowy brush. "Or alone."

Tiller chuckled. "It's been many years since this rutted trail was known as the Devil's Backbone, sir. Not since Robinson Road pulled the starch right out of her spine." He winked. "More to the point, you're riding alone."

One gnarled finger tapped the pearl handle of the six-barreled Remington revolver. "Your eyesight's failing you, son. My little friend here don't talk much, but he's pretty fair company in a pinch." His flashing stare demanded answers. "If you like Robinson Road so much, what are you doing out here?"

Slapping his thigh, Tiller laughed with delight in his most charming and persuasive manner—and if anyone could be charming and persuasive, it was Tiller McRae. "You've got me there, mister." He nodded toward the rising band of orange sky on the horizon. "I guess a fellow has to get up earlier than daybreak to pull one on you."

A smug grin lifted the wrinkled cheeks. "You got that right. Now, commence to telling me what you're up to a'fore I dot your eye with this pistol."

Paying careful attention to the man's surprisingly steady hand, Tiller raised the brim of his hat and scratched his head. "Truth be told, sir, I'm a little embarrassed to say."

His new friend sat forward on the seat, his rheumy eyes bulging. "You'll be a sight more embarrassed with air holes in that Stetson and a part in your taffy-colored hair."

Bright smile waning, Tiller swallowed hard, resisting the urge to glance over his shoulder at the empty trail. What was taking them so almighty long? "All right, mister. Keep your suspenders fastened and

I'll explain." Grimacing, Tiller shifted in the saddle while his mind scrambled for a likely account. Quirking one brow at his edgy audience, he released a shaky laugh. "The sad truth is I got hitched a couple of days ago. Up Carthage way, where I'm from." He cocked his head and beamed a sweet smile. "Married the girl of my dreams."

"Married?" The saggy eyelids fluttered. "You don't say."

Tiller drooped his shoulders and sighed. "Our bliss was short-lived, I'm afraid. We'd barely doused the lights in our bedchamber when her brothers knocked down the door. They dragged her from my loving arms, kicking and screaming, and carted her out." He stared off in the distance and shook his head. "Still in her dressing gown."

The gun barrel dropped a quarter inch. The old man gulped and leaned closer, curiosity burning in his eyes. "What'd they go and do that for?"

Tiller cut his gaze to the ground. "Her pa in Jackson ain't so fond of me. He didn't approve of our union, so we ran off together. The scoundrel sent his ill-mannered sons to fetch her."

A long, slow whistle followed. "That ain't hardly right, young fella'. . . not with you hitched to the gal. Why didn't you stop 'em?"

"I tried my best, sir, but her three brothers are as stout as oaks. I was no match for the burly brutes. They loaded up Lucinda and whisked her away before I could catch my breath."

"Lucinda, huh? That's a real nice name."

Tiller waved his hand across the sky, as if painting a picture he saw in his mind. "I can still see her delicate arms reaching for me. . .tears shining in those big, doe eyes."

The old man lowered the revolver to his lap. "Now that's a dirty shame. The poor little thing. What do you plan on doing about it, son?"

Sitting tall in the saddle, Tiller squared his shoulders. "I'm bound to bring her home, if I have to waltz clear to Jackson and dance right up to her daddy's door."

"That's tellin' him, boy!"

Tiller nudged back his hat. "So you see. . .that's why I'm fool enough to brave the Trace alone. I'm on a quest to rescue my darlin' bride. I figured on shaving some time by cutting through on this old stretch of road. Might even catch them before they make it home."

Softness eased the lines of the traveler's face as he holstered the

Remington. "I was engaged once myself. To the sweetest little thing this side of the Mississippi Delta." He worked his jaw, trying to contain his grin. "But her pa was a horse's rear end." Giving in to mirth, he beamed and lifted his chin. "Tell you what, boy. I'm headed to Jackson, myself. Why don't we ride on down together?"

Tiller angled his head. "You mean it, mister?"

"Well, sure I do." His toothless smile seemed childlike. "The good Lord makes fine company on a long trip, but it's nice talking to a fella' wearing skin for a change." He motioned to the rear of the wagon. "Tie that animal to the back and sit up here with me. Two brains ciphering your problem may hit on a plan to bring your little wife home." He leaned closer and lowered his voice. "You ain't mentioned if you're a religious man, but if you'd like, I'll ask God to help you out." He winked. "Him and me are fairly close friends, you see."

Shame—Tiller's constant companion of late—surged in the pit of his stomach. He stole a quick look at the line of brush and young magnolias on the opposite side of the gulch. Except for a few leaves caught in a sudden breeze, the trees were still. "Listen, old-timer"— Tiller nodded at the furrowed road winding in the distance—"maybe you'd best get on without me. It's not safe to lollygag for too long in these parts."

The stranger scooted over and patted the seat. "All the more reason for you to join me. Why, together we could fend off—" He swallowed the rest as his head jerked to the side.

A flurry of masked riders swept over the steep slope, bearing down on him like all wrath.

His mouth gaped in shock, and his palsied hand groped for his holster. Caught off guard, the old man's draw wasn't fast enough.

"Don't try it, grandpa," the lead rider's voice growled. "Twitch a finger, and you'll lose it."

Digging in his heels and yanking his reins to the side, Tiller bolted, the sound of gunfire and the old man's pleas ringing in his ears. At the top of the rise, a bullet slammed into his Stetson, spinning it into the air.

He wove through the woods alongside the road until he no longer heard the shouting voices of the ambushing men. Ducking into a clearing, he dismounted and secured the horse to a branch then plopped down on a fallen pine log.

With his arms hugging his head, he didn't hear a rider approaching, didn't realize he wasn't alone until someone tapped his shoulder.

Fire surged through his limbs. Fists clenched, his chin came up.

His oldest friend in the world, Nathan Carter, stood over him holding his hat. "I reckon this belongs to you," he said, passing Tiller the Stetson.

Tiller snatched his favorite hat, turning it over in his hands and poking his fingers through the bullet holes. "What were you thinking, Nathan? You cut it a little close that time, don't you think?"

Nathan's booming laughter flushed a covey of bobwhite quail. They scattered to the sky in a rush of brown speckled wings. "Don't you believe it, son. That bullet found its mark." He hitched up his pants. "We have to make it look good, don't we?"

Tiller tossed the hat at Nathan's feet. "You owe me thirty dollars."

Nathan grinned, his brown eyes dancing. "That shouldn't be a problem, once we split the take. The old buzzard was sitting on his life savings. Under his seat there was a fortune in—"

Tiller's hand shot up. "Spare the details."

Pushing long strands of his black hair behind his ears, Nathan smirked. "Ignorance makes you innocent, is that it? You don't seem to mind when you're sitting around patting a full belly."

With a devilish grin, he drew back and kicked. The Stetson sailed in the air, landing upside down in the cold, gray ashes of the campfire. "Tiller boy, the cost of new headgear seems a small price to pay for a lily-white conscience."

Tiller tensed. "Nate, that's enough."

Nathan slapped his shoulder. "After ten years, you're still not cut out for this game." He leaned close to Tiller's face. "Don't think I didn't see what you tried to do back there."

Warmth crawled up Tiller's neck. "I don't know what you're talking about."

"Oh, I think you do."

Noticing his hands wringing like a washerwoman's, Tiller clenched them and slid them along his trouser legs. "They didn't hurt that old man, did they? I mean. . .he was all right when you left?"

Nathan gave a harsh laugh. "He'll have a sizable knot on his head, but I expect he'll live."

Tiller scowled at the rugged face he knew so well. "They hit him? Why'd they go and do that?"

Nathan shrugged. "Reckon he asked for it. Or else Hade got one of his urges to hurt something. I didn't hang around to see." He jerked his thumb at Tiller. "I lit out after you."

Propping his sizable foot on the log, he leaned to study Tiller's face. "While it's just you and me, there's something I've been meaning to ask."

Less than eager to hear, Tiller cocked his head. "Well, go on. Get it out of your system."

Nathan's brows rose. "I'm wondering how that mind of yours works, is all. How you can twist the truth around to suit you." His smile turned cold. "Don't you get it, pardner? You may not wear a bandanna or wave a gun, but your part in this operation still makes you a thief." He paused to spit, his mocking gaze pinned to Tiller's face. "The way I see it, owning up to what you are is better than what you looked like just then."

Tiller scowled. "And what's that?"

"Instead of the raider who robbed an old man on the Trace, you're the coward who rode off and left him."

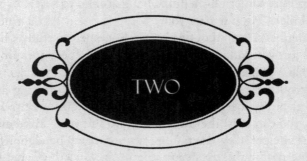

TWO

Mariah beat the sunrise to the house, but just barely. The surrounding forest blocked her view of the horizon for most of the way home, but the glowing sky over the treetops meant the first bright sliver of the sun would soon appear.

Casting a nervous glance at the inn, she wheeled the rig into the barn and leaped to the hay-scattered floor. Grunting from the effort, she wrestled Sheki free from his harness, a worrisome task with the stubborn beast straining his neck for the feed bucket.

Mother did well to name him the Choctaw word for buzzard. The greedy animal nuzzled for every morsel in his trough and never missed a chance to scavenge for a bite of grass.

Sheki pawed the ground and nickered softly. Mariah patted his freckled back and smoothed his white mane. "You're ready to eat, aren't you, friend?"

Urgency surged in her limbs at the reminder of food. For the cost of a night's stay at one of the last working stands left on the Natchez Trace, her father promised his lodgers a fine, hearty breakfast. She'd inherited the promise, if not the inn, and had less than an hour to fulfill her end of the bargain.

Mariah left the horse eagerly chewing a mouthful of oats. Sidling up to the barn door, she made a quick check of the house before stepping outside and heading up the path.

God was with her. Early morning gloom still cloaked the first floor, despite the glimmer of a lamp burning in a back room upstairs. Up front, Miss Vee's tasseled shade was blessedly dark.

She had to rush. Before long, Dicey Turner would trudge out of the woods beside the house, dragging her apron as well as her behind, dreading the workday before it started. Rainy Boswell would come, once the dew dried, to cut the grass.

Crossing the yard, the nagging dread returned to tug at Mariah's spirit. With Father's death, she could lose all claim to Bell's Inn—what should be her rightful inheritance and the only home she'd ever known. It would take a miracle for a Choctaw man in Mississippi to hold on to such valuable property. A miracle wouldn't help a lone, half-breed woman.

In the desperate early hours at Father's bedside, the answer had come. Despite the body she'd rolled into a hidden grave, her father could not be dead.

Whatever it took, Mariah would keep the proprietor of Bell's Inn alive in the world's reckoning until she found a suitable man to marry. What an English father could not do for her, even in death, a pale-faced husband could.

She had plenty of would-be suitors among the sons of her tribesmen, those who stayed behind after the Treaty of Dancing Rabbit Creek and the exodus of her people. Handsome young braves who vied for her attention.

There were even some who'd caught her eye, such as Christopher and Justin Jones, the sons of the tribal physician. Either brother would make Mariah a fine husband. Each had made his interests known, but they couldn't change the biggest mark against them. Indian blood coursed through their veins.

As she mounted the rickety steps, a loose board moaned beneath her feet and paint chips from the rail came off in her hand. The two-story house was a far cry from its humble beginnings, a lean-to run by her grandfather, strewn with bearskins for the lodgers to sleep on. Still, it needed some upkeep.

Minding the inn kept Mariah too busy for outside chores, and most of the jobs were too much for her to tackle. Another reason to find someone to marry as soon as possible.

She'd find a husband with a strong back and feeble mind, an item in ready supply in her opinion. With such a man in tow, no one would question her claim to Bell's Inn, and she could go on running things the way she had since Mother died.

Mariah knew just the man.

Gabriel Tabor had made his interest known by less than subtle glances. One crook of her finger, and he'd be down on one knee pleading for her hand.

Unfortunately, Gabe was coarse and dimwitted. Distasteful traits at best, but he was the only eligible man around for miles.

Tiptoeing across the wobbly porch, she eased through the door, cringing when the hinges squealed. A little oil was in order, a matter she'd make time for after breakfast.

She eased off her boots and started for the stove, but her fleeting image in the speckled mirror stopped her cold. Backing up, she peered into the wavering glass. In the hours since finding her father's body, grief had aged her, stress etching lines in her youthful face. Shock and sorrow had washed the woman in the glass as white as her English ancestors.

Mariah gazed at her high cheekbones and the bump at the bridge of her nose. Odd how a nice dress and upswept hair disguised the truth. Barefoot, dressed in riding britches and a cotton shirt, there was no denying her Indian roots.

"You're a chameleon," she whispered, fingering her long black braid. "One day the lady of the manor, the next an Indian princess. Can't you decide who you want to be?" Thanks to her parents, Mariah was both, stuck in between two vastly different worlds—the Pearl River clan of the Choctaw Indian and her blue-eyed British relations.

The ugly name "half-breed" pressed at her lips. She'd had it whispered in her direction all her life and loathed the sound of it.

"Mariah?"

She whirled, clutching her chest.

By the dim glow of the lantern gripped in Miss Vee's dimpled hand, her tall red curls seemed to hover on the stairs. Turning sideways to maneuver the narrow passage, she took the last two steps to the kitchen and held up the light. "Did I startle you? I'm not surprised, with all this creeping about before dawn." Frowning, she tugged her dressing gown tighter. "What have you been up to?"

"I—"

"Where's your father?" Miss Vee interrupted, leaning to peer past Mariah. "Did you leave him in the barn?"

Jolted, Mariah nearly choked. "Y–you saw me take him?"

Miss Vee's ginger head came up. "I saw an empty room when I stepped inside to check on him, and the wagon just pulled into the yard. I can add two and two all by myself."

Weak with relief, Mariah hurried to change the subject. "I'm pleased you're finally home, Miss Vee. We've missed you something terrible."

"John, too?" She beamed. "Oh, I'm glad. I've sorely missed you both. I came as soon as I could."

"I heard you come in last night."

Her thinning brows peaked. "Impossibly late, I'm afraid. I hope I didn't disturb your poor father."

Mariah hid her twisting hands behind her back. "No, ma'am. You didn't disturb him." That much was achingly true. "How are things in Natchez?"

Miss Vee waved her hand. "Natchez never changes."

"And your sister?"

"Still weak, but on the mend. When I got your wire saying your father had taken ill, I left at once." She stretched her chubby neck to see over Mariah's shoulder. "Where is John, honey? He needs me."

Pity surged in Mariah's heart. The chance to nurse Father, to hover at his bedside, would've meant so much to Miss Vee. She'd loved him for years, a fact that everyone knew but Father.

When Mother died two years ago, the feisty widow turned up on the steps of Bell's Inn, suitcase in hand, to offer him comfort and consolation. Blind to her motives, he hired her on the spot as a chambermaid. She patiently made beds and scrubbed floors, waiting for his mourning to end. Father never seemed to notice her yearning glances across the breakfast table. Now he never would.

Mariah's breath caught on a strangled sob, and she cleared her throat to mask the sound.

Distracted, Miss Vee shuffled to the window to search the yard. "I don't see him. Shouldn't he be in bed?" The concern shining from her faded green eyes made the secret even harder to bear.

"Father's not out there, Miss Vee. He's gone." Pain squeezed her chest. Would she survive such heartrending deception?

"Gone?" Miss Vee pushed away from the window. "I don't understand." Luckily, she was too upset to notice Mariah's brimming tears.

Mariah blinked them away and cleared her throat. "Yes, ma'am. To. . .a place where he'll be well again. Healed once and for all."

Miss Vee's shoulders sagged and her face soured. "But I rushed home to nurse him back to health." Her brows drew together. "What sort of *place?*"

"Umm. . .well, the reverend told us about it. He assured us Father will be much better off there."

Red splotches tinged Miss Vee's cheeks. "Better off than in my care?" She sniffed and shook her head. "I assure you, Mariah, no one else will afford John Coffee Bell more tenderhearted compassion."

Mariah couldn't help but smile. *You're mistaken, dear lady. There's One other, and my father rests in His hands.* So far, she hadn't told a lie, but it was time to change the subject. "Run up and put on some clothes while I start breakfast. We have guests this morning. You don't want to meet them on the stairs in your dressing gown."

Miss Vee absently clutched her bodice. "No, I—Mariah, are you certain John is all right?"

"Gracious, don't fret so," Mariah called on the way to light the stove. "Father will be just fine. I. . .saw him off to his destination myself."

"I see." She touched her plump bottom lip. "He took the train then. Did he say when he might return?"

Mariah shooed her with an apron. "Go along now, and don't worry." She turned away and made a wry face. "It won't do Father a speck of good to worry yourself sick."

Heavy footfalls overhead stifled the persistent woman's next question and sent her scurrying to the foot of the stairs. She paused on the squeaky bottom step and turned. "Mariah, how did John look when last you saw him?"

Mariah cracked another egg into the bowl, stirring briskly with her fork. There'd be no turning back, with the eggs or the scheme. Both were too far along to unscramble. She smiled brightly over her shoulder.

"I've never seen him more at peace."

The roiling fear cooled in Miss Vee's green eyes, and her fuzzy chin rose on a sigh. "Good." She nodded firmly. "That's good to hear." As she lumbered out of sight, her final words tumbled down the stairwell behind her. "Still, it's a crying shame. No one on earth could tend that man better than me."

Tiller's body went as stiff as the pine log where he sat, and a rush of hot air fired through his nostrils. He slapped the fallen tree so hard the notched bark stung his palm. "I know you didn't call me a coward, old friend, since that would make you a careless fool."

He struggled to his feet and pressed his heaving chest close to Nathan, his breath coming in labored gasps. "Take it back fast, and I won't bust your mouth."

Before Nathan could react—or Tiller make good on his threat—the gang rode into the clearing like a raiding muster of crows, their spirited shouts and cackling laughter echoing off the trunks of the loblolly pine.

Hade Betts, the rowdy band's leader, slid off his saddle and gathered his reins. "McRae," he announced with a grin on his face, "you're one talented liar, son. You had that old badger so fixed on your yarn we were cuddled in his lap before he saw us coming."

Tiller shot Nathan one last challenge with hooded eyes and stepped away. "I'd thank you for the compliment, Hade, but I'm not sure lying is an admirable skill."

Hade's jowly face crinkled with glee. "Dodge the praise all you like, but I call it a gift. Your tales get taller each time I hear one. Especially when there's a woman involved."

The men chuckled with Hade. Climbing down from the stolen rig, a beat-up satchel under his arm, young Sonny Thompson slapped his skinny leg. "Ain't it the truth? And this time he gave the gal"—he tipped his hat at Tiller—"excuse me, his *wife* a name."

"Lucinda McRae, with her loving arms stretched wide and her big doe eyes filled with tears." Laughing, Hade wrapped one arm around Tiller's shoulders and shook him. "Where *do* you get your wild imagination, boy?"

In a flicker, Tiller was seated at Uncle Silas's feet in a misty Scuffletown swamp, listening to stories about a ten-foot giant who picked his teeth with railroad ties and fed Carolina lawmen to gators. He shrugged away the painful memory. "Can't say where I get my stories. I reckon they just come to me on the spot."

Sobering, Hade wiped his eyes on his sleeve. "For a second there, you had me believing. Poor fellow, left all alone on your wedding night. I was starting to feel sorry for you." With a loud snort, he bent over howling again.

Tiller gave in to a grin. "That's all right, Hade. Sometimes, I believe it myself. I get to feeling a little sad when I remember I'm telling a yarn."

Overcome by Tiller's remark, Hade eased his broad behind onto a nearby stump, his potbelly shaking.

Nathan sauntered over, a knowing smile on his face. "Tiller boy, I'm wondering if all your talk of marriage lately might be wishful thinking. Maybe you have it in mind to find some pretty little gal, get hitched, and settle down to a respectable life."

A scowl erased Tiller's grin. He shot Nathan a glare, wondering what had come over him. "What are you saying, Nate?"

Nathan shrugged. "You're not planning to split trails with us, are you?"

Sonny squatted in front of Hade and laid open the satchel at his feet, delight on his rawboned face. "Don't worry. Tiller ain't going nowhere. Not while we're pulling in this kind of loot."

Grinning, Hade leaned over to pull out a double handful of bills, the bundles tied up with string. "It's been slim pickings lately, boys, but cast your eyes on the fruit of our patience. Belly up and get your share."

The bright-eyed gang gathered around, their faces lit with anxious greed.

Licking his fingers, Hade counted out equal piles, the thrill in his voice building to a pitch as the stacks got taller.

"Wooeee!" Sonny cried. "Would you look at that?" He glanced over his shoulder. "Tiller, you struck a wide vein this time."

The blissful men jostled closer with outstretched hands to get their share while Hade divided the spoils. Reaching deep into the bottom of the bag, he brought up a leather-bound book, its pages crimped and worn. Opening the cover, he smiled and cleared his throat. "'This Holy Book is the property of Otis Gooch of Tallahatchie County,

Mississippi.'" Beaming, he tossed it into the doused campfire where it landed in a smoky cloud of white ash. "Much obliged, Mr. Gooch. We'll spend your money wisely." He cocked his head. "Well, quick anyways."

The camp erupted in riotous laughter.

Chuckling, Hade lifted his chin at Tiller. "Come get your money. I gave you the extra five dollars."

Hade's wide smile blurred into the traveler's toothless grin.

Cursing, Tiller whirled for his horse.

"Hey, where you going?" Hade spun on the stump. "Come take your split. You earned every cent."

Ignoring him, Tiller swung into the saddle. "What I've earned is some time off. I'm going away for a few days."

Nathan smirked from the ground. "What about your cut?" He snatched the wad of cash from Hade and held it up to Tiller. "A man on a spree could have a high time with this kind of dough."

Tiller plucked Nathan's slouch hat from his head and put it on. "I'll take this to even our score for now. You keep the money. Share it with the boys." He nudged the horse with his heel. "Lay it on those ashes and use it for kindling. I don't rightly care."

Sonny pushed to his feet and came to stare up at Tiller as he passed. "Where you going, Tiller? When will you be back?"

"I can't answer those questions, Sonny. I don't know myself."

"Kin I come?" He waved a wad of cash in both hands. "We could have us a high old time down in Natchez."

"Not this time."

"When will we see you again?"

With a halfhearted salute at the circle of gaping men, Tiller rode out of the clearing. Out of earshot, he drew up his shoulders and jutted his chin. "Tell you what. . .look for me when you see me."

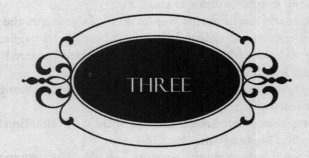

THREE

Choctaw Nation, Oklahoma Country, Indian Territory

Joseph Nukowa Brashears stilled in his tracks. With the ruins of Fort Towson at his back, he gazed northward along the old military road toward Gates Creek, as sure as spit that a fat buck rabbit had just scurried past. The taste of Myrtle's stew teasing the back of his tongue, he held his breath and trained his gun on the brush.

"He's gone, Joe."

The barrel leaped toward the sky, along with his surging heart. Spinning, he gaped at his woman.

Myrtle stood a few paces behind, her fingers toying with the plaited black hair over one shoulder. Her skirt moved as she swayed, the turned-in toes of her moccasins peeking from under the hem. She looked like a naughty child instead of his wife of many moons. She shrugged. "I saw him go. Don't waste your lead."

"You saw nothing." Joe sniffed and turned up the wide brim of his hat. "And you just loud-mouthed yourself out of a fine supper."

She gave an answering snort. "I know what a cottontail's behind looks like, old man. Something's gone off with your vision, and I suppose it's old age. Once you were a lively young brave, one who wouldn't let a meal slip through his fingers." With a strangled laugh, she tugged on his sleeve and pointed. "Hop through in this case."

In the distance, the long-eared critter bolted past a pawpaw tree, bounded thirty yards, and ducked into a knot of flowering staggerbush—stopping once along the way to nibble a dandelion.

"Forty years is not old, wife. My eyesight's keen. There's a pressing weight on my shoulders today, is all."

Myrtle made a sunshade with her hand and gazed at the horizon. "It's early to be wound so tight, Joe. The day has hardly begun."

"Never mind." He yanked his arm free and shouldered the gun. "His furry behind will be mine yet. Wait and see."

Tilting her face, she peeked at him. "I'd ask what's hung in your craw, but I fear you'll tell me."

He stared into the sunrise and pursed his lips. "You'll find out soon enough—when I ride off after breakfast tomorrow."

She shot him a wobbly grin. "So you're leaving me here to pull corn by myself? How long will I be shed of you this time?"

If a stranger happened along to hear the teasing in Myrtle's voice, see the carefree set of her mouth, he'd swear Joe's wife didn't mind his going away.

Joe knew better.

He wound her arm through his and patted her hand. "I'll be gone for a good while, I'm afraid." Urging her forward until her shuffling feet caught up, he started her down the road toward what was left of the fort and their humble cabin beyond. "Don't worry about bringing in the corn. Our neighbors will help."

She trudged alongside him in silence before slipping her hand free and fisting it at her side. If he bothered to look, he'd find the other hand clenched, too, the knuckles of all ten fingers a matching shade of white.

Joe steeled his spine and prepared for battle. "I don't want you to fret, Myrtle. I'll be home before the days grow short. You can count on it."

"Where you thinking to go?" The angry glint in her downcast eyes said she knew the answer before she asked.

Squirming under the scorn in her voice, he glanced to the side of the road. "Thought I'd ride east for a spell."

"Joe." His name hung in the air between them, splitting their hearts like an ax on kindling. "There's nothing left for you in Mississippi."

His brows bunched. "I'm duty-bound to my sister's memory."

Myrtle pinched her lips and blew a long breath through her nose.

"You'll do as much good as you did before. John Coffee won't change his mind."

Joe winced at the sound of his enemy's name. Why had his sister married an ignorant *nahullo* then up and died? And not just any white man. The most stubborn paleface in Mississippi.

To drive the thorn deeper in Joe's side, his sister's husband was named for Colonel John Coffee, a United States representative at the Treaty of Dancing Rabbit Creek, the day that marked the end of the Mississippi Choctaw Nation.

Because of John Coffee Bell, Joe had taken the name Nukowa, or "fiercely angry," in the white man's tongue.

Myrtle prattled on, as if he hadn't growled and set his jaw. "John doesn't hold with the ways of our people. He will never accept that Mariah became your charge the day she was born."

She lifted one shoulder. "Besides, if your niece cared to live with us, she'd be walking this trail with us now. The girl has made her wishes known."

"I can't help what she wishes."

"Mariah's not a child, Joe. She's well past marrying age."

"All the more reason to bring her among her people. John will see her wed to a nahullo, one as stubborn as he is. Then Mariah and her children will abandon our traditions forever." Joe gripped the stock of his gun until his fingers ached. "Every day she becomes more of John and less of her mother. My sister's spirit wails to me in my sleep."

Blinking away stinging tears, he gazed over his shoulder at Fort Towson, abandoned by the military at the close of the Civil War. Once a thriving garrison, the broken-down row of buildings was little more than a burned-out shell.

Joe took Myrtle's arm and led her down the path that branched away from the stark reminder of the past. There'd been enough wars fought in the nation to suit him, yet he found himself crossing swords with his dead sister's man.

With a mind shut tighter than a gulf clam, John ignored Joe's pleas where it came to Mariah's welfare. Joe had swallowed his bitter anger and allowed John to force the white man's way over Onnat, but his heart had stirred at her death.

The time had come to bring Mariah Bell to live where she belonged, under the watchful eyes of Joe and the other men of the tribe. John Coffee's pride would not stand against generations of Choctaw wisdom.

Distant voices brought Joe's head up.

Three boys loped toward them on the lane, their sun-washed faces the color of acorn tops. The oldest balanced a shotgun over his shoulder. The beaming lads flanking him carried bobbing cane poles and a can likely filled with fat worms. They nodded as they passed, no doubt headed for Gates Creek to jerk fish for the family table.

Their laughter and happy chatter pulled at Joe. He longed to swivel on the ball of his foot and fall in beside them. He'd missed so much by never having a son.

"Did you hear me, Joe? You can't force Mariah to come."

He grunted. "I heard."

"But you won't change your mind." Her defeated sigh pricked his heart.

Digging in his heels, Joe gripped her arm and pulled her around. "I've chosen Mariah's husband, Myrtle. A nephew of the tribal chief. It's what my sister would want for her daughter." He blew a frustrated breath. "The girl's future is here now."

Myrtle shook her head. "Your sister embraced John's way of life, especially where Mariah was concerned. How do you know that Onnat—" Her gazed dropped, shame bright in her eyes. "I mean. . .how can you know it's what she wanted?"

He shot her a warning scowl. "You utter aloud my dead sister's name? In your eagerness to keep me here, you abandoned our ways, too?"

She bit her bottom lip. "I'm sorry," she whispered. "I didn't mean—"

A blast rang out, the echo sounding through the nearby trees.

Joe's head whipped around, a sudden thought tensing his jaw. "The boys. They've bagged something."

Sullen, Myrtle nodded. "Sounds that way."

"You don't suppose they crossed paths with my cottontail?"

The hint of a smile teased the corners of her mouth. "I'd say it's more than likely."

Biting back a grin, he tugged on her arm and started down the trail. "In that case, let's go home so you can cook me something tasty. Those three will have my rabbit stew for supper tonight, and it's your fault."

She sniffed. "Since you're bound to leave, I'll cook you something better than stew, a meal to fill your stomach and see you off right."

He nudged her with his elbow. "Not too much for you, huh? Your belly looks full enough these days, and your behind's getting broad in old age."

She ducked her head, pressing the palm of her hand to her middle. "I've grown heavier, I admit. But I'm barely forty, Joe Brashears, and I can still best you in a footrace."

He cocked back his head and laughed, then grabbed her and hugged her close. "You're forty-one years, Myrtle Brashears, but don't fret. You're a fetching woman still. Besides, I don't mind a little extra to hold on to. You were always too scrawny for my taste."

Myrtle's soft chuckle lifted his spirits. She didn't want him to leave, but she'd see him off with a kiss and a smile. A knapsack filled with corn cakes, if he was lucky.

Joe drew a deep, cleansing breath. It was enough.

Mariah slid a plate piled high with steaming flapjacks to the center of the table.

Greedy, grasping hands emptied the Stanley platter before it came to a stop, clear down to the bright bluebirds perched in the center. The four men seated around the kitchen had already cleared a large bowl of scrambled eggs and most of a slab of bacon.

Dicey bustled behind them with a jug of cold milk in one hand, a chilled pitcher of water in the other. She'd arrived to work a half hour late, dragging onto the porch with a frown, her black curlicues braided in haste by the look of her crooked rows. Sighing, she'd fumbled into her apron and set to work mixing the batter. For reasons unknown to Mariah, the girl despised her job.

The steady *whir* of spinning blades drifted under the windowsill. Between the slats of the blinds, Rainy crisscrossed the yard, cutting a swath in the tall grass with the push mower. His bare, skinny wings stuck out behind him, glistening with sweat despite the early hour.

"Any more of them eggs, miss?"

She turned with a smile. "Coming right up."

The patrons of Bell's Inn were a few faithful regulars and those who found their way by word of mouth. Occasionally, daring souls who still braved the overgrown Trace stopped in, but the stretch that passed in front of the inn saw far less traffic these days. For the most part, the men who wound up on her doorstep were of a kindly sort, friendly wayfarers on their way to unknown destinations.

At times, tight-lipped, shifty-eyed strangers arrived, rough and tumble men who looked like trouble. To keep the peace, Father allowed them rooms if he had any free, but Mariah always fed them fast and sent them on their way. It wouldn't do for those types of men to find out she and Miss Vee were running the inn alone.

Thankfully, the group that hunkered over the table, elbows working, seemed as harmless as nursing pups.

Back at the stove, Mariah poured six more beaten eggs into a pan with sizzling butter. Eagerness to see the men fed and out the door sped her hands. Their crude chorus of smacking lips and belching set her teeth on edge.

"These are mighty-fine vittles, ma'am. Most especially these here biscuits."

She craned her neck to nod at the skinny young man smiling up at her with blackened teeth. "Why, thank you. Make sure you get enough, now, you hear?"

The scruffy companion perched beside him nudged his side. "She ain't no ma'am, Jack. That there's *Miss* Mariah Bell. Her daddy owns the place."

At the mention of Mariah's father, tears blinded her. Biting her lip, she blinked them away.

She caught the glint of admiration in both men's eyes and fought a shudder, cautioning herself to be nice. With the scarcity of business, she needed these poor, bedraggled souls and others like them. Resting her spoon, she turned with a weak smile.

The prim gentleman seated across the table smoothed his vest and straightened his cuffs. "This girl's no ma'am or miss, you half-wits." He sniffed as if he'd caught a whiff of the chamber pot. "She's an Injun squaw."

Pain jolted Mariah's heart, and her head reeled as if he'd struck her with his deerskin gloves. Dicey's huge eyes flickered to Mariah's before she slanted her heated gaze to the floor.

The two dullards' interest turned to mischief as they snickered and sparred with their elbows.

A fourth guest, the big man traveling with the prissy boor, bent over his plate with glassy eyes, shoveling eggs in his mouth. He showed no interest in the antics swirling around him, and Mariah suspected the sour smell of stale liquor came from him.

"If you lot are done stuffing your guts, it's time you were on your way."

Heads spun toward the irate voice on the stairs.

Miss Vee always did like to make an entrance. She stood on the bottom step, her cheeks softly rouged, her lashes darkened, and mounds of hennaed curls pinned beneath a small white cap. A crinoline petticoat, out of fashion for years, puffed the skirt of her crisp black dress, and a starched white apron stretched fit-to-split over her ample bosom. With a warning scowl and clenched fists on her hips, she made a daunting figure.

Glaring at the fancy man, she sauntered to the table. "For your information, this lovely girl is the mistress of our establishment, and I'll ask you to treat her accordingly"—she pointed behind her—"or you can hit the road out front, finished with breakfast or not."

The large fellow, who had minded his business so far, gaped up at Miss Vee. Abandoning his eggs and skillet cakes, he spun on the chair and wrapped his arms about her waist. "Look what I got me, Herman. This big heifer's my kind of woman."

Miss Vee gasped and slapped his hands away. Making a run for the counter, she whirled with a war cry and a rolling pin.

Dicey screamed and pressed her back to the wall, both hands clutching her face.

Mariah slid between the vengeful redhead and her drunken suitor just in time to prevent a battered skull. Easing the flour-dusted weapon from Miss Vee's hand, she smiled to calm her rage. "Steady, now. I'll take it from here." Steeling her spine, Mariah faced the disrespectful dandy. "I'll appreciate the removal of your overzealous friend. Even squaws recognize beastly behavior toward a lady."

Avoiding her eyes, he stood wiping his mouth and laid his napkin beside his plate. "Of course." He caught the swaying brute by his collar and hauled him down the hall with Mariah, Miss Vee, and Dicey close on their heels. In the parlor, he collected their waiting bags and escorted his companion onto the front porch. With a tip of his hat and a slight bow, he shoved him past the gaping yard boy to a wagon at the end of the walk.

Rainy nudged his hat toward one ear and scratched his head. "Everything all right, Missy Bell?"

Mariah flicked a sweat-dampened curl from her forehead. "It is now."

Miss Vee shook her head. "Not quite." Spinning on her heel, she led them back the way they came and waltzed up to the table, her crinoline petticoat swaying. With a meaningful glance at her rolling pin, she gave the two remaining guests a pointed look. "I believe you gents were about to take your leave as well?"

Her question ignited a frantic struggle to shove back their chairs and stand. Black Tooth snatched his hat from the hook on the wall and shoved it onto his head. "Yes ma'am. I can see it's about that time."

Still chewing a bite of food, his partner's head bobbed. "We'd like to thank you ladies for a most pleasant stay."

Miss Vee narrowed her eyes. "I'd invite you back, but you won't be coming within ten miles of here ever again." She smiled sweetly. "Ain't that right?"

"No, ma'am," said one man.

"Yes'm," croaked the other.

Swatting with their hats and stumbling over their feet, they battered each other soundly while racing for the back door, clattering off the porch in a sprint.

One glance at Miss Vee's face, red blotches standing out against her rouge, and Mariah doubled over laughing.

Dicey yanked her apron over her mouth, but a giggle escaped.

Miss Vee sputtered a bit then joined in, howling until she gripped her sides.

Eyes shining, they dropped into the empty chairs and stared across the messy table, still grinning.

Mariah sobered first. Leaning her head to stare at the ceiling, she sighed. "Oh, Miss Vee. . .there go four paying customers who won't be coming back. With travel along the Trace so scarce these days, perhaps we should've handled things differently."

"Oh, piddle," Miss Vee said. "There are still plenty of men who'll cross over from Robinson Road just to have one of your breakfasts." She patted Mariah's hand. "Don't fret, honey. We'll be just fine without the likes of those vermin."

She slapped the table, rattling the sugar bowl. "If your father was here, it never would've happened. John Coffee commands respect." Tilting her head, she smiled. "Folks like him on sight. It's a gift."

A leaden weight settled in Mariah's stomach. "You're right, Miss Vee. If only my father was here. . ."

FOUR

The cheerful morning had disappeared. Storm clouds roiling in from the gulf met the afternoon sun overhead, sweeping across it like a giant snuffer dousing the light.

Tiller raised his collar against the sudden gusty wind, glanced up, and winced when the first chilly raindrops began to fall.

A little farther south and the Trace angled close to the Pearl. A few miles past the river bend, the road grew nearly impassable. He had decided to bypass that point, ride cross-country to Canton, and hide out for a few days, but then the squall blew in. With thunder rattling the treetops and lightning lifting the hairs on his arms, finding shelter was the only thing left on his mind.

Faint whistling pricked his ears. He flicked his collar away from his face, tilting his head to listen. Scared to blink, he watched the road ahead, his stomach hot, hands clammy.

He'd never waited in the shadows for an approaching stranger without the comforting presence of his men lurking nearby. It occurred to him that fate may have turned the tables—the bait used to lure unsuspecting prey would find itself ensnared. A part of him knew it'd be justice served.

Tiller reined his horse behind a cluster of oaks and watched, grateful for the cover of the darkening sky.

A gangly boy in a floppy straw hat ducked from the woody canopy, all dusky arms and skinny legs. Humming now, he picked his way down the slope into the misty ravine and ambled toward Tiller with a burlap sack slung over his shoulder.

In the manner of a soul who believes himself alone, he closed his eyes and sang with all his grit, so loud he flushed a chattering squirrel.

"Dat gospel train's a comin',
I hear it jus' at hand,
I hear the car wheels movin',
And rumblin' thru the land.
Get on board, childr'n,
Get on board, childr'n,
Get on board, childr'n,
They be room for many a mo'."

Taking his first easy breath, Tiller nudged his horse onto the road. The boy's head jerked up, and he spun for the opposite rise.

"Hold up there," Tiller called. "I mean you no harm."

Chest heaving, the lad stilled with one foot braced on the grassy incline, watching over his shoulder.

Tiller rode closer. "Did you hear what I said? Don't be afraid. I'm not going to hurt you."

A nod. His scrawny throat worked furiously, as if he found it hard to swallow. By the size of the budding Adam's apple, he couldn't be more than twelve, but his small stature made it hard to tell.

Inching closer, Tiller flashed his brightest smile. "How are you faring on this dismal afternoon?" He ducked his head at the empty sack on the boy's bony shoulder. "About to pick a mess of berries, I see."

The boy twisted around to face Tiller, both thumbs shoved in the waistband of his tattered trousers. "Nawsuh." He stared at Tiller with darting eyes. "Cain't pick nothin', now. We 'bout to get us a drenchin'."

Tiller grinned. "I reckon we are at that." He softened his voice. "Where you bound for, young man? You have someplace to go to get in out of the rain?"

Despite the protection of Nathan's hat, Tiller's wet shirt stuck to his back. Rivulets of water ran along his spine beneath his braces, soaking him down to the skin. It would take a mighty hot fire to dry him out and ease the chill from his bones. He shivered, waiting for an answer.

Say the right thing, boy. Tell me you live close by, somewhere warm and dry with plenty of room by the fire.

The little fellow stammered and slid one foot behind him. "Well, suh. . .you see, we. . .that is, we ain't—"

Together, they spun toward the rustle of footsteps. A taller, meatier version of Tiller's new friend rounded the bend, halting fast when he saw Tiller. The boy's brother. No doubt about it. Gathered brows and a quick flick of his head summoned the smaller one to his side. "What you doing consortin' with strangers? Pa gon' take a switch to yo' behind."

"I ain't consortin', Rainy. I jus' run up on him, same as you."

Like a puppy, the older boy hadn't quite grown into his oversized paws. Lifting wary eyes to Tiller, he spread long fingers over his little brother's chest and urged the child behind him. "Hush up, and come on with me. We going home."

"Wait." Tiller's upraised hand stopped them cold. "I'm hankering to get out of this weather. You know of a place close by where I could hole up for a spell?"

Two sets of eyes studied Tiller, as dark and brooding as the angry clouds rolling in behind them. Jagged shards of lightning scattered overhead followed by violent thunder.

At last, the elder brother nodded. "Yessuh, Bell's Inn." His arm shot out to point behind him. "A short piece that way. Mastah John and his Injun daughter run the finest stand on the Natchez Trace."

Tiller nodded. "I know just the one you mean, but I thought the new road shut down all the stands on the Trace."

"Bell's Inn shut?" The boy wagged his head. "Nawsuh, it ain't no such."

Tiller's gaze flicked up the hill. "Am I close?"

The boy nodded, steadily easing his brother up the slope. "A good gallop will get you there in a tick. Watch for a split rail fence and a whole mess of magnolias out back." At the top of the rise, he flashed a toothy grin. "You cain't miss it. Jus' look for the best tended grounds in Madison County."

Sighing with relief, Tiller lifted his soggy hat. "Much obliged."

But they were gone. Nothing left where they'd been standing but the wind-whipped branches of a young hawthorn tree.

Grinning, he spun his horse into a trot up the Trace, his heart set on a soft bed and the warmth of a roaring fire.

Mariah gripped her forehead and fought to see the swirling digits scrawled across the ledger. She'd come close to crying over the dismal numbers in the past, but today the persistent threat of tears had little to do with the state of her accounts.

Laying aside her dusting cloth, Miss Vee swiped her palms on her apron. "Are you all right, Mariah?" She leaned to look out the window, drawing away again as thunder shook the pane. "You're about as gloomy as this awful weather, and you didn't touch your lunch."

Mariah summoned the will to answer. "I'm fine, thank you."

Miss Vee crossed to the desk and pressed the back of her hand to Mariah's forehead. "You feel a bit warm, child. You don't have a temperature, do you?"

Across the room, Dicey rounded her eyes and slid along the wall to the parlor door, ducking out of sight around the corner.

The yellow fever epidemic of 1878 had ravaged the state of Mississippi, creating ghost towns and wiping out whole families. Four years later, folks still got jumpy around any threat of sickness.

Mariah supposed suffering would resemble the Yellow Jack if no one knew a body was grieving. It would be difficult to hide the bitter ache in her heart, but she'd have to try harder. She drew a shaky breath and glanced up. "I'm a little tired, is all. Got up too early, I guess."

Pulling the accounting book from Mariah's hands, Miss Vee closed the dusty cover. "This mess will keep, honey." Bending, she tossed it into the small safe beneath Mariah's desk and closed it with her foot. "Go upstairs and have yourself a lie-down. There are still a few hours before suppertime."

"I really should—"

"No arguments." Miss Vee, who no one would describe as delicate, had surprising strength in her determined hands. She curled her fingers around Mariah's wrist and pulled. "Come along, now. Don't make me try to tote you up the stairs. We'd both wind up regretting it."

Smiling, Mariah allowed her spunky friend to tug her toward the landing. As they neared the bottom step, a knock came at the door. Miss Vee jumped then stumbled, nearly yanking Mariah's arm from the socket. Her frantic grab for the newel post was all that saved them from falling. Wobbly, they clung together, breathing hard.

Dicey raced into the front hall and stood gaping at the door. "Who you s'pose that gon' be?"

Miss Vee's throat rose and fell. "You don't think it's those same fools?" Her hoarse voice cracked. "Returning to get revenge?"

Glancing toward Miss Vee, Dicey shuddered. "Who be addled enough to go out on a day like this. . .'less they up to no good?"

Thunder rattled the house, and the three of them shrieked.

Feeling ridiculous, Mariah pulled free of Miss Vee's clutches. "For pity's sake, we're behaving like schoolgirls, scaring ourselves silly with ghost stories. Those men are halfway to Jackson." She brushed wayward strands of hair from her eyes. "I'm sure it's just some poor soul hoping to get out of the rain."

The rapping came again, louder this time.

Mariah fought to still her pounding heart. Why did ordinary things suddenly feel so scary? Knowing Father was gone had knocked the braces from under her. Resenting the fact, she balled her fists. Onnat Bell's daughter wouldn't give in to fear. "Answer the door, Dicey."

The girl whined and wrung her hands. "Me, Miss Mariah? Oh, no. Let Miss Vee."

"Go on, now," Mariah said. "We're right behind you."

Dicey inched forward. Pausing, her trembling fingers stretched toward the knob, she pleaded over her shoulder with her eyes.

Mariah urged her on with a nod.

Swallowing hard, the girl eased the door open a crack and peered through. "Um, y–yessuh?"

"Afternoon." The booming voice dripped with sass as thick as country gravy. "I've come to see about a room."

Tension melting from Mariah's shoulders, she released her breath. "Ask him in, Dicey."

Dicey stepped primly aside. "She say come on in."

Framed by the doorposts—his beaming face out of place against a backdrop of driving rain—stood the most curiously handsome man Mariah had ever seen.

Drenched from head to heels, his hair clung to his face in soggy strands, a light orangey red, even darkened by rainwater. Along with soaked-through britches and a damp cotton shirt, he wore a practiced grin and the forced cheerfulness of a man used to having his way.

He ducked inside but kept to the rug, his anxious gaze on his muddy feet. Spotting Mariah, he whipped off his hat. "Good day, miss." Mischief flared in his roguish green eyes like sparks in a hearth.

Smoothing her skirt, she approached the door, glad she'd donned a dress and swept up her hair. For reasons she had no time to ponder, she wanted this man to see the lady of the manor and not the Indian princess. "May we help you, sir?"

He pointed his hat at Dicey. "I was telling your gal here that I need a room for the night. Nothing fancy, mind you. I'd curl up in the pantry to get out of that rain."

Mariah smiled. "I'm certain we can do better than that. As a matter of fact, you're in luck. We happen to have a vacancy." No sense admitting he could have his pick of the empty rooms.

Relief washed over his face. "Well, I'm much obliged." He offered his hand. "The name's McRae. Tiller McRae."

"Mariah Bell, at your service. I own—" Her breath caught at what she'd nearly uttered. "That is, my father is the proprietor of Bell's Inn." She dipped her head at Miss Vee. "This is Mrs. Ashmore. She helps us run the place."

Miss Vee colored like a blushing girl. "Call me Viola. Or better yet, Miss Vee."

He all but bowed. "Honored to meet you both." Handsome or not, a grin that forced couldn't be trusted.

"Your accommodations are down the hall, the first door on the left. We serve an informal breakfast in the kitchen, promptly at six. If you're not seated around the table by then, you stand a fair chance of going without."

He cleared his throat. "Promptly at six. I'll be there."

Mariah touched Dicey's arm. "Bring a towel for Mr. McRae then mop up this mess."

His smile waned, and the merry eyes dimmed. "Sorry, ma'am. If you ladies will excuse my sock feet, I'll shuck these boots and leave them outside the door."

She studied his boyish face, even more striking up close. In the space of a minute, he'd gone from calling her miss to ma'am. He must think her a cranky old matron. Contrite, she relaxed her crinkled forehead and softened her mouth. "Don't you want to settle your horse first?"

He arched his brows. "I hope you don't mind. I left him in the barn sharing oats with your paint."

Irritated afresh at his cocky assurance, Mariah spun on her heels and headed for the stairs. "We require full payment up front, Mr. McRae. For the care of your horse, as well. Miss Viola will take your money."

"Yes, ma'am."

Unwilling to scare off another guest with gold in his purse, she paused halfway up the steps and forced her gritted teeth into a halfhearted smile. "I do hope you'll enjoy your stay, Mister. . .McRae, was it?"

The smile tugging the corners of his mouth seemed genuine, but the insufferable twinkle had returned to his eyes. "Miss Bell, I get the feeling I'll enjoy my stay very much."

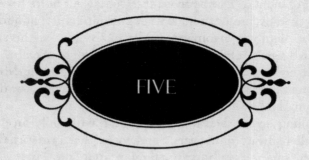

FIVE

Grinning at the thought of Mariah Bell blushing fiery red and flouncing up the stairs, Tiller flopped on the mattress so hard he bounced. After too many days on the road, it felt good to be in the company of a pretty woman—a feisty one, at that—and blasted good to be in a real bed again.

He bunched the quilt beneath him with both hands and sighed. A bed with sheets so clean, the scent of lilac water and sunshine rose in a pleasurable cloud. Turning his nose to the feather pillow, he drew in deep, fairly sure Miss Bell would smell just as sweet.

The trusting, toothless smile of the kindhearted traveler merged in his head with Miss Bell's fetching face—not a pleasing picture to be sure. He shook his head to clear it, the motion sending the pretty parts to the rafters in a wisp, leaving him to stare vacantly at the scraggly, white-haired man named Otis Gooch. Without a doubt, the poor coot wouldn't sleep in a clean bed that night—if the gang had left him alive to care.

In all of Tiller's years in Nathan's company, he'd watched the ambush of many a hapless prey, putting them out of his mind as fast as he rode away. So why did the thought of this old gentleman, slumped in a heap at the side of the road, tear at his heart like a pickax?

What Nathan said was true. Tiller couldn't go on ignoring the fate of the folks he charmed into trusting him. He dangled the carrots that lured the poor rabbits into Hade Betts's perilous snare, so whatever happened next was his fault as much as the men who wielded the guns and struck the blows. Maybe more so.

Along with the realization came the aching truth that he'd never be worthy of a fine, decent woman like Miss Bell. Rolling to his side, Tiller clenched his fists, the admission a searing pain in his gut.

The harsh life of a raiding thief wasn't the adventure he'd expected as a boy, wasn't the path he wanted as a man. He'd grown more discontent with each passing year but didn't know how to escape.

Nathan's vaunted tales of a bandit's life along the Trace had once tickled Tiller's grimy young ears. Somewhere along the way, the dismal truth wore the shine off Nathan's stories.

After a few months of dodged bullets and empty bellies, Tiller was ready to go home.

Nathan, who took to the drifter's life like a tick to a hound, dug in his heels and stayed put. In the early days, two things kept Tiller at his side: the misplaced loyalty of youth and the fear of striking out on his own. Lately, he wasn't sure what held him.

Staring into the past, he sighed, and a stray goose feather shot to the sky. As always, the swirling mists of Scuffletown's swamps lured him. Memories of his brief stay there throbbed in his heart like a sore tooth. Never sure if Aunt Odie's cooking was as fine as he recalled or Uncle Silas's stories as grand, he only knew his longing to return was the closest thing to homesick he'd ever felt.

Tiller jumped at the light knock on the door.

"Mr. McRae?"

He bolted upright, swiping at the tears wetting the hair at his temples. Jogging to the door, he swung it wide, his smile firmly in place. "Yes, ma'am, Miss Viola. What can I do for you, lovely lady?" Gazing at her delighted face, he cringed inside. Remorseful or not, it hadn't taken him long to return to his practiced charm.

Fanning briskly to cool her cheeks, Mrs. Ashmore blushed to her graying roots.

Tiller's gaze wandered to her curls, wondering what she used to turn them the bright shade of copper. The reason she might do so confused him even more. If he could find a concoction to turn his hair a less garish color, he'd shell out the money for a crate.

"Mr. McRae, how you do flatter." She winked and shifted a stack of clean linens to her hip. "Your smooth talk could make a girl forget sagging jowls and wrinkled cheeks." Her tinted lashes fluttered down. "Until she passes that blasted looking glass in the hall."

Compassion nudged his heart. "No mirror reflects a woman's true beauty, Mrs. Ashmore."

Beaming, she touched his arm. "Now, I told you to call me Miss Vee."

"You sure did." He patted her hand. "I won't forget again."

She tilted her head toward the end of the hall. "I came to say I'd be happy to run out to the kitchen and fix you something to eat, seeing you arrived too late for the noon meal."

Tiller's growling stomach answered before he had the chance.

She smiled and nodded. "I'll go put these things away then bring you something light. Don't want to spoil your supper."

He held up his hand. "You'd be hard pressed to spoil my supper, ma'am. When they handed out appetites, I stood in the line twice."

A tender smile softened her face. "John's the same. Can't seem to get the man fed."

"John?"

With a quick breath, she returned from her distant thoughts. "John Coffee, Mariah's father. Such a lovely family, the Bells." Her sagging eyes widened. "Mariah in particular. Wouldn't you agree?"

Tiller's cheeks warmed. "Miss Vee, a man would be blind not to."

Watching him closely, her head slowly bobbed. "I see." A glimmer of something birthed in her eyes, like a scheme beginning to hatch. "How long are you planning to stay with us, Mr. McRae?"

Amused, he lifted his chin and met her calculating stare. "I can't say exactly, but I'm in no hurry to leave." A fact he wasn't aware of until he'd said it. "I suppose you'll have to put up with me until I can't peel off any more greenbacks."

She brightened. "I hope you're well off then. We need a strong young man around this place." She nodded firmly. "One we can trust." With a backhanded wave and a promise to return with some grub, Miss Vee rounded the corner, humming a merry tune.

Tiller closed the door, white-hot needles of guilt piercing his sides.

A trustworthy man? He hardly qualified.

As for his money running out— Wincing, he patted the scrawny drawstring purse at his side. In precious little time, he'd be busted.

His thoughts jumped to the safe in the parlor where Miss Vee stashed the money he'd paid for a night's stay. By the meager few dollars he spotted before she closed the door, they needed his cash to hold out for as long as possible.

Odd how he hadn't remembered the safe until now. Glancing at his reddening face in the mirror, Tiller smiled. For the first time in many years, a pretty woman tempted him more than an easy take.

Mariah slipped down the back stairwell, yearning for a cup of hot tea and a few stolen moments of blessed quiet. Halfway to the kitchen, Miss Vee's tuneless song drifted up to meet her, which meant time alone to grieve wasn't to be. Feeling guilty, she paused at the turn in the stairs to ease her frown and pray for pleasing manners.

Miss Vee often lapsed into singing as she went about her chores. Unfortunately, she sang badly and fractured her lyrics, combining two or three songs at once. Today she croaked out a medley of "Bonnie Blue Flag" and "Dixie," doing justice to neither piece.

The squeaky board at the bottom announced Mariah's arrival.

Miss Vee spun. The corners of her mouth turned down, but her eyes were smiling. "That wasn't much of a nap, young lady."

"I couldn't sleep." A kettle steamed on the stove, and Mariah's tin of favorite tea leaves perched on the counter. She quirked her brow and nodded. "How did you know?"

"That rotted old landing isn't the only board in this house that squeals. I tracked you crossing your room and halfway down the hall."

Mariah's heart sank at the reminder. The inn was falling apart around them. "I'm going to have to lay aside enough money to pay a carpenter. Only the Lord knows how much it will cost this time, and that just for urgent repairs."

Miss Vee returned to her task on the counter. "You know what the Bible says. 'No man putteth a piece of new cloth unto an old garment.'" She shook her head. "I fear you'll find no end to patching this old place.

You need to tear it to the ground and start fresh."

Mariah lifted the lid of the kettle and sprinkled tea over the simmering water. "Well, I don't have that choice, do I? It's far too costly." She settled the pot off the fire. "I can't sit idly by while the walls collapse on our heads."

Miss Vee stepped closer to pat her back. "Of course you can't, but that won't happen, will it? Your father won't allow it." Pulling a knife from the tray under the counter, she slathered butter onto fresh-cut slices of bread. "You bear far too much on your shoulders, honey. Repairs and the like are a man's concerns. I'm certain your father has a plan in mind, and he'll tend to this inn the minute he comes home." She beamed over her shoulder. "After all, he'll be returning right as rain. Healed once and for all, just like you said."

Her cheery words were a blow. Swallowing her pain, Mariah poured the steaming tea while her mind struggled for something to say. "Y–yes. Right as rain."

Miss Vee laid down the knife. "Gracious, what's wrong? You've gone pasty."

The hedge around Mariah's heart began to slip. She lowered her head and let the tears fall. "I miss him so much."

The comforting arms she expected surrounded her. Miss Vee held her, crooning in her ear. "Go on and cry, honey. I've shed many a tear since he's been gone."

Briefly, Mariah pretended Miss Vee knew the truth. She allowed her heart to grieve her father's death with another soul who loved him. Only for a moment, and then she got hold of herself.

She pushed Miss Vee to arm's length and wiped her eyes on a napkin. "Forgive me. I'm acting childish. Go on with what you're doing. I'm all right now." Her gaze slid to the cold meat sandwich Miss Vee had sliced and arranged on a plate. "Oh my, are you hungry?" She leaned to peer at the hall clock. "Have I rested longer than I thought? Where's Dicey? She should be peeling potatoes."

Miss Vee smiled sweetly. "This isn't for me, dear. I fixed it for that nice Mr. McRae. The poor man's so hungry, his insides begged to be fed."

Pursing her lips, Mariah drizzled honey in her cup and stirred. "I'd be careful of 'nice Mr. McRae' if I were you." She tapped the edge of her spoon on the cup so hard the porcelain rang like a gong. "I'm not sure he's the innocent he seems."

Miss Vee's brow puckered. "Mariah! If you can't tell the difference between Tiller McRae and the pack of wild dogs we rousted earlier, then I've lost all hope for you." Grinning, she set a glass of lemonade beside the toppling sandwich and hefted the tray. "And if you can't admit he's the handsomest catch to cross your path in years, well then, you're blind, to boot."

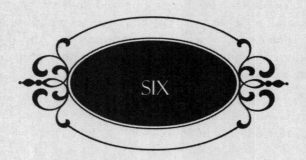

SIX

The sandwich Miss Viola brought had tamed the gnawing in Tiller's stomach, but the smells drifting from the kitchen, oozing under his door like a beckoning finger, watered his mouth like a drooling pup's.

Miss Bell's instructions about breakfast were clear, but no one said a word about supper. Tiller strained his ears for the sound of a gong or a call to the table, but nothing came.

Lured to the hallway by the scent of roasted beef mingled with onions and potatoes, he decided to mosey on down and scout out the kitchen. Just in case they forgot him.

Outside his door, he glanced to the right toward the dim parlor and across the way into what must be another guest room judging by a glimpse of a vanity and a bed made up with a blue and green quilt. No one in sight.

Creeping on the toes of his boots, he moved stealthily toward the kitchen. Halfway there, he sniffed the air and smiled. The first item on his list to explore would be the bread basket. The way he had it figured, hot rolls were the source of the warm, golden-crust aroma filling the house.

Tiller peered around the arched doorway into the dining room, empty except for a long table covered in an eyelet cloth and a place setting for one in silverware and white china. He frowned and tilted his head. If only one guest would be eating, he hoped he was the one.

Crossing the hall to the kitchen, he knocked on the wall before entering. "Miss Viola, are you in there?" A few more steps brought him next to the pantry door. "Hello? Miss Vee?"

The object of his raid beckoned from the sideboard, a metal basket lined with a red-checkered cloth. Tiller lifted away the folds, releasing the steamy baked bread smell into the air. Leaning over the heaped-up rolls, he drew a deep breath through his nose.

Ah! Pure pleasure.

His fingers closed around one of the light brown tops, so soft it gave at his touch. Closing his eyes, he brought the roll to his lips, savoring the moment briefly before he shoved it in whole.

Warm, yeasty flavor melted to the roof of his mouth.

Butter. He needed butter.

Rummaging inside the cold box, he brought out a full bowl, creamy and fresh-churned, then reached back in for a jar of strawberry jam. Placing them on the counter beside the rolls, he scurried across the room to search the cabinets for a plate. "Now where do you suppose they—"

A scream ripped the air.

Whirling with an iron skillet, Tiller backed against the sink.

The young woman cowering in the doorway bellowed louder. "Come quick! Miss Vee! Miss Mariah! He a thief."

Taking a step toward her, Tiller held up his hands, skillet and all, in protest. "Now, wait a minute—"

She let go another ear-piercing screech. "Lord, he'p me! He gon' bash in my head."

Over the girl's shoulder, Miss Bell lurched into sight with Miss Vee on her heels. Sliding to a halt, Miss Bell drew the trembling girl behind her skirts. "Mr. McRae?" Her sultry brown eyes opened wider than Tiller thought possible. "What are you doing in here?"

Frantic, he took in their suspicious glares. "I'm sorry. I was"—he squinted at the food spread over the sideboard—"hungry?"

Miss Bell's silent stare raked him with doubt.

The high-strung girl turned up her nose like something foul had crawled inside. "I s'pose you about to eat the frying pan?" She pursed her lips. "Don't believe him, Miss Mariah. He after the good silver."

Now that the girl's mouth wasn't cocked wide and screaming, Tiller recognized her as the one they called Dicey, who answered the door when he came. Even then, she'd been hesitant to let him in the house. Poor thing must be the nervous sort.

Tiller glanced at Miss Vee, watching him with brooding eyes. "Ma'am, I'm no thief. Just impatient, I reckon. The house is full of the scent of good cooking, and my appetite got the best of me." He shuffled his feet. "It's not the first time, I'll say that much, but this lapse of good sense isn't my fault. Judging by the smell, someone in this house has an inspiring talent for shaking a skillet." For emphasis, he shook the one in his hand.

Dicey ducked and clutched her bodice with both hands, pressing her back against the wall.

A smile edged the corners of Miss Vee's mouth then melted into rowdy laughter. She patted Dicey's shoulder. "Stop it, now. You're wasting a good conniption. He's not going to hurt you."

Dicey moaned. "How you know?"

Miss Bell glanced over her shoulder. "Good question, Dicey. I'm wondering the same."

Slipping one arm around Miss Bell's dainty waist, Miss Vee hugged her close. "Honey, this boy's harmless, as long as we keep him fed."

She jutted her chin at Tiller. "Go into the dining room and tuck in your napkin. We'll be right in to serve you."

Tiller glanced toward the rolls.

Grinning, Miss Vee handed him the basket. "Take it along with you. Dicey will fetch the butter and jam."

He started for the hall with Miss Vee barking orders behind him.

"I've seen men like this before, Mariah. Pile a platter high with beef and ladle ample gravy in the bowl. If we don't get his belly full, he'll be back in the kitchen by nightfall."

Dicey followed Tiller into the dining room with mincing steps. She slid him the butter and jam from across the table, and then lit two tapered candles and poured water from a frosty pitcher. By the time she finished her duties and backed out the way she came, he had finished half the basket of rolls.

"If you eat many more of those, you'll pay the piper. Yeast breads bloat the stomach."

He beamed up at Miss Vee crossing the room with a serving dish.

"I'll take the risk. Who makes these? They're the best I've ever tasted."

She nodded over her shoulder at Miss Bell. "This little thing, that's who. Mariah's the finest cook in Mississippi state."

"Don't believe her, Mr. McRae. My dear departed mother held that honor." Blushing a pretty shade of pink, Miss Bell placed a steaming bowl of corn within Tiller's reach. "I place a distant second to her."

Smiling, Tiller held up one of the rolls. "Not in my opinion." He sobered and cleared his throat. "Though I mean no disrespect to your mama."

Miss Bell seemed pleased. "Of course you don't. I thank you for the compliment. Now eat up, Mr. McRae, before your food gets cold."

"Tiller."

She raised one brow. "Sorry?"

He shot her a winsome grin. "Call me Tiller, if you don't mind."

Mariah stiffened. *You'd like that, wouldn't you?* The man was entirely too forward. Each time she softened the slightest bit toward him, he made a reckless blunder that pulled her guard up again.

Most likely, Dicey had him rightly pegged. Hungry or not, no man was foolish enough to go plundering about where he had no right. Was he?

Flustered, she got busy carving the roast, lowering her lashes to shield herself from his toothy smile.

"Tiller it is," Miss Vee crowed, evidently forgetting herself.

Irritation laced through Mariah. The woman became a simpering girl around this man.

Another roll in one hand, a forkful of roast in the other, Tiller stilled. "Wait a minute. Why am I eating alone? Aren't you gals hungry?"

Miss Vee giggled. "Don't worry about us. We'll have a bite when you're done."

He stood and pulled out a nearby chair. "No time like the present, I say." He made a sweeping gesture. "Please join me."

She blinked at him then raised her brows at Mariah. "Well, I guess it couldn't hurt."

Narrowing her eyes at Miss Vee, Mariah slapped a second hunk of beef in front of him. "Thank you, but we don't take meals with our guests."

Miss Vee propped her fist on her hip. "We certainly do."

Mariah cleared her throat. "An occasional breakfast, but never lunch or supper."

Tiller frowned. "Well, you should, if you don't mind my saying. It's a pitiful waste of this nice, long table."

She opened her mouth to firmly decline, but he held up his hand.

"Miss Bell, I insist." The sugarloaf smile again. "It ain't fittin' for a man to eat alone."

Miss Vee snatched two china plates from the mahogany hutch and plopped one on each side of Tiller McRae. "He's right, Mariah. It's bad for his digestion." Seating herself, she reached for the basket of rolls. "You wouldn't want to be responsible for this poor boy's discomfort, would you?"

Outmatched, Mariah wiped her hands on her apron then tugged on the strings and pulled it off. Handing it to Dicey with a grimace, she walked around the table and perched at the edge of a chair. "This is highly unusual, but I suppose a quick bite won't hurt." She turned her brightest smile on her cunning boarder and shook out her napkin. "Now the stomachache you're certain to have can rightly be blamed on all those rolls."

He raised one in the air, drenched in butter. "Like I said before. . . some things are worth it." He dragged the bread through his gravy, leaving streaks of strawberry jam behind.

Mariah cringed.

Miss Vee beamed at her from across the table, nodding and winking as if his words held special meaning. "You're not the first man willing to take the risk. Men around these parts make utter fools of themselves for a taste of Mariah's cooking."

Playing along with her silly game, he leaned toward Miss Vee and lowered his voice. "Are you're certain it's the food they're after? Miss Bell's a mighty handsome woman."

Her cheeks warming, Mariah hurriedly changed the subject. "Where are you from, Mr. McRae?"

A touch of sadness flickered on his face, gone so fast Mariah wondered if she'd imagined it. "Who me?" He toyed with a kernel of corn on his plate with the tines of his fork, taking his time to answer. "I suppose you could call me a drifter. I try not to stay in one place for too long. The minute roots start to sprout from my toes, I hit the road again." He stabbed the kernel and popped it in his mouth. "Can't have anything pinning me down."

Mariah's glass paused in midair. "That's a dreadful way to live. . .if you don't mind my saying," she added, borrowing his earlier phrase.

"Mariah Bell!" Miss Vee shamed her with a glance. "Mind your manners." Bristling, she ladled him another serving of potatoes. "The very idea."

"Well, I'm sorry, it's true." She took the bowl Miss Vee passed to her, tilting her head at Mr. McRae. "Don't you miss having land or family? I thought such things were important to men."

He rolled his shoulders as if casting off a weight. "Too confining. When I get ready to light out, I don't want anything riding my coattail."

His lowered lids were hiding something. When trouble plagued Mariah, she'd saddle Sheki and race along the bank of the Pearl, drawing strength from the rushing water. Tiller McRae seemed more like a man swimming upstream.

Another glance at his forced brightness pierced the shell of his posturing. The handsome young man's swagger covered a deep well of discontent. Mariah's heart stirred with unexpected pity.

Tittering, Miss Vee raised her goblet of water. "Here's to living free."

Strident knocking on the front door startled Miss Vee so violently she jumped. The glass slipped from her hand, hit the table, and tipped over, landing in front of Mariah on its side. A ring of moisture spread in a wide circle from the mouth, soaking the tablecloth down to the wood.

The pounding came again, louder and more persistent.

Squealing, Dicey spun toward the sound, her fingers twisting the dishcloth in her hand.

Mariah folded her napkin and stood. "It's all right, Dicey. I'll go."

Wiping his mouth, Mr. McRae half rose from his chair. "Is there a problem?"

She shook her head. "Not at all."

"Are you sure?" He straightened, watching her. "Would you like for me to go with you?"

"Of course not." The lie raised a knot in her throat. Swallowing hard, Mariah hurried from the room and down the hall. She'd answered the bell to lodgers countless times in her life. Why did it suddenly seem so frightening?

At the entry, she turned the lock and gripped the knob. Holding her breath, she opened the door.

Four strange men stood on her porch, two of them supporting the weight of an old man. Rusty blotches stained his shirt, and dried blood darkened the tuft of white hair on his head, stiffening the wiry strands.

Mariah's breath quickened. "What happened?"

A tall gentleman standing behind the others took off his hat. "We're not sure, ma'am. We found him huddled on the road blubbering and talking out of his head. He's been whacked plenty hard on the noggin."

She stepped aside. "Bring him in, please."

They bundled him over the threshold and followed her to the guest room across the hall from the parlor. Mariah pulled back the quilt and stood wringing her hands while they laid him against the pillows.

She glanced at the two who had carried him. "Stay with him, if you don't mind. I'll be right back." To the others, she nodded toward the hall. "You must be tired and hungry. Won't you join us for supper?"

The big man smiled kindly and shook his head. "A tempting offer, ma'am, but we need to be on our way."

"Very well," Mariah said. "Wait inside the parlor, and I'll pack you something to take with you." Excusing herself, she scurried down the hall, sliding on the plank floor as she turned the corner. "Come quick, Miss Vee. I need your help."

"Heavens," Miss Vee said, clutching her chest. "What is it? You're as pale as a haint."

"Good Samaritans have come bearing an injured man. They've asked for our help."

Mr. McRae yanked his napkin from around his neck. "Do you know them?"

She shook her head. "Strangers traveling the Trace. I've never seen them before."

He seemed edgy. "It might be a trick."

"I'm certain it's not. They found the old man alongside the road a few miles from here. He's hurt badly. A nasty blow to the head."

Mr. McRae's eyes rounded. "An old man?"

She nodded. "Quite elderly, I believe. He's white-haired and toothless as a babe."

Miss Vee shoved back her chair. "I'll find clean cloths for bandages. Mariah, go heat some water. Dicey, take the wagon and find a doctor."

Dicey worried the hem of her apron. "Ride clear to Canton by myself?"

"Of course not. We need him now, not sometime tomorrow. Fetch Tobias Jones."

"That ol' Injun healer?"

"Yes."

"No'm, Miss Vee! All his chantin' and dancin' make me feel all-overish. I'm sorely 'fraid of Tobias Jones."

Miss Vee caught her arm and urged her forward. "Be more scared of me. Now get on with you, and no dawdling."

"I'll put the water on then pack provisions for those nice men in the parlor," Mariah said. "They're exhausted and damp from the rain, but they want to press on."

She followed Miss Vee out, pausing under the arched doorway to glance curiously at Mr. McRae. Judging by his sagging jaw and sickly pallor, the stomach bloat they'd warned him of had hit him full force.

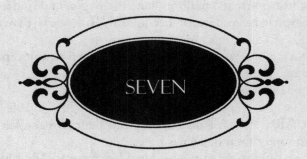

SEVEN

Fear nailed Tiller to the chair.

The flurry of clicking heels and swishing skirts finally swept from the room, plunging him in silence. Dread climbed up his throat and swirled over his head like rushing water. He struggled to draw a breath.

The helplessness was the same he felt while lurking in the shadows of the Trace without the protection of his gang. The heavy cloak of misdeeds weighed him down and sin crouched on his shoulders. He was tired of running but too scared of what would happen if he stopped.

Miss Bell ducked her head around the corner. "Come quick. We need you."

Stunned, Tiller's head shot up, but she had gone.

Panic gripped his gut. How could he traipse down the hall, stroll into the room, and say, "How do," to the man he'd helped put there? Yet how could he refuse?

At best, he'd brand Tiller a coward in front of the women—unless he'd figured out Tiller's part in the robbery. Either possibility meant trouble.

Before he could cipher what to do, Miss Bell rushed past and hurried into the kitchen, quickly returning with a basin of water. She paused to stare. "Are you just going to sit there?"

For as long as it takes, he thought. Nevertheless, his traitorous legs straightened, bringing him upright. Gritting his teeth, he followed her to his doom.

Movement inside the parlor caught his eye, and he glanced inside.

Four scruffy men, as jittery as fleas on a hairless dog, hovered near the fire. One at a time their hollow, weary eyes rose to his.

Satisfied he didn't know them, Tiller nodded and stepped across the hall to the guest room. Lingering outside the door, he watched the women tend to the huddled lump on the bed.

Miss Bell placed the pan of hot water on the bedside table. Miss Vee dipped a cloth, wrung it out, and bent over her patient. Tiller winced when she returned it to the water dark with blood.

Glancing up, Miss Bell caught his eye. "Come in, Mr. McRae," she said in a soft voice. "It's all right. You won't disturb him. I'm afraid he's delirious. Poor man doesn't even know we're here."

Tiller's knees sank with relief. Awed by a streak of luck or grace he didn't deserve, he eased into the room. "How can I help?"

"I've brought down one of my father's old nightshirts." She blushed ruby red and stared a hole in the floor. "Once we get his wound bandaged, we're going to need you to undress him."

"I'll help," Miss Vee announced. "After raising nine brothers and a husband, he can't have much I haven't seen before." She dunked the gory rag and squeezed it out again. "Mariah, go assist those pitiful souls in the parlor. Tiller and I will take care of this one."

Gathering her skirts, Miss Bell dashed for the door.

"Bring fresh water when you finish with them," Miss Vee called. "We'll need it clean to sponge him off."

Miss Bell returned and lifted the soiled container. "I'll do it now, so you can get him settled."

By the time she got back, Tiller had the old man shucked down to his long underwear.

Rosy-cheeked again, she stopped outside the door.

He hurried over, and their eyes met over the steaming basin.

"I want to thank you, Mr. McRae."

"Tiller."

She swallowed delicately. "Tiller. It's very kind of you to help. I realize you don't have to."

"It's my pleasure, ma'am."

She smiled stiffly and lowered her eyes. "I suppose you may call me Mariah. . .if you'd like."

He studied her sweeping lashes. "I'd like it very much."

Miss Vee bellowed for the pan.

They jumped apart, sloshing water over Mariah's hands.

Grinning, Tiller took the basin and hurried to set it beside the bed. When he looked toward the threshold again, she was gone.

He worked beside Miss Vee for the next half hour, ministering to their patient. They washed him head to toe, wrestled him into the long white nightshirt, and redressed his seeping wound.

Caring for him soothed Tiller's aching conscience a little, but the gray, lifeless face against the pillow seared his guilty heart.

Miss Vee pressed her palm to the ashen forehead then straightened with a tight smile. "No fever. That's a blessing, but we sure need the doctor. I can't imagine what's keeping Dicey with Tobias." She rested her hands on her hips. "Where did Mariah run off to?"

Miss Vee wasn't the only one who missed Mariah's company. She ducked in once to say she'd aided the strangers and sent them on their way, but hadn't returned since.

Pointing to the corner, Miss Vee patted his back. "Pull up that chair and sit with him whilst I go scout things out."

She left the room, and Tiller hauled the chair close to the bed—just not too close. Sitting stiff as a plank, he gripped his knees and studied the injured man's face.

His bushy brows bunched in sleep, and his toothless mouth gaped as if to cry out, but no sound came. Tiller wondered if he suffered much pain.

It squeezed his chest to watch, so he turned his attention to the shuttered window. Between the slats, the moon shone from a puddle on the ground, and no raindrops stirred the bright reflection. The storm had passed.

Mariah's pleasing face tugged at his thoughts. In all his rambling years, he'd seen a passel of pretty gals—fetching saloon girls, shopkeepers' daughters, and the painted ladies down on Silver Street in Natchez, crooking their red-tipped fingers from the shadows as he passed.

Mariah was beautiful in a different way, from inky black hair piled on her head to hot coffee glances from under sleepy lashes. She seemed wild in the way of a broken stallion, subdued but never tamed.

"Where am I, boy?"

The shock jerked Tiller to his feet.

Bleary eyes studied him from the bed. "Are you folks caring for me?"

Feigning a sudden itch, Tiller's hand shot up to cover his face. His other hand groped for his head, but without his hat, he couldn't hide his auburn hair. "Y–yes, sir. We are."

The old fellow nodded then winced and probed his bandages with shaky fingers. "I'm hurt bad?"

Tiller set the chair out of his way and backed up several steps. "Not sure yet. We're waiting for the doc."

The man drifted in and out, mumbling garbled words.

Anxious to know whether he was making sense or talking out of his head, Tiller walked to the bed and leaned over.

The wrinkled eyelids shot open, jolting Tiller's heart. The stranger pointed a bony finger, his watery gaze locked on Tiller's face.

Dread pitched his stomach. Now would come the anger. The accusation. A fast run to the door and a frantic ride out.

"Thank ye for helping me, son. I'm much obliged." Spent, his hand fell to the mattress, and his head lolled to the side, out like a candle in a draft.

Relief spreading warmth through his limbs, Tiller slumped in the chair. The old man didn't remember him. Not this time. Would that change when his head cleared?

Tiller should run, no doubt about it. Roll up his pack, roust his horse, and get far away as fast as he could ride. So why couldn't he bring himself to move?

Did he want to be caught? With his secret in the open, the threat of discovery wouldn't loom like a guillotine blade.

He scrubbed his face with his hands then laced his trembling fingers behind his head. What kind of game was he playing, gambling with his life?

A need he didn't understand held him within the comforting walls of Bell's Inn. Something greater than common sense, stronger than fear. He glanced at his pale face in the dressing table mirror. *Something, Tiller boy, or someone?*

Either way, he wasn't ready to saddle up and hit the long, lonely road outside. Until the injured traveler sat up in bed and called him out, Tiller had no plans to leave.

Mariah sprawled across her bed and sobbed. The sweet-faced old gentleman lying wounded downstairs stirred painful memories of her father writhing in pain for weeks.

She sent for Dr. Moony against Father's wishes when a terrible cough began to wrack his thinning frame. Doc slipped from the room after the examination, peered into Mariah's soul, and shook his head. He told her to allow Father his pipe. It wouldn't matter.

Helpless, she stood by and watched as the burly man who raised her disappeared.

Clenching her fist, she gave her pillow a vicious whack. His death was a waste! The cruel disease an unwelcome guest stealing him pound by shocking pound, breath by gasping breath.

Mariah barely had time to accept his illness before he was gone. She wasn't ready to lose him.

Startled, she sat up in bed, surprised she hadn't thought of it sooner. Before long, Doc would ride out from Canton to check on Father's condition. Dr. Moony would never believe the story she'd told Miss Vee.

Gripping her face, Mariah lay back in bed to figure a way out of her latest predicament. Except she couldn't think straight with her heart and mind overflowing with memories.

No matter, she'd work out something before the doctor came nosing around. Whatever the cost, she'd find a way to keep Father's death a secret for as long as possible.

"Tobias is here," Miss Vee called through her door.

Wiping her eyes, Mariah sat up and scooted off the bed. She opened the door, surprised to find Miss Vee still there.

Her penciled brows arched. "I'm getting a little concerned about you, honey. It's not like you to hole up in your room."

Evidently, her efforts to hide her heartache were still lacking. "I'm fine. Just a little tired tonight, I suppose."

Miss Vee frowned. "You said the same thing earlier." She reached to cup Mariah's cheek. "No fever. Still, you must be coming down with something. I could pack for a trip to Natchez in the bags under your eyes." She peered closer. "Sugar, have you been crying?"

Ducking her head, Mariah eased from her grasp. "We'd best get downstairs. If we don't watch him, Tobias will bust up the headboard for kindling and build a ceremonial fire at the foot of the bed."

Miss Vee caught her hand as she passed. "A girl needs her mama, and I know how much you miss yours." Her smile brimmed with compassion. "If there's anything you need to talk about, I'm a good listener."

Guilt an elephant on her chest, Mariah squeezed her fingers. "I'm grateful."

"Grateful for what? I love you like you're my own." Longing softened Miss Vee's features, subtracting years from her eager face. "I know your father might never want me, considering he's so partial to slender women." She sighed. "After all, your mother was as thin as a twelve-year-old boy, and I've been plump all my life." She blushed slightly. "I'm a silly old woman. I shouldn't be saying such things to you."

Mariah squirmed inside but patted her hand. "It's all right."

"No, it's not, but what I'm trying to say is this—if John Coffee ever did take a shine to me, if we were to actually get married, I'd be honored to call you my daughter." She ducked her head and drew in her shoulders. "That is, if you didn't mind."

Bile rose in Mariah's throat. She swallowed and forced an answer. "You know I wouldn't mind."

"Really?" Miss Vee lit up, and a brilliant smile replaced the uncertain set of her lips. "Well, that means so much. God chose not to bless me with a child of my own, but I've always wanted a daughter. Of course, I'd never be able to take Minti's place." She sighed so hard she shuddered. "Not for either of you." Her haunted gaze swept the room in a wide arc from floor to ceiling. "I still feel her presence in this place. In every board, every nail, the very air we breathe."

"The inn was such a large part of who Mother was."

She nodded, her voice barely a whisper. "And she'll always be part of the inn."

"Miss Vee? Miss Bell? Anybody?"

With a shared look of surprise, they hurried from the room and rushed to the head of the stairs.

Tiller stared up from the bottom step. A spate of freckles Mariah hadn't noticed before stood out on his whitewashed face. "I think you ladies might want to come down here."

Mariah took the stairs two at a time. Respectability be hanged. Tobias Jones was in her house.

Behind her, Miss Vee moaned. "What is it, son?"

Tiller shook his head. "I can't rightly say. I've never seen anything like it before."

It was all Mariah needed to hear. Clutching her skirts, she sprinted for the sickroom.

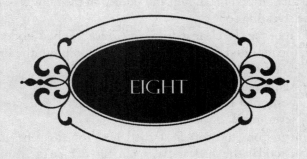

EIGHT

Mariah spun out of the parlor and across the hall, lurching to a stop outside the guest room. She stared at the scene before her, dumbstruck.

Their patient, as bare as the day his mother bore him except for a sheet draped over his middle, sprawled on the floor in front of a blazing hearth. His skinny arms were stretched out to the sides. His pasty legs and knobby knees were on display.

The Choctaw healer knelt at his side with puckered lips pressed to his forehead like a child drawing juice from a lemon.

Too shocked to look away, Mariah found her voice. "Stop it this instant."

Ignoring her, Tobias lifted his mouth and spat in his cupped palm, then gracefully rose and shook an unseen substance off his hand into the fire. A bright red mark appeared on the old man's brow.

Mariah had heard of the Indian practice of dry cupping, but she'd never witnessed the procedure. Most felt it a silly superstition, with no real power to heal. After seeing it in action, she tended to agree.

"We brought you here to care for his injury. To clean it and apply healing herbs." She waved her hand over the scene. "Not for all this nonsense."

"Sucking near the wound draws out the poison."

"So will a poultice of cotton-tree root."

Tobias's glare held scorn. "Old way better."

Mariah cautiously approached the poor soul stretched out on the floor. Moisture beaded his top lip and pooled in the hollow of his chest. "Why is he sweating so?"

"China root tea. To cleanse from *isht abeka*." Tobias nodded firmly. "Infection," he repeated as if she hadn't understood him the first time.

She frowned. "How'd you get it down him?"

He crossed his arms, his scowl deepening.

She'd questioned his skill, insulting him. Her shoulders drooped. "All right. Never mind."

Movement from the corner startled her. Tobias's sons, Justin and Christopher, stood in the shadows, trying in vain to hide their amusement.

Recalling what Miss Vee said about her black-ringed eyes, Mariah lowered her head and touched her burning face with her fingertips.

Tiller pushed past and stood over the man on the floor. "What's he done to Mr. Gooch?"

Mariah's head came around. "You know him?"

Tiller blanched like beans in hot water. "Just his name."

"But, how?"

"He, um. . .came to for a minute. Thanked me for taking care of him. Before he passed out again, he said his name. Otis, I think it was." He nodded and backed toward the corner. "Otis Gooch."

Miss Vee swept inside and took command. "Whatever his name, with him sweating like this, we should cover him. He'll catch a draft." She motioned to the younger men. "Help me get him back in bed."

Grinning and casting furtive glances in Mariah's direction, Chris and Justin took Mr. Gooch's arms. Tiller hoisted his legs. They carried him with ease and gently placed him against the pillows.

Miss Vee hustled to his side with a dry towel to wipe his face. "He'll stink now. After all the care we took to get him washed."

Tobias stood his ground in front of the fireplace, mumbling under his breath. As always, despite his irritation, he watched Miss Vee closely from under veiled lids.

Mariah propped her fisted hands at her waist. "Are you quite finished?"

He grunted. "All done. He'll be better now."

She shot him a doubtful look. "What do I owe you?"

"Corn bread."

She tilted her head. "Did you say corn bread?"

He nodded. "Whole pan. Butter, too. Big tub."

Miss Vee paused from tucking the quilt under Mr. Gooch's chin. "See, Tiller. I told you this girl was known for her cooking."

Mariah sighed. "I don't have any corn bread prepared, and it's too late to start. Can you come for it tomorrow?"

Tobias quirked his mouth then gave her a solemn nod. "By noon. No later. My boys will fetch it."

"I'll have it ready."

The Jones men filed past her out of the room. Chris winked as he passed, and Justin smiled and touched her arm, both so handsome up close her toes curled.

Cursing her twisted fate, she groaned inside, wishing with all her might that they weren't Choctaw.

Tiller's brows lifted. Tilting his head, he took another look to be certain of what he'd seen.

Mariah stood in a trance, ogling the cumbersome broad backs and prissy long hair of the departing braves. She watched them go, the dreamy look turning to pouted lips and an angry scowl.

Tiller cleared his throat. "Mariah?"

Her shoulders twitched and she spun. "Yes? I'm sorry."

He smirked. "Forgive me for interrupting your musings."

A crimson blush swept up from her collar. "Not at all. I was just—"

His eyes held hers until she lowered her lashes. He couldn't contain his knowing smile.

"Is there anything else before I turn in?"

Her gaze flickered up then dove to her feet. "Thank you, no. Miss Vee and I plan to take turns sitting with Mr. Gooch. You've done more than enough, and it's very late. I'm sure you had a tiresome day on the road."

He offered a small bow. "I'll say good night then."

"Just a minute, please," Miss Vee called in a hushed tone. Hurrying over, she ushered them into the hall. "Actually, I need to talk to you both. Now seems as good a time as any."

"Our guest said he's tired," Mariah protested. "Can't this wait until morning?"

Miss Vee cocked her head at Tiller. "Are you too bushed for a little chat? I have a business proposition." By the eager glow on her face, she had something big to say.

He grinned. "I suppose I can fend off sleep, now that you've piqued my interest."

"That's what I thought." Ignoring Mariah's furrowed scowl, she pointed at the parlor. "Take a seat inside. I'll fetch us some tea."

Tiller raised his hand. "None for me, ma'am. Keeps me awake."

"Don't worry"—she waved him off—"I'll brew a pot of chamomile."

They crossed the hall, and Tiller stepped aside to allow Mariah into the room. She hadn't met his eyes since he'd embarrassed her, and he couldn't help but wonder what thoughts swirled in her head while she stared at the two young men with such admiration.

The possibilities churned his gut and lit a small fire of jealousy in his heart. Surely, she wasn't interested in those two showy braves.

Don't be a fool. You have no right.

He'd just met her, after all, though it seemed he knew her well. He felt a kinship with Mariah. An easy bond greater than simple attraction. Greater and more enticing by far.

She settled into a chair across the low table and folded her hands in her lap.

Tiller studied her, taking advantage of the fact that she refused to look up.

In her frenzied rush to deal with the Indian healer, a few locks of hair had escaped from the topknot on her head. Long and bountifully black, the wispy strands gleamed in the firelight coming from the hearth. Her eyes were the color of chestnuts. This he recalled from memory since only her sleepy lids were visible. Dark brows with a delicate arch set off her sweeping lashes. His meddling appraisal moved to her full lips, and his pulse surged.

Mariah's hand fluttered to her mouth, waking him from his daze. She'd caught him at the very thing he'd mocked her for doing.

Clearing his throat, he shifted his attention to the hearth.

"I apologize for Miss Vee," she said lightly. "She gets worked up at times."

He glanced at her. "I don't mind. She seems to have a good heart."

Mariah tucked in one of her loose strands. "It's very astute of you to notice." She angled her head. "Considering you've known her for such a short while."

For the first time, Tiller took note of the slight crook in her nose. An imperfection, some might say, but it took nothing from her beauty. No more than the pleasing slant to her eyes.

He blinked as the realization hit. The boy he met on the road had said, "Mastah John and his Injun daughter run the finest stand on the Natchez Trace." Little wonder the Choctaw brothers would appeal to her. The elegant mistress of Bell's Inn was an Indian, too.

Did it matter? He'd have to think on it awhile.

"Mr. McRae?" Mariah said softly. "Have I lost you?"

He covered his wayward thoughts with a wide grin. "What happened to calling me Tiller?"

She gave him a shy smile. "Your name bears getting used to. It's very unusual."

"Just think of tilling the ground, and you won't forget. That's why folks started to call me Tiller in the first place. I suppose I'm good with the soil."

Mariah leaned closer. "So it's not your given name?"

He shook his head. "Reddick's on my birth papers, but I doubt I'd remember to answer to it. No one's called me Reddick in years."

She thoughtfully mouthed the name. "I think I like it. Reddick has a nice ring." Her chin came up. "Though Tiller's nice, too."

"I agree." Miss Vee swept into the room on the tail end of their conversation, placing a tray filled with teacups and little cakes on the table. "Tiller's very nice indeed. Why would there be any question?"

Mariah shot him a grin. "Never mind, dear. Let me help you with the tea."

Miss Vee handed Mariah a delicate cup, which she passed on to Tiller. Once she'd served them, they settled down to watch each other over the steaming rims of their drinks.

Tiller's first sip coated his top lip with creamy foam, the warm liquid so pleasant he hated to swallow. He held up his cup. "What did you say this concoction was?"

Miss Vee beamed. "Chamomile. I doctor it to my own peculiar taste. I hope you like it."

He chuckled. "You could say so. What makes it so good?"

Miss Vee set her saucer on the table. "Oh, I'm glad you like it. I brew it like everyone else then add a dollop of beaten cream and a teaspoon of honey. Sometimes I scrape in a little cinnamon, but I didn't this time."

Tiller shook his head. "I like it fine the way it is."

"Tastes positively cozy, doesn't it? It'll help you sleep, too."

"Is that a fact?"

Mariah sat forward. "Speaking of sleep, it's well past everyone's bedtime, so if you will, kindly get on with it."

Swiping foam off her lip with the back of her hand, Miss Vee nodded. "You're right. I'll come to the point." She shifted toward Tiller. "Were you serious when you said you were in no hurry to leave?"

He glanced at Mariah. "Well yes, but—"

"Good, because we're in no rush to see you go."

Mariah's cheeks colored. "Dear lady, what are you suggesting?"

Miss Vee seemed not to hear. "Like I told you before, Mariah's in need of a strong, trustworthy man."

Mariah's pretty face paled and she gulped air.

Still ignoring her, Miss Vee tilted her head at Tiller. "At supper you said there's no family to speak of, correct? No wife and passel of kids tucked away, waiting for you to come home?"

"Miss Vee!"

The lady finally glanced over her shoulder. "Keep your garter fastened, honey. It's not what you think."

Tiller came to the rescue. "Listen, I'm not sure what this is about, but I can only stay until my pockets dry up." He raised his hands and shrugged. "And the truth is I'm not carrying that much cash."

Miss Vee clapped her hands. "Perfect. My idea may be the solution to both your problems."

Standing so fast her teacup sloshed, Mariah scowled at Miss Vee. "I don't know where you're going with this nonsense, but I've heard quite enough." She set her saucer on the table. "If you'll excuse me, I'm going to bed."

Miss Vee caught her wrist. "Hear me out." Her pleading gaze seemed to hold Mariah tighter than her restraining hand.

Mariah sniffed. "With the way you started, I don't think I want to hear the rest."

Wringing her hands, Miss Vee colored. "Oh fiddle! That's because I'm not saying it right. Sit down and let me start over."

Easing into the chair, Mariah picked up her cup. "Very well, but make it quick." She narrowed her eyes. "And choose your words carefully."

Miss Vee grimaced. "Yes, of course. I'll try." She raised her chin. "I've been mulling over the facts in my head, honey. About the inn being so neglected."

Mariah colored and shot her a warning scowl. "A few things may need a hammer and a coat of paint, but—"

"You said it yourself, the walls are collapsing on our heads." She followed Mariah's pointed look at Tiller. "No need in posturing. I doubt the state of this place has escaped his notice."

Mariah huffed her frustration and fell against the back of her chair. "What's your point to all this?"

The older woman's face lit up. "I'm proposing that Tiller stay on and make the repairs in exchange for room and board—with a few buttered rolls thrown into the bargain." She winked. "If you think her yeast bread is good, wait till you taste her pies."

Her eyes darting between them, Mariah scooted to the edge of her seat. "Oh my, you really should've run your plan by me first. You see, I already have the repairs worked out."

Miss Vee crossed her arms. "Let me guess. You intend on tackling them yourself, don't you?"

Mariah opened her mouth to speak, but Miss Vee's hand shot up. "Young lady, you have more than enough to say grace over. Dash your pride and accept Tiller's help." Her bottom lip trembled. "For pity's sake, accept my help. I feel responsible for you in your father's absence."

Pulling a handkerchief from her waistband, she wiped her eyes. "I'm suggesting this idea for John's sake as much as yours. He'll still be recuperating when he comes home. I won't have him climbing ladders and toting lumber." She shook her finger in Mariah's face. "One thing's certain, he'd roll over and die before he'd allow you to do it."

Mariah's cup shattered in a spray of milky-white tea and shards of porcelain. Flinching, she dropped the jagged remnants at her feet.

Miss Vee struggled to stand. "Oh, honey! I'm so sorry. It must've cracked when I poured in the hot water. Are you hurt?"

Tiller snatched a folded towel from the tray. Skirting the table, he inspected Mariah's hands and found a cut, small but deep enough to bleed. He wrapped the cloth around her wound while Miss Vee shook the broken pieces from her frock and blotted creamy splatter from her chin.

"I'm all right," Mariah said quietly. "It's nothing. Please don't fuss."

"We're going to make sure, if you don't mind." Miss Vee peered at her face. "I pray no glass flew inside your eyes. Do they sting when you blink?"

Mariah shook her head. "Really, I'm fine." She swiped at her wet skirt. "Though I would like to get upstairs and change."

"Of course, dear." Miss Vee slid her arm around Mariah's waist. "Come, I'll help you."

"What about Mr. Gooch?" Mariah asked.

"Don't fret," Miss Vee said, urging her forward. "I'll take first watch."

Concerned, Tiller followed them to the landing.

At the foot of the stairs, Miss Vee paused. "We'll all sleep better if we get this thing settled." Biting her bottom lip, she raised her brows. "Will you do it, Tiller? Will you stay on at Bell's Inn and help us?"

He studied Mariah's face, but it offered no hint to her thoughts. "If I were to agree, would it be all right with you?"

Her sigh, sweet with the smell of honey, stirred the air between them. "I can't think of a good enough reason to say no."

Tiller smiled. "Tell you what. . .I'll chew on it overnight and let you know my decision in the morning."

Winking, Miss Vee pointed at the tray on the table. "While you ponder, chew on one of Mariah's iced cakes. If you decide to hang around, there will be plenty more to follow."

Once they'd gone, Tiller bit into the confection, rolling the buttery goodness over his tongue. Delicious. Only sweetness didn't set right in a mouth filled with questions. The proud mistress of Bell's Inn, hard to figure from the start, just became a delightful riddle.

Mariah may have Miss Vee fooled, but not Tiller. Hot water had nothing to do with the broken cup. Some word or deed clenched the girl's fingers so fiercely she'd crushed it to bits.

Was it Miss Vee's reminder of Mariah's responsibilities? The rebuke about her pride? Perhaps the mention of her father, wherever the absent man might be.

Snatching one more cake, Tiller munched on it as he made his way to his room. He intended to replay every second of the evening in his mind until he figured out what thistle had so sorely pricked Miss Mariah's winsome hide.

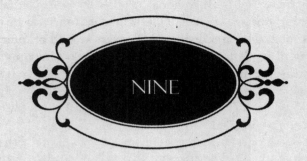

NINE

The sun began a slow crawl up the far horizon as Joe reached the end of his rutted lane. By nightfall, it would slide down the backside of the sky and sleep closer to Myrtle than he would.

He had a long ride ahead to reach Mississippi, and the same distance to come back. In between loomed the time it would take to convince John Coffee to release Mariah.

Joe halted his pony and shifted in the saddle to stare behind him. His ancestors left their Mississippi homeland in tears, but the place Joe had carved out of the vast Indian Territory was *apookta*. His happy place. Long, lonely days stretched ahead before he could return.

Gray smoke swirled from the crooked stovepipe, reminding him of the pleasant morning spent with his wife. Myrtle had slipped out of bed early or else hadn't turned back the covers at all, since she'd managed to wash and pack all of his clothes, load his rucksack, and prepare a breakfast fit for three men.

In light of the fact Joe was leaving, and considering the news she'd served alongside his eggs and fried bread, she probably hadn't slept a wink all night. Tears had brightened her eyes in the firelight—tears of joy or fear, he couldn't tell—before she lowered her chin to her chest and whispered the words he'd waited twenty years to hear.

Myrtle would bear him a son, for surely a male child wrestled for life beneath her bosom. He'd been too patient, too hopeful for the babe to be anything else. They'd call him George after George Hudson, the first principal chief under the new Choctaw constitution. Joe would teach him to hunt and fish, to honor his mother, and to sit tall at tribal council.

Myrtle said the miracle came to her in November, near the time of the white man's Thanksgiving. For the first time in Joe's life, there would be cause to celebrate the season.

He couldn't help but wonder why fate waited until all hope had dimmed. Why the gift had come at a time when he wouldn't be home to share its unfolding.

In the distance, Myrtle stepped out of the front door with a dishpan in her hand, hustled to the edge of the porch, and let the water fly in a silvery arc that caught the morning light.

Watching her dart inside, Joe sighed with contentment, a smile lifting the corners of his mouth. His wife had carried the child and the secret close to her heart for nearly six months, which meant the boy would come by the dawn of the Mulberry Moon.

Sudden pain squeezed his chest and worry tickled the back of his mind. Myrtle was spritely for her age but hardly a girl. Fretting drove her to bustle about, looking for work to fill her hands and occupy her troubled mind. She'd toil hard, sleep few hours, and eat too little until he returned. He imagined her lumbering about the cabin, hauling water, chopping wood, bent over the washboard, her body swollen with his child.

The picture set his teeth on edge. John would not stand in his way this time. Mariah would be a comfort to her aunt in her condition and a great help with the baby. With his niece settled in his home, his obligation to his sister fulfilled at last, Joe could relax and enjoy his new son.

Ghostlike, Myrtle appeared again, drifting across the porch with one hand on her stomach, the other splayed over her heart. She stared toward the southern pasture, her back to him. Joe knew she wept even before she leaned into the rail and gripped her face.

He clenched his jaw and fought the urge to turn the dun pony and race to her side, take her in his arms, and soothe her fears. With a leaden heart, he forced his eyes to the front and tapped the horse's flank with his heels.

Home wouldn't be apookta for Myrtle until Joe returned, but his spirit couldn't rest until he settled his business with John Coffee. The sooner he began the journey, the better for all concerned.

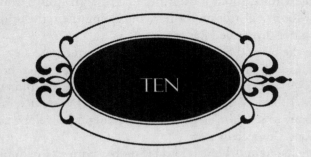

TEN

To the honorable Dr. T. Moony
Canton, Mississippi

Dear Dr. Moony,
    This letter serves to inform you of my father's recent demise.
As you predicted, his condition worsened day by day until, on the
evening before last, shortly before the midnight hour, he lost his
feeble hold on this life and passed into blessed rest. I want to thank
you for your kind administrations in our hour of need.

Respectfully,
Miss Mariah Minti Bell

P.S. The enclosed should cancel the balance of my debt.

Mariah laid down her pen, the tightness in her chest beginning to ease. She would seal the letter and hire Rainy to deliver it first thing this morning. The money tucked inside should satisfy her debt in full and cancel her prior arrangement to make payments for Father's care. Once she'd paid her bill, Dr. Moony would have no reason to return to the inn. They had no friends or relatives in Canton, no close connections in town, so the good doctor wouldn't likely mention the death of John

Coffee Bell to anyone there.

Her shoulders tensed as Mr. Gooch's pain-wracked face drifted into her mind. She and Miss Vee had taken turns sitting with their battered guest throughout a fitful night. The right thing would be to bring Dr. Moony out to care for him, but doing the right thing would roll the boulder that sealed her tomb.

Unlike the blessed Savior, there'd be no resurrection.

If Mr. Gooch took a turn for the worse, she'd have no choice. For now, everyone seemed perfectly content with the Indian healer. Thankfully, Tobias accepted goods in trade for his services since she had no money to pay him—she patted the bulging envelope addressed to Dr. Moony—especially now.

Mariah stared out the window, biting her bottom lip. Which need would get the meager few dollars she had left? The help's salaries or stocking the pantry? Feeding Sheki or repairing the loose boards and chipped railing?

Jutting her chin, she counted out the few dollars she owed Miss Vee, Dicey, and Rainy and set them aside. Those dear ones wouldn't suffer lack because of her deception. She'd find some way to cover the other needs.

A knock on the door brought her hand up to hide the letter. "Yes?"

Miss Vee peered in. "Are you awake?" She stepped inside, her brow etched with concern. "You're usually downstairs brewing coffee by now."

Crumpling the letter, Mariah hid it in the folds of her skirt. "Gracious, I know. I'm dawdling worse than Dicey this morning. A lingering touch of spring fever, I suppose."

"We're two days into June, Mariah. The time for spring fever is past." Mariah shot her a pointed look, and she held up her hand. "All right. I won't hover." At the door, she paused and smiled. "But hurry along, will you? We have to fill Tiller's stomach in case he's decided to accept your proposition. He'll need strength to tackle all those repairs."

My proposition? Hardly. Miss Vee and Tiller had worked out the terms of the arrangement across the top of her unwilling head. "I'll feed him, though I have doubts about filling his stomach. Go on down. I'll be right along."

Laughing, Miss Vee pulled the door closed behind her.

Mariah glanced up and frowned at her anxious face in the mirror.

With Miss Vee's reminder, the web of deceit tightened. If Tiller accepted the job, he would need building material. Lumber, shingles, and nails weren't free.

The thought of her redheaded guest quirked her mouth to the side. Tiller had wriggled under her skin on several different occasions. So far, this day fared no better. How dare the insufferable man ride into her life and provoke such angst?

First, he'd positively leered at her in front of the Jones brothers, implying with his crooked grin that he'd read her private thoughts. Last night he'd tracked her up the stairs with a knowing gaze that peered right into her soul.

She cringed. Tiller couldn't possibly know why she broke the cup, but she had been admiring Christopher's flashing eyes and Justin's dazzling smile, so he wasn't far off the mark on that score. Even so, a gentleman wouldn't blatantly accuse her. Blast his foul manners!

How dare Miss Vee ask him to stay on against Mariah's wishes? Could she bear having Tiller McRae and his bloated self-assurance underfoot every minute of the day? With a man like him around, a woman's secrets weren't safe.

A shudder took her, and she slanted her eyes from the mirror. One secret he mustn't guess. She determined to bear the weight of it with more care, no matter how heavy it lay on her shoulders.

Tiller fastened the last button on his shirt then plopped on the bed to pull on his boots. The familiar rattle of a woman in the kitchen drifted down the hallway, along with the unmistakable smell of brewed coffee.

Whatever breakfast came of the clanging pots and pans would be welcome, but Tiller needed the coffee. He had flipped like a gambler's nickel half the night, twisting the quilt around his legs and dragging his sheets from the bed.

Once he admitted he wasn't ready to leave Bell's Inn whatever the risk, the decision to accept Miss Vee's offer came easy. After that, so did sleep, what little he got before the sun peeked through the blinds.

He pulled the snaggletoothed comb from his pocket and smoothed back his hair, grateful the bright orange color of his youth had mellowed some to match his beard. Fingering the two days' growth on his chin, he decided shaving could wait one more day.

Feeling refreshed but a little reckless about the decision he'd made, he ducked out the door and made for the kitchen. He didn't feel foolish about staying on to help two women in need, more for the reasons he couldn't make himself leave.

For one, he felt at home in the aging, broken-down inn in a way he hadn't since the day he left Uncle Silas's house. When he turned the corner, his second reason stood barefoot at the stove stirring gravy in a cast-iron skillet.

"Where's Dicey?" Mariah asked without turning around.

"She's late," Miss Vee fired over her shoulder. "As usual." She spun again, staring at Mariah's feet. "Where are your shoes? These old boards are bound to be cold."

Miss Vee noticed Tiller lurking on the threshold and smiled. "Well, good morning. Take a seat. You'd best be hungry. We're stirring up a feast."

Mariah stiffened, tucking in her chin. She didn't offer an explanation about her shoes or a greeting for Tiller.

Winking at Miss Vee, he pulled out a chair. "I could do serious damage to a feast, but let's start with a mug of hot coffee." He cleared his throat to dislodge the lump. "Um. . .morning, Mariah."

She glanced over her shoulder. "Good morning."

From the glimpse at her swollen eyelids, she hadn't rested so well herself. Or she'd been crying. After the way she smashed her teacup to bits, his bet was on the tears. The thought stirred his heart to pity and stoked his curiosity to a flame.

Miss Vee swung around from the counter and set a heaped-up plate in front of him. He shot her a grateful smile before she returned to buttering biscuits. "How's Mr. Gooch this morning?" she called to Mariah.

The sound of the old man's name lodged so tight in Tiller's craw, he choked on his first bite of food.

Miss Vee laughed and pounded his back. "Gracious, son. Did that griddle cake take the wrong chute?"

Hacking furiously, he nodded.

Mariah picked that moment to come to the table, casting alarmed glances at his burning face and streaming tears.

Recovering somewhat, Tiller blew his nose on the napkin by his plate.

"Let me just get you a new one of these," Miss Vee offered, pinching the corner of the cloth and tossing it in a basket behind her.

Mariah set two more plates on the table. "Do you mind if we join you?"

Unable to answer, he waved for her to sit.

She pulled out a chair and tucked into her food, thoughtfully giving him time to recover.

Miss Vee took her place opposite Mariah. "So Mr. Gooch is all right this morning?"

Unfolding her napkin, Mariah dabbed at the corners of her mouth. "Actually, our patient seems much improved. He awoke twice during the night, asking questions and thanking us again for helping him." She smiled across the table. "I believe he did the same with you, right, Miss Vee?"

She beamed. "He sure did. The old fellow seems a kindly sort." A sudden frown creased her brow. "Not the type to deserve a whack on the head, that's for sure. Such a shame that evil men roam the earth taking advantage of innocent souls like him."

The buttery bite of pancake melting on Tiller's tongue swelled to cotton. He swallowed carefully and pushed aside his plate.

Mariah's startled gaze jumped to his food. "Is something wrong?"

He tried to smile. "Not at all. It was delicious."

"But you've hardly—"

He pushed back his chair and slapped his legs. "I've made my decision, ladies. I'm ready to get to work on your repairs. If you'll direct me to the proper tools, I'll get started."

Miss Vee leaned across the table. "You mean you'll stay on and help?"

Tiller pasted on his finley tuned grin and saluted. "For as long as you can stand me."

She whooped and clasped her hands. "Mariah, isn't that the best news?"

Mariah's brows gathered. "Yes, wonderful." She pointed at Tiller's full plate. "He hasn't eaten his breakfast. How can he work on an empty stomach?"

"I'll grab something later. I'm pretty anxious to get started." Standing, he clutched a fistful of bacon in one hand, his coffee cup in the other. "I'll just take this with me, if you don't mind."

The kitchen door flew open, yanking Tiller's heart to his throat. He leaped back so fast he sloshed his coffee in splatters around him.

The girl, Dicey, stood panting on the threshold. "It's Rainy's fault, Miss Mariah, his and my daddy's. Rainy's always late, and Daddy's bullheaded."

Miss Vee crossed her arms and scooted her chair around. "Good *afternoon*, Dicey. Do go on with your latest excuse. This one has the makings of an imaginative tale."

"No'm, Miss Vee. This ain't no kind of tale. Daddy say I cain't walk myself to work no mo'—not with some ramblin' fool going about busting folks in the head. So Rainy say he gon' walk me out here, and I say, 'How nice, Rainy!' Then he say, 'For a penny of your wages every day.'" Her fists balled at her sides and she scowled. "I don't hold with paying that shiftless boy nothin', but Daddy say it's the only way I'll be keepin' my job." Dicey pinched her mouth, breathing through her nose in short blasts. "Only Rainy jus' now showed up to fetch me." She cast a sinister glare over her shoulder. "Those big feet mired up in molasses."

In the distance, a tall boy ambled away, both hands shoved deep in his pockets. With a second look, Tiller recognized him as the young man who first directed him to the inn.

Mariah stood in a rush. "Rainy's out there?" She raised her skirt past her bare ankles and whirled around the table. "I have an errand for him."

Pouting her lips, Dicey stepped aside. "He headed home lickety-click. Runnin' away from my scolding, I s'pose. I lit into him all the way here." Her angry scowl became a simper. "You can see it ain't my fault I'm late, Miss Mariah. Now cain't you?"

Without pausing to answer, Mariah hurried past her calling Rainy's name.

Miss Vee jumped up and crossed to the door. "For pity's sake, Mariah Bell. You're barefoot!" She flapped her dishcloth so hard it popped. "The bottom of that girl's feet must be tanned hide."

Tiller pressed in behind Miss Vee as Mariah caught up with the boy and handed him what looked like a thick letter. "I reckon a person with natural leather soles wouldn't see the necessity for shoes."

She snorted. "Not exactly proper, is she?"

Tiller suppressed a grin. *Proper? Maybe not, but decidedly intriguing.*

Miss Vee stared after Mariah with a puzzled frown. "What do you suppose that's all about?"

"I was about to ask you the same," he said.

She shrugged. "We don't have time to find out, do we? Dicey has a kitchen to clear, and I have a box of tools with your name on it." She wiggled her fingers. "Come along, I'll show you where they're kept."

Tiller followed her down the back steps, so intent on watching Mariah he nearly ran into a stump.

With a knowing smile, Miss Vee took his arm and steered him clear.

The early summer day promised to be a mild one, considering the dew still wetting the ground and the faint chill in the morning air. He glanced around, admiring the well-kept grounds. "Who keeps up the yard?"

She snapped off a low-hanging magnolia blossom and held it to her nose. "Young Rainy. The boy loves working outside. He has a gift."

Tiller thought back to Rainy grinning from atop the rise. *'Jus' look for the best tended grounds in Madison County.'* Chuckling, he shook his head.

"Rainy keeps the vegetable garden, too."

"You have a garden?"

Miss Vee smiled over her shoulder. "Just the best in the county. We turn out a fine, healthy crop every year, and it's a special blessing. Without a good harvest, we couldn't keep the customers fed." She veered toward the corner of the yard. "Follow me, and I'll show you."

She led Tiller to a nice-sized patch with rows of green beans climbing sticks and big heads of lettuce sprawling around the outer edges. Young melons, tomato plants, peas, and squash would soon be bursting for harvest.

Reminded of himself at Rainy's age, and of his own skill in working the soil, Tiller swallowed a sudden knot crowding his throat. He longed to linger in the inviting garden, to drop to one knee and bury his fingers in rich, black dirt. It had been too long since he'd soiled his hands in worthwhile pursuits instead of deception and crime. "The boy does a fine job."

Miss Vee nodded. "He sure does. With Rainy's knack for growing things and Mariah's gift for cooking, they make a tasty combination." Laughing, she tugged on Tiller's sleeve. "You've tricked me into dawdling long enough. Let's get to those chores."

Instead of heading for the crooked little lean-to, Miss Vee led him to the barn. Lifting the bar from across the heavy doors, she yanked them open with a grunt. "Mariah keeps her thingamajigs in here to protect them from the dampness of the shed. The girl is more particular with these old wrenches and hammers than most men are with their wives." She winked. "Count yourself among the privileged few she allows to touch them."

Miss Vee crossed the shadowy barn and ducked into a small storeroom in the corner. From inside a built-in cabinet with squeaky doors, she pulled a wooden box with shiny tools of every sort nestled beneath the curved handles like eggs in a basket.

Tiller glanced at Miss Vee. "These are Mariah's?"

She held them up for a closer look. "Every oiled and polished piece."

He cleared his throat. "I thought they'd belong to her pa."

A grin lit Miss Vee's face. "Not hardly. Mariah's the handy one. At least when she has the time." Her eyes warmed. "For all his talents, John Coffee's not so good when it comes to repairs." Her bosom shook with laughter. "Chores either, for that matter."

By her smitten look, Mr. Bell's failings didn't bother Miss Vee one bit.

"If you don't mind my asking, ma'am. . .where is Mariah's pa?"

She motioned with her head for him to take the toolbox. He obliged, and she closed the cabinet with a squeal of hinges. Pausing for several long seconds, she studied him, the love-struck shine faded to worry. "Poor John is sick, I'm afraid. Gravely ill, the last I heard. Some ailment afflicting his lungs."

"Well, I'm sorry to hear it," Tiller said. "Will he"—he cleared his throat—"recover soon?"

Her apple cheeks swelled with glee. "Yes, he will," she said, stressing each word. "The doctor sent him away to get better. 'Healed once and for all,' to quote Mariah." She sobered. "It burdens my heart that he's gone who-knows-where, depending on who-knows-who to care for him, but he'll be home soon, just as feisty as always." Her thoughts busy elsewhere, she stared mindlessly at Tiller's chin. "Then all the folks who love him can get on with living again."

Tiller gave her a knowing smile. "Yes, ma'am. I expect you will."

Oblivious, she drew up her shoulders and returned to the present. "Here you go again, distracting me to get out of doing your work." She jabbed him in the chest with her finger. "Well, it won't work, mister. Come with me." She ducked out of the storeroom and led him across the barn. "I figure you'll start from the top and work your way down, which means the roof comes first."

"Yes, ma'am."

"If you look in the shed, you'll find enough shingles to get you started. For the rest, I'm going to ask your help with a minor duplicity."

Tiller angled his head. "Ma'am?"

"A little harmless deceit for a good cause."

He shoved the door open. "What are you up to?"

She gave him a playful wink. "Starting tomorrow, you'll have the supplies you need. If Mariah asks, you say you stumbled across them in the shed or behind the barn." She grinned. "As in fact you will, once I give Rainy the funds to run into Canton. I just need a list from you and your promise to keep my secret."

Tiller shoved back his hat. "Lumber and nails are expensive."

She shrugged. "What else do I have to spend money on?"

He ducked his head to catch her eye. "It's very generous."

"Oh, pooh." Miss Vee waved him off. "After all, I live here, too." She hooked her arm through his. "Let me show you where to find the ladder. Then I'd best go see about Mr. Gooch. We've left him untended far too long."

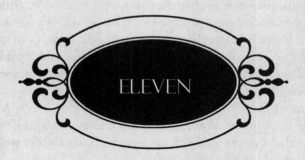

ELEVEN

Scuffletown, North Carolina

Hooper McRae tightened his fingers on the reins and eased the wagon to the right, dodging a gaping muddy rut straddling the middle of the road. Warmth stole over his heart, despite his aching shoulders and stiff hands. Soggy lanes and swampland were the first signs of nearing home.

Glancing at his sleeping wife curled on the seat beside him, he grinned and nudged her awake.

She moaned and stirred then squinted up with a drowsy smile, her pretty face dappled by the sunrise peeking over the horizon. "Hello, handsome stranger."

Hooper smoothed her red hair. "How do you sleep all bunched in a knot?"

Dawsey scratched her nose with the back of her hand. "It's not easy, I can tell you that much. In fact, I'm not really sleeping. . .just dozing a little." Her groggy voice faded. "Merely resting my eyes."

Leaning closer, Hooper's grin widened. "Were you planning to *doze* clear to Scuffletown?"

She yawned. "Don't be silly. I intend to keep you company along the way."

"I appreciate the effort, honey, but you're too late. We're here."

Her startled eyes flashed open. Bolting upright, she stared around her. "We're in Scuffletown? Hooper, that's impossible." She spun to gaze at him. "You drove all night?"

He laughed around the yawn he'd caught from her. "I didn't go to. The wheels kept turning while the road unfurled in front of me. Next thing I knew, we were pulling into Lumberton. No sense stopping twelve miles short of home."

Dawsey scooted closer on the seat and gripped his hand. "You're no longer a Scuffletown resident, Mr. McRae. Hope Mills is where you hang your hat now and has been for more than ten years."

He shook his head. "Sorry, dumplin'. If I live in Hope Mills fifty more years, this bogged-down swamp will still be my home."

She giggled and stretched. "Oh Hooper, I can't believe we're here. I can hardly wait to see Dilsey and the twins."

He held up a warning finger. "Ellie, not Dilsey. If you insist on calling her that name, you'll only make her mad."

She shot him a pout. "I do wish we could've brought our daughters to see your parents."

Hooper shook his head. "We made the right decision, Dawsey." He held up his fingers to count off the reasons they'd discussed. "It's a long trip, and we don't know when we'll see Hope Mills again. The girls are in school. All their friends are there. They're better off staying with Aunt Lavinia this time.

"Besides"—he winked—"a few days with their Aunt Ellie and your prissy daughters would be done up in britches, toting rifles, and tracking hogs through the swamp."

Dawsey's laughter echoed off the passing trees. "You're right, they would. I've always said it's a blessing Dilsey had sons."

Hooper raised his brows. "Two sets of twin boys born less than a year apart? Is that a blessing or double trouble? Those four scamps run their mother aground."

"And provide endless joy for your pa," she added, laughing harder. Sobering, she squeezed his hand. "I wish my father had lived to see the last two born."

"So do I." He patted her hand. "I really miss the old man."

Dawsey tilted her head. "Do you ever wonder what might've happened if the Wilkeses and McRaes hadn't found each other? I'd never have known I had a sister." She pointed between them. "Or that we share a sister, as madly improper as it sounds unless you know the story. And—the most amazing part of all—that you and I would fall in love and get married, forever blending our families."

He laughed. "Take a breath before you grow faint."

She fanned her flushed face. "I'm sorry, but after all these years, I'm still awed by the way God worked out the details."

Hooper smiled. "If you think about it, our families were blended from the day Pa brought our Ellie home."

Dawsey wrinkled her forehead. "You mean the day he kidnapped *our* Dilsey Elaine to raise as his own." She seemed to stare into the past. "I never thought I could forgive your father, but as it happens, Silas McRae is an irresistibly charming man."

Familiar tightness stung Hooper's throat. "I'll always admire the Colonel for forgiving Pa. It meant so much to him."

Glancing at his brimming eyes, Dawsey fished for her hankie and wiped tears from her cheeks. "I was awfully proud of Father. Showing mercy to the McRaes didn't come easy for a man like him."

They rode in silence until Dawsey nudged his shoulder. "If you think about it, God used Tiller to bring us all together. If I hadn't taken him under my wing, and if you hadn't come to Fayetteville on a mission to return him to Scuffletown, we never would've known such joy."

Hooper chuckled. "You're right. One skinny, carrot-topped boy set the whole thing in motion. Only Tiller ran away before he saw how well things turned out."

She inhaled sharply. "And we never got to thank him."

Hooper draped his arm around her and tugged her close. "Don't despair, Dawsey. Our visit home could change all that." He squeezed her shoulders. "And speaking of home, look. . .we're here."

Spirits soaring, Hooper turned the wagon down the lane to his old homestead. Peering to see in the early morning light, he could just make out the cabin in the distance. As they drew closer, a dim light shone from the open doorway, and milling shapes were gathering on the porch.

"They've heard us coming." He swallowed the lump in his throat. "Won't they be surprised to see it's us?"

A fact Hooper would soon make clear if he had to call out their names. Despite the few years of relative peace throughout the swamp, there would be half a dozen guns trained on the rig.

Dawsey shifted her weight impatiently. "I still say you should've wired ahead."

He shook his head. "The old man knows I'd never leave our farm this time of year. He'd have worried fit to bust until we arrived." He blew a long breath through his nostrils. "I wish we were here on a pleasure trip instead of this distasteful business."

"We'll get the unpleasantness out of the way first," Dawsey said, patting his hand. "Then we can enjoy ourselves with the family." She peeked up at him. "What do you think Silas will say when he hears the shocking news we're bringing?"

Hooper's stomach lurched. "He'll start all over again blaming himself that Tiller ran off." He tightened his jaw. "I don't relish causing him hurt, but I have to tell him, Dawsey. I have no choice."

She squeezed his fingers. "Of course you don't." Her eyes sparkling, Dawsey pointed at a slim figure standing on the porch. "Oh, Hooper! I think that's Dilsey." She leaned to squint. "Yes, Dilsey's here, and so are Wyatt and the boys."

He shot her a pained glance. "Do you plan to call her that the whole time we're here? If so, tell me now while there's still time to turn around. I'm not in the mood for Ellie's temper."

Her darting eyes trained on the cabin, Dawsey dragged her attention back to him. "Don't be silly. I'm the only person Dilsey tolerates on that score, but she allows me the one small indulgence." She gave him a look from under her lashes. "It's her real name, after all."

"Try to convince Ellie. . .only wait till I'm out of the house."

Smiling, Dawsey pointed with her chin. "Speaking of the house, I don't believe it's changed one whit."

Hooper gazed toward the ramshackle cabin. Smoke poured from the skinny stovepipe on the sagging roof. Firewood stacked high on the rickety front porch nearly covered the dirt-smeared windows. Shimmering puddles in the waterlogged yard mirrored the surrounding trees.

"You're right." He beamed at Dawsey. "Not a whit."

A high-pitched scream followed by a dancing, bobbing ruckus meant the family had identified the wagon.

As Hooper pulled to a stop a few yards from the beaming hoard on the porch, Dawsey leaned to whisper. "Don't say anything right away. It'll spoil their fun."

He lifted one brow. "What happened to getting the unpleasantness out of the way?" Climbing down, he winced from the stiffness and turned to help her to the ground.

She puckered her face at him, but anything else she thought to say got swallowed up in Pa's welcoming shouts and Mama's sloppy kisses.

Dawsey flew into Ellie's waiting arms, both women laughing and crying at once.

Pa squeezed between them and yanked Dawsey into his burly arms. "Little Dawsey. You're a delight for these old eyes. How's my boy treating you?"

"Hooper still pampers me like a bride, Silas."

"Well, he'd better," Pa shouted. "Else I'll twist his ears."

He spun. "Hooper, blast your hide! You don't come home near as often as you should."

Hooper winked at Dawsey. "See? Pa knows where home is."

With tears streaking her rosy cheeks, Ellie gave a war whoop and slung herself at Hooper.

He lifted and twirled her around, then set her on the ground, his arm crooked around her neck. "Have you given Wyatt plenty of trouble, little sister?"

She gave a solemn nod. "Every day."

Hooper gripped Wyatt's offered hand. "It's been awhile."

Wyatt's fingers tightened. "It sure has."

Ellie's four boys shoved closer, the elder twins waiting their turns with silly grins. When the grown-ups gave them room, they bolted for Dawsey and Hooper, clinging until Wyatt plucked them off.

One of the younger twins gaped at Dawsey, his brow furrowed under the cowlick in his hair. Squeezing between his parents, he tugged on her skirt. "Hey, you look like our ma."

His identical brother curled his lip. "She ain't nothing like our ma. She's too prissy and girlie."

Ellie gripped their necks, ignoring their howls. "This prissy lady is your Aunt Dawsey, sprouts. Go on and give her a hug."

Dawsey knelt in front of them. "Don't you remember me, boys? You've seen me many times before, though I'll admit it's been awhile."

Never one to let the point of a matter ramble in the dark, Papa ushered them toward the steps. "Let's move this shindig inside, family, so they can tell us why they've come." He clamped his meaty hand on Hooper's shoulder, a tiny frown gathering on his brow. "I get the feeling there's far more to this visit than a long overdue howdy."

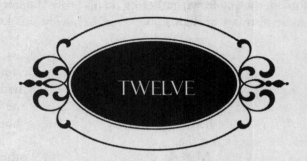

TWELVE

Mariah knelt in the cold, wet patch of grass covering her father's grave, the ground beneath her lumpy from unsettled clods of dirt.

With no windbreak on the rise, the morning breeze flapped her scarf against her face. The whistling wind in the overhead branches sang a haunting song, an endless tale of loss and broken hearts.

Contrary to the rest of God's creation, trees slipped into bright green coats to brave the sweltering heat only to shed their clothes and dance naked through the winter, waving their bare arms and groaning in protest. The foolish practice made as little sense as the mess Mariah had made of her life.

"Aki, tell me what to do. I'm lost without you." She sniffled and wiped the back of her hand under her nose. "I'm hurting Miss Vee, though I never meant to, and I know her sorrow would not please you."

Mariah had watched over the past months as her father had warmed toward the spunky, determined redhead. He'd begun to watch Miss Vee fondly as she went about her chores, a secret smile on his lips and a growing tenderness in the lines of his face.

How could Mariah tell her? *Father did care, dear lady. He'd come to admire you greatly, only now I'm afraid he's quite dead.*

She leaned over and gripped her face. "Miss Vee will be so angry when she finds out I've deceived her. Robbed her of the chance to grieve."

Mariah's head came up and snapped around to the other grave as if Mother had stepped across and caught her by the chin.

Promise, daughter. You must promise. Mother had pleaded until Mariah swore an oath to keep the land. Then she'd closed her eyes and slipped away, leaving her only child with a pledge she didn't know how to keep.

Mariah buried her fingers in the thick Mississippi grass, the land her mother's people had owned for decades under article fourteen of the Treaty of Dancing Rabbit Creek. Since then, her tribe had suffered indignities at the hands of greedy settlers. Hoping to drive the Choctaw off their land, these men had taunted them, burned their homes, torn down fences, and driven out their cattle.

They succeeded with Mariah's Uncle Joe and many others of her family. Father's name had protected her mother. Mother loved Bell's Inn and loved Father all the more for securing it for her. Running the inn made her feel like a great lady, not a mongrel only fit for the reservation.

A proud member of the Pearl River Clan of the Choctaw, Onnat Minti Bell loved the land even more. As a child, she raced along the same sandy bank as Mariah. Ran barefoot through the same backyard. Visited her mother's grave on the same grassy knoll.

Mariah cast a sheepish glance behind her. On the high bluff where she knelt lay the bones of generations of her ancestors, their unspoken hope a pressing burden.

Spinning, she scowled at Mother's tombstone. "It was Father's promise to make, yet you asked it of me?" She brought her fists down on her legs. "Why charge it to me? It's too heavy."

Oh Aki, why indeed?

Mariah knew the answer, one she'd never speak aloud. Her lighthearted father took one day at a time and lived as carefree as possible. He left responsible matters for Mother to tend, and when she died, the burden fell to Mariah. If Father had sworn to protect the land for Mariah and her children, he'd have died a failure. Mariah was her mother's only chance.

Gabriel Taber's jowly face and slack mouth flashed in her mind. He wasn't a God-fearing man, a fact that grieved her. No matter. She'd have to stop putting him off. The time had come to put her plan into motion.

With a shuddering sigh, Mariah pushed to her feet. Shading her eyes, she watched the Pearl River meander past on its way to places she'd never been. She wondered what it would be like to sail off the bank into the rippling brown water and go along for the ride. She'd cross her arms behind her head and float belly-up along the mud banks and sandy shores, the groves and cypress swamps, on past Jackson and down to the open seas—the inn and her promise be hanged.

Instead, she did what she'd always done. Girding herself under the oppressive weight of duty, she hoisted her lie and the promise to her shoulders and trudged to the tree where Sheki waited, his neck stretched so far toward a tasty bush his reins were taut enough to strum.

"Leave it, beast." Mariah pulled him around to a stump and mounted him bareback. "If you had your way, there'd be nothing green left in Madison County except for buttonbush, and then only because they're poison." She smiled to herself. Lucky thing they were bitter, or the gluttonous pony would wind up on his back, belly bloated, and stiff legs aimed for the sky.

Tangling her fingers in Sheki's mane, she whispered in his ear. He lifted his head and broke into a trot. Tensing her legs, Mariah tightened her hold on the little paint's neck.

"*Kil-ia!*"

Sheki's nostrils flared and his muscles gathered beneath her. He bolted, and Mariah curled close to his body.

Cold air blasted her face. She gulped and ducked her head. The wind tore at her scarf, the knot working loose from under her chin. The flimsy cloth trailed behind her until a sudden gust wrenched it away. She didn't dare turn loose to catch it.

They thundered past the birch grove and roared into the yard, scattering chickens and raising dust. Mariah slid to the ground bubbling over with a jumble of laughter and tears—until a flash of color caught the corner of her eye. Peeking over Sheki's back, she cringed and ducked her head.

Miss Vee and Tiller stood gaping at her from just inside the barn.

The ladder slid to the ground with a clatter, but Tiller hardly noticed. In all his years, he'd never seen a more fetching sight.

Mariah's dark eyes flashed and her chest heaved. Waist-length hair, tangled by the wind, puffed like shiny black tumbleweed around her delicate seashell ears. The deep flush of high spirits tinted her mouth and cheeks a glorious rosy hue. The genteel daughter of the innkeeper had become a wild and beautiful creature.

Defiantly meeting his stare, Mariah gathered her hair over one shoulder and lifted her chin. "I see you're finally starting to work."

Startled from his trance by her voice, he realized his lips had parted. He clamped them shut and nodded. "Miss Vee showed me where you keep the tools."

As if sprung into action by the sound of his voice, Miss Vee bustled toward Mariah. "Gracious, child. What have you been tromping through?"

Leaving the ladder, Tiller followed, stealing a peek at Mariah's feet. Clumps of mud clung to them in thick gobs, and red clay oozed between her toes. At least four inches of her hem was soaking wet.

"I—went for a walk," Mariah stammered. "Along the river."

Miss Vee's forehead crinkled. "Last we saw, you were talking to Rainy."

"Yes, I finished with him and decided to take Sheki out for a while."

"At this time of day?"

"I had a sudden impulse. It's such a nice, cool morning."

"Before your chores?" The older woman pressed, ignoring her explanation. "What were you thinking?"

Mariah's delicate brows lowered. "I was thinking to take a ride. Why are you questioning me?"

"Because it's not like you. With your father away, you have added responsibilities."

Mariah's fiery gaze flashed hotter. "I'll thank you to mind your business. I'll run this inn as I see fit."

Miss Vee's temper ignited to meet hers. "I don't understand your behavior, young lady. Something is quite off kilter." She scowled. "Just look at you, straddling a horse in a dress, showing off your knees to half of Mississippi. You have mud up to your ankles and grass stains covering the front of your skirt." She bent to dust off Mariah's garment. "Have you been crawling on the ground?"

With a sharp inhalation, Mariah yanked the fabric out of her reach. "Certainly not."

Straightening, Miss Vee's chest heaved. "Mariah Bell, if your father was here, why he'd—"

Mariah glared. "Well, he's not! And try to remember you're not my mother."

Miss Vee drew back, flushed as bright as her hair. Shock and pain darkened her green eyes. "I hardly recognize you." Clutching her blotchy face, she whirled for the back door.

Snatching up her pony's leads, Mariah stomped inside the barn.

Captive, Tiller followed.

At the stall, she flung the door open and slapped the animal hard on the rump. "Hurry up, you worthless fat horse."

The pony startled then hustled through the gate like a chastened child.

Mariah slung the door closed, fastened it, then spun around—stopping with a muted cry at the sight of Tiller. "What are you doing in here?" She narrowed her eyes. "Why are you following me? Don't you have work to do?"

As surprised to be standing behind her as Mariah was to find him there, Tiller couldn't answer the first question. The second seemed a whole lot like the first, so he let it pass and went for the third. "I reckon I have plenty to do." He held up the hammer still clutched in one hand. "At the moment, I'm supposed to be up on your roof, but I wanted to make sure you're all right."

"Why wouldn't I be?" Her scowl would blister paint.

He shrugged. "I get the feeling you women don't usually go at each other like that." He nodded at the pony. "Or you and the horse."

Mariah's gaze dropped to the ground, and her pretty mouth puckered. Tears brimmed perilously close to spilling, and she chewed her bottom lip so hard Tiller winced.

He took a step closer. "Mariah?"

With a moan, she lunged to open the stall door and fling her arms around the horse's neck. "Oh, Sheki. I'm so sorry. Did I hurt you?"

Obviously deciding to forgive, the handsome animal stood still while Mariah pressed her forehead against the side of his face.

"Miss Vee's right. I don't recognize myself either."

Tiller took off his hat. "Is there. . .anything I can do?"

Mariah shook her head against the pony. "There's nothing anyone can do." She peeked at him. "Though I'd appreciate your pardon for our behavior. I'm ashamed we aired our grievance in front of a guest."

Tiller grinned and wiggled the hammer. "I don't qualify as a guest anymore. I'm officially part of this operation."

Mariah lowered her lashes, a faint smile softening her lips. "So it's all right to rail like shrews as long as we confine it to the staff?" She straightened, staring toward the house. "I suppose I'd best go mend things with Miss Vee, or she'll mourn herself sick. I do regret saying those things to her. She's been good to me since my mother died."

Tightening the grip on his hat brim, Tiller ducked his head. "I'm real sorry."

"Thank you." She smiled. "It's been two years, but I miss her every day." Mariah left the stall and brushed past him to lean against the rail. "Miss Vee's been the closest thing to a mother ever since. I can't believe I spoke so harshly to her."

Tiller nodded. "I suspected you two were more like family than anything else. I know she can't take your ma's place, but she sure does fret like one."

Mariah studied his face. "What about you? Is it true you don't have a family? A wife or mother somewhere who worries about you?"

"A wife?" He drew back. "Hardly. No one will have me." The familiar ache filled his chest. "As for my ma"—he quirked his mouth—"she'd run me off with a broom if I stepped one foot on her porch."

Mariah laughed. "I doubt that."

Grinning, he gaped at her. "Well don't. It's a fact." He sobered and shook his head. "I have family up in North Carolina that used to care about me a little. My uncle Silas and aunt Odell plus a few rowdy cousins and a handful of friends." He sighed. "But I haven't seen them in a good long while."

Mariah tilted her head. "How long?"

"Oh, about ten years now."

"Gracious. Why?"

Tiller offered a shaky laugh. "That's a long story, and I won't bore you with it."

Her steady gaze said he hadn't fooled her. "Tell me about them."

He tucked his chin. "Really?"

She nodded.

Crossing his arms, Tiller leaned against the stall in deep thought. "My folks are Lumber River Indians from a place called Scuffletown." He shrugged. "Come to think of it, I suppose I am, too. At least a part of me."

"You're Indian?" The fact seemed to please her. "With that crop of red hair?"

Tiller grinned. "That's the other part, I suppose." He feigned an accent. "The Irish."

With an air of fascination, she scooted closer. "Keep going."

"You're sure you want to hear all this?"

"Positive."

Her earnest answer stirred his heart. "I suppose Uncle Silas sticks out in my memory the most." Warmth he'd not felt in a while made him smile. "The old man could spin a yarn from here to China. Far-fetched tales about warriors, giants, and magic lanterns." He laughed. "I was nearly sixteen. Old enough to know better, but he had me believing most of the things he said."

Mariah giggled. "What about your aunt Odell?"

Tiller stared at the ceiling. "Ah yes, Aunt Odie. She worked magic with a frying pan the way Uncle Silas did with his stories."

He shot her a sidelong glance. "If I remember right, her cooking was almost as tasty as yours." He winked. "Not quite, but close."

She bumped him with her shoulder. "And what of the cousins?"

Tiller called out their names, ticking them off with his fingers. "There was Hooper. His brother, Duncan. Their little sister, Ellie." He grinned. "And Miss Dawsey Wilkes, who was Ellie's twin sister, but no kin to the rest."

She frowned. "That makes no sense at all."

"You're right, it doesn't, but I'll try to explain. You see, Ellie was raised by my aunt and uncle instead of her real parents, so the girls never knew they had a sister until they ran into each other by accident."

Mariah angled her head. "Are you making this up?"

Laughter bubbled up from Tiller's belly, the first genuine glee he'd felt in a while. "That story's a doozey and would take all day to tell." He waved his hand. "Don't get me started."

Mariah joined in the laughter. "It sounds fascinating. You'll have to make time one day to fill me in."

The warmth of her arm pressed against his. Sobering, he turned his head toward her, wondering how she wound up so close. "I sure will, if you want me to."

"I want you to." Her big brown eyes, inches away, lured him.

His breath grew shallow, and he couldn't draw air. The floor seemed to tilt, and his ears buzzed like they were stuffed with honeybees. He longed to stroke her cheek with the back of his hand, and his fingers twitched with the urge to touch her bottom lip. "Mariah, I—"

Behind them, the pony snorted and pawed the ground, jolting Tiller's heart. Blushing, he leaped to his feet. "Look at me dawdling again. I suppose I'd best get going. I've got a roof to mend."

Mariah glanced up with a shy smile. "By all means. Now that you're part of this operation, you'll have to toe the line. I can't have an idler on my payroll."

With ease that came of much practice, Tiller slid into his cocky role as smoothly as slipping on his boots. "Well, if you'll excuse me, ma'am. . ." He tossed his hat on his head, bowed, and turned to go.

"Tiller?"

He pivoted on one heel. "Yes, boss?"

"You should go up to North Carolina. Pay your folks a visit. Sounds like you're long overdue."

Tiller worked to keep his roguish grin in place, but his traitor mouth trembled. Drawing in his bottom lip, he scraped it hard with his teeth. "Nah, it's too late. After all this time, they don't remember my name."

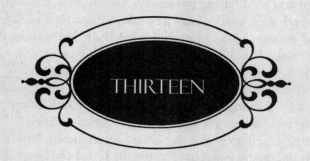

THIRTEEN

Tiller's mama is dead?"

Hooper tensed. "I'm sorry to say it's true, Pa." For a moment, he wished they'd heeded Dawsey's inclination to wait a bit before they sprang the news, but with Pa sniffing around, the story was bound to come out.

Despite the dismal report, Hooper rejoiced at being home. Inside the tiny cabin, the folks he loved most in the world huddled in a tight circle around Papa's rocking chair. The cheery fireplace crackled, stoked by Ma to ward off the morning chill. The smell of breakfast hung so thick in the air, he could almost taste crispy bacon and golden, flaky biscuits. The only thing missing from the familiar scene was his younger brother, Duncan, who married a Lumber River girl and moved across the swamp.

Papa gripped the arms of his rocker. "So my poor brother's widow passed on?"

"Yes, sir. Aunt Effie's neighbors found her five days ago. We had to bury her right away." He glanced at the twins playing a board game around the table and lowered his voice. "She'd been gone a day or so when they found her. She died all alone, though I think she might've preferred it that way."

His eyes red-rimmed and moist, Pa sat forward in his rocker. "Effie perished more than a week ago, and I'm just now finding out?"

Hooper swallowed against the tightness in his throat. He hadn't shared the worst yet. "There were. . .complications, Pa. This is the quickest we could come."

"You couldn't send a wire?"

Hooper and Dawsey exchanged glances.

Before Hooper could answer, Pa lost interest in the question. "Poor old soul." He reached over his shoulder for Ma's hand. "Effie never had much of a life, did she, Odie?"

Mama shook her head. "She did without things most folks take for granted. Her plight grew even worse after Sol died, God rest him."

Papa's jaw tightened. "If he's resting, I don't see how. I'm ashamed to speak ill of the dead, but the truth is my brother didn't provide well for his family. He left Effie and Tiller penniless, living off the kindness of strangers and begging for crumbs of bread. It's no wonder Effie sent Tiller to live with us. She didn't want the poor lad to starve."

With a quick look at Dawsey for courage, Hooper waded in. "You've got it all wrong, Pa. The only one starving Tiller was Aunt Effie. She lived poor all right, but she didn't have to."

Papa frowned. "Don't talk foolish. No sane person would live Effie's life if they had a choice."

Ma nodded in agreement. "Papa's right. What are you saying, son?"

Hooper stared at their puzzled faces. "I'm saying Aunt Effie wasn't sane. Tiller's plight grew worse when his pa died, because Uncle Sol wasn't there to stand between the boy and his mother's greed."

The high color faded from Pa's wrinkled cheeks. "Come again?"

"I'm saying Aunt Effie was a miserly old woman who never spent a nickel she didn't pinch. She died richer than Ma's apple potpie."

Mama gasped, and Pa swung his chair around and stared.

"It's true," Hooper said. "The bed Aunt Effie died on was stuffed to bursting with money." They gasped, and he nodded. "A treasure in greenbacks and gold coin."

Ellie touched Hooper's arm. "How is that possible? Tiller was a bag of bones when he came here to live."

Hooper patted his sister's hand. "I remember. He couldn't keep his trousers on without a tight pair of suspenders."

A purple vein stood out on Papa's neck. "Effie's been squirreling away money since my brother died?"

Hooper snorted. "A far sight longer, considering her bulging nest egg. The old skinflint tucked nearly every dollar Uncle Sol earned in her cotton tick mattress. Besides being tight with her family's purse strings, she inherited a sizable fortune from her parents when they died. I doubt she spent a dime of it."

Papa stared around the circle with bulging eyes. "Which means. . ."

"Tiller's a wealthy man," Mama finished, her brows lifted to her hairline. "And he doesn't even know it."

Hooper nodded. "I've deposited the money in a Fayetteville bank in Tiller's name. It's sitting there waiting for him." His fists clenched. "When I think how Aunt Effie starved that boy, made him go without, I get mad all over again."

Lowering his face to his hands, Papa groaned. "All these years I've judged my brother a shiftless no-account, begrudging his wife and son the necessities of life. When all the time, his sin was not having the backbone to stand up to Effie."

"In fairness to Uncle Sol," Hooper said, recalling his own daunting encounters with the fearsome woman, "she was a mighty hard person to stand up to."

Papa began to cry quietly, the only evidence his quivering shoulders.

Mama glanced at Hooper, and he stepped behind the chair and wrapped his arms around his papa's neck. "Don't weep, sir. I feel mighty bad to be bringing you this news. I know how you've grieved for that boy."

"And shouldn't I grieve? It's my fault he ran off. At the first spell of trouble between us, I threatened to send him back to Fayetteville, straight into Effie's stingy arms."

He gazed up at Hooper with tears wetting his cheeks. "Son, it all makes sense now. No wonder the boy ran away. In his shoes, I'd be done with the lot of us, too."

Pa wiped his face with his sleeve. "I wish he was standing here now, so I could tell him he'll never have to go without again."

Ellie squeezed in behind him and kissed the top of his head. "You tried to find him, Papa. We all did."

He raised tortured eyes. "But we quit looking. We never should've stopped until that boy was home again."

Wyatt slid his arm around Ellie's waist. "Sir, my family searched for Nathan right alongside you. It's tough to find someone who doesn't want to be found."

Ma patted Wyatt's back. "Forgive us, dear. We get so caught up in mourning Tiller, we forget your brother's missing, too."

Wyatt shot her a wry glance. "You're being kind, Miss Odie. We all know Nathan's not missing. He ran away and hauled your nephew with him." He sighed. "Tiller was just a boy. Nathan was old enough to know better." He gripped the arm of Papa's chair. "Mr. Silas, if anybody's at fault, it's my little brother."

Pa wagged his grizzled head. "I suppose the days for blame is past, son. Ten years have come and gone since those two left the swamp. God forgive us, what did we do with the time?"

Ellie knelt at his side. "We built homes and bore children, pitched in to help Scuffletown recover from the war. It's been a busy time for us all, but things are quieter now." She glanced around the room. "Why can't we start our search again?"

Hooper gave her a tender smile. "Actually, that's why we're here. I aim to do just that. And this time I'm going to look until I find them."

Ellie's face lit up, and she shot to her feet. "I'll go."

Leaning to see around her, Hooper widened his eyes at Wyatt. "What do you say, old man? I'd like for you and Ellie both to come."

A tiny frown rippled Wyatt's forehead. "But, sugar. . .what about our boys?"

Hooper nodded at his wife. "That's one reason Dawsey's here. She's willing to stay behind and care for the twins."

Wyatt flashed Dawsey a grimace then pushed back his hair with both hands. "I don't know, Hoop. We could be gone for weeks. Dawsey doesn't realize what she's signing on for."

Ma pushed into the circle, worrying a tattered dishrag. "I'll help out, Wyatt. I'll go over to your place every day to untie her and put out the fires."

Dawsey's wide eyes swung to the boys. All four wore angelic smiles.

Hooper absently patted her shoulder, his attention turning to Ellie. "It's a long time to be away from your boys, little sis. I wouldn't ask if you didn't track a man better than a hound dog."

Pa shook his head. "There's nothing left to track. The trail is long cold."

"Maybe not." Hooper squatted in front of the rocker. "Aunt Effie's neighbor spoke of a local fellow who went to see Effie a few months before she died. This man had just returned from a trip to Mississippi. He swore he saw Tiller strolling along the boardwalk in a town by the name of Canton."

Pa's eyes lit up. "You don't say?"

"Aunt Effie called him a fool among other names. She said he had to be drunk or seeing things because Tiller was dead and gone. That got him mad, so he's had plenty to say around town. I looked him up and talked to him myself."

"And?" Pa asked.

"I believe him. I think the man he saw was Tiller."

"Why do you set such stock in a stranger's opinion?"

"Because"—Hooper's gaze jumped to each of them in turn—"when the stranger called Tiller's name, he spun around to look and then ducked down an alley."

Excitement surged in the room like the tension before a storm.

"And Nathan?" Wyatt asked, his tone hopeful.

"Sorry, buddy. Tiller appeared to be alone, but if he's in Canton, Mississippi, you can bet Nathan's close by."

The corners of Papa's eyes crinkled the way they did when he was thinking. "I know where Canton is. About twenty. . .thirty days' ride on a good horse."

"Thirty days," Ma said. "That's a long time."

Hooper nodded. "Yes, it is. That's why we're taking the train. We'll book passage to Jackson then hire some horses. If we have to, we'll ride every inch of the state until we find a good lead."

Wyatt worried his bottom lip, his brow creased in thought. "Suppose Nathan and Tiller don't want to be found, Hoop? Did you consider that possibility? We're not looking for boys this time around. They're grown men and likely to be settled somewhere. Raising families."

Pa slapped the arm of his chair. "No sir, I don't believe that for a minute. Those two have been up to no good. Only shame will keep a man away from home and family this long." He sighed. "Still. . .we can't let that stop us."

He shifted his gaze to the glowing hearth. "Tiller may not want to be found—that wouldn't surprise me—but if the boy ever decides to come home, it'll start by learning he's welcome."

FOURTEEN

Mariah stuck her muddy foot under the spout and worked the pump's squeaky handle. Ice-cold water shot out in a burst, splashing her bare ankles. She squealed and jumped back then forced her toes under the flow, wiggling to wash the thick, dried clay from between them.

Next she washed the basket of lettuce she'd cut from the garden. She told herself she might as well pick a few heads while she was dressed for grubbing in the dirt. In truth, she was stalling while she found the right words to apologize to Miss Vee.

Shading her eyes, she scanned the rooftop until she found Tiller kneeling next to the side gable. As hard as she tried, she couldn't stop watching him.

He had rolled up his sleeves and unbuttoned his shirt since leaving the barn, probably once he climbed onto the sun-baked shingles. A dark circle of sweat moistened his back, and his shirttails flapped in the breeze.

She admired the pleasing way his chest appeared chiseled and his tanned skin glistened in the sun. Even more, she liked how he'd laughed like a small boy in the barn and then gazed at her so boldly. In his own way, Tiller McRae was more fetching than the sons of Tobias Jones.

Stop it, Mariah! Embarrassed, she tugged her attention back to washing her feet.

She may as well get such thoughts right out of her head. No matter how striking she found him, she needed a weak-willed nahullo. One she could lead by the nose and persuade to do her will. Swaggering, self-assured Tiller simply wouldn't do.

By his own admission, he lived the life of an aimless drifter with no family ties. Not exactly the sort of man to trust with the reins to Bell's Inn. Or with her heart.

Balancing on one foot at a time, she dried them on her dress. Giving the handle one last crank, she leaned to the spigot for a drink and saw Tiller from the corner of her eye, watching from the roof. By his appreciative stare and the way his hammer slowed, Tiller found her just as much the distraction. Mariah hid her smile and pretended not to notice.

Straightening, she started across the yard, glancing up in time to see Tiller miss the nail and hit his thumb. With a howl of pain, he shook the battered appendage then stuffed it in his mouth.

She covered her mouth to suppress a giggle and scurried across the yard to the back porch. Ducking through the door into the kitchen, she paused at the mirror to gape at her dirt-streaked chin and messy hair, mortified that she'd sat with Tiller in the barn acting the grand lady when she looked like a windblown wretch.

She needed to change her soggy, mud-splattered dress, but first she'd find Miss Vee and beg forgiveness.

"Mornin' again."

Mariah spun, clutching her bodice, and glared at Dicey grinning from the pantry. "Dicey Turner! Must you creep around all the time?"

Dicey tilted her head. "Since when is fetching the lard creepin'? Folks in this house mighty jumpy." Her startled gaze leaped to Mariah's tangled locks and filthy dress. Pointing as if Mariah might not be aware of her bedraggled state, she gasped. "Look here what the cat dragged in. What done happen to you?"

"Never mind. Just get on with the piecrusts then start kneading the bread. It'll be lunchtime soon."

Still staring, Dicey heaved the lard bucket to the counter. "Yes'm, but I hope you plan to wash up and change 'fore you start messin' about this kitchen."

Mariah smiled. "I'm going upstairs to clean up, but I'll come right back in to help." She started for the hall then turned. "When you're done with the dough, run out to the smokehouse and get a ham. If I'm not back in time, trim the fat for a pot of beans and put the rest in the oven. While you're there, bring in a link of venison sausage." Remembering Tiller, she glanced toward the roof. "Best make it three."

"Miss Mariah, you sure?" Dicey blinked her confusion. "It ain't like we got us a full house. Who gon' eat all that?"

Mariah sidestepped to the mirror again to wind a coil of hair at the base of her neck. "They'll come. I'm praying hard for guests."

"You praying for miracles."

"We need one," Mariah said over her shoulder. "The coffers are on their last breath. In the meantime, we have meat in store and a man on the roof working up a healthy appetite."

Dicey rolled her eyes. "Ain't nothin' healthy 'bout the way he eat. For a tall, skinny man, he got a reckless hunger."

Mariah's fingers stilled on her hair. "You really think he's too thin? I don't find him the least bit skinny."

Dicey cocked her head to the side and grinned. "Uh, huh. It's like that, is it? Jus' how does you find him?"

Tugging her eyes from the mirror and the slow flush crawling up her neck, Mariah turned. "Miss Vee's been reading to you from those trashy dime novels again. Now, where did she get off to?"

"She tending that old man. He finally decide to wake up."

"He did? Oh, Dicey, why didn't you say so?"

Dicey cocked her hip. "I jus' did."

Mariah hurried down the hallway to what she'd come to think of as the sickroom. Pausing at the door, she cautiously peered inside.

Miss Vee had a chair pulled up to the bed, her back and shoulders rounded as she leaned to feed her patient spoonfuls of what appeared to be oatmeal.

Otis Gooch sat up in bed, dutifully opening his mouth. He gummed the cereal with pursed lips, smacking disgracefully.

"Last bite," Miss Vee said then wiped his mouth as if he were a child. Standing, she placed the bowl on the nightstand.

Mariah slipped up from behind and caught her hand, stretching to whisper in her ear. "Forgive me?"

Miss Vee's rigid body relaxed. Her fingers twined with Mariah's and squeezed. "Look, honey. Our patient's on the mend."

Mr. Gooch lay propped against two pillows, a weak but contented smile on his face. "If my head didn't hurt so fierce, I'd swear the Almighty sent two ministering angels to escort me home." He chuckled. "But I reckon I'm still earthbound. If'n I was in heaven, you wouldn't be covered in muck, little missy." The man peered closer. "Though I'm thinking this one might be one of your angels, Lord, muddy or not. She sure looks like one."

Mariah smiled down at him. "No angel here, sir. Just a flesh and blood woman, uncommonly prone to frailties and faults." She glanced over her shoulder. "Just ask my dear friend."

Mr. Gooch winked. "Honey, you'll do just fine."

He held out his trembling hand and Mariah took it, settling in Miss Vee's vacated chair. The bony fingers felt fragile in her grip, and the wrinkled, paper-thin skin softer than silk to the touch.

"I can't tell you how grateful I am," he said. "You folks are like the Good Samaritan come to life right out of the scriptures."

Mariah shook her head. "Not at all. We're just the innkeepers. The real Samaritans were the men who brought you here and left without telling us their names. They saved your life."

He frowned and tilted his head. "One of them a red-haired fella? I seem to remember someone. . ."

Mariah patted his hand. "You must mean Mr. McRae. He's a guest here." She glanced at Miss Vee. "At least he was until we hired him on. He works for us now, so you'll be seeing him again."

"Well, that's good because I—" He grimaced, and his wobbly hand rose to his temple. "I want to thank him, too."

Miss Vee touched Mariah's shoulder. "Come along, sugar. We're tiring him."

Standing, Mariah stepped aside to let Miss Vee move closer to the bed. She pulled the extra pillow from behind Otis's head, easing him down. "You rest up, now. I'll brew a cup of feverfew tea for that headache."

Wincing, he shaded his eyes against the light. "I don't want you ladies fretting about the cost of my keep. I can pay you for your trouble. You can count on that." Struggling to sit up again, he waved his skinny arm. "I have money. Lots of it. My whole life savings is"—he strained forward, craning his neck to search the room—"s–somewhere."

His bleary gaze focused on a point across the room, and he lifted one bent finger. "There he is. That's the man I was talking about."

Miss Vee and Mariah turned toward the door, but no one was there. They gave each other knowing looks.

"Well, I'll be." The poor man seemed confused. "The fella' disappeared. Just like that." He blinked at Mariah. "Why's he all wet?"

Squeezing past Miss Vee, she gripped his shoulders and urged him against the bed. "Just rest, Mr. Gooch."

Grinning, he waved her off. "I ain't never been mister nobody, honey. Call me Otis."

Moaning, he relaxed as if suddenly spent, and then his eyelids flew open again. "Say, did I ever thank you nice girls for helping me?"

"I'll fetch that tea," Miss Vee said, backing away. She motioned for Mariah to follow and hurried from the room. In the hallway, she pulled Mariah toward the kitchen, whispering in a low voice. "I swear, that old man is a caution. Do you reckon he was already crazy, or can a bump on the head bring on insanity?"

Mariah bit back a smile. "Shame on you, Viola Ashmore. How can you speak so harshly about such a kindhearted old gentleman? I don't think Mr. Gooch is crazy." She shrugged. "A bit peculiar perhaps."

"A bit?" Miss Vee clutched her arm. "One minute he's talking to God like He's perched at the foot of the bed, the next he sees Jesus peeking around the corner."

"Is that really so bad? We should all be having more talks with God."

"Maybe so, but he's seeing things that aren't there and forgetting the rest."

Mariah glanced behind them and shushed her. "Mr. Gooch has a nasty bump on the head. I'm sure he'll be fine in a few days." She frowned. "I'm more concerned about the other thing he said."

"What other thing?"

"Didn't you see? He was searching for his money." Mariah pressed her fists to her temples and groaned. "Evidently, his attackers robbed him of all he had." Hot tears stung her eyes. "The poor old soul. He said it was his life savings."

Miss Vee shook her head. "It's a pitiful shame, that's what it is."

They reached the entrance to the kitchen, and Mariah followed her inside. Tiller glanced up from the table where he sat draining a tumbler of lemonade.

Dicey stood over him, ready to pour another glass as soon as he finished. "It must be blazing hot on that roof," she said, fanning him with a dishcloth. "This poor man be drenched in sweat."

Tiller had stumbled into Otis Gooch's room, looked fate in the eye, then tucked tail and ran.

The old man had recognized him. Pointed him out. Instead of numbering his days at Bell's Inn, Tiller could count his stay in minutes, maybe seconds, depending on what Otis told Mariah.

His hand shook as he raised his glass for another long swig of the tart drink. Looking everywhere but straight at them, he waited for the ruckus sure to come.

Climbing off the roof after he made the repairs for Mariah felt good. For the first time in years, he'd used his hands for something useful. Leaving meant she'd be back in the same rough patch where he'd found her, burdened with a broken-down inn. And he'd be back on the Trace, running from what he'd become.

Funny how the work he wasn't sure he should take on suddenly seemed like the most important job in the world.

"Miss Mariah, why you still sashaying around in them filthy clothes?"

Tiller stole a peek out of the corner of his eye. Dicey was right. Mariah wore the same dirty dress, the mud splatter dried to light patches and her hem a stiff gray circle around her feet.

He might've smiled if his situation weren't so dire. He'd never seen a woman so opposed to wearing shoes.

"I'm going up now to change, but lest I forget"—she tapped his shoulder—"Mr. Gooch would like to see you when he wakes up."

Tiller's heart sped up and his mind raced. So, that's how much time he had, as long as it took an old man to take a nap.

Odd how Mariah didn't sound angry. Maybe she handled things differently than most.

He scratched his head, trying to think. Could it be that Gooch didn't tell them what he knew, so he could run Tiller off himself?

Miss Vee chuckled, the sound grating on his taut nerves. "He wants to thank you, Tiller." She shook her head. "Again."

His puzzled frown bounced between them. "For what?"

The women laughed.

"He thanks us over and over for helping him," Mariah said. "Each time he wakes up, he repeats himself again. Poor soul can't remember a thing."

The mirth disappeared from Miss Vee's face. "I'm telling you, Mariah, he's worse off than we thought, and that whack on the head could be the cause." She pointed toward Otis's room. "The old codger has lost his memory right along with his good sense."

Tiller raised his head. "Mr. Gooch can't remember?"

Ignoring him, Miss Vee took a sugar spoon from the counter to scratch up under her mound of red curls. "You reckon we should fetch Doc Moony after all?"

Mariah's body tensed and her hands fisted. If she'd been drinking from a cup, the inn would be short another piece of china. "Oh, I don't think that's necessary. Not just yet. Let's give him a chance to heal. He's bound to be as good as new in a day or so."

With a strained laugh, she clutched the skirt of her dress and stared at the smear of grass stains. "For heaven's sake, I need to get out of this silly thing."

"Been telling her that all mornin' long," Dicey pointed out.

As Mariah rushed up the winding stairs, Tiller wondered why she'd picked that particular moment to listen.

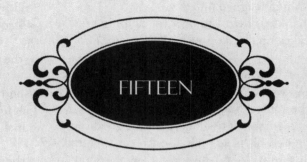

FIFTEEN

Mariah stripped off her dress then splashed her mud-freckled legs and sweaty face with cold water. Going downstairs to heat more would take too much time from her mission.

After washing off, she fumbled with the strings of a clean petticoat and barely laced her corset. Pulling on her stockings and a clean frock, she hurried out the door.

Five paces from the stairs she remembered her blasted shoes and ran back to slip them on. Taking the steps by twos, she raced across the parlor, not slowing until she reached the door to Otis Gooch's room.

In the light of Miss Vee's fears, she had to see him again to reassure herself that he was all right. If not, did she have the courage to call Dr. Moony?

Outside the door she spun, pressing her back to the wall. *Mother, what have you done to me?*

"Who—who's out there?"

There was nothing wrong with his hearing.

Mariah drew a deep breath and pasted on a smile. "Only me, sir," she trilled, edging into the room. She approached the bed, her trembling hands behind her back, praying Miss Vee was wrong. "Am I disturbing you?"

Otis seemed groggy, the effects of the feverfew tea. "Not at all."

He struggled to sit up, but Mariah hustled to his side and touched his shoulder. "Please don't rouse yourself. I won't stay long."

He smiled. "Stay as long as you like, missy. I'm grateful for the company." With a shaky finger, he pointed to the bowl and pitcher on the dressing table. "You wouldn't mind wetting a rag, so's I could wash my face?"

Mariah hopped up. "Of course not." Dipping a cloth in the steaming bowl, she wrung it out and handed it to him.

Otis buried his face in it and moaned. Concerned, she bent over him, but he emerged with a toothless grin. "There. Don't that feel better? I was getting a mite crusty." When he finished washing, including his neck and ears, he returned the rag with a contented sigh.

Relieved to see him acting so spry, Mariah sat back in the chair and crossed her arms.

Watching her, Otis leaned back and crossed his, too. "Whatever you're itching to say, you might as well get it said."

She launched forward, resting her hands on her knees. "How are you, Mr. Gooch? I mean, how do you really feel?"

His brows knitted. "Well, my headache seems lessened today." He reached for his bandage. "Still hurts to push on my wound, but I expect that's normal."

"Do you believe you're on the mend?"

Otis shrugged. "I ain't no doctor, little lady, so I'm not smart enough to say." He motioned her closer. "But I had me a talk with God, and He reminded me I'm in good shape either way." He pursed his lips and winked.

Mariah tilted her head. "It's interesting that you should mention a doctor because I was wondering—"

"If you're asking if I'm about to breathe my last, the answer is no. I'm too miserable to die." He gazed around the room. "And too hungry. Got any more of that oatmeal?"

The burden lifting from around her heart, she reached for his hand and gave it a squeeze. "We can do a whole lot better than oatmeal, if you think you're up to it."

He rubbed his stomach. "I'm up to it, all right."

"How does a bowl of beans and a link of venison sausage sound?"

He sat up straighter and rubbed his hands together. "With a square of buttered corn bread?"

She preened. "The best in Mississippi, or so I've been told."

His eyes lit up, the twinkle so bright it chased Mariah's fears to the shadows. "Fetch me them vittles," Otis said. "See if I don't make quick work of them."

Laughing, she patted his hand. "Give us a while to get it ready, and we'll give you a chance to prove yourself."

Plain tired of running.

Tiller braced his hands on each side of the washstand and leaned to stare at his ashen face in the mirror. The green striped walls of the cozy room, more like home than any place he'd slept in years, closed in around him, urging him to make a decision.

If Otis Gooch planned to accuse him, he'd just as soon have it done. Waiting for the gallows floor to drop from beneath him had his stomach twisted in knots. The old man had asked to see him, and it seemed like the perfect time.

"March down to that room," Tiller ordered his reflection. "Take a front row seat, and give Otis a good long look to be certain."

If the old man sat up and pointed the finger, Tiller had two options worked out in his mind. He could apologize. Lay his hand on the Bible Mr. Gooch set such stock in and swear he'd mended his ways. He'd confess that meeting him on the road had triggered a change of heart. He'd throw himself on Gooch's mercy and promise to repay every cent if only he'd keep his mouth shut to Mariah. If that didn't work, he'd deny the charge and swear the man's injury had addled his mind.

Tiller stilled as the second idea turned to soot and sifted away, leaving him nowhere to hide. What was happening to him? How could he consider confronting his doom? He must've fried his own brain on that blasted hot roof.

"Like I told you before," he said to his image, "I'm plain tired of running."

He dried his face so hard his whiskers chafed, threw the towel in the laundry bin, and smoothed back his hair. A haircut and shave were in order. He'd ask one of the women first thing in the morning. . .if he was still around.

With the slow easy pace of a man who'd made peace with his fate,

Tiller strolled down the hall to the last room on the left and peered inside. Clutching the doorpost, he drew back and stiffened to bolt.

"This is my lucky day," Mr. Gooch crowed. "Two visitors at once. Come in here, boy. Don't be shy."

Too late to escape, Tiller gritted his teeth and shifted back into sight. "How do, sir."

Mariah peered over her shoulder. "You'll be happy to hear Otis is much better today."

Sweating like Judas on judgment day, Tiller's courage waned. "I'll come back later. I don't want to barge in."

Otis waved his scrawny arm. "You ain't barging into nothing, and that lintel don't need you to hold it up. Get over here."

The urge to duck his head tugged at Tiller's chin. *No sir. No more hiding.* He raised it high instead and strode to the foot of the bed.

The closer he came, the wider Mr. Gooch's welcoming smile.

Tiller tried to smile in return, but his lips felt like wood. "How are you feeling, sir?"

"A sight better than yesterday, thank ye. I was just telling the little missy here that I'm feeling mighty hungry." He quirked his brows. "That's a good sign, ain't it?"

Mariah's merry laugh eased the tightness from Tiller's shoulders. "You're making up for lost time, I suppose."

Mr. Gooch nodded. "I don't remember the last thing I ate until those few paltry spoons of oatmeal."

Mariah squeezed his knobby hand. "Poor man." Her tone hardened. "Heaven knows how long those ruffians left you lying there helpless."

Tiller's stomach flipped, squashing his resolve. His shuffling feet itched to race for the door.

"I've been pondering that myself," Mr. Gooch murmured, scratching his balding head. "Do you suppose the men who brought me here could be the same gang who ambushed me to start with?" He bobbed his head. "You know, riding for help once their consciences started throbbing?"

Mariah spun with a little gasp. "Do you suppose Otis could be right, Tiller? Did we entertain the very devils who beat and robbed him?" Her pretty brow creased. "By the grace of God we didn't wind up sharing his fate." Realizing what she'd said, her hand rushed to her mouth. "Oh, Otis. . ."

All the starch seemed to drain from his wasted body. His shoulders slumped against the headboard, his watery gaze fixed on the ceiling while he stared down the awful news. "They got my money?" He flinched. "My horse and wagon, too?"

Her fingers pressed to her lips, Mariah nodded. "You had nothing when they brought you here. I'm so sorry."

Staring overhead, he gnawed the inside of his cheek. "Well, sure they took it. I'm a fool to think otherwise." He touched his head. "That's why they gave me this knot." He cut his eyes to Mariah. "Don't feel bad, little missy. I'd have figured it out for myself once my head cleared."

Regret twisted his features. "It took me the better part of my days to save that stash. All gone in a wink."

Shame torched Tiller's gut. Swallowing an apology along with rising bile, he decided on the spot to pay Otis back every dollar, however long it took.

Mariah scooted closer and caught Mr. Gooch's trembling hand. "I don't want you worrying about all this right now. Rest assured that you have a place here as long as you need one. If you decide to go home when you're able, we'll make sure you get there."

Otis shook his head. "I've been a traveling merchant for years. That rig was my home."

Tears spilled onto his gaunt cheeks. "I'll never understand how greed and pure raw meanness can drive one man to hurt another for gain." His swimming gaze sought Tiller's. "Then I run across a kindhearted saint like you, and my hope is restored." He smiled through his tears. "Young fella', I know you washed me, dressed me, sat by my sickbed, and I want to thank you."

Tiller's hand shot up. "You don't need to thank me." He quickly checked the bitterness in his voice and tried again. "Anybody would've done the same."

Mr. Gooch wagged his head. "Not with the care I sensed in your hands." He lifted his chin. "You're truly sorry about what happened to me, aren't you? I felt it in your touch."

Startled by the need to bawl, Tiller blinked and shoved his fists in his pockets.

"That's all right, boy," Mr. Gooch said. "I didn't mean to embarrass you. Just mighty grateful is all."

He pulled free of Mariah's grip and patted her hand. "I'd like to be alone for a spell if you youngsters don't mind. I need to ask God for strength to forgive before a root of bitterness springs up to defile my soul." He paused. "Fair warning from the book of Hebrews if anyone cares to look it up."

Mariah stood. "We'll leave you now. I'll come back soon with your lunch."

Tiller couldn't wait to get out the door. He didn't have the guts to look at Mariah, but he felt her watching him. Head down, he stepped aside at the threshold so she could go first.

"By the way," Mr. Gooch called in a frantic voice. "Did I ever thank you nice folks for helping me?"

Stopping so fast she skidded, Mariah cast a worried glance at Tiller. "Oh my," she whispered hoarsely then turned to Mr. Gooch with a weak smile. "Y–yes, sir. You sure did."

Otis released his breath on a ragged sigh and lay back in the bed. "Good. That's real good to hear."

Mariah's shoulders drooped as low as Tiller's as he followed her from the room.

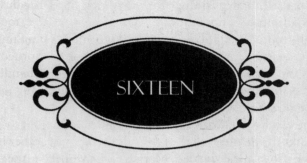

SIXTEEN

Tiller drove a nail into the final board of the new porch and stood up to survey his work. For a man more suited to working the soil than plying a hammer, he had to admit the even rows of cedar planks looked smart. Lifting his hat to wipe his brow, he glanced at his helper. "What do you think, Rainy?"

"Yes, suh." The boy grinned and bobbed his head. "Ain't nothin' wrong with this porch. We make a fine team, don't we, Mista' Tilla'?"

"You certainly do," a voice said from inside the back door. Mariah stepped out with a tray in her hand and tiptoed across the porch like a cat on coals.

Tiller chuckled. "It's all right to walk on it, Mariah."

She beamed. "I can't help it. It's too pretty."

Shrugging, Tiller laid aside the hammer. "I never thought of a porch as pretty, but I suppose this one will do. It'll look a lot nicer once we add the steps and get the rails up."

Mariah handed the tray to Rainy. "I can hardly wait to see it finished. What a wonderful surprise to find all this beautiful lumber behind the barn. Why, it's practically brand new."

Tiller glanced at the boy.

He smiled and ducked his head.

"I've brought you two your lunch," Mariah said. "You deserve a special treat after all your hard work."

Tiller reached for a mug of cold lemonade and held it up. "I don't know if I deserve it, but I sure am grateful." He took a long swig then held out his hand to help Mariah down, brushing away sawdust to clear a place for her to sit. "Those sandwiches look mighty nice, too."

Rainy nodded. "Mista' Tilla' took the words right out of my mouth."

Tiller lifted one corner of the thinly sliced bread. "Corned beef?"

"Spread with fresh dressing I made myself." Mariah handed one to each of them and took one for herself.

Tiller took a hearty bite then winked at her. "Good."

She ducked her head and smiled. "Thank you."

They settled along the edge of the porch, eating together in silence. Tiller stole glances at Mariah, wondering how it was possible he'd known her for such a short while. It took him years to build a fortress around his heart. She'd scaled the walls in six short days.

He'd tried to fight his tender feelings, but the time for turning back was past. He was utterly besotted with her.

"Missy Bell, my sunflower patch be coming up nice," Rainy said. "They poppin' out now, so they'll have nice-sized heads before long."

"Budding already?"

"Yes'm." He gave her a timid smile. "I thank you for letting me plant 'em this year."

"I thought it was a fine idea." She wiped the corner of her mouth on a napkin. "I'd love to see them."

Rainy shoved the last quarter of his sandwich inside his bulging cheek and hopped to his feet, swiping crumbs from his baggy trousers. "I can show you right now."

Tiller laughed. "Rein it in, son. The lady's not done eating." He understood the boy's eagerness. He remembered the joy he once felt from growing a nice head of lettuce or a pretty rose.

Wrapping her sandwich in a napkin, Mariah stood. "I can finish while we walk." She motioned to Tiller. "Come go with us."

They crossed the backyard and took the little stone path to the garden gate. Rainy led them inside, past the tomato stakes and raised beds to the neat row of sunflower plants in the corner. A dozen flowers, each with new buds, stretched proudly toward the sky.

Mariah sighed. "They're going to be beautiful, Rainy."

He seemed to grow taller. "Much obliged, ma'am. Only I don't mind what they look like. I'm in it for the seeds."

Squeezing his shoulder, she laughed. "I sort of look forward to those myself." She gently stroked one of the small green and yellow knots. "Isn't it wonderful how they all face the same direction?"

Tiller took a second look. "How about that? I never once noticed."

"It's a mystery," Mariah said. "From the time the flowers form, they follow the sun across the sky, all in step like tiny dancers."

Evidently as ignorant of the facts as Tiller, Rainy leaned closer to stare. "Well, I'll be switched. They sho' is."

"Each morning they wake up facing east," Mariah said. "By evening, they're watching while the sun sets in the west. Then overnight their little heads swivel around again to greet the sunrise."

Rainy looked duly impressed. "Do tell?"

She nodded. "Once the flowers reach full bloom, they bow to the eastern sky until they die. My father told me they're watching for Christ's return." Sadness darkened her eyes. "He said the sunflower is our example to follow Jesus throughout our lives then go to our graves awaiting his return."

Silence stole over the garden.

Rainy glanced at the distant, haunted stare on Mariah's face and promptly squatted to pull weeds.

Tiller fought the urge to reach for her. Confused by her sudden gloominess, he cleared his throat. "Your father sounds like a fine man. I hope I'll get to meet him someday."

Her baffling sadness turned to great, swimming tears. Brushing them off her cheeks, she spun away.

"Mariah?" He touched her shoulder. "Did I say something wrong?"

"No." She sniffed and shook her head. "It's just a lovely memory, that's all. I suppose I'm missing him."

Shading his eyes, Rainy peered up from the ground. "I didn't go to make you sad, ma'am."

She held out her arms. "Oh Rainy, come here." He came, flushed and shuffling his feet, and she wrapped him in a tight hug. "You didn't do one thing wrong. In fact, it's a compliment to your skill." She held him at arm's length. "Your flowers are pretty enough to make a lady cry."

He flashed a pleased grinned. "Yes'm, Missy Bell. Thank you kindly, ma'am."

She released him and started back up the row. "You've outdone yourself with the rest of the garden, too. It's simply wonderful this year."

"That's on account of it ain't just me," Rainy said, falling in behind her. "Mista' Tilla' been out here, too. Most every day."

Mariah stopped short and turned. "You've been helping in the garden?"

Tiller released a shaky laugh. "Yes, but I take no credit. All the praise goes to Rainy."

"Ain't so, ma'am. Mista' Tilla' got sap for blood. This old patch rise up and clap when it see him coming."

Beginning to squirm under her bold stare, Tiller's cheeks warmed.

"I don't understand," Mariah said. "With all you've accomplished lately, how have you found the time?"

"It only takes a minute here and there."

Concern tightened her mouth. "You really don't have to take on the gardening, as well. It's too much."

He shrugged. "I do it because I like it. Of course, if you mind. . ."

"Mind?" A happy smile lit her face. "Of course not. As long as you two are happy with the arrangement."

"Don't bother me none," Rainy said, winking at Tiller. "We make a fine team."

The back door slammed, turning all their heads at once. Dicey walked to the edge of the porch, the back of one hand resting on her hip and the other shading her eyes. She scanned the yard in a slow arc, stopping when she faced the garden. "There you is, Rainy Boswell," she bellowed.

"She lookin' for me?" Rainy asked in a shrill voice. "Curse my no-account luck. I cain't get away from that burdensome woman."

Tiller chuckled. "What have you done now?"

"It ain't what I done. It's what she want. I wish I'd never struck no bargain to walk her home. She a heap more than a penny's worth of trouble."

Dicey sailed to the earth and bore down on them, her calico dress and white apron flapping in the breeze. She blew past the gate and chugged toward them in a rolling gait. "My daddy gon' be fit to bust, waitin' all day for his lunch. Where you been hidin'?"

"You know where I been. . .helping Mista' Tilla' with the porch."

She ground to a stop and cocked her hip. "I don't see no porch out here. If you growing one, I want me a peek at it." She snatched his sleeve. "Now come on." At the gate, she paused. "You done a fine job building that new porch, Mista' Tilla'. A mighty-fine job."

Tiller ducked to hide his smile. "Thank you, Dicey."

"You welcome."

Their bickering voices echoed across the yard until they slipped past the tree line and disappeared.

Mariah's lilting laugh eased Tiller's heart. "If Rainy was a bit older, they'd make a nice couple."

He laughed with her. "What are you saying? Those two would kill each other before the 'I do's' were said."

"Oh, I don't know." She grew thoughtful. "My mother was spirited, too. Not in the same way as Dicey, but at times she led my father a merry chase."

Tiller followed Mariah outside the gate to a wrought iron bench under a tall maple.

She sat and motioned for him to join her. "My parents were happy though." Her mouth softened and the corners quirked. "They loved each other very much, but I suppose they had to with all they fought to be together."

Tiller slid closer. "What do you mean?"

"Their union was frowned upon by both her tribesmen and my father's people. In fact, his grandparents in England got wind of the marriage and disinherited him."

"That hardly seems fair."

She shook her head. "It wasn't. These days, people are slightly more accepting. Back then, it was very hard."

Tiller couldn't stop watching Mariah worry the folds of her dress nestled in her lap. He itched to reach for her fingers, to cradle her hand and see if it felt as soft and warm as he imagined. "I'm glad folks are more agreeable now," he murmured.

"You are?"

Pulling his gaze from her hands, he squirmed on the seat. "Well, sure. Like I said, it's not fair to treat people so harshly. A person can't help who they love."

She straightened proudly. "It doesn't bother you that my mother was Choctaw?"

"Not a whit."

Tucking her chin, she tilted her head closer and lowered her voice to just above a whisper. "I'm pleased you feel that way, Tiller. I'm glad you're fair-minded and kind and not prejudiced against other cultures."

He swayed to meet her. She smelled of sawdust and tea leaves, green garden shoots, and the wind in her hair. "Mariah. . ." His hand inched toward hers. "Would you mind if I—"

A series of whistles split the air, like the call of a nearby bird.

Mariah leaped to her feet as if she'd been fired on, whirling to stare at the woods behind them.

Laughing, Tiller stood and steadied her shoulders. "Relax. It's just a silly mockingbird."

Still watching the verge, she shook her head.

Two men strode from the woods, one as tall as an oak, the other sturdy and broad.

Mariah stiffened beneath his hands.

Tiller took a second look and saw they were the sons of the Indian healer.

They strutted across the clearing with the sun on their faces, as proud as buck deer and confidence in every step. Two worthy specimens. The pride of the Choctaw.

Fisting his hands, Tiller clenched his teeth and exhaled his frustration.

Mariah watched the brothers come with mixed emotions. Though always happy to see them, their pleasing manner and striking looks affected her good sense.

She usually found herself staring at one or the other, hanging on their words, and laughing too loud at their jokes. Whatever power they had over her behavior, she felt uncomfortable to have Tiller in the mix—especially since he'd caught her at it once before.

"*Halito!*" Christopher called as they drew near.

"Halito!" Mariah shouted.

Justin's handsome face broke into a grin. *"Chim-achukma."*

"I am well. *Chishnato?"*

"Can't complain."

"What brings you? To barter for more corn bread?"

Chris laughed. "Our father sent us to ask about the old man."

"His name is Otis Gooch," Mariah said. "And thankfully he improves more each day." She frowned. "Though I wish Tobias had come himself. There is the matter of his forgetting things. His memory seems a little shaky."

Justin, in training to be the tribe's next healer, tilted his head. "He's well on in years, Mariah. I doubt it has much to do with his injury, but I'll mention it to Father."

Chris placed his arm around Mariah. "How are you, Lotus Flower? Looking lovely, I must say." He leaned to peer at her feet. "I see you're wearing your shoes today."

Mariah's cheeks warmed. She'd grown up alongside the brothers and their familiar behavior, but Tiller had no way of knowing Chris meant no harm. She lowered her shoulder and let his arm slide away. "Do you remember Tiller McRae?"

"I believe so." Justin stretched out his hand. "You're staying at the inn, aren't you?"

"Yes." Tiller shook both their hands. "But not as a guest. Mariah put me on the payroll."

She nodded eagerly. "Tiller's making our repairs, and doing a wonderful job. Wait until you see the new porch."

Chris pointed over their shoulders. "Right here at the back door? Well, let's go see."

"It's not finished," Tiller said. "It lacks steps and a rail."

Mariah glanced at him. He seemed less than eager to show off his work.

She smiled at the brothers. "I'd ask if you're hungry, but it's a pointless question."

"Well. . ." Justin rubbed his stomach. "It's a mighty long walk from our place to yours."

Mariah laughed. "Follow me, and I'll make you a corned beef sandwich. While you're here, I'll introduce you to Mr. Gooch. He's a very nice man."

"Sure," Chris said. "But will he remember meeting us?"

Mariah punched his arm. "Oh, stop."

Tiller lagged behind on the walk to the house, so Mariah wound up flanked by the burly brothers, sparring and vying for her attention as they always did. Sensing Tiller watching their backs, she didn't enjoy the flattery as much as usual.

She showed off the porch, careful to brag on Tiller's workmanship.

Chris and Justin ran their hands over the wood then climbed up and tested the strength of the braces with little hops. They seemed fittingly impressed by Tiller's skill.

As Tiller helped her onto the porch, he leaned close to her ear. "No one ever taught those two how to button their shirts?"

She pushed down the laughter bubbling inside. Self-assured Tiller McRae was jealous!

"Be thankful they're wearing shirts," she whispered back then led the procession to the kitchen.

Tiller pulled down a glass from the shelf. "I'll just grab another serving of lemonade then get back to work."

Mariah shot him a little frown. "Can't it wait? We'd love to have you join us, and I know you have room for more corned beef."

"Nah," he said, pouring from the pitcher. "I'd like to finish that porch before nightfall."

"Are you sure?"

His mouth a grim line, he tipped his hat and backed out the door.

Watching the brothers devour the rest of the beef, Mariah mulled over Tiller's downright unfriendly behavior. She'd never seen him less than charming, though she'd learned to spot when it wasn't genuine.

Her first guess, that he resented her relationship with the boys, was the only explanation she could conjure. The thought made her smile.

Chris slapped the table in front of her with his broad hand, the sudden noise nearly firing her out of her corset. "What's so funny, Lotus?"

Leaping, she gripped her pounding heart. "Christopher! You mustn't do that."

Justin shot Chris a wicked grin. "That wasn't a funny smile, brother. More of a cunning smile. Tell us, Flower. What evil thoughts were you thinking?"

Heat flashed up her neck. "Oh, stop. You two are scandalous." She stood and faced the counter with a whirl of her skirts. "Besides, a woman never tells, Justin. I should think you'd know that by now."

She poured three glasses of lemonade while regaining control. By the snickering and shoving behind her, the boys seemed certain her smile had something to do with them. Wouldn't they be surprised to know it didn't this time?

Busying her hands at the counter, Mariah pondered her distressing predicament. Three special men within the sound of her voice—thoughtful Justin, with his strong arms, broad chest, and beautiful brown eyes that pierced her soul; uncommonly handsome Chris, confident and daring, lighthearted and funny with a winsome smile; and Tiller—

Her breath caught remembering the yearning in his light green eyes, his boyish face so close she counted blond whiskers mingling with the dark red beard on his chin.

All pleasing suitors, all interested, yet she wasn't free to choose any one of them.

Tiller's irresistible allure frightened her the most. She needed a man she could count on to stay and protect the inn, one she could bend to her will. His need to float high and free like a dandelion seed clashed with her sense of family and strong ties to the land.

Even if Mariah could ground him long enough to marry her, she had no hope of holding him down. At the first strong wind, he'd lift to the sky and drift away again.

She took a deep breath and forced a bright smile before turning to serve the drinks. Her head should be busy with more pressing matters than fending off the wrong beaus. Like feed for the livestock and food for the guests she fervently prayed would arrive. Providing the necessities for her household, for that matter.

Not to mention persuading Gabriel Tabor to marry her before her dreadful secret blew up in her face.

SEVENTEEN

Six noisy men crowded around the breakfast table, never knowing God had used them to answer Mariah's prayers.

They'd checked in the night before, cash in advance, and she quickly sent Rainy to buy eggs, shortening, and a rack of bacon. The merchant had only scraps of sowbelly left, but the box of ends and pieces would have to do. So far, she'd heard no complaints. They were eating too fast to notice.

She set the platter of biscuits on the table, hoping there'd be enough to go around. Glancing at the meager bowl of scrambled eggs, made without cream or butter, she winced. Father's boast that a room at Bell's Inn came with the finest breakfast in the state echoed in her mind, flooding her with shame. The inn's reputation centered on her cooking skills. Whatever the cost, she had to find a way to get the supplies she needed.

It was an unjust cycle. With the last hog slaughtered and the cows sold, she needed money to buy most of her provisions. How could she fulfill her father's promise if there weren't enough lodgers to fill the coffers, especially now that she'd emptied her savings to ward off Dr. Moony?

Mariah grew weary with barely scraping by. Breakfast was the hardest meal to come up with, and the situation got worse every day.

Rainy's garden helped with lunch and supper, but the smokehouse was nearly empty. Miss Vee and Dicey had started to watch her with anxious eyes.

Even worse, Tiller had noticed the lack. He took skimpy portions at every meal, covering his plate when she offered him seconds, insisting he couldn't hold another bite. Yet she caught him in the garden after supper, peeling and eating cucumbers.

Mariah chastened herself again for not riding out to see Gabe. She'd have to stop putting it off. Nothing would change until she did.

"Little lady, you got any more of these larruping good biscuits?"

She dropped a dishcloth on the three she'd saved for Tiller and turned with a pretty smile. "Mr. Lenard, it does my heart good to see such hearty appetites, but you've eaten the last one available, I'm afraid."

Scooping a spoonful of eggs onto his plate, she added a few extra pieces of bacon. "See if this won't fill up your last hollow spot."

Mr. Lenard grinned as if she'd offered him treasure, his bushy mustache fanning. "Much obliged, miss." He took two bites of the eggs and glanced up. "Any chance there might be more biscuits tomorrow morning? If so, I'd be willing to stay one more night."

Mariah's heart soared. "If you gentlemen are here in the morning, I'll make you a double batch." She patted his back. "Along with butter and homemade peach jelly."

"You've got a bargain," he said, his eyes lighting up. "Put us down for one more night."

His companions, their faces buried in their plates, mumbled agreement around mouthfuls of food.

Near tears at the unexpected blessing, Mariah busied herself at the sink. Maybe her cooking was the key to saving Bell's Inn after all.

Once she got her guests fed and out the door to Father's favorite fishing hole, she crossed to the larder and took her last three eggs out of a wicker basket for Tiller. Pouring in the few drops of cream she had left in the house, she beat them good and poured them over bacon fat in the skillet.

By the time she had them nicely set, Tiller breezed through the back door.

She met him with an eager smile. "Good morning. It's about time you showed up. Hurry and wash your hands. Your breakfast is getting cold."

Tiller hooked his thumb behind him. "Already washed up at the pump." He gazed around the empty kitchen. "Where is everyone?"

She quirked her brows. "Dicey's late again. I'm sure she'll turn up eventually. Miss Vee's upstairs cleaning. Our guests are down by the Pearl, yanking catfish for supper."

Happier to see him than she ought to be, her heart felt as light as the wind. She laughed. "With the stampede through here this morning, you almost lost your share."

Concern tightened his face. "If someone else is hungry, I can wait till lunchtime."

Mariah bit her lip, wishing she'd picked her words more carefully. "As hard as you work, mister? No one in this house deserves a hearty breakfast more than you."

In the time Tiller had been at Bell's Inn, he'd transformed the place. No more loose rails. No squeaky boards, upstairs or down. Chipped paint was gone and a new coat applied. Gray, crooked posts had turned to shiny, whitewashed columns. With every day that passed, he brought the inn nearer its former glory.

"In fact"—she nodded for him to sit and handed him his plate with a grin—"you're the only one who got cream in his eggs."

His green eyes flashed with alarm. "You're out of cream, aren't you?"

Heat rising to her cheeks, Mariah lowered her lashes. "That's not your concern." Trying hard not to cry, she twisted her mouth to the side and nibbled the inside of her cheek.

Tiller stood and gripped her shoulders. "It might be true that it's none of my business, but don't tell me what to be concerned about." He lifted her chin. "Or who."

Mariah met his eyes. "I'm no stranger to lack, but we always pull through." She wriggled free and brought his biscuits, placing them on his plate. "It's always a little tight through winter and spring. Once the roads dry up, I won't have a single empty room to let."

Not easily put off, Tiller caught her wrist and gently turned her around. "I believed you when you said I'm part of this operation now. To be honest, Mariah, it feels grand to be part of something good." He lowered his head to make her look at him. "So, if there's anything I can do to ease that frown from your pretty brow; say the word, and I'll bust a gut trying."

His tender words spread warmth through her heart. "Oh, Tiller. That's the nicest thing to say." Despite her resolve, she leaned into him. Nestled close to his chest, she felt safe, comforted.

The nearer she pressed, the tighter Tiller's arms drew her. His fingers touched the base of her neck and slid to her chin, pulling her face up to his. His searching eyes consumed her, and the warmth of his quick breath fell on her lips.

Mariah slid from his arms, keenly aware of a sudden emptiness. "I can't do this."

Worry creased his brow. "I didn't mean to. . . I wasn't—"

She spun away. "I can't be with you."

On her heels, he followed her to the counter. "Why not? You like me—I know you do."

She stepped away and crossed her arms. "It's not enough."

"It's a start." He ducked low to see her face. "I'm not asking to marry you, Mariah. I just want to court you a little. Find out if we're suited for each other."

She tightened her lips and turned her head to the side.

Tiller teased the top of her hand with his finger. "Do you want me to wait and ask your pa? Is that it? Because I don't mind waiting."

Frowning, she jerked away. "You're wrong for me, Tiller McRae."

Anger flashed on his face. "Why do you think so?"

"Because you're a dandelion," she spat.

"A what?" His voice came out shrill. "Woman, you're not making any sense."

Her fury rose to meet his. "You live like the wind, with no ties to anything. The roots you shun have me bound to this place heart and soul."

Understanding softened his eyes. "Mariah, there's more to me than an aimless drifter. If you'd take the time to get to know me—"

Tears washed over her cheeks in an unexpected flood. "That's just it. I'm out of time." Darting past him, she bolted for the door.

Tiller watched Mariah go with sickening dread. Every step she took pounded deeper regret into his wounded soul. He'd felt the same empty sorrow while fleeing Scuffletown, a sense of sudden, irreplaceable loss.

What had she meant by "out of time"? It could only mean she planned to send him packing now that he'd finished most of the repairs.

Tiller slapped the counter so hard his palm stung. He'd miss the hard work. The garden. The little room he'd made his own. Teasing talks with Miss Vee and Dicey. Long walks along the Pearl with Mariah.

Without her, he'd miss the childlike pleasure of a new porch. Bible lessons from a nodding sunflower. Bare feet and muddy toes.

In a rush of certainty, Tiller knew he couldn't leave her. He belonged with Mariah as surely as they both belonged at the inn. He had to find a way to make her believe it.

Reaching the back door in purposeful strides, he yanked it open.

Mariah stood on the top step, watching a big man climb down from his wagon.

Tiller tensed, his eyes jumping to the hammer he'd laid outside the door.

Mariah didn't seem threatened, though she drew back her shoulders and stiffened her spine. "Morning, Gabe. Did you read my thoughts?"

The man's bulging stomach reached the steps before him, his large, drooping mouth seconds later. Hauling the rest of him closer, he hitched up his pants and tilted his head to the side. "I ain't read nothing, Miss Mariah." His bushy brows drew to a frown. "You know I can't read."

She laughed as if he'd said something funny. "Oh, Gabe. I just meant that I was thinking about you, and here you are."

"You was?" He drew in his fat bottom lip, no small feat, and slurped, catching a string of drool before it escaped down his chin.

"I was indeed."

"Well, I'll be." A leer replaced his befuddled stare. He didn't have enough sense to hide his lurid thoughts. "I've been thinking about you, too."

The garden gate squealed on rusty hinges, and Mariah's head swiveled toward it.

Miss Vee puttered along the path with a basket of vegetables, headed for the house. Raising her head, she missed a step then came to a full stop, staring at Mariah and her guest.

With a quick glance at Tiller, Mariah took the steps to the ground and linked her arm with Gabe's. "Walk with me."

"Sure thing." His heavy gaze fixed on Mariah like she'd asked him to supper and she was the bill of fare. "Where to?"

Tugging his bulk into motion, she ignored his question and hurried him along beside her. "I've been meaning to ride out and check on you and Mr. Tabor. How is your father's health these days?"

They strolled past Gabe's rig, their voices still carrying but not their words.

Miss Vee reached the porch, stopping with one hand on the rail to stare after them. "My eyes tell me Mariah just left with Gabe Tabor hanging off her arm like a bloated tick. My common sense can't believe it."

Tiller blew out a breath. "Your common sense lost the bet."

"What's she doing hugged up to the likes of him?"

Leaning for the hammer, Tiller wiped it clean with the tail of his shirt. "I was wondering the same. Who is he?"

Miss Vee pursed her lips like she wanted to spit. "Little vermin owns the neighboring farm. At least he will when his ailing pa dies. More's the pity. Won't be long before Gabe runs that place underground."

Tiller took the basket from her hand. "Why's that?"

"He's simpleminded. Lacks the sense to keep his boots strapped. His daddy does all but wipe his nose for him." She shook her head. "Gabe makes it hard to feel sorry for him though. He's full to the brim with mischief."

Tiller stiffened and stared toward the river just as their bobbing heads disappeared down the sloping bank. "Should I go after her?"

"Mariah can take care of herself. She knows how to handle Gabe."

Miss Vee frowned over her shoulder as if battling second thoughts. "But if she's not back soon, you and that hammer might want to take a stroll." Patting Tiller's shoulder, she pulled his gaze from the Pearl. "Have our fishermen returned?"

"No ma'am. Not yet."

She grinned. "I hope that means catfish for supper. I think I can scratch up enough meal for a nice creel of fish. Enough for a batch of corn fritters, too, if we're lucky."

"That sounds pretty good on an empty stomach."

Her green eyes widened. "Mariah didn't fix your breakfast?"

"She did." He glanced toward the river. "I got a little distracted from my plate."

With a sympathetic smile, she tugged on his sleeve. "Let's go see if it's fit for warming. After you eat a bite, you can help me give Otis a bath. It's been a week since his last one. The poor man's ripe as a split fig."

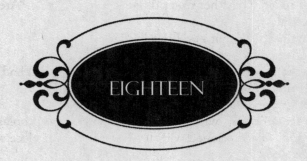

EIGHTEEN

Still wary around Otis Gooch, Tiller followed Miss Vee inside his room with a sloshing pan of water. Each time Tiller saw him, he wondered if that would be the day Otis remembered.

He slept drawn up on his side with his face to the wall, his scrawny behind jutting halfway off the bed. They drew near, and Tiller decided Miss Vee was mistaken. Otis had passed ripe days ago. Warmed by the fire they kept stoked for the thin-skinned old man, the air sagged with the smell of rotted armpits.

Miss Vee made a face.

Tiller grimaced and shook his head.

She nudged the side of the mattress with her knee. "Come forth, Lazarus. It's time for your bath."

Otis rolled toward them, his toothless mouth a gaping maw. Drawing in a wheezing breath, the tail end of a snore, he coughed and mumbled.

When his body relaxed into sleep again, Miss Vee banged the bed harder. "Come on, now. Time to wake up."

One eye opened a slit; then the other followed suit. "Mornin', good lady."

"Morning is said and done. It's nearly lunchtime."

He frowned and scooted up on his pillow. "Did I miss breakfast?"

She shook her head. "You ate hearty and enjoyed every bite. Don't you remember?"

He didn't answer, but doubt swam in his eyes.

Tiller scooted past her to set the water on the table. "Are you ready to get clean?"

His wrinkled face lit up. "Howdy, Tator."

"It's Tiller, sir."

He held up his crooked finger. "I was close. I knew it had to do with growing things. How are ye, son?"

Tiller grinned. "I can't complain."

Otis scratched his wiry head. "I sure could, but complaining don't do any good." He motioned with his fingers. "Come close and I'll tell you a secret, boy."

Trying not to breathe through his nose, Tiller leaned in. "Yes, sir?"

Otis squinted at him. "Did you say your name was Tiller?"

Biting back a smile, he nodded.

"Well, Tiller, I learned some time ago that a grateful heart will take you miles farther than grumbling." He nodded firmly. "I'll tell you something else, too. This old heart has plenty to be grateful for."

Tiller stared in disbelief. The man was penniless and sleeping in a borrowed bed. He was dressed in another man's nightshirt with his head bashed in and strangers tending his needs. As far as Tiller could see, he didn't have one thing going his way. What could he possibly have to be thankful for?

"Let's get on with the washing," Miss Vee said, throwing another log on the fire.

While Otis chattered endlessly, Tiller got him shucked and scrubbed down the best he could. Discreetly holding her nose, Miss Vee traded him a clean union suit for the soiled nightshirt.

Holding the one-piece garment in front of Otis, Tiller opened and closed the button-flap drop seat in back, as if demonstrating the ease of use. He glanced toward Miss Vee, who was warming her hands by the fire, and they shared a quiet chuckle before Tiller helped him to slip it on his frail body.

Otis beamed. "I reckon nightshirts are more in fashion, but there's nothing like a union suit for keeping a body warm." He stretched to see around Tiller and called to Miss Vee. "All done, dear lady. You can turn around."

She crossed to them and lifted the pan of dirty water. "Will you be needing anything else?"

"Not a thing. I'm much obliged for the clean clothes." He cut grateful eyes up to Tiller. "And the bath."

Tiller smiled down at him. "It's nothing. No trouble at all."

He reached to take the dirty water from Miss Vee, but Otis caught his arm. "The Lord wants you to know He don't see all you've done for me as nothing, and He's in charge of settling accounts. He said to tell you so."

Tiller's head began to roar. The gnarled fingers circling his wrist shot sparks to his flesh like cotton socks on a wintery morn. Unable to move a muscle, he stilled, watching Otis.

"When you do the will of God from your heart, you're doing service to the Lord, not to men. And God will reward each of us for the good we do." Otis nodded and released him. "It's true. The Good Book says so."

Warmth flooded Tiller's body, and weakness shook his knees. He reached for the tub Miss Vee held out, fearing he might not have the strength to carry it.

She seemed unaware of his distress, but the old man's kind eyes followed him across the room.

Miss Vee paused at the door. "I'll be back in a while with your lunch. We'll make it something so special you're not likely to forget."

Otis smiled, but he still watched Tiller. "You come back in here after lunch, boy. We'll continue our little chat."

With a hesitant half nod, Tiller followed Miss Vee into the hall.

"What was that?" he asked breathlessly once he'd put some distance between himself and the room.

She lifted her brows. "What was what?"

He pointed. "You didn't hear? Didn't feel. . ."

"All I could manage to do in there was smell." She chuckled. "We'll have to do better by him from now on, or we'll miss that reward he keeps crowing about." Turning the corner into the kitchen, she laughed aloud. "I'm just glad it's God who's keeping score and passing out prizes. Left to Otis, he wouldn't remember long enough."

Dazed, Tiller jumped when Mariah opened the back door.

Ashamed that he hadn't thought of her well-being once they got busy with Otis's bath, he breathed a relieved sigh that she'd returned safely.

She stepped over the threshold, a basket overflowing with bright red berries on her hip. "Look what we found. A big patch of wild strawberries. Aren't they nice?"

Miss Vee grunted. "I saw that deplorable Gabe Tabor. What did he want?"

Mariah dunked her basket in a pan of fresh, cold water, drew it out and shook it, then rested it on the counter. "Did you know the fields in the South were once covered by these? Like a great red blanket spread out for miles. Mother told me about seeing them as a child. She called it a glorious sight." She gathered a double handful and dropped them into a bowl. Bending under the counter, she rummaged in the cutlery jar and withdrew a paring knife.

"What were you thinking to go off alone with that man?" Miss Vee persisted. "What was he doing here?"

Mariah ducked her head. "If you must know, he asked me to go on a picnic."

Miss Vee's mouth fell open. "For heaven's sake. I hope you told him what bank of the Pearl to jump off."

Mariah turned the color of the glistening fruit in her hand. "I told him I'd love to go." She began to cut thick slices into a bowl on the counter. "In fact, I'm making a pie for the occasion."

Rendered speechless, Tiller stared. He could almost accept the Choctaw brothers as rivals. Any fool could guess what a woman might see in them. But the gangly, potbellied dullard with a lustful glint in his eye? Impossible.

Evidently, Miss Vee shared his thoughts. "Mariah Bell. Please tell me you jest."

Mariah frowned. "Oh, stop. He's not so bad. His father's an unreasonable old toad, but Gabe can be quite nice when he wants to be."

Miss Vee hissed through her teeth. "Gabe Tabor couldn't be nice tied up and knocked unconscious. That son of a toad is twice as warty as his father. At least the elder Tabor has some semblance of morals."

Mariah wiped her hands on her apron. "For pity's sake. It's just a picnic. Besides"—she shot an angry glance at Tiller—"I won't discuss my personal life in front of the hired help."

He winced and started for the door. "I'll just get on back to work."

Miss Vee clutched his sleeve as he passed. "No, you won't. We all know you care about this thick-headed girl as much as I do." She glared at Mariah. "Tiller stays. I want him here with me to help talk sense into you."

Mariah whirled to the sink. "There's nothing more to talk about."

Miss Vee gripped her arms from behind. "Honey, can't you see how much you've changed? Overnight you've become a stranger. The sensible girl I know wouldn't let that horrible man stand in her shadow, much less court her." She gave her a little shake. "Tell me what happened. What crawled under your skin? You can tell an old friend." She glanced back at Tiller. "And a new one who seems mighty concerned about you right now."

Mariah stood in silence.

Miss Vee tried to turn her around.

Drawing in her shoulders, she shrank farther away. "I simply refuse to talk about this."

Going red in the face, Miss Vee gave Mariah's back a determined nod. "Very well. Your father will be home soon. We'll see what he has to say about Gabe as a fitting suitor." Grit in her fiery glare, she pursed her lips at Tiller. "Mark my words. John Coffee will set this mess to rights in a Mississippi minute."

Avoiding the back door, Mariah hurried around to the front of the house and slipped inside on tiptoes.

She'd heard Tiller hammering in the barn as she passed. Her six sunburned guests sprawled on benches near the garden, resting their full stomachs after lunch and swapping fish stories. Dicey's high-pitched chatter drifting from the kitchen told her Miss Vee must be with her, the two of them clearing the dishes.

The only one left was Otis. She'd slip by him then sail to her room and scour the hand Gabe Tabor held, scrub the cheek his wet lips kissed. On second thought, she'd strip and scrub from head to toe, since there wasn't an inch of her his roaming eyes and leering grin hadn't bared.

Mariah crossed her arms protectively and shuddered. Easing past

Otis's room, she lifted her skirts and prepared to dash for the parlor stairs.

"Whoa, missy. Could I trouble you for a minute?"

Groaning inside, she froze. She considered pretending she hadn't heard, but her conscience wouldn't allow it. Taking three steps back, she peered into the room. "Yes, sir? Do you need something?"

He motioned her inside. "Just a spare second, if you have it."

She wavered, every nerve in her body screaming for the comfort of her room.

Otis smiled and motioned again. "Just a smidgen of your time. I won't keep you long."

Pushing aside her distress, she approached the bed with a weak smile. "All right, I'm here. Now what can I get for you?"

"Nothing for me." He flashed his gaping grin. "This here's about you, little missy."

Mariah frowned and cocked her head. "Me?"

Sobering, he nodded and gripped her hand.

The room dimmed, despite the sudden flame that roared up in the hearth. She tried to glance toward the fire, but Otis's somber gaze held her.

"The burden you carry ain't your load to bear. I'm supposed to tell you so."

A rushing sound filled her ears. "W–what?"

His kind eyes glowed with compassion. "Like a tender shoot pushing to the surface, truth always seeks the light." He shook his head. "You can't keep the secret you guard so close, honey. It's bound to come out."

She fought to look away from him but couldn't. Stumbling backward, her grasping hands searched for the bedpost to hold her up. "What makes you think I have a secret?"

With a knowing smile, Otis pointed up in the air. "'Blessed be the name of God for ever and ever: for wisdom and might are his. . . . He revealeth the deep and secret things: he knoweth what is in the darkness, and the light dwelleth with him.'"

Following his finger, Mariah gaped at the low ceiling. Tingly hairs rose on her neck and the backs of her arms, and her heartbeat pounded in her ears. "That's impossible. How could you know anything about me?"

Otis shrugged. "I don't. Not really. God don't always provide me with the details." He gave her a wink and a warm smile. "Just enough to pass on the message. . .and to pray." He held out a trembling hand. "Can I pray for you, little missy?"

Afraid to take her eyes off him, Mariah backed to the door. When her groping fingers closed around the frame, she launched her body into the hall and streaked for the parlor. Taking the stairs by sets of two, she hurled herself into her room and bolted the door.

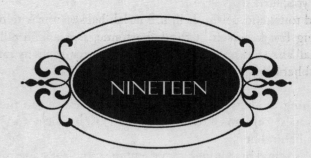

NINETEEN

Rowdy laughter and a curious commotion drew Mariah to her bedroom window for a peek.

The men had carted the dining room table outside under the big oak and spread it with a tattered white tablecloth. Like a colony of ants, they paraded single file between the table and the house, bringing chairs, napkins, and sloshing pitchers of drinks. The last item to arrive appeared to be a brightly colored relish tray, sectioned by green pickles and olives, purple beets, and quarters of sliced red onion.

Mr. Lenard, the lodger she'd promised a double batch of biscuits in the morning, settled a fiddle to this chin and raised his bow. Music filled the air, and Dicey, on her way from the house with a platter of sliced bread, broke into a little jig. Smiling, she danced across the yard to the table and delivered her tray.

Mariah leaned to search the yard for Tiller. She found him standing over the fire pit, tossing catfish fillets into a kettle of roiling fat.

Miss Vee appeared, trailing Dicey, and guilt struck Mariah's heart. She'd claimed to be ill when Miss Vee poked her head in asking why she hadn't started supper. Knowing how the woman worried, Mariah felt downright cruel to add to her fears. With a full house, Miss Vee worked half the day cleaning and washing linens. Now she bore the added burden of Mariah's kitchen duties, and the strain showed in her slumped shoulders and halting steps.

With a determined sigh, Mariah closed the curtain and hurried from her room. She could face anything as long as she didn't have to see Otis Gooch.

At the back end of the hall, she slipped down the kitchen stairs. Stopping to check herself in the mirror, she gasped. The pillows had mussed her hair, and her eyes were red from crying. She straightened her topknot the best she could, but only time would ease her swollen eyelids.

Snatching the bowl of peeled potatoes, she moved to the counter for her sharpest knife to cut them into slices just as Dicey and Miss Vee breezed in behind her.

Dicey's excited prattle ended midsentence, and she gaped at Mariah with startled eyes.

Mariah laughed. "Don't fret. I'm not sick in the body. It's my mind that's vexed, and that's not contagious."

There were many things Miss Vee might have said at that point, but she thankfully declined. "I'll finish cutting those, Mariah. Take this batter out to Tiller, if you will. You look like you could use the fresh air."

Mariah wasn't eager to face Tiller, but she didn't know how to refuse gracefully. Her unbearably trying day had taken another foul turn. Wiping her hands on a cloth, she slid it under the bowl to catch any spills and pressed open the door with her shoulder. Her teeth gritted, she stepped out to the lively strains of Mr. Lenard's fiddle and his friends singing "Turkey in the Straw" at the top of their voices.

"Met Mr. Catfish comin' downstream.
Says Mr. Catfish, 'What does you mean?'
Caught Mr. Catfish by the snout,
And turned Mr. Catfish wrong side out.
Turkey in the straw, turkey in the hay,
Roll 'em up and twist 'em up a high tuckahaw
And twist 'em up a tune called Turkey in the Straw."

A gentle breeze lifted her hair as she crossed the porch. With the early summer sun resting on the treetops and a wide patch of shade under the oak, it was a perfect evening to take a meal outside in the yard.

The aroma of golden fried fish reached her before she reached Tiller, and a deep, hungry growl rumbled her stomach. During her lunchtime picnic, Gabe's determined advances kept her too busy to eat a bite of her lovely sandwich or taste a nibble of her strawberry pie.

"Any room in the pot for these fritters?" she called.

Tiller glanced up from the iron kettle, the thoughtful frown on his handsome face warming to a delighted smile.

Mariah's heart stirred. The man seemed achingly glad to see her—unexpected after the way she'd treated him.

"Miss Vee said you were feeling poorly. I was just weighing the consequences of sneaking upstairs to check on you."

She handed him the batter. "You mean the threat of catching my illness?"

He grinned. "The threat of a skillet upside my head if Dicey caught me skulking near your room."

Tilting her head, she laughed into his merry eyes, but the familiarity of the moment sobered them.

Mariah lowered her lashes. "It's kind of you to be concerned about me. Especially after I. . .well, you know."

He plopped a dollop of batter into the hot fat, jumping back when it sizzled and splattered. "After you set me on my swaggering ear. . .and rightfully so?"

She searched his face for the cocky manner he used to cover his feelings. There wasn't a trace.

"I mistook your kindness and offer of friendship for something else." His features softened, and he smiled. "I apologize. It won't happen again."

She longed to cover her ears, to stretch out her hand and cover his mouth. Instead, she touched his arm. "Oh, Tiller."

The fiddler reached the end of his song and swiveled in his chair. "Smells mighty good, young fella'. Got any samples of that fish yet?"

"I'd even taste a bite of fritter," another man called. "Whatever you've got, bring it over."

Laughing, Tiller hefted the heaping tray of catfish. "I'll go tame them down with this batch. You'd better hurry Miss Vee along with the rest of the meal. I'm not sure how long I can hold them off." He stepped toward the table then spun on his heel. "Mariah, Miss Vee may have the right to frown on the man who courts you. I reckon I don't, only. . ." He chewed his bottom lip then released it. "Please be careful, won't you?"

Squirming, she couldn't hold his gaze.

"If you ever need to talk, I make a pretty good listener," he said then turned to go.

Mariah clutched his arm. "If you don't mind my saying, you seem different."

He laughed softly. "I'm not surprised. I feel different. I had a long talk with Otis after lunch. I can't explain it, but the old man knows things about me no one is supposed to know."

Her heart surged. "He does?"

Tiller nodded thoughtfully then blushed. "He said not to worry about the way I feel about you. Said he couldn't tell me the outcome, but he promised everything would turn out right in the end." He gave her a slow smile. "Once he finished praying, I believed it, too."

Mariah watched him go, holding the platter high over his head and whistling "Turkey in the Straw." Spinning, she tripped over the exposed roots of the oak then stumbled for the house.

First Otis, who seemed to hear directly from God, had read her secret thoughts. Then Tiller, without a whiff of deceit or false charm, had wormed his way deeper into her heart. Now the two seemed in cahoots on some scheme concerning her.

Like it or not, the time had come to persuade Gabriel Tabor to propose.

Tiller stole a peek over his shoulder and smiled. Mariah lurched toward the house, her mind clearly on something besides walking. He felt a little underhanded because he hadn't told her everything. A gambler kept a few cards close to his chest.

Waving the platter under their noses, he centered the fried fish on the table in front of the men. "Here you go, boys. This ought to hold you until we get the potatoes done."

Returning to the cooking fire, Tiller dropped a few more spoonfuls of batter into the steaming fat. They bobbed and danced before settling to the bottom in a ring of bubbles. In the same way, his insides had bobbed and danced before settling in to hear the rest of what Otis had to say.

After Tiller shared his fears about the black-hearted Mr. Tabor's intentions, Otis sat straight up in bed and promised with glowing eyes that God would deliver her out of the rascal's clutches. Then he winked and patted Tiller's hand, promising to pray every day that Mariah would one day be his.

As Tiller told Mariah, Otis knew things. His messages were cloudy but seemed miraculous for a man who couldn't remember a name past five minutes. His peculiar insight into people's hearts convinced Tiller that the gift, talent, or whatever a man might call it, came from a higher source.

Tiller might not be cozy with the Almighty, but he believed. As a frightened boy in Fayetteville, dodging broomsticks and scratching for crusts of bread, he'd felt God's sheltering arms many times. Living with a half-crazy mama will get a boy searching for something to believe in.

Rescue came when his ma sent him to Scuffletown to live with Uncle Silas. When Tiller heard he'd be leaving her house, he sensed the hand of God reaching down to pluck him from a terrible fate.

Yet with the rash self-centeredness of a foolish boy, he'd managed to spoil everything. He fell in with a group of unruly youths in Scuffletown and barreled headlong into his own destruction.

The women's voices pulled his head up from the bobbing fritters and his thoughts from the dreadful past. He shuddered as his mama's shrill taunts faded to 1871 where they belonged.

"Here are the potatoes," Miss Vee said, handing over a large bowl brimming with thin slices.

Tiller took up the crisp fritters then dropped the potatoes by double handfuls into the iron pot. "It won't take these long to fry." He nodded toward the men hunched over the platter of fish. "And even less time to eat them." He chuckled. "It might be a good idea to cut the pies. You'll be dishing them up before long."

Dicey swung around to a smaller table where they'd lined up rows of Mariah's fresh-baked desserts under a low, shady bough of the oak.

Miss Vee gathered a stack of small plates. "Wait, Dicey. I'll help."

Mariah seemed wary and fretful. Keeping her distance, she watched him from under her lashes.

He'd said too much. Turned her skittish.

Laying aside his tongs, Tiller turned with a smile, but the reassuring words he planned to say turned bitter in his mouth.

Over her shoulder, Tobias Jones and his nuisance sons strolled toward them with wide grins.

Mariah spun to follow Tiller's gaze, and her shoulders stiffened.

Tobias reached them first. He took off his battered slouch hat and nodded. "Halito, Mariah. Thank you for inviting us to supper."

A tiny frown gave her away. Mariah had no idea she'd extended an invitation. "You're always welcome, Tobias." She accepted the hand he offered. "All of you."

Miss Vee scurried over. "My, my. Ain't this a nice surprise?" A surprise to everyone but her.

Chris slipped up beside Mariah and gently touched her back. "Hello, Flower." His warm eyes and affectionate tone were as familiar as a kiss.

Tiller glared, but basking in Mariah's answering smile kept the brash boy too busy to notice.

Miss Vee turned a bright smile on Tobias. "I hope you're hungry."

Beaming, he nodded eagerly.

Wringing a napkin into a knot, Mariah's anxious gaze flitted between her newest guests and the six boarders.

Tiller guessed what had her jumpy. The meal kept the men too busy to cast more than a few curious glances, but if Tobias and his boys pulled a chair alongside them, it could become a problem.

Tipping his chin, Tiller grinned. "Not much room over there, and it looks like they'll be busy for a spell. Why don't we move the kitchen table out to the porch?"

Mariah gripped his arm and whispered her thanks as she passed. "Dicey, you and Rainy drag out the table. Miss Vee, fetch a clean cloth and help with the chairs, please. I'll see if our fishermen can spare a few pieces of their catch."

Grinning, Tiller handed her a plate and a pair of tongs. "Careful. You may wind up with a few less fingers."

She winked. "Not if I trade them for a slice of my strawberry pie."

With her bright smile and coy glances, it didn't take her long to charm a heaping plate of food right out from under the beguiled men.

Passing Tiller without a backward glance, she handed the plate to Dicey and took Chris's and Justin's arms. "I can't decide which of you I'd rather sit by, so let's set a place for me in between you, shall we?"

Watching her go, Tiller's temper flared as hot as the bubbling grease.

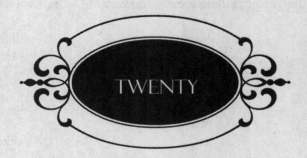

TWENTY

Mariah sat at her dressing table dragging a brush through her hair, her riotous thoughts sure to cost her a night's sleep.

She scowled at her reflection, seeing Miss Vee's self-satisfied smile. The meddling woman knew exactly what she was doing when she invited the Jones boys to supper. She figured if Tiller wasn't enough to distract her away from Gabe, then Chris or Justin might.

Grumbling to herself, Mariah focused her anger on the real conniving female in the room. How could she have played those simpering games—shamelessly flirting with the boys in front of Tiller just to test his reaction? It wasn't like her to toy with men's affections. Such behavior was indecent, especially since she planned the shortest engagement ever with another man entirely.

She slammed the brush down hard on the vanity. Why should she feel guilty for engaging in the harmless fun considered normal courting behavior by most Southern girls?

Yet wasn't that her problem? A Pearl River Indian fighting to save her ancestral land was far from a normal girl.

Besides, Tiller was guilty of toying with her affections, too. Whatever nonsense had gone on between him and Otis, Tiller wasn't the marrying kind. He had plainly stated the fact down in the kitchen. *"I'm not asking you to marry me, Mariah. I just want to court you a little."*

Blast his slippery hide. She needed a sight more than a "little" courting, and she needed it now. In her weakened state, her yearning heart betrayed her. If only Tiller intended to stick around, if he'd make his intentions clear, she could lay aside her fears.

She could lay aside most anything for him.

The admission pained her stomach. Gripping her middle, she rested her flushed cheek on the tabletop, weary from battling her muddled emotions.

"Mariah? Are you all right?"

She raised her head. If she didn't answer, perhaps Miss Vee would go away and leave her in peace.

The door creaked open, and Miss Vee's wide eyes peeked around the edge. "I heard a ruckus. Is something wrong in here?"

Mariah sighed and spun toward her. "Nothing's wrong. Come on in."

Miss Vee entered wearing her faded dressing gown, a tasseled nightcap, and a worried frown. "What on earth was that banging? I could've sworn it came from in here."

Mariah slid her brush into the top drawer. "You can see for yourself that I'm fine." She managed a grudging smile. "Go back to bed. You must be worn to a frazzle."

"Who, me?" She blinked. "I'm no worse off than the rest of you. We all worked hard today."

"On the contrary." Mariah lifted one brow. "You took on the added weight of managing my personal life."

Miss Vee's shoulders slumped. "So you caught me." Shuffling to the bed, she plopped down with a grimace. "I'm not very skilled at trickery, am I?"

"At least have the grace to seem contrite."

She leaned to squeeze Mariah's knee. "I don't mean to meddle, honey. Please understand, I feel responsible for you in your father's absence." Her eyes widened. "What would John say if he came home to find his daughter rubbing cozy shoulders with the likes of Gabriel Tabor?"

"I think Father would find my interest perfectly reasonable. After all, Gabe stands to inherit his father's plantation one day."

Startled, Mariah realized it hadn't stung to speak of her father's homecoming. Did it mean she'd grown callous in her deceit? Or had she pretended so long she'd started to believe it herself?

Disgust flickered in Miss Vee's eyes. "That's what this is about? With a man like Tiller McRae pining after you, you'd sell yourself for a patch of Mississippi dirt?" She shook her head. "Minti Bell's daughter or not, I wouldn't have believed it in a hundred years." Standing, she gazed at Mariah in disbelief. "It's possible that what I said earlier is true. I don't suppose I've ever really known you."

Tiller glanced at the ceiling then back at Otis.

Otis stared overhead, his brows raised so high he looked owlish. "That's a lot of throwing things and slamming doors, even for a couple of women."

Tiller scooted to the edge of his chair. "Should I go see what's going on up there?"

Otis grinned. "I wouldn't. You might get your ears handed to you."

They listened together as a set of stomping feet reached the end of the hallway. After a last wall-rattling slam that shook the oil fixture above their heads, silence fell over the house.

The old man blew out a breath. "See what I mean?"

Tiller couldn't help but chuckle. "For two people whose hearts seem so close-knit, Mariah and Miss Vee go at each other with shocking regularity."

Otis nodded. "Just means they've passed up friends and turned into family." His smile dimming, he shivered suddenly and tugged his blanket up around his shoulders.

Tiller helped him tuck the covers around his thin frame then patted his bundled arm. "Sit tight. I'll throw on another log."

They were into the second week in June, but the weather hadn't bothered to check the calendar. The days were mild enough that the meager daytime heat didn't carry into evening, so at night Miss Vee had Rainy bank fires in all the hearths. Otis's burned all the time.

Before long, the extra wood ignited to a roaring blaze. They sat quietly in the close little room, so warm and cozy Tiller felt drowsy.

The glowing fire wasn't the only thing that set his heart at ease. Sitting beside the strange little man beneath the quilt soothed Tiller without a word ever passing between them. When they did share long talks, especially when Otis spoke his God-words, Tiller's heart soared to receive them.

The only blight on their peculiar friendship was the dreadful truth. Tiller's part in the terrible thing that happened to Otis was a leaden weight around his shoulders.

He sat forward and patted Otis's arm. "Are you sure there's nothing else I can get for you tonight?"

Otis shook with laughter. "Not since the last time you asked. Or the time before." He cocked his head. "You ain't gettin' befuddled same as me, are you?"

Tiller longed to confess his sins and purge his sore conscience, but a streak of yellow held him back. He forced a grin. "I'm just trying to make sure you're comfortable."

Otis sat up in bed. "You know, boy. . .there is one thing I sure would like, if it's not too much trouble."

Eager to please, Tiller leaned closer. "Anything at all. Just name your poison."

The rheumy old eyes darted past the foot of the bed. "I've been locked inside these four walls for quite a spell. I'd sure like to see what's outside that door."

Warmth flooded Tiller's heart. "You know what that means, don't you?"

Childlike, Otis glanced up and shook his head.

"It shows you're getting better."

"Sure enough? Well, how about that?"

Tiller slipped one arm around his shoulders and helped him sit up. Otis swung his feet to the floor and scooted to the edge of the bed.

"Take it slow, now," Tiller warned. "Are you ready?"

He nodded. "A little shaky, but I think I can make it. . .as long as you don't turn me loose."

"There's not a chance of that happening. Let's go."

With a grunt, Otis pushed to his feet. He'd grown so thin and frail, holding him took no more effort than steadying a child.

Tiller guided him across the room and through the door. He paused in the hallway to study Otis's face. "How are we doing?"

Otis grinned. "Not sure about you, but I'd take kindly to a seat in that nice parlor yonder."

They passed under the archway and made it to the settee in mincing steps. Tiller changed his mind at the last minute and steered him to a set of overstuffed chairs pulled close to the crackling hearth. "How's this?"

"Fine, son. Just fine."

Otis reached for the padded arm, and Tiller eased him down. "Can I get you anything?" He wished he knew how to make Miss Vee's foamy white tea. "A cup of coffee or a slice of pie?"

His movements a bit wobbly, Otis leaned to pat the opposite chair. "I just need you to sit right here beside me."

Tiller slid dutifully into the seat.

With a contented sigh, Otis nestled into the soft, tufted fabric. He sat quietly for so long, his mouth ajar, he appeared to have fallen asleep.

The heat from the blazing flames toasted Tiller's arms and face. Before long, his own eyelids grew heavy, and he drifted in a pleasing fog. Resting against the pillowed headrest, he thought to doze awhile himself.

"She needs you, boy."

Tiller startled awake at the voice. He spun his head toward Otis, certain he'd dreamed the grim words.

Firelight danced in Otis's eyes. "Mariah's in a frightful mess." He shook his head, the weight of sadness sagging his cheeks.

Terrified, Tiller's breath stilled while he waited for Otis's Godwords about the woman he loved.

"The Lord didn't tell me." The old man pointed up the stairs. "I got this from the little missy herself."

Swallowing hard, Tiller nodded. "She told you something?"

"Not in words." Otis leaned to prop his chin, his thoughtful gaze fixed on the floor. "We were having a little talk. I gave her a message from God about some secret she's keeping, and well. . .it hit her hard." He glanced at Tiller. "Poor girl jumped like she'd stepped on a darning needle. Nearly shook her right out of her skin."

"A secret?" His interest piqued, Tiller scooted to the edge of his chair. "What did you tell her exactly?" He blinked. "If you're free to say."

Otis thoughtfully scratched his cheek. "That's the trouble, son. I don't know if I'm free to say or not. I can't remember what I said."

Frustrated, Tiller pressed him. "Try harder, Otis. It could be important."

A pained look crossed his face. "It's no good. I've strained my thinker since it happened. Nothing comes to me. Not a whiff."

Tiller patted his trembling hand. "Easy. Don't rile yourself. We'll find another way to help her."

Otis pulled his hand free to squeeze Tiller's fingers. "I know you'll bust a gut trying, son. Because there's nothing but good in you."

The flames grew unbearably hot, and the room closed in on Tiller. He ducked his head. "Please don't call me that, sir. I'm a long way from good."

Otis smiled. "Ain't we all when you get right down to it? The Good Book says, 'For all have sinned, and come short of the glory of God.' We're all sinners, boy. You've done no worse things than me."

Tiller swallowed hard, but the painful knot refused to budge. He slid out of Otis's grasp. "I reckon that's not so. I'm afraid I've done far worse. In fact, there's something you need to know about me, and it's time I told you the truth. Otis, I—"

Footsteps over their heads stemmed his words. Angry at the interruption, he scowled up at the stairwell.

Mariah stood a few steps off the top landing, her hand clutching the neck of a white dressing gown and her flowing hair draping her shoulders like a lustrous black cape. She was a vision straight from a man's dreams.

Her expression was the only flaw, and the most striking thing about her. Sheer panic had frozen her features and paled her beautiful face.

Gaping at Otis as if she'd stumbled onto a ghoul, she spun on her heels. "I'm sorry. I didn't mean to interrupt."

Otis stirred and reached his hand toward her. "Little missy, don't go."

Leaping from his chair, Tiller started after her. Before he reached the bottom stair, she was gone in a whirl of white lace.

"There, you see?" Otis said, wonder in his voice.

Stunned, Tiller stared over his shoulder. "For pity's sake. She was scared stiff."

Otis pointed a shaky finger. "That's the same look she had when I gave her the message from God."

TWENTY-ONE

The road home had changed. Not because of overgrown trails or washed-out bridges—things a man might expect. Joe felt the difference in his spirit, a restless sense of going in the wrong direction.

On other trips to Mississippi, the past lured him. Each step closer to the land of his ancestors stoked an eager fire within. This time the miles drained him as he rode away from the cabin he shared with his wife.

The full moon overhead lit his way. After the first long day, Joe had traveled at night when most of the world rested. At first light, he sought hidden places to sleep before the roads filled with travelers. This way, he fell asleep knowing he would see trouble before it spotted him.

He followed a winding, scum-coated creek for miles until the water ran fast and clear again. Reining the horse beside a mayhaw thicket, he eased his aching body from the saddle and lay on his belly for a drink from the rushing stream.

After tending the animal's needs, he built a fire to heat a tin of beans. With his bones warmed and belly full, he spread his bedroll in a clutch of trees as fiery orange rays from *hvshi* peeked over the tall grass on the horizon, setting it aflame.

Overhead, a spiraling cyclone of buzzards rose and fell over a distant carcass. The birds reminded him of an ancient tale, the day the animals held a powwow to decide who would steal fire for their tribe.

Brave buzzard volunteered to fly to the people of the east and return with fire, which he did without delay. Swooping close to the flames, he hid a burning ember in the long, beautiful feathers on his head. For his trouble, he got a bald, blistered skull to wear for the rest of his days.

Smiling at the old legend, Joe yawned and smacked lazily, the pleasing taste of beans lingering on his tongue. He closed his eyes, wondering if his skirmish with John Coffee would earn him the same fate as the poor buzzard. In previous battles, they'd parted company with the stench of burning feathers in the air. He doubted this time would be different.

Joe loved Mariah, felt a pressing weight of duty to see her marry well. He couldn't deny that the promise of three fine horses and a passel of land sweetened the deal.

With his niece wed to the chief's son, Joe would move into a choice position within the tribe. With little George coming, it was a fine place to be. These things he wouldn't bother telling John. The man seemed blind to their traditions.

For all his trying ways, John's love for Mariah was great. John's devotion to his daughter was Joe's biggest hindrance, but this time he wouldn't leave Mississippi without her.

He drew the musty blanket over his eyes to shut out the rising sun. Just a few more days to reach the Mississippi crossing. Less than a week and he'd arrive at his destination. He still had plenty of time to work out a plan to steal John Coffee's fire. For now, his biggest need was rest.

Hooper dashed the dregs from his coffee cup into the fire and kicked dirt over the ashes. They'd slept too long, but after days of hard riding, they were a sore and sorry lot—with a lot more ground left to cover.

Wyatt approached, a bleary-eyed version of himself. "I've packed the horses, and Ellie's scouting the trail. You about ready to go?"

Hooper groaned. "Not in the least. What happened to us, Wyatt? Our gang used to ride the swamp for days, short on sleep and provisions with muddy water lapping our stirrups and a posse on our tails." He reached to rub the small of his back. "I don't remember once feeling this stiff."

Wyatt grinned. "Good thing you mended your ways, old man." He tightened the neck of his flask and slung it over one shoulder. "Hoop, that was ten years ago. We're not that band of raiders anymore."

"Still, it don't make a lick of sense," Hooper said. "I work as hard as any man running my farm."

"Not the same. It's not easy sleeping on a train for days or riding the overgrown trails around Jackson. These saddles bore in deep after so many miles."

Hooper lowered his voice. "Don't let on to Ellie, but I miss my feather bed."

Wyatt burst into laughter. "Ellie's hero? Missing his comforts? You can bet I won't tell her that."

Ellie ducked out of the trees behind them. "Tell me what?"

Wyatt spun. "Take my word, honey. You're better off not knowing."

Hooper nudged him. "Why doesn't my sister look any worse for wear? She woke me up at dawn, scurrying around camp like a youngster on an outing."

Wyatt slipped his arm around Ellie's waist. "This stuff is in her blood." He gave her a little shake. "Besides, running after our boys keeps her able-bodied. I doubt those sweet cherubs of yours give much of a chase."

Ellie grinned. "Things will change when they're courting age, Hoop. You'll stay fit chasing suitors from your door."

He frowned. "No lop-eared boy will come closer than shotgun range. Not a second time, at least."

Wyatt slapped him on the back. "Best keep a good stock of shells around the house. As pretty as your two gals are, half the boys in Hope Mills will be plucking buckshot from their behinds."

Hooper hefted his pack and nodded toward the sun. "Let's get going. We should've been on the road two hours by now."

Ellie pulled away from Wyatt to straighten Hooper's collar, an obvious excuse to search his eyes. "Do you think we'll have any luck this time?"

Hooper ran his hand along the back of her head. "We have a good lead. If Tiller's alive, we're bound to stumble onto more information." He squeezed her shoulder. "Don't fret, Ellie. We'll search Mississippi until we find him."

TWENTY-TWO

The blustery weather seemed the right setting for the storm brewing within the walls of Bell's Inn. Since Tiller opened his eyes, the house had echoed with deafening silence. The kind wrought by the mutual cold shoulders of quarreling women.

If not for their angry steps on the stairs and their scornful snorts as they passed in the hall outside his room, Tiller would swear no females lived in the house—until a ruckus commenced in the kitchen.

His stomach growled, but with the alarming clatter of dishes and the banging of pots and pans, he didn't dare venture out to fill it. He worried about the poor men who'd paid to spend another breakfast with Mariah and Miss Vee. He doubted Mariah's biscuits were worth blundering into that skirmish.

Another glance past the curtains at the swirling cloud bank drew his concerns to a more pressing matter—whether or not they'd wind up running for cover. He didn't relish spending the morning huddled in the cellar with Mariah and Miss Vee. Considering the whole house didn't seem big enough for their spat, he'd sooner take his chances with a twister.

Lightning flashed outside his window, filling the yard with brilliant light. The peal of thunder that followed and the way it shook the house made the cellar seem like a good idea after all.

Braving the tempest in the kitchen was unavoidable. He had to warn the women.

Tiller snatched his hat from the hook on the wall, reliving for a moment how he'd swiped it right off Nathan's head. Pushing aside the prickly memory, he swept out the door and down the hall.

At the kitchen door, he took a deep breath and boldly stepped inside. Gloom hung from the rafters like cemetery fog. Just as he feared, the poor lodgers hunkered over their plates picking at their food in silence, their wary eyes skittering between Miss Vee and Mariah.

Formidable, stiff-shouldered Miss Vee scoured a cast iron skillet so hard she'd soon wear through the bottom. Scowling, straight-backed Mariah scrubbed the silver off her utensils, tossing them on the counter with a loud, careless clatter. Dicey lurked inside the dim pantry, staring out with frightened eyes.

Mr. Lenard, the wretched fellow who'd requested more biscuits, nibbled on the corner of one, frowning like a man forced to eat sawdust. Bickering women could sure ruin a man's day.

Noticing Tiller on the threshold, his face lit up as if he'd spotted a lifeline. "Look, boys. Here's our fish fryer. How are you this morning, son?"

Tiller nodded. "I'm fine, sir. At least for now." He lifted the curtain from the back door to peer out. The oak tree seemed to reach for him, pleading with wildly waving limbs for a rest he couldn't give. It wouldn't do for a tree that size to be split by lightning or hurled by the wind. If the big oak fell on the house, there'd be nothing left to repair. "Hasn't anyone noticed it's blowing up a powerful gale?"

All three women glanced his way.

"There's been a little thunder and wind," Miss Vee said. "I just figured it for another rainstorm."

Tiller's somber gaze moved from her to Mariah. "If we're lucky, rain is all we'll get."

Mariah opened the wooden blind over the sink with her thumb. "It's that bad?"

Dicey crowded beside her to peek out. "Mercy sakes, them pines swaying right for us."

"It's not the pine I'm worried about," Tiller said. "If the wind kicks up a notch, that oak will be joining us for breakfast."

Dicey tried to smile, but her chin wobbled. "Mista' Tilla', you funnin' us."

"I wish I was." He met Mariah's frightened stare. "Is the root cellar fit for company?"

She looked dazed. A white ring of fear lined her mouth. "I honestly don't know. I haven't been down there in so long." Drying her hands on her apron, she tugged the strings and laid it aside. "What will we need?"

Tiller shrugged "Water, I suppose. A lantern or two." He opened the door, and the wind rushed in, wildly billowing curtains, tablecloths, and the ladies' skirts.

"Shut it, Mista' Tilla', please!" Dicey screamed, stooping to the floor and covering her head.

Ignoring her shrill cries, Tiller held Mariah's gaze. "I'll go down and check things out. Wait here unless I call you."

She nodded.

"Hold up, son." Mr. Lenard wiped his mouth and stood. "I'll go with you."

Miss Vee stood on tiptoe to pull down a candle and a box of long matches. "Take these. You'll need them."

Mr. Lenard fisted them and scurried out the door on Tiller's heels.

Tiller had spotted the cellar doors from the roof when he made his repairs. Clutching his hat, he ran to that side of the house. With his free hand, he latched onto the handle and motioned for Mr. Lenard to take the other side. They pulled together, and dirt sifted like flour into the dark hole in the ground.

Tiller went first, feeling his way down the slanted ladder. Before ducking inside, he paused for another quick look at the storm. The sky held a greenish cast, and the peaks of the tall, dark clouds were churning.

Mr. Lenard stood above him staring at the fearsome sight, his clothes flapping around his large frame. He glanced at Tiller with an ominous shake of his head.

Tiller descended into the darkness, batting away spider webs and crumbling dirt dauber mounds from the rungs. At the bottom, he moved aside for Mr. Lenard, who sprang to the ground and turned his back on the drafty opening to light the candle. Shielding the flame with his palm, he held it aloft.

Evidently, the cellar had gone unused for some time. Tiller supposed the women preferred the comfort and convenience of their roomy indoor pantry. Looking around, he couldn't say he blamed them.

The musty smell of damp earth rose with every footfall, mixed with the pungent odor of spoiled onions and rotted potatoes. A long abandoned termite nest took up one corner, explaining the crumbling boards he had replaced throughout the house.

A raised platform along one wall stood off the dirt floor about two feet, stacked with crates and assorted old canning jars filled with blackened food. Mr. Lenard bent over the shelf and dripped wax to set the candle. "Over here, son. Help me clear this ledge. If the boards are sound, it'll make a good place for the women to sit."

Together, they filled the crates with the ruined preserves and other assorted rubbish and set them in the opposite corner.

Tiller dusted his hands. "With a couple of quilts for padding, this should do fine."

Smiling, Mr. Lenard opened his mouth to answer, but a strong gust doused the candle, plunging the corner into darkness.

They made their way to the dim square of light atop the ladder and climbed outside to a shower of hail.

"This is bad," Tiller shouted. "We'd best hurry." He bailed for the house with Mr. Lenard on his tail.

Halfway to the porch, a muffled roar hauled them to a stop. Tiller stared in disbelief as the boiling black clouds pitched a monster to the ground. The twister seemed a hundred acres wide. He couldn't tell how close, but it surged toward them, a black devil on a ruthless path.

"Let's go!" he cried, but Mr. Lenard had already run ahead.

A line of anxious faces awaited them inside the kitchen. With the memory of what he'd just seen spurring him on, Tiller wasted no time. "Dicey, fetch all the quilts you can carry. One of these men will help you. Miss Vee, take the others and open as many windows as you can.

Mariah, bring lanterns, oil, and plenty of matches. Now hurry!"

Covering her ears, Dicey backed into Miss Vee, her wild gaze darting from face to face. "What's that noise I hear? What's out there?"

Miss Vee gripped her arm and thrust her forward. "Doomsday. Unless you want it to get you, you'll do like you're told."

With a high-pitched squeal, Dicey shot out the door and skidded toward the guest rooms.

Frightened people scattered in every direction, leaving Tiller and Mr. Lenard alone in the kitchen. "How can I help?" he asked.

Tiller tugged his sleeve. "Come with me."

They raced down the hall to Otis's room. Curled in his usual position, face to the wall and his rear jutted over the mattress, he slept like a carefree baby.

"Can you believe this?" Tiller asked Mr. Lenard.

They shared a quick smile.

Tiller shook the bed. "Otis, wake up."

Mumbling, he waved them away.

Tiller took his arm and gently pulled him over. "On your feet or carried, Otis? It's your choice. We have to get you to safety."

Startled awake, he blinked up at Tiller. "What's the trouble?"

Bracing his back, Tiller helped him to his feet. "Twister. A big one headed right for us."

Mr. Lenard took his other arm. "There ain't a minute to spare, old-timer. Let's get you underground."

The roar closed on the house, rattling the walls. The churning rumbled like madly rushing water one minute, howled like an angry, squalling beast the next. Mariah's heartbeat thundered.

The wild-eyed parties finished their appointed tasks and met at the back door awaiting orders from Tiller. Motioning over his head, he and Mr. Lenard led the way with Otis's skinny legs dangling between them. Mariah and the others followed, cowering like children.

Halfway to the cellar, overwhelming curiosity drove her to raise her head. Fear like she'd never known brought her to a standstill.

The twister bore down on them, a moving explosion. Wide at the top, engorged, it narrowed to a whirling cloud of debris at its base. In the distance, a herd of panicked deer darted out of its course, leaping and soaring to escape.

The hail had stopped, but rain pelted her like a shower of bullets. The wind shrieked, whipping past her eyes until they stung. A force tugged at her body, her hair, her clothes, as if the nightmarish, spinning top sought to draw her, to feed on her along with everything in its path.

Mariah steeled herself, but the pull was too strong. Terrified, she stumbled forward, longing to cry out for God's protection. To her shame, she didn't feel worthy. When had she stopped praying?

In a rush, Tiller's arms engulfed her from behind. Digging in his heels, he held her while the twister danced just over the Pearl.

Breathless, her gaze darted to him. "It stopped moving?" The wind ripped the words from her mouth, and she didn't think he heard.

His throat rose and fell. "I think so," he shouted in her ear.

"Is that possible?"

Tiller laughed. "It must be. It's happening right in front of us." He tugged on her arm. "It won't last. Let's go."

Bowing into the wind, she let him drag her to the cellar. Clinging to his comforting arm, she swung her legs over the top of the ladder.

Tiller stood over her, his hair whipping, his shirttail beating wildly. Reaching past her, he handed the oil and lanterns down to Mr. Lenard.

As Mariah's head cleared the opening, Tiller lowered the door.

Startled, her hand shot out to stop him. "What are you doing?" she shrieked. "Come inside."

"I'll be back."

"No! Where are you going?"

He jabbed his thumb over his shoulder. "The horses. I have to turn them out."

Sheki! How could she have forgotten him?

In the moment where she almost forbade him to save her horse, her feelings for Tiller became clear. She lowered her lashes, certain her love for him shone from her eyes.

Tiller glanced over his shoulder, the set of his jaw grim. "Get inside," he yelled. "It's on the move again." He shouted something else before he ran, but building pressure in Mariah's ears muffled his voice.

Mr. Lenard climbed up beside her to help close the doors. Her muscles strained from the effort, and still the handle jerked up repeatedly, nearly pulling her arms from the sockets.

One of the other men tugged her down and took her place. Between the two, they managed to force them shut, blotting out the meager light and some of the noise.

Miss Vee met her at the bottom rung. "Honey, please forgive me. I can't die at odds with you." Her voice shook with fear. "If we survive this, I promise never to meddle again."

Mariah forced a wobbly smile for Miss Vee's sake and leaned into her, so frightened for Tiller she couldn't speak.

A lantern flashed to life in the corner. Then another, casting long flickering shadows on the floor. Miss Vee wrapped a quilt around Mariah's wet, shivering body and led her to a nest of blankets spread over a low storage shelf.

Crawling across on her knees, Mariah pressed her back to the wall, her gaze fixed on the overhead doors. She covered her ears to drown out the hideous moaning wind and prayed. For Tiller, Sheki, and the lives of those around her.

To plead for the safety of the inn entered her mind, but the words never formed in her heart. If the tornado ripped Bell's Inn from the face of the earth, the promise would go up with it, along with the burden she carried. Good riddance to all, as long as it spared those she loved.

Dicey yelped and hid her face when the doors sailed open.

Mariah's spirit soared to meet Tiller on the stairs.

This time it took all the men to shut out the storm. Then Tiller beat a path to her side. Clearing the platform on one knee, he pulled her close as if he knew she needed his strength.

She'd been wrong about her dandelion seed. The first strong wind hadn't whisked him away. Instead, it blew him straight into her arms.

The cellar groaned and rattled as the house danced over their heads. A deafening crack brought shrill screams from Miss Vee and Dicey. Mariah clung tighter to Tiller's chest.

The twister sucked one of the doors free and spun it away. With a wrenching squeal of metal, the second spun crazily on one hinge before it shot straight up in the air. The tempest raged overhead, a leering black wolf belching threats down a rabbit hole.

Sheltered in Tiller's arms, Mariah gazed in terrible awe as the world spun past in a dizzying blur.

TWENTY-THREE

Faster than it came, the twister was gone. The danger had passed, but Tiller couldn't turn loose of Mariah. His jaw ached from clenching, and his muscles bunched in knots.

But for the groan of settling boards and a quiet sniff from Dicey, eerie silence filled the cellar. The square patch of sky overhead was deathly still.

No one seemed able to move—until Dicey began to wail.

Miss Vee patted her back. "Now's not the time to cry. It's over. We made it."

Tears wet Dicey's rounded cheeks. "I ain't bawlin' for me." Her frantic gaze darted over their faces. "I'm worryin' 'bout my daddy."

Understanding dawned in Miss Vee's eyes. "Don't fret, honey. I'm sure he'll be fine."

"But it's headed our way, and we ain't got no root cellar." Wriggling to the edge of the platform, she struggled to her feet and started for the ladder. "I gots to run home and see."

"Wait," Tiller called. "It could be dangerous."

She stilled and turned, wringing her hands. "What you mean by dangerous?"

He ducked his chin at the opening. "There's no telling what we'll find up there. Let the menfolk go first. We'll have a look around, and then I'll walk you home to check on your pa."

She retraced her steps and settled obediently on the rim of the shelf.

Realizing he still held Mariah, Tiller glanced down. "Are you all right?"

Her face tilted up, trust shining from her eyes. "I think so."

A smile twitched his lips. "Let me know when you're sure."

She ducked her head and nodded. "I'm sure."

He gave her a little squeeze then released her to let her sit up. Gazing around in the flickering light, his eyes lit on Otis. "How are you faring, sir?"

Otis chuckled and pulled the quilt tighter around his shoulders. "Missing my bed and my hearth. And this empty belly's asking for lunch."

Dicey spun to gape at him. "How you gon' eat after all this?"

Otis beamed. "Hand me a drumstick, and I'll show you."

Miss Vee snorted. "Let's pray there's still a kitchen left to fry a drumstick."

Tiller heaved himself off the ledge. "Who wants to go up top with me and find out?"

Mr. Lenard and his troop stood one at a time, shaking the dust off their clothes. Two of the older men looked a bit shaky.

Tiller nodded at them. "I'd be obliged if you'd wait here to keep an eye on the women."

He didn't have to ask them twice.

First at the ladder, Tiller climbed, dreading what he might see. The loud crack they'd heard could've been anything, but his money was on the oak. He hoped it hadn't split Bell's Inn down the middle when it fell.

His anxious gaze cleared the opening. Groaning, he couldn't believe the devastation.

A blanket of debris covered the backyard in a patchwork of mismatched rubble. Brightly colored quilts tangled with splintered tree limbs. A feather pillow peeked from under a wagon wheel. Shredded wallpaper and cracked lumber mixed with twisted tablecloths, busted frames, and shards of china dishes. Large sections of walls, ceilings, and broken gables scattered the grounds, along with a ripped-out kitchen sink.

Tiller spun.

Bell's Inn stood untouched behind him, except for two whitewashed planks jutting from the wall. The wood, once part of the garden fence, had impaled the house without breaking, driven in like a hammer drives a nail.

The oak tree, its twisted roots jutting to the sky like gnarled rope, had rolled the dice, and the house won. The barn hadn't been so lucky.

"Is it bad, son?" Mr. Lenard called.

"Well, sure it's bad," Miss Vee said beside him. "Can't you see the man's dumbstruck?" She tugged on Tiller's pants leg. "The house is gone, ain't that right? Everything is gone."

He ducked his head inside. "You don't get off so easy, Miss Vee. You'll still be frying chicken."

Miss Vee cheered and clasped hands with Dicey. Whirling, she drew Mariah into a smothering hug.

Tiller sought Mariah's worried brown eyes. "It's a shocking mess up here, but you still have a roof over your head." He cocked his head. "I can't say the same for Sheki."

"The barn?"

He tried for a comforting smile. "You'll need a handyman for a while longer."

"Do you see Sheki?"

After a quick scan of the property, he shook his head. "No sign of any of the horses, but don't fret. When they calm down, they'll come home." Clearing the top of the ladder, Tiller peered below. "Come on out, but watch your step."

The men came first, followed by Miss Vee, gasping and clutching her chest.

Then Dicey, moaning and sobbing.

Mariah came last, drawing in a quick breath as she reached the top. She tented her hands over her brow and whirled in a circle. "Oh my. It's inconceivable. Where did all of this come from?"

Tiller grimaced. "The storm dumped half of Mississippi in our lap."

Staring across the backyard, Mr. Lenard heaved a sigh. "To think that just last night, I sat over there playing my fiddle and eating fish." He pointed. "Look. The cook pot's still there." He chuckled, wonder in his voice. "Took the tree but left the kettle. Fickle old thing, weren't it?"

"Oh no, Mista' Tilla'." Dicey tugged his sleeve. "Look what else it took."

He turned to follow the direction her finger pointed, and his heart seemed to stop. "By thunder, it's gone. Ripped up down to the soil."

Mariah clutched his arm. "Even the sunflowers. What will I say to poor Rainy?" She lifted dazed eyes. "We'll have nothing to eat. Nothing to feed our guests."

Tiller gripped her taut knuckles. "I'll set all this right, Mariah. You'll see." He swept his arm over the wreckage. "I'll clear the yard, repair the barn, and with Rainy's help, I'll replant the garden." He squeezed her hand. "In a few weeks' time, you'll forget this ever happened."

She tilted her head up, and Tiller cupped her chin. "Bell's Inn will be even better than it was before. I give you my solemn word."

Though Dicey's ramshackle house stood directly in its path, the twister had jogged off course long enough to spare her home and family. She returned to the inn, smiling and singing, to help with the cleanup.

Mariah was grateful for the effort, since every muscle in her body ached and hysterical tears threatened to surface.

The beast had spared the inn but demanded a high price for the favor. The destruction inside looked much the same as the yard. The storm had roared through the windows, turning the rooms upside down.

Tiller assured her the inn hadn't taken the twister's full force. "If it had," he said, "you wouldn't have a mess to clean because you wouldn't have a house."

Mariah tried hard to be grateful.

Even Otis's room on the opposite side suffered damage. The wind sucked his curtains out the window, soaking them through, and rain had wet his mattress.

Otis didn't want to give up his cozy den, so Tiller hauled the bedding from an upstairs room then changed the sheets and blankets himself. He pulled down the wet curtains, hanging a quilt in their place. Once he had a roaring fire going, he dressed Otis in a clean nightshirt and put him to bed.

Mariah took note of how affectionately he cared for Otis, and it warmed her heart.

After he had the old man tended, Tiller appeared at the parlor door. "Here you are," he said from the hallway.

She glanced up. "Did you get Otis settled?"

"I think so." He hurried to help her pull the settee away from the open window. Tossing out leaves and small branches, he pulled down the sash. "Mr. Lenard and his men are cleaning their rooms as best they can. Only one of them took in water. We may have to move that man to a different bed for the night."

She bit her bottom lip. "I thought they were leaving."

"They offered to stay one more night to lend a hand, and I agreed. We can't afford to turn down the help.

"Although"—he winced—"I don't think you can charge them in this case."

Her mind jumped to the near-empty pantry. "No, of course not."

He gathered her hands and squeezed. "Don't worry. We'll manage."

She nodded. "Except I don't have another empty room. Otis has the mattress from the last one."

Tiller bit the corner of his lip. "I know. I'm willing to give up my bed." He nodded at the settee. "I can bunk in here, if you don't mind."

Mariah shook her head. "I won't allow it. That's your room, Tiller. You've earned it with the sweat of your brow." She blew a determined breath. "One of them can sleep out here. Or they can double up. I'm sure they'll understand in the circumstances."

Tiller winked and saluted. "Whatever you say, boss." He took her hand and led her to the sofa. "I know you have plenty to do, but will you sit for a minute? There's something I want to say."

Curious, she perched on the edge of her seat.

Sitting beside her, he ran his hands through his hair. "I know with the repairs almost finished, my time here was nearing an end. I figured any day you'd hand me my bedroll and send me down the Trace."

She pulled in her lips and struggled to keep the truth to herself. Sending Tiller away hadn't entered her mind.

"But now"—he waved his hand to take in the chaos around them—"I think you need me more than you need my empty room."

Mariah started to agree, but his hand shot up.

"Hush, and hear me out." His lively grin reminded her of the Tiller she'd first met.

"When I promised to put this place right, I meant every word." His dancing eyes glowed. "I looked over the wreckage of the barn. It won't take much to rebuild."

She had to stop him. "I can't afford the lumber, Tiller."

As eager as a boy at Christmas, he scooted closer. "You won't need to buy a single board." He pointed behind them. "There's enough wood on your felled oak to build a small town."

Her chin came up. "Gracious, I forgot about the oak."

He nodded. "It's a fine, sturdy tree. A lot of them are hollow in the center, but yours is solid through and through."

"But how will we cut it?"

He patted her shoulder. "Leave the details to me. I have a few friends in Canton."

She stared at her hands, twisting in her lap. "But I can't pay you."

He widened his eyes. "Sure you can. In room and board and the best hot rolls this side of the Mississip'."

Catching his mood, she giggled. "I don't feel so helpless now." She beamed at him. "How can I ever thank you?"

He shrugged, a mischievous glint in his eyes. "Just keep those rolls coming, I guess." He picked up her hand and squeezed. "And let me help Rainy replant the garden. I can't think of anything I'd rather do."

For a man who boasted of wanderlust, he was certainly in no hurry to leave. In fact, he seemed to care about Bell's Inn as much as Mariah did. She tightened her fingers around his. "I think it's a wonderful idea."

He released her and stood. "It's all settled then. I'll let you get back to work. Miss Vee asked me to help sweep up in the kitchen."

As he strode away, Mariah couldn't help glancing at his boots. The carefree drifter once claimed to hit the road before roots sprouted from his feet to pin him down. Grinning, she sensed the presence of little green shoots between his toes.

Tendrils of hope broke the surface of her despair. Like Rainy's sunflowers chasing the sun, they yearned after Tiller as he loped out the door.

TWENTY-FOUR

Mariah stepped out on the porch and searched the sundrenched yard for Tiller. In the six days since the storm, he'd wrought miracles. The green grass gleamed in the bright daylight, picked up and raked free of every scrap of trash.

Piece by piece, the huge oak had disappeared, hauled off by wagonloads and returning as stacks of lumber. Most of the wood, gleaming in the afternoon light, jutted bare and skeletal over the barn, a sturdy frame awaiting wallboards and shingles.

The furious winds had carted off the two magnolia trees beside the pump, and good riddance. Since the morning when she'd carried Father's body from the house, the sweet-smelling blossoms had reminded her of his death.

The storm had spared the wagon, one of the many miracles for which Mariah was thankful. Sheki, nickering outside her window the morning after the twister, was another.

At first, Mariah thought he'd come home begging for oats, but the shameful horse was bloated from a rampant eating spree and returned in need of a stomach cure. Thankfully, Rainy knew a thing or two about horses and fixed him right up.

Sheki and Tiller's gelding slept in the corral for a few days, but once Tiller raised and braced the walls, they returned to their stalls to oversee the rest of Tiller's handiwork.

Shading her eyes, Mariah spotted Tiller high on the roof of the barn, his sun-toasted back and shoulders gleaming with sweat. She hurried down the steps with his lunch, waving when he raised his head. The warmth of his smile crossed the distance.

She entered the newly set doors, peering up through the unfinished gap. With a grizzly growl, Tiller leaped from behind, howling and spinning her around when she screamed.

Mariah clutched her heart. "You fiend! I almost threw this tray at you."

Laughing, he lifted the corner of the napkin and sniffed. "What a shame that would be."

He lifted his shirt from a hook in the corner and slipped it on. Straddling a hay bale, he patted the one next to him.

She cocked her head. "Is this your way of inviting a lady to lunch?"

Nodding, he held out his hands for the tray. "If a lady will do me the honor."

Mariah smoothed her skirt and sat, watching him eagerly plunder the food. She accepted a spoonful of potato soup and a roll stuffed with a bite of pork roast. It seemed only fair since she'd brought him her share to begin with to make sure he filled his stomach. Besides, it smelled too good to resist.

The small roast was the last of a wild young pig, the rolls from her last cups of flour. After Otis and Miss Vee ate their fill, there wasn't much left in the kitchen. Thank heavens Rainy and Dicey took their midday meals at home with their folks.

Mariah wiped her mouth on the corner of the napkin. "How are things in town? I heard you drive up and wondered why you never came inside the house."

Tiller had left for Canton the day before on more business with the sawmill. He returned in a rush then went straight up on the roof and set to work.

He glanced at the sky through the gaping hole. "Rain clouds chased me most of the way home. I wanted to get the roof finished before Sheki got his ears wet, but I got fooled. It looks like the bad weather took a turn." His ears reddened. "Just because I didn't come say hello doesn't mean I didn't think about you."

Mariah's cheeks warmed and her hand came up to stifle a giggle. Ten minutes in his presence, and she'd turned into a blushing girl.

Tiller's eyes widened. His throat made a choking sound, and he stood so fast he nearly upset the tray. "Curse me for a blasted fool. I can't believe I let this slip my mind."

Steadying his soup bowl, Mariah gaped at his eager face. "Gracious, what are you blathering about?"

"I have something for you." He shoved his hand deep in his pocket and came up with a bulging white hankie tied up with all four corners. Grinning, he held it out to her.

Mariah took the bundle and the weight sagged her arms to her lap. One knot loosened and bright coins spilled out in her hands.

Her head shot up. "What is this?"

His toothy smile lit the barn brighter than the sunbeam pouring through the roof. "Maybe it's been quite a spell since you saw any, darlin', but that's money."

She shoved it toward him. "I can see that much, but it's not my money."

He withdrew his hands, refusing to take it from her. "It's yours, all right. Every dollar."

Her heart pounded. "I'm scared to ask where you got this, Tiller, but it doesn't belong to me. Take it back this instant."

He wrapped his big hands gently around hers and guided them, handkerchief and all, back to her lap. "Our friend, the twister, cleared a path from here to Yazoo city and points north, creating a serious demand for lumber."

Tiller let go and straightened with a hesitant smile. "The oak wasn't the only tree down on your property. With Rainy's help, I've been hauling them to the mill and selling them. I took the last one this trip. Apart from a few dollars to Rainy for his trouble, you're holding the profits." He shoved back his hat and quirked one brow. "I hope you don't mind."

Stunned, Mariah's gaze dropped to her hands. One finger twitched and more coins tumbled across her palms, more money than she'd ever seen in her life. Enough to run the inn for a year, maybe more, if she didn't have a single paying guest. "It's really mine?"

He nodded.

"I don't know what to say." Laughter bubbled up in her throat. "I thought it took you an unreasonable number of trips to haul one tree." She glanced up. "Miss Vee said it seemed like the miracle of the loaves and fishes. God multiplying the oak." Awed, she shook her head. "I suppose in a way He did."

Tiller tucked his chin. "So it's all right?"

"It's more than all right." She shot up with a squeal and threw her arms around his neck. "I'm so grateful I could burst!"

Remembering his shirt was unfastened, she pulled away blushing. "How forward of me. Please forgive me."

His hands fumbled with the top button. "No, it's my fault."

She couldn't contain her joy for long. "Oh, Tiller. We can eat again."

He gave her a crooked smile. "Why do you think I went to all the trouble?"

Leaning across the distance she'd put between them, she stretched to kiss his cheek. "Because you're the dearest man in the whole world."

"What's this?" an angry voice snarled behind them.

They spun, still beaming brightly.

Gabriel Tabor loomed on the threshold.

Mariah stepped away from Tiller. Fisting the money, she dropped it with a jangle into her skirt pocket. "Gabe. What a nice surprise. I didn't expect you today."

His bottom lip hung looser than usual, and fury blazed in his eyes. "I can see you didn't." He pointed a murderous finger at Tiller. "Why's he half naked and pawing at you?"

Mariah had a moment to consider the absurdity of the charge. How preposterous for a man with a dozen untamed hands to accuse decent, respectful Tiller. She drew herself up. "I assure you he did no such thing."

Gabe took three steps closer, his hulking size a tad frightening. "Don't you lie, Mariah Bell. Maybe I ain't real smart, but I ain't stupid."

His bulk shifted to Tiller. "Mister, you trying to steal my girl?"

Tiller held his ground as Gabe approached. "Can a man steal a girl who wants to be taken?"

"Huh?" Gabe balled his fist. "Don't think you can get out of a thrashing by fast talk and riddles."

Easing into a swaggering stance, Tiller clenched his hands at his sides. "I'm saying Mariah's free to choose. If she wants you, I'll step out of your way. But if she wants me, I'm staying right here." He jutted his jaw. "And you'll have to kill me to keep me away from her."

Tiller's brows raised to question marks as his eyes sought hers past Gabe's shoulder. "Mariah?"

The last ounce of resistance slid from around her heart. Tiller McRae had braved starvation, twisters, giant oak trees, collapsed barns, and now the ugly, big fists of Gabe Tabor. He'd more than proved himself worthy of her trust.

With a teasing smile, she lifted her head higher to see over Gabe's broad back. She didn't need words for the message her eyes sent Tiller.

Gabe stiffened and swung around to blink at her. "Well?"

She lifted her chin. "Gabe, I think it's time for you to go."

"What?" He frowned and jabbed himself in the chest. "You're giving me the boot? After you done kissed me and everything?"

Blushing to the roots of her hair, Mariah lowered her lashes. "Your memory fails you, Mr. Tabor. You kissed me, and without an invitation." She glanced at Tiller. "And only on the cheek."

Gabe shuffled toward her. His meaty, meddling hand snaked around her waist and slid to the small of her back, lingering too long to be respectable. "But you liked it, didn't you?"

Tiller blustered and lunged, but Mariah held up her hand. "Say good-bye, Tiller. Gabe was just leaving."

"You really want me to go?" Gabe hooked his thumb over his shoulder. "I could go on and kill him like he said."

Mariah couldn't hold back a grin. "Killing Tiller won't be necessary, but thank you for the offer." She caught his sleeve and led him to the threshold. "Say hello to your father for me, won't you?"

"Well, sure, but I—"

"Watch your step past those loose boards. You might trip and take a nasty fall."

His droopy eyes bugged. "Mariah!"

"Good-bye, Gabe." Reaching for the barn door, she nodded before pulling it closed.

Leaning her head against the rough wood, she tried to still her thudding heart. Where would she find the courage to face Tiller after she'd just declared her love? Turning slowly, she stood across the barn from him, one hand over her mouth.

He slouched with both hands on his hips, giving her a sideways look and a teasing smile.

A dusty beam of light filtered through the open rooftop, the bright ray anointing his red head with fire. The unearthly glow seemed like the warm kiss of God's approval.

Tiller crooked his finger.

Mariah's stomach flipped. She crossed the barn into the sunbeam and the warmth of his embrace.

Sliding his hand up her neck, he tangled his fingers in her hair and pulled her to his chest. "It's high time you came to your senses, woman."

Breathless, she laughed against his shirt. "I'm inclined to agree."

His arms tightened. "I love you, Mariah Bell."

"I love you, Tiller McRae."

"Enough to skip all that silly courtship business and marry me?"

A thrill shot through her. "I don't see why not." She leaned to frown up at him. "You've taken quite a leap from courting me a little to a proposal. What changed?"

He kissed her forehead and snuggled her close again. "I wanted to marry you from the first. I thought if I told you, it might spook you."

Her joy boundless, she tightened her fingers on the front of his shirt and smiled to herself. "And you really plan to stay on here at Bell's Inn? What about your carefree coattails? Those roots you find so binding?"

Tiller chuckled, the sound a rumble in his throat. "You believed the words of a shiftless drifter?"

She laughed aloud. "A point well taken."

He held her, swaying as if rocking a cherished child.

Mariah swayed too, dizzy with loving him.

Abruptly, Tiller stilled, dragging them to a stop. "What about your father? We need his blessing, don't we? He'll want to be here for the wedding, too." He patted her back. "I understand that you'll want to put things off until he returns."

Her heart surged and fluttered in her chest. "Father will be gone a very long time."

A groan escaped his lips. "How long do we have to wait?"

She shook her head. "I don't think we can. It wouldn't be practical."

He brightened. "So we'll be married right away?"

She nodded and rested her head on his shoulder. "The sooner the better."

Mariah braced for another squabble with Miss Vee. The poor woman would never understand, and Mariah couldn't imagine how to convince her. Most likely, the time had come to tell her the truth.

Tiller sighed in her ear. "You're taking a gamble, aren't you? You don't know much about me." His heartbeat thudded against her cheek. "About my past, I mean."

Caught in her own guilty thoughts, hot tears stung her throat. "You don't know everything about me either."

He cradled her head in his hands and raised her face to his. Determination, heart-stirring affection, and a touch of fear swirled in his eyes. "You won't like some of what I've done."

She bunched her brows. "It can't be that bad."

"I'm afraid it is," he said firmly then drew a deep breath. "But I swear to make it up to you." His throat rose and fell. "To everyone."

He looked so grim. What dastardly deeds could sweet-faced Tiller McRae possibly be guilty of? Mariah shuddered and lowered her lashes. Whatever he'd done, she didn't want to know. Not with their love just confessed.

Besides, she wasn't ready to lay her secrets on the table. There'd be plenty of time later for baring their souls. "Don't say anything else, Tiller. We'll discuss it later." She pushed out of his arms and backed away, despising herself for the pain that flashed in his eyes.

Skirting past him, she picked up the tray. "Miss Vee will be wondering where I am."

He caught her arm as she passed and held her, searching her face.

She summoned a weak smile. "Don't fret. Nothing's changed."

Gnawing his bottom lip, he nodded. "Let me walk you to the house then. I'll get cleaned up and go for supplies."

Crossing the yard, he cleared his throat. "Can we tell the others? Miss Vee, Dicey, and Rainy?"

She grinned. "I suppose so."

A delighted smile lit his face. "Miss Vee first. As soon as we reach the house."

She touched his arm. "Don't mention how soon we plan to marry, Tiller. I'll break that news to her myself."

Nearing the porch, she halted, clutching Tiller's sleeve.

A horse lumbered up the rise bearing a lone Indian. The big man slouched in the saddle with a broad, battered hat tugged low over his face.

Mariah strained to see what the dread in her heart had already confirmed. The worst problem imaginable rode toward her on the sun-dappled Trace. She groaned. "Oh, no. It's really him."

Tiller stared with her. "You know that man?"

"He's my uncle, Joe Brashears. But please don't call him Joe. It enrages him. He prefers Nukowa."

"Nu-who?"

"It's pronounced Nook-o-ah. It means 'angry' in our tongue. He took the name when my mother died." She sighed. "It fits him well, I'm afraid."

"I like Joe better."

Ignoring him, she danced with frustration. "I adore my uncle, but I dread his visits. These days, they're never pleasant."

"I suppose not, if he's angry all the time. What made him mad?"

"He wants something, and he can be very stubborn about it."

"What does he want?" Tiller asked, shading his eyes.

She shrugged. "Me."

"You?" He shot her a glance. "What for?"

"To take me back to the Indian Territory."

Tiller's head whipped around. "What? No!"

"He's chosen a husband for me there."

He growled low in his throat. "I can see I'm going to love Uncle Joe."

Mariah pasted a welcome smile on her face. "Hush. He's almost here."

Tiller slung his arm around her shoulders. "Just in time to share our happy news."

"No!" Mariah whispered harshly, shrugging off his arm. She moved a few paces away. "You mustn't breathe a word of our engagement, Tiller. Not a word, do you understand?"

"Why not?"

She narrowed her eyes. "If you do, I'll be on my way to marry the son of a chief, and you'll be left here scratching your head."

He gaped at her. "I can handle Uncle Joe, Mariah."

"Nukowa," she hissed. "And please leave him to me." She frowned. "Maybe you should go on back to the barn."

"No." Scowling, he closed the distance between them. "If it's all the same to you, I'm staying right here."

TWENTY-FIVE

Joe squinted against the afternoon sun. Surely his tired eyes deceived him. The nahullo beside Mariah had drawn her beneath his arm as if he'd bartered for her and won.

His stomach tightened. Who was the red-haired man at his niece's side, his welcoming smile as forced as hers?

Slant-eyed glances fired between the two. The feud of a couple in love. What mischief was afoot in John Coffee's house, right under his nose?

Joe snorted. He'd arrived just in time to help Blazing Hair find the road.

Mariah strode to meet him. Pink tinged her cheeks, but the warmth of her greeting seemed more fitting. "Halito, *amoshi!*"

"Halito, *sabitek.*" He swung his aching body from the saddle. "*Chim achukma?*"

"I'm fine, Uncle. And you?"

"I need water." Joe swiped his hand across his dry mouth. "I have miles of dusty road in my throat."

"Of course you do," Mariah said. "After such a long ride. Come up to the house, and we'll do even better than water."

Joe dragged his pack off the horse. "You have whiskey?"

Mariah's laugh was as false as her smile. "No, and you have no business drinking strong spirits." She handed the reins to the nahullo without a second glance in his direction. "I'm sure Miss Vee has a fresh pitcher of lemonade."

Joe wasn't fooled by the girl's deliberate shun. She could go on treating the tall young man as if he didn't matter, but Joe had spotted a fox in the henhouse. A lanky red fox.

Over his shoulder, Joe watched the man lead the horse to the barn at an angry stride. He smiled. It wouldn't be the last time he walked away mad, if Joe had his way.

He turned his attention to Mariah. "Your father is well?"

She stumbled a bit and lost her footing.

Joe's quick hand caught and steadied her. "Now I see why you have no more whiskey. Have you been sipping firewater this morning?"

She wound her arm through his and continued walking, but her strained smile didn't reach her eyes. "I'm drunk with happiness to see you, I guess."

He patted her hand. "Is something wrong, sabitek?"

Staring at the ground, she bit her bottom lip. "Father's not here, Uncle."

Joe peered at her. "John's in town today?"

"Not in town. He's. . .gone away."

Joe stopped so fast he pulled her off balance again. "What do you mean 'away'? Where did he go?"

Mariah angled her head so he couldn't see her eyes. "I'm not sure. Not exactly. He left so suddenly." She looked everywhere but at Joe. "He became very ill and had to leave."

"To the white man's hospital?"

"Not a hospital."

"Then where? Don't talk riddles, Mariah. I've come a long way. When will he return?"

She raised her chin. "He'll be gone for a very long time."

Joe narrowed one eye and tried to read her. The girl's tight mouth and sulky eyes were a black-watered pool.

To what lengths would John Coffee go to outwit him? What trick had he put his daughter up to? Mariah wanted to stay in Mississippi— she'd made this no secret—but it wasn't like her to deceive.

Impatient, he stalked ahead of her. "No matter. I can wait. For as long as it takes." His bold words were a lie. He'd left Myrtle to pull corn and work crops, to grow a son for him, alone and frightened. John Coffee had the upper hand before the battle had ever begun. Furious, Joe reached the porch and spun to scowl at her. "Who is the red-haired nahullo?"

The truth flickered in her eyes but skirted her mouth. "Tiller? He's a drifter we hired to make a few repairs. He works for room and board."

Peering past the haze of anger that had him blinded, Joe gazed around the inn's backyard, seeing it for the first time.

A careless giant had strolled through the familiar grounds. He'd plundered the garden, used the fence posts for toothpicks, and ripped up the oak for a parasol.

Joe's wandering gaze stopped at the half-finished barn. "What happened here?"

"A twister." Mariah closed her eyes and shuddered. "It was awful. We hid in the root cellar."

He whistled. "All this damage and the house still stands?"

Mariah nodded. "The inn shook above our heads like a wet dog, but it held together."

Smiling, Joe took in the old house from the eaves to the foundation. "She's faced down worse in her time."

He patted the railing on the new porch. "Nice job." He glanced at Red Hair scaling the barn like a nimble goat. "His doing?"

Mariah nodded. "Tiller made all the improvements to the inn." She slid her fingers along the smooth wood with the pride of a mother caressing her child. "He built this porch in two days."

Joe stuck out his jaw. "I thought you planned to quench my thirst."

She swept past him to the back door. "Right this way, and I'll pour you that lemonade I promised. You must be starving, too."

Grumbling, he followed her through the kitchen door. Tossing his wide-brimmed hat at the rack, he glanced across the hall. An ugly white stain marred the hardwood floor where the dining room had taken in water. The curtain rod hung by a loose nail, and the drapes were missing. More damage from the twister, no doubt. Thankfully, the kitchen, with the broad behind bending over the stove, was just as he remembered. "Woman, you haven't changed a bit."

Viola glanced around then sprang up and slammed the oven door. "Joe Brashears. You old rascal." She scurried toward him, wiping her hands on her skirt.

Joe braced for her smothering hug.

"How are you, Joe?"

He'd given up on her calling him anything else. "It's been awhile."

Viola released him, just barely, her painted lips stretched in a smile. "If you're not the last person I expected to see in my kitchen. . ." She pulled out a chair. "Here, sit down. Let me fix you something to eat."

Mariah hurried for the pitcher. "He's more thirsty than hungry, Miss Vee."

Joe shifted the weight of his pack. "Right now, I'd like to put this down somewhere." He glanced toward the hall. "Is my room empty?"

Mariah paused, the lemonade she poured slowed to a drip. "I'm afraid it's taken." Her eyes flashed a warning at Viola, but it came too late.

"That's Tiller's room now," Viola said. "It has been since he got here. I doubt you could blast him out with a scattergun."

The best plan Joe had heard all day. Scowling, he dropped the heavy pack with a thud. "I always take that room."

Mariah finished filling his glass with shaky hands. "But Uncle," she said with a nervous laugh, "we didn't know you were coming."

"You do now. *Tiller* can move."

"Oh, but it wouldn't be fair, would it? He's all settled, and—"

"I have an idea," Viola interrupted. "We'll move young Tiller upstairs to your father's bedroom, Mariah." She shot the girl a look Joe couldn't read. "You know. . .the one right across the hall from yours."

Handing her wide-eyed uncle his drink, Mariah bit back a smile. "What a wonderful idea, Miss Vee. After all, it's the largest room in the house, and a big man like Tiller McRae needs room to stretch his legs."

Uncle Nukowa cleared his throat. "On second thought, there's no reason for the boy to move his things." He set the glass on the table, grabbed his pack, and started up the kitchen stairs. "If John's room is empty, I'll take it."

Miss Vee winked at Mariah. "Get washed up, Joe. I'll have you something fixed to eat before you can say. . ."

His footsteps faded up the stairs.

"Bamboozled," she whispered.

They fell against each other laughing.

"What's he doing here?" Miss Vee asked.

"Do you need to ask? I'm surprised he's not in war paint."

Miss Vee's hands fisted at her waist. "Joe needn't think he can start badgering John the minute he returns. I won't have it, you hear me? I just won't."

Mariah released a weary breath. "Let's not borrow trouble, dear. 'Sufficient unto the day is the evil thereof.'"

Miss Vee sniffed. "Now you sound like Otis."

"Speaking of Otis, where is he?"

Since the storm, Mariah's terror of the little man had eased. She avoided being alone with him, but otherwise things had returned to normal.

Otis had started to venture out of his room more often, always supported by Tiller's ready arms, but he still had a way to go toward regaining his strength.

"Last I saw, he was napping. He sleeps more than a newborn babe."

"I suppose he's still recovering." Mariah glanced toward the stairs. "I need to explain Otis to my uncle before he trips over him in the parlor in his union suit."

Miss Vee's laugh came out a snort. "Especially since the poor thing can't keep his flap fastened."

They giggled together like naughty children.

Sobering, Miss Vee tied on her apron and opened the pantry. "Now then, what am I going to feed Joe? I've never seen the larder so bare."

Mariah grinned. "It won't be empty for long. Tiller's taking me to town to buy supplies."

Her casual announcement caught Miss Vee's attention. "Granted, you and Tiller are a handsome pair, but I doubt the merchants will trade your looks for goods. How do you plan to pay for these supplies?"

With a saucy wink, Mariah jiggled the pocket of her skirt, letting the coins clink together.

Miss Vee's eyebrows soared. "I know the sound of money when I hear it. Where'd you get those coins?"

"Isn't it wonderful?" Mariah kissed her cheek. "Tiller's been selling trees downed by the storm. He surprised me with a handful of gold."

Miss Vee clasped her hands toward the ceiling. "Hallelujah! Our troubles are over. I knew that boy was a blessing in disguise."

Mariah longed to share the rest of the morning's good news, but with Uncle Nukowa around, she didn't dare trust Miss Vee to keep it quiet.

"I can hardly wait to get to town and fill the pantry." She parted the kitchen blinds, searching the roof of the barn for Tiller. "Where is that man? We need to be on the road. It's getting late."

Miss Vee shooed her with her hands. "Go roust him, honey. The sooner you leave, the quicker you'll get back."

Mariah hurried to the back door. "Prepare a list of all we need. I'll tell Tiller to hitch up Sheki and pull the wagon around."

"Where are we going?"

Her startled gaze jumped to Uncle Nukowa on the stairs. He had washed the gray film of grime from his face and loosened the cords that held his long braids. Gleaming hair draped his shoulders, still as black as when ten-year-old Mariah dogged the heels of her handsome young uncle, learning to hunt, fish, and trap on their Mississippi land. Watching his stern, rigid face, it seemed a long time ago.

"It's just a supply run, sir. We'll be back tonight."

"We?" He reached the bottom landing, his face drawn to a pucker. "Do you mean you and that. . .Tiller?"

She nodded.

He raised a staying hand. "I don't think so. It's a long drive, and you've waited too late to strike out. We'll go tomorrow."

Mariah shifted her weight impatiently. "But Uncle, we're out of supplies. I don't have eggs or meat for breakfast."

He shot her a warning glare. "A matter you should've already tended. It's settled. We go in the morning."

To defend herself would mean revealing more than she intended about the inn's waning business. He didn't need more ammunition in his war to make her leave.

She raised her lashes to peek at him. "We, Uncle?"

"It's been awhile since I've seen Canton." He picked up his empty glass and strolled casually to the waiting pitcher. "Now then, Viola. Where's this fine meal you promised?"

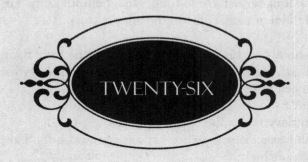

TWENTY-SIX

Tiller pounded the head of the nail until it disappeared inside the splintered wood. Growling, he forced himself to stop before the board split in two.

As long as he could remember, life had been an unlucky hand of poker. Any reasonable man would admit he'd suffered an unjust childhood. The mess he'd made of things since could be pinned squarely on his own shoulders, but not the way he got started in the unsavory way of life.

Just when he'd taken steps to turn the game around, fate had dealt him a marked card in the form of Uncle "I'm angry" Joe. Tiller tightened his grip on the hammer. "Thanks to you, I'm not so happy myself, old boy." He took another hard swipe at the nail and stood—spinning toward the river so fast he nearly tripped over his boots.

A lone rider sat on the far bank of the Pearl, dappled by the shimmering reflection off the water. By the easy forward slump in the saddle, his arms crossed over the horn, the dim outline could very well be Nathan Carter.

Tiller's heartbeat raced in his ears. Shading his eyes, he squinted. If the sun didn't shine so bright on the river, he could see that it wasn't so. As soon as he caught his breath, he'd tear across the field and relieve his scattered mind.

Before he could move a muscle, the specter from his former life straightened in the saddle and fired a snappy salute. Reining his horse, he rode off the backside of the rise and disappeared.

Tiller's legs turned to shifting sand beneath him. He lowered himself to the beam and clung to the braces.

Was it Nathan?

Impossible. Nathan wouldn't ride away. If the hazy figure was his old friend, he'd have found a low crossing and rode across boasting about how he'd found him.

"Tiller?"

He whirled, nearly pitching himself to the ground.

Mariah gasped and stretched her arms toward him. "For goodness' sake, be careful."

He swiped his mouth with his arm. "You shouldn't be sneaking around like that."

She leaned to see out the back window of the barn. "What do you see over there? You're the color of cotton."

"It's nothing. Too much sun on my head, I guess." He scooted across the beam to the ladder and made his way down. "Are you ready to go? It's getting late."

She made a face. "That's what I came to tell you. We have to wait until morning."

"Why?"

"Uncle Nukowa doesn't want me out so late."

Irritation crept up Tiller's spine. "Since when does he make the decisions?"

She took a deep breath. "Since the moment he rode into the yard."

Tiller propped his hands on his hips. "Does he think you sit on a shelf and twiddle your thumbs until he shows up? You've managed just fine without him."

Mariah gripped his arms. "I know it's hard to understand, but please try. In the tradition of my people, my uncle believes I'm his responsibility. Of course, my father never held with the Indian ways. He's never allowed Uncle Nukowa that sort of access."

Tiller set his jaw. "Good for him."

"When Mother died, my uncle assumed I'd be returning with him to the Indian Territory. He became enraged when Father forbade it."

Twirling the soft hair beside her ear, Tiller frowned. "You're not exactly a child anymore. Shouldn't the tug-of-war be over?"

She gave a somber shake of her head. "Not until my wedding day. It's up to my uncle to make sure I marry well."

"I'll be happy to relieve him of that obligation." He leaned to see her face. "And very soon, I hope."

Her gaze shifted to his. "Within our tribe, Tiller. After Mother broke with custom and married an outsider, he'll be extra vigilant to see it doesn't happen to me."

Mariah reached for his hands. "That's why you must promise to keep our engagement a secret." She tightened her grip. "Uncle Nukowa will go to any lengths to make sure we never wed."

The passion in her plea struck sudden fear in Tiller's heart. "What's to keep him from whisking you away from here?"

"He won't. Not against my father's wishes." She shook her head. "My uncle's not here to kidnap me. He's here to settle a feud and win a longstanding war of wills."

Tiller pulled her close. "Suppose your Father comes back and agrees to let you go? Do you hold enough sway to talk him out of it?"

With a weary sigh, Mariah leaned into his chest. "Believe me, that's the last thing we have to fret about."

He caressed her head, the silky feel of her hair making it hard to stay mad—until the unmistakable moan of a hungry stomach sprang them apart.

"Yours or mine?" he asked.

She blushed and shrugged.

"Blast it! You're hungry. Joe should credit me with enough sense to get you to Canton and back so you can eat tonight."

"It's not so different in any culture, is it? Show me an uncle who wouldn't be concerned about his niece traveling the roads at night. Alone with a man, at that."

Tiller blew out a frustrated breath. "This is different. We need food." He pushed back the dread of another long, lonely ride so soon. "If there's no changing his mind, I'll just go by myself."

"I'd rather you didn't." She jingled her bulging pocket and smiled. "I've got my heart set on going into town."

Tiller drew back and laughed. "You're still carrying that money around? Shouldn't it be tucked away in the safe?"

She rattled the coins again. "Would you deprive me of my music? I'm rather enjoying the sound of plenty."

Unable to resist, he drew her into his arms. "All right, maestro. We'll go in the morning. But in the meantime, what will you eat?"

"I think we'll be fine. Miss Vee is a wonder at making something to eat out of scraps. She's inside now turning a basket of wilted potatoes into soup and the leftover meal into fritters."

"And in the morning?"

"We found an old tin of flour in the back of the pantry. I'll make flapjacks and cover them in honey so we won't miss the butter. And I still have a few pieces left from the box of bacon." She gripped his hand. "We'll make do, Tiller. Then we'll leave first thing after breakfast."

He rubbed his forehead. "I wish I'd brought some things back with me from Canton."

She cocked her head. "Why didn't you?"

"It wasn't my money to spend." He cupped her chin. "I want you to always be able to trust me, Mariah. No matter what you may hear in the future, just know you can trust me."

A tiny frown appeared between her brows, but she smiled. "I do trust you, Tiller. Someday you'll know just how much."

He smoothed the soft skin of her chin with his thumb. "Then there's the other reason I didn't bring home supplies. . ."

"Yes?"

He gave her his best roguish grin. "The thought never entered my mind."

She shoved him away. "Oh, you!"

Laughing, he gathered her close. "The more I think about it, the more I like the idea of waiting for daylight." He winked. "That way I can stare at your pretty profile all the way into Canton."

She lowered her lashes. "I hope you find as much pleasure in staring at my uncle."

Tiller's brow shot up. "Joe's coming?"

"I'm afraid so."

He groaned. "Can't you talk him out of it?"

"I dare not try, or he'll be suspicious."

"If it's a chaperone he's worried about, we'll take Miss Vee. Or Rainy."

Mariah patted his chest. "I'm sorry, Tiller. He's coming along, and that's the end of it. My uncle's a very stubborn man. Once he gets an idea in his head, you can't drive it out with your hammer."

Tiller glanced at the tool in question, hefting its weight. "It wouldn't take a forceful blow. Just enough for an afternoon nap."

"Tiller McRae!"

He grinned. "You know I'm teasing, but the idea is tempting." He softened his eyes. "There are things I'd planned to say to you, but the matter won't bear your uncle's prying ears."

Blushing, she nodded. "I'll admit I looked forward to those hours alone with you to talk about our future."

" 'Our future.' That has a nice ring to it." He gave her a lazy smile. "Hours alone with you sounds even better."

Planting her fingers against his chest, she pushed away. "I'd best get back, or he'll come looking for me."

Tiller walked with her to the barn door. "I'll do like you say, honey. I'll keep our secret as long as it takes." He dropped a soft kiss on her ear then lingered to whisper. "I only hope it won't be a lengthy wait."

Watching her go, he recalled Otis's God-words promising that things would turn out good in the end. Maybe his ill-fated life had taken a lucky turn at last. If he had to be patient for a spell, Mariah was worth the wait.

A shadow crossed the floor, and Tiller spun.

Just the wind dipping a branch past the window.

He shook himself and released a shuddering breath. It wasn't the time for seeing ghosts. He had his hands full enough with the old warhorse setting up camp inside Bell's Inn.

TWENTY-SEVEN

Tiller tugged the reins and eased Sheki around a miry hole in the Trace, leftover from the relentless summer rains. As long as he avoided the low places, the going was easy. His frequent trips into Canton had reestablished portions of the road, pushing back the heavy overgrowth threatening to reclaim the old trail.

He headed west as soon as he could and followed the trail into town. As Mariah predicted, Uncle Joe's stern profile, nowhere near as pleasing as hers, glowered beside Tiller on the front seat of the rig.

Mariah made small talk, pointing out the wild herbs and strawberries and commenting on the greening of the hillsides, helped along by the recent downpours.

Joe answered in grunts, meeting Tiller's few comments with a raised brow and harsh stare. Even when the old coyote nodded off, his head bobbing to his chest, he slept with one ear open, raising his head to glare when Tiller spoke quietly to Mariah.

The miles and hours dragged. Tiller sagged with relief when the tall white spires of Canton's Grace Episcopal Church came into view over the treetops. He decided to speak his mind whether Uncle Joe liked it or not. "I'll drop the two of you in the square then take the wagon to have the wheels looked at. The way they're squealing, the rear axle needs greasing."

"Will you be joining us soon?"

The hopeful lilt in Mariah's voice spun Uncle Joe around so fast it's a wonder his neck didn't squeal.

She ducked her head. "I just meant that it's very close to lunchtime. I thought we might sit for a meal before we start shopping."

Tiller turned aside to hide his grin. If Mariah wasn't careful, she'd give up her own secret. He leaped to the ground and handed her down before Uncle Joe had a chance, raising both brows and winking when Joe turned his head. She rewarded him with a blush and a shy smile.

Tiller tipped his hat. "I'll drop off the rig then meet you in front of the courthouse. There's a café next door that serves fork-tender roast and fairly respectable rolls." He winked. "Though not as good as yours."

Joe swept around the back of the wagon. "We don't have time for such dawdling, Mariah. There are many supplies to buy, and it's a long way home. We'll find some hardtack and jerky."

Mariah's bright smile slid away. "Oh, Uncle, please. I'm starving. Our breakfast didn't have enough substance to stick." She tucked her dainty chin. "It would be such a treat to have someone else do the cooking for a change."

Joe's resolve wilted under the spell of Mariah's big eyes. He gazed toward the courthouse. "Where is this place you speak of?"

Grinning, Tiller ducked his head. They had something in common after all. He pointed out the narrow building with the checkered curtains in the windows. "Go on over. I won't be long."

"Maybe they have coffee fit for a man to drink," Joe mumbled as Mariah took his arm. "The slush John Coffee has Viola trained to make tastes like swamp water."

Shaking his head, Tiller climbed aboard the wagon and turned Sheki toward the smithy. He couldn't get shed of the horse and rig fast enough. After giving instructions concerning both, he hustled up the boardwalk, eager to belly up to the table. Even the strong coffee Joe mentioned sounded good.

Tiller couldn't remember the last time he'd eaten his fill. His shirts were baggy, his ribs stuck out, and his trousers drooped down past his waist. "The lean times are over," he told himself, loping toward the café. The checkered curtains were just ahead, and his darlin' waited inside with a pocketful of money. One thing was certain—he wouldn't leave Canton hungry.

The waitress frowned at the empty basket. "Dreadful sorry, folks." She picked it up. "I thought I just filled this with rolls."

Mariah laughed. "Oh, you did. My friend here enjoyed them very much. Bring us another basket if you don't mind."

Tiller's cheeks were too full to speak, but he nodded his agreement.

Uncle Nukowa shot him a contemptuous scowl. "Just like the greedy white man, always taking more than he needs."

Mariah seethed. He spoke in their language, but she answered in English. "Yes, he has quite an appetite, doesn't he? It's the hunger of a hardworking man." She let the fire in her eyes say the rest.

Her uncle's hand swept over the stack of empty dishes and the slice of apple pie in front of Tiller's plate. "Who pays for all this?"

Mariah wished he'd stuck with Choctaw. Her patience at an end, she decided the time had come to set her uncle straight. "My understanding with Tiller is between us. Please don't insult him again or dishonor me by questioning our arrangement."

He shrugged. "I was just asking."

Tiller calmly pulled the pie plate toward him and poured a dollop of cream over the top. "It's all right, Mariah. Your uncle's looking out for your interests." Leaning over the table with a bold stare, he raised his chin. "Sir, if there's ever a day when I don't earn my keep around Bell's Inn, I hope you'll invite me to leave." He nodded. "Are we understood?"

Before her uncle could respond, Tiller continued. "I'm not in the habit of allowing a woman to fight my battles, but since Mariah has opened the can, let me stir the worms." He laid down his fork. "On the subject of battles, I'm not sure why you've declared war against me. Since you hardly know me, I don't feel you have just cause."

Uncle Nukowa watched Tiller with guarded eyes.

"That said, if I've done anything to rile you, it wasn't deliberate, and I apologize." Turning on the full force of his charm, Tiller offered his hand. "So I say we shake and start over."

Nibbling at her pie, Mariah held her breath.

The sullen wall Uncle Nukowa had erected crumbled twitch by twitch on his proud face, toppling with a grudging smile. "I suppose we could do that," he said, reaching across the bread basket.

Before their palms met, a light touch at Mariah's elbow spun her around.

"I thought it was you, dear." The tall, gaunt man behind her smiled warmly. "It's good to see you, Mariah."

Blackness swirled. Mariah gulped for air to clear the murky fog. Her chest thundered and her tongue forged to the roof of her mouth. She tried to bolt from her chair and flee, but her limbs wouldn't budge.

"How have you been holding up?" Dr. Moony asked, his eyes a sea of compassion.

She made a strangled sound, followed by a guttural moan, worsened by the bite of spiced apple hung in her throat. Frantic, she silently pleaded with Tiller across the table.

Staring back helplessly, his freckles stood on tiptoe.

TWENTY-EIGHT

Mariah was choking. Or having some sort of a spell.

Tiller's gaze jumped to the tall man at her side. Somehow, it was this geezer's fault.

He half rose from his chair. "Mariah?"

She struggled to swallow as if something had her by the throat and then sucked in a breath of air. "D–Dr. Moony," she finally managed, blinking up at the stranger. "How nice to see you." Pulling her napkin from her lap, she dabbed the corners of her mouth, the starched cloth no whiter than her face.

Relief settled Tiller against his chair.

"I planned to ride out and check on you," the man was saying. "Then I got your letter." He patted her shoulder. "I was sorry to hear that John Coffee was gone."

Mariah shot to her feet, loudly clearing her throat. "Doctor. . ." She pointed at the door. "May we continue this conversation outside?"

He held up his finger. "In a moment." With a warm smile, he nodded at Joe. "I'm happy to see you've come to stay with your niece. I hated to think of her all alone out there."

The pallor of Mariah's cheeks rose to a fiery mottled red. "Please, sir?"

"The onset of John's illness was sudden," the doctor continued. "Of course, his leaving us so quickly was no surprise."

"Didn't surprise me, either." Joe swung his chair around and casually crossed his legs. "It's just like my brother-in-law to run off and leave his responsibilities on someone else's shoulders."

Flustered, the doctor stared. "Forgive me, Joe, but it's not like the poor man had a choice. John was quite ill, you know."

Joe folded his arms over his chest. "Just so he returns stronger than when he left. I have a few things to say to him."

The doctor's throat bobbed a few times before he nodded. "Of, course. You mean when he"—he twirled his finger in the air and rolled his eyes—*"returns."* He gave a nervous laugh. "I must say, you people have the quaintest customs."

Mariah hooked her arm in his and urged him toward the door. "If you don't mind, I have something of a delicate nature to discuss. In private."

Nearly pulling the lanky man off balance, Mariah hauled him over the threshold.

Tiller's puzzled gaze met Joe's across the table. "What do you suppose that was about?"

Joe shrugged. "The mind of a woman is a deep river. I try not to fish there."

Nodding thoughtfully, Tiller cut the rest of his pie in half and slid a portion onto Joe's empty plate. "That was Mr. Bell's doctor?"

Joe pulled the offering in front of him and took a bite. "Yes. For many years."

Tiller nodded. "Do you know what sickness he has?"

Joe shook his head. "I suppose I should've asked."

His motives a mite selfish, Tiller posed a thought. "To hear him and Mariah talk, Mr. Bell could be gone a long. . .*long* time."

"You're right." Joe craned his neck to stare at the door, the concern Tiller had hoped to rouse creasing his forehead. "Maybe I should go ask him."

"So you see, doctor," Mariah said, "among my people the subject of death is forbidden, so the less said about the departed, the better. Once we've completed the mourning ritual, we're not allowed to utter their names again."

Dr. Moony took both her hands and squeezed. "I'm a blundering old fool, dear. I'll be more careful next time."

She tightened her fingers. "It's my fault. I should've said something before now. And I'm very grateful for all you've done."

He flashed a warm smile. "I'm happy to see you're all right. I watched you suffer right along with your father."

A cleansing rest flooded Mariah's soul, and grateful tears welled. She felt comforted to speak openly of her father's death, especially with someone who understood the depths of her pain. She tugged a hankie from her waistband and wiped her eyes. "Thank you, sir."

Despite how good it felt to grieve, to linger would be folly. She pointed over her shoulder. "I'd best get back inside. They'll be wondering where I am."

"Yes, and I have patients to see." He leaned to kiss her cheek. "You know how to reach me and the missus. If you need anything, don't hesitate to call on us." Mariah clung to his hand as he backed away smiling. "Anything at all, you hear?"

She nodded, letting his fingers slip from her grasp. "I won't forget." A throbbing ache in her chest, she watched him stroll to the corner and disappear. With a shuddering sigh, she returned to the café and met Uncle Nukowa on the doorstep.

He pushed past her and peered up and down the boardwalk, his bushy brows drawn to peaks. "Where's the doctor?"

"Gone," Mariah said, clutching his sleeve to draw him inside. "He had patients to tend."

Avoiding Tiller's curious stare, she approached the waitress to pay the bill. Once she'd counted out enough coins, she tucked the leather pouch away. "Miss, where is your. . .?"

The girl pointed. "Through there and out the back to your left."

Nodding her thanks, Mariah headed down the long hallway, forcing herself not to run. At the end of the longest walk of her life, she yanked open the door of the cramped little building. Slumping against the roughhewn wall, she allowed the bitter tears to fall.

Joe had a newfound respect for Tiller McRae. The boy stood in the wagon bed shifting boxes of canned foods and shoving crates of dry goods aside to make room, attacking the job with the same strength of character he'd shown while defending himself in the café.

Tiller had a strong back and willing hands when it came to hard work, qualities Joe prided himself on. Unfortunately, the brash buck couldn't hide his desire for Mariah.

The two thought him a witless fool. A blind man could see their lingering looks, the quick twining of their fingers when she handed up her bundles, his thumb stroking the back of her hand each time they passed.

Clearly, Mariah loved him. Despite Tiller's charm, or maybe because of it, Joe hadn't decided if he loved her, too.

Maybe greed clouded Tiller's vision. The chance to own Bell's Inn and acres of Mississippi farmland would tempt a man even with an ugly woman thrown into the bargain. Mariah, her father's only heir, was as lovely as a spotted fawn.

Hadn't Joe suspected the same of John Coffee? But his sister had closed her love-struck ears and married the spineless man despite Joe's warning.

Mariah handed the last bundle to Tiller, her eyes twin stars of admiration. Leaning to take it from her hands, he winked.

Joe ground his heel in the dirt and gritted his teeth. Whatever it took to prevent it, Mariah wouldn't make the same mistake as her mother.

Tiller kicked the end of a box, wedging it between a crate and the side of the wagon. "There now. Maybe we can close the tailgate." He jumped to the ground, tilting his head at Mariah. "You must be finished shopping since you've emptied all the stores."

She glanced up from checking things off her list. "I suppose that's all we need. Can you think of anything we may have forgotten?"

He raised the gate and shoved home the latch. "I don't see how. There's at least one of everything in town back here."

Her cheeks colored. "Oh, you."

Already they sparred like husband and wife. Angry with himself for making peace with Tiller, Joe tugged down his hat to hide his glowering face. "Are we ready to go? It's a long way home."

"Yes, Uncle." With a flourish, she scratched off the last item on her list. "We're ready."

They climbed aboard, Mariah giggling the way she had as a child when Joe held her down and tickled her. "I can't wait to see Miss Vee's face. It's been a while since our cupboard was full."

Tiller shifted around to look at her. "With all these different foods, I can't wait to taste whatever you two come up with."

Joe couldn't help frowning at him. The bottomless man couldn't be hungry.

"I promise you fine meals for your patience, Tiller," Mariah said gleefully. "And baked goods in abundance. Have you ever seen so much flour and sugar and butter?"

Grinning, Tiller glanced over his shoulder. "I'll get the meat straight into the smokehouse. Those salted hams and racks of bacon should last a good while."

"Yes, and I bought extra meal. In case we catch more fish."

"More fish sounds good. With Rainy's help, I'll make sure that happens." His smile widened. "Which reminds me. . .the garden is coming along fine. In no time, we'll have plenty of fresh vegetables again."

"That's enough," Joe growled, sweeping off his hat and slapping his leg with the brim. "What's going on here?"

Two sets of stunned eyes blinked at him.

"What do you mean, Uncle?"

He spun around. "The two of you talk like you've been starving. Why is the pantry and smokehouse so empty?"

Squirming like a guilty child, her gaze jumped to Tiller.

Joe lifted his hand. "I don't want my answer from him. You tell me, Mariah. Why has John Coffee allowed my only niece to go hungry while the rest of her tribe prospers?"

TWENTY-NINE

It took the better part of the ride home to smooth Uncle Nukowa's ruffled feathers. Mariah explained that in the aftermath of the storm, and with the usual decline in travelers during the winter months, the coffers had dwindled. Now, thanks to Tiller's fine head for business, she had enough money to last a good long while.

She didn't dare mention the cost of father's illness. Weary of half-truths and careful omission of details, she neglected to explain how she'd emptied her safe into Dr. Moony's pockets to avoid the very confrontation she'd just faced.

Uncle Nukowa vented his frustration on Tiller by hinting the money would last longer without the price of his appetite.

Mariah jumped to Tiller's defense. "That's highly unfair, Uncle. While it's true that he enjoys his food, I've watched this poor man go without until every last member of the household was fed."

Her uncle cut his eyes to Tiller. "Is that true?"

"Maybe." He shrugged. "I reckon it is."

Uncle Nukowa sat against the side rail, watching Tiller as if he didn't quite know what to make of him. "Then I owe you an apology."

Tiller slapped her uncle's knee. "I wouldn't fret, Joe."

Mariah cringed, but Uncle Nukowa didn't bat an eye.

With the extra weight of the load on poor Sheki, the journey back

515

took longer. Dusk had settled over the land as they turned off the Canton road onto the Trace. So close to home, Tiller didn't bother with the lantern. Mariah supposed they were all relieved, especially the horse, when the warm glow of lights from the inn appeared between the trees.

They pulled into the backyard, and Miss Vee met them on the porch with a lamp. "Hallelujah! I've never been so happy to see three faces in my life. Excuse me, Sheki—make that four." She grinned. "I can hear Otis smiling from here. The poor man's hollow as a gourd."

She ran down the steps and peered over the side of the wagon, running eager hands over the boxes. "How did you sneak up on me, Tiller? I've been straining to hear those squeaky wheels for hours."

"Had her greased, Miss Vee," he said.

"So you tricked me, you rascal." Her dimpled cheeks were shadows in the dim light. "Never mind. You're here now. Let's get this load in the house and go to cooking."

Guilt fell heavy on Mariah's shoulders. While they'd frolicked and feasted in town, poor Miss Vee and Otis suffered hunger. She scurried down. "We'll unload, Miss Vee. Go warm up the stove."

"I've had a fire in the oven for hours. The burning wood was starting to smell tasty."

Mariah passed a ham over her shoulder. "Take this inside. Get it sliced and put it on to fry. I'll be in to make skillet bread as soon as I can."

Tiller unhooked the latch and lowered the tailgate. "Go ahead, Mariah. Me and Uncle Joe can handle things out here."

Cringing, she waited for her uncle's flash of anger at Tiller's familiar tone. Instead, he eased his body stiffly to the ground and took the first heavy crate from Tiller's hands. "Don't worry," he said, huffing up the steps to the back door. "I remember where everything goes."

Miss Vee took a box and followed him inside.

Flashing Tiller a grateful smile, Mariah held out her hands. "I may as well take one on my way."

He reached for her, drawing her into his arms with a quick intake of air. Checking over her shoulder first, he lifted her to her tiptoes and kissed her soundly. Not the bare brush of lips against her cheek, but a crushing, dizzying kiss that robbed her of her senses.

Setting her on her feet, he handed her a box of canned goods and gave her a gentle shove toward the house. Glancing back, she found him grinning smugly. "What was the meaning of that, Tiller McRae?"

He lifted one shoulder. "Just collecting my due."

"Your due?"

He hefted one of the heavier crates, nodding at her to get moving. "The price of keeping your secret against my will. The penalty for making me wait when I'd marry you tomorrow."

She hurried onto the porch then turned. "Was it sufficient payment? I like my debts paid in full."

"Oh no, ma'am." One foot on the bottom step, he raised a teasing brow. "Consider it the first of many installments."

She jutted her chin. "It's hardly chivalrous to make a lady weak in the knees and then hand her a load to bear."

Amusement danced in his eyes. He opened his mouth to speak, but the squeal of the back door stifled his answer.

Uncle Nukowa bustled past. "Viola's watching for you, niece. She's anxious for you to finish the bread so she'll have something to wrap around her fried ham."

Fatigue seeped into Tiller's bones, and sweat dampened his shirt. Unable to pass another kitchen chair without resting his throbbing feet, he sank into the next one he came to. He'd lost count of the trips it took from the wagon to the pantry and then the smokehouse, but they finally found the bottom of the rig.

The well-stocked larder filled him with a happiness he hadn't felt in years—and not for the reason Uncle Joe might think. Tiller savored the knowledge that his idea to sell off the downed trees had filled Mariah's little safe with money. A good stash of coins promising ample food and a measure of security that lifted a burden from her shoulders for a good long while.

It felt good to take care of Mariah. Right somehow. He planned to spend the rest of his days looking after her.

Watching her bustle near the stove, flipping crisp golden circles of skillet bread, Tiller couldn't stop thinking about their kiss. He'd meant no disrespect. In fact, he'd set out to give her a teasing peck on the cheek. At the last second, her lips had drawn him like cool water on a summer day. He'd held his breath and taken the plunge, drowning in her sweetness.

As if she felt him watching, she looked over her shoulder and smiled. "You look tired."

He leaned forward and gripped his knees. "I suppose I am, but we're all exhausted. Especially poor old Sheki." He forced himself to stand. "I'll go get him tended for the night."

Mariah caught his arm as he passed. "No, I'll go. I haven't just unloaded a month's worth of supplies." She handed her spatula to Miss Vee and untied her apron. "Finish the bread, please. I'll be back in time to set the table."

Pausing at the door, she winked at Tiller. "You might want to follow my uncle's lead and freshen up before supper."

Aware of how he smelled after toting all the boxes, he stumbled toward her with his arms outstretched. "All right, but hug me first."

She squealed and darted outside while Miss Vee shook with laughter.

Tiller passed his room by and ducked in on Otis. "How are you this evening, sir?"

Otis waved merrily then rubbed his stomach. "Ready for grub." His eyes widened. "Is supper about ready?"

Tiller grinned. "It won't be much longer. Can I do anything for you before I clean up?"

Otis sank against his pillow. "Keep a close watch over little missy," he said. "Something's weighing on my spirit where she's concerned. Been praying for her all day."

Thinking of Mariah's cantankerous uncle and his determination to take her out of Mississippi, Tiller nodded. "Keep praying, sir. I think I know what it's about."

A dazed look in his eyes, Otis shook his head. "This ain't about her secret. I'm sure it's something else."

Leaning against the doorjamb, Tiller stared at Otis as the truth sank in. He knew Mariah's secret. In fact, he *was* her secret—the truth she couldn't tell her uncle Joe. How did God and Otis see a thing coming before it happened?

"You listening to me, boy?" Otis seemed upset. "You watch her close, you hear?"

Dazed, Tiller nodded. "I will, sir. I promise." He entered the room and eased Otis down on the bed. "Just rest until we bring your supper." He pointed behind him. "I have to go get cleaned up now."

Stopping on the threshold, he turned to look back, worry gnawing the back of his mind.

Otis shook his skinny finger. "Watch her."

Tiller fretted the whole time he washed up and changed his clothes. Was the old boy trying to tell him their secret was bound to come out? Was he warning Tiller that her uncle was about to steal her away?

Otis knew things, after all. God-things too wonderful for Tiller's mind to grasp.

The whole thing reminded him of the lie he'd told Otis that first day on the trail. His made-up story of a wife named Lucinda and her brutish brothers, who came in the night to snatch her from his arms.

It seemed a hundred years ago he'd spun the fanciful tale. Could it be coming to life in the form of Uncle Joe taking Mariah out of Tiller's arms, catching him in his own deceitful web?

He left his room determined to be more cautious, to guard Mariah's secret with more care.

Miss Vee had already set the dining room table then graced it with heaping platters of ham, fried eggs, and skillet bread. Lifting a hefty plateful, she placed it on a tray with a cup of coffee. "Sit down, Tiller. I'll take this to Otis and come right back to serve you."

Uncle Joe, lounging at the head of the table, stabbed a piece of bread with his fork and started eating.

Tiller pulled out a chair beside him. "Mariah's not back yet?"

Joe raised his head, his bulging jaw working. "From where? I thought she was in her room."

Tiller poured them both a cup of coffee. "She's tending Sheki."

Adding a cube of sugar to his cup, Joe stirred and took a long sip. "Counting my nag and your gelding, there are only three horses out there. She could've tended a stable-full by now."

Tiller shrugged. "You know how she is about Sheki. She's likely brushing his teeth and reading him a bedtime story."

Uncle Joe spewed a bit of coffee then swallowed and laughed with Tiller, wiping his mouth with his sleeve.

Miss Vee hurried into the room rubbing her hands together. "Now then, where were we?" She settled in her place and forked a pile of ham before passing the silver charger. "I'm not sure what's keeping Mariah, but I say we go ahead without her. If she was as hungry as I am, she'd be here by now."

Tiller took a slice of meat then handed the platter to Joe. "Share the bread, will you, Miss Vee. I can smell it from here."

Miss Vee balanced the butter dish on the tray of fried rounds and stretched the whole thing toward him. "Anything else before I get busy?"

"Tiller!" Otis swept around the corner panting hard. "You ain't watching."

Miss Vee's shoulders jerked, and she dropped the tray, scattering bread like savory place mats over the table. The careening butter dish upset the coffee urn, spilling rich, dark liquid in a puddle that soaked the bread.

Tiller leaped to his feet.

Still in his nightshirt, Otis clung to the doorpost, his mouth sagging and his eyes glazed with panic.

The hair on Tiller's arms tingled. "Something's wrong?"

Otis nodded frantically.

Tiller hurled himself past Otis and out the door.

THIRTY

Two steps inside the barn, and Tiller knew. His stomach a quivering jumble of mush, he whirled to face Joe and Miss Vee. "She's gone."

Miss Vee smoothed her hair with a shaky hand. "What do you mean 'gone'? She's somewhere on the grounds. Maybe down by the river. The girl does that sometimes." She started for the door. "I'll just walk out here and call her."

Joe caught her arm. "She won't answer, Viola. Tiller's right. Mariah's gone."

She stamped her foot. "Now blast it, how do you know?"

He pointed at Sheki, still wearing the unbuckled harness and nuzzling Tiller's hand for oats. "She brought him to the barn, but that's as far as she got."

Miss Vee spun to face Tiller. "I don't understand. Mariah wouldn't just walk away."

He shot her a pointed look. "She didn't."

Pale and trembling, Joe lurched to a nearby post and clung to it. "Any ideas, son? We need to know where to start looking."

A high-pitched ringing shrilled in Tiller's ears. He rubbed his forehead. "Give me a minute to think."

Joe glanced between them. "Did John Coffee have any enemies?"

Besides you? Tiller shook his head, panic climbing his throat. "She never mentioned anyone."

"A drifter?" Joe persisted. He gripped Miss Vee's shoulders. "Think, Viola. Who might have taken her?"

She licked her lips. "We get all kinds at the inn. Just a few weeks ago, we had a right rowdy bunch. They made trouble, and I ran them off." Her wide eyes flashed with fear. "Maybe they came back to take revenge."

Tiller glanced at Joe. "There was another band of rough-looking strangers after that." He pointed toward the house. "The men who brought Otis."

"That's right," Miss Vee said, snapping her fingers. "We realized once they'd gone they could've been the very ones who robbed poor Otis and left him for dead."

Remembering his ruthless gang, the real culprits, Tiller shuddered and cast her a doubtful look. "I never held with that idea. Believe me, the animals that hurt Otis wouldn't have turned right around and helped him." A picture came to mind of the strange man on the far bank snapping a jaunty salute. "Let's face it, folks. This is still the Natchez Trace. The Devil's Backbone. There's never been anything but greed and mischief along this road." Tiller swept past them to saddle his horse. "Are you going with me Joe? We've got to hurry."

Spinning, Joe grabbed his tack and carried it inside the other stall.

Miss Vee paced and wrung her hands until they led the horses out. "Where will you go?" Her voice shook. "You don't know where to look."

Tiller swung onto the gelding and gathered the reins. "Pray, Miss Vee. Pray that God will give me a taste of what He gives Otis before it's too late."

She clutched his leg and handed him her lamp. "I'll pray. And I'll ask Otis, as well. I promise."

He lifted his chin at Sheki. "Take care of him for Mariah, would you?"

Tears in her eyes, she nodded.

Side by side, Tiller and Joe barreled from the barn in a flurry of hooves and dust. By lantern light, they combed every trail and stand of brush in a ten-mile sweep around the inn, searching until Tiller's eyes burned from the strain.

Joe dismounted twice. Once to study a clutch of broken twigs near the house and now to crouch and stare at the print of a boot heel in a low spot off the road. "No Indian has her. This man is a clumsy fool."

Tiller squatted beside him with the lamp. "I suppose there isn't one clumsy Indian in Mississippi?"

Joe shrugged. "Among the Chickasaw, maybe."

Tiller watched to see if he was joking. He didn't smile. "If he's such a fool, why don't we know which way to ride next?"

Joe stood, his hands on his hips. "Because it's dark and we're tired." He lifted one shoulder. "Because I'm not the Choctaw I used to be." He sounded close to tears.

Glancing up from the dim circle of light, Tiller sighed. "I'm no Choctaw, but I think I know which way to ride." He stood and pointed toward the horses. "We've got to get these animals to the barn before they drop from under us." Holding up the lamp, he shook it. "Besides, we're almost out of oil." Passing Joe, he gripped his sagging shoulder. "Maybe you should take them home and get some rest. If you know where I can find oil and a fresh horse—"

Joe shoved his hand away. "A woman needs rest. I won't stop until I find Mariah." He sniffed. "We ride back together. You can take Sheki. I'll find myself another horse."

Tiller gazed at him with new respect. "All right then."

A bobbing lantern swept toward them in the pitch darkness as they reined off the Trace into the yard. Miss Vee ran toward them shouting Tiller's name, her shrill voice echoing off the trees.

His heart dared to hope. He laid his heels into the gelding's side and galloped to meet her. "Did she come back?"

Panting, she held her side and gasped for breath. "No. But I know who took her."

Tiller leaped to the ground and gripped her shoulders. "Who?"

"I've been thinking for hours, and it came to me just now. I was about to saddle Sheki and go after her myself."

Joe reached them, jumping to the ground. "You know something, Viola?"

Losing patience, Tiller shook her. "Where is she, Miss Vee?"

Her eyes glowed like an angry cat's. "I don't know why we didn't think of it sooner. Gabriel Tabor's got her."

Shock fired through Tiller. Loose-lipped, potbellied Gabe who couldn't keep his hands or his dirty thoughts to himself?

Joe pushed between them. "Julian Tabor's son? Why would Gabe take Mariah?"

"To get revenge." Miss Vee started to cry. "To ruin her if he can. Mariah's all he's ever wanted, and she spurned him."

Gathering his reins, Tiller smoothed his horse's neck. "Hang on for just a while longer, can you boy?" He slid his boot into the stirrup and threw his leg over then reached for Miss Vee's lantern. "How do I get there?"

"I know the way," Joe said, pulling his horse around. "We'll go as the crow flies. Follow me." He swung into the saddle, shouted a command in Choctaw, and thundered toward the Pearl.

They picked their way over the nearest crossing. At the Tabor's fence line, Tiller kicked an opening in the leaning pickets. "What if we're wrong, Joe?" he asked, guiding the horses through.

Joe glanced up. "We'll owe this man a new fence."

Mounting up, they skirted a pecan grove then sailed over rows of young cotton in a field that seemed to stretch on forever, until the shadowy outline of a stately plantation house rose in the distance. Despite the late hour, lights burned in most of the tall windows.

Joe glanced at him. "Something's stirring, that's for sure."

Tiller nodded grimly. "It's about to get a whole lot worse."

They rode up to the porch and slid to the ground. Tiller strode up the steps with Joe at his heels. Together they pounded with their fists, showing no regard for the hands on the clock and no mercy for the rattling door frame.

A shouting voice ordered them to keep their trousers on, and then the door jerked open. "What's the meaning of this infernal hullabaloo?"

Could the scowling little sprout be Julian Tabor? Tiller had braced for big Gabe or a slightly older version, so the tiny, stoop-shouldered gentleman caught him off guard. Thin and frail, a high wind would carry him off without the weight of his full, gray beard to hold him down. If the man was Gabe's father, Mrs. Tabor hailed from sturdy stock.

Leaning closer, he squinted. "Joe Brashears, is that you? How dare you beat on my door at this hour?"

"Julian, we're looking for Gabe," Joe said through clenched teeth.

Mr. Tabor stood up straighter. "Well, that makes two of us."

Joe narrowed his eyes. "What do you mean?"

"I mean my boy's not here."

Tiller edged closer and peered over his shoulder into the house. "You need to let us in, mister. We're bound to find him."

His hollow eyes flinched, fixing Tiller with a murderous gaze. "I told you my son ain't home. You hard of hearing?"

Joe cleared his throat. "Gabe took Mariah, Julian. He ran off with her."

Interest flickered on his face. "Ran off? You mean to get hitched?"

Tiller shook his head. "No hearts and flowers, sir. He slipped inside the barn and carried her out against her will."

The old man winced. "That's the craziest talk I ever heard. Gabe wouldn't hurt Mariah." His tongue flicked out to wet his bottom lip. "You boys have the wrong man."

Joe glanced at Tiller and heaved a sigh. "I guess it's time to ride for the sheriff in Canton. A posse will ferret him out."

Mr. Tabor's hands shot up. "Now Joe, there's no call to bring in the law. We sweep our own doorsteps out here."

Joe clenched his fists and leaned threateningly. "Then start sweeping."

Backing away from the door, Mr. Tabor motioned them in.

The moment Tiller crossed the threshold, his anxious gaze flitted over the high-ceilinged entry and the fancy parlor off the hall, searching for any sign of Mariah.

"You're wasting your time looking, boy. She hasn't been here." He swallowed hard. "And neither has Gabe." Sadness dulled his eyes. "He's been missing all night, and I'm worried sick. It ain't like him not to come home."

Tiller nodded at Joe over Mr. Tabor's head. "Do you have any idea where he might've taken her?"

The old man's hand shot up. "I never said he did." Breathing hard, he leaned one hand on his hip, kneading his shaggy brows with two fingers of the other. "Let's say for argument's sake that Gabe's your culprit. My boy wouldn't pluck a hair from Mariah's head. He's quite fond of her."

A knot rose in Tiller's throat. "A little too fond of her, isn't he, Mr.

Tabor? Surely you're not blind to your own son's heart."

"The boy's right," Joe said. "There's more than one way to harm a decent woman."

Mr. Tabor glanced away.

Joe shifted in front of his face. "You know something, don't you, Julian? I can see it in your eyes." Clutching his arms, Joe gave him a shake. "Come on, man! This is Mariah at stake. The same little girl who groomed your horses, played in your cornfield, brought soup to your sickbed."

Mr. Tabor groaned and spun toward the parlor. "Come this way."

They followed him inside the well-appointed room, every nerve in Tiller's body yearning for the chase. "We don't have much time, sir."

He stopped in front of the mantelpiece. "This won't take long." Rummaging in an ornately carved box, he turned with a folded paper in his hands. "This is the map to a little cabin I own up near Cypress Swamp."

Tiller lifted his brows at Joe.

"Ten miles from here," he said.

Mr. Tabor leaned against the mantel and crossed his arms over the paper. "If I know my son, Gabe's headed one of two places." He cleared his throat. "If he plans to do right by Mariah, they're bound for Canton and a justice of the peace." He paused. "But if his mind's gone twisted, he's taking her to this cabin."

Tiller watched his weathered face. "Make the call, Mr. Tabor."

Gripping the back of a chair for support, the man seemed to age ten years. His chin slumped to his chest, and he held out the map. "Please don't hurt him, Joe."

Joe's fingers lingered on his hand. "I'll do my best to prevent it."

Mr. Tabor's agony over his son echoed Tiller's dread for Mariah. He touched his sleeve. "Thank you, sir."

One glance at Joe and they bolted for the door.

Mr. Tabor's voice stopped them at the threshold. "Keep a sharp eye. Gabe's bound to be armed, and he won't give her up without a fight."

Outside on the steps, Joe caught Tiller's sleeve. "It's time to bring in some help."

"From where?"

"The same place we'll find fresh horses. Follow me."

Riding hard, Tiller chased him across the river again. Instead of turning left toward the inn, Joe angled right and rode along the sandy bank for about two miles. Cutting into the woods, they rode another half mile before wending past chicken coops and pigsties then up to a rickety back porch.

Joe gave a sharp whistle, holding the lantern close to his face.

A light came on in the house, and a squinting Tobias Jones appeared at the door. "Halito, Joe Brashears! A long time has passed since we've seen you."

"We need your help," Joe said simply. He dismounted and ambled to join Tobias on the porch. In the flickering glow, they continued their conversation in the language they shared.

Tiller caught Mariah's name, and then Gabe's name paired with a foul curse. Sometime during Joe's rant, Christopher and Justin tumbled outside pulling on trousers and shirts. They crowded behind their pa with menacing dark scowls.

Without a word, Tobias lifted his arm. Chris vaulted the rail to his left and disappeared into the shadowy pine. Justin squeezed between them and tore across the junk-cluttered yard to the barn.

Tiller waited while Joe and Tobias plotted quietly in the haunting rhythm of the Choctaw. He didn't understand the words, but their stern, serene faces gave him confidence in the plan.

Justin reappeared, leading two paint ponies from the barn. Tiller pulled the saddle from the gelding and threw it on the closest horse while Justin fixed Joe's saddle to the other. Before Tiller had tightened the cinch, Chris marched out of the woods by torchlight with a cluster of Indian braves.

At least thirty men converged like an army set for battle. Concern tightened some of the faces, anger twisted others, reminding Tiller that these were Mariah's people.

A chill shot along his spine. Would Joe be able to honor his promise to let no harm come to Gabriel Tabor?

THIRTY-ONE

A ballet of tiny green fireflies danced between Mariah and the quaint little cabin. Clusters of glowing mushrooms, their snow-white tops bathed in moonlight, dotted the rustic yard. In the distance, a low-lying mist hung over the swamp, weaving in and out between fat cypress trunks. Her ears rang with the deep-throated croak of bullfrogs and the frenzied shrill of crickets.

In other circumstances, the scene would be a magical dream. Astride a horse, wedged against Gabe's big belly with her wrists bound and his foul breath in her ear, it was a ghastly nightmare.

Gabe climbed out of the saddle and lifted her down beside him.

Shuddering, she shrank away from his beefy hands. "Touch me like that again, and I'll kill you quicker than a dry horse sniffs out water."

Gabe braced his hands on his knees and laughed like a fiend. "I can't help it, Mariah. You're like a sickness to me. A fever in my blood. I cotton to you like a child to a sweet."

She raised her chin. "You're hardly a child, Gabe, except in your mind. You should be ashamed of yourself. Bringing me here against my will is the meanest, mangiest thing you've ever done."

Fury flashed in his eyes. "Hush, gal. Don't talk to me about mean after the hateful thing you done." He shoved her shoulder. "Get on up to the cabin."

She held her ground. "Untie me first. I can't see a thing." She softened her voice. "You don't want me to trip and hurt myself, do you?"

He turned her, fumbled with the ropes, then stilled. "Wait a minute. You'll run."

Mariah crossed her fingers. "I won't. I promise." *Not until the first chance I get.*

Mumbling, Gabe seemed to mull it over then spun her around. "I won't do it. But don't worry, I've got you." Linking his arm through hers, he herded her for the door. She stumbled a few times on the way, but his grip was a cruel vise that held her upright.

Their booted feet thundered on the loose boards of the porch, the echo bouncing off the sagging overhang and resounding in her head. Gabe released her while he fumbled for the knob then shoved the door open in front of them. Before he pushed her over the threshold, he groped along a shelf on the inside wall and pulled down a lantern. Striking a long match, he lit the wick then nudged her in the back with his elbow.

The charm of the cabin ended past the front wall. The moldy odor of dampness reached her first, followed by the stench of unwashed chamber pots and dirty laundry. Mariah turned her face to her shoulder and gagged.

When she recovered enough to speak, she turned watery eyes to Gabe. "Please untie me. I can't stand being bound another second."

Watching her, Gabe fumbled for a long brass key hidden over the door frame. Hanging the lamp from a hook, he inserted the key in the door and turned the lock. Hurrying across the room, he lit another lantern in the center of a small round dining table.

More light was both a blessing and a curse. The dimness made the musty cabin gloomy, but the light revealed the filth and diminished her hope of escape. The tiny cabin had a single door with a window to one side. Watermarked curtains over the sink offered hope of another exit. The rest of the walls were solid cypress logs, set together like interlocking fists to hold her inside.

"Now then. I suppose I could unknot your rope." He gave her a long, searching look. "As long as you promise to behave."

Mariah nodded fiercely. "I promise."

"If you go she-cat on me, I'll tie you up again, only tighter. You won't get loose no matter how much you squawk." He shook his finger in her face. "I swear on my ma's grave."

She lowered her lashes. "I'll behave myself." *As long as you do the same.*

The bulging knot in his throat rose and fell. "First, let me tell you how it's got to be." His hands moved to rest on his broad hips. "I'll hunt up some food in that pantry yonder"—he jutted his chin toward a door in the corner—"whilst you clean up a little in the kitchen. There ain't been no female around here in a spell, so it lacks a woman's touch."

Mariah glanced over her shoulder at the appalling mess. "Yes, I can do that." Anything to keep his mind off her.

"I'll build a cozy fire, and you can make us a nice little supper." He ducked his head, the shy gesture almost human. "I heard how good you cook."

She forced a smile. "I'll do my best."

His tongue darted out to lick his bottom lip. "You set the table real nice, and we'll eat together like a happy married couple."

Her stomach jerked. "Th–that sounds nice."

"Once our bellies are full and the fire burns down to embers, we'll be ready for a little nap." His head made a slow, deliberate turn toward the small rumpled cot in the corner. "How's all that sound?"

Straining against her bonds, Mariah swallowed a scream. She longed to rail at him. Pummel the lurid grin from his drooling mouth. Show him the difference between a she-cat and a she-devil.

Instead, she forced her muscles to relax, her breathing to ease. Pushing Gabe to action would be a huge mistake. She would stay calm and bide her time. Mariah had two important things on her side—her mind and body were quicker than the dimwitted oaf who held her captive.

Gabe slipped around behind her. The rope tightened at first then released in a rush of warmth spreading to her tingling fingertips. She almost cried in relief.

Rubbing her hands to restore them to life, she moved a few steps closer to the stove and held them up. "See? Isn't this better? Now I can get this old kitchen ready for our meal."

He toddled after her. "Can I help?"

She waved him toward the pantry. "Go scout our provisions. I'll be fine."

He glanced toward the exit then back at her.

Mariah tilted her head. "It's locked. Remember?"

Innocent as a lamb, she lifted a broom from the corner and started to sweep, the meager bristles stirring a cloud of ancient dust around her feet. "I'll need a bucket of fresh water once I'm done here."

He raised one finger. "Don't you worry, darlin'. I'll fetch one as soon as I find our grub."

Pausing with his hand gripping the pantry door, he gazed at her with sad, droopy eyes. "You ain't mad at me, are you?"

The trussed-up she-devil surged. "Do you mean because you kidnapped me and brought me here against my will to play house in the middle of the night?"

He nodded dumbly.

Mariah tightened her grip on the broom, entertaining thoughts of beating him with it. "You'll understand if I'm just a little out of sorts? I'm sure I'll get over it in time."

His mouth pouted like a sulky boy's. "Well, don't stay mad too long, you hear?"

The second his bulk ducked inside, Mariah lunged for the kitchen window.

Locked.

Feeling around the casing with trembling fingers, she found the latch and tried it. The sliding metal squealed.

She froze, checking over her shoulder.

Another push and the lock gave, but she didn't dare try to crack the window. The rush of fresh air would give her away.

Fumbling under the curtain, her hand slid across the glass from corner to corner. The opening was small, but when the time was right, she'd find a way to squeeze through.

Dusting rusty grime on her skirt, she resumed her sweeping just as Gabe stumbled out with a crate in his hands.

"Here." Still pouting, he slid the box across the table. "You ought to be able to whip up something with all that."

Mariah put the broom aside to rummage in the box. One part of her mind devised a possible meal from the ingredients. The sensible part reminded her to take her time.

Hours had passed since she stood at the stove frying skillet bread for Tiller's supper. She should be snug in her feather bed, freshly bathed with a full stomach. Instead, she had a greasy kitchen to clean and a full meal to prepare.

No matter. If it took until daybreak to get it done, even better. The longer she stretched out Gabe's cozy meal, the longer she could scramble to escape what came next.

With the tin of beef, cubes of pocket soup, onions, carrots, and potatoes, Mariah would stir up a slow-simmering stew. With the Indian meal, she'd make johnnycakes. Better yet, hasty pudding—just not too hasty.

She'd flood the cabin with smells Gabe would find more enticing than her and fill his barrel belly so full he'd grow sluggish and drowsy in front of the fire. If her plan failed? She had the broom handle and enough white-hot rage to put him to sleep with it.

Either way, Gabe would wake up to find her gone.

Riding the moonlit Trace alongside a somber band of braves, Tiller imagined himself part of a raiding war party. The men, some with paint smeared across their high cheekbones, sat their saddles with the grace born of an ancient treaty with their ponies.

Watching how they rallied to the common call for help, Tiller had gained a new respect for the beleaguered Indians. He glanced around at the silent tribe of warriors, each man lost in his own grim thoughts. By the determination etched in their faces, they would find Mariah. The only question—would they find her in time?

With the new evidence of Gabe Tabor's twisted mind-set, his passionless offer to kill Tiller at Mariah's bidding took a dark and ominous turn. Even if the man wasn't capable of taking her life, his lingering hands and slant-eyed glances left no doubt of the ugly offense he'd be more than willing to commit.

Tiller shuddered and struggled to clear his head. Such thoughts would have him gnashing his teeth and braying at the moon. He needed a steady mind when they reached Julian Tabor's cabin. What they found there would determine the need for snarling fangs.

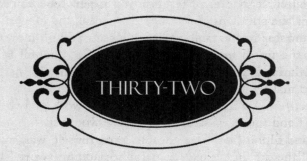

THIRTY-TWO

Gabe reclined in a chair by the hearth, his arms crossed over his head and his legs stretched out in front of him. He had slipped off his boots and made himself at home.

Mariah couldn't tell whether his relaxed state stemmed from her show of submission, his droopy-eyed fatigue, or the warmth of the fire on his feet. Heating up his holey, disgusting socks had done nothing to improve the smell of the cabin, but the revolting man seemed oblivious.

"You sure have this place smelling good," he called over his shoulder.

More than I can say for you, she thought.

"I don't hear those pots rattling much. Does that mean you're almost done?"

Mariah picked up the spoon and stirred, clanging the sides of the pot for effect. "It shouldn't be long now."

She'd actually pulled the hasty pudding off the fire and drizzled honey over it a half hour ago. The stew she'd finished even sooner.

The drowsier Gabe got the better. Then the meal ought to finish him off.

The hasty pudding began to dry out and crack, and Gabe's anxious glances turned to scowls, forcing Mariah to finish setting the table. She hadn't thought she could swallow a bite around the angry lump in her throat, but the stew looked good and the pudding even better.

Ladling a heaping serving into each bowl, she gritted her teeth and clenched her fists. "Supper's ready."

Gabe's head, rolling groggily on his thick neck, snapped up, and he stared through bleary eyes. "Breakfast, you mean. Took you all blessed night to make a pot of vittles."

He stumbled to the table and took a seat. Still grumpy, he pulled the sloshing bowl in front of him and slurped a spoonful of the rich, savory broth. He grew still, and his face lit up. "This ain't bad, woman. Not bad at all."

Hunkering over the dish, he made quick work of two helpings, asking for a third before Mariah had finished her first.

She warmed inside. Her idea to save herself was working as planned. "Be sure and leave room for something sweet." His head slowly rose, a lewd smile on his face, and Mariah wished she'd minded her tongue.

She shot to her feet and leaned over the pudding. "Let me fix you a hearty serving." Scooping out enough for three men, she poured more honey on top and pushed it toward him. "I made it special just for you."

He dug in, eating far too fast. She had to slow him down. "May I ask you something, Gabe?"

He shifted a wad of food to the other cheek. "I reckon so."

"Well"— she rested her hands on the table, twiddling her thumbs— "I'm having a bit of an argument with myself about why you brought me out here."

His fisted hand, the one shoveling food to his mouth, stilled.

"One side of me," she continued, "the part that's known you since we were children, says you could never hurt me. Especially when we're such good friends."

Gabe glanced up, a touch of anger twitching his brow.

Careful, Mariah! "The other part, the girl you crept up on and snatched from the barn, is scared half out of her wits."

Gabe's mood darkened. He leered, enjoying her discomfort. "Which of those little gals you reckon you ought to listen to?"

The fireplace popped, showering sparks up the flue. Mariah had hoped to talk sense into Gabe, shame him into releasing her. Instead, she'd somehow incited him. "Why the first one, of course. The one who reminds me that you're a true Southern gentleman. A faithful friend and neighbor who's going to take me home the minute we're done with our meal."

Shaking his head slowly, Gabe leaned over the table and snatched her wrist, his wicked eyes aglow. "Don't believe a word that one says. She's a bare-faced liar."

Riding the lead with Tobias, Joe suddenly pulled up his horse and swung out of the saddle. He waited for Tiller to join him then pointed through the heavy tangle of trees. "According to Julian's map, the cabin is close by, and I see lights up ahead of those woods. We'll go the rest of the way by foot."

The other men dismounted, crowding around to await their orders.

"Circle the house," Joe said. "Make sure the dog can't escape."

His voice shook with anger that chilled Tiller's spine. At the same time, it spoke to his own seething rage. "What's the plan to get inside?"

Joe shook his head. "No plan to get inside." He led his horse off the road and tied him to a reedy bush.

Tiller stalked after him. "What do you mean?"

Joe fixed his brooding eyes on a point in the distance. "We bring him out to us."

With an overhead wave, he started to run. The tribe sprang after him, thirty swift arrows nocked and shot as one. A few yards out from the cabin, they scattered in all directions, running on quick, silent feet. Bathed in pale moonlight, they merged with the brush and disappeared.

Tiller followed Joe and Tobias, mirroring their stealth as best he could. Without a twitch of a muscle or a whisper of sound to give them away, they closed in on the little house. A lantern's glow in the single window lifted Tiller's heart. The dark scheme he imagined Gabe plotting seemed unsuited to the light.

As if to prove him wrong, Gabe roared inside the house. Mariah screamed, her shrill, frightened cry echoing in Tiller's heart.

He broke past Joe, running for the door.

Tobias caught him, spinning him around as a shower of stones pelted the house.

A rock struck the window, shattering the pane. A storm of rocks rained down on the roof, rolling off with a jarring clatter. The relentless attack continued for several minutes, and the noise inside the cabin would be deafening.

The onslaught finally over, Tiller spun to stare at Joe. He motioned with his hand for Tiller to stay put and ran to crouch behind a water trough. "Gabe Tabor!" he shouted. "Send my niece out that door."

The butt of a rifle busted the remaining glass from the window. "I'll kill her first."

"An eye for an eye, Gabe. If that's what you want."

A long silence, then Gabe called in a wobbly voice, "I don't know what you mean."

"You have Mariah. We have your pa."

Gabe's pasty face appeared in the flickering light. "My pa?"

Movement overhead caught Tiller's eye. Shadowy silhouettes were topping the roof, inching toward the front eaves.

"You touch a hair of her head," Joe warned, "and we'll scatter his brains."

"I don't believe you," Gabe roared.

"Well," Joe said calmly, drawing out the word, "that won't make him any less dead."

The door opened a crack. Gabe stuck out his head and peered around the yard. "Pa?"

He inched a few steps over the threshold. "I don't see him, Joe." His voice trembled with fear. "Why won't he answer?"

"You come out a little further, boy," Tobias cooed. "You'll see him, all right."

Holding a lantern aloft, Gabe stumbled to the edge of the porch. The shadows above him pounced like big cats, taking him down in a huddle of blows and curses.

With no further invitation, Tiller sprang for the house.

THIRTY-THREE

Mariah huddled beneath a sagging shelf, scared to breathe. When the barrage of gunfire exploded against the house, Gabe had her by the hair, dragging her back inside the cabin.

Despite his vile threats, he'd drifted off at the table after the second serving of pudding, his head resting on folded arms. When his mouth sagged, releasing loud snores and drool that ran down his arm, Mariah made her break. She got halfway out of the window before he awoke with a bellow and lunged.

When the shooting started, breaking the window, he released her, and she'd scrambled inside the dark pantry to hide. She cowered there, her ears tuned to every sound and her thrashing heart in her throat.

A muffled commotion shot ice to her veins. A man screamed, followed by loud, angry voices. Footsteps and a flickering light paused outside the door.

She pressed closer to the wall, cursing herself for setting her own trap.

"Mariah! Where are you?"

Relief flooded her soul. She shot from the corner and threw open the musty larder. "I'm here!"

In one motion, Tiller slid the lantern onto the table and gathered her into his arms. He clung so desperately, she had to wiggle loose to catch her breath. "Please say you're all right."

Crying too hard to answer, she nodded against his chest.

"I heard a scream."

She rubbed the back of her head. "He yanked my hair."

Tiller stiffened, his voice barely above a whisper. "Did he. . .hurt you?"

Mariah pressed her cheek to his and let their tears mingle. "No."

"Thank God." He slid his mouth to kiss the hollow of her chin then gave a ragged sigh. "Thank God."

They sprang apart as the door swung open behind them. Uncle Nukowa stood on the threshold with tears in his eyes. "Sabitek?"

"Amoshi." She ran to him, throwing her arms around his neck. "I was so frightened."

He smoothed her hair then held her at arm's length. "Chim achukma?"

"I'm fine."

"Do you speak the truth? If not, I will gut that swine and feed his entrails to the hogs."

She patted his cheek. "I speak the truth." Frowning, she rubbed the back of her head. "I'm short a few strands of hair. Apart from that, I'm untouched."

Yipping and chanting from the yard drew her uncle's attention. Tobias ducked his head in the door, a grim look on his face. "She all right?"

Uncle Nukowa beamed over his shoulder. "Yes, I believe so."

Tobias shot Mariah a crooked grin. "I'm glad. You ready, Joe?"

Her uncle waved him on. "Go ahead. I'm coming." Ignoring the question in Tiller's anxious eyes, he nodded at Mariah. "Take my niece home, please."

"What's going on, Joe?"

"Take her home." He raised one brow. "Or shall I ask the sons of Tobias?"

Tiller cleared his throat and slid his arm around Mariah's waist. "Are you up to the ride?"

"Of course."

"All right, let's go."

Outside, Justin led his pony to the porch. "She can take my horse, Joe."

Her uncle nodded.

Concern swam in Justin's thoughtful eyes as he helped her into the saddle. Gazing up at her, he smiled sweetly. "I'm glad you're unhurt, Flower."

She gripped his hand. "Thank you." Raising her head, she glanced around the yard.

Gabe sat on the ground in a tight circle of her people, blubbering into his hands. He glanced up and stretched a pleading hand toward her as Tiller led her past. "Tell 'em I'm sorry, Mariah. I wasn't really going to do nothing. I swear it." His voice rose with hysteria. "Don't let these savages hurt me."

Straightening her spine, she lifted a regal chin and raked him with slanted eyes.

At the edge of the yard, Tiller jerked the reins and pulled her to a stop. Behind them, Gabe's sniveling had turned to babbling shrieks.

Off the far corner of the house, a clothesline stretched from a nail to a leaning pole. The men were dragging him to the post where they'd stacked a pile of kindling. Binding his hands behind him, they tied him to the stake and shoved a dirty rag in his mouth. Gabe went on screaming with his eyes.

Tiller gaped at her. "Merciful heavens! They mean to burn him." With a strangled cry, he let go of the horse and ran.

Uncle Nukowa stepped out of the circle with a lit torch in his hand. His fierce glare held a warning for Tiller. "Don't interfere, nahullo. Go find your horse and ride away."

Mariah's stomach tensed as several men closed in on Tiller, ugly scowls on their faces.

Backing away with clenched fists, he pleaded. "Come on, Joe. You can't." His hands raked his hair. "You'll never get away with it. Julian Tabor will hunt you down." He waved his hand. "All of you will hang."

Fearing for his safety, Mariah slid off the pony and ran. Catching his sleeve, she pulled him along behind her to where the horse stood pawing the ground. Climbing into the saddle, she scooted to make room. "Mount up, Tiller. Please."

He stared at the men in horror. "You're going to let them do this?"

"I can't stop them, and neither can you. Let's go."

Swinging up behind her, he urged the paint through the scatter of young cypress and entered the thick pine forest. In the clearing where they'd left Tiller's horse, he couldn't switch saddles fast enough. Spurring his mount, he trotted ahead, pushing the animal too fast along the unfamiliar ground. They rode toward the Trace until the echoing shouts faded, so distant they were hard to pick out from the other night sounds.

With several miles between Mariah and the dreadful cabin, she pulled up the pony and slid to the ground. A few yards ahead, Tiller did the same. They met in a bright patch of moonlight.

He groaned and crushed her to his chest. "I should've stopped them, Mariah. If they killed me for trying."

She clung to him, comforted by the strength of his arms. "I'm so sorry."

He cupped her face with trembling fingers. "For what? It's not your fault."

Mariah caressed his hands, turned one to kiss the hollow of his palm. "For this. Look how you're shaking." She tilted her head to peer up at him. "I wanted to tell you sooner. I just couldn't until we got away from the cabin."

Tiny lines appeared between his brows. "Tell me what?" Sudden alarm rocked his features. "Oh, honey. . ." Pain glazed his eyes, and his body shook beneath her hands. "Gabe did hurt you, didn't he?"

Her heart skipped a beat. "No, Tiller. I wouldn't lie to you, even for a moment."

"Then what haven't you told me?"

She smoothed his face with her fingertips. "That my uncle and his men won't really burn Gabe."

He drew in his bottom lip, gave his head a little shake. "But they did. I saw them."

She smiled. "They made you think you saw them. Just as Gabe will believe it so surely his blood will run cold each time he sees a fire in the hearth. But they won't go through with it."

Relief washed Tiller pale in the meager light. He spun away from her laughing. "Of course. They were punishing him."

She nodded. "And making sure it won't happen again. For the rest of his days, Gabriel Tabor will cross the street if he sees me coming."

Tiller slapped his knee. "It's brilliant." He chuckled. "And effective.

But suppose Gabe tells his pa? Won't the tribe land in trouble with the law?"

She raised her brows. "Believe me, Gabe won't tell."

He spun her around the clearing then reeled her in close. "Remind me to never get crossways with your folks."

Standing on tiptoe, she kissed his cheek.

He grinned. "What was that for?"

"For rescuing me."

"I had a little help." He nodded toward the cabin. "Mariah Bell's avenging angels."

"My people stick together. I'm afraid we've had to." Ducking her head, she covered a yawn. "What time is it? It must be nearly dawn."

Tiller took her wrist and led her to her horse. "Let's get on the road. You're exhausted, and Miss Vee will be frantic."

The long ride home was harder than Mariah expected. She dozed when she could; her head bobbing like a fat bird on a skinny limb. She stirred, her heart surging with relief when the horse's weight shifted to his haunches to climb the rise into the yard.

Drifting off again, she awoke to Miss Vee's soft clucking and Tiller's gentle hands lifting her from the saddle. He carried her up the stairs, nudging the door open with his foot. Miss Vee pulled the covers back, and Tiller laid her on the bed. She lolled against her pillows, her head spinning like a whirligig.

"Our girl will be just fine now that she's home," Miss Vee said, as if trying to convince herself. She lowered her voice. "She is all right, isn't she, Tiller?"

Mariah fumbled for her hand and squeezed. "Tiller saved me," she mumbled, too drowsy to open her eyes.

Miss Vee's sigh came out on a sob. "Heaven be praised," she said, her voice cracking.

Her footsteps crossed to the door and the hinges squealed. "Your work is done, young man. So if you please. . ."

Tiller's gentle touch on her cheek was as soft as a butterfly kiss. "Rest well. I'll see you in the morning."

Smiling into the fog was the last thing Mariah remembered.

THIRTY-FOUR

Tiller closed the garden gate behind him and strolled to the pump. He felt good enough to whistle, but his mouth was too dry. Working the handle, he waited for the spit and gurgle then plunged his hands under the clear, cold water, washing away the dirt from his late summer plot.

He hadn't seen Mariah all morning. Miss Vee had her safely tucked in bed, resting after her ordeal with Gabe.

The situation might've gone really bad. Suppose Gabe had carted Mariah off to Canton and forced her into marriage? Even worse, he might've succeeded in his cruel plan to take advantage of her. Considering the possibilities soured Tiller's stomach all over again and gave him second thoughts about burning Gabe at the stake.

What thoughts swirled in old Gabe's head that bright, cheery morning? Tiller doubted they centered on Mariah. More likely, he pondered the blessing of uncharred flesh.

Chuckling, he pumped more icy water into a cup and took a long drink. According to the sun, perched high over the house like a joyful smile, it would soon be lunchtime. Mariah would surely be awake by now. He hung the cup on the pump and started for the back porch, pausing when he saw the Jones brothers lounging around the new steps.

Joe sat in Miss Vee's rocking chair, staring toward the barn, his deep bass rumble carrying over the yard. "I'll hear your terms, of course," he was saying to Chris. "Your brother's, too."

He sat forward in the chair. "Perhaps you might consider combining your offers."

The boys shared a glance.

"How would that work?" Justin asked. "Mariah can't marry us both."

Feeling a chill down his back, Tiller held his ground and listened.

Joe laughed. "You'll work it out between you. Compete for her. The one who wins the prize will vow to repay his brother's share."

Chris sneered. "Even if I lost, which I won't, I wouldn't help this cur take my girl."

Justin shoved him with his shoulder. "Mind your tongue. Mariah's my girl."

They sprang off the porch, all long hair and sputter, flexing their muscles and jutting their chests. They took turns shoving each other backward, but neither boy swung a punch. As it should be between brothers, the true urge to fight seemed to be missing.

Joe cackled, obviously entertained by their mock sparring.

Justin rushed Chris. Chris spun to shake him off, and they both tumbled over the steps and sprawled in the dirt.

Joe raised his hand to end the skirmish. "I don't mean compete for her now." He dismissed them with a wave. "Take this match home and present your case before the elders. You won't settle things here in my yard."

Still glaring, they nodded toward Joe then trotted across the yard and disappeared down the sandy slope.

Joe sat back in the rocker, still chuckling.

Harnessing his rage, Tiller swung around the hedge to the porch and sat on the top step. "Afternoon, sir."

Scratching his chin, Joe nodded. "How's your patch of ground coming along?"

Tiller glanced toward the garden. "Mariah will soon have vegetables on her table again."

Joe blew out a breath. "She won't be here to eat them."

Tiller watched him quietly. Lowering his head, he focused on scraping a line of dirt from under his thumbnail. "You're a peculiar man, Joe."

Joe grunted. "You're not the first to say so."

"Is it a game for you?" He nodded toward the path. "Dangling false hope before their eyes? And before mine with your friendship?"

One bushy brow twitched, but Joe held his somber expression. "Neither boy loves my niece. They only think they do. By the end of the challenge I've given them, they'll know the truth in their own hearts."

"And if they don't?" Tiller glared. "Will you sell Mariah to one of them or wait for a higher bid? What was the offer back home?" He sneered. "Pretty high, I'll wager. Since it brought you all the way to Mississippi to fetch her."

Joe gripped the arms of the rocker. "Be careful."

Tiller stood clenching his fists. "I love her, Joe. She loves me, too, and I think you know it." He shifted his weight. "I'm not Gabe Tabor. You can't scare me out of her life."

Joe stood and shoved past him down the steps. "Stay away from her, nahullo. I won't tell you again."

"If you want me away from Mariah," Tiller shouted at his retreating back, "have the guts to light the kindling. That's the only way you'll ever be rid of me."

Groaning, Mariah sat up groping her head. She rubbed the spot where Gabe had yanked, expecting to find it bald. Despite the covering of hair, the skin her fingers probed sorely ached.

She frowned at her reflection across the room. Looking down, she found what the mirror had reported was true. She'd slept fully clothed and in her stockings with her hair pinned up on her head. If it didn't feel so scandalous, it'd be comical.

Mariah grinned. She certainly looked funny with her rumpled clothes, sleep-creased face, and wildly tangled hair. Not unlike a discarded rag doll—played with by dirty hands then tossed aside.

Her bright smile vanished. Gabe had meant to do that very thing. If Tiller and her uncle hadn't come in time, she'd find no humor in the day.

She shuddered at the memory of Gabe's foul touch. How different from Tiller's soft caress on her cheek.

A knock on the door fired her heartbeat to life. Frantic, she stood, ready to hide. Tiller couldn't see her in such an unkempt state.

"Mariah?" Only Miss Vee.

Relieved, she swiped wisps of hair off her forehead. "Yes, come in."

The door opened a crack. Miss Vee peeked in and smiled. "She's decent, Tiller. Go on in." Swinging the door wide, she stepped aside.

In one leap, Mariah landed on the bed and pulled the covers over her head.

Tiller's footsteps paused just inside the room then quietly approached. "Mariah? Are you all right?"

Blushing and fuming beneath the quilt, she wondered how Miss Vee would like salt instead of sugar in her next cup of tea. Maybe soap flakes mixed with her powdered milk? "I'm not presentable this morning. Could you come back in just a while?"

"I need to talk to you. It's important."

Miss Vee cleared her throat. "On second thought, a lady's boudoir ain't the proper place for chatting with a gentleman. You go wait in the parlor. I'll get our girl prettified and send her down."

In Tiller's long pause, Mariah felt him beside the bed, staring down at her. "All right, I suppose. But hurry, please. This won't keep."

When the door closed, Mariah shot upright and gaped at Miss Vee. "How could you?"

Red-faced, she hung her head. "I thought he had in mind a sickroom visit, not an important talk visit."

Mariah huffed. "That's ridiculous. I'm not sick."

"No, but you had quite a shock."

Mariah crossed her arms. "No more startling than the one you just gave me."

Miss Vee hurried to pour water in the basin. "Come wash up while I fluff a clean dress. I don't think Tiller's in the mood to wait."

He paced in front of the settee when Mariah reached the bottom step—feeling much better in a proper frock with her hair pinned. Crossing the room in broad strides, he pulled her close.

Mariah peered up at him. "Aren't you going to tell me how nice I look?"

"I thought you looked nice before."

She frowned. "You didn't see me."

"I didn't have to."

"Oh, Tiller. How sweet."

He pushed her to arm's length. "You won't find me sweet for long." His throat worked furiously. "I have a confession."

The dread on his face frightened her. "Go on."

"I told Uncle Joe that I love you."

Her arms slid from his shoulders and dropped to her sides. "Please say you didn't."

"I told him you love me, too, and he can't keep us apart."

She gripped her brow. "No, Tiller."

Cupping her chin, he raised her eyes to his. "I broke my promise, and for that I'm sorry. You have to know I had good reason."

She turned her back. "I hope so, since you've ruined everything."

Tiller squeezed her shoulders then eased her around. "Joe already knew, honey. He's known since the day he arrived. The only person you've been fooling is yourself."

Mariah shook her head. "He would've left soon. I just know it. Now that you've challenged him, he'll die first." She searched his troubled face. "What reason was so important that you broke our trust?"

Tiller's face flashed red. Indignant, he pointed behind him. "I caught him bartering with Tobias's sons, offering your hand in exchange for goods."

"Chris and Justin?" She lowered her head to hide her smile. "They both asked him?"

Tiller angled his head. "You find this funny? They're out there now, trying to gather enough mules and chickens, whatever they think you're worth, to come back and make a trade. Meanwhile, Joe is sitting back, waiting to see who comes with the best offer."

Mariah gathered his hands. "Yes, I know."

"You know." His angry scowl deepened. "Well, you're pretty calm about your own kin selling you off for livestock."

She laughed. "It's not quite like you make it sound. It's our custom, Tiller. . .my uncle's way to make sure I marry well. He'll weigh several offers, but the value of goods won't be his main concern. My position in the tribe, his position, too, will sway his final decision."

"Position? What about your heart?" Tiller stalked away from her. "It's nonsense, Mariah. You talk like you're just a. . .a. . ."

"A squaw?"

He spun to face her. "I didn't mean that."

"What did you mean?" Pulling free of him, Mariah bit her lip, trying to think.

Tiller cocked his head, his eyes fearful. "Where does all this leave us?"

"After you betrayed me to my uncle?" She hung her head. "I don't know."

He touched her hair, his voice thick with emotion. "Please don't say that."

She turned her face aside.

"You could stand up to him," he said quietly. "Tell him what you want."

Mariah shook her head. "Have you forgotten how fast the tribe came to his aid? One crook of my uncle's finger, and we'd both be headed out of Mississippi. . .in opposite directions." She sighed. "Besides, I won't openly defy him. It would shame my mother's memory."

"Then how can we ever marry?"

She took a deep breath. "If I can get him to leave without me, he'll go on with his life and forget. It's happened before."

Tiller snorted. "Good luck with that. Uncle Joe seems to be settling in for good."

Her temper flared. "Don't mention anything else to him, Tiller McRae. Maybe I can repair the damage." She shook her finger in his face. "Don't speak of our love to anyone in this household, do you understand? Not even to me."

He held up his hands. "I promise."

Mariah jabbed his chest. "Keep your word this time."

Gathering her skirt, she flounced out the door.

THIRTY-FIVE

Six days had passed since Tiller spilled Mariah's secret to Joe. She worked so hard to convince her uncle they weren't really in love, Tiller had started to wonder himself.

Even when they were alone, in the hallway or passing in the yard, she shrank from his touch and pulled away if he tried to whisper in her ear.

She seemed to be a different woman, and it scared him, made him long for her with a passion he'd never known. He hoped her coldness was borne of determination to trick Joe and not a picture of her true feelings.

Pushing aside his worrisome thoughts, Tiller lowered Otis into the cane-bottomed chair on the front porch and tucked a blue knitted shawl beneath his chin. The view toward the river in back was nicer, but it took so much out of Otis to walk the long hallway, he had little energy left to take pleasure in his time outside.

He settled against the cushion and gazed around the yard with a satisfied smile. "Yes sir. Just what the doctor ordered."

Tiller pulled the matching chair around and lowered his lanky body, enjoying the cool breeze on his face. His gaze wandered the grassy yard from Rainy's climbing roses to Mariah's herb garden set off by a border of white stones. Bright green ivy sprawled across the latticed arbor, stretching from the road to the house. Seated beneath its shade and tucked into the shadows of the portico, it wasn't long before he wished he'd brought out an extra shawl. "You warm enough, Otis?"

He nodded. "It's a mite cool for this late in June, ain't it?"

Tiller rubbed his arms. "I suppose we'd best enjoy it while we can. We'll be fuming about the heat come August."

"What sort of weather you reckon Scuffletown is having, son?"

Tiller had shared everything he could remember about his Carolina home and the family he'd left behind. The old man loved the stories and seemed willing to listen for hours.

Time spent with Otis was the most relaxing Tiller had ever spent and the most distressing. The peace in Otis's eyes stirred an emptiness long denied and a yearning Tiller couldn't shake. He longed to purge the guilt that clawed his mind during long, sleepless nights, but he'd found some rest in a recent decision.

It would be selfish to clear his conscience at the little man's expense. Otis needed him, at least for now. When he regained his strength, Tiller would lay the ugly facts on the table and plead for pardon. Whether Otis forgave him or not, Tiller would beg him to stay on at the inn and allow them to care for him.

Mariah would have to agree, but he couldn't discuss this or anything else of importance with her until Joe left Mississippi. Of course, there was still the matter of coming clean with her.

Tiller groaned inside. He'd made such a mess of his life. How would he ever set things right?

Feeling Otis watching, he eased back and unclenched his fists.

Otis continued to stare. "Got something to tell me, boy?"

Squirming, he shook his head.

"Well. . .maybe I got something to tell you."

Tiller spun to the edge of his chair, hoping Otis would bring up the subject of Mariah. He needed assurance that Joe would leave, that things with Mariah would return to normal. He wouldn't tell Otis their secret, but he sure hoped God would.

Otis swiveled to face him. "I sense you're ripe for turning your life over to God, and I reckon it's time you stop putting it off."

The simple words dashed Tiller's hopes and made him uneasy. "I don't have enough church in my background to know exactly what you mean, but I have an idea." He stole a quick glance. "You're talking about baring my sins." He tried to smile. "A thing like that could take awhile."

Otis waved his hand. "There's no need to air your trespasses one by one. God's already acquainted with each of them since they nailed Jesus to the cross." He patted Tiller's hand. "A whispered plea for mercy will cover it."

The ache inside Tiller's heart swelled to bursting. "That don't sound fair to God. Besides, there are a few things I need to set right first."

Otis lifted his chin. "You reckon there's anything in your life He can't handle?"

Tiller glanced away from his searching gaze. "There are deeds I've done that are too dark to bring to Him. I need to mop up behind me before I'll be fit to talk to God."

Setting his lips in a firm line, Otis shook his head. "That's hitching the horse on backwards, boy." He gripped Tiller's wrist. "You think I was lily-white when God found me?"

His words swirled Tiller away to the day Nathan accused him of trying to protect his lily-white conscience. Blinded by the glare of God's righteousness, the notion seemed absurd. He lowered his head to his hands. "My life's been broke for so long, I don't know how to fix it."

A warm, trembling hand touched his shoulder. "You can't."

Embarrassed by his swimming eyes, Tiller shot Otis a troubled frown. "Then what's the use?"

"That's what I'm trying to tell you, boy. None of us have the power to make things right again." His face glowing, he pointed to the sky. "But He can."

The emptiness inside Tiller couldn't be denied a second longer. Guilt weighed him to his knees. "Please, Otis. Tell me what I need to do."

Gnarled fingers rested on Tiller's head. "You just made a good start, son. Repeat this prayer after me, and I'll lead you on home."

Otis's gentle voice overhead, thick with unshed tears, washed over Tiller in waves like warm molasses, the graceful ebb and flow pulling out the years of lonely heartbreak, rushing in with tides of peace.

When they finished praying, Otis hugged him. "You'll never regret this decision."

Patting his bony back, Tiller withdrew and smiled. "I don't see how

I could." He chuckled, deep and free, unlike any laugh he'd had before. "I feel different."

"Because you are." Otis gave a satisfied nod. "That just proves it took."

They beamed at each other like carefree boys trading secrets.

Otis tugged on his arm. "Get up from there before the cold seeps into your bones."

Tiller returned to his chair, wiping tears on his sleeve. "I don't know how I'll ever thank you."

"Don't talk foolish. After all you've done for me?"

"This doesn't come close to anything I've done, and you know it." Tiller stared in the distance. "I suppose I'll always think of you as a father of sorts." He lifted one brow. "I hope you don't mind."

"Mind?" Tears tracked his ruddy cheeks, but he grinned. "I'm honored to know you feel that way." He winked. "But I'm more like a grandfather, don't you think? On account of I'm older than thunder."

Tiller patted his knee. "You're not so old."

Otis snorted. "You must need a pair of spectacles." Scooting to the end of his seat, he held out his arm for Tiller to grasp. "Take me inside before I rust."

Hauling Otis to his feet, Tiller took one last look around. Whether from the haze of recent tears or the freedom of a burden lifted, the front yard blazed with brilliant color. The grass was greener. The roses redder. Patches of sky peered through the ivy-covered trellis, as clear and blue as a newborn's eyes.

"One more thing," Otis said before Tiller opened the door. "You'll need a Bible so you can study on the scriptures." He scratched his head. "I'd give you mine, but it was in my pack when those mangy scoundrels stole it."

Tiller's heart sank, but not with the sickening thud of before. He felt certain God had removed the terrible deed from his account, but if it took the rest of his days, he'd make it up to Otis. "Don't worry," Tiller said. "Next time I'm in town, I'll get us both new ones." He guided Otis inside the house.

Men's voices and heavy-booted footsteps sounded from the dining room, along with the smell of serious cooking.

Otis stared down the hall. "Sounds like Mariah has a passel of new guests. I didn't see them come in off the road, did you?"

Tiller frowned and shook his head. "I suppose they came downriver. I'd best get you settled and go lend the women a hand."

Plopping on the side of his bed, Otis grinned. "We stayed outside longer than I thought if it's already lunchtime." He lifted his finger. "But I ain't complaining."

Patting his stomach, Tiller smiled. "That makes two of us."

When he reached the door, Otis called his name. "Tiller, little missy's better acquainted with God than you were before this morning, only she's lost her way." Lying back on his fresh-plumped pillows, his eyes twinkled. "But don't you worry. He'll reel her in before long."

The details were sketchy, but it was the reassurance Tiller needed. After the morning's encounter with God, it was enough.

He saluted and Otis returned it.

"I'll go see if I can hurry those vittles."

Otis raised his thumb. "Now you're talking."

Smiling, Tiller strolled toward the back of the house whistling a merry tune. He didn't see how life could get much better. Following the lively voices of men enjoying good food and better company, he turned the corner into the dining room—and rocked back on his heels.

The mocking eyes of Nathan Carter, Sonny Thompson, and Hade Betts lifted to greet him, mischief in their depths.

Nailed to the spot, Tiller stared, his blissful joy paled to hopeless loss.

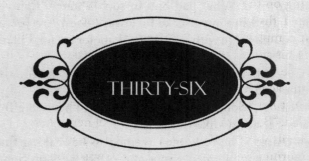

THIRTY-SIX

The sudden stillness in the room brought Mariah's head up from the bowl of mashed potatoes in her hand.

A whitewashed version of Tiller slumped in the doorway, his bottom jaw unhinged.

"Tiller?"

His wide eyes darted to her.

"Won't you greet our guests?"

The youngest of the three men stood quickly and offered his hand. "How-do, sir. I'm Nathan Carter." His friendly smile lit up a handsome face. With his swarthy complexion and dark hair, he looked to be Indian, though not from a local tribe. "Did she say your name's Tiller?"

Tiller nodded dumbly.

The other two beamed up at them. Nathan introduced them by turn. "That skinny, ugly soul to your left is Sonny Thompson."

Sonny's smile revealed a gap in his front teeth. "Nice to know you, Tiller."

"And the old man to my right is Hade Betts."

Mr. Betts stretched his arm past Nathan. "I can't tell you how pleased."

Prying himself from the wall that seemed to hold him up, Tiller allowed Mr. Betts to shake his limp hand, but he didn't seem to put much effort into it. Wiping his palm on his pants leg, Tiller lifted his vacant stare to Mariah. "I'll just"—he hooked his thumb—"go on out and take care of their horses."

Mariah frowned. What had him in such a state? "Rainy's tending them." She bugged her eyes. "Like he always does. Are you all right?" She shared a quick smile with Mr. Betts. "I apologize for Tiller. He's not himself today."

"We can see that, Miss Bell." He winked at Tiller. "Your boy seems a little tongue-tied."

"He sure does," Sonny said, his dancing gaze bouncing from Tiller to Mr. Betts. "He always like this?"

Mariah tensed. The rude men seemed to be making fun of him. None too gently, she plopped a spoonful of potatoes on Sonny's plate and picked up the carving knife. "Care for more beef, Mr. Thompson?"

Swallowing his simpering grin, he sat back in his chair and shook his head.

Glancing up, Mariah found Tiller gone. His behavior, so unlike him, churned her stomach. The way she'd treated him for the past week, his sullen mood had to be her fault.

"Enjoy your meal, gentlemen," she said, untying her apron. "Miss Viola will be in soon with your dessert."

"Where'd Tiller fly off to?" Miss Vee asked, meeting her at the doorway.

Mariah handed her the apron. "Have Dicey bring in the apple pie, Miss Vee. I'll be right back."

"You're leaving me, too?"

Out the door so fast it slammed behind her, Mariah scurried across the yard.

Tiller paced the barn. Sheki, hoping for a treat, followed with his head each time Tiller passed the stall.

Rainy glanced up from brushing down Hade's bay. "Mista' Tilla', you're bound to hit water soon in that ditch you're digging. You got something peckin' at you?"

The barn door squealed open.

Tiller's breath caught at the sight of Mariah. What did she know? How much had the blackguards told her?

"I thought I'd find you here." She pulled the door shut and hurried toward him.

He lifted his chin at Rainy.

Glancing at the boy, she slowed her steps. "Rainy, leave that for now, please. I need to have a private word with Mr. Tiller."

Shoving his hands in his pockets, Rainy pushed the stall open with one shoulder, hiding his grin with the other. He ducked out the door whistling the tune his little brother had sung the first time Tiller laid eyes on them. A lively song about a coming gospel train rumbling through the land.

Tiller's heart squeezed. Something was rumbling toward him all right, and it wasn't the gospel train. Weak in the knees, he felt powerless to stop it.

Mariah's chin shot up. "What happened to you in there?"

She didn't know. Not yet, at least. He shrugged and leaned against Sheki's stall. "I don't like the look of that bunch around the table."

She frowned. "I'll admit they're rude and uncouth, but we've seen worse, I assure you."

Tiller longed to grab her shoulders and shake her, tell her she'd never seen the likes of Hade Betts. He wanted her to promise to watch her back every second the men were in the house. Since he could do no such thing, he vowed to watch her every second himself. Until he found out the purpose of Hade's deceitful game, he'd guard his own back fairly close, too. "Did they pay up front?"

"Of course."

"How many days?"

"Two, but Mr. Betts said they might stay longer." She caught his arm. "What's this about? I've never seen you this way."

"Don't trust them, Mariah. I've got a bad feeling."

She smiled. "Now you sound like Otis. They're just guests, Tiller. In a few days they'll be moving on."

He drew a deep breath. "Let's hope it's a short visit."

Mariah took a step closer. "Are you sure that's what's bothering you? I sense you're angry with me." She reached to finger a button on his shirt. "I've only acted the way I have because I had to. But you should know—"

Tiller brushed her hand away and stepped back.

Pain glazed her eyes until Joe's voice growled behind her. "Mariah, come inside. The guests are fed; now it's time to feed me."

"Coming, Uncle." She whirled away, slipping past Joe at the door.

He glared a warning at Tiller.

Smiling brightly, Tiller raised his chin and winked. "Save me some mashed potatoes, Uncle Joe."

His craggy face stiff with rage, Joe spun on his heel and followed Mariah.

Sheki bobbed his head, and Tiller laughed and patted his neck. "You liked that, didn't you, boy? I really put the old man in his place." The thing was he shouldn't have. Mariah wouldn't approve, especially after Joe had just caught them together.

Tiller's desperate sense of swimming upstream had returned. Now with Hade and Nathan showing up. . .

He smoothed his hand along the horse's soft muzzle. "Ah, Sheki. I can't just give up and run. She's too important."

"Well, well."

Tiller's head swiveled to watch Nathan saunter toward him.

"You're slipping, Tiller boy. With that pretty little thing in the house, you're out here snuggled up to a horse?"

Tiller nodded toward the river. "That was you the other day, wasn't it? Across the Pearl."

Nathan grinned and snapped a salute. "That hair of yours stuck out like a red flag atop this roof."

Dread knotting his stomach, Tiller leaned against the stall while Hade and Sonny strolled up behind Nathan.

Sonny ran up and slapped his arm, a huge grin on his face. "I knew we'd find you! Mississippi ain't big enough to hide you from us."

Tiller scowled. "Keep your voice down."

Hade watched him with admiration shining in his eyes. "This is some arrangement you fell into. What's your angle?"

"There's no angle. Just taking some time away."

Hade sneered. "Come on, now. This is old Hade you're talking to. If you want to keep the profits to yourself, go ahead, but at least fill us in."

Nathan spat in the straw at his feet. "I think it's the girl."

"Whooee!" Sonny cried. "She sure is a looker."

"Nah." A lewd smile curled Hade's lips. "Tiller has his pick of the gals. There's something else he's after."

Forcing himself to relax, Tiller crossed his ankles. "More to the point, what are you boys after? What's the reason for pretending you don't know me?"

With a rowdy laugh, Hade slapped him on the back. "Just having a little fun with you. Besides, we're not here to throw a polecat at your picnic." He tightened his arm around Tiller's neck. "We were starting to miss having you around is all."

Sonny sniffed and hauled up his pants. "Hadn't been the same in camp without you and your stories. I suppose you've missed us, too. Ain't that right, Tiller?"

"After all," Hade continued, "I've been like a daddy to you." He reached for Nathan, pulling him into a clumsy three-way hug. "And old Nate has been like your elder brother." He gave them both hearty pats on the back. "I reckon we've been the closest thing you've ever had to a family."

No doubt about it. Hade was up to something.

It didn't take long to flush it out. "I don't mean to sound impatient"— he bumped heads with Tiller—"but how long will it take you to fleece this lamb and come home to our loving arms?"

A rock in the pit of his stomach, Tiller laughed softly and casually drew away. "What if I said I may not be coming back?"

Hade's gleeful eyes hardened to glassy stones. "Well, that won't do, will it?" His fatherly grip became a vise around Tiller's neck. "Not by a jugful. I've lost a lot of revenue since you left, McRae." His rattled exhalation, reeking of roast beef and raw onion, warmed Tiller's cheek. "An unfortunate turn I'm willing to forgive if you'll stop all this foolishness and come back to the camp."

Struggling to stay calm, Tiller steadied his voice. "How have I cost you money?"

Hade gave a breathy laugh. "Look around at these ugly mugs. Would you stop on the road to have a friendly chat with one of us?"

Tiller tightened his jaw. "I'd start shooting and ask questions later."

Loosening his hold, Hade chuckled. "Then you see my problem." He gripped Tiller's chin and shook it. "This pretty-boy face is worth a gold mine."

Nathan, quiet until now, moved closer to the stall. Smoothing Sheki's mane, he cleared his throat. "Look, Hade. . .if Tiller wants out, there's really no way to make him stay. He'll just hang up the fiddle again, first chance he gets." He glanced over his shoulder. "Besides, it ain't smart to place all our bets on one man." He grinned at Tiller. "Little brother here won't always be good-looking."

Hade frowned. "So, I should just let our meal ticket walk out?" He shook his head. "No sir."

Nate drew himself up and strutted a few paces. "I've been doing some pondering. I think it's time we found us a new game. The word's out on the Trace. Folks are leery. Trigger-happy."

He turned. "If we're going to risk getting filled with lead, it's time we thought bigger." His eyes glowed. "Richer."

Hade joined him near Sheki. "Keep talking."

"Boss, I'm thinking banks. . .trains. Real jobs yielding big money."

Sonny's eyes bugged. "Like the James brothers?"

Nathan pointed. "Exactly like the James brothers."

Tiller frowned. "May I remind you that Jesse was shot dead two months ago?"

Greedily rubbing his chin, Hade ignored him. "I think this merits more discussion. How about we grab a cup of coffee and meet around the fire in the parlor to draw up some plans."

Sonny rubbed his stomach. "I'm hankering for another piece of that fine apple pie."

Nathan nodded at the door. "You two go on but save me a slice. I'll be right along."

Tiller drew a deep cleansing breath as Hade and Sonny left the barn. His heart filled with warmth for Nathan, and he shot him a grateful smile. "Thanks, Nate."

Nathan waved him off. "Nothing to it."

"Why'd you step out like that for me?"

Nate glanced up, his eyes shimmering in the dim light. "I suppose I'm trying to make amends for how I've messed up your life." He offered a wry laugh. "Including telling Hade where I found you."

"Then why did you?"

Nathan crossed to where Tiller stood and chucked him on the chin. "I looked for you because I missed you. I wanted you riding with us again. You're the only family I have left."

"And now you've changed your mind?"

"You changed it for me. When I saw you, saw the way that pretty gal looks at you, I knew you were happy."

They shared a long look; then Tiller grinned and swatted his arm. "I'll miss you, pardner."

"Not for long. I'll be stopping by."

Tiller frowned. "Unless you find yourself chained to Hade and Sonny on a Mississippi prison farm. Or worse, wind up like Jesse James."

He gripped Nathan's arm. "Stay here, Nate. Mariah won't mind, and we could use the extra hands."

Nathan gazed around the barn. "Trade my carefree life on the road for this?" He shook his head. "Tilling soil and pitching hay won't cut it for me, I'm afraid."

Staring at his feet, Tiller nodded. "Be careful, won't you?"

Nathan flicked the brim of Tiller's hat—his until Tiller snatched it from his head the day he left. "Nice headgear. Keep it free of holes, won't you?" At the door, he turned. "I'll try to get those two to leave as soon as possible. Until then, keep a close watch on them."

Tiller nodded. "You can count on it."

THIRTY-SEVEN

Hade, Sonny, and Nathan huddled around the settee hatching dastardly schemes until suppertime. Pretty worked up about their new plans, they gobbled Mariah's soup and corn cakes like pigs on slop and hustled right back to the parlor.

Tiller loathed knowing the gang was sowing the seeds of a crime spree around Mariah's cozy hearth, but if it took them away from the inn, he'd have to live with it for now.

His heart soared at how God had used Nathan to rescue him from Hade's clutches. He longed to do the same for Nate, but one man couldn't force his viewpoint on another. The life Tiller found empty and degrading, Nate's reckless nature seemed to feed on. Tiller would chose pitching hay over robbing banks any day.

Seated at the kitchen table playing a game of Dr. Busby with Mariah and Miss Vee, he tried not to focus on the excited voices floating down the hall. Thankfully, Otis slept like the dead, but he prayed the ruckus wouldn't disturb him. The last thing he needed was Otis awake, itching to socialize with the new guests.

Having Otis's attackers in the same house set Tiller's nerves on edge. He'd carefully avoided mentioning to them who Otis was and kept them away from the old man's room by telling them he was sick. If Hade thought Otis might recognize him, he'd kill him with less remorse than swatting a fly.

Miss Vee leaned across the table, interrupting his grim thoughts. "Mariah, I need the Dairymaid's Lover."

She pulled the card from her hand and slid it across to her. "You're good, Miss Vee."

"Okay. . ." Miss Vee touched her chin. "How about Dr. Busby's Wife?"

Mariah shook her head. "Your luck just ran out."

"Oh, pooh. All right, it's your turn then."

The twinkle in Mariah's brown eyes gave her away—she remembered the last card Tiller had lured from Miss Vee.

Grinning, she held out her hand. "Mr. Ninnycometwitch, if you please."

He passed it to her, along with a little squeeze to her pinkie finger.

Blushing, she tapped his shin with her toe. "I'll just take Spade the Gardener, too."

Miss Vee squealed and bounced in her chair. "Watch her, Tiller. She's trying to win this game." Sobering, she rested her chin on her hands and stared over Tiller's shoulder. "I wish John Coffee was here. He loves to play Dr. Busby."

Sadness dropped like a tasseled shade over Mariah's smile.

Tiller hurried to change the subject. "Where's Joe tonight?"

She scrunched her face. "Won't you ever call him anything but Joe?"

He quirked his mouth. "I have no plans in that direction."

Mariah swatted his arm with her cards. "Why not? You know it frustrates him."

"Well, it shouldn't. What sort of name is 'I'm angry' for a grown man? Suppose I took a name based on how I felt?"

"I see your point." She batted her lashes. " 'I'm hungry' doesn't suit you."

Beaming, he returned her swat. "So where is Mr. Mad?"

"Playing cards and drinking ale with Tobias. He said not to wait up."

Miss Vee snorted. "I doubt they're playing Dr. Busby."

They shared a laugh, cut short by the downstairs clock striking the ten o'clock hour.

Mariah stretched and yawned. "Gracious, I'm tired. It's been a long day. I forgot how hard it is to chase after a houseful of guests."

Miss Vee stood to put the kettle on. "I'll make those noisy yahoos a pot of my chamomile tea. Maybe it'll put them to sleep. Or at least calm them down before they wake Otis."

By the time Mariah won the hand of Dr. Busby, Miss Vee had three cups of tea sweetened and spiced, foaming over on a silver serving tray. She handed it to Tiller with a wink. "I hope this works. Take it in for me, will you?"

The men in the parlor had wound down a bit. Sonny sat in Otis's chair, stretching his legs toward the fire. Hade slumped in the seat beside him, chewing a fat cigar. Nathan had slipped off his boots and reclined on the settee, his stocking feet hanging off the end.

"Well, look here," Hade said. "Tiller, you make a pretty little maid."

Sonny laughed wildly, and the other two grinned.

"I'd curtsy," Tiller said, "but then I might spill your tea."

More rowdy laughter from Sonny.

Nathan made a face. "Tea? Has it got whiskey in it?"

Tiller handed him a cup. "You'll think it did, once it hits your belly. Drink this, and you'll sleep like a man with no conscience."

Nate grinned. "By cracker, I'd better have me a double portion."

Mariah swept in, beautiful by firelight in a red dress cinched tight at the waist. Everything else forgotten, the men's hungry eyes tracked her across the room. "Don't let me disturb you, gentlemen. I won't be a minute. I just need my ledger."

Tiller had no inkling of what she was about to do, or he'd have found a way to stop her. Caught up in her charms himself, he stared like a witless boy while she swung open the door of her safe, revealing the bulging leather bag of gold coins.

Whirling, he watched Hade's slant-eyed desire turn to wide-eyed greed.

Hurrying to Mariah, Tiller slid his arms around her waist and drew her upright, slamming the safe with the toe of his boot.

Guileless, trusting, she stared at him. "Tiller? What in the world?"

"Just lending a hand."

Blushing, glancing at the men, she gave him a scathing look and shook off his hands. "Well, thank you, but I can manage." Snatching a pen from her desk, she tucked the ledger under her arm and nodded around the room. "I'll bid you all a good night. Don't forget, breakfast promptly at six. If you're not seated around the table by then, you stand a fair chance of going without."

Tiller followed her to the foot of the stairs. "Where are you going?"

"To bed, if you must know," she whispered. "What's come over you?"

He glanced toward the safe. Surely she had a key somewhere. "I need to speak to you."

"In the morning, if you don't mind. I'm tired. Now, good night."

The room crackled with strain, waiting for her footsteps to reach the top of the stairs and down the hall. When her bedroom door closed, Tiller spun. Stalking to stand in front of them, he pointed at the safe. "Forget you ever saw that, you hear?"

Hade slouched in his chair, puffing his cigar through a delighted smirk.

Sonny's gaze darted around the room like a child with a secret.

Nathan, defeat sagging his face, sat on the edge of the couch twiddling his thumbs.

"Well, now," Hade said. "Who would've thought a dump like this would pull in that kind of dough?"

Sonny giggled like a girl. "I reckon Tiller knew. Ain't that right, Tiller boy?"

Hade leaned forward to rest his arms on his knees, flicking a long white ash on Mariah's rug. "In light of this new development, I'll have to change my mind about the hardship your mutiny caused the gang." His steely gazed fixed on Tiller. "It's time to pony up. I'd say a sixty-forty split in my favor is more than reasonable."

Tiller's chest heaved. "I don't intend to take any of that money."

"Suit yourself." Glancing from Nate to Sonny, Hade breathed a throaty laugh. "I have no problem with taking it all."

Tiller balled his fists and made a move toward the safe. Nathan leaped up to block him. "Don't be stupid, Tiller," he warned, his voice laden with gloom. "Go to bed. By morning, we'll be out of your hair for good."

Tiller shoved closer to Hade, but Nate held him.

"Better listen to big brother," Hade growled. "That is if you want to see morning." He lifted his chin toward the top of the stairs. "More to the point, if you want your friends to wake up tomorrow."

Tiller backed across the threshold into the hall, his eyes flashing a warning. Storming to his room, he swore under his breath that Hade Betts would steal Mariah's money over his cold, dead corpse.

THIRTY-EIGHT

Mariah's eyes shot open. Raising her head from her pillow, she stared over her shoulder into the pitch darkness of the room, listening.

The house had been silent for hours, her guests all tucked into bed. Now a muffled ruckus drifted to her from downstairs.

She swung her legs over the side and quietly lowered her feet. Easing the door open, she crept down the hall in her nightgown to peer over the banister.

Her heart surged. Harsh whispers quarreled, and tall shadows danced a jerky waltz on the parlor walls.

Passing by her room, she paused long enough to lift her wrap from the hook by the door. Grateful that Tiller had fixed the squeaky boards, she slipped across the hall to Father's room.

His scent overcame her as she entered. Standing dazed, she realized she hadn't been inside the room since the morning she carried out his feeble body. The ache in her chest was crippling, but she lingered with the memories anyway, like the tip of a tongue jabbing a sore tooth.

Tears blinding her, she brushed them away. She had no time to surrender to grief. Opening the drawer bedside Father's bed, she carefully lifted the revolver, the weight a comfort in her hand.

In the hall again, she cocked her ears and heard a thud. Scurrying on tiptoe, she took the back stairwell down to the kitchen, her pounding heart drawn to Tiller. The bottom stair creaked under her weight. Wincing, she made a mental note to have Tiller repair it—if they lived through the night.

Tightening her fingers around the handle, Mariah lifted the gun and skulked to Tiller's door, pressing her face against the cold wood. She whispered his name and strained to hear him answer.

Afraid the intruders would hear if she called out again, she gripped the knob and turned, stepping warily inside another room she hadn't visited lately. Here, too, she breathed the familiar scent of a man she loved. The woody, fresh-air scent of Tiller gave her strength.

The sound of his voice spun her around. Tiller argued fiercely in an ugly tone she'd never heard before, but not inside this room.

Her stomach pitched with fear for his safety. Bolting, she dashed for the parlor, one hand cocking the hammer, her finger tensed on the trigger.

Tiller lunged for the bag of coins in Hade's white-knuckled hand. Hade whirled, and his shoulder collided with Tiller's jaw. Tiller fell to one knee and blackness threatened.

The haze took him under briefly, but a high-pitched, wavering voice tugged him back to consciousness. "Hold it right there. . .and I mean you."

Fearing the "you" Mariah threatened could be him, Tiller froze. The way the barrel shook in her hand, she might've been aiming at any one of them.

Blinking up at her from the floor, he reached out his hand. "Mariah? Honey, be careful with that thing."

Sonny's mouth gaped. "Did you just call her honey?" His shocked expression slid into a grin. "Nathan was right. She's your girl, ain't she, Tiller boy?" He reached to pull Tiller to his feet. "I reckon she's the ripsnortin'est gal you ever romanced."

Mariah's wide-eyed stare packed ice around Tiller's heart. "You know these men?" Her gaze shifted to her drawstring bag in Hade's clenched fist. "These are friends of yours?"

Hade leered. "Not just friends, little lady. We're partners. Tiller here is a member of our gang."

Her aim steadied on Hade. "I don't believe you."

Shame seeped from Tiller's pores. "It's a lie, Mariah." He had to talk fast. She was backing away. "I'm not one of them. Not since I—"

"Hey! What's going on in here?"

The roomful of people spun to the door.

Otis tottered on the threshold in his nightshirt. "I woke up hankering for a slice of apple pie, but I see I'm missing a party." He spotted Tiller across the room and smiled. "I called out for you, <u>son</u>, but you couldn't hear me for all the fun you're having."

His merry eyes lit on Hade, and his smile waned. Leaning forward, he squinted. "Wait a minute, now. I know you, mister." His trembling fingers reached for the wound on his head. "You're the no-good rascal who bashed in my skull."

His foggy gaze slid to Sonny and Nathan. "You fellas were there, too." He nodded at Nathan. "You rode up the rise chasing—"

He pivoted in his socks, his shaky finger aimed at Tiller. "Chasing you! By Job, I remember it all now. You're the varmint who left me alone in the hands of these devils."

Mariah's troubled scowl fixed on Tiller. "You? You're the men who hurt Otis?"

Otis stared vacantly for several seconds before his face softened. "I won't hold it agin' you, Tiller. You were thinking of your little bride." He scratched his chin. "What was her name again?"

Tiller took a step toward him. "No, Otis. . ."

One finger shot up, and Otis flashed his toothless grin. "Lucinda! Sweet Lucinda with the big doe eyes." The smile died on his lips and confusion took its place. "But that can't be, can it? Where is she, son? And what are you doing here with little missy? Couldn't you convince Lucinda's pa that your wife belongs with you?"

Tiller's gaze swung to Mariah.

She stood pale and trembling, the big gun dangling at her side. "Your wife?"

Stumbling across the room, Tiller latched onto her arms. "I can explain all of this."

She tried to shrug his hands away, but he held on tight. "Mariah, please."

"You're hurting me." Her voice was steely-calm, and the fire never left her eyes, but her wince of pain cut him to the core.

Nathan lunged and grabbed his collar. "The jig's up, Tiller boy. Let's go."

Tiller's soul cried out to stay and fight for her. Shame spun him for the door.

Bumping shoulders, they bolted, Hade and Sonny fast on their heels. Like the cowards they were, they tore down the hall and out the back door.

And like ten years before in Scuffletown, Tiller's traitor feet followed Nathan from the only place he really wanted to be.

Dazed and speechless, Mariah stared at the door. Whatever madness had just come to light, one truth broke through her shock. Tiller was leaving, taking her battered heart with him. If he rode away from Bell's Inn, she might never see him again, might never understand what he'd done.

Miss Vee appeared on the stairs, tugging her dressing gown around her bosom, her hennaed hair an orange sunburst atop her head. "What the devil's going on down here?"

His eyes clearer now, Otis toddled to Mariah's side and touched her arm. "You're just gonna let him leave?"

"He's already gone." Her voice sounded hollow in her ears.

Otis shook his head. "They're still saddling the horses. But you'd best hurry."

With an anguished cry, Mariah dashed out of the parlor and raced for the kitchen door. Tiller said there was an explanation. She wanted to hear it, needed him to deny the ugly things she'd just heard.

Clutching the knob, she yanked, rattling the doors on its hinges. Pounding hooves sped past, kicking up dust and uprooted grass. She sprang off the threshold, but strong arms caught her in midair. "Whoa, not so fast."

"Let go, Uncle," she cried. "I have to catch him."

Uncle Nukowa set her down, his narrowed eyes boring into her. "Not just yet. You have some explaining to do."

She struggled against him. "Please! They're getting away."

His fisted hand loomed before her face, his raw knuckles blotting out the darkness of the yard. One by one, his fingers opened. Lit by the flickering kitchen light, Mother's bead necklace slid out in a clicking rush, jerking to a dangling stop from the end of his thumb.

The necklace Mariah last saw when she tucked it under her father's gravestone.

Stunned, she cut her eyes to him.

Watching her reaction, he nodded slowly then nudged her toward the door. "Go back inside, Mariah. It's time you start telling the truth."

Tiller rode hard behind Nathan, the rush of wind in his face a harsh reminder. How many times had he fled with the gang, running from the bullet, beating, or noose they deserved?

The unwanted miles stretched between Tiller and Bell's Inn. With every beat of his heart, he longed for Mariah. The sight of her proud face slack with shock, her eyes brimmed with pain, had broken him. To know he caused it rocked his soul.

His only comfort was the horse galloping beneath him—solid proof that he had every intention of returning. What would Mariah think when she found Sheki gone?

She'd add it to his list of sins and curse him for a soulless devil.

No matter. When he returned with her horse and money, it might be enough to convince her to listen. He'd be praying every second for God to work a miracle in her heart.

How to pry the gold from Hade's greedy fingers?

Tiller still had to work that part out, but he planned to succeed if he had to loosen those fingers by death.

THIRTY-NINE

Uncle Joe caught Mariah's wrist and sat her down hard on a kitchen chair. Standing over her, he swung the jasper pendant strung between the wooden beads like a pendulum past her eyes.

She tried in vain to look away, but they held her mesmerized.

"I found the grave, Mariah."

"Mother's grave?" She licked her lips. "You've always known where she rests."

He slapped the table hard. "Enough! The time for lies is past."

Mariah's heart dove as Miss Vee hurried in, her face as pale as her white collar. "What's going on in this house tonight? First that ruckus in the parlor, now this?" She tugged on his arm. "Come away from her. Joe. You're scaring her to death."

His head swiveled. "That's an interesting choice of words, Viola, when death is what we're dealing with."

Mariah shot him a warning glance. "Please, Uncle." She shook her head. "Not like this."

"Death?" Miss Vee repeated. "I don't understand."

Otis appeared behind Miss Vee, his eyes wide and darting. Uncle Nukowa's gaze bounced between them. "I stopped to pay respects to my sister tonight, and what do you suppose I found?"

They blinked at each other. Otis shrugged.

"A fresh grave in the family plot," Uncle Nukowa said. He glared at Mariah. "A hidden grave, though not hid well enough."

"What?" Miss Vee shuddered and rubbed her arms. "Whose, for heaven's sake? We've had no recent deaths."

Her uncle's gaze seared Mariah to her chair. "You can answer her question, can't you?" He raised his chin toward Miss Vee. "Go on. Tell her who's buried beside your mother on the hill. With a rock for a headstone"—he rattled the string of beads—"and these for a marker."

Miss Vee's hand snaked around to take them. "Your mother's necklace?" Her bewildered stare lifted to Mariah. "You placed your prized possession on a grave?" She shook her head. "But whose?"

Otis wagged his head sadly and patted Miss Vee's arm. She glanced down at him and started to wobble.

Mariah lunged for her. "For heaven's sake, Uncle, get a chair."

They sat her down just before she swooned. The men held her upright while Mariah brought a cold cloth to wipe her face.

"Slap her wrists," Otis said. "I hear that helps to bring 'em around."

In the time it took to revive Miss Vee, the events since Father's death tumbled through Mariah's mind like scenes before a drowning man— every chance to change her mind, every missed opportunity to confess.

She hadn't once paused to admit she'd stopped talking to God along the way. If she had, she would've realized she'd veered far from His will.

Forgive me! her heart cried.

The rage in Miss Vee's glance and the fury in her uncle's stance told her God's was the only forgiveness she could ever hope to get.

"Why?" Miss Vee's single word held a bitter accusation.

"I wanted to tell you so many times. Can you imagine how difficult it was to keep it from you?"

Tears flowing, Miss Vee shook her head. "I can't imagine a single thing about the terrible deed you've done."

Sinking to one knee, Mariah reached for her hands.

Miss Vee yanked them free and turned away.

Mariah sighed. "At least let me answer your question. I did it because I had no choice. Mother made me swear never to lose our ancestral land. Her burial place."

Uncle Nukowa crossed his arms. "It was a promise you couldn't keep."

Her mouth as dry as cotton, she nodded firmly. "But I could, Uncle. If I married a nahullo like she did."

Otis nodded grimly. "Which explains all the nonsense with that wicked Gabe."

Grateful for one ally, Mariah spun. "Yes. Only Tiller came along and we fell in love. He's already asked me to marry him."

She stood and reached for her uncle's arm, relieved when he didn't pull away. "Don't you see? You became the only thing standing in my way. If you hadn't arrived, I'd be Tiller's wife right now, and Mother's land would be safe."

Stunned, Mariah gripped her forehead to still the spinning room. "What am I saying?" She swallowed hard to ease the pain crowding her throat. "How could Tiller marry me? He already has a wife."

Her uncle's head snapped around. "What?"

She tucked her chin. "He deceived me all along. As it happens, Tiller's married."

Otis tugged at her arm. "Little missy, I've been thinking, and I don't think it's true because—"

"I'll kill him." Uncle Nukowa balled his fists, murderous rage coloring his face. "I'll boil the flesh from his rotted bones."

"Stop!" Miss Vee stood, as if waking from a trance. "John Coffee's gone. That's all that matters now." Clinging to the back of her chair, she lifted her chin. "I loved him from the first day I laid eyes on him." She smiled softly. "At first it seemed John might grow to love me, too." Moaning, she clutched her stomach. "Then Minti came along and cast her spell." Her mouth twisted. "I'm not a bit surprised to learn all this grief leads back to her."

Closing her eyes, she let her head fall back. "Well, they're together now, and so be it. Even from the grave Minti's won. If you listen close, you can hear her laughing."

Uncle Nukowa reached to steady her. "Viola. . ."

Miss Vee glanced his way. "Forgive me, Joe, for speaking ill of the dead." Gazing around the kitchen, she gave an eerie laugh. "But she's not really gone, is she? This is Onnat Minti Bell's inn. Always has been. Always will. Just like John Coffee was hers, and she'll never turn loose of either one." She staggered to the stairs with Otis clinging to her arm.

Longing to comfort her, Mariah edged closer. "Go up and rest,

Miss Vee. Tomorrow we'll sort all this out."

She raised her brows. "Can you undo your lies?" Her laugh was chilling. "Can you bring John back?" Stiffening her spine, she patted Otis's arm then pulled away. "I'm going to bed. Tomorrow, when I come down these stairs for the final time, I'll have my belongings with me."

She glanced around the room as if Mother flitted there. "This is the last night I'll sleep in her blasted house."

Joe caught Mariah's sleeve before she escaped up the stairs. "Where do you think you're going? We're not done."

She whirled, her eyes spitting fire. "How could you be so cruel?"

Otis backed into the hall. "I'm a mite tuckered, myself. Reckon I'll get back to my room." Reeling away, he disappeared.

Gritting his teeth, Joe pointed at his chest. "Me cruel? Do you muddy the pond to avoid your own reflection?"

She hung her head. "I have a lot to make up to her. But you could've been more considerate in how you broke the news."

He raised one brow. "You had plenty of time to tell her any way you saw fit."

"I told you why I couldn't. You know how Mother was. Surely you of all people can understand."

"You lied to me, girl. To everyone in this house." He shook his head. "Such behavior I'll never understand." He tightened his mouth. "And now I learn the dog who urged you to defy me has a wife?"

She held up her hand. "Believe me, I didn't know. Not until tonight."

Biting off a blistering curse, he glanced toward Tiller's room. "Is he in there? Sleeping under my roof?"

Tears spilled onto Mariah's cheeks. She let them flow unchecked. "He's gone. He rode out with his gang as you came in. After they robbed the safe."

"His gang?" Stunned, Joe gaped at her. "Are you saying *Tiller* robbed us?" He wouldn't admit it, but none of the things he'd heard matched what his heart believed about the boy. Taking her by the arm, he led her to the table. "I think you'd better start from the beginning."

Sinking into a chair, Mariah covered her face with her hands. "I still can't believe it myself. My head is reeling."

Joe patted her trembling shoulder. "Do your best, but I need to know what happened."

When she finished her tale of burglars in the parlor, Otis regaining his memory, her stolen gold, and Tiller making a getaway with his band of thieves, Joe was madder than he'd ever been in his life. He stood and lifted Mariah to her feet. "Go to bed and try not to fret. I'm going to round up some men and go after them."

She touched his arm. "Rest first. You haven't slept all night."

"I dozed awhile at Tobias's house."

"Helped along by a few pints of ale?"

He lowered his eyes.

"It's not enough, amoshi." She squeezed his hands. "It's nearly daylight. Rest until then."

He scowled. "This can't wait."

"At least while I pack food and water for your trip? Besides"—she shrugged—"you've said it many times, nahullos are easy to track."

He twisted his mouth to the side and nodded. "I suppose another hour can't hurt."

"Thank you. I'll feel better knowing you've had some sleep." Mariah turned toward the counter, her shoulders slumped in defeat. "Go on up. I'll call you when everything is ready."

Hurting for her, Joe pulled her around and tugged her to his chest. She buried her face in his shirt and wept. "How can you forgive me?"

He grunted. "Because you're right. I know how your mother was."

Raising her head, she searched his face. "You won't hurt him?" She knitted her brow. "When you find Tiller, you won't harm him, will you?"

The ways of women were a deep river indeed. "I should think you'd want his scalp."

She shook her head. "Maybe someday. Not now."

He swiped the tears from her cheeks with his thumbs. "Go upstairs and wash your face before you ready my pack."

"Yes, Uncle."

He walked her to the bottom step, and she climbed as if her legs were made of stone. Halfway up, he called her name.

"Yes sir?"

"I'm sorry about your father. I know how you loved him."

"Yes, very much." Her voice broke, and her red nose flared.

"And Mariah?"

"Yes sir?"

"I want you to call me Uncle Joe now. The time of my anger has passed."

FORTY

Tiller reined Sheki beside the other horses and slid to the ground. Every inch of him hurt as if they'd dragged him the last grueling miles. He supposed in many ways they had. His head throbbed, his heart ached, and his muscles strained to return to Mariah.

Hade lit the lantern then tossed his pack against the trunk of a river birch tree. Sliding to the ground, he propped his back against the worn leather bag, groaning when his knees cracked. "Sure is soon to be setting up camp. We should at least ride until daylight so they won't spot our fire. There may be a posse behind us, and I'd like to see them before they see us."

"I doubt there's a posse," Nathan said. "It would take too long to round one up. The nearest lawman's in Canton." He kicked a rock toward the Pearl. It landed with a *plunk* and a splash. "Besides, I'm tired of running."

Hade yawned and stretched. "I'm just plain tired. I sure could use some coffee. You boys go see what you can do about it."

Sonny pushed off the ground where he'd sprawled to dig a fire pit. "Yes sir. I'll round up some wood."

Nathan pulled a battered coffeepot from his saddlebag then squatted by the riverbank to fill it.

Tiller sat on a log and slid his knife from the scabbard to dig up a piece of chicory root to roast. Anything to add flavor to Nathan's strong, bitter grounds.

He paused, turning the bone handle over in his hand while memories flooded his mind.

The day he fled Scuffletown, he took the time to grab his Christmas gifts from under the tree. The knife, the only gift he'd kept up with over the years, came from his uncle.

Uncle Silas, a gem of a whittler, spent hours carving fine statues and trinkets, and he'd promised to teach Tiller to do the same. If he'd stayed in North Carolina, he'd be carving something besides chicory root and sassafras and might've carved something better out of life.

Uncle Silas once told him, "The blunders you make as a youth can chase you into old age. Don't make a mess of your life while you're still damp behind the ears."

Anger surged in Tiller's heart, and he squinted toward Nathan. He'd been a child when the older boys led him out of town by his soggy ear. For ten years, he'd stumbled along behind a ruthless gang, feeling lost and out of place—years spent away from his family that he could never get back.

Tiller appreciated what Nathan tried to do for him in the barn, but it wasn't enough. He didn't know if anything ever could be. He felt as if a fog had lifted in his head. Otis, Mariah, and the inn had awakened him from a bad dream, and he wasn't about to roll over and go back to sleep.

Lantern light glinted off the knife in Tiller's hand. His searing gaze jumped to Hade, snoring under the tree with Mariah's coins tucked inside his makeshift pillow.

Planted by impatience, watered by desperation, the idea grew, slipping into Tiller's head the way sap oozed from greening bark. He saw no reason to wait any longer.

Fighting tears, Mariah slung eggshells at the sink. Scrambled eggs, his favorite food, reminded her of Tiller. The cream she poured into the eggs he liked stirred into his coffee. Coffee summoned memories of sipping cups together at the breakfast table. The table brought to mind their Dr. Busby games.

How could she forget Tiller McRae when he'd invaded every corner of her life?

Miserable, Mariah's heart lifted to Miss Vee's room. She longed to race up the stairs and knock on her door, but she'd find no comfort there.

Why hadn't she realized how much she loved Miss Vee? She only prayed she hadn't lost her for good. Life would be unbearable if Miss Vee left the inn. The loss would be like losing a mother all over again.

"Little missy?"

She glanced around.

Otis stood behind her wearing the stiff gray shirt and baggy trousers he wore when they first carried him to her door. He'd slicked back his hair and shined up his boots, as well.

"Otis." She blinked at him. "You're dressed."

He grinned. "Well, not quite, thanks to you and Miss Vee. I can't seem to fasten the top button of my drawers, and I don't even need my suspenders."

She hid a smile behind her hand. "I was about to ask if you were ready for your breakfast."

He patted his bulging stomach. "Well, sure. It may be big, but it's empty this morning."

She nodded at the table. "Have a seat. It's almost ready."

He swung into a chair and glanced around. "Your uncle ain't left yet to go hunt Tiller, has he?"

Mariah glanced up. "How did you know he was going?"

"It don't take much figuring to know a man like Joe will go after those men."

She went back to stirring her eggs. "I'm about to wake him. He's eager to get on the road."

"That makes two of us."

Laying aside her ladle, Mariah turned. "You can't go. You're not strong enough."

The banister creaked, jolting her heart. She prayed to see Miss Vee lumbering down to slip on her apron and help with breakfast as she did every morning, her threats to leave forgotten.

Uncle Joe's heavy footsteps descended instead.

Otis lifted his head. "I'm going with you, Joe."

Her uncle smoothed back his hair and tied it with a leather strap then crossed to the coffeepot. "I don't think you can keep up, Otis. We'll be riding hard."

"I'll keep up. I'm stronger than I look."

Uncle Joe poured his coffee and stirred in a cube of sugar. "Why do you want to go?"

Otis swung around in his chair. "I've been mulling over the day I first ran into Tiller on the Trace. The day they took my money and busted my head." He glanced at Mariah. "When Tiller told me he had a wife, he was outright lying."

She gave her head a little shake. "Why would he lie about a thing like that?"

Otis tapped his nose. "Tiller was the bait, you see. Those ruffians used his boyish face and winsome ways to lure folks. Then they'd swoop in and skin their prey." He nodded. "The story Tiller told me that day he made up on the fly. He meant to sidetrack me, get me feeling sorry for him, and take my mind off the danger." He chuckled. "It worked, too."

Hope surged in Mariah's heart, but her anger squashed it. She slid a plate of food in front of both men and pulled out the opposite chair. "If it's true, it's still a crime. And a terrible thing to do."

Otis leaned across the table and peered into her eyes. "You're right, honey. It don't sound like the man we know, does it?"

Mariah bit her bottom lip and shook her head. "Not at all."

He touched her hand. "Why do you reckon Tiller came here in the first place, snuggling in and making himself at home?"

She'd never once asked herself that question. "I. . .don't know."

"He was running from those men because a life of pure meanery and shecoonery never set right in his heart. Tiller rode away and left me that day for the same reason. He's not the kind of man to take part in what happened next."

"He did have a part in it," Uncle Joe said. "He set you up to be fleeced."

Otis stared at his breakfast. "I'm not excusing him for that. He was guilty as sin." He glanced between them. "But Tiller brought that sin to the cross."

Silence settled over the table.

"It's the truth," Otis said. "Yesterday, he knelt at my feet and sobbed his heart out to God. He got up a brand-new man." He reached for

Mariah's hand. "Little missy, Tiller came here for a fresh start, and now he's had a true change of heart."

"Then why'd he run?" Uncle Joe growled.

Otis scratched his head. "I ain't figured that part out yet. That's why I intend to ride along, Joe. I mean to ask young Tiller myself." He squeezed Mariah's fingers. "There are two things I know for sure. One, Tiller didn't go willingly, and two, he loves you, honey."

Mariah got up and faced the counter, her napkin pressed to her mouth. "Then why didn't he tell me about his past? Why did he keep secrets from me?"

Otis cleared his throat. "I seem to remember another secret." His quiet voice soothed and convicted her at the same time. "Did you share all yours with him?"

Dicey swept through the back door, her high-pitched voice shattering the stillness like busted glass. "Sorry I's late. It ain't my fault. That tomfool Rainy ain't been on time one day in his life." Unaware of the strain in the room, she snatched her apron off the hook and set to washing the dishes.

Mariah wiped her eyes and brought another serving of eggs to Uncle Joe. She held the ladle suspended over his plate when Rainy ducked in the back door.

"Missy Bell?"

She glanced up.

"When Mista' Tilla' be back? We s'posed to build fences this mornin'."

She swallowed hard. "You'd best go on and start without him."

He frowned. "Yes'm."

As he ducked out of sight, a thought niggled at Mariah's mind. "Rainy, wait," she called.

He poked his head in again.

"How did you know Tiller's not here?"

Rainy, pointed. "Well, there's you and Mr. Joe. Mr. Otis and Miss Vee don't get on no horse." He grinned. "*Somebody* ridin' Sheki, so it got to be Mista' Tilla'."

Mariah dropped the ladle with a clatter, and Uncle Joe lurched up from his chair.

It felt like Rainy punched her in the stomach. She had to suck air before she could speak. "Sheki's gone?" It came out a croak.

The boy's eyes rounded. "Y—yes'm. Horse, bridle, and saddle."

Mariah shook her head at Uncle Joe. "He wouldn't take Sheki."

Uncle Joe slammed his fisted napkin to the table. "Well, he did," he roared.

Dicey screamed and dropped a plate with a *crash*.

Rainy made himself scarce.

The trembling in Mariah's chest flamed into rage. Of all the betrayals, this one stung the worst. Tiller knew what Sheki meant to her. His actions stank with bold assumption, the cocky action of a man with no conscience and no capacity for love.

In that moment, her heart closed on him and turned a lock. From here on, any reminders of Tiller McRae would taste of bitter swill.

Otis half stood, his eyes pleading. "Now, little missy. . .don't jump to conclusions."

Her hand shot up. "Don't you dare defend him. If Tiller took Sheki, he can't be who we thought he was." She turned to Uncle Joe. "I don't care about the money. Just find my horse."

He nodded. "I'll saddle up and come back for my provisions."

Otis watched Uncle Joe stalk to the door. "I'm going too, ain't I, Joe?"

Her uncle chewed inside his cheek for a moment then sighed. "Against my better judgment, Mariah, pack enough for two." He wagged a warning finger. "I won't slow my pace for you. If you can't keep up, I'll send you back alone."

Otis gave him a quick nod. "Fair enough."

A knock on the front door pulled them around. Staring at the hallway, Mariah clenched her fists. "Oh please, not today. I have no patience for lodgers."

Dicey set the dish towel filled with broken china aside and scurried past. "You want me to send them away?"

Mariah sighed. With her money stolen, she couldn't afford the luxury of her wishes. "Just answer the door, Dicey. See what they want."

Uncle Joe returned to the table and picked up his coffee. "I'll wait here until we find out who they are."

Exhausted, Mariah sank down at the table to wait. The breakfast she'd labored over had looked so good just moments before. Now its smell turned her stomach.

Dicey appeared wringing her hands. "They say they don't need no room for the night. Jus' a hot meal and coffee, if we please, and to fill their canteens at the pump. They willing to pay."

Mariah shared a look with Uncle Joe.

"I need to get on the road," he said. "I won't leave you alone with a rough bunch of strangers."

"We need the money." Mariah bit her lip. "I can handle them. I've done it before."

"Not without Viola." He nodded at Dicey. "Bring them in so I can have a look at them."

She bustled away, returning quickly with two men and a woman trailing behind her. The beautiful redhead was definitely a woman, though she wore jean pants and a youth's checkered shirt. She strutted into the kitchen ahead of her companions with the quiet confidence of a man.

Dust from the road covered them in a fine layer, and fatigue lined their faces, but the unmistakable light of decency shone from their eyes.

"Morning, ma'am," the striking, dark-eyed man said then nodded at Otis and Uncle Joe.

Uncle Joe shook hands all around. "Mariah, these folks look hungry. See what you can do to fix it."

"Yes sir," she said, turning to the stove.

"We need to clean up before we sit at your nice table," the woman said. "We've got many a long mile clinging to our hides."

"Show them to the pump, Dicey," Mariah said. "Take a towel for each of them when you go."

They returned refreshed and sat at the table, eagerly pouring cups of steaming coffee.

Mariah found the oddly attractive group so pleasant to look at she could hardly keep from staring.

Otis, gaping from one to the other, seemed to suffer the same affliction.

Heaping plates with eggs, bacon, fried potatoes, and buttered biscuits, she passed them around. Grinning, her guests shared a pleased look then tucked into the food.

The handsome man, his cheeks bulging, beamed at Mariah. "Ma'am, this is the best spread we've had in weeks."

His friend nodded. "Not since we pulled out of Scuffletown."

Otis shot to his feet. "I knew it! I know just who you are."

The dark-eyed man sloshed his coffee.

His friend seemed to bite his tongue.

The forkful of food headed for the woman's mouth fell to her plate.

They stilled, as if scared to move, gazing stupidly at Otis.

Uncle Joe scowled. "Man, have you lost your senses?"

Ignoring him, Otis pointed to each of them in turn. "You're Hooper. You're Duncan. And you're Dilsey."

Staring blankly, the woman slowly shook her head. "No sir. I'm Ellie. And this here's my husband, Wyatt. But how—"

"Close enough," Otis crowed.

Mariah gasped. No wonder these folks struck a chord in her heart. Like Otis, she already knew them from her long talks with Tiller. The family he hadn't seen in ten long years sat for breakfast around Mariah's kitchen table.

FORTY-ONE

Mariah held her breath and waited, a pulse pounding in her throat. The man Otis claimed to be Hooper didn't deny it. Waking from his daze, he stood. "Tiller's been here," he announced in a steady voice, his eyes brimming with hope. He glanced at each of them, settling on Mariah. "Is he still?"

She wondered if he saw the same bond to Tiller she sensed in him.

"No sir," Otis said. "You just missed him."

Ellie squealed and sprang up to hug her brother. Turning from the crook of his arm, she swiped at her tears. "Tell us where he is. We'll go right now."

Otis cleared his throat. "Well, ma'am, that part's a little tricky."

"If he's coming back, we'll wait," Hooper said. "No matter how long it takes."

Uncle Joe's mouth tensed to a thin white line. "You'll wait a long time. Tiller's not welcome here."

Ellie spun, her green eyes flashing. "Why is that?"

"Tiller McRae is a thief and a liar," he said. "And a no-account beguiler of women."

The three stared in disbelief.

Uncle Joe jutted his chin. "Not to mention a horse thief."

"Who says?" Ellie demanded, her fists clenched.

Wyatt's arm shot out to hold her. "Let him talk, Ellie. It's been a long time since we've seen Tiller. He's not the young whelp you remember."

"I don't care. Tiller's our kin. He couldn't be all those things." Her voice wavered. "He just couldn't."

"Ask my niece," Uncle Joe said, pointing at Mariah. "The swindler proposed marriage to her when he already has a wife."

Ellie gasped and covered her mouth.

Hooper and Wyatt shot troubled frowns over her head.

"Not only that," Uncle Joe continued, "he robbed our safe last night of every cent we owned. I'm on my way this morning to form a posse and go after him."

Showing strength Mariah didn't think he had, Otis pushed between them. "Now blast it! Hold up a minute, Joe. You're only giving them part of the story. Tiller's family deserves the whole truth."

Ellie's hand slid away from her mouth. "If it's any worse than what we've heard, kindly keep it to yourself."

Hooper gripped his shoulder. "Tell us what you know, old-timer."

Otis pulled out a chair for Ellie then gave Mariah a brisk nod. "Brew up more coffee, little missy. This might take a minute."

Uncle Joe fumed. "I don't have time for stories, Otis. If you want to stay behind and flap your jaws, that's up to you. I need to call out a manhunt."

Mariah gripped his wrist. "Please, Uncle Joe. Otis is right. These folks are Tiller's family. They have a right to hear everything and decide for themselves."

Hooper nodded. "I'd be much obliged if you'd wait, sir. Since we're both looking for the same man, I'd like to ride along."

Uncle Joe looked doubtful. "I don't know if that's a good idea."

"We might be of use," Hooper said. "My sister is quite gifted at tracking."

Looking down his nose, Uncle Joe scoffed. "I have no need of her. I can trail a goose in a southbound flock."

Ellie's brow puckered. "I can track a flea in a sandstorm."

They challenged each other across the room.

Mariah sought his hand and squeezed.

With a whispered curse, Uncle Joe nodded and plopped in his chair.

They settled around the table while Otis talked about the kind-hearted Tiller, the man who hovered over his sickbed, bathing and feeding him with gentle hands when he was too weak to care for himself. He spoke of the Tiller devoted to Mariah, rescuing her from the twister and its aftermath and from crazy Gabe Tabor.

Otis told them how Tiller loved the inn, rebuilding it from roof-top to foundation then doing it all over again after the storm. He mentioned the garden, how Tiller spent long hours coaxing green shoots from the ground, determined that Mariah have fresh vegetables despite the destructive tornado.

In a voice filled with fatherly pride, he told of Tiller chopping up trees for days and hauling them off to sell, so proud of bringing every cent to place in Mariah's lap. He ended with the story of Tiller in tears, kneeling on the porch to lay down his sins and invite Jesus into his life. "If there's one thing a man can't fake, it's a repentant heart."

Ellie crossed her arms on the table and lowered her head to cry, strands of her long hair falling in the butter dish.

Dicey lifted her apron to cover her face and ran sobbing into the pantry.

Ducking his head, Hooper wiped his face with his sleeve.

Even Wyatt, Ellie's husband, had shimmering eyes. "That sounds more like the boy we knew."

"So what happened after all that?" Hooper asked. "And what's this about a wife?"

Otis opened his mouth to answer, but Mariah gripped his shoulder. "No. Let me."

Otis glanced up with a sweet smile. "Go ahead, honey."

Taking a deep breath, she told how Tiller had been riding with a raiding gang of thieves. She made it clear that he took off when the real crimes were committed because his tender conscience drove him to. She said Tiller didn't really have a wife, that sweet Lucinda was a story he made up on the fly to gain Otis's trust.

In a proud voice, she explained how Tiller broke with the gang to seek a fresh start, but they followed him to Bell's Inn. She assured them Tiller took no part in robbing the inn. He'd been in the parlor to protect her money from his former gang, not to steal it.

Mariah said all these things to Tiller's family because she knew without a single doubt they were true.

"Then why did he run?" Joe demanded.

Mariah hung her head. "I'm certain Tiller ran from the doubt in my eyes." Her heart breaking, she glared. "But he didn't run for good. Tiller would never steal my horse, Uncle Joe. Leaving on Sheki proves he has every intention of coming back."

"That's it!" Otis cried, slapping the table. "He's planning to ride back here with your money and make you proud. It lines up with everything else the boy's done since he got here."

Mariah crossed her arms over the sudden ache in her stomach. "That could be dangerous, couldn't it? Those men won't let him get away with all those coins. They'll kill him first."

Uncle Joe raised his chin, staring down his nose at her. "You really believe in this red-haired nahullo?"

She smiled through her tears. "With all my heart."

Standing, he offered his hand to Hooper. "Looks like our manhunt just became a rescue."

Ellie's husband seemed anxious. He stood with Hooper, wiping his trembling hands on his trousers. "This thieving gang," he said in a voice filled with dread, "did you happen to catch their names?"

"Yes." Mariah gave him a thoughtful nod. "The one with cold eyes was Hade Betts. The lanky man with a ready smile was Sonny Thompson."

She turned to Otis. "I can't recall the quiet one's name."

"Nathan somebody," Otis said.

Wyatt turned as pale as the tablecloth. "Carter? Nathan Carter?"

Mariah pointed. "Yes, that's him."

Ellie wrapped her arms around Wyatt's neck, and Hooper gently patted his shoulder.

Compassion squeezed Mariah's heart. "You know him?"

Wyatt gave a somber nod. "He's my brother."

"I'm so sorry."

Hooper hooked his arm around Wyatt. "Don't worry. We'll find them both and bring them home."

Wyatt shook his head. "I'd like to believe you, Hoop. Nathan's pretty headstrong."

"Nonsense," Ellie said. "He's bound to be tired of drifting." She smiled. "We'll tell him he has a passel of nephews back home just dying to meet their Uncle Nate."

Wyatt grinned and squared his shoulders. "That might chase him off for good."

Uncle Joe grunted. "I hate to rush you folks, but it's time to ride." He crossed to the rack and shoved his big hat on his head. "The longer we sit here, the farther away they'll get."

He motioned to Otis. "I'll saddle Tiller's horse for you and meet you outside."

Otis waved his hand. "Aw, go on without me, Joe. I'd just slow you down."

Mariah smiled to herself. Funny how fast Otis lost his zeal to go once the tide of Uncle Joe's anger switched off Tiller.

Swiveling on his chair, Otis gazed up at Hooper. "I have one more question, if you don't mind."

"Not at all, sir," Hooper said.

Otis's eyes crinkled in thought. "Why have you come looking for young Tiller?"

Hooper shot him a warm smile. "We've come to take him home."

Mariah's breath caught. "Home? You mean to North Carolina?"

"That's right." Ellie beamed. "Back to Scuffletown where he belongs."

Otis swung around to her. "Why now, after ten long years?"

Pulling on his leather gloves, Hooper lowered his gaze. "It's not the first time we've searched, I can tell you that, but we finally got a good lead." He grinned. "Looks like it paid off."

Beaming, Otis glanced around at them. "I'm glad to know you care about him. Tiller don't know that, you see."

Ellie clenched her hands and fixed determined eyes on Otis. "He'll know soon enough, sir."

Mariah pushed up from the table. "What if Tiller doesn't want to go back with you?"

Hooper's mood seemed to lighten. "He'll want to." He glanced at Ellie. "Once we tell him what's waiting there for him."

Before Mariah could ask what he meant, Uncle Joe herded them out the door.

She called Dicey out of the pantry, and together they finished tying up bundles of food and filling canteens with water. As they carried them out the back door, the rising sun broke through the trees by the river.

Uncle Joe and the others rode up to the porch, and Dicey helped Mariah load their packs and tie on the full canteens.

Feeling her uncle watching from the saddle, Mariah glanced up at him.

He gently caressed her cheek. "Your mother loved you very much."

A lump rose in her throat. "Yes, she did."

"She loved your father, too."

Unable to speak, Mariah nodded.

Straightening, his thoughtful gaze swept his surroundings in a wide arc, from the Pearl River to the Natchez Trace stretching out of sight in the distance. "I'll help you keep your promise, niece. I'll bring home your Tiller so you can keep your mother's land."

Her grateful tears blurred his dear face. "Thank you, Uncle. I love you with all my heart."

He nodded. "I'll stay for your wedding, but then I must go home."

"Already? There's no rush to leave."

A teasing glint sparked his eyes. "There is if I want to be home for the birth of my son."

A hush fell over the yard. "Aunt Myrtle is with child?"

He grinned. "Yes, at last. With my son, George."

Laughing, she reached up to give him a hug. "I'm so happy for you."

Pulling free, he took up his reins. "Enough of this dawdling. Let me go find your nahullo."

They rode down the slope of the yard and onto the Trace, turning left toward Jackson.

Mariah clung to the porch rail and watched as long as she could spot any sight of them flickering past the trees. Her heart felt somewhat lighter, but an unsettled matter weighed heavy on her mind. She had to face Miss Vee. The sooner the better.

There hadn't been a peep from her all morning, despite her determined threat to pack and leave. Sudden fear struck Mariah's heart. Miss Vee didn't seem the type to harm herself, but—

Whirling for the door, Mariah burst into the kitchen and dashed for the stairs.

"She's over here, little missy."

She froze, her trembling hand clutching the rail.

Otis sat across the table from a bleary-eyed Miss Vee, her face bare of makeup, her hair an unholy mess. Through bloodred eyes, the lids puffed like risen dough, she stared at her hands twisting the tablecloth.

Mariah cautiously approached. "Miss Vee?"

Otis stood. "Here, take my chair. She's ready to talk." He backed toward the door. "I'll just. . ." Then he was gone.

Unsure what to say, Mariah slid into his surrendered seat and laced her fingers in front of her, her knuckles white.

Her chest ached when Miss Vee groped for her hand. "I always knew, Mariah. Deep inside, I knew."

A lump crowded Mariah's throat. "That Father was gone?"

Miss Vee shook her head. "That I wouldn't be allowed to have him— not with how bad I wanted him." She raised her eyes. "I'd have lured your father straight from your mama's arms if he'd given me the chance." She shook her head. "Such a thing should never go unpunished."

"Please don't." Mariah squeezed her hand. "Father's death wasn't to punish you."

Miss Vee shrugged. "I reckon I know that in my head. My heart's not so sure." She lifted tortured eyes. "It was an awful lie you told. A terrible, cruel secret to keep." Her gaze held Mariah captive. "You understand that now, don't you?"

She nodded. "To my shame, I understood all along. That's why I have to beg your forgiveness." She lowered her cheek to Miss Vee's hand. "I knew how much it would hurt when you found out."

Miss Vee sat quietly for a moment then caressed Mariah's bowed head. "Pretty girl, you're all I have left of your father. I couldn't bear to lose you, too."

Mariah sat up and flung her arms around Miss Vee's neck, basking in the warmth of her pardon. Clinging together, they sobbed for the heartbreaking loss they shared.

FORTY-TWO

Sonny's boisterous mood and Nathan's loud rustling never stirred Hade. The man slept like the dead and always had. A dangerous inclination for a criminal, but it would work in Tiller's favor. He'd find a way to distract Sonny, and then he'd pounce on Hade.

Licking his lips, he looked around, trying to get some idea of what to do with the gawky court jester who stayed loyal to a fault to Hade Betts.

"What you up to, Nate?" The clown in question leaned over Nathan's shoulder while he rummaged in his saddlebag.

"Going fishing," Nathan said, holding up the hooks and ball of twine he kept in his pack. If not for Nathan's knack with catching fish, many days on the trail the gang might've gone hungry.

Sonny danced with excitement. "Hey, I want to go."

Nathan shrugged. "Sure. Go dig up a mess of worms. I'll rig the poles."

The tension in Tiller's shoulders eased. *Thanks, Nate.* Without knowing it, he'd just solved Tiller's problem.

Squirming with impatience, Tiller wiped his wet palms on his trousers while Nathan cut and trimmed two limber oak branches and rigged them with the makeshift tackle. Pulling his hat low over his face, he saluted Tiller and lumbered upriver, Sonny bounding behind him like a flop-eared hound.

Now that Tiller's chance had come, he couldn't seem to move. His heart pounded and sweat broke out on his top lip. He swiped it away, his nervous gaze fixed on Hade.

In the years since Nate had coaxed Tiller to join Hade's gang, he'd never trusted the man. Never respected his spiteful tactics. Savage as a meat ax, Hade's unpredictable cruelty was the reason Tiller rode away from every ambush. Still, what he was about to do wouldn't be easy.

He stood, flexed his fingers at his side. Raised his head and sought the heavens for courage. Unsheathed his knife and squatted in front of Hade.

His mouth sagging, one arm flung over his head, Hade snored like the call of a bull moose. The leather pack under his neck forced his head back, exposing his fleshy throat like a formal invitation.

His first try, Tiller shook so hard he had to withdraw, taking deep breaths through his nose to settle his nerves.

Biting his bottom lip, he inched the blade forward again.

"Just. . .back away, Tiller boy." Nathan's hoarse whisper jolted Tiller so close to Hade's jugular, he nearly severed it. A firm grip on Tiller's hand guided the knife away from the man's throat. Dropping to his knees beside them, Nathan cocked his head and raised his brows to question marks.

"What's going on?" Hade mumbled, struggling to sit up.

Nathan pried the knife from Tiller and swept moldy leaves from the base of the tree. "Just digging for worms, Hade," he said, twisting the knife in the exposed dirt.

"Worms?" Hade blinked his bleary eyes then hurled a foul curse. "Don't dig them from under me, you fool." He waved his arm. "Go over yonder and dig the blasted things."

"Sorry, pardner. Go back to sleep," Nathan cooed, rising to his feet.

He pulled Tiller up by his collar and marched him across the camp to the river. Smiling brightly, he waved at Sonny, perched on a rock about fifty yards away, dangling his pole over the water. Hauling Tiller around, Nate punched his arm. "Are you crazy? It's a good thing I forgot my cork."

Tiller frowned. "Where did you learn to be so quiet?"

"I'm a Lumbee, remember? We learned to be quiet or be dead."

He shoved Tiller's shoulder. "What did you think you were doing?

You'd never get away with killing Hade Betts. Besides, with your tender conscience, you couldn't live with yourself."

Tiller lifted his chin. "I wasn't going to kill him."

Nate flung the knife, burying it to the hilt in the ground. "I don't know if you know this, Tiller boy, but if you slit a man's throat, he dies."

Bending to yank the blade free, Tiller wiped it on his trousers and shoved it in the scabbard at his side. "I didn't intend to cut him, but Hade had to wake up believing I would."

"If he believed it, he'd kill you even deader." Nathan pointed at the knife. "Do me a favor and leave that Mississippi toothpick in its sleeve. I know what you're trying to do, but you're going about it all wrong." He patted Tiller's back and strolled ahead. "Just sit tight and leave the scheming to me. Trickery's not your style."

Tiller ran up and caught his arm. "What are you up to?"

Nate winked. "Watch and learn." Pulling free, he nodded toward camp. "Go fetch my corks and bring an extra hook for yourself. We need to land a few catfish and get them frying before the old man wakes up again."

After rounding up Tobias and a few able-bodied men, Joe led the party down the Trace toward Jackson. The plowed soil, churned up by pounding hooves, left no doubt which way the fleeing men had gone. They'd burned a path into the rain-soaked dirt for several miles before slowing to a walk. A few yards later, their tracks faded into higher ground and disappeared.

Before Joe could dismount, the red-haired woman, as small and spry as a boy, slid off her horse and scrambled up the grassy knoll. After a spell, she trudged into view at the top of the rise and pointed behind her. "They came up here then veered off downriver."

Joe caught her horse's reins, and the riders climbed the sloping earth wall that bordered the sunken road, cut out by years of rolling wheels, plodding hooves, and determined shoe leather.

Hooper nudged up the brim of his hat. "They wouldn't go much farther without resting the horses. Not after riding them so hard."

Watching Hooper's calm, determined face, Joe saw a man of power, a leader of men. He sensed in him the same strength he couldn't deny in Tiller McRae.

Joe nodded. "Keep watch for signs of a camp along the bank. They'll be long gone by now, but we'll be able to pick up their trail from there." He twisted in the saddle and repeated the charge in Choctaw.

"Hoop, what if the old man and Joe's niece are wrong about Tiller?" Wyatt asked, his throat working. "From what she said, Nathan's in tight with this gang. We could be walking into a gunfight with our own kin."

Hooper wound his reins around his hand. "Once they know it's us, I doubt they'll take a shot." His jaw shifted. "If they do, we'll get out of Joe's way and let his men settle their hash."

Respect for Hooper surged in Joe's chest. The dark-eyed man's spirit was indeed strong and good. "I make you this promise," Joe said. "My men won't harm Tiller unless he strikes first."

"And Nathan?"

Joe raised his chin. "We'll fire if we're fired on. Not before."

Hooper nudged his horse closer and held out his hand. "Thank you, Joe. I couldn't ask for more."

The skillet sizzled over the fire, and the smell of seared catfish hung in the air. Nathan boiled a hunk of venison jerky in water from his canteen, stewing up a savory broth. Flicking weevils from sheets of hardtack, he busted them up in the broth and left it to thicken.

Tiller peeled and roasted the chicory he'd dug earlier, and Nathan brewed a fresh pot of coffee. For the first time since they'd fled the house, Tiller realized his belly was empty.

Fingering the tin plates Nathan kept in his pack, he leaned to peer into the pan. "Is the grub almost ready?"

"Just about." Grinning, Nathan lifted the biggest fish from the grease. "Hand me your shingle. I know it's hard for you to wait."

Hade sat up moaning and briskly rubbing his face. "I smell food."

Nathan glanced behind him. "Almost ready, boss."

Hade gazed around with a blank look until deep furrows marred his brow. "What time is it, Nathan? Why the devil didn't you wake me?"

"Well, good morning to you, too, sunshine," Nate said. "You woke up in a fine pucker."

"Why are you boys hanging around here? There ain't near enough road stretched between us and that blasted inn." Grunting, he struggled to his feet. "You hear me, Sonny? Get this mess cleared up, and you plug-uglies break camp. It's time to get a move on."

Nate went on stirring the hardtack slop. "Load your plate first, Sonny. We eat before we do anything else."

Sonny stood, his hesitant gaze jumping from Nathan to Hade.

Hade stalked to the fire, nervously working his fingers. "I'm telling you, we need to pull foot. Tiller's spunky little innkeeper will have the law on our tails."

Nathan laughed. "She won't turn in our boy. Didn't you see the way she looked at him? The little lady is well smitten after a taste of Tiller's charm."

"Nate's right," Sonny said, dishing up his grub. "Tiller must've poured it on thick."

Tiller's hands tensed until his plate shook. Forcing himself to relax, he squatted in front of the fire. "Don't worry." He turned steady eyes on Hade. "Mariah won't turn me in."

Hade snorted. "I wouldn't be so sure, pretty boy. You know what they say about a scorned woman."

"'Heaven has no rage, like love to hatred turned, nor hell a fury, like a woman scorned.'"

Their heads swiveled to Sonny.

Fried fish clutched in his dirty hand and grease smearing his cheeks, he blinked. "What? You think I got no culture?"

Hade shook a warning finger at Nate. "Eat up then, but make it quick. If we get set on by the law, I'll row you up salt crick." Filling his tin plate to overflowing, Hade settled against the tree to grumble and eat.

Nathan showed no fear of Hade rowing him up a creek. By the time Hade put away his usual three helpings, his bulging gut would be too heavy to give chase, much less give anyone a beating.

Tiller raised his brows at Nathan. His answering smile meant his scheme, whatever it was, must have been going according to plan.

FORTY-THREE

Mariah walked Miss Vee to her room and tucked her in bed, plumping the crocheted pillows at her back. Sitting in a chair beside her grief-stricken friend, Mariah held her hand while they shared memories of the man who was father to one, cherished love of the other.

At last, Miss Vee slept. Her every shudder, every hitching breath laid the finger of blame on Mariah's aching heart. Unable to bear another minute, she slipped from the room and closed the door.

Downstairs, she had Rainy fetch meat from the smokehouse and gave instructions to Dicey about preparing lunch, though she wondered who would have the stomach to eat. The thought of food put sawdust in her mouth, and she doubted Miss Vee would touch a bite.

And with Tiller gone—

The sound of his name in her head shot pulsing waves of pain to her chest. With Tiller gone, the house would go on feeling empty, the food tasteless, her once cheery table a soulless place.

Losing Father had robbed her of the ties to her past. Losing Tiller would mean the loss of her future, a loss she couldn't bear.

She pushed onto the back porch, his spirit rising from every board and nail. Sitting on the top step, she ran her hands along the smooth cedar rail.

How blind they'd been in their innocence. Blissful, content, falling deeply in love—unaware of disaster approaching from three different directions.

Hooper McRae from the east, coming to cart Tiller home to Scuffletown.

Uncle Joe from the west, intent to carry Mariah away, over his shoulder if need be.

Hade Betts and his gang from out of nowhere, determined to lure Tiller back to their degrading lifestyle.

Angry, she brought her clenched fist down on the porch. "Why couldn't they all just leave us in peace?"

"Life seldom works that way, little missy."

She raised her head. "I'm sorry. I didn't see you there."

Otis ambled to the porch, wiping his hands on his baggy britches. "Just washing up at the pump." He glanced heavenward. "One of God's greatest gifts is water. Did you ever consider what a stinking lot we'd be without it?"

Mariah tucked her chin at the mention of the God she'd sorely neglected. "I thought you were resting. What are you doing outside?"

He pointed over his shoulder. "I thought I'd lend Rainy a hand in the garden."

"Oh?" She angled her head. "I didn't know you liked to work the soil."

"You'll find most men do. There's nothing more healing to the soul than the promise of new life." Otis patted her hand. "It's the reason we're awed by a woman ripe with child." He chuckled. "We can't pull that off, but we can give birth to a fine crop of tomatoes."

Mariah's cheeks warmed, but she couldn't hold back a smile.

He leaned back to study her. "That's better. I don't like to see you fret. It paints lines betwixt them pretty eyebrows."

Mariah sniffed. "Lately I've had my share of things to fret over. But the most pressing burden I'm relieved to have off my chest." She stole a glance at him. "How did you know? That day in your room, I mean."

He crooked one brow. "You mean your secret?"

Lowering her gaze, she nodded.

"Well, I didn't really know, did I? God gave me just enough to get

His message across." He laughed. "If I'd known the particulars, I may have turned you over my knee."

Mariah covered her face with her hands. "I'm so ashamed. I don't suppose I'll ever forgive myself."

With palsied fingers, Otis lifted her chin. "It starts with asking God's forgiveness."

She shook her head. "Oh, I couldn't. I can't even find the words."

"Well, that's different." Otis withdrew his hand. "Sorry, gal. I mistook you for one of His."

Her head whipped around. "But I—I am. At least I was."

"Was?" He quirked his brow. "The Book says, 'I have loved thee with an everlasting love.' "

Mariah braced her forehead with her palms. "Otis, I ache for God's pardon. For everyone's."

"What are you waiting for? God says to fess up then bet on Him to forgive. He goes the extra mile and washes us clean." He nudged her with his shoulder. "Why are you making it harder than He did?"

Tears squeezed between her tight lashes.

Otis pulled her close. "Oh, lamb. Why is it easier to accept mercy from your uncle and Miss Vee when God loves you most of all?"

She wiped her nose. "I don't feel worthy."

"None of us are. Don't you see?" He took her hands and peered into her eyes. "Godly sorrow pleases Him because it leads to repenting. Condemning yourself does just the opposite."

She nodded. "I think I understand."

"Good." He stood and hitched up his pants. "I'll leave you alone so you and God can have a little talk."

Mariah stretched out her hand. "Before you go, I have to ask you something."

"Anything, child."

She searched his gentle eyes. "Will Tiller be all right? Will he come back to us?"

A shadow crossed his face. "I can't see the future, honey. But I can tell you one thing—Tiller left here fully intent on coming home."

At the door, he turned. "While you're talking to God, ask Him to be a stone of stumbling and a rock of offense to those disobedient men for Tiller's sake."

Hade lounged across the fire from Tiller, shoveling hardtack mush in his mouth with a wide spoon. After two helpings, he laid aside his plate and pulled the pan off the fire to wolf down the rest.

Sonny tried to elbow in next to him for a share, but Hade turned aside, growling like a dog on a bone. "This here's fine mush, Nathan," he said with bulging cheeks. "Best you ever made."

"You ought to share, Hade," Sonny whined. "I'm still hungry."

He tossed the empty pan at Sonny's feet. "Here, I'll share the washing up. Take that down to the river and rinse it out before I beat you to a jelly."

Sonny bent to grab the handle. "Aw, Hade. That ain't no way to do."

Cackling, Hade watched him go, the corners of his eyes crinkled with glee. "I hope he don't fall in and drown. It wouldn't be near as much fun around here without old Sonny, would it?"

Dodging Hade's grasping fingers, Nathan slid the last fish on Tiller's plate. Hade leaned over and snatched it before Tiller could take a bite. "Let's don't be greedy, boys."

Leering, he took a deliberate bite then tilted his chin. "So, what do you say, Tiller? Are you ready to ride with us again? We've got big plans, and I think you'd fit in real nice." He swiveled to Nathan. "Don't you think so, Nate?"

Nathan shrugged. "I'm not sure Tiller's cut out for robbing banks."

Hade licked his fingers then wiped them on his britches. "Sure he is." He pointed. "With that guileless face, he could spin one of his yarns while we emptied the safe. They'd be so caught up in his tale, they wouldn't notice until we were long gone." He winked. "How about it, Tiller boy? Can we count on you?"

Tiller slowly set his plate aside. "I don't know, Hade. It's like Nathan said. I wouldn't be good at robbing banks."

Hade's features hardened. "Now you listen up. . . . I've invested years in training you. I don't take kindly to folks running out on me."

Tiller gnawed the side of his lip. "I'm not running out on anybody. It's time to split the sheets, that's all."

Chest heaving, Hade pushed to his feet. "We ain't splitting nothing but the take, you hear?" He loomed over Tiller with his fists clenched. "You owe me, boy."

His fury raging to the surface, Tiller stood, but Nathan stepped between them. "Settle down, boys. There's no call to get riled."

Shoving him aside, Hade advanced on Tiller.

Tiller took a step toward him, his hand on his knife.

The frying pan sailed toward them from the brush, spinning across the dirt and landing at their feet.

Wide-eyed, Hade stared dumbly at the greasy skillet. "What the—" He glanced around. "Where's Sonny?"

A large rock arced from the other side of the camp, landing three feet away and rolling past them. Then another that struck the fire, flipping a burning limb into the air and raising a spiral of glowing embers.

With a shout, Hade spun in a circle as a storm of sticks, stones, and pinecones showered from the sky.

Tiller grinned. A familiar storm.

"It's come-to-judgment-day, pretty boy," Hade roared. "They're on us, and it's your fault."

Down and up so fast Tiller couldn't react, Hade drew back the skillet and swung. With a shout, Nathan leaped, shoving Tiller out of the way. The heavy pan hit the back of Nate's head with a sickening thud. He dropped without a whimper.

The clearing erupted with running feet and loud voices just as Hade pulled the pistol at his side. "You've been both blessing and curse to me, son. I should've cut my losses and let you go."

Tiller braced for a bullet, his soul crying out to God, his heart to Mariah.

Four hundred pounds of mad Indian sailed at Hade, knocking him to the ground. The gun went off, firing harmlessly into the trees.

Uncle Joe strolled up and ground his heel into Hade's hand until he howled and turned loose of the gun. Justin and Christopher scrambled off Hade's winded body, standing over him with clenched fists.

Feeling sick, Tiller knelt over Nathan's prone body. He called his name and heard an anguished echo from behind him in a stranger's voice. Shading his eyes against the sun, he glanced up.

The man gazing down at Nathan, his face white with concern, stirred distant memories of mud and misty swamps. "Who—"

The familiar stranger went down on one knee and touched Nathan's back. "Is he alive?"

Tiller stared, afraid to blink. "Wyatt Carter? It can't be."

Nathan groaned, and Tobias Jones pushed close to see to his wound.

Standing on shaky legs, Tiller gaped in disbelief as Nathan's long-lost brother hovered by his side. "Where. . .where'd you come from?"

Against the shouting voices circling Hade and Sonny, a woman's quiet sobs reached Tiller's ears. Heart pounding, he spun. "Mariah?"

A tall man with pitch-colored hair held a slight figure against his chest, her long hair the color of a redbird. Clenched fist pressed to her mouth, she wept as one who mourned.

Dazed, Tiller tilted his chin while scenes from another life rushed through his head.

The two moved toward him, enveloped him, and he knew for sure. "Hooper?" Tears blurred his vision. He blinked to see them better. "Ellie, it's really you?"

Wailing, she wrapped both arms around him and clung with all her might.

Hooper, one hand resting on Ellie's neck, the other gripping Tiller's, gazed at him with streaming eyes. "Thank God we finally found you."

"You've been looking for me?" He didn't realize he was crying, too, until he heard his wavering voice.

Hooper nodded. "For most of the last ten years."

Tiller wiped his eyes on his sleeve. "But why?" he whispered.

Ellie lifted her head and smiled sweetly. "Why do you think, silly boy? We're your family, and we've come to take you home."

FORTY-FOUR

Mariah yanked the pins from her hair, kicked off her shoes, and rolled off her stockings. She longed to climb on Sheki's bare back, bury her fingers in his mane, and soar along the river until the rushing wind eased her fears.

She settled for a barefoot run through the cool grass in the backyard then over the weedy verge to the distant riverbank. Padding across the warm bank, she relished the swishing sand between her toes. Gathering her skirt, she lowered herself to the ground and swung her legs into the cold water.

The loose soil swirled, disturbed by her toes, and silvery minnows shot in every direction. Mariah held very still. Soon the water cleared and the curious minnows returned to peck at her skin for a taste.

The Pearl had always been a refuge from the shunning she endured from both sides of her bloodline. As a child, she spent hours exploring along the banks, listening to the mockingbird's song, and watching eagles soar overhead.

Today her haven withheld its comfort. The water felt too cold on her feet, the sun too hot on her head. The water lapping the hem of her chemise wicked clammy moisture to her skin. Leaning back on her arms, she closed her eyes and let the promise of the Lord's enduring love still the pounding of her heart.

Mother's influence had endowed her with a strong spirit. How else could a girl of her tender age endure what she had? Yet through those trials, she'd learned the depths of her weakness and her desperate need for God.

"Great Father, bring my love safely home."

The words were barely past her lips when a distant, tinny voice called her name.

Mariah's head jerked up. Shading her eyes from the water's glare, she squinted down the meandering ribbon of water. The shimmering outline of approaching riders quickened her pulse. A waving hat and a thatch of orange hair brought her to her feet in a stumbling run.

Tiller spurred Sheki to a gallop and raced to meet her. They reached her fast, and Tiller leaped from the saddle before Sheki came to a full stop.

His arms and shoulders cloaked her, his fingers tangled in her hair. He held her so near she felt a part of him, his racing heartbeat pounding in her ears. Pulling her head back, he kissed her, smoothing damp strands of hair from her face with gentle hands.

Lifting his head, he breathed a shaky laugh. "Does this mean you don't despise me?"

Too overcome to speak, she nodded helplessly.

He frowned and shook his head. "You're letting me off too easy. I lied to you. To all of you."

"You didn't lie. You withheld the truth. I'm guilty of the same."

He furrowed his brow but continued. "It's my fault Otis got hurt."

She lowered her lashes. "I hurt Miss Vee."

"I hid things from you about my past."

"I hid worse things from you."

Tiller held her at arm's length. "Why does my apology sound like yours instead? Maybe you'd better tell me what's going on."

Clinging to his hands for courage, Mariah confessed the ugly story of Mother's deathbed promise. She didn't spare herself any sordid detail, from rolling her poor father's body into an unmarked grave, to tricking simpleminded Gabe, to deeming Tiller an unfit prospect to marry.

She ended with how she'd deliberately deceived poor Miss Vee, robbing her of grieving for her lost love.

Listening quietly, Tiller didn't interrupt, though he blinked a few times in disbelief. Before he could respond, Uncle Joe rode up with his family. Tiller stepped away from her and beamed up at Hooper, Wyatt, and Ellie.

These people, strangers before now, held the power to put such joy on Tiller's face? To bring a peace and rest of soul she'd never seen in his eyes before?

Her heart skipped a beat, and she felt a surge of jealousy. What would Tiller choose? Would he stay with her at the inn or return with them to North Carolina? Might he possibly ask her to go with him, and could she make the heartrending choice?

Hooper shoved back his hat. "When you're done here, we need to wash up and meet around the table. We still have a lot to talk about."

Tiller placed his arm around Mariah's shoulders. "We'll be up in a minute." He raised his face to Uncle Joe. "If that's all right with you, sir."

Uncle Joe smiled and nodded, and the four of them rode toward the barn.

Turning Mariah to face him, Tiller's lively green eyes darted over her face. "Everything we've done will right itself with God's help and time to heal, on one condition."

She drew back. "And that is?"

"If you agree to marry me because you love me, not just to save the inn."

This time Mariah grinned. "You doubt my feelings after that kiss?"

Tiller chuckled and pulled her close. "Maybe we'd best have seconds and find out for sure." Before their lips met, he released her and plunged his hand in his pocket. "First, I have something for you."

He came up with the cloth bag that held her coins and dropped it into her hand. "I never meant to leave you, Mariah. Going with Hade was the only way to get this back."

Mariah touched his cheek. "I had assurance of that truth from a couple of witnesses."

He frowned his confusion, and she laughed. "Otis for one. My heart for another."

Recalling Hade Betts's lifeless eyes, she couldn't help glancing over her shoulder. "What happened out there, Tiller? Won't those men come riding back for you?" She shook the coins. "For this?"

"Not for triple the amount." His eyes glowed with mischief. "In fact, they'll cross the street when they see me coming."

She gasped and covered her mouth. "No they didn't!"

He chuckled. "I've never seen two men so scared."

Her brow rose. "Two men?"

The teasing left his voice. "Nathan Carter's hurt. We brought him as far as Tobias's house. They're treating him there."

She touched his face. "Your family explained about Nathan. Is he hurt badly?"

Tiller caught her hand and pulled it to his lips. "We don't know yet." Pain shone from his eyes. "Nathan jumped between me and Hade, Mariah. He got hurt trying to save me. I don't know what I'll do if he doesn't make it."

Holding hands, they led Sheki to the barn. While Tiller saw to the horse's food and water, Mariah brushed his coat to a glossy sheen with loving hands, stopping often to smooth his neck and nuzzle his silky face.

"Mariah?"

She glanced at Tiller over Sheki's back. "Yes?"

"I know you could tend this old feedbag all night, but I'm so hungry his oats are starting to look tasty."

"All right," she said, focused on Sheki's grooming. "Just one more minute."

Tiller ducked beneath the horse's neck and caught her hand. "If I prance and whinny and let you throw a saddle on my back, will you come inside and feed me?"

Laughing, Mariah hung up the brush and traced the faint sprinkling of freckles across his nose. "Granted, you bear the markings of a fine Indian pony, and you do share Sheki's love for food." She patted his cheek. "We'll forgo the prance and whinny and do without the saddle, but you may carry me if you'd like."

With a growl, he swept her off her feet and whirled her out of the barn. Staring into her eyes, he carried her to the house.

Stopping by the pump to wash up first, they hurried onto the porch. At the threshold, she paused to search his face. There were still many questions, and she'd put them off for as long as she could. Mariah sensed the answers, good or bad, waited beyond her kitchen door.

Tiller turned the knob and led her inside.

The back door opened to the sound of laughter and the smells of home. Never so glad to be in a place in his life, Tiller hung up his hat and ambled into the dining room.

His usual place next to Joe sat empty, as if in welcome. He swung into the chair and smiled at Hooper, Ellie, and Wyatt, shaking his head at the miracle of breaking bread with family.

Mariah and Dicey bustled in to ladle stew. Parading in and out from the kitchen, they passed bowls filled with seasoned green beans, buttered squash, sliced tomatoes, onions, and bread, the bounty from their shopping trip to Canton.

The sights and smells of a meal from Mariah's kitchen tempted a man like few things could. His stomach moaning in protest, Tiller laid aside his napkin and pushed away from the table. "I hope you'll all excuse me; I can't eat a bite until I have a talk with Otis."

"Looking for me, boy?"

Blood surged to Tiller's head as Otis rounded the corner, his dancing eyes searching the room. They landed on Tiller, and he beamed his toothless grin.

Standing, Tiller took a hesitant step, but the joy on the old man's face lured him forward.

Otis reached out first, wrapping him around the waist in a warm embrace.

Staring down at his wiry, white head, Tiller's chest swelled with unshed tears. "You should despise me."

Otis grunted. "Pshaw! How could I despise my best friend?"

Tiller pushed him to arm's length. "You have every right to turn me in to the law, and I'll understand if you do. Either way, I promise to repay every cent they stole if it takes me the rest of my life."

Otis shook his head. "I don't expect it."

Tiller gripped his shoulders. "Consider it done, sir. Can you ever forgive me?"

"I forgave before you asked." Otis winked and offered his hand. "It might've been a sight harder if I hadn't got to know you for the fine lad you are. I thank the Lord I got the chance."

Soaring with the freedom born of pardon, Tiller clasped both hands around Otis's hands and shook so hard he nearly pulled him off his feet. Grinning, Otis pulled free and nudged him aside. "You won't find me so forgiving if you didn't save me a bowl of Dicey's fine stew."

Smiling, Mariah slipped off her apron and took her seat across from Tiller. Otis slid into the chair next to her. Her face red and swollen, Miss Vee slipped quietly into the room, patting Tiller's back before taking her place. His heart went out to her, and he reached across to squeeze her hand.

The meal seemed the best he'd ever tasted. The lively conversation and the presence of people he loved etched a notch in Tiller's soul that promised to rival his memories of Scuffletown.

Shoving in his last forkful of blackberry cobbler, Hooper pushed aside his plate and cleared his throat. "Tiller, can we go somewhere and talk?"

God's peace settled around Tiller with the warmth of a quilt. "Whatever you came to say, go on and say it."

Hooper glanced around. "Are you sure? It's of a personal nature."

Gazing at each familiar face, Tiller nodded. "These folks are my family, too. I don't mind them hearing."

Hooper leaned forward. "I'm afraid the first part of our news is bad." His eyes darkened. "It's about your mama, son."

Ellie reached across to take his hand. "Aunt Effie died, Tiller."

Mariah gasped and came around the table to stand behind him, her soothing fingers on his neck.

The words touched his heart but didn't penetrate. He tried to feel sadness but couldn't feel much of anything but regret. "When?" The single word was all he could muster.

"Weeks ago," Hooper said. "I saw to her burial myself."

So they hadn't come to pack him off to a funeral. "What happened?"

"She had an illness." Hooper seemed to squirm in his chair. "A stomach problem worsened by her. . .inability to eat."

Tiller cringed, the stew a surge of bile in his throat. His mother slowly died of hunger while he ate his fill of good food, most of it bought by stolen money. He understood for the first time the depths to which he'd fallen. "I failed her." Defeat washed over him and he closed his eyes. "I left her to die."

"No." Ellie tightened her grip. "You surely didn't." Her strident voice softened. "She failed you."

His gaze shifted to her. "Ellie, don't."

"Let her talk," Hooper said. "What she said is true. Don't you remember? Your ma sent you away."

Tiller leaned back in his chair. "What choice did she have? I was shiftless and troublesome. Couldn't earn enough for my keep. It was either send me to Uncle Silas or watch me starve, too."

Hooper wasn't listening, just watching and shaking his head. "Your memory is skewed. You worked hard tending other folk's lawns and brought home every cent." His face red, he slapped the table. "You were a skinny, starving child who could never do enough to avoid her strap."

"What is this?" Tiller hated that his voice cracked. Wishing he'd agreed to talk in private, he gaped at them. "Did you come all this way to speak ill of my ma?"

Releasing his breath on a sigh, Hooper folded his hands in front of him. "I'm sorry. I just can't bear to hear you blame yourself."

Determination surged in Ellie's gaze. "There are things you still don't know."

Tiller pulled away from her. "Then tell me, blast it. That's what you came for, isn't it?"

Sympathy oozed from the circle around him. Wyatt patted his back, tears wet Mariah's cheek when she leaned to embrace him, and Miss Vee clutched a napkin to her trembling mouth.

"All right, I'll tell you." Hooper sighed. "But there's no easy way to say it." As if an idea just came to him, he pointed at Otis. "Let's start with him."

Fear nudging his heart, Tiller's gaze flickered to Otis sitting across the table, wiping his eyes on his shirtsleeve. "What's this got to do with him?"

Hooper patted Otis's shoulder. "I heard you swear to honor a debt to this man."

"That's right, but—"

"We're here to say you won't have a problem keeping your promise."

Desperate to understand, Tiller blinked from Hooper to Ellie. Her eyes danced and a smile tugged the corners of her mouth. "You have money, Tiller. That's the good news we came to tell you."

Hooper nodded. "Your ma hoarded every cent she ever got her hands on. She lived poor but died rich. Aunt Effie left you a fortune."

Uncle Joe leaned forward and cleared his throat. "How much?"

"Plenty," Hooper said, glancing at him. "Thousands of dollars deposited in a Fayetteville bank in the name of Tiller McRae."

FORTY-FIVE

A solemn procession worked its way down the Natchez Trace to the southwest corner of Mariah's land, the family burial grounds. Her mind flooded with memories of the night she rode the back way along the Pearl with Father's poor ravaged body. Far better to be in the company of loved ones, with the bright sun in her face, than picking her way alone and afraid by moonlight.

Sheki pulled the rig up the bluff overlooking the bend of the river. Uncle Joe hauled back on the reins and parked near the broad oak next to Mother's grave.

Mariah reached for Miss Vee's hand. "Are you ready?"

Dressed in mourning clothes, she pressed a black hankie to her lips and nodded.

Tiller climbed down and offered them a hand, then joined Uncle Joe at the tailgate to help shoulder the weight of Father's headstone.

John Coffee Bell, Husband of Onnat Minti Bell, Loving Father of Mariah.

His name engraved in the cold stone settled the fact in Mariah's heart more surely than carrying his lifeless body. Father was gone. She wouldn't see him again this side of heaven.

Clinging to Miss Vee and Dicey, Mariah led them to the unmarked patch of ground, his final resting place. Pulling off their hats, Tiller's

Scuffletown family and a few of Father's close friends gathered around them. Rainy, along with his father and little brother, held to the back of the crowd. Tobias, his sons, and the rest of the Pearl River clan stood in hushed silence.

Mariah drew strength from their quiet presence, and a load lifted from her shoulders. At last, those who loved her father could honor him in death, as he deserved.

Pulling shovels from the rig, Uncle Joe and Tiller dug a trench and set the gravestone in place.

Miss Vee knelt and placed a handful of wildflowers next to the marker, her fingers caressing the letters of his name. "Oh, John. How I'll miss you."

Crying softly, Dicey patted her shoulder. "He was a fine man, that Mista' Bell. A real fine man. I'm gon' miss him, too." She sniffled and spun away.

Tiller's comforting warmth slid behind Mariah, his hand on the small of her back. "You all right?"

She shook her head. "Not yet."

Raising her trembling chin, she faced the circle of mourners. "I want to thank you all for coming to say farewell to my father. And while you're here"—she forced herself to look up—"I want to apologize for the terrible thing I've done. I pray you can forgive me." She couldn't make out every word from the mumbling, shuffling group, but she felt the healing balm of their acceptance.

Tiller gripped her hand. "While we have your attention, I'd like to make another announcement."

He raised his brows at Uncle Joe who nodded. Mariah clutched his arm to stop him, but his loving smile eased her heart.

"Mariah Bell has consented to be my wife," he said. "We'll be married right away, before we leave for North Carolina."

The wide eyes of the Pearl River clan swung to Uncle Joe.

He squared his shoulders. "It's a good match," he boomed in a loud voice, forever settling the question.

Nudging elbows and broad smiles followed, especially from Tiller's family. Only Chris and Justin Jones cast dark, brooding scowls at Tiller.

Tiller bowed his head respectfully. "Given the circumstances, we'll have a quiet ceremony with just the family as witnesses. I know you'll understand." His voice grew louder. "But after a respectable amount of time, I promise to throw a rousing good party to celebrate."

Amid a curious mix of warm condolences and sincere congratulations, the mourners filed away to their conveyances and scattered.

Mariah leaned her head against Tiller's chest. "Are you certain the time was right to announce our wedding?"

He shrugged. "Looked like the only chance since tomorrow you'll be my bride."

Tobias, the last to leave, paused to give Miss Vee's shoulder an awkward pat. "Miss Viola, if there's anything I can do to ease your grief, you let me know."

Still kneeling at Father's grave, she reached to squeeze his hand.

"Well, I'll be pickled," Uncle Joe whispered, his eyes twinkling. "Did you see that?"

Mariah shook her head. "See what?"

"Tobias is sweet on Viola."

Mariah shushed him with a finger to her lips. "For pity's sake, keep your voice down. Are you certain?"

He raised one brow. "As sure as I'm standing here. I saw it all over his face."

Watching Tobias shuffle across the yard, his shoulders bowed, Mariah recalled how he always grew flushed and tongue-tied in Miss Vee's presence. Was it possible Tobias had pined for Miss Vee while she carried a torch for Father?

Mariah smiled at the thought. She prayed Miss Vee's heart would quickly mend and she'd finally see poor Tobias. It comforted her to hope her friend wouldn't wind up all alone.

Turning to help Miss Vee off the ground, Mariah patted her puffy, sagging cheek. "Let me take you home."

She nodded. "I'm ready."

Mariah wrapped an arm around her waist. "I'll make you a pot of your special tea."

She smiled weakly. "I'd like that."

At the wagon, Tiller gave Miss Vee a boost up while Mariah climbed in the other side. Wrapping a shawl around her, Mariah pulled it snug while she searched her pale face. "Perhaps it would be best if we postponed the wedding."

Miss Vee's head snapped around. "You'll do no such thing. Why would you even consider it?"

Mariah raised one shoulder. "It doesn't feel quite right. You know... so soon after."

Miss Vee's trembling fingers locked on Mariah's chin, and her darting eyes roamed her face. "Haven't you learned anything by watching my plight?" She gave Mariah a gentle shake. "Every second is precious, dear. Don't waste a single breath." She released Mariah and slid on her gloves. "Take us home, Joe Brashears. A pot of chamomile tea is sounding better by the minute."

FORTY-SIX

Mariah pinned the last dark curl atop her head then slid her brush in her vanity drawer. Turning her face to the side, she smiled. If she squinted, the strong chin, straight nose, and almond eyes were her mother, gazing back proudly from the glass.

Today Mariah would fulfill her promise. Under the protection of Tiller's name, no one would try to lay claim to her land. In the freedom of his love and care, she'd be able to run the inn exactly as she saw fit. She gave her image a saucy grin. "As long as my husband approves."

Standing, she appraised her gown of black satin with its applied beading, chenille tassels, and needle lace. In the dress, she would marry the man she loved and still respect her father's memory. It pleased her to honor the two most important men in her life on the same day.

Satisfied with her appearance, she slid on her mother's delicate wedding slippers, set aside for this day, and crossed the hall to her father's room. The familiar smells rushed at her. Instead of allowing grief to take her breath, she inhaled deeply, drawing comfort from his presence in the room. "*Chi hollo li,* Aki," she whispered, the love she swore an ache in her chest. "Very, very much."

The beaded necklace her mother had left her, last seen dangling from Uncle Joe's angry fist, hung from a corner of the mirror. Lifting it with shaky fingers, Mariah slipped it over her head and patted the jasper stone at her chest. "I love you, too, Mother. I wish you and Father were here today. I know you would be happy for me."

There would be many more times in Mariah's life when she'd miss her parents' presence. Birthdays, anniversaries, the births of her children. She squeezed her eyes tight against the tears. A bride shouldn't cry on her wedding day.

"Mariah? Where are you?"

She ducked her head out the door. "In here, Miss Vee."

Standing with her head poked into Mariah's room, she spun and gasped. "There you are. You're a vision, honey. Joe's back with the minister." She laughed. "And Tiller's pacing holes in the parlor rug."

Stepping over the threshold of Father's room, Miss Vee's breath caught. "It's the first time I've been in here. You can still feel his presence, can't you?" Gazing around sadly, she wrapped her arm about Mariah's waist. "I wish he could be here to give you away."

Mariah smiled and leaned her head on Miss Vee's shoulder. "I was just telling him the same thing."

Miss Vee pushed her to arm's length. "We'll lay aside our grief and all regret for now. John Coffee wouldn't have it any other way."

Wiping her eyes, Mariah beamed. "To quote Otis, 'This is the day which the Lord hath made; we will rejoice and be glad in it.'"

"Amen!" Miss Vee grinned. "But I'm pretty sure Otis borrowed that from somewhere."

They stood together for a few more minutes, Mariah gazing at the painful reminders of her parents. Would it always be hard to come inside this room?

As if she'd read her mind, Miss Vee walked to the bed and ran her hand along the quilt. "If you don't mind, I'm going to pack away their belongings while you're gone." She glanced over her shoulder. "And move yours and Tiller's in here." She smiled weakly. "After all, you're the lord and mistress of the inn now."

The idea surprised Mariah, yet in a way pleased her. She felt her parents would approve. "Won't that be hard for you so soon? I can always tend to it when I return."

Miss Vee waved her off. "I can manage. I'll have this room so spruced up you won't recognize it." She glanced up. "And don't fret. I'll take great care with their things."

On the way to the stairs, Mariah caught her arm. "Are you sure you'll be all right until we return from North Carolina?"

Miss Vee swatted the air. "Don't be silly. You'll only be gone for a few weeks, and I can run this inn in my sleep. Besides, I still have Dicey and Rainy, if they don't kill each other first." She made a face. "And if they can ever be on time."

Mariah laughed. "Now you're spinning miracles."

Downstairs, Uncle Joe waited in the parlor with the minister of Grace Church. Immediately after Father's memorial service, Uncle Joe had ridden to Canton to fetch him.

Otis stood beside Tiller and seemed to be holding him up.

Uncle Joe had invited Tobias. Mariah was stunned to see Christopher and Justin standing stiff as posts at his side.

The most pleasant surprise was the dark-haired man chatting with Tiller's family. Spotting Mariah, he broke free of the group and approached her. "You're a lovely bride, Miss Bell."

"Thank you, Nathan." She held out her hand. "I'm so happy to see you're all right."

He rubbed the back of his head. "I'm too hardheaded to let an iron skillet keep me from Tiller's wedding." His gaze fell. "That is, if you don't mind."

"Of course not. Tiller told me how close the two of you are."

He winced, his eyes filled with regret. "I haven't been a very good friend, but I plan to change. Starting with asking your forgiveness."

Mariah drew a cleansing breath and gripped his hand. "It's been a season for seeking mercy. How could I offer you less than I've received?"

He ducked his head. "I don't deserve it, but I'm grateful. Thank you for tolerating my presence at your wedding."

She patted his arm. "I'm happy you're here. Will you be riding to North Carolina with us?"

He grinned. "My brother and Tiller won't have it any other way."

"I'm glad," she said. "We'll have a chance to get acquainted. Now, will you excuse me?"

He nodded and Mariah slipped past.

Christopher lowered his gaze as she approached.

Justin turned his head.

Mariah reached for their hands. "I'm so glad you came."

In a sulk, Justin pursed his lips. "Don't be. Our father made us."

Chris nudged him.

Hiding her smile, Mariah squeezed their fingers. "Please be happy for me, boys. It would mean so much."

Justin glared. "Why would you choose the nahullo over one of us?"

She crossed her fingers behind her back. "Dear Justin, how could I ever decide between you? The problem gave me many sleepless nights. I found the only possible solution in giving both of you up. Don't you see? It was the only way."

The boys shared a startled glance.

"Of course." Chris smoothed her hair. "Poor Lotus Blossom."

Justin puffed his chest. "Still, it's a shame you were forced to settle."

"Mariah?"

She turned at the sound of Tiller's voice, so handsome with his fresh-shaved cheeks and wet-combed hair he took her breath. "Yes?"

"It's time to start." His grin held no trace of the rogue she first met. "If you're still agreeable."

She smiled and wiggled her fingers. "I'll be right along."

Uncle Joe caught her hand as she passed. "I'll be leaving right after the ceremony, niece."

She made a face. "So soon?"

Glowing with happiness for her, he patted her face. "What need has a new bride of a cantankerous old uncle underfoot?"

She leaned into his chest. "Won't you at least wait until morning?"

"No, sabitek. I travel best at night." He wrapped a tendril of hair behind her ear. "Besides, you leave soon for North Carolina with your husband, and I'm long overdue at home."

"Mariah?" Tiller stood behind her, worry crowding his brows. "Have you changed your mind?"

Turning, she latched onto his hand. "After all I've been through to snare the proper husband?"

"Then you'd best get a move on. You know our policy here at Bell's Inn"—he glanced at the parlor clock, about to strike the hour—"if you're not standing before the minister promptly at six, you stand a fair chance of going without."

Tiller awoke to find Mariah staring down at him. Propped on one arm, she'd been watching him sleep by the moonbeam filtering through her bedroom window.

With her dark hair loose and flowing and the soft white fabric of her nightdress draped over one shoulder, she looked like an angel.

Tiller pushed up on his elbows and blinked at her. "Honey? What are you doing?"

She smiled sweetly. "Counting my blessings."

"At this hour?" He squinted. "Can't we count them in the morning?"

Mariah threw back the covers and crawled out of bed. "I'm glad you're awake." She held out her hand. "Get dressed and come with me."

Grinning, he allowed her to pull him to his feet. "Where are we going?" he asked, knowing it didn't matter. He'd follow her anywhere.

She held her finger to her lips. "You'll see."

He slid into his trousers while she slipped behind a screen, emerging in a buckskin dress he'd never seen before. Stunned, he stared at his wildly beautiful wife.

She caught his hand when he reached for his shirt. "You won't need it."

Ducking into the hallway, they tiptoed to the kitchen stairs. At the bottom, she skipped the last step and whispered for him to do the same.

They crept out the back door and across the yard to the barn. Catching their scent, Sheki nickered softly before they ever opened the door. Mariah ran to throw her arms around the paint, nuzzling his neck.

Tiller caught up and hugged her from behind. "Do you think you'll ever love me as much?"

She turned into his embrace. "Maybe. Someday." Laughing, she opened the stall and bridled the horse. Leading him next to the rail, she climbed on his back and motioned for Tiller to join her.

"Without a saddle?"

"You won't need it."

He chuckled. "What else won't I need tonight?" Swinging up behind her, he grimaced. "Hopefully I won't need a doctor."

She giggled. "Just tighten your knees and hold on to me."

They trotted into the moonlit yard and veered toward the Pearl. Sheki seemed to need no direction. They'd taken this ride before.

Down a sandy slope, they leveled out on a long stretch of the riverbank. Reaching behind her, Mariah tightened his arms snugly around her waist. "Are you ready?"

He pressed his cheek to hers. "For what?"

"Hold on," she said then leaned toward Sheki's ear. "Kil-ia!"

The pony bolted. Mariah clung to his mane and Tiller clung to her.

They soared past the shimmering water, the wind rushing in their ears. Emotion swelled in Tiller's chest, and prickly hairs stood up on his neck. His heart broke inside him like a hammer on a clay pot, spilling tears down his cheeks and beauty inside his soul.

Anchored tighter to a person than he'd ever been in his life, Tiller McRae had never felt so free.

FORTY-SEVEN

Every bruised muscle and strained sinew crying for relief, Joe urged the nag down the road that led to his lane and his little house at the end. He'd driven himself hard to cut time from his trip, stopping only when he had to and riding half asleep in the saddle.

He felt as old as the crescent moon overhead. So old that the idea of chasing a feisty young son didn't seem quite as appealing as it had at the start of his journey.

He couldn't help but wonder again why fate had played its trick on him and Myrtle. Though they neared the age for bouncing grandchildren on their knees, their firstborn would soon be nursing at her breast and teething on Joe's thumbs.

A sudden thought threatened to choke him. Suppose little George became the first of many? Would their quiet little cabin swarm with crawling babes? Groaning, he pushed the exhausting thought out of his mind.

As selfish as the desire might be, he longed to reach his wife's nimble, comforting hands so she could soothe him back together. Joe held no manly delusions. Myrtle's courage and strength far surpassed his. She would be glad to see him, but Joe needed her.

He turned down his lane, sighing with pleasure at the sight of lights burning in the windows. She wouldn't be expecting him, but it wouldn't take her long to prepare him something to eat. Myrtle could make an old boot taste like a Sunday roast.

The front door eased open, and she peered out, steadying the barrel of his shotgun.

His heart squeezed at the sight of fear on her face. Still a few yards out, he whistled.

Setting aside the gun, she burst out the door and sailed over the porch, wearing nothing but one of his nightshirts.

Laughing, he lowered his stiff, aching body to the ground.

Myrtle flew at him, all tangled hair and white cotton, the feel of her in his arms welcome and familiar despite his sore muscles.

Familiar except for one thing.

Joe held her away and ran his hand over the bump that stood between them.

Crying, clinging to his neck, she fought to press close again.

"Look at you," he cried, his strength renewed and silly fears forgotten. "You've done a fine job of growing our son."

Laughing through tears, she placed a gentle hand over his. "A son is it? You sound quite sure of yourself." She glanced behind him. "Where is Mariah?"

He sighed. "You'll have to manage without her. Mariah is where she belongs."

Myrtle cocked her brow but didn't speak.

Joe pulled his pack off the horse and slung it over his shoulder. "I'm tired and hungry. Feed me well and let me rest, and I'll tell you the legend of the buzzard that journeyed far from home to steal fire."

She nudged him with her shoulder. "You foolish man, I've heard that story many times."

He pulled her close to kiss her forehead. "But my tale has a happy ending. The buzzard makes it home with all his feathers—and learns the fire was there all along."

Smiling, Myrtle tucked her hand in his and led him toward the house. "I'm glad you're hungry. I made rabbit stew." She reached the porch first and grinned over her shoulder. "The fat old thing is a little tough from all your chasing him, but he still tastes good."

Joe stilled with one foot on the bottom step. "Woman, tell me you didn't."

With a gleeful laugh, she scurried inside.

Pausing, Joe patted the doorpost. The sun would rise to find him under the same roof with Myrtle and George. It felt good to be home.

Tiller strolled out of the Fayetteville haberdashery decked in finery from head to foot. He doffed his bowler hat at Mariah, and she covered her mouth and laughed.

There wasn't a speck of pomp or pretense in his decision to buy new clothes. It started with his desire to buy her something nice. Once he had, he didn't feel properly dressed to walk her down the street.

Neither did he intend to put on airs with their mode of transportation. It wasn't his fault the last conveyance available for hire was a garish, pretentious carriage. "Well, we need a rig," he'd murmured, drumming his fingers on his chin. "I can't have you straddling a horse in that getup."

Looking down at her dress of black taffeta and velvet, she nodded. "Yes, it would be difficult."

"Then we'll do it," he announced. "It might be fun. Lord knows I can afford it," he added with a wink.

Handing her aboard, he started to laugh. "It's a good thing the others decided to wait in the hotel. Can you imagine Ellie riding in this contraption?"

Mariah laughed. "Actually, no. I can't."

He angled his head. "If you don't mind, I'm going to ride past the old house before we go to the cemetery."

She patted his hand. "I think it's a fine idea."

Heads turned as the carriage rolled through the narrow alleys of the poor part of town. Gaunt, hungry faces stared up as they passed, striking a chill in Mariah's heart. Wishing they'd given the fancy clothes and high-flown rig more thought, she tightened her grip on Tiller's arm.

They pulled up to a broken-down shanty, a study in hopeless gloom. The sagging roof had caved in places, allowing the weather to rot the eaves. The outer walls—what was left of them—were a dirty, paint-chipped gray. Weeds had sprouted through and overgrown the walkway from the porch to the street.

Mariah couldn't imagine anyone living inside, and it saddened her to think Tiller once had.

Climbing down, they made their way toward the door. Tiller pulled to a sudden stop and caught her hand. "This is far enough. I don't think I want to go inside."

Concerned, she studied his pale, sickly face. "Of course."

His gaze roaming the dilapidated house, he sighed. "I could've done so much to help her."

"No, Tiller." She squeezed his fingers. "We both know how expensive repairs can be. She wouldn't have let you spend the money."

He bit his lip and nodded.

Glancing around, Mariah saw they'd drawn a crowd of curious people, closing in from all sides. Nervous, she drew closer to Tiller and nudged him with her elbow.

Awaking from his daze, he took off his hat and nodded. "Afternoon, folks."

An older man, short in stature, stepped up and held out his hand. "Reddick McRae. I'd know you anywhere."

Tiller beamed. "Mr. McLean. How are you, sir?"

The little man enveloped Tiller's hand in both of his. "Not as well as you, I see." His remark held no resentment. Instead, he smiled warmly. "I'm happy to see you've done well for yourself."

Mariah held her breath, waiting to see if Tiller would mention where his fortune had lain hidden for years.

He smiled graciously. "It was none of my doing, sir. I fell into a blessing is all."

Mr. McLean laughed. "Just like when you were a boy. Everything you touched turned to a blessing." He pointed. "I still have the finest roses in the neighborhood, thanks to you."

Tiller introduced Mariah as his new bride. Thrilled each time she heard the words, she accepted the round of well wishes.

Mr. McLean scooted closer and nudged Tiller. "My cousin is the one who first spotted you in Canton, son." His brow furrowed. "We tried to tell your ma. She just didn't believe us."

Tiller fingered his hat brim. "I'm real sorry about that, sir."

The man pounded on Tiller's back. "That's all right. I'm just happy to see that other fellow looked you up." He blinked uncertainly. "This is what happened, ain't it? You do know your ma is. . .well, no longer with us?"

"Yes, I heard. And I'm obliged to your cousin. You'll tell him for me, won't you?"

"I sure will, son."

Shading his eyes, Tiller stared down the street. "As a matter of fact, we're on our way to the cemetery now to pay our respects."

Awkward silence fell over the crowd. Backs straightened and feet shuffled. Smiling faces turned to frowns, and some looked away in disgust.

Excusing themselves, Tiller and Mariah climbed aboard the carriage and drove away.

Tiller sat so quietly in thought, Mariah began to worry. Leaning on his arm, she peered into his face. "Will a penny buy some of those weighty thoughts?"

He flashed a weak smile. "You were with me at the bank, Mrs. McRae. You have a sight more than a penny to barter with."

She stretched to kiss his cheek. "Are you all right?"

Tiller sighed. "Just sorting a few things out." He tipped his chin. "Those folks back there want me to be mad at Ma. I reckon paying her respect was the last thing they'd want me to do." His gaze softened. "Most likely, if I hadn't had me that talk with God, I'd feel the same."

She nodded. "We've both had a few lessons in mercy lately."

"That's true, but it's more than mercy I feel. My ma wasn't mean for meanness' sake. She was different when I was younger. Outright kind and gentle. She turned into a stranger after pa died."

The pain in his eyes took Mariah's breath.

"But I think I understand now that it wasn't my fault she treated me bad. After all I've heard, I realize Ma was sick. Sick in body, mind, and spirit." He smiled through his tears. "Knowing that truth, I intend to pay respect to my ma and tell her good-bye. I'm going to lay flowers on her grave then walk away from Fayetteville, free of bad memories once and for all."

Grinning, he wrapped his arm around Mariah's shoulder and sat taller in the seat, shifting the bowler to a jaunty angle. "Free of my past and ready for the future with the woman I love."

FORTY-EIGHT

Tiller's breath caught as they turned their horses toward the lone cabin in the distance. His anxious mind flooded with old memories of his first sight of the tiny house. Looking around that day at the crooked porch, swampy yard, and flooded rain barrel, he'd refused to believe they were at his uncle's house in Scuffletown.

"I'm too tired for teasing," he'd said to Hooper. "What is this place?"

Despite what the outside lacked in charm, once past the front door, that sad, frightened boy knew he'd come home at last. Within those unassuming walls lived good times, great stories, welcoming arms, and love that stretched the seams.

"Home sweet home," Hooper said beside him, speaking Tiller's thoughts aloud.

Frowning, Mariah pointed. "That's the house?"

Tiller smiled. He knew just how she felt. "Don't worry, it's cozy inside," he said, offering the same assurance Hooper had given him that day.

The jumble of thoughts in Tiller's mind was nothing compared to how his insides felt. Though he'd finally accepted that his mama's plight was not his fault, he couldn't say the same for his uncle's pain. He'd rehearsed a dozen times what he'd say to Uncle Silas.

Glancing at Nathan riding tense and tight-lipped beside Wyatt,

Tiller knew he must have been dreading his own reckoning.

Neither of them would be putting it off for long. The door burst open, and a dozen shouting people spilled onto the front porch.

Tiller's eager eyes searched for Uncle Silas. Grayer than Tiller remembered, moving a little slower, he tottered down the steps behind a whole passel of squealing youngsters with Aunt Odell at his side.

"Look at that," Hooper said, smiling from hither to yon. "My girls are here."

Ellie leaned in the saddle and stared. "Blast it, Hooper, I knew it. What has your wife gone and done to my boys?" She sped up and rode ahead, reining her mount in front of two sets of dapper boys standing quietly with folded hands.

Hooper laughed so hard he almost fell out of his saddle.

Grinning, Tiller pointed. "Ellie had twins?"

Wyatt groaned. "Two pair as rowdy as they come." He chuckled. "At least they were when we left."

The prettiest little things Tiller had ever seen scampered, dainty and giggly, toward Hooper's horse. He slid to the ground and swung them up, one at a time, for a kiss on the cheek. "Girls, come meet your cousin, Tiller."

Pausing to draw his smiling wife under his arm, he led his family to where Tiller and Mariah stood holding their reins.

"I'd like you to meet our girls." He placed his hand atop one chestnut head. "This here is Della, named after Ma, and the younger one"—he patted her curly head—"is Olivia. We call her Livvy after Dawsey's aunt."

Tiller bowed and kissed their hands. "I'm happy to meet you, ladies."

Blushing, they ducked behind their mother's skirt.

Beaming into his eyes, the woman reached for his hand. "I can't tell you how happy we are to see you again. I do hope you remember me."

He smiled. "Of course I do. . .Dawsey." Tiller knew Hooper's wife as Miss Wilkes, the young woman he'd worked for in Fayetteville, so it was hard to think of her as anything else.

Ellie caught Dawsey's shoulder from behind. "All right, Dawsey McRae. What have you done to them?"

Dawsey turned and gathered her into a hug. "Sweet Dilsey. I'm so glad you're home."

Ellie pushed away her hands. "There will be none of that until you've explained yourself." She pointed over her shoulder at the docile boys. "I want you to take away these charlatans and bring back my young'uns."

Wyatt squatted in front of his sons, smoothing their slicked-back hair and patting their rosy, scrubbed cheeks. "I don't know, Ellie. I could get used to them like this."

In the hubbub, Tiller learned the elder twins were Silas and Gerry, named for their grandfathers. The younger set were Duncan and Hooper, named for Ellie's brothers—but Hooper, the quiet one with serious green eyes, they called Tiller because of his uncanny knack with the soil.

Quiet throughout the how-dos and welcomes, Uncle Silas nudged through the crowd to stand in front of Tiller. As solemn as a deacon, he quietly took his hand.

The years had been hard on him. His shoulders stooped, and deep creases marred his weathered face, but the bright eyes were the same. Roguish eyes, twinkling with a thousand untold stories.

Tiller pulled Mariah forward. "Uncle Si"—he nodded—"Aunt Odie, I'd like you to meet my wife, Mariah."

His aunt, as pretty as ever despite her age, wrapped them both in a tearful hug. "We missed you, Tiller. I prayed every day for your safe return."

Uncle Silas released Tiller and reached for Mariah's arm. "Let's go inside by the fire, pretty lady."

Mariah smiled and let him lead her away.

On the porch, he stopped and waved his hand. "You children find something to do outside while the grown-ups have a little talk."

His grandchildren scattered for the woods.

Nathan hung back as everyone crowded for the door. Frowning, Wyatt tugged on his sleeve. "It's all right, Nate. Let's go inside."

He shook his head. "I don't think I'm welcome. The old man never glanced my way."

"It doesn't matter," Wyatt said. "You can allow him a little anger. You owe him that much."

Tiller grasped Nathan's shoulder. "I've made up my mind to offer an apology whether he accepts it or throws me out on my ear." He tightened his grip. "It's like Wyatt said. We owe him."

Wyatt pointed toward the house. "If you can't stand up to that little man in there, how will you face our parents?"

Doubt wavering on his face, Nathan glanced toward his horse.

Tiller shook his head. "Don't do it, Nate. If you run now, you'll be alone for the rest of your life."

"Nathan Carter!"

They swiveled toward the house. Uncle Silas meandered across the yard, dodging scattered kindling by the porch and mud holes near the rain barrel.

Unable to read the expression on his uncle's face, Tiller held his breath.

He glanced at Nathan. The poor man's hands shook, and he stared like a cornered animal. Backing up two steps, his body tensed to run.

Uncle Silas reached them, his smile a little shaky, but the hand he extended to Nathan was steady. "It's been awhile, young fella'. In all the ruckus, I didn't get to tell you how glad I am to see you."

Nathan pulled off his hat, wadding it in his trembling fingers. "Mr. McRae, it's good to see you, too."

"You weren't leaving, were you? I know you're in a hurry to see your folks, but I was hoping you'd stay for a cup of coffee at least. We can catch up on old times."

Nate's throat worked up and down. "I don't want to intrude, sir."

"Intrude? It'll be a sorry day when I don't enjoy the company of an old friend."

Tiller and Nathan had grown too tall for Uncle Silas to reach around them, so he rested a hand on each of their arms and led them to the house.

Crossing the threshold felt like stepping back in time. Glancing around, Tiller saw that nothing much had changed. Aunt Odell had spread the kitchen table with food, Uncle Si's rocker faced the crackling hearth, and the mats they used for extra beds were rolled up against the wall. He almost expected to see the one he'd slept on years ago spread for him in the corner.

"If anyone's hungry, there's plenty. Just grab a plate and fill it."

Aunt Odie didn't have to offer a second invitation. The hungry travelers bustled close to the table, laughing and rubbing shoulders.

Uncle Silas caught Tiller's arm and pulled him aside. "I know you're probably starved son, but I reckon we need us a talk first."

Tiller nodded. Best to get the apology over so he could stomach the food.

They watched each other with wary eyes. "I'm sorry," they blurted at the same time.

Tiller drew back with a puzzled frown. "What do you have to be sorry for?"

"I let you down, son. I wanted you to feel welcome here, then I threatened to send you back to your ma the first time you made a mistake." Tears spilled onto his cheeks, tearing at Tiller's heart.

"You don't owe me an apology, sir. I owe you one. I gave you nothing but trouble from the first day I came."

Hooper squeezed in between them. "I say you call it a draw and come to supper."

A squeal from outside sent Wyatt stumbling for the door. "Mercy, it sounds like somebody's getting skint out there."

Hooper and Dawsey shared a grin. "You're not used to the way girls express themselves, Wyatt," she said. "Livvy's just excited, that's all."

"About what, I wonder?" Hooper said, peering over Wyatt's shoulder.

The rest of the children set to squealing, too—Ellie's boys the loudest. She shot Dawsey a look of pure disgust.

Hooper spun with a grin. "I see what has them worked up. Their Uncle Duncan and his family are riding this way."

Wiping his eyes, Uncle Silas beamed at his wife. "The Lord has blessed this day, Odell McRae. All of our children will sleep under one roof tonight."

She clasped her hands. "It's been a long time since that happened."

As was their custom, the family rushed outside to greet the newcomers. Tiller took the chance to pull Mariah aside for a kiss. "What do you think of your new family, Mrs. McRae?"

Wrapping her arms around his neck, she rested her head on his shoulder. "I can see where you get your humor, goodness, and amazing gift for love." She angled her head. "Not to mention your irresistible charm."

He raised her chin with his finger. "You see all that in this rowdy bunch?"

She nodded. "They're wonderful, Tiller."

"I'm glad you think so because there's one more to meet. You'll like Duncan. He has a bigger appetite than me."

"Oh my." She regarded the table with a worried frown. "Will there be enough to feed you both?"

Laughing, Tiller tugged her toward the door. Clinging to each other's waists, they squeezed onto the porch like true McRaes to be part of the welcoming party.

FORTY-NINE

Mariah followed Tiller off the Trace and into the yard, her muscles tired and sore from riding the train. Rainy had met them at the station in Jackson and brought their mounts. Rounding the house, they found Otis, Miss Vee, and Dicey smiling from the porch. It reminded Mariah of huddling in the mists on a different porch with her Scuffletown family.

After hugs and kisses all around, Dicey and Rainy went back to work, and Mariah led the horses to the barn, thrilled with the familiar routine. It felt wonderful to be home.

Later, seated around the kitchen table with their loved ones, she and Tiller shared stories of their journey, including one of Silas's tales that had Otis bouncing and clapping his hands—until Tiller shot out of his chair, wiggling his finger. "I almost forgot, Otis. I have something for you."

Spinning, he hurried to the pack he'd tossed into a corner. Rummaging inside, he came up with a bundle wrapped in newspaper and tied with a string. Handing it to Otis, he straightened with a smile.

Otis blinked up at him. "What's this?"

"Go on, open it."

Otis seemed unsure whether to look at Tiller or the package in his lap. With trembling fingers, he yanked the end of the string. The paper fell away to reveal legal tender in large denominations, stacked on top of a fat leather book. Otis gasped and cut his eyes to Tiller. "This here's my money." He gently ran his thumb along the spine of the book. "And my new Bible."

Tears in his eyes, Tiller nodded. "I got one for myself, too." He glanced up at Mariah and Miss Vee. "One for each of us, in fact."

Otis shook his head. "It's too much currency, son. I never had this much stashed in my life." He peeled off more than half of the wads of cash and handed it up to Tiller. "Take this back."

Tiller wrapped his hands around Otis's and guided the money to his lap. "I won't be taking anything back, sir. Consider it interest on a loan."

Sniffing, Otis wiped his eyes on his sleeve. "It's a blessing you didn't get shanghaied on the trail, carrying this much loot around."

The irony of his words struck the group at once, and laughter rang out.

When the room grew quiet, Miss Vee reached for Mariah's hand. "I don't want to spoil your good mood, honey, but I suppose you have to know." She glanced at Otis. "There wasn't a single boarder the whole time you were gone."

Mariah smiled at Tiller. They'd spent time on the long trip home discussing the future of the inn. "I'm not surprised, Miss Vee."

She blew out a breath. "Well, I am. We always pick up in the summer."

Mariah smoothed a wrinkle in the tablecloth. "The Trace is fading into disuse. I expect there will be less and less traffic in the months ahead."

Miss Vee seemed near tears.

Her own eyes filling, Mariah smiled at them both. "Would it be so bad if Bell's Inn became just a house where people live and raise a family?"

Disbelief narrowed Miss Vee's eyes. "You mean close our doors?"

"We'll accept weary travelers who wander by," Tiller said, "but in the meantime we'll go on like we have."

Otis sat so quietly, Mariah nudged Tiller.

"Is something troubling you, sir?" Tiller asked.

Otis barely glanced up. "Nothing important."

Mariah leaned across the table. "Go on, tell us."

His mouth worked, but nothing came out."

Miss Vee wiped her eyes. "Otis was thinking to ask for a job and stay on here. But now, well. . ." She shrugged.

Tiller couldn't contain his glee. Jumping from his chair, he knelt beside Otis. "I think that's a fine idea, considering I planned to ask you to stay on and help me around the place."

Otis perked up. "You reckon there's enough to keep us both busy?"

Tiller patted his back. "I'll make sure of it." He gave Miss Vee a firm nod. "Both of you have a home here as long as you want."

As if she couldn't take it in, Miss Vee stared at Mariah. "So we'll all just go on living here?" She blinked. "Like a family?"

Tiller smiled. "We are a family, Miss Vee."

She pressed her fingers to her quavering mouth and nodded.

Mariah reached for her hand. "One day, I'd like for Tiller to build me a big house on this spot." She winked at him. "To make room for dozens of little McRaes. For now, I'm quite happy where we are."

Miss Vee pushed up from the table. "That reminds me. You two come see your surprise."

They filed up the kitchen stairs and followed her down the hall. At the door to Father's room, Mariah had to stop and remind herself that it was hers now. Hers and Tiller's.

Miss Vee swept inside then stood back to await their reaction.

Tiller looked stunned then roared with laughter.

Mariah gasped and spun in a circle, trying to see everything at once.

Miss Vee had worked a marvel. The space was a perfect blend of their personalities. Tiller's hat rack stood in the corner beside his washstand. Mariah's vanity with all her favorite trinkets on top had replaced her mother's. Miss Vee had repapered the walls, half with the pattern from Mariah's room, half with Tiller's. Even the bedspread was an expression of their union. She'd cut their quilts in two and sewn the pieces down the middle.

Mariah ran to hug her neck. "It's the most perfect surprise ever. Thank you so much."

Obviously pleased with herself, she beamed proudly. "I put a lot of love in it, honey. I hope you'll be able to feel it."

"We already do, Miss Vee," Tiller said, kissing her cheek.

Otis tugged on her sleeve. "Let's go, Viola, and let these young people rest and enjoy your gift."

"Hmm? Oh yes, of course." Blushing, she backed out the door behind Otis.

Melting into Tiller's arms, Mariah breathed deeply of the new smell in the air. No longer the stench of death, the scent was a pleasing blend of wallpaper paste and new rugs, her rose water and Tiller's hair pomade.

Mariah made a vow on the spot to forget the suffering she'd witnessed inside the room. Instead, she'd cherish her parents' memories and honor them by taking joy in her new life.

She would remember to be grateful for every breath she breathed, and to thank God every day for His mercy.

JOHNNYCAKE

Scald 1 pint of milk and put to 3 pints of Indian meal, and half pint of flour—bake before the fire. Or scald with milk two-thirds of the Indian meal, or wet two-thirds with boiling water, add salt, molasses and shortening, work up with cold water pretty stiff and bake as above.

INDIAN SLAPJACK (Skillet Bread)

One quart of milk, 1 pint of Indian meal, 4 eggs, 4 spoons of flour, little salt, beat together, baked on gridles [*sic*], or fry in a dry pan, or baked in a pan which has been rub'd [*sic*]with suet, lard, or butter.

Amelia Simmons, *American Cookery*
(Hartford, CT: Hudson and Goodwin, 1796)

HASTY PUDDING (circa 1833)

Boil water, a quart, three pints, or two quarts, according to the size of your family; sift your meal, stir five or six spoonfuls of it thoroughly into a bowl of water; when the water in the kettle boils, pour into it the contents of the bowl; stir it well, and let it boil up thick; put in salt to suit your own taste, then stand over the kettle, and sprinkle in meal, handful after handful, stirring it very thoroughly all the time and letting it boil between whiles. When it is so thick that you stir it with great difficulty, it is about right. It takes about half an hour's cooking. Eat it with milk or molasses. Either Indian meal or rye meal may be used. If the system is in a restricted state, nothing can be better than rye hasty pudding and West India molasses. This diet would save many a one the horrors of dyspepsia.

Lydia M. Child, *American Frugal Housewife*,
facsimile 12th ed. (Boston: Applewood Books), 65.

CHOCTAW RECIPES:

PASHOFA

1 pound cracked corn, pearl hominy
2 quarts water, add more if needed
1 pound fresh lean pork, meaty backbone
Salt

Wash and clean corn. Bring water to boil and add corn. Cook slowly, stirring often. When corn is about half done, add the fresh pork. Cook until the meat and corn are tender and soft. The mixture should be thick and soupy. Cooking time is about four hours. Add no salt while cooking. Each individual salts to his/her own taste. (If meaty backbone is not available, use fresh chopped pork, small pieces. Pork chops are good to use.)

BANAHA

2 cups cornmeal
1 teaspoon salt
1 teaspoon soda
1½ cups hot water
Corn shucks, boiled 10 minutes

Mix dry ingredients. Add water until mixture is stiff enough to handle easily. Form small oblong balls the size of a tennis ball and wrap in corn shucks. Tie in middle with corn shuck string, or use oblong white rags (8x10 inches) cut from an old sheet. They are much better boiled in shucks. Drop covered balls into a deep pot of boiling water. Cover and cook 40 minutes. Serve.

Article from the Choctaw newspaper *Bishinik,* unknown date.

HUNTER'S PRIZE

DEDICATION

To Dorothy Faye, George Edward, and Nancy Jane—my siblings. Thoughts of you call to mind pulled hair, skinned knees, and chinaberry fights. Mud pies, cardboard forts, and side-lot baseball. Poodle skirts, miniskirts, and bell-bottom jeans. Brenda Lee, Elvis, Chubby Checker, and the Beatles. It passed too fast! I wish we could live it all over again. Never forget that I love you.

Lay not up for yourselves treasures upon earth, where moth and
rust doth corrupt, and where thieves break through and steal:
But lay up for yourselves treasures in heaven. . .
For where your treasure is, there will your heart be also.
MATTHEW 6:19–21

ACKNOWLEDGMENTS

Thank you, Lee, my husband, friend, and very own Superman. It's nice to have your broad shoulders to lean on.

Special thanks to Mr. John Winn of Caddo Outback Backwater Tours, my Caddo area expert, knowledgeable historian, and all-around great guy. Bless you, John, for allowing me to pick your brain. I acknowledge freely that yours are some of the best lines in the book. Find out more about John and Caddo Lake at: www.caddolaketours.com.

As always, my heartfelt appreciation goes to Elizabeth Ludwig, the first responder to my first draft carnage and the reason my Barbour editors don't tear out their hair. Lisa, dear friend, thank you for dotting my i's, crossing my t's, and chasing me down rabbit trails. I salute you!

Speaking of Barbour editors, thanks and blessings to Aaron McCarver for your knowledge, talent, and razor-sharp eye. It is a genuine pleasure to work with you.

And speaking of Barbour Publishing, Rebecca Germany and the rest of the crew, you guys are my heroes. Thank you for your unmerited favor and gracious support.

PROLOGUE

Pretoria, South Africa, November 1904

A raspy, hissing *zzzzzzZZTT* spun Cedric Whitfield toward the lone African swift soaring overhead. Whimpering, he covered his ears and stumbled away from the jarring sound. Lips tightly sealed to spare his parched throat, he ran along the hard-packed road, the hot, dry air burning inside his nose with every breath.

He skittered past Denny Currie and Charlie Pickering, arching his back and shivering at the thought of touching the scary men hired to drive them to town. In his haste, he blundered into one of the great beasts Charlie led behind him like hounds on a leash.

"Mind the oxen, sonny." The big man caught his collar, lifting him off the ground. "Unless you fancy being trampled."

Fixing Ceddy with a bulging eye, the huge animal flared his velvet nostrils and snorted.

With a shrill scream, Ceddy struggled free and shot away.

"Blimey, he's off again!" Mr. Currie shouted. "Mrs. Beale, can't you keep the lad close at hand?"

At the mention of Aunt Jane, Ceddy slowed to a trot and spun, his heart thudding against his ribs. Shuffling backward, feeling the sun on the backs of his bare legs, he watched her top the rise.

"He's frightened of your team, Mr. Currie," she called, her brows rising to peaks.

Shifting his weight, Mr. Currie dried his forehead with his sleeve. "Appears to be frightened of most things, now, don't he?"

Panting hard, Auntie pressed a silk hankie to her mouth and plodded up the uneven path, the grasping branches of the sweet thorn brush tangling with her hem as she passed. "My nephew is a child, sir. A child with uncommon debilitations. Must I remind you of that?"

Charlie frowned. "He seems right fit to me."

Mr. Currie jabbed him with his elbow and spoke from the side of his mouth. "She don't mean weak in the physical sense, you twit."

"Nor do I mean weakness of the mind, sir," Aunt Jane said. "Please don't twist my words."

Mr. Currie's smile slid away. "Whatever ails him, if he persists in playing about, we won't see Pretoria by nightfall." Spinning on his heel, he forged ahead. "Never mind catching the train."

Ignoring his growly threat, Auntie fell in behind him, dabbing her beaded forehead with the cloth. "How much farther? This pace is a bit much, I'm afraid."

Drawn to her strong, steady voice, Ceddy lagged to wait for her. . . until the long, silver wings of a snout bug teased away his eyes.

"A couple kilometers," Mr. Currie said.

"Oh my," Auntie shrilled. "Did you say *two* kilometers?"

He quirked his mouth. "Yes, m'lady, thereabout." He dragged off his battered cap to scratch behind his ear then used the hat to point. "If memory serves, once we round that distant grove, it's but a few steps more."

Staring across the rolling grassland, Auntie sniffed. "I'll try to remain optimistic."

Glancing around, she lowered her voice. "Could there be predators lurking in the brush? I'd prefer to survive this unscheduled trek."

Ceddy longed to chase the darting snout bug, but his aunt's frightened tone pained his stomach. Holding his breath, he passed the men and their oxen then fell back to match her steps.

"Predators in South Africa?" Mr. Currie's laugh rang hollow like a gourd. "There are lions in these parts, no doubt." He patted the long-handled pistol at his side. "But you need fear no four-footed creature, Mrs. Beale. It's the bloodthirsty lot who creep around on two limbs we hope to avoid."

Stopping so fast she tripped on the uneven path, Auntie lifted her eyes. "Would you care to elaborate?"

His stubby fingers cradled his sidearm. "Soulless devils lurk in the veld. The sort who slip up without warning and straddle your back. . .slit you from ear to ear without so much as a 'how do.'"

Moaning, Ceddy curled into the folds of Aunt Jane's skirt.

She clutched his shoulder with a trembling hand. "What could such men want with us?"

"Not an invitation to tea, that's for sure."

She drew Ceddy closer. "*Really*, Mr. Currie. If that's the case, I should think checking the hitch for damage before we left would top your list of priorities."

Mr. Currie scowled at Charlie Pickering. "You have my blundering assistant to thank for our present fix. He's in charge of the rigging."

"Quite right, missus." Charlie lifted his sweat-stained bush hat and bowed. "An unforgivable lapse on my part."

Guiding Ceddy with a firm grip on his neck, Aunt Jane continued up the road toward them. "You'd both better pray the train to Port Elizabeth hasn't left without us. If we don't make the coast in time to board the steamer for England, you'll be explaining your lapse to my husband."

"I'll drop to me pious knees on the spot, you daft cow," Mr. Currie muttered as she passed.

Frowning, Auntie paused and lowered her hankie. "Beg your pardon?"

"I say it's a pleasant day for a walk, anyhow."

She snorted. "Perhaps. . .if one considers a stifling greenhouse pleasant." She blotted around her mouth. "Peculiar weather for mid-November, I must say."

Charlie grinned. "Not in South Africa. November's the first month of summer 'round here."

"Is that a fact?" She tilted her head. "This time of year in London they're banking fires and airing heavy wraps."

He swiped his damp forehead. "Wish we had cause to bank a fire today. By the feel of things, we're due a scorcher."

Aunt Jane patted Ceddy's back. "I suppose the American climate will be quite the adjustment for this young man."

"The Americas, missus? I thought you were bound for England."

"We are. But I will accompany Cedric to Texas in a few months.

Should be quite the adventure"—she leaned to smile at Ceddy—"with all the buckaroos and Indians and such."

"Blimey," Charlie said, stroking his bristly chin. "I'd sorely love to see a buckaroo."

Frowning, Mr. Currie elbowed past. "We can stand about chatting all day, if you like. Only don't blame me when you miss your train."

"You're quite right, Mr. Currie," Aunt Jane said. "Let's soldier on, shall we?"

Ceddy clutched her skirt with both hands, allowing her steps to jerk him forward. Closing his eyes, he let his head drift back as he ambled along the path—listening.

The jumble of sound, at once frightening and familiar, settled around his shoulders like a favorite quilt. Resting in it, he picked out the rumble of a lioness calling her young to a meal, a yipping jackal, the trill of a sunbird, a huffing white rhino in the distance. Howls, barks, and calls that awakened him each morning and lulled him to sleep every night.

Mr. Currie sniffed, dragging Ceddy from his trance. Clearing his throat, the horrid man spat. "I understand his parents were missionaries?"

"Yes, the both of them." Auntie's voice drifted behind her, quivering like a sedge warbler's song. "Peter and Eliza devoted themselves to sharing the Gospel in this godforsaken region." Slowing, she looked up. "How thoughtless of me to speak so harshly of your country. Forgive me, gentlemen."

"Quite all right, mum," Mr. Currie said. "I find their efforts downright inspiring." He glanced behind him. "Your husband said they drove right off a cliff?"

Auntie gasped and eased Ceddy in front of her. "Mr. Currie, please!"

He tipped his grimy cap. "Sorry, missus. Just making conversation."

"Sadly, it's true," she whispered. "My poor sister and her husband lost their lives in a terrible accident."

Ceddy squirmed. Adults often talked quietly around him, as if his ears were dull. He could hear quite well, in fact, and her words rang in his head like a gong.

"The crash of a motorcar, of all things! In the wilds of South Africa. Can you imagine the folly?" she shrilled. "The silly contraption slid off-road in a muddy downpour. What was Peter thinking to bring that accursed machine to a place with naught to drive upon but rutted ox trails? For all his good intentions, Peter Whitfield had more money than good sense."

Charlie slid off his hat and clutched it in front of him. "More's the pity, that. Dreadful sorry."

Aunt Jane let go a rush of air, tickling the top of Ceddy's head. "The news came as quite a shock. The poor dears perished the way they lived—side by side in service to our Lord. Now they're together for eternity." She dabbed the corners of her eyes with her hankie. "That hope is my only comfort."

Charlie tapped Ceddy's shoulder with a bony finger. "What will happen to this poor little mite?"

Ceddy drew away with a grunt.

Gathering him close, Auntie draped her arms around his neck. "I requested the privilege of raising him, but"—her clipped words sounded stern—"his parents made other arrangements in their will. He'll spend Christmas with my family in London. Come spring, he's off to live with Aunt Priss in Marshall, Texas."

Charlie cleared his throat. "Forgive me boldness, missus, but ain't you his aunt?"

"Priscilla Whitfield is the boy's great-aunt on his father's side. To honor his parents' wishes, the old girl will take him in." Her mouth twisted. "It's what they wanted, though I can't imagine why they preferred that dried-up old spinster to me."

The lead ox stumbled on a mound of clods, nearly going down. Denny Currie cursed and stuck it with a rod, prompting the creature to bellow in protest.

With a loud wail, Ceddy broke free and ran.

"Oy! Not again," Mr. Currie groaned. "Where's he off to now?"

"It's your own fault," Aunt Jane cried. "The boy has no tolerance for sudden noise or violence of any sort."

"Violence?" Mr. Currie said. "We 'aven't—"

"Stay close, dear," Aunt Jane called, as if from the bottom of a well. "It's dangerous on your own."

"Mrs. Beale, this won't do!"

The packed dirt pounded beneath Ceddy's feet, sending vibrations along his spindly legs.

"Cedric, love, please come back," a lilting voice warbled in the distance. "Where are you going, darling?"

He stretched his arms to the sides and flew. He was a blue crane soaring over the rippling grass. A spoonbill searching for water. Cresting the hill, he shot down the other side, counting his jarring footsteps.

"He's gone!" The angry words echoed overhead. "What are we supposed to do now?"

"Don't just stand there." The fury in Auntie's tone drew Ceddy's shoulders to his ears. "Earn your money, gentlemen. Go after him."

Heavy footsteps thundered behind him on the trail as the men closed in, muttering fierce curses at his back. Cruel fingers lashed out, closing around his neck. "Come back 'ere, you little—"

Squirming, Ceddy spun and bit down hard.

Mr. Currie howled. Gripping Ceddy's arm with his other hand, he shoved him along the path. "Oy, Charlie," he growled. "When we reach the top of the ridge, mate, distract the old girl whilst I nudge this brat over the side."

"Tempting, boss," Charlie whispered back. "But we can't kill off clergy's seed. We'll roast in perdition."

Denny snorted. "I'd risk the fiery flames to be shed of 'im."

Scowling, Charlie swiped a bony finger across his neck. "Shut it. She'll hear you."

"Let her hear. I don't give a monkey's behind."

"'Ere she comes," Charlie hissed. "Get a handle, mate. It's the only way we'll see our wages. We'll be shed of them for good and all once they board the train."

Ceddy covered his ears and moaned to escape their vile whispers.

"Did you hear me, Mr. Currie?" Aunt Jane's panting cry came from behind the hill. "Catch hold of my nephew this instant."

"Catch hold of my nephew."

"Nudge him over the side."

Ceddy's breath caught as he pulled free of their grasping hands and shot around them. Veering to the right, he tripped over a tussock of wool grass, the smooth bottoms of his shoes slipping on the bright green blades.

Flailing his arms, he scrambled for a hold, but the long fronds slid through his fingers, leaving a sharp sting. He toppled, moving so fast the ground shot past in a blur. Shrieking in fear, he dug in his heels, plowing twin rows in the earth as he slid.

Halfway down, his feet hit a rock, flipping him again. He tumbled to the bottom in a blinding rush, rolling to a stop on his back, next to the bank of a stream.

Ceddy screwed up to cry, but the wide expanse of a cloudless blue sky drew his gaze. He stilled, watching the gray belly of an osprey soaring overhead.

Arching his body, he drew away from the sharp stones biting into his shoulders. Stirred by pain and frantic voices calling his name, he rolled to his elbows and stared at the scatter of rocks and stones he'd unearthed.

One of them glinted in the sunlight. Ceddy made a grab for it as the brush parted and long shadows fell, blocking the light.

Glancing up the hill, he tensed to flee, but Aunt Jane pushed between the men, her face bright from the heat. "Heavens, child! Are you all right? Come to me, dearie. That's it, now. No more games, right? You're a good boy, then, aren't you, lamb?"

Pushing off the ground, Ceddy hobbled to the safety of her skirts.

Mr. Currie cursed aloud. "Well ain't that just ducky. Dusts 'im off and pats 'is head, she does, and after he nearly got us killed. That brat needs a strap to 'is backside."

Auntie spun. "Mind your tongue and your business, Mr. Currie. And I'll thank you to abstain from vulgar language around Cedric. He understands every word."

Mr. Currie snorted. "That ain't likely."

"It's true," she huffed. "Ceddy's quite intelligent. Brighter than most, in fact."

Charlie laughed, a muffled sputter from behind his hand. "Pardon, missus. I don't mean to make sport. I'll give it to you that he's a right handsome child. But smart?" He fell to chuckling again.

Her arms tightened around Ceddy. "Let's get something straight before we take another step. This is no ordinary youngster."

Mr. Currie elbowed his partner. "We worked out that bit for ourselves."

"Well, you've worked it out all wrong. Cedric's brighter than the two of you lumped together. A bit of a genius, really. He has difficulty expressing himself, that's all, and he's easily distracted." Her voice faltered. "It's why he's so flighty."

Auntie's white-gloved fingers closed around Ceddy's clenched fist.

Glancing down, she frowned. "What have we here, lovey?"

Prying the stone from his grip, she turned it over in her hands. "Oh my. Another rock? I should think you've gathered plenty for your collection. They're weighing us down as it is."

He whimpered and scrambled for it.

Pulling away, she poised to toss it into the stream. "Leave it behind, dear. It's filthy."

"Nuh!"

"Yes, 'tis, Ceddy." She brushed her hand against her skirt. "Look how it soiled my nice, clean gloves. Let's throw it down, shall we? You have so many."

Bouncing on his heels, he tugged on her arm. "Mm-muh!"

With a sigh, she knelt at his side. "Yours? Is that what you're trying to say?"

He worked for the word. Fought for it. "Muh."

Auntie peered at him with narrowed eyes then pulled a hankie from her bodice. "Oh, all right. I suppose you've suffered loss enough for a lifetime. You may keep it." She wrapped the jagged stone, shoving it deep inside his pocket. "See that it stays tucked in here until we can wash it, right?" Pausing, she caught his chin. "If you run off again, I'll take it from you. Do you understand?"

He drew in his shoulders and turned away, curling his fingers around the bulging pouch at his side.

Auntie faced the angry men. "Shall we go back to the trail now?"

"Right," Charlie growled. "If we can find it."

Mr. Currie crossed his arms. "Listen up, Mrs. Beale. I ain't signed on to be no baby-minder. For all the trouble the lad's been, I've a notion to carry on without you."

She gasped. "You'd leave us at the mercy of wild animals and prowling natives?"

He held his bleeding hand toward Ceddy. "Five minutes with 'im and they'd set you free."

She stiffened. "He won't stray again. I give you my word." Her fingers tightened on Ceddy's arm. "He certainly won't be biting again. I'll see to that."

Charlie slapped Denny on the back. "Come along, old man. You've come this far; now see it through." He puffed his cheeks and blew a breath. "Let's get topside and mind the team before they're set upon by lions."

"No worries, mate," Denny grumbled, falling in alongside him. "If a lion dares to show his hairy face, we'll just sic that rabid boy on 'im."

Denny had never been so happy to see Church Square. Coming into Pretoria from the acacia karoo always startled him at first. The town, sitting square in the middle of nowhere, sported a richness that didn't belong in the valleys and rolling plains of the thornveld.

South Africa afforded plenty of room to sprawl in, and the capital of Transvaal Province had taken advantage of the space. The streets were wide, the buildings several stories high. Church Square, at the center of it all, was vast and gaudy.

Blindfolded and carried into Pretoria, Denny would recognize the town at once when the blinders came off. One glance at the Jacaranda trees lining the shaded lanes and the rambler roses climbing the walls would give it away. The City of Roses was a fitting name for a town strewn with colorful petals.

Drawing a deep, fragrant breath, he rested his hands on his hips. "Charlie, take the oxen and have them looked after. Once they're settled, unstrap the baggage from the beasts and meet us at Pretoria Station."

"Right, boss," Charlie said, turning the team.

Mrs. Beale sought Denny's eyes, her mouth set in a stern line. "There's no need for you to accompany us to the station. Ceddy and I can find our way from here."

Denny shook his head. "I was hired to see you safely onto the train, and that's what I mean to do."

She tugged on the fingers of her glove. "Very well, Mr. Currie. As you wish." Resting her hand on the boy's back, she struck out down the street—in the wrong direction.

"Mrs. Beale?"

She turned.

"It's that way," Denny said, pointing.

"Of course." She raised a haughty chin and pranced up the sidewalk.

Denny grimaced at Charlie in the distance then grudgingly followed the silly cow and her impish nephew.

A bicycle careened around the corner, frantically pedaled by a businessman in a suit coat and dapper straw hat.

In a burst of speed, Denny yanked the troublesome child and his aunt out of the road.

Ceddy jerked free with a sullen pout and plodded woodenly toward the station platform.

Denny ran his thumb over the ring of teeth marks on his hand. "S'aright, you cheeky little beggar," he whispered to the back of the boy's head. "I'll be shed of you soon enough."

The 132 wending its way toward them on the tracks—its big engine primed to take Cedric Whitfield out of his life for good—was a sight to warm the cockles of Denny's heart. If he never saw the wicked lad again, it would suit him fine.

"Wait up, dear. You'll be lost."

Ignoring his aunt's harried warning, the boy scurried onto the platform and ran to a row of windows. Folding his legs beneath him, he sat on the ground and reached inside his pocket. Unwrapping the stone she'd given him, he commenced to scratching on the wall of the station.

Mrs. Beale sighed then shook her finger. "Stay put, yeah? The train's almost here."

Turning to Denny, she held out a fat wad of bills. "I've decided to pay extra for your trouble."

"Not extra, lady." He raised one brow. "Double."

She drew back, narrowing her eyes.

Denny wiggled his fingers. "I earned every copper."

Releasing a huffy breath, she counted out a few more pounds. "Very well. Done."

Loud tapping pulled their attention to the boy. Kneeling before a window, he rapped hard on the glass with his silly rock.

"Oh bother. What's he doing?" Denny waved his arms. "Hullo there, sonny! Stop that, now."

Fidgeting, Mrs. Beale stared down the track, deaf and blind to the child in her charge.

"Call the lad away, Mrs. Beale, before he breaks something."

She glanced over her shoulder. "Leave him be, Mr. Currie. He's not hurting anything."

Gritting his teeth, Denny turned aside in disgust. "Right," he whispered. "What's it to you? You'll soon be rolling south, free as the wind. I'll be left to square the tab."

Charlie appeared as the hulking engine rumbled past, the squeal on metal piercing as the engineer braked to a stop.

Denny hooked his thumb in Ceddy's direction. "I'll load their bags. You go fetch the brat so he can board. We can't have her leaving without 'im."

Nodding, Charlie dropped his burden then hustled to the boy and leaned to speak to him.

Cedric pushed to his feet and ran to join his aunt.

As they climbed the steps of the passenger car and disappeared inside, Denny drew a deep, cleansing breath. He didn't relax until the rods on the massive wheels began to pump, rolling the bothersome blighters out of his life. Patting the wad of money in his pocket, he grinned and strolled to join Charlie. "Looks like we scored a profit after all."

"Maybe not, boss," Charlie said as he approached. "Take a gander at what he's done."

Denny groaned. So much for the few extra quid. "The window's cracked, ain't it?"

Charlie shook his head. "Not cracked. The little beggar left his calling card."

"What are you on about now?" Curious, he bent to stare at the pane. What he saw fired a rushing sound inside his ears.

"Blast me! Will you look at that?" Heart racing, he ran his finger over the jagged letters of Ceddy's name etched into the glass.

Charlie scratched the wiggly lines with his thumbnail. "He's done it now, ain't he? It's ruined." Standing, he tugged on Denny's sleeve. "There's still time to do a runner. No one's noticed yet."

Denny jerked off his cap and whacked Charlie on the head. "Don't you know what you're looking at, you mindless dolt?"

Clutching his reddening ear, Charlie frowned and shook his head.

"Use your loaf, mate. Nothing will cut into glass like that except. . ." His voice rose on the end, inviting Charlie to finish.

Wheeling, Charlie stared toward the train, the last car glinting on the horizon. "You mean that hulking great rock is a. . ." His words trailed off, but his eyes bulged from their sockets.

Denny gripped his arm and spun him around. "Where was that silly woman taking the boy?"

"To London for Christmas." Charlie flapped his hands as if it helped him to remember. "Then somewhere in America. Texas, I think."

"Ah yes," Denny said, the satisfying *hiss* befitting his slanted eyes. "I remember now." He whirled and stared down the tracks. "They're bound for a place called Marshall."

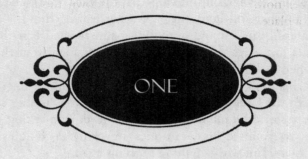

ONE

Galveston, Texas, December 1904

Salty spray blasted Pearson Foster as he hurdled the side of the dinghy and hauled the boat to shore. Cold, wet clothes clung to his body, and gritty sand chafed his shivering frame.

Bone-wracking fatigue wasn't new to Pearson. Neither was the disappointment weighing his heart. The latest promising lead to the treasure of Jean Lafitte had him combing deserted beaches again to no avail—after he'd sworn never to fall for the legend again.

This time he'd been so sure.

If "the Terror of the Gulf" had hidden a stash of gold on Galveston Island, he'd buried it well. The only things Pearson had unearthed in his relentless pursuit of the pirate's treasure were painful memories and deep feelings of utter failure.

Harsh sea breezes lifted his damp shirttails, waving them like flags of surrender. He couldn't suppress a shudder and a quick glance at the horizon. Since the terrible day four years ago when the worst hurricane in history swept all he held dear into the sea, he'd kept a nervous watch on any threat of foul weather.

Pearson gritted his teeth until his jaw ached. "I should've been here," he whispered for the thousandth time. If he hadn't taken a jaunt off the island the day before the storm, he'd have perished alongside his family and the six thousand souls lost that dreadful night. Some days, when

653

loneliness and guilt came in crushing waves, he wished he had.

At times, he tortured himself with thoughts of their final moments. His mother's frightened face as the rushing water swirled under the door, higher and higher, until it lapped at the eaves. . .and beyond. His jovial little brother and innocent baby sister fearing that the shrieking wind, splintering houses and uprooting palms, would tear them from their parents' arms. Hardest to bear, his father's anguish at the terrible moment when he knew he couldn't save them.

Jutting his chin, Pearson scowled into the bank of angry clouds, staring down the Creator Himself. As sure as the pounding surf at his back and the shifting sand at his feet, he'd never stop asking why God spared him yet counted his loved ones unworthy. As long as he lived, he'd never trust Him with anything precious again.

"Ahoy, brigand!" Theodoro Bernardi's familiar voice drifted up the beach followed by his lanky body.

Wincing, Pearson pretended not to hear. He itched to push off again, steer past the breaking waves, and set sail. He'd sooner battle the restless sea than admit defeat to his closest friend. Instead, he put his head down and dragged the boat farther inland, away from the rising tide.

Grinning, Theo hustled to lend a hand, his oversized feet leaving great sucking prints in the sand. "Well?" he asked, the question Pearson dreaded evident in his raised brows.

"Nothing," Pearson said calmly, as if declining jam with his morning toast.

Theo's eyes echoed Pearson's frustration. "Too bad, Pearce. I know you were hopeful."

Abandoning false indifference, Pearson pursed his lips and sighed. "It was a good lead this time around. I really thought—"

"I told you to wait till I could join you, no? With both of us looking, the outcome might've been different."

Pearson shook his head. "Once I locked onto the site, nothing felt right. That blasted storm turned this whole island upside down."

"Then how are you sure you found the spot?"

Pearson fired him a pointed look.

Theo lifted his hands. "Sorry I asked. I still say you should've waited."

Flipping the dinghy with one heave, Pearson gritted his teeth. "Some battles a man has to face alone."

Theo hooked his neck with the crook of his arm. "Well, you don't have to drink alone. Let me buy you a stiff swig at Rosie's to warm your mulish bones."

Pearson stiffened. "I appreciate the offer, old boy, but my stand on strong drink still holds."

Questions swirled in Theo's veiled eyes, but he wisely bit them back. "In that case, I was referring to Rosie's coffee. A shot of her stout brew should thaw you out." He thumped Pearson's chest. "And grow hair on this bald, girlie carcass."

Pearson chuckled and knocked his hand away. "That's different. When have I ever turned down Rosie's coffee?"

Grinning, Theo pointed him away from the approaching wall of rain, guiding him up the beach to the outline of the wagon waiting in the distance.

Pearson understood Theo's confusion about his ethics. His life was a contradiction that baffled him as well. Consuming rage kept him from communing with the Lord, yet he carefully maintained godly standards. It made little sense, but he couldn't seem to walk another path. His upbringing by Christian parents had marked him.

By the time the buckboard pulled in front of Rosie's Café and Theo set the brake, dusk—helped along by the imminent storm—had settled over the island, and the whipping wind had nearly dried Pearson's clothes. To dry his thick, matted hair would require a bench close to Rosie's glowing hearth.

Welcoming light from the window drew them past the double doors. Pearson relished the familiar comfort of babbling voices and soft laughter, the mingled odors of good food and men who smelled of the sea. Shouts of greeting melted the lead from his careworn heart. Grinning, he shook hands all around, returning warm smiles and hearty pats on the back.

"What foul breeze blew your ugly mug across the bay?" Cookie cried over the noise. Shoving through the kitchen door, the ruddy-cheeked cook poured a steaming cup of oily coffee from a blackened pot on the counter and slid it across to Pearson. "And after we'd set our hearts on never seeing you again."

The gathered circle of men hooted, pounding on the bar until the dishes rattled.

"I never meant to come, that's for sure." Pearson pinched the man's scruffy cheek. "But I couldn't get your handsome face out of my mind."

The room erupted in catcalls and gales of laughter.

Cool fingers tightened around Pearson's arm. "What about my face?" Pearl, Rosie's daughter, had slipped in from the kitchen and pressed against him, the smell of her hair and curve of her neck headier than any sip of ale. Her sultry gaze lingered on his arm while she caressed the swell of his muscle. Pearson cleared his throat, and she pulled her eyes to his, bold appreciation flickering in their depths. "Did you think of me while you were gone?" A slow smile tilted the corners of her plump, inviting mouth.

"You know I did." He lowered his voice. "Almost every day."

She pouted her lips. "Almost?"

Beaming, he winked at her mother who had come to stand behind her. "The other days were taken with thoughts of my own sweet Rosie." He held out his arms to the portly older woman. "Come to me, vixen."

Startled, Pearl glanced over her shoulder, stepping aside as Rosie coolly slid into her place.

"Don't fret, little Pearl," Theo teased, snaking his long arm around her shoulders. "I promise to think of you every minute."

"A likely pledge, Theo Bernardi. You'll think of me alongside ten other girls." She flashed him a shy smile, but her longing gaze slid to Pearson.

Rosie held Pearson's face with both hands, planting a kiss on his lips. "What wretched folly kept you from us, darlin'?" she demanded, her booming voice rattling the rafters. "The island mourns in your absence." She tilted her head and winked. "And so does this old woman."

He grinned. "You know me, Rosie. I've been chasing my fortune to the four corners."

"The four corners of Galveston, maybe," one of the laughing men shouted to the room. "We're stuck with the great adventurer while Lafitte's gold has a hook set in him." Nodding at Theo, he gave Pearson a wicked grin. "Since your friend here hasn't offered to buy a round of drinks, I'm thinking old Jean outsmarted you again."

Pearson cringed, and a blush warmed his neck. Despite his secrecy, word had gotten out that he'd come home chasing another blind lead. Worse, that he'd be slinking off again in defeat. He flashed a look at Theo, who shrugged and shook his head.

"Don't bother denying what I saw with my own eyes, matey," the fellow pressed. "There's only one reason you'd pitch that bobbing cork of yours onto rough seas." He flashed a wicked grin. "And no mistaking the thatch of seaweed on your head, not even from a distance."

The man's companion lifted a strand of Pearson's hair. "Looks more like tentacles to me. With all the time he's spent in water, the lad's more sea beast than man."

Rosie's glare wiped the smirks from his tormentor's faces. Swiveling on their bar stools, they rounded chastened shoulders over their mugs.

Lifting her chin, she graced Pearson with a sunny smile. "Don't mind those two simpletons. They still think the earth is flat. Grab your coffee, and come take your ease by the fire." Hooking her arm through his, she led him to a table near the hearth.

Sliding onto a bench worn smooth by the backsides of faithful patrons, Pearson scrubbed his weary eyes with calloused palms. "Trouble is, the simpletons called it right. I'm a dolt to keep chasing an old fable. There's no hidden treasure on this island."

Rosie and Theo's jaws dropped as if wired by a single hinge.

Falling into a seat across from Pearson, Rosie gaped. "I never expected those words to come out of your mouth."

"Me either." Theo plopped into a chair next to her. "What's gotten into you?"

Pearson gripped his cup to still his shaking hands. "They're feeling more and more like the truth."

"Nonsense, dear boy. You just need something else to think about for a while. Something to whet your appetite. . .stir your sense of adventure." A spark of mischief lit the depths of her eyes. Lurching forward, she held up a knobby finger. "And I know just the thing."

Twisting to search the café, Rosie's roving gaze jerked to a stop on an elderly stranger hunched over an empty mug at the end of the bar.

"Hoy, mister!" She whistled and waved her arm.

The man's head came up and he frowned. Slowly, warily, he stole a peek over his shoulder.

"I'm talking to you," she called.

His throat rose and fell, and he pointed at his chest.

Rosie nodded. "That's right. Come over here, please. We'd like to speak to you."

He slid off the stool, nearly toppling, and shuffled across the room. Five feet shy of the table, he stopped and licked his thin lips, so dry they were cracked and white. His darting gaze swept Pearson and Theo, but the need driving him proved stronger than his fear. Venturing two steps closer, he pleaded with his eyes. "Miss Rosie. . .you reckon you might allow me one more on the tab?" His trembling fingers fiddled at his pockets. "I've come up a little short this week." His mouth strained at a smile. "Well, I never been tall, truth be told. What I mean to say is my thirst stretched farther than my earnings this month."

Rosie's round face softened. "I have a better idea. Pull that chair around, and we'll serve you a bite to eat on the house." Resting her arm on the back of the bench, she scanned the room for Pearl. Spying her, she beckoned. "Honey, dish up a bowl of beef stew for our friend here, with a big slice of sourdough bread."

Pearl stirred from her thoughts and slunk toward the kitchen.

Halfway there, Cookie waved her toward three newcomers sidling up to the bar. "Wait on them fellows first, gal, while I ladle the stew."

"On second thought," Rosie called, wiggling four fingers in his direction, "bring a round for the table."

"Coming up, boss," he said, spooning meat and potatoes into crockery bowls.

The old sailor's weathered face relaxed. "Well, thank you, ma'am. Don't mind if I do." A new spring in his step, he dragged up a slatted chair and straddled it, crossing his wrists atop the back. "That's mighty nice of you folks."

Rosie leaned across the table, her mischievous smile in place. "I want you to tell these gents the story you told me last night."

He tugged his anxious gaze from Pearl, who watched from the bar as she filled tall glasses with frothy ale. His brows drew to a knot. "Story?"

"You know," Rosie offered, "the sunken steamboat?"

He withdrew to arm's length, his eyes wary. "I never said nothing about a steamer."

"Sure you did. The *Mary* or *Tillie*, or some such thing. She went down carrying a fortune in gold."

Evidently, when he'd shared the tale with Rosie, his pockets had jingled with plenty of coin to quench his thirst. Whatever he'd told her, he hadn't meant to let slip. Batting bleary eyes, he gnawed his bottom lip. "You've got the wrong man," he finally blurted. "I don't know anything."

She touched his trembling hand. "It's all right. These fellows are friends of mine."

He tucked his chin and gave a firm shake of his head.

Pearl finished her appointed task then snatched the heavy tray from the counter and hoisted it over one shoulder. Dodging tables and grasping, leering men, she wove toward them.

Straightening, Rosie took the tray from her and slid it under the old man's nose. Lifting a bowl, she handed it to him with a smile. "There we go. Nice and hot."

Brightening, he lifted his head and beamed. "Much obliged, ma'am."

Pearl stood watching Pearson, her hands twisting her white apron to knots. "I made a fresh pot of coffee for you." She pointed at the steaming cup on the tray. "I hope it's strong enough."

Pearson laced his fingers behind his head and shot her a playful wink. "If you made it, I'm sure it's fine."

Blushing, she flitted away.

Rosie's careful gaze trailed her daughter to the bar. "Sorry, Pearson," she muttered over her shoulder. "She's so blinded by how she feels, she can't see you don't feel the same."

Pearson gripped her shoulder. "It's all right, Rosie. I don't mind."

She sighed. "I need a good man to marry her and take her out of here. She's better suited to raising babies than drawing ale."

Rosie watched Pearl until she disappeared inside the kitchen. Propping her arms on the table, she jutted her chin at the old man. "Now then. . .about that shipwreck." Her finger shot forward, pointing at him. "I remember now. You called her the *Mittie*." She slapped the wobbly table. "The *Mittie Stephens*."

He flinched and drew up his shoulders. "Have a heart, Miss Rosie. I don't know much about that old legend. Just an ear-load of wayfarer's drivel."

Rosie patted his trembling hand. "Go on, now. Tell my friends what you told me."

Releasing a weary sigh, he picked up his spoon and nodded. "If you say so, ma'am."

Details emerged with each careful bite of the hearty dish. As his stew cooled and the bowl emptied, he warmed to the story with the bright-eyed eagerness born of a worthy tale. Darkness settled over the room as he spoke, broken only by distant flashes of lightning outside and the dim, flickering candles burning in blackened jars.

Thunder boomed overhead, rattling the windowpanes. A brilliant flash exposed startled faces, followed by a violent, piercing crash as lightning struck something close by. A few of Rosie's patrons hustled for the door to seek another port in the storm.

A handful of regulars, with no better place to be, found their way to the table, curiosity getting the best of them as the old fellow's hushed voice carried across the room.

He spoke of a "lost world" in the northeastern reaches of Texas and the dreadful fate of a doomed side-wheeler steamboat. "February, it was, in 1869. The *Mittie Stephens* left Shreveport with her guards flat in the water."

"What's that mean?" Rosie whispered hoarsely.

"A full load," Theo explained, his spoon clanking. Oblivious to the patrons hanging on the old sailor's words, he chased dregs of brown gravy around his bowl.

The old man nodded. "Under command of Captain H. Kellogg, the ship pulled away from the Commerce Street wharf with her cargo, forty-three passengers, and sixty-six crewmen. Stacked on board were two hundred seventy-some bales of hay, a dozen kegs of gunpowder, and enough gold to make payroll for the Reconstruction troops in Jefferson. Now mind you"—one bushy brow peaked as he stared around the circle of rapt faces—"this shipment of hay, stacked four tiers deep on the guards, weren't just any old bales."

Pearson swallowed a sip of his coffee, the liquid hot and bitter all the way down. "What was so different?"

"Government issue, that's what. The stuff was parched as powder on account of being kiln dried."

"I've heard of this," Theo said. "They dry the hay to fight off mold."

The old boy nodded. "The water was high that night, so it was clear sailing through the channel on Caddo Lake. At the midnight hour, just below Swanson's Landing, a steersman alerted the pilot that he'd caught a whiff of smoke. Sure enough, they hadn't properly snuffed the torch baskets on the bow before setting sail. The wind lifted sparks from the basket, carrying them across to the dry bales. They went up as if doused with coal oil. The crew kept their wits about them and tossed the gunpowder overboard, but it was too late."

He leaned across the table, his haggard face ghoulish above the flickering candle. "Better than sixty folks lost their lives that fateful night. Some because they couldn't swim but most because they plain lost their bearings." He shook his head. "Blinded by the flames, the poor souls swam away from the bank. Turns out the *Mittie* was less than twenty feet from shore. She ran aground with her cargo of gold and sank into Caddo's murky depths." He shuddered then grew silent, his haunted eyes staring into the blazing hearth.

"And?" Rosie prompted.

Without warning, his chin sank to his chest and his bottom lip sagged.

Rosie clutched his bony shoulder and shook him awake. "Is that it? Nothing else about the gold?"

Jerking upright, he fixed her with bloodshot eyes. "I've blabbered all I know, though I'm sure there's more to tell." He yawned and wiped his slack mouth on his sleeve. "I'm bone-weary, Miss Rosie. Can't go no more. Ain't found a place to sleep since I left my ship." Folding his arms for pillows, he slumped to the table, resting his grizzled head.

Compassion softened her features. "Poor, wretched thing, you have now." Signaling Cookie, she gave him instructions to help the fellow to the storeroom.

Towering over him, Cookie sighed. "He's playing you for a mark, Rosie. You should charge him rent. He spends more time on free cots than he does at sea."

Rosie tilted her face up to him. "I'm surprised at you, Cookie. Where's your Christian charity?"

"Christian charity?" He snorted. "He should be keelhauled."

She frowned. "I won't turn away a man in need."

"Suit yourself, but don't expect him to appreciate it none. And while you're at it, forget any notion of collecting his tab. You won't see a nickel." He circled the fellow's chest with both arms and hauled him to his feet. "Toe the mark, you old beggar. No night watches for you."

They took a few shuffling steps before the man's drooping head lolled to the side. "There's a fellow on Caddo Lake," he said, his voice surprisingly strong for a bone-weary man. "An old fishing guide they call Catfish John. Ask for him around Marshall, Texas."

"Yes?" Theo said. "What about him?"

"Find him. He can tell you anything you want to know about the *Mittie*." He and Cookie disappeared beneath the low archway.

Rosie turned twinkling eyes on Pearson. "Well then?"

He shrugged. "Well, what?"

"It's a good lead. Why aren't you running out the door to book passage on a northbound train?"

Pearson stifled a grin and winked at the spellbound circle of men. "Sorry, honey, but he's not the first drunken sailor with a far-fetched yarn." He hooked his thumb toward the mainland. "There's a tale like his in every port of call."

Dazed, she shook her head. "No, sir. Not like this one. I sense he's telling the truth."

Pearson laughed softly. "Oh, he is. . .the truth as he believes it to be."

Rosie slapped the varnished table so hard, coffee sloshed over the rim of his cup. "How can you treat this so lightly? When first he told it to me, I wanted to round up some men and go search for the *Mittie* myself."

Pearson calmly wiped up the spill with his napkin and took a slow swig of the tepid brew. "I understand your passion, little Rosie. I used to get worked up about these old legends myself. After a while you get a feel for what's real"—he nodded toward the raspy snores coming from the back room—"and what isn't." He shot the uninvited spectators an amused glance. "Right, boys?"

Several grinned and nodded. A couple patted Rosie affectionately on the shoulder. Others shared winks and knowing glances with Pearson before drifting to the bar, their murmuring voices sprinkled with good-natured laughter.

She stared after them with blazing eyes.

Pearson slid his chair around to make room to stretch out his legs. With a wide yawn, he fisted his hands and kneaded his temples. "Are you ready to take me back to your place, Theo? I'm so tired I won't mind your lumpy couch." He grinned and winked at Rosie. "Or the musty quilt he pulled out of mothballs just for me."

Stirring from her pout, she blinked at Pearson. "Still can't bear the thought of staying in your house, honey?"

Not willing to talk about his parents' big house on Broadway Street, he shook his head.

"Well, that's all right." She patted his hand. "There's no need to suffer Theo's distorted idea of hospitality. We have the spare room upstairs." She pointed with her chin. "It's not much, but it's clean. . .and free of lumps and moths."

Pearson's stomach tightened the way it did only while on the island. The prospect of sitting upstairs alone with his thoughts seemed far less appealing than a tattered blanket. He squeezed Rosie's hand. "I appreciate the offer, sweetheart. I really do." He ducked his head at Theo. "But I'll stay with my old friend there, so his feelings won't be hurt. I hate to see a grown man cry."

Stepping gingerly over his booted feet, Pearl stopped in front of him, her crossed arms hugging her chest. "Are you sure, Pearson? It's a nice little room, and the windows face the ocean. You'd wake up to a beautiful sunrise." Blushing, she reached to fiddle with her apron again. "I washed and ironed the curtains myself." She cleared her throat. "They're yellow."

An uncomfortable silence settled like dew.

Pearl's bright flush deepened, and she lowered her lashes.

"It's no use, honey," Rosie said, coming to her rescue. "You know how stubborn men are, and I'd say his mind is made." Grunting from the effort, she pushed up and stood behind Pearson, gathering long strands of hair off his shoulders. "Do you have any plans to cut this moldy mess?" She tugged hard on a lock. "I've seen sheep with less matted wool."

Laughing, he straightened in his chair. "Speaking of hurting a man's feelings. . ."

She pulled his head back and stared upside down at his face. "There are topics I dare to raise out of love"—she scowled at the two scoundrels who were teasing him before—"and those I won't tolerate from anyone else." She grinned. "But you have to admit it's a peculiar mess."

Theo snickered. "His hair has always twisted into knots, and people have always taunted him. That's how he learned to fight like a badger."

Rosie held out a snakelike strand and tried to pull it straight. "You couldn't drag a rake through this. How do you comb it?"

Pearson preened. "Go on and scoff, but in your hands you hold the fruit of careful and deliberate neglect."

They shared a hearty laugh, except for Pearl. Casting a shy glance at Pearson, she frowned. "I think your hair is nice. It suits you."

Holding her gaze, he gave her a warm smile. "Thank you, Pearl."

Grinning like an unbalanced dolt, Theo stood and pulled Pearson from his chair. "Let's get you home so you can wash up. Lumpy or not, you can't sleep on my sofa without a soak in the tub. You stink."

Pearson sniffed his shirtsleeve. "It's not so bad. I smell better than your quilt."

Theo tugged him toward the door. "Not unless it reeks of sunbaked codfish." He grimaced. "Or the stench of a rotted octopus."

Rosie's high-pitched cackle followed them out the door.

The storm had passed, leaving a light drizzle behind and trailing dark, wispy clouds across the moon. The dim glow of the streetlamp lit their path to the wagon and the poor, wilted horse standing in a puddle of rainwater.

Stopping short of the rig, Theo slapped his forehead and groaned. "Stupido! I forgot about him."

"So did I," Pearson said. "Maybe he'll forgive us if we get him to the barn and rub him down. If not, a few oats might do the trick. A little love and care goes a long way."

Tittering like a child again, Theo nudged him. "I think Pearl would like to give you a bit of loving care. With very little encouragement, she'd have you broken and stabled before you could whinny."

Pearson balled his fist and delivered a sound blow to Theo's arm. "That's why I won't be encouraging her. I'm not ready to be gentled." He shuffled sideways to dodge the return punch. "Besides, when I'm ready to be strapped to the feed bag, I'm not looking for Pearl's brand of oats."

"Particular, aren't you? Exactly what are you looking for?"

Grabbing the wagon post, Pearson tensed to pull up on the seat. "I suppose I'll know when I see her."

Theo caught his arm before he could board. "How long will it take you to pack for East Texas?"

Pearson stifled a grin. "I never unpack my bags in Galveston. You know that."

"So when are you leaving?"

"When are *we* leaving is the question." He gripped Theo's shoulder. "I want you to go with me."

Theo's beaming face glowed in the streetlight. "I've been waiting for you to ask. Let's go!"

Pearson chuckled. "Not so fast, boy. The *Mittie's* been at the bottom of Caddo Lake for thirty-six years. She'll be there in a few more months."

"Why waste time?"

"It's the dead of winter, Theo. Too cold to dive. Besides, we need supplies. Special gear. Let me get back to Houston and pull a plan together. I'll wire you when I'm ready to leave."

"How long?"

Scratching his sandy scalp, Pearson ticked off the facts in his head. "Well. . .it's mid-December, isn't it?"

Theo chuckled. "You don't know?"

"It's hard to keep track of the date when you're riding the Gulf in a dinghy."

Theo patted his shoulder. "Point made. It's December 15th, to be exact. Nearly Christmastime."

Pearson nodded. "Then I say we slow down and enjoy the holidays. Let the weather warm up a tad. Come spring, plan to celebrate my birthday in East Texas."

"End of April?" Theo's voice cracked with excitement. "Sounds right to me."

Pearson searched his eager face. "So it's settled? You're on board?"

Hitching up his pants, Theo frowned. "Try and stop me. What town did the old man mention before? The place where we'll find Catfish John?"

"He said Marshall." Staring toward the mainland, Pearson's blood surged hot and fast in his veins. A familiar pull in his chest urged him toward the lure of treasure. "We'll find what we need in Marshall, Texas."

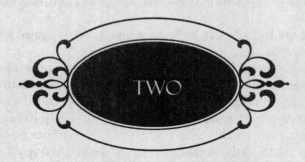

TWO

Canton, Mississippi, March 1905

Addie McRae clutched the letter to her heart with both hands. The scent of lavender wafted up from the page and teased her nose, but the smell of freedom flared her nostrils. Determination surged, and excitement gripped her chest. Placing the delicate stationery onto her desk, she smoothed the creases from the dainty bluebonnet border and stared hard at the graceful scrawl.

> *Therefore, with the tragic demise of my young nephew and his*
> *wife, I will soon find myself in dire need of a reliable governess for*
> *my new charge, their only son, Cedric. As you know, our Ceddy is*
> *an unusual child and will need special handling. My fervent prayer*
> *is that you will arrange for your lovely granddaughter to come to*
> *our aide. If this isn't possible, perhaps you know of a suitable girl of*
> *a sober and responsible character to come in her stead. In my hour of*
> *need, my thoughts turned to you, Thomas Moony. Might you help*
> *an old friend?*

Miss Priscilla Whitfield of Texas had written of her urgent need for a governess to Addie's dearest companion, Hope Moony, the granddaughter of Canton's distinguished doctor. Hope's recent engagement forced her to decline, so Dr. Moony passed the offer to Addie with a promise to recommend her for the position. From the first reading, Addie felt a sense of destiny spark in her veins.

Movement at the edge of the garden drew her eye. The abandoned kittens, a little calico and her tabby brother, crouched near the woods, watching her.

Placing the letter beside her on the bench, she wriggled her fingers close to the ground.

The kittens launched themselves past the azaleas and over the bricks lining the flower bed, tumbling over each other in their haste. Tiny claws extended, they climbed her skirt and huddled in the folds of her dress, lapping the saucer of cream she held ready. Eyes slanted in bliss, they took turns arching their bony backs toward her caress.

Addie smiled. Only weeks ago, they'd darted away each time she stepped out the door. After days of baiting them, placing bits of food a little closer each time, they'd come as near as the hem of her dress, but no farther—until the evening she'd offered bits of leftover fish from supper. Unable to resist such a tempting treat, they'd conquered their fear and crawled into her lap to eat.

The pair shared the final drop of cream in the dish then curled together, diligently cleaning their whiskered mouths on furled paws.

Addie set the empty saucer aside and took up the troubling letter. Spreading her slender fingers over the flowing script, she swallowed the lump rising in her throat. The idea of a child so brutally torn from the safety of his mother's arms, rendered an orphan by one fateful turn of events, brought her to tears. A little one left to fend for himself without the guidance and tender care of his parents seemed a tragic and lonely soul.

She glanced at the helpless creatures in her lap, waifs and strays themselves. Their plight and the boy's rose in stark contrast to her own dilemma. By comparison, struggling against the wishes of overprotective parents was infinitely better than not having them at all.

She smoothed her knuckle over the boy's name on the page. "I'm deeply sorry for your loss, dear Ceddy. Poor little tyke."

Miss Whitfield wrote that her nephew's son was unusual. Despite any sort of "special handling" he might need, Addie had never met a child who didn't respond to love.

Recalling the impish youngsters she'd encountered as a governess, she nodded thoughtfully. With a gentle hand and understanding heart, she'd taught all of them to trust her and eventually brought them into line. Cedric Whitfield would be no different.

The back door opened, and the housemaid's strident voice shrilled her name.

Addie blinked away the moisture in her eyes and spun. "Yes, Dicey?"

Chin raised, Dicey scanned the garden until her gaze fell on Addie, sitting in her favorite spot on the bench under the wicker arbor. "Breakfast, Miss Addie. Drop them flea-ridden critters and come inside. Yo' sistahs already gathered at the table, and yo' folks say hurry. They hungry."

"Tell them I'll be right along."

"All right now. . .but don't make me be tellin' no lies."

Before the screen clicked shut at Dicey's back, Addie returned the letter to its envelope and tucked it deep inside the pocket of her skirt. She'd carry it to breakfast and allow Miss Whitfield herself to sway them. The woman's expensive stationery and lovely handwriting would help drive home her impassioned plea, but reading firsthand of Ceddy's plight would go a long way in persuading them.

Addie would need all the help she could get.

Rousting the drowsy kittens, she deposited them at her feet. The tabby mewed in protest, and the calico stole a peek with one slanted eye. Sluggish from full bellies, they snuggled on the spot and fell straight back to sleep. Steeling her spine, Addie arose and crossed the yard to the steps.

At the end of the hall, she paused to eavesdrop on the family's conversation, hoping to assess the mood. By the sound of Father's gentle teasing and Mother's gleeful laughter, it appeared to be the perfect morning to state her intentions. Closing her eyes, she imagined their reactions—her horrified gasp, his disbelieving stare—when she told them she planned to move to Texas. Gathering her skirts along with her courage, she breezed around the corner.

"Here she is," Father announced, looking up from his breakfast. "Hurry and pass the corn cakes, Carrie Beth, before Addie catches sight of them." He grinned and winked at Mother. "Take some for yourself, Mariah, if you plan to have any. Once your eldest daughter gets a taste of corn cakes, it's 'Katy, bar the door.' "

Carrie and the twins, Father's preferred audience when it came to tormenting Addie, tittered like a nest of baby mockingbirds.

"I like corn cakes, too, Papa," Marti crowed, crossing her arms.

Mattie stuck out her bottom lip. "Well, so do I!"

Father grinned at his matched set of pouting little girls. "And you shall have some, my doves. I'll see to it Addie shares."

"Hush, Tiller McRae," Mother said. "There's plenty to go around. I baked extra this morning."

Addie leaned to kiss his cheek, noticing for the first time the strands of silver hair mingled with the rusty red of his sideburns. "What's this?" She fingered the smattering of gray. "Heavens, it can't be. My handsome father, losing the battle with time?"

His big hand closed over hers. "Time isn't turning my hair, Addie Viola. Fretting over your constant stream of suitors is to blame for bleaching it white."

Mother liked to boast that she'd borrowed Addie's forename from Adelina Patti, highly acclaimed opera singer. The source of Addie's middle name made her prouder. Viola Ashmore Jones was Addie's old governess and Mother's longtime companion, and Addie loved her dearly. Rendered feeble by age, poor Miss Vee seldom made it to breakfast these days.

Addie feigned shock. "What's the harm in a few suitors? A girl has to weigh her options."

Father squeezed her fingers, drawing them to his lips for a kiss. "None of the addlepated options I've chased from the porch lately are good enough for you. I'd lock you in your room until your curls grayed if I thought it would do any good."

Addie laughed, but her stomach lurched. Time to steer him to less troublesome ground. "You'd best douse your temples with Miss Vee's henna if you want to keep up with your wife." Pressing her face close to his, she pointed across the table. "Look at Mother, as young and lovely as ever. She could pass for my sister."

Father huffed. "A stinging injustice, considering she worries over you girls more than I do."

Mother blushed and ducked her head. "My Indian ancestry keeps me youthful. The Choctaw age quite gracefully."

Smiling, Father winked at her. "You're only half Indian, Mariah. The British half should have the manners to grow old alongside her husband." He tugged on Addie's arm, pulling her from behind him. "Sit down so I can ask God's blessing on our food." He chuckled.

"Especially these poor corn cakes. They're not long for this world."

Addie's giggle echoed back at her from around the breakfast table. Grinning at her sisters, she folded her hands and slipped off her shoes. She may as well make herself comfortable. Most of Father's prayers turned to long-winded chats with God.

That morning proved no different. His heartfelt pleas touched on each of them in turn, asking protection and direction for each life. When he reached Addie's name, thanking the Lord for his dutiful daughter, she squirmed in her chair.

Longing to blurt her news, she held herself in check. He'd be more receptive with a bellyful of Dicey's ham, doused with a ladle of redeye gravy.

After a heartfelt "Amen," Father shook out his napkin and smoothed it on his lap. He finished the first half of his breakfast in silence, except for quiet murmurs of appreciation for Mother's biscuits and grunts of approval for the meal in general. Her father loved to eat as well as any gentleman of the South and kept his zeal for Southern cooking finely tuned. Stabbing a forkful of ham, he tilted his chin in Addie's direction. "What's on your dance card for today, little miss?"

The endearment irked a bit. Addie might be short in stature and small-boned, but he needn't treat her like a child. "I thought I'd run into town for a spell." *To ask Dr. Moony to wire Miss Whitfield of my decision to accept—just as soon as I've broken the news.*

"What manner of mischief are you and Hope planning for our townsfolk?" Father leaned across the table and winked. "And how gravely will it impact my wallet?"

Addie's heart stirred with pride. Silver hair and outrageous appetite aside, she had the handsomest father in all of Mississippi. "Mischief indeed." Pouting her lips, she pretended to sulk. "I could stroll these streets for weeks and not find a smidgen of trouble. Canton is, without a doubt, the most boring place on earth."

Mother's fork stilled, her large brown eyes lifting to meet Addie's. "Do we need to discuss your values, Adelina? When did safe and respectable become boring?"

Since the beginning of time, at least, but it wouldn't be prudent to say so. "How's Miss Vee this morning?" she asked, wisely changing the subject.

"Feeling frail, poor old love. Her joints pain her worse every year."

Father chuckled. "If you believe half her complaints, she'll be joining

Otis in eternal rest any day now."

"Was Otis Miss Vee's husband?" Carrie asked.

"No, dear," their mother said. "Miss Vee wed Tobias Jones, God rest his soul. Dear departed Otis was Papa's closest friend. Both men passed on before you were born."

Turning, she touched Addie's arm. "I hope you'll duck in on Miss Vee before you leave for town. You always seem to cheer her."

Addie nodded. "Yes, ma'am, I will." She cleared her throat. "First, there's something I'd like you both to see." She pulled the envelope from her pocket and handed it to her father.

Creases formed between his brows, but he pulled his spectacles from his vest pocket and unfolded the letter.

The onionskin paper was so thin, Addie read along with him, her eyes following the backward letters across the page.

He finished and handed the missive across the table to Mother. As she read, he reached for Addie's hand. "I know how this must feel, sugar. It'll be hard to manage without young Hope around." He smiled softly. "We'll miss her, too, considering she's been underfoot since the age of ten. She's practically part of the family."

Taking off his glasses, he tucked them away. "Take comfort in knowing she's providing a worthy service."

"Poor little boy." Wiping her eyes, Mother placed the letter on the table. "I don't understand, Addie. How can Hope consider the offer when she's getting married soon?" She frowned. "Will her young man accompany her to Texas?"

Addie clenched her fists in her lap. The time had come. "Hope won't be accepting the position." She swallowed hard. "I will."

Stunned silence pressed her down in her chair. Wide-eyed, she watched the looks that passed between her parents.

His said, *"Here we go again."*

Hers said, *"Relax, I can handle this."*

Tightening her lips, Addie gathered her resolve. *I won't be handled. I simply won't!*

"Well?" she demanded. "Won't one of you say something?"

Mother placed her hand over the folded sheet of stationery, as if she couldn't bear to look at it. "Who gave you this letter, Addie?"

She jutted her chin. "Dr. Moony."

Father's mouth tightened. "Wait until I see Thomas Moony in town. . ."

"Now, Tiller," Mother soothed. "It's not his fault." Tears still glistening in her soulful eyes, she turned the force of them on Addie. "I feel for this poor orphaned child, dear girl, but my first concern is for you. With all the children in Mississippi, you can't find a position closer to home?" A tiny frown wrinkled her brow. "*Texas*, Addie. Do you know how far away that is?"

Addie sighed. "I didn't look for this opportunity, Mother. It fell into my lap. And I don't want another position. I want this one." Hearing a whine in her voice, she cringed. It wouldn't do to act like the child they thought her to be.

She sat forward and tried again. "I won't shrivel by degrees in Canton with never a chance to see the world. I can't settle for a loveless marriage like half the girls in town, groomed to live a dutiful life while pretending to be ignorant of intellectual opinion. I need to prove I'm capable of making a decision besides which day of the week should be washday." The final impassioned word squeaked out on her last bit of air. Drawing a fresh breath through her nose, she glared. "Surely God gifted me with talent beyond how to mend socks and maintain an organized pantry."

Her mother lowered her head. "Tending a family to the best of your ability is a gift of God, too. One that I treasure."

Her heated stand doused with guilt, Addie's hand flew to her mouth. "Oh Mother, I didn't mean to imply—"

Father cleared his throat. "We'll let this offer pass, Addie. There will be others, I'm sure."

Lurching to her feet, Addie strode to the door and spun. "I would never deliberately defy you, Father, but I feel led of God to go. I'm not asking your permission. I'm announcing my intentions."

Speechless for several seconds, Father closed his startled mouth and wagged a finger in Mother's direction. "This is your fault, Mariah Bell McRae. She inherited your willful spirit."

Mother sat back in her chair and calmly placed her napkin beside her plate. "Caroline, Martha, Matilda, go to your rooms."

Carrie, Marti, and Mattie likely couldn't understand the reason for the breakfast-hour skirmish, but the use of their proper names sent them scrambling. Carrie turned back long enough to make a face at Addie and snatch a slice of jellied toast.

Wincing, Addie glanced at her mother, bracing for a glimpse

of her fiery temper.

Respect shone from her dark eyes instead. She touched Father's arm. "The words sting because they're coming from Adelina. You look at her heart-shaped face and delicate features and see your five-year-old daughter. She's a woman now, Tiller. One who's been more than patient with us." She reached across and patted his hand. "It's time to let our little bird fly."

Addie bit her trembling lip and shot her mother a grateful smile.

Father steepled his hands on the table and sighed. "I get the distinct feeling that I'm outflanked." He quirked his mouth to the side. "I guess this means you're bound for Texas?"

Squealing, she crossed the room and hugged him around the neck. "You won't be sorry. I promise."

Standing, he gripped her shoulders. "Don't be so sure. I already regret my decision. And on one point I won't compromise. You can't leave until after your birthday. Otherwise, you'll break your father's heart."

"But sir, my birthday is over a month away."

Mother stood, her arm circling Addie's waist. "We'll write Miss Whitfield of your intention to interview. If the position is filled by the end of April, it wasn't meant to be."

Addie bit her bottom lip. She didn't view it the same way, but after the concession her parents had made, it wouldn't be fair to say so. Excitement bubbling in her chest, she turned to go. "I'll run upstairs now and write her when to expect me."

Father caught her wrist and hauled her back. "Not so fast, young lady." His green-eyed gaze searched her face. "Sometimes, with the best of intentions, we misread God's voice. That said, your mother will be traveling with you to meet your Miss Whitfield. If she doesn't approve of the arrangement, you'll feel led of God to take the next train home. Is that clear?"

Addie lowered her head and nodded. "Quite."

Mother held out the letter. "You'd better take this, honey. You may need it."

"One second," Father said, snatching the envelope. "I want to see exactly where my womenfolk are going." He stared at the return address then lifted puzzled eyes. "I've never heard of this place, Addie. Where in blazes is Marshall, Texas?"

THREE

Marshall, Texas, April 1905

Ceddy trudged up the walkway to Aunt Priscilla's two-story house. Clinging to Auntie Jane's skirt, he counted the soaring white columns stretching from the porch to the rooftop like bars on a giant cage. *One, two, three, four* across the front. He couldn't see those extending around the sides of the house, but he counted them from memory. *Five, six, seven* on one side. *Eight, nine, ten* on the other.

The door swung open before they reached it, and Aunt Priscilla appeared on the stoop. It wasn't right. Wasn't right. Lilah should've answered, wearing her white ruffled cap.

"Cedric, my dear child, how tall you've grown! You're as brown as pork pie, precious." She leaned close and smoothed his hair the way she'd always done with Daddy. The skin of her face sagged, and her breath reeked of lemon tea.

He stiffened and flapped his hands, grunted, and spun away.

She sighed and stood up straight. "Hello, Jane. So nice to see you again. I suppose some things never change, do they?"

"Ever so sorry, Priscilla," Auntie Jane said. "He's in a right foul mood. Thoroughly knackered, I suppose."

"Think nothing of it. I'm used to him. You must be exhausted as well."

"That I am. It's an endless trip across the Atlantic. Days of nothing but ocean on all sides. It's enough to drive you quite insane after a time."

"Yes, it's maddening," Aunt Priss murmured. "Before the dawn of transatlantic steamers, it took months to cross. You can't imagine the ordeal."

Aunt Jane moaned. "I'd perish."

"I'm surprised you didn't, poor thing."

The driver struggled up the walkway with two bulky trunks then returned to the buggy to fetch two more. "Where shall I put these, ma'am?"

"Heavens!" Aunt Priss cried. "Are they yours, Jane?"

She shook her head and pointed at a small green case. "I won't be staying that long. I have to be back in England soon or Richard will summon King Edward's Guard."

Aunt Priss's skirt swished as she spun toward the luggage. "Then whose. . ."

"Those are Ceddy's things."

"All of this for one small boy?" Her voice grew shrill at the end.

Ceddy cowered and covered his ears.

"I'm afraid so. I had the man swing by my sister's house to pack the boy's belongings, as you requested. You can't imagine the odd assortment of toys, books, and such. I tried persuading him to leave most of it behind, but he fell into such a panic, I gave in."

Auntie continued talking as Aunt Priscilla herded them inside the great hall, their footsteps echoing overhead. "He became most unreasonable about a collection of rocks and stones." She waved her hand at the trunks as the driver carried them over the threshold. "They weighed us down until I feared the poor horse might collapse."

"I wish you'd sent for my carriage, Jane."

Auntie waved her hand. "There was no need to trouble you. Ceddy and I have traversed the African continent." Her laugh was like jangling bells. "Mostly on foot. Traveling from the station required far less effort." She lowered her voice. "At least there are no *lions* in Marshall."

Aunt Priss gasped. "You can't be serious! You'll have to tell me all about it once you're settled."

Lilah hurried down the hall and bent to hug Ceddy, her smiling cheeks smooth and dark. "How you, Little Man?" she whispered in his ear. "I'm mighty pleased you here. We gon' have us a high old time."

Ceddy pressed closer to her baked-bread smell.

675

Handing her shawl to Lilah, Auntie tugged off her gloves. "It's unseasonably warm in Texas, isn't it? I hardly needed my wrap."

"I wouldn't put it away just yet," Aunt Priss said, bending to help Ceddy take off his jacket. "The weather here can be quite unpredictable."

Aunt Jane glanced toward Ceddy. "Speaking of unpredictable, there are things we need to discuss about the boy. Can we talk in private?"

Aunt Priss paused with Ceddy's arm still halfway up his sleeve. "But Jane. . .there will be plenty of time for that later. Won't you have a lie-down first?"

"I'd rather not. I need to speak my piece before I can relax."

Aunt Priss blew a shaky breath. "As you wish. We can retire to the study."

Handing Lilah Ceddy's coat, she guided him into her hands. "Delilah, show the boy upstairs and entertain him for a spell. This won't take long."

Lilah shoved back the brim of her cap and smiled. "Yes'm, Miss Whitfield." She nudged Ceddy toward the stairs as the study door closed with a loud click. "Let's us go see your new bedroom, Little Man."

Ceddy frowned. His room was on North Washington Avenue from where they'd just left, not here in Aunt Priscilla's big house. Shying away, he ran his fingers along the white rail on the wall, following the smooth, shiny board to the end of the hall.

Lilah's soft footsteps trailed at his heels. "What's this, now? You don't care none to see your quarters? Well, suit yo'self, but your toys and such be there. Miss Priscilla done bought you a shiny new book. . .filled to bustin' with pictures of rainbow-colored rocks."

Spinning, Ceddy took her hand. Halfway up the staircase, the study door opened, and angry voices filled the downstairs hall.

Lilah stopped so fast she jerked Ceddy's arm.

"You're being stubborn and unreasonable, Priscilla Whitfield," Aunt Jane spat.

"I rather think *you* are, Jane. Don't you wish to honor your sister's wishes?"

"Don't bring my sister into this. Matters of earthly import can't trouble her now. This is about Ceddy's welfare." Aunt Jane's voice softened. "I'm thinking of you as well, dear lady. Do you have the faintest idea what a handful he can be? His parents shamelessly indulged the lad's whims, and it hasn't improved his behavior. You're not getting any younger, you know."

Aunt Priss huffed. "While I thank you for your concern, it's misplaced. Doddering old fool that I am, I can handle a little boy."

"Can you?" In the quiet that followed, the two words danced in Ceddy's head, bouncing, twisting, changing places until they'd lost all meaning. He counted the click of shoe heels across the floor until the door opened with a whoosh of air. "I'll take a room at the Capital Hotel. You can reach me there if you come to your senses."

"Dear Jane, is that necessary?" Aunt Priss's angry tone had eased. "You'll be far more comfortable here."

"I'm leaving tomorrow afternoon, Priscilla. Think long and hard about the choice you're making. Meanwhile, I pray to hear from you before I board the train. Afterward, it will be too late to change your mind. I won't be coming back to the States."

"Save your prayers, dear. I won't change my mind."

The door banged shut, and Ceddy tugged on Lilah's hand. With a low whistle, she squeezed his fingers then led him to the top of the stairs.

North Atlantic Ocean, April 1905

Cursing his fetid luck, Denny Currie leaned against the rail and let the brisk Atlantic wind buffet him the way life had always done. Despite months of odd jobs, pinching every farthing with grasping fingers, the run-down ship he'd managed to book would take twice as long to cross the ocean as any modern steamer, since the outdated engines still required the use of sails.

By his reckoning, he and Charlie had another week to ride the pitching, dilapidated tub before reaching New York Harbor. Another week for the ghastly boy's family to discover what he'd smuggled home in his pocket.

Denny had spent sleepless nights staring at the ceiling of his ramshackle flat, weighing the odds that the treasure might be undiscovered after so long a time. In its raw state, the big stone little resembled a diamond. Only a practiced eye would ever figure it out.

If memory served, the boy had gone to live with a dotty old aunt—a fact that increased his odds tenfold. The old girl could be using it as a paperweight and be none the wiser. After all, it had happened before.

On the banks of the Orange River, in the spring of 1866, children of Boer settlers played about with sparkling rocks picked up from the ground, tossing them aside like worthless trinkets when they were bored. A roving peddler took more than a casual glance at one of the brilliant stones then passed it along to a government mineralogist. Denny's gut-twisting quest to better himself began with the diamond rush that followed.

Since that day, he'd followed strikes across South Africa, from the Orange River to the Vaal. Griqualand. Kimberley Mine. The strike in Pretoria—his own backyard, for pity's sake.

For endless years, his weary soles had trod upon the answer to life's problems, his clumsy big feet tripping over his own destiny. Roaming the rich African soil, he'd dug, burrowed, and scoured the ground for diamond pipes until his fingers bled and muscles ached. The relentless search became obsession, aging him beyond his fifty-three years and netting him little more than frustration and dishonor.

How could there be diamonds on every farm in Africa, yet always just out of his reach?

Now a simple-minded heathen on his way to the docks in Port Elizabeth had stumbled onto a king's fortune, only the dolt and his foolish aunt hadn't realized what he held.

Blast it all! Could every blithering fool find himself a diamond? Everyone but him?

His chest swelled to draw a hopeful breath. With a clarity he'd never felt before, he sensed the earth tilting, shifting a bit of good luck his way.

Stand aside, world. It's Denny Currie's turn at last.

"Hoy, Denny!" Charlie shouted, jerking him back to the present. Clinging to his cap, the big man staggered along the rail. "I've looked everywhere for you."

"Not everywhere, have you, mate? I've been 'ere all along."

"Listen up, Den. We need to 'ave us a chin-wag."

"Go on then," Denny growled. "I'm listening." He gulped as the wind whisked the words right out of his mouth. Lowering his head, he waited for the gust to pass, but the next one plastered his thinning hair to his scalp and whipped his lashes like bloomers strung on a line.

Charlie leaned into the squall, gripping his hat with one hand and clutching his worn coat with the other. "It's cold out, boss," he yelled. "Come inside, will ya? It's important."

Denny waved him on, and they staggered along the pitching deck to the stairwell. Shielded from the bitter wind, they descended into the belly of the ship and made their way down a long corridor to the tiny, one-room cabin they shared.

Charlie led the way inside. "This is better, yeah? A man can't hear himself think out there."

"I could hear meself fine till you turned up." Wrinkling his nose, Denny glared at the dusty corners, dingy blankets, and water-stained curtain over the porthole. "Blimey, the ocean smelled less of fish."

Chuckling, Charlie plopped on the bottom bunk. "You get used to it over time."

Denny pulled out a rickety chair and perched on the seat. "There's where you're wrong, old boy. I won't ever get used to living in dustbins and fish stalls. That's why I'm bound to change my luck." He propped his ankle on his knee and leaned forward. "Now, then. . .what's all this about?"

Charlie blinked up at him. "Well, I. . ."

"Go on, Charlie. You dragged me away from fresh air to choke in this stinking hole, so where's the house on fire?"

"Ain't no house on fire." Twisting his fingers in knots, Charlie stole a guilty glance. "But our bellies may be burning once we reach land."

Denny cocked his head, staring dumbly at the squirming man. "What are you on about, mate?" His stomach coiling with dread, he stalked to the bed, shoved Charlie aside, and raised the mattress. Snatching the drawstring purse, he knew it was empty before he ever peered inside. The pleasing bulge in the bag was gone; the cloth draped his hand like a dead cat. He glared ferociously. "Where's the money?"

Charlie grimaced, drew in his shoulders, and sank deeper into the moldy mattress. "Gone."

The word thundered in Denny's head. "What happened to it?"

"Now don't go spare on me, Den. I'm awful sorry. I happened onto a game of five-card loo down in the hold. Just a couple of damp-eared deckhands, so raw I had to teach them the rules of the game." He spread his hands. "I figured to double our stakes, see? But they skinned me." He shrugged. "A streak of beginner's luck, I suppose."

Denny glared through a heated tunnel while the shabby little room whirled in a haze. They were riding the lurching barrel in the first place to save a few quid to get them to Texas. "They took you for a mug, Charlie!" he roared. "They saw you coming, you witless nit."

Confusion twisted Charlie's pasty face. "You're wrong, mate. They didn't even know—"

"Do you really think you found two sailors who couldn't play a round of loo?" Struggling to breathe, Denny jabbed at the air with his finger. "The first trick they played was on you."

Charlie frantically shook his head. "Nah, Den. I don't think so."

Denny lunged and gripped his collar, jerking him to his feet. "There's your trouble, bloke. You never think. You've got 'idiot' scrawled across your forehead. Those boys cut their teeth on dolts like you." He shoved him toward the door. "Now, go on with you. Haul your worthless bum topside and replace every shilling."

Charlie widened his eyes. "H—how am I supposed to do that?"

"Rob a few cabins. Pick some fat pockets. I don't care how you do it—just get it done."

Eyes downcast, Charlie slumped across the threshold.

Catching his arm, Denny spun him around. "You get nicked, and I'll deny ever knowing you. They can toss your rotted corpse off the starboard bow for all I'll care." He wrinkled his brows and scowled. "Mind you, it's a long swim to shore."

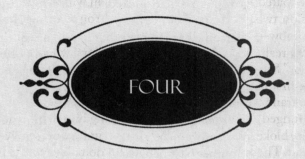

FOUR

Marshall, Texas, April 1905

Addie stepped down from the T&P railway car and took her first shaky steps on Texas soil. Nervous fingers clutching the moss-green fringe on Mother's shawl, she felt like a toddling child traipsing behind her mother on the first day of school. She couldn't pretend that if Mother weren't there, leading her wherever she went, she wouldn't be frightened out of her wits.

The porter handed down their luggage with a broad-toothed smile, tipped his cap, and moved on.

Lifting her chin, Addie stole a peek over her mother's shoulder.

The platform teemed with people of every description, all in a terrible hurry. Most ignored them, brushing blindly past in their haste. Others, all of them men, stared rudely. One young fellow, sporting pointy-toed boots and a bold smile, raised his broad-brimmed hat and winked.

Ducking her head, Addie swallowed the lump in her throat and stepped closer to Mother.

Texans are ill mannered and full of themselves, she thought—and felt like saying so.

Miss Whitfield had forwarded several points of interest about her town, neglecting to mention the improper conduct of its male residents. Marshall, known as the Gateway of Texas, was a regional education center, a major railroad hub, the cotton-marketing center for East Texas, and the first city in the state to have electricity and telegraph service—not to mention boasting a population of more than ten thousand souls.

Evidently, all ten thousand had picked that day to cluster at the depot.

Shifting the cumbersome bags to her other hand, she squirmed with irritation. "I don't know why you refused Miss Whitfield's offer to send her driver, Mother. Now we're totally at the mercy of strangers."

"We are no such thing. The Lord will be our guide."

"Can you at least tell me why you didn't wire ahead?"

Mother raised her strong chin and stared down the street. "Your father thought to catch her off guard. If the lady knew exactly when we were coming, she'd be on her best behavior."

Addie fumed inside. She had the notion there was little chance of catching a woman like Miss Whitfield at anything but her best behavior. When would her parents allow her to trust her own instincts?

Mother leaned to squint past Addie's head. "Over there, dear. The G—Ginocchio." She smiled. "An odd-sounding name for a hotel, if I've pronounced it correctly, but it looks very nice." A determined set to her mouth, she gripped the handles of her cases and straightened her spine. "Come along. We'll find a bite to eat before we hire a ride to our destination. It's bad manners to arrive hungry if we're going to show up unannounced."

Worse manners to show up unannounced, Addie decided, but chose to bite her tongue.

On the walk to the hotel, weighed down by heavy bags and wearing dusty, rumpled clothes, Addie feared they resembled a pair of common laborers. Blushing, she tucked her chin close to her chest and followed the swish of her mother's skirt.

As they reached the path leading to the impressive, well-appointed building, two men rushed them from behind.

Startled, Addie spun, tightening her grip on her luggage.

A stranger towered over her, staring confidently into her eyes. "May I?" he asked, slipping her belongings from her fingers with ease.

Stifling a cry, she gaped helplessly, too captivated by the arresting figure to do otherwise.

The man was as tall as a Mississippi magnolia. His eyes were warm and smiling, the outer lashes so long they curved close to his expressive, dark brows. The skin of his face glowed smooth and dark, sunbaked to a golden brown. A narrow line of fine-whiskered hair grew from a dimpled recess beneath his full bottom lip, extending down his strong chin. But his most striking feature by far was the matted hair tumbling past his shoulders, the tips bleached by the sun.

"I—I—" Addie stammered, unsure whether to swoon or shriek for help.

"Why, thank you," Mother said, her voice sounding far away.

Addie whirled to see her blithely pass her bags to a small, swarthy man. "Mother, for heaven's sake," she hissed, "what are you doing?"

"Allowing these nice young men to render aid." Turning the force of her considerable charm on the lanky man at her side, she smiled her brightest. "And not a moment too soon. I couldn't have carried those things another step."

The fellow beside her tipped his odd little hat, freeing a dark tumble of curls. "Happy to serve, *signorina*."

Mother's laughter floated back to Addie. "That's *signora*, if you don't mind."

Swinging her gaze upward, Addie fell once more into haunting brown eyes. The color of burnt-sugar candy and as clear as a handblown demijohn, they latched onto her, and she couldn't pull away.

"We frightened you," he said. "I apologize." Some men's voices didn't suit them, despite a pleasing appearance or manner of dress. This man's deep rumble served him well, melting in Addie's ears like a match on candle wax.

Her traitorous mother had moved on, chatting with her new companion like an old friend. Addie scowled after them, her brows drawn to a tight knot.

"After you," the man behind her said, interrupting her pout.

She lifted her glare to him, and he waved his hand with a flourish, his once-friendly smile now more of an amused grin.

Before Addie reached the entrance of the hotel, her mother had disappeared.

The stranger stepped onto the boardwalk in front of Addie to hold the door.

Careful to avoid brushing against him, she slipped past and hurried inside. As she gazed around the high-ceilinged lobby, her heart sped up. Instead of weaving through the milling crowd or waiting her turn to speak to the clerk, Mother was nowhere in sight. Frantic, Addie searched the big room, her head spinning and panic crowding her throat.

The stranger touched her shoulder, nodding toward an arched doorway. Inside the dining hall, the dark-skinned man held a chair for her mother as she settled gracefully against the padded cushion.

Weak with relief, Addie reached for her bags. "Thank you. I can manage from here."

He held them out of her reach. "They're pretty heavy. Go on, and I'll carry them to the table for you."

"That won't be necessary."

"It's really no trouble."

Her jaw tightened. "I wouldn't dream of detaining you. I'll take them now, so you and your friend can be on your way."

He tilted his head, the effect on his appeal mesmerizing. "This is on my way. We were headed to the Ginocchio to eat." He glanced toward her mother, holding a menu and conversing with a waiter. "I'm guessing the two of you were, too."

Defeated more by his searching gaze than his answer, she bit back her objections and made her way to the table.

Mother seemed to miss the quizzical look Addie fired as she crossed the room. Instead, she nodded and smiled at something her new friend had said.

Incredibly, he had pulled out the chair next to her, draped a napkin over his arm, and proceeded to pour her a glass of water from a cut glass pitcher. Setting the container aside, he lurched to his feet as Addie approached.

"Say hello to Theodoro Bernardi of Galveston, dear," Mother said. "By way of Sicily, that is. Theo's family owns a restaurant near the shore. Isn't that wonderful?"

Explains his accent, Addie thought. *And his finesse with a pitcher.* She returned his nod of greeting, fighting the urge to shake her head in disbelief. Given three minutes or less, her mother had unearthed the man's family history.

Mother lifted a dazzling smile to the man at Addie's side. "According to Theo, this gracious fellow is Pearson Foster from Houston. It was his idea to help us, Addie." She held out her hand. "Allow me to offer our thanks."

Cupping her slender fingers in his palm, Mr. Foster gave a slight bow. "Like I told your sister here, it's no trouble at all."

Raising her hankie, Mother sought to hide a pleased grin. "Gracious, you do flatter. I'm her mother." She blushed prettily. "But of course, you knew that."

Genuine surprise flashed in his eyes. "On the contrary. It's obvious you're related, since you favor, but I'd never have guessed."

Mother had met her match.

She withdrew her hand. "I'm Mariah McRae from Canton, Mississippi. The pretty and much younger girl at your side is my daughter, Adelina Viola."

Addie cringed at the use of her formal name but stifled the urge to correct it. It didn't matter what name he called her.

"Sit down, dear," Mother said, "so these poor gentlemen can rest their feet."

A twinkle of amusement in his eyes, Pearson held Addie's chair while she reluctantly sat. With wide grins and a boisterous scraping of chairs, the blatant interlopers followed suit.

"There. You see, Addie?" Mother nodded firmly. "I asked God to provide in our hour of need, and He sent us these nice young men. I'm so grateful. Aren't you?"

Addie focused on shaking out her napkin but couldn't prevent her brows from rising. "Um. . .yes, ma'am. I suppose so."

"You know," Mother said, "there's a passage in the Bible that reads, 'Be not forgetful to entertain strangers: for thereby some have entertained angels unawares.'" She winked. "You two aren't angels by any chance?"

Theo chuckled, the sound so merry Addie smiled despite herself. "Mrs. McRae, I assure you, angelic behavior is a thing we'll never be accused of."

Pearson pouted his lips. "Speak for yourself, old man. You're dangerously close to hurting my feelings."

Theo burst into laughter, joined by Mother and Pearson.

Glancing around, Addie blushed.

Nearby patrons looked on, some with amused expressions, others laughing along with them. Anyone passing the table would think they were dear old friends enjoying each other's company instead of strangers who hadn't been properly introduced.

"By the way," Mother said, "Theo and I took the liberty of ordering for you both. I hope you won't mind."

Addie's cheeks warmed. Of course she minded. Only a child needed its mother to order lunch.

Pearson grinned. "I don't care, as long as he doesn't try to eat it for me, too."

Curious, Addie stole a peek at his face.

Glancing her way, he lifted one expressive brow. "Theo's well acquainted with my likes and dislikes. We've been friends since his parents first came to this country. He didn't speak a word of English for the first six months." He shrugged. "Somehow we managed to communicate."

"How long has it been?" Mother asked.

Theo pinched his bottom lip. "Let me see. . .we came to Galveston in April of '91, on Pearson's tenth birthday. I remember because his mother crossed the street to invite me to his party." He winked at Pearson. "I was his favorite birthday present."

Pearson folded his arms on the table, a relaxed smile on his face. "My only present that year, as I recall. I've tried to return him ever since."

"Your birthday's in April, then? What day?"

Addie shot a warning scowl across the bread basket. "Mother, please."

"The twentieth," Pearson said, ignoring her.

Delight lit her mother's pretty face. "For goodness' sake! You share birthdays with Addie. Isn't that a wonderful coincidence?"

Leaning back in his chair, he flashed Addie a warm smile. "I think it is."

"Of course she's a bit younger," Mother continued. "You're twenty-four by my calculations. She just turned twenty-two."

Compelled to stop her before she revealed the color of their bloomers, Addie swiveled toward Theo. "When will you be returning to Galveston?"

A hush fell over the table, magnifying the murmur of voices and the clink of eating utensils in the room. Before she could recover from her inappropriate question, the waiter delivered four lovely salads to the table, bowed at the waist, and backed away.

Addie licked her lips and tried again. "I meant to say, are the two of you here on business?"

Theo picked up his napkin. "Well, miss, the length of our stay is up to the boss here." He jabbed a forkful of lettuce and got it halfway to his mouth before Mother cleared her throat. With a startled glance, he lowered the food to his plate.

Mother tilted her head and shot Pearson a winsome smile. "Do you mind if we say grace?"

Drawing a deep breath, he folded his hands in his lap. "Not at all, ma'am." The words were right, but the slight buckling between his brows said otherwise.

His reaction surprised Addie so completely she scarcely heard the prayer. She found his discomfort so unexpected, her unruly eyes wouldn't stay off him throughout the rest of the meal—a meal that passed in a blinding flash of lively conversation and pleasant laughter.

Pearson explained that they were in the wrecker business—adding "sort of" in a most mysterious tone—and in Marshall on an expedition to raise a shipwrecked steamboat from nearby Caddo Lake.

Mother asked a few polite questions, but their answers were vague, so she tactfully steered the conversation to safer ground.

Once Addie relaxed, she began to enjoy herself. The Ginocchio salad was a first for her, but she vowed it wouldn't be her last. Both men seemed content to focus on conversing with her mother, so Addie was free to sit back and savor every bite.

"I'm mostly a meat and potatoes man," Pearson said, talking around a generous bite. "But this is really good."

Theo shoved in the last bit he could scrape from his plate. "I'm a pasta and sauce man myself, but I have to agree."

They laughed together while Pearson signaled the waiter and handed him several wrinkled bills.

Mother held up her hand. "No, dear. It's my treat. It's the least I can do after you two came to our rescue."

"Sorry, ma'am, it's taken care of." He ducked his head at the waiter. "Go ahead, sir, and keep the change."

"Well then—" Mother pushed back her chair and stood while the others followed suit. She held out her hand to Pearson with a big smile. "I don't know what to say, except thank you. You're very kind."

A faraway look crossed his face, and a tinge of sadness darkened his eyes. "You're very welcome, Mrs. McRae. I'd like to think someone would offer the same courtesy to my mother and sister." His throat rose and fell. "If they were still with us, that is."

Mother's chin jerked up. "Oh Pearson. Do you mean—?"

"Yes, ma'am. I lost them, along with the rest of my family. Almost five years ago now, in the great storm on Galveston Isle."

Addie's heart stirred to pity. She knew which storm he meant. News of the terrible hurricane that swept over the island, washing hundreds of people into the sea, had spread quickly. Shocked by the dreadful report, the citizens of Canton mourned the tragic loss for days.

Her mother reached for Pearson's hand, gripping so hard her knuckles turned white. "I'm so sorry, dear boy. It must've been a devastating loss. But how fortunate that you were spared."

Blushing, he blinked rapidly and turned his face aside. "Thank you, ma'am."

Catching Theo's sleeve, he shook him gently. "Are you ready, old boy? We have work to do, and we'd best get at it."

Mother gave his hand a final pat then turned him loose. "Yes, we need to get started ourselves. We're running late for an appointment."

Addie glanced at her. How could one be late to an appointment they'd never set?

She leaned to pick up her bags, but Pearson's long fingers closed over the handles. With a combination smirk and challenging smile, he hoisted them and nodded at the door.

Theo collected Mother's two cases, and they followed her out to the street.

Fishing in her handbag, she brought out the letter from Miss Whitfield and held up the envelope. "I realize you're new in town as well, but do you have any idea where we might find this address?"

Theo shoved back his cap and whistled. "You don't have to be around Marshall long to hear of Whitfield Manor. It's the grandest place in town."

Mother brightened. "Is it close by? Within walking distance?"

Pearson shook his head. "It's not too far, but you'll have to hire a ride." He pointed. "The house is built on a rise a few miles outside of town. You could see it from here, if not for the trees."

Theo flagged a passing carriage and announced their destination to the driver. While he loaded the luggage, Pearson offered his arm to help them board. Grinning and waving merrily, the men stood on the street and saw them on their way.

As soon as she could speak without being heard, Addie spun on the seat. "Heavens, Mother, what were you thinking? Those two weren't the sort of men we should take up with in a strange town. What would Father say?"

Mother drew back and frowned. "Theo and Pearson? What was wrong with them?"

"They were entirely too forward for one thing. And far too familiar for strangers."

She laughed. "Nonsense, Addie. I'm a fair judge of character, if I say so myself. And I believe I proved it just now." She nodded firmly. "My instincts about those two bore out. They were wonderful young men and perfect gentlemen."

Addie widened her eyes. "But they looked so. . .so coarse, for lack of a better word." The warning glance from under her mother's lashes wilted Addie's smug indignation.

"Character isn't always reflected on the surface, young lady. One look at Theo's bright smile and the sincerity in Pearson's brown eyes, and I knew we were in safe hands." She nudged Addie with her elbow. "Don't act as if they didn't intrigue you. Especially Pearson. I didn't miss how closely you watched him."

Addie's gaze leaped to the back of the driver's head. "Mother! Keep your voice down. I was only—"

"Pearson's a very attractive man, which you can't deny. If I'd judged your father on his rough-and-tumble appearance, I'd never have given him a second glance." Smiling, she stared across Addie's shoulder into the past. "I saw straight through his cocky boasts and swaggering posture to the wonderful man that he is." Back in the present, she winked at Addie. "In the nick of time, too. He almost got away."

Addie shrugged, feigning interest in a passing stand of trees. "Please don't compare your courtship with Father to a brief encounter with a strange man." She rolled her eyes. "And I emphasize *strange*." She focused on her lap, twirling a loose string on the index finger of her glove. "Besides, they'll finish their business in Marshall and go back to where they're from. Chances are I'll never see Mr. Foster again."

A knowing look on her face, Mother tilted up Addie's chin, her slender fingers adjusting the brim of her hat. "I wouldn't count on it, honey. I saw the way he looked at you, too."

Shifting away to hide the flush that warmed her face, Addie fiddled with the row of pearl buttons on her sleeves. "Don't be silly. How could he look at me when he never took his eyes off you?"

Pearson's handsome profile swam in Addie's mind, with his straight nose and strong chin, his peculiar hair, and the haughty smile he gave her—infuriating yet titillating at the same time.

Flustered, she dismissed him with a shake of her head. "I'd prefer we change the subject. I have more important things to occupy my mind." She settled against the seat with a sigh. "Besides, the whole conversation is ridiculous."

"Premature, perhaps," Mother said. "Hardly ridiculous." Her almond eyes softened. "Don't misunderstand. I'm not suggesting you cavort with strange men while you're in Marshall. Your father would have our hides." Reaching for Addie's hand, she squeezed. "Just don't limit God's ability to bring two people together." She held up one finger. "In a proper and respectable way, of course. After all, He managed things quite nicely for your father and me." Nudging Addie again, she chuckled. "Lucky for you, as it turns out. Otherwise, where would you be?"

Addie laughed and leaned her head on her mother's shoulder. "I wouldn't be, I suppose."

"The ways of God are wonderful," Mother said, caressing her cheek. "His generous heart unsearchable. It's important to keep watch at all times, allow Him to orchestrate your destiny. You never know what amazing gifts He has in store, and you don't want to miss a thing."

A large house loomed as they crested the hill, its tall white columns stark against the bright blue Texas sky.

Addie's breath caught and her stomach tensed. "Oh Mother, that must be Whitfield Manor. I can hardly believe we're finally here."

The driver took the sharp curve at the top of the rise then turned into the circular driveway and pulled up in front. The two-story, redbrick building sat off the back side of the gently sloping lot, the crawl space concealed by white lattice. Matching windows fronted the house, four on the bottom and four on top, each as tall and wide as the door and framed in bright white borders. Another lofty casement sat atop the door, with more windows and columns lined up around the corner.

Her mother sighed with pleasure. "It is quite impressive, isn't it?"

Addie inhaled sharply. "More grand than I could've imagined."

The driver helped them down to the stone walkway then scurried to the rear to unload their baggage.

Mother turned with a stern look on her face. "Now remember,

Adelina, let me do the talking."

Would there be any way to stop her? Addie wondered.

Of course, she didn't say so.

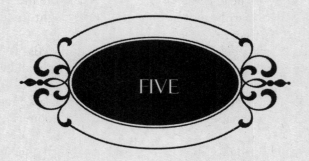

FIVE

The air in Miss Whitfield's spacious study smelled of starched curtains and leather chairs. Each time the kind-faced lady shifted in her seat, a hint of lavender-scented soap drifted across in pleasing waves. She smiled sweetly at Addie then tilted her head at Mother. "Thomas's letter overflowed with praise for your daughter, Mrs. McRae, but never once mentioned how lovely she is."

Mother sat up straighter and preened. "Why, thank you. Addie's our firstborn, the eldest of four girls. Their father and I are proud of each and every one."

Miss Whitfield clasped her hands at her chest. "Four wonderful daughters. My, who wouldn't be proud?"

The women beamed at each other across the heavy oak desk, and Addie felt the first surge of hope. If things continued to progress so pleasantly, Mother would soon be on her way back to Canton, and Addie could begin her life in Texas as Cedric Whitfield's governess. Consumed by curiosity, she had craned her neck from the moment a maid in a ruffled cap admitted them into the cavernous front hall. So far, there'd been no sign of a little boy.

"How long have you known our Dr. Moony?"

The translucent glow of Miss Whitfield's cheeks turned bright pink. "Thomas and I attended school together up north. He went on to pursue a higher education, and I wound up in Marshall. We haven't seen each other since, but we never lost touch." She smiled wistfully. "You might say we're kindred spirits."

"Oh, what a shame," Mother said. "You know he's a widower now."

Miss Whitfield's head came up. "Yes, Thomas wrote me."

Addie inhaled sharply and sat forward. She'd caught the meddling spark in her mother's eye.

The rascal reached across the desk and patted Miss Whitfield's hand. "If you enjoyed each other's company so much, why did you allow a separation?"

Groaning inside, Addie clenched her fists in her lap. Her coveted position—and the shade of Miss Whitfield's bloomers—was in jeopardy.

"What brought you to Marshall, ma'am?" she asked quickly, hoping to steer the conversation to safer ground. "Do you have family here?"

Pulling her startled gaze from Mother, a bit of color returned to the poor woman's face. "I did at the time. My father was a shrewd businessman, you see. Forty years ago, Marshall was the fifth-largest city in Texas." She lifted her chin. "A prosperous Confederate city. Somehow, despite the eventual occupation by Union forces, Daddy maintained control of his vast holdings. He built this old house, and we've been here ever since."

"He did well for himself," Mother said. "He's made a lovely home for you here."

Miss Whitfield smiled. "I haven't confessed the whole story, I'm afraid. My father didn't amass all of his fortune from that unfortunate war. We're old money, as pompous and posturing as it sounds. Daddy brought his fortune with him when he came to this country. He was quite the philanthropist, however, and I'm quite proud of the good things he accomplished with our wealth." A faraway look crossed her face. "We had hoped Cedric would one day fill his shoes. He stands to inherit all of this one day, only—"

She sniffed demurely and folded her hands on top of the desk. "Speaking of Ceddy, I suppose we should begin the interview."

Thankfully, Mother stood, gathering her parasol and gloves. "The two of you have quite a lot to discuss, and I'm sure you don't need me. If you'll direct me to the parlor, I'll wait there for my daughter."

"You'll do no such thing," Miss Whitfield said, reaching for a small brass bell.

The pleasant jangle brought a polite knock at the door, and the maid in the white cap peered inside. "Yes'm?"

"Delilah, will you show Mrs. McRae—" Her eyes widened as a small figure in khaki shorts and a striped percale waist staggered into the study, clinging blindly to Delilah's skirts.

Addie's first glimpse of Ceddy Whitfield took her breath. The boy was achingly beautiful.

Clear blue eyes dominated his delicate pixie features, and flyaway blond wisps fell over his forehead to tangle with his sweeping lashes. His graceful bottom lip dimpled, and his rosebud mouth turned up a bit at the corners. A beam of light from the hall shone through his hair, illuminating the top of his head like a kiss from God. Swinging his head dreamily from side to side, he seemed cut off from the presence of mere mortals.

Irritation marring her pleasant face, Miss Whitfield cleared her throat. "I asked you to keep him occupied until"—she glanced at Addie and her mother—"after."

Delilah caught Ceddy's shoulder to guide him from the room.

Whether her touch set him off or he'd noticed the company of strangers, Addie couldn't tell, but he moaned and grimaced, straining toward the far corner.

"I done jus' like you say, ma'am," Delilah said, scrambling to hold on to him. "I kept right on his heels the whole time, only I heard you ring the bell."

Ceddy's moans became shrill screams as he struggled to escape her grasping hands.

The older woman bent close to the hysterical boy's face. "It's all right, precious. Won't you please go with Lilah? She has a cookie for you, I'm sure. After a while she'll take you out back to dig for rocks." She glanced at the maid. "Won't you, Lilah?"

"I sho' will." She stretched out her hand. "Come along, sugar."

Ceddy eased from the corner and ambled out ahead of the maid.

Before she left, Delilah glanced over her shoulder. "I'm real sorry, Miss Priscilla."

Pulling an embroidered handkerchief from her waistband, Miss Whitfield blotted her top lip. "Never you mind. Take Ceddy to the kitchen; then come show Mrs. McRae to her quarters. Make her comfortable and bring her refreshments. It's awhile yet before suppertime."

"Yes, ma'am."

The door closed, and Mother smiled at their hostess. "That's very kind, Miss Whitfield. I'm grateful."

She waved the hankie. "No trouble at all."

Mother's dark eyes softened. "He's a lovely boy. You must be so proud."

Their hands clasped briefly. Miss Whitfield's damp lashes fluttered. "Thank you."

Mother had made another conquest.

Their heads tucked close together, the women chatted quietly until Delilah returned. With a last encouraging wink, Mother backed from the room, shutting the door on Addie and her prospective employer.

Priscilla Whitfield cleared her throat, bringing Addie to the edge of her seat. Despite the gracious smile on the lady's face, there was a change in her demeanor. "I suppose you have questions. About Ceddy, I mean."

Addie sat straighter and modestly folded her hands on the desk. What could be said to explain the wild behavior they'd just witnessed? "I'm sorry, ma'am. I'm not sure what to ask."

She nodded. "That's understandable. I'll just begin, then. Shall I?"

"Yes, please."

She settled against her high-backed chair. "As I mentioned in my letter, my nephew's son is an unusual child."

Unusual or unmanageable? If only Addie had taken the warning to heart. . .

"He was a beautiful infant. Positively angelic. People noticed he was special and commented often on his appearance." She smiled. "Peter and Eliza doted on Ceddy from the second they laid eyes on him and loved showing him off around the community." Her smile waned. "I suppose that's why they noticed his differences so early."

"Differences?"

"He didn't smile like most babies or respond to their voices. He wouldn't meet their eyes and became easily distracted."

Addie nodded thoughtfully. "I can understand their concern."

Miss Whitfield pursed her lips. "We tried to comfort them, told them the child just needed time to develop properly. When Ceddy got older and his. . .*unique* behavior grew more noticeable, his parents took him around the globe searching for answers. The closest we came to understanding his illness was in a London hospital. Doctors there diagnosed him with nervous mental disease."

Addie frowned. "What does it mean?"

Miss Whitfield glanced up from the desktop and whatever else held her anguished gaze. "I have no idea, to be honest. I can only describe his current behavior."

Addie leaned closer. "Please do."

"Well. . .he still avoids eye contact, still resists smiling. Loud noises, strong odors, and the like startle him. Any change in routine angers him. When he's upset, he flaps his hands or rocks himself. Often he sits on the floor and spins like a top. Left alone, he entertains himself for hours, with no need for human interaction."

She stared out the window at the manicured lawn, profound sadness etched on her face. "He forms attachments to objects yet won't allow cuddles or hugs." Tucking her bottom lip, she dug in her teeth so hard the skin turned white. The attempt to contain her grief failed. Large tears pooled at the corners of her eyes. "I find the last trait the saddest of all, and the hardest to accept."

"I can imagine how difficult that would be."

"No, dear," Miss Whitfield said, wiping her eyes with the tips of her slender fingers. "I'm sorry, but you can't." Her trembling voice held no rebuke. Taking a quick breath, she regained her composure. "One last thing. Ceddy becomes preoccupied—obsessed, if you will—with certain items. Rocks and stones in particular."

Remembering the mischievous charges from her past, Addie grinned. "It seems a harmless obsession for a boy. At least it's not frogs and snakes."

A smile tugged at the woman's lips. "Except he won't throw them away. His room resembles an excavation site."

Addie chuckled. "I see your point."

"As you may have noticed, he will not speak."

"No speech at all?"

Miss Whitfield sighed and shook her head. "Not for a very long time, though he spoke quite well in the beginning."

A lump swelled in Addie's throat. "So he's mute?"

"Not according to my understanding of the word. *Webster's International* defines *mute* as 'unable to speak' or 'lacking the power of speech.' Ceddy meets neither criterion."

"I'm not sure I understand."

"The doctors say he still has the faculty of speech. He simply won't use it." She shrugged. "I suppose he doesn't see the necessity."

Addie shook her head. "How could that be? Speech is the greatest tool for communication."

Miss Whitfield sobered. "You're beginning to catch on, dear. With the exception of meeting his most basic needs, Ceddy hasn't the slightest desire to communicate."

Addie struggled with an urge to abandon the conversation. She longed to bolt from the chair and join Mother for refreshments, where she'd find the topic of conversation no weightier than adding one lump or two to her cup of tea. The pretense of appearing knowledgeable on the matter of broken children left her drained. Uncomfortable, Addie squirmed in her chair.

Miss Whitfield's probing gaze flickered away. "Of course, these are just parts of his complex personality. With the passage of time, you'll discover the rest on your own." She angled her head. "If you accept the position, that is."

Staring at her hands twisting in her lap, Addie cleared her throat. "What are the predictions for his future? I mean, what are Ceddy's prospects?"

Lips pursed, Miss Whitfield studied her for several moments then slid open the shallow drawer in front of her. "I can best answer your question with an article Eliza discovered shortly after Ceddy's diagnosis. Along with our faith in God's plan, this story inspired us to hope."

Unfolding a yellowed sheet of newsprint, the creases so worn they'd torn in spots, she spread it carefully on the desk. "A child born in Dalston, London, in 1835, was labeled a deaf-mute and developmentally disabled. They called him Poor James, an appropriate name considering his family gave up on him when he turned fifteen, committing him to the Earlswood Asylum. James nearly succumbed to the bleak environment, lapsing into terrible mood swings and exhibiting violent episodes of rage."

Addie cringed. "I'm not the least surprised. How awful for him." She'd heard horrid tales of such institutions, and the thought of a helpless child locked away in a hospital for the insane pained her chest.

"Awful indeed," Miss Whitfield said. "Until a discerning employee suggested a handcrafting session for the boy. The staff introduced him to woodworking tools, and he took to it wholeheartedly, designing intricate figurines and elaborate pieces of furniture as if he'd been born with an awl in his hand. Before long, Poor James became the "Genius of Earlswood Asylum"—from discarded child to celebrated artist." She smiled. "In fact, his lovely masterpieces are on display in England still today."

Pleased with the ending, Addie sat back in her chair. "It's a wonderful story, but I don't see a connection to Ceddy's plight."

"Cedric has a similar gift in relation to rocks and stones. His father first saw it when he brought home a volume on gems and minerals. From that day, Ceddy spent hours poring over the book. At first, Peter supposed the pictures fascinated his son—until he realized Ceddy had lined up his entire collection of colorful pebbles according to the classifications in the book. He was six at the time."

"Amazing."

"From that moment, Peter began searching once more for cures. Eliza, God rest her, made the wise and heartfelt decision to stop chasing miracles and accept her son as he was. Over the protests of my brother and nephew, she ceased all interference from outside sources and began to raise Ceddy according to her instincts and God's direction. In their bumbling fashion, both men raised a stink, along with the rest of the Whitfield family, but the darling girl held her ground."

She carefully folded the article and put it away. "Once Ceddy relaxed, he flourished. His nervousness improved and his appetite picked up. For the first time in years, he seemed happy. This fact alone won my nephew over to his wife's way of thinking." She sighed. "That's when he agreed to leave Ceddy to me, should anything happen to them."

Addie leaned forward. "Because?"

"I stood in wholehearted agreement with his mama. Eliza knew she could trust me to keep the swarming horde from descending on the poor little thing." Her jaw tightened. "And I shall. As long as I draw a breath, Ceddy will be safe from those who seek to poke and prod at his fragile spirit."

"I should think the family would honor his parents' wishes."

Anger clouded her features as she struggled with unseen foes. "Certain of them feel compelled by duty to 'fix' Ceddy. I'm afraid, despite their good intentions, they'll never see him as anything but flawed."

Relaxing her chin, she drew a breath. "You're very young, Addie. I'll understand if you find our plight too much to bear, but I hope you'll consider the position. I sense in you the same loving spirit that embodied the boy's mother."

Addie lowered her eyes. "Thank you. That's a heady compliment." Heady but undeserved. She couldn't possibly accept the demanding position. Glancing up, she wrung her hands and searched for something to say.

Miss Whitfield held up her finger. "Don't answer yet. You need ample time to decide about such an important matter." Nodding as if the issue were resolved, she continued, "I'd like you to stay on at Whitfield Manor for a few weeks. You can observe Ceddy's day-to-day activities and get a better idea of what's expected before you commit."

Startled, Addie shook her head. "I'm afraid that's impossible. Mother can't stay away from home for long." She blinked rapidly, struggling to find a way out. "My father and sisters need her."

Miss Whitfield's knowing eyes studied her closely. "I'd love to have her, dear, but I'm certain a bright young woman like you can manage without her mother."

Embarrassed, Addie tucked her lips. "And if I choose not to take the position?"

"I'll arrange your passage home and accompany you straight to your doorstep. Your parents have my solemn word."

Before Addie could protest further, Miss Whitfield swiveled in her chair and stood, signaling the end of the interview. "Talk it over with your mother, dear. She appears to be a very wise woman."

Addie struggled to her feet, her knees trembling. "Yes, I'll speak to her." She held out her hand. "And thank you for considering me."

The woman squeezed her fingers, determination burning in her eyes. "I believe God brought us together for a reason, Addie. Let's sort out what He has in store for us, shall we?"

Ceddy shoved the last bite of cookie into his mouth then pulled the wooden box from under the bed. Running his thumbnail over the rows of square sections, he counted each time he passed a divider. Twenty-five across. Twenty-five down. Grunting, he hefted the case, struggled into the window seat, and settled the collection onto his lap where a ray of sunlight lit fires inside the bright stones.

There were other boxes under his bed, filled with igneous, sedimentary, and metamorphic rock. These were his favorites, the gemstones, each labeled and tucked into the special box Papa built for them.

Wriggling at the thought of his father, he started his count. *One, agate. Two, alexandrite. Three, aquamarine. Four, chrysocolla. Five, chrysoprase.*

Pausing, he smoothed his fingertips across the next one in the box. The side facing him was the color of milk mixed with water, rough and cloudy like white alum. Traces of kimberlite still clung to the edges.

He lifted the stone from the velvet lining and turned the smooth side to the dusty sunbeam. The hidden sparkle inside blinked up at him, and the words from the big book in the library trailed across his mind. *Gemstone. Mineral species. Crystallized carbon. Hardest known naturally occurring mineral.*

With a contented sigh, he returned it to its place, climbed down, and shoved the collection box into the deep shadows under the bed.

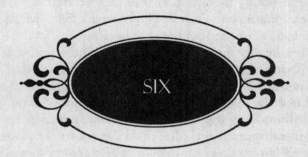

SIX

Pearson held the door of the Ginocchio Hotel for Theo then followed him onto the wide porch, the drum of their heels on the cedar planks loud in the morning air.

After seeing the women off to Whitfield Manor the day before, they'd booked a room in the hotel. Pearson had looked forward to a restful evening after traveling three hundred miles, but he'd spent a fitful night instead.

The cheerful clerk at the desk said they'd find supplies and information about Caddo Lake at a nearby store, so they'd set out early to find the place.

Yawning, Pearson gazed around with bleary eyes. "Which way, *paisan*?"

Theo shook his head. "You navigate the Gulf of Mexico in the dead of night but can't follow simple directions?"

Pearson chuckled and gazed overhead. "There are no stars to chart my course."

Theo's brows drew together. "The only stars are in your eyes. You're distracted by the pretty *bambolina* we met yesterday, aren't you? Your big feet haven't touched the ground since Miss Addie McRae wrestled you for her bags." He nudged Pearson with his elbow. "A fight she nearly won, I might add."

Pearson slanted his eyes at his irksome friend. "Which way, Theo?"

701

His cheeks round with glee, Theo pointed. "Dead ahead, Christopher Columbus. Washington Street to the town square." He cut his gaze to Pearson. "She was mighty pretty, though."

Catching him by the collar, Pearson herded him down the steps. He wouldn't admit it, but Theo was on the mark. Miss McRae and her dainty face had stolen precious hours of his sleep.

"Sure is a mighty fine day." Long-legged Theo strolled beside him at a leisurely pace, as if he hadn't a single care—or a sunken ship to raise.

"It is indeed," Pearson agreed, gazing at mounded white clouds suspended in a blue sky. "I'm ready to come out of this jacket."

Varied shops lined the boardwalk, and fine carriages transporting dapper men and spruced-up ladies filled the streets. The women wore tall, feathered hats and colorful wraps. Their escorts sported brushed derbies, turned-down collars, and canes.

A well-heeled couple approached from the opposite direction. The gentleman hurriedly switched sides with his lady, placing himself between her and Pearson. Lifting their noses, they offered a wide berth.

Pearson tipped his hat, giving them a devilish grin, and then nudged Theo. "Looks like we failed inspection."

Theo swatted his back. "This isn't the island, *paisano*. We stick out like knots on a whittling stick."

"Did you see all the finery they were trussed up in? It's not Sunday, is it?"

"Today's Wednesday, but I think every day's Sunday here. We'd best hurry and find our way to the swamp where we belong."

A few blocks from the hotel, Theo slowed his steps and whistled. "Would you take a look at that?"

Pearson glanced over his shoulder, expecting to see another pretty girl. Instead, the oddest contraption he'd ever seen raced along the street, darting easily between mounted horsemen and dodging rigs. It resembled a fancy wagon, complete with four wheels and a buggy top but missing a pony. Mouth agape, Pearson stared until it bounced around a turn and disappeared from sight.

Theo wagged his head. "Brother, that was something to see."

"A horseless carriage they're called. All the rage up North."

"Maybe, but I wouldn't trade in my horse for one. I can't see them ever taking hold in the South."

Pearson sniffed and shook his head. "I'm sure you're right. Still. . .it would be grand to drive one." Nudging Theo's shoulder, he jutted his chin at the building across the street. "We've arrived, my friend. There's the store we're looking for."

They crossed the rutted road, Theo reading aloud the large, painted letters on the sign. "J. WEISMAN & COMPANY—THE FIRST DEPARTMENT STORE IN TEXAS. What do you reckon a department store has for sale?"

Pulling a slip of paper from his pocket, Pearson grinned. "Hopefully, some of the items on our list." Theo reached for the doorknob, but Pearson brushed aside his hand. "I'll go first, thank you. And let me do the talking."

Theo scowled. "Why?"

"Don't you remember that time in Amarillo?"

A sheepish look crossed his face. "You're right. You'd better do the talking."

Leaving the pleasing warmth of the early spring sunshine, they strolled beneath the bell jingling over the door. The morning chill lingered inside the store, so Pearson pulled his jacket tighter, thankful he'd left it on.

The cavernous shop was like nothing he'd ever seen before. Equal parts general store, hardware store, and clothing boutique, there seemed to be something for everyone. Potent odors wafted from the four corners—familiar smells such as tobacco, spices, and soap. One wall held the usual items sold in a general store—straight razors, shaving cups, eyeglasses, hairbrushes, and looking glasses. Another offered churns, coffee mills, iron kettles, dishware, and silver utensils. Behind the glass counter, folded neatly in stacks, were woolen socks, handkerchiefs, wallets, cravats, and suspenders. In a corner along the back wall sat a brightly colored display of fabrics, buttons, and ribbons. Along the upstairs rail were racks of hats, high-top boots, ladies' shawls, and fancy dresses.

Even toys for children, Pearson thought, dodging the handle of a wagon with brightly painted slats for sides.

A stately gentleman with a heavily waxed mustache approached the counter. "Help you fellows?"

Pearson took off his hat. "Yes, sir. We're in need of a few supplies."

The proprietor swept his arm to take in the room. "I'm sure we can accommodate."

Pearson grinned. "I'm inclined to agree."

Looking eager to please, the man pulled out a pad and the stub of a pencil. "What can I get for you?"

Holding the list beneath a dusty beam, Pearson started from the top. "We'll need a healthy coil of rope, a couple of lanterns, coal oil"—he pointed to a high shelf over the man's head—"three or four of those oilcloths." He scanned the room. "You don't carry lumber by any chance?"

The clerk bobbed his head proudly. "Sure do. Stacked out back in the shed."

Properly impressed, Pearson nodded. "Well, that's fine. We'll need enough to build a platform over the water." Tapping his chin, he gazed around the room. "I suppose that's all for now. Later we'll need a couple of rowboats, oars, and a sturdy lift rig, if you have one."

The man pointed to a storage bin. "Like that Yale & Towne hoist and pulley over there?"

Pearson grinned. "Yes, sir. Exactly like that one. Now, if you can point me to a wagon for hire so we can haul all these goods, I'd be much obliged."

The man stopped tallying their purchases and straightened. One hand on his hip, he gazed from Pearson to Theo, his eyes alight with mirth. "You're headed out to Lake Caddo, am I right?"

Pearson shared a look with Theo.

Before they could answer, he chuckled. "I know what this is about. You boys are set to try your hand at the *Mittie*."

Theo squirmed, shuffling his feet like a schoolboy.

Pearson swallowed, taking his time to answer. "What makes you say so?"

Bending behind the counter, the clerk brought up a lantern in each hand and slid them toward Pearson. "You're not the first to try it, believe me." He cocked his head. "Say, where are you fellows from?"

"Down Galveston way," Theo said, grabbing a bottle of oil and adding it to the items on the counter.

"You're seamen, then?"

"Sometimes," Pearson said, dodging his eyes.

"What makes a couple of young sea dogs think they can find the *Mittie Stephens* when experienced men have searched for thirty years?"

"Well, we—"

"Your mariner skills may help you dodge sharks but won't do you a bit of good in a nest of cottonmouths." He flashed a knowing wink. "Unlike the alligators you'll meet in the swamp, you boys have bitten off a little more than you can chew." Laughter shook his body. "You'll wrestle a few gators, too, before you've earned your right to the *Mittie*."

Pearson leaned against the counter. "Well then. . .since you're onto us, maybe you can tell us where to find Catfish John."

The clerk stilled, his eyebrows lifted. "I see you've done your homework."

"How about it?" Pearson pressed. "Can you tell us where he is?"

The man opened his mouth to speak, but the overhead bell jangled, dragging their attention to the door.

An elderly gent shuffled inside, pulling off his sweat-stained hat with gnarled fingers. He moved in the slow, measured gait of the aged, men with stiff joints and nothing but time on their hands. "Mornin', folks." Wincing, he patted the door. "Ought to prop this thing open, Sam. Warmer outside than it is in here."

"That's a good idea," the clerk called. "Go on and brace it, then." Lowering his voice, he nodded at Pearson. "Must be your lucky day. There's the man you need to see."

"Catfish John?"

He grinned. "Not *that* lucky. This here's Mr. Robb, a plantation owner on the Caddo. If you ask him real nice-like, he just might tell you where John can be found."

SEVEN

Addie stood at the full-length mirror adjusting the sash at her waist and marveling at the furnishings surrounding her. Her room in the big house Father built in Canton was grand, to say the least, but unimpressive compared to the opulence of Whitfield Manor.

She ran her fingertips along the gilded frame of the looking glass, touched the bronze bust of William Shakespeare on the desk. Every detail shouted wealth aplenty—with impeccable taste, of course. Yet for all the manor's lavish comforts, Addie wouldn't trade a home filled with little girls' laughter for the heartache sleeping in the room next door.

How could one endure such pain and disappointment? How did Miss Whitfield manage Ceddy every day?

At the lady's forceful suggestion, Addie slipped into his room after the meal to offer a plate of treacle tart and clotted cream. The experiment produced disastrous results, ending with the child cowering in the corner and Addie splattered with cream.

A tap on the door jolted her heart. She prayed it wasn't Miss Whitfield with another plot to help Ceddy warm up to her. She wasn't up to the task, and besides, she didn't plan to stay. When her mother left on the afternoon train, Addie would be sitting beside her, shoulders slumped in defeat.

The door opened before she reached it, and Mother peered inside. "There you are, *sioshitek*. Look at you, already dressed. I feared my knock might awaken you."

Alarm tightened Addie's stomach. Mother seldom addressed her in Choctaw. When she did, dire news often followed. She watched her mother's serene face carefully as she approached. "Oh my," she said, one hand over her heart. "What's wrong?"

Mother blinked at her. "Why, nothing, dear."

Addie shook her head. "You don't speak Grandmother's language unless you're troubled."

She chuckled and pulled Addie close. "How clever of you to notice this about me."

Drawing back, Addie tilted her head. "I've had years of practice."

Caressing her hair, Mother offered a wobbly smile. "Actually, I am quite distressed, but I have every reason to be. I'm leaving here today, traveling three hundred miles away from my firstborn."

Addie lowered her chin. "Well, cheer yourself, Mother, because I'm going with you."

"No, darling." Her knuckle curled beneath Addie's chin and raised her head. "No, you're not."

Addie had expected stunned silence. A disappointed pause. Mother's quick answer meant she anticipated the announcement. Pulling away, Addie busied herself at the mirror, adjusting her hair. "I've given it a lot of thought. I was up half the night, in fact. I regret putting everyone through all this trouble, but I'm absolutely certain it's the right thing to do."

"Addie. . ."

She spun. "I don't belong here, Mother. I have no special training for this sort of thing. I'm not the right person for the job."

"Nonsense. You're exactly what that poor child needs."

"You saw for yourself how difficult he is. I'm not sure if I. . . I don't know if I'm—"

Mother lifted one hand to cut her off then crossed to sit on the bed, patting the spot beside her. "Come over here."

Slouching like a disciplined child, Addie slunk to join her.

Mother caught her hands, wringing in her lap, and held them still. "I've watched you win the trust of innocent creatures in the past, from hurting children to feral cats. It's your gift."

"But don't you see? That's the problem. Ceddy Whitfield is both. He's a wounded boy but wilder than any beast I've ever seen."

"Not really. Unsettling behavior seems more extreme from a cherubic child."

"If you offer food to a wild animal, it won't shriek and sling it in your face." She touched her still-damp curls. "I don't think I could bear that happening again."

Mother had the nerve to laugh. "A touch of clotted cream is good for the complexion, honey. Don't underestimate yourself. You can bear more than you think."

"I'm not so sure anymore."

"Then I'll be sure for you," Mother insisted. "This is your chosen vocation, Adelina. All your work with children up to this point was to prepare you for this position. You won't tuck tail and run when it counts the most."

Tears spilled down Addie's cheeks. "You have entirely too much faith in me, and I fear it's misplaced." She met the familiar brown eyes, seeking comfort in their depths. "I'm frightened, Mama."

"Of course you are. We're all afraid when confronted by our destiny." Reaching beneath her high-buttoned collar, Mother's searching fingers emerged with the beaded necklace she wore so often it seemed a part of her. Pulling it over her head, she slipped it around Addie's neck and patted the speckled stone dangling at the end. "There now."

Addie gripped the polished bloodstone. "What are you doing? Not your mother's jasper necklace. I couldn't."

"Hush, now. They don't belong to you yet. That privilege comes on your wedding day." She squeezed the hand that held the pendant. "Just wear it for courage until I see you again. When you feel the weight against your heart, think of your grandmother. She was the bravest woman I've ever known."

Lifting damp lashes, Addie searched her face. "Are you sure?"

"I'll feel better knowing you have it."

With a ragged sigh, Addie shook her head. "I haven't decided to stay."

Mother gave her hands a final squeeze then stood and walked to the door. "I want you to pray before you make up your mind. That's all I ask. If you feel you should leave on the afternoon train, I'll help you pack."

Addie gave her a grudging nod and watched the door close at her back. Mother had best be ready to help because she'd already made up her mind. She just hadn't the nerve to say so.

Grinning like a fisherman with a bobbing cork, Mr. Robb's head wagged. "Why, sure I have time to talk to these young fellows about Catfish John." The twinkle in his eyes deepening, he motioned toward the door. "If you don't mind waiting whilst I make a quick purchase, we'll sit outside and chat a spell. These old bones can't abide the chill in here for long."

"Very good, sir," Pearson said. "We'll wait for you there." He opened the door to the accompanying overhead jingle then followed Theo out of Weisman's into the warm sunlight.

Theo braced his hands on his hips and stared down the street. "You suppose that old coot knows anything?"

Pearson shrugged. "We'll have to take our chances, won't we? Right now he's our only lead."

Theo pivoted toward the door. "I think they're playing us for ninnies." He pointed. "Listen at them in there. They're laughing at us."

Pearson pulled a wood-slatted chair around and took a seat. "Let them laugh. As long as Mr. Robb steers us in the right direction, I don't care."

"Well, I just might," Theo groused, straddling the chair beside him.

A rowdy group of young men crossed the street and hurried along the storefront, talking loud and jostling for position with their elbows. Two men in tall hats and pretentious suits strolled from the other direction, lost in a hushed conversation. A flirtatious couple rounded the corner of the building, the giggly girl blushing at being caught by Pearson's gaze, the boy intent on grasping for her hand.

The boisterous commotion in the street hadn't faded since they'd been inside the store. The denizens of Marshall hustled past in droves, oblivious to strangers in their midst, hatching a plan to snatch a prize from under their noses.

Pearson nodded at the milling throng. "Don't you wonder why they're not looking for the *Mittie*? Why they haven't already found her? She can't be hidden that well, can she? Finding a great hulking thing at the bottom of a lake is not like searching the ocean floor."

Theo nodded. "It would be something, wouldn't it? If we came all the way from Galveston and pulled up a fortune in gold, when all the time these folks were sitting right on top of it?"

Pearson leaned forward and laced his fingers. "I've wondered the same about Lafitte's gold. Why aren't there leagues of men contending with me for it? How could a man hear of a lost bounty and lack the heart to search?" He shook his head. "It's not in me, Theo. I'm not made that way."

Theo nodded thoughtfully. "I suppose most people are busy chasing the fire in their own chests. Just because a man works for years baking bread for someone else doesn't mean he's not burning inside to own the bakery."

Pearson bit his lip and nodded.

"Look at Rosie," Theo continued. "For years she served slop up and down the Strand, saving every penny she earned. Now she has a little place of her own. It took most of her life, but she chased her treasure and found it." He nudged Pearson's arm. "It's just that your idea of treasure is a tad more literal than most."

Grinning, Pearson sat back and crossed his arms. "So what about you? What hidden riches do you covet?"

Before Theo could answer, a bevy of young women sashayed toward them, their sweeping skirts, mounded curls, and brightly colored parasols crowding the boardwalk. Tittering and cooing, they danced past, lovely preening birds on display.

His attention snared, Theo tipped his cap at each smiling girl as she went by. Only when their retreating backs turned the corner did he pull his gaze around to Pearson. "I'm sorry. What did you ask me?"

Shaking his head, Pearson laughed. "Never mind, paisan. I think I have my answer."

Mr. Robb tottered out of Weisman's, paused by the door to summon his best offering for the spittoon, then joined them with a broad smile.

Pearson stood and offered the old man his seat, stepping over Theo's long legs to slide into the chair opposite him.

"Turning into a mighty fine day, ain't it?" Mr. Robb said.

Pearson leaned to nod at him. "It surely is. And Marshall's a real nice town."

Mr. Robb raised his chin. "Yes indeed. Thanks to Mr. Gould and cotton."

Frowning, Pearson glanced at Theo and shrugged. "Come again, sir?"

"Jay Gould, president of T&P Railroad. He moved his operation to Marshall in the '70s. The town grew rich overnight. Before long, we were one of the South's largest markets in cotton."

Theo smiled. "Jay Gould and cotton. I get it now."

Mr. Robb leaned over and nudged him. "Speaking of money and cotton, I could use your strong backs and nimble fingers on my farm. I'd pay you a fair picker's wage." Grinning, he lowered his voice. "You'll get rich a lot quicker that way than looking for sunken gold."

Theo slapped his knee. "The clerk told you. I knew it!"

Grinning, Mr. Robb patted his back. "He did, but he didn't have to. Why else would two strangers come asking for Catfish John?"

Pearson scooted his chair so he could see the man better. "Well then? Now that our secret's out, can you tell us where to find him?"

His unruly brows rose to peaks. "Mind you, catching up with Catfish John could be as hard as raising the *Mittie*."

Pearson shot him a slant-eyed challenge. "Try me. I'm fairly skilled at finding things." Theo cleared his throat, and Pearson scowled. "Most things, that is."

"Well, all right," Mr. Robb said, settling his back against the slats of his chair. "He lives on an island out on the lake—no one knows exactly where. He only comes to shore to sell fish and store up supplies. You could wait around one of the landings until he comes off the lake with a stringer of catfish. Otherwise, the chance of running across him is slim."

"I'll take that chance," Pearson said.

Mr. Robb shook his head. "You're on a fool's quest, you know, one even John can't help you with. Many a man has scoured the Caddo looking for that ship, men who've lived their lives working the steamboats. They know the routes, some even lived on the lake, but none of them has ever found her. What makes you think you can?"

"To be honest, sir"—Pearson winked—"I'm more determined."

Mr. Robb blinked, his jaw going slack. Sudden laughter bubbled up his throat, first as a wheezing sound then tumbling from his mouth in belly-shaking glee.

Theo joined in, draping one arm around his shoulders and patting him.

Except for the hint of a smile, one he quickly bit back, Pearson fought to stay sober lest the old man doubt his sincerity.

When Mr. Robb finally caught his breath, he clutched his knees with both hands and swiveled toward Pearson. "Son, you've given me the best laugh I've had all year. For that, and because I admire your gumption, I'm going to tell you what you want to know. You take the Port Caddo road, the Old Stagecoach Road they call it, heading east out of town. It's a good long ride. Go to old Port Caddo or the old Uncertain Landing and talk to some of the dockhands who used to work with the steamboats, loading and unloading goods. Those that are left are commercial fishermen now, guides and so forth."

He paused. "Who knows. . .you might find a leftover Caddo Indian still lurking in the woods. Then you'd have a bona fide tracker." He snorted. "You'll need one to find that ol' *Mittie*."

Theo's big eyes held a question. "Did you say you were uncertain about which landing? Because if you don't know, how can we hope to find it?"

Mr. Robb's shoulders shook again. "No, son. Uncertain is the name. The old steamboat captains had the dickens of a time mooring their vessels there, so it became known as Uncertain Landing." Beaming, he tilted his head. "Come to think on it, it's right comical that you two are headed out there seeking an uncertain treasure on the wreckage of a ship whose location is the most uncertain part of all."

Standing, the old man stretched then scratched his midsection. "If I can help you boys with anything else you're uncertain about, come out to the house and see me." The twinkle had returned to his eyes. "It's not too late to change your minds, you know. My offer to pick cotton still holds."

Smiling despite himself, Pearson stood and offered his hand. "I'm pleased you find our plight so entertaining, Mr. Robb. I've enjoyed meeting you, sir, and thank you for the information. I guess we'll pass on your generous offer, though."

"Suit yourself, young fella. You all be careful, you hear?" With a jaunty salute, Mr. Robb shuffled away, still chuckling as he turned the corner.

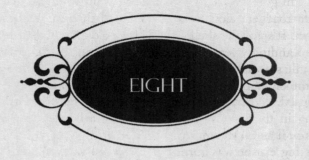

EIGHT

Breakfast passed in an uncomfortable blur. Every word Miss Whit-field said, every topic broached, held the erroneous assumption that Addie would stay. Her own mother behaved the same way.

Watching them, Addie squirmed in discomfort. How would she break the news to the two gaily chatting women that her clothes were already tucked inside the trunk waiting just inside her bedroom door? Resisting the urge to sit on her wringing hands, Addie stole a glance at the tall clock in the corner. Would it ever be time to leave for the station?

Miss Whitfield leaned to touch her arm. "I see you're quite fascinated by the longcase clock, Addie. It was a gift to my parents from Alfred, the Duke of Edinburgh."

She stared wistfully at the old timepiece as if remembering grander days. "Did you know they're becoming known as grandfather clocks?"

She smiled. "And all because of a song penned in 1876 by Henry Clay Work. As the story goes, there was an inn down in Piercebridge on the border of Yorkshire and County Durham called the George Hotel. Mr. Work visited this establishment and learned the legend of the elderly Jenkins brothers who once owned it. The lobby of the inn had a longcase clock that kept perfect time until one of the gentlemen died—at which point it began to falter. When the other brother joined him in death, the old clock stopped for good."

"How fascinating," Mother said.

"Henry Clay Work went home and set the story to music." She inclined her head toward the ceiling. "If you'll indulge me, it's a quaint little ditty that goes like this:

"My grandfather's clock
Was too large for the shelf,
So it stood ninety years on the floor;
It was taller by half
Than the old man himself,
Though it weighed not a pennyweight more.

"It was bought on the morn
Of the day that he was born,
And was always his treasure and pride;
But it stopped short,
Never to go again,
When the old man died."

Mother beamed over the top of her cup. "You have a wonderful voice, Miss Whitfield."

The blushing lady busied herself with the delicate lace bordering her place mat. "Oh heavens, not really, but thank you. And please. . .call me Priscilla."

"I will, if you'll call me Mariah."

"I'd be honored."

Mother glanced toward the window. "I stepped out onto the porch earlier. It's a lovely morning."

Miss Whitfield smiled. "Texas weather is as fickle as a debutante, so don't forget the whereabouts of your wrap. In all possibility, we could wake up tomorrow to a cold front." She laughed. "Then face a heat wave by Tuesday. We endure a hot summer here in Marshall once it sets in. Enjoy the cool while it lasts."

With a dainty clink, Mother set her teacup in the matching saucer. "Doesn't Cedric join you for meals? I noticed his absence last night at supper and again this morning."

Miss Whitfield lowered her chin and shook her head. "It's not possible, I'm afraid. Ceddy is far too disruptive. He takes his meals in the kitchen with Delilah." She raised her head and smiled. "I join them occasionally. . .when he's feeling calm."

Delilah slipped quietly into the room, collecting Miss Whitfield's empty plate with one hand while sliding a platter of rounded cakes onto the table with the other.

"What's this?" the elder woman asked. "Scones?"

"Buttermilk scones," Delilah said proudly. "Dotted with currants and slathered with peach jelly."

"Oh, how lovely." Miss Whitfield reached for one then paused, her cheeks ripening to apples again. "I know what you two are thinking. We eat entirely too many sweets around this house."

Giving in to temptation, she fumbled for a scone then jabbed her knife into a pat of butter. "I blame it all on Delilah. She's the best cook in town. I count myself lucky to have her"—she chuckled merrily—"until I consider the girth of my hips." She took a bite then swooned. "Light as a cloud." Picking up the platter, she held it out to Mother. "Where on earth are my manners? I should serve you first. Go on, have one, Mariah. You won't be sorry."

"They look lovely," Mother said, reaching for one of the golden-brown quick breads.

"Addie?" Miss Whitfield said, waving them under her nose.

Addie reached for one, but her hostess pulled them back. "On second thought, why not partake of yours in the kitchen with Ceddy?" Oblivious to Addie's discomfort, she placed two servings on a small plate and handed it across the table. "He's much fonder of these than he is the tarts. I'm sure he won't throw them."

Her pleading look touched Addie's heart, but that only increased its pounding. "I don't know, ma'am. He, um. . .he's not very receptive to me."

The offered plate didn't budge.

Mother quietly cleared her throat. "Go ahead, Addie. Take it."

Wishing her hand didn't tremble so visibly, Addie reluctantly reached for the treats. With a last pleading glance at her mother, she excused herself from the table and followed Delilah down the hallway to the kitchen.

Easing the swinging door open, Delilah peeked inside. "Always make sure he's not sitting right in front," she explained over her shoulder. "Many a time, I've busted inside without looking, and he wound up with a goose egg."

She stepped aside, and Addie entered the kitchen.

Ceddy lay on his stomach with his chubby cheek pressed against the floor, running one stubby finger along a polished wood plank. In his other hand, the arm crooked over his head, he held a jaunty little cap, black-rimmed velvet with a double row of silk cords stitched to the front.

"We just come in from outside," Delilah said brightly, taking the cap from his lifeless fingers.

Engrossed in tracing the line, he didn't seem to notice.

She snatched his jacket from the back of a chair and swept past. "I'll go put his things in his room."

Lifting her hand toward Delilah's retreating back, Addie swallowed the urge to ask her to stay. An ache starting low in her stomach, she pressed against the counter and watched him.

She couldn't call the noise he made a proper hum, more of a rhythmic grunt, but it was the first sound he'd made that might've come from a little boy.

Encouraged, she moved closer. "Ceddy?"

The slightest pause—then his tracing resumed.

Swallowing hard, she squatted to the floor. "I've brought you something nice, see? One of Delilah's scones."

No response.

"There's jelly inside. Peach, I think." She put the plate on the hardwood floor and nudged it toward him with the backs of her fingers. He continued to ignore her, so she edged it bit by bit until it bumped into his hand.

With barely a break in concentration, he shoved it away with the heel of his palm.

Addie sighed and sought the heavens. What was Miss Whitfield thinking? She could barely reach her great-nephew herself. How could she expect a stranger with no training in his unusual behavior to get through?

She dropped to her behind and crossed her legs in front of her, absently reaching for the strand of beads around her neck. Instead of lending her courage, they pressed against her heart with the weight of her mother's expectations.

A scurrying sound from Ceddy raised her head. He had straightened his arms and pushed up, his wide-eyed stare locked on her necklace.

Startled, Addie dropped the clattering beads to her chest.

As though mesmerized, Ceddy's gaze followed them.

Struck by sudden inspiration, she gripped the strand and rattled it.

In a flash, he scampered across the floor and scrambled into her lap. Wonder lit his delicate features as he placed his hand over hers, gently tugging them out of the way. Palming the jasper pendant, he lifted it close to his face and smiled.

Of course! Addie thought. *I've been using the wrong bait.*

In a surge of understanding, she saw the orphaned kittens snuggled in the folds of her skirt, straining toward her caress as if desperate to be touched. Just as bits of cold fish drew them against their wills, Ceddy, responding to what he loved most, couldn't resist her. He perched close to Addie, allowing himself to be touched by the only thing that moved him.

What had Mother said? That winning the trust of innocent creatures was Addie's gift? For the first time since she'd heard the words, she began to believe them.

Unable to stop herself, she smoothed wispy strands of hair off the child's forehead with trembling fingers. She expected him to withdraw, but the stone held him transfixed.

"Ceddy?" she whispered, desperate to have him look at her.

He batted his long, tangled lashes but didn't glance up.

In a blinding flash, in a jumble of thoughts coming so fast she couldn't have put them into words, she saw the parallel to God cut off from His creation by a yawning gulf of sin, shut off in the same way Ceddy had locked out the world around him. Her breath caught on a sob. Compassion welled in her chest, so deeply felt her untrained heart could only express it as love for a feral creature who couldn't acknowledge it—at least not yet. But she knew in her heart that he would.

Just as certainly, she knew that when the northbound train pulled out of Marshall with her mother aboard, she wouldn't be sitting beside her.

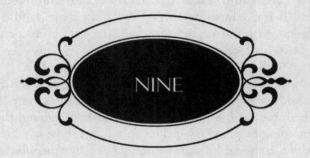

NINE

Pearson stood on the dilapidated dock overlooking Tow Head, where the Big Cypress River fed into Broad Lake, and stared into the murky depths of the Caddo. Surrounded by acres of cypress swamps, bayous, waterways, channels, and sloughs, the enormity of the task he'd so boastfully shouldered hit his stomach like a blow.

Beside him, Theo whistled. "Now I see why that old sailor called this region a lost world."

Pearson nodded. "And why the clerk at Weisman's said we'd bitten off more than we could chew."

Theo's gaze jerked to his face. "Are you thinking we have?"

Giving his head a little shake, Pearson squatted close to the water. "I'm not ready to quit just yet."

Kicking a pinecone off the end of the dock, Theo sighed. "Everyone we've talked to today said we'll be lucky to find Catfish John. Without him, we're as sunk as the *Mittie*."

"We asked each of them to pass the word to John if they see him. That's all we can do for now. Besides"—he glanced over his shoulder—"we may not need him. All of the old hands agreed that this is about where she rests."

Theo pointed with his chin at the widening rings fanning out on the surface of the water where the pinecone went down. "You heard them, Pearce. That overgrown sinkhole is twenty feet deep in some places."

Pearson gave him a sideways glance. "But it averages eight. And it won't be that deep where we'll be searching. The *Mittie* sank close to the bank, near the shallows."

Twisting his mouth, Theo tapped his bottom lip. "Hmm. The shallows. Where the gators live?"

"Only the babies. The big ones go deep."

"Except when they're hunting a meal. And why are you ignoring what the one fellow said?"

"Which fellow?"

"The man at Port Caddo who told you the *Mittie* burned to the waterline. That her safe, bell, and boilers were salvaged right after she sank."

Pearson waved him off. "That man didn't believe the words coming out of his own mouth. Besides, they never recovered the gold. So if the safe was found, the gold wasn't in it." Pushing past him, Pearson stalked off the dock to the water's edge. "Ready to get wet?"

"What?" Theo whirled, his voice cracking. "Now?"

"We might as well take a look while we're here. Find out what we're dealing with."

"Don't we already know what we're dealing with?" Grasping Pearson's shirtsleeve, he pulled him around. "Nests of angry cottonmouths." His eyes bulged. "Remember?"

Hiding a smile at Theo's hysterics, Pearson spoke calmly. "I intend to give this lake every ounce of respect it deserves, buddy boy, especially the cottonmouths. Now come on." Pearson strode along the shoreline for several yards to a spot where the bank sloped gently to the water.

Theo ran along behind him, still fussing like a flustered woman.

Sitting on the ground, Pearson slid off his boots and socks then stood and peeled off his sweat-dampened shirt. The wind felt good on his bare chest.

Walking into the water up to his ankles, he sighed. If he closed his eyes, ignoring the dank smell and the mud squishing between his toes, he could almost imagine himself back on the coast. After two more steps, bringing the frigid lake up to his calves, he stopped and glanced behind him.

Theo still dawdled on the bank, fully clothed.

"Aren't you coming?"

He licked his lips. "I realize your skin's like a whale's. You can't live long without getting wet." Breaking eye contact, he gazed at the dark water lapping his boots. "But I'm not like you, Pearson. I wasn't born with gills."

"You don't like getting those prissy curls wet is all. Stop grousing. You sound like your grandmother."

"Nonna is a wise and cautious woman. It's why she's lived so long." He shook his head. "I'll wait here this time."

"Suit yourself, sissy boy."

Theo gawked. "You're really going in there? What do you hope to accomplish?"

In up to his waist now, Pearson looked over his shoulder. "I'll let you know the answer when I figure it out. But I can truthfully say I prefer sand and salt water." With a sharp inhale, he dove.

So this was how it felt to be blind. Opening his eyes in the pitch darkness got him little more than a burning sensation from silt and debris. Feeling his way along the bottom was none too pleasant either, with slime so deep, his groping fingers buried to the wrists, never hitting solid ground.

Aware of small fish darting in all directions, Pearson kicked his legs, skimming the lake bed for several feet until it dropped sharply from beneath him. From somewhere below a bubble rose, tickling his stomach as it bounced off him. The exhale of a large animal, one that would soon rise for another breath.

Spinning, he fought through a tangle of underwater plants, swam as far as he could, and then forced his way to the surface. Gasping for breath, he pushed back his hair and sought the bank.

Theo paced like an anxious mother, biting what was left of his stubby nails.

Grinning, Pearson paddled toward him until he found his feet, emerging from the swirling water with mud up to his knees.

"There you are," Theo said. "What took so long?"

"It seemed only seconds to me." He pointed behind him. "It's dark and cold down there."

Crossing his arms, Theo slouched to one side. "What did you expect?"

Pearson laughed. "That it would be dark and cold, I suppose." He sobered. "We're going to need a drag, Theo, and it won't be easy going. We'll have to find a couple of rough-and-tumble men with strong arms and backs, preferably as familiar with this lake as we are with the Gulf."

"Men like Catfish John?"

He nodded. "Exactly like him."

"How do you plan on finding them? We've been asking around since we got here. No one seems interested."

Gripping Theo's shoulder with a muddy hand, he shook him. "Let's worry about the details later, all right? For now, I'm anxious to get back to town and clean up."

"And have dinner?" Theo rubbed his stomach. "I'm starved."

Pearson nodded, leading him to where they'd tethered their rented horses. "I could eat a bite myself." He patted Theo's back good-naturedly. "As long as it isn't catfish."

Smiling and waving, Mother boarded the train out of Marshall, her eyes red from crying, her chest puffed with pride.

Standing beside Miss Whitfield at the station, Addie struggled with all her might not to cry. She wasn't a child anymore, for goodness' sake! Her parents had sheltered her far too long. She'd fought hard for independence and the respect due her twenty-two years. Standing on the train platform, waving good-bye to her mother, she had it at last. Why then did it seem so hard?

"Oh Adelina," Miss Whitfield said, her arm circling Addie's waist, "you have the most forlorn expression. Don't worry, dear. You'll see her again."

Addie swallowed the growing lump in her throat. "I know I will. It's just that. . .well, it's the first time we've ever been apart."

"I know how you feel, honey. I remember when my parents sent me away to school for the first time. I thought my heart would break." She sighed. "Soon I made new friends, met your Dr. Moony, and before long, my father was scolding me for neglecting to write home." She tittered. "I got so wrapped up in my new life, the pull of my old one lessened."

Addie shook her head. "I can't imagine that happening."

"It will though." Miss Whitfield patted her waist. "You'll see."

Addie stood on tiptoe at the edge of the platform, watching the train until there was no longer even a speck visible down the track. Shoulders slumped, she rejoined her new employer, waiting patiently with her hands clasped and a fringed reticule dangling from her wrist.

"Are you ready now?" Miss Whitfield asked.

"I suppose so." She tucked her bottom lip. "I want to thank you for coming with me, ma'am. I didn't relish facing this alone."

Clucking her tongue, Miss Whitfield tapped her hand. "Nor should you. I was more than happy to be here. Let's get back to the carriage and we'll take you home."

Home? Addie's heart sank. The word had taken a whole new meaning. Instead of the two-story house in Canton, Mississippi, with her loved ones gathered inside, home meant a stately manor house in Marshall, Texas, where she dwelled with utter strangers.

"Are you hungry, dear? Delilah will have supper about ready when we arrive. I believe she's frying chicken for us tonight. Won't that be nice?"

Addie's mouth felt as though she had cotton bolls tucked into her cheeks. She grimaced. "Oh yes, ma'am. It sounds lovely."

Miss Whitfield prattled on about all the foods she hoped Delilah would serve alongside the main dish.

Not sure how she could stomach one bite, since the mere mention of supper made her queasy, Addie tuned out her chatter and gazed around at the nearby shops and houses.

Marshall's a pretty town, she thought as they neared the carriage. A prosperous town by the look of it. People dressed very nicely and kept their homes and yards in first-rate conditions. She would miss the familiarity of her hometown but decided on the spot to give Marshall a fair shake.

Two horses approached, trotting side by side along the opposite edge of the road. The riders' merry voices carried on the afternoon breeze—one shrill with mock indignation, the other gently teasing.

Addie's breath caught even before she glimpsed the tanned face and tangled hair beneath the hat. She couldn't mistake his smooth, rich voice.

Despite Pearson Foster's wet shirt and a layer of dried mud on his bare feet and rolled-up pants, he sat the saddle with the self-assured grace of a man in frock coat, button boots, and cashmere trousers.

He didn't see her at first, so she got a good long look at his handsome profile as he passed. At the last second, he whirled in the saddle and stared.

Addie blushed and ducked her head. Then, unable to resist, she met his gaze.

Pearson's eyes lit up, and a wide smile graced his face. He lifted his hat and nodded. "Well, well. Good afternoon."

Before she could think how to respond, or if indeed she should, Miss Whitfield took her arm and spun her around. "Shameless rabble," she muttered. "No better breeding than to address strange women in the street?" She rushed Addie into the carriage and tapped the driver's shoulder with her parasol. "Drive on, please. The streets aren't safe for decent women these days."

The man flicked the reins, and the horses moved away from the station. As they made the turn, Addie stole a peek.

Pearson and his funny little friend pulled up to the hotel and slid off their horses. Halfway up the walkway, he turned, bumped his hat off his forehead, and gazed in her direction.

Theo continued walking then stopped and doubled back. Clutching Pearson's sleeve, he hauled him toward the door.

Covering her smile with two fingers, she forced herself to focus on Miss Whitfield and whether candied yams or mashed potatoes were the best complement to Southern fried chicken. Unfortunately, she couldn't offer much to the conversation, considering the only accompaniment to supper she desired wasn't welcome at the table.

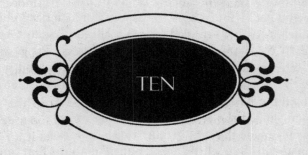

TEN

Pearson dried himself off then wrapped the towel around his waist. Despite the endless pitchers of water he'd poured over his head, muddy streams still dripped from his hair.

He'd sloshed through sludge as thick as gruel over the past three days in Caddo Lake, but today was the worst. He didn't look forward to doing it again, but he'd have to if he wanted to raise the *Mittie*.

"Won't you hurry, *principessa*?" Theo called.

Grinning, Pearson peered around the doorway, choking on laughter at the sight of Theo, his impatient dance rattling the boards of the bathhouse floor. Mud covered his face like a mask with cutouts for his mouth and eyes. "I'm the princess? I'm not the one who was afraid to go into the water for the last two days."

"I was afraid today, too," Theo countered, "but I went. I'm not accustomed to swimming with alligators, you know."

"The trick is in the dodge, my friend."

Theo chuckled, but his voice rose in irritation. "Hurry out of there, Pearson. The mud is beginning to harden on my skin. Pigeons are circling my head." He slapped his arms. "And I'm cold! What fools we were to come so early in the year. The warmth of the sun is deceptive. Two feet down in that lake and you'd swear it was winter."

"I'm almost done." Pulling on his britches and lifting his shirt from a hook, Pearson glanced at the tub. "Have the chambermaid bring a fresh bath. You don't want to dunk yourself in this muck soup. You'll come out worse off than you went in." He slipped on his boots and rounded the corner, settling his hat on his head. Lifting it again, he nodded at the fetching young maid crossing the courtyard of the Ginocchio Hotel. "Afternoon, miss."

She shot him a sweet smile and lowered her lashes.

Tossing the towel across his shoulder, he tipped his head at Theo. "I hope you'll excuse my grubby friend. He's been making mud pies again."

Theo shot him a threatening look then bowed to the maid, his smile bright against his mud-smeared face. "If it's not too much trouble, pretty lady, I'd appreciate a fresh tub of water. I make it a rule not to bathe after hogs."

She ducked her head and giggled.

Pearson yanked the towel from around his neck and swatted Theo with a loud *pop*.

"It's true," Theo insisted, dodging the end of the towel. "He cleans up well, but this man isn't kosher."

"Whatever you say, sir," she managed through her laughter. "I'll bring your water right away." Tittering, she scurried down the walk toward the back door of the hotel.

Watching her go, Theo yawned and stretched. "I hope she hurries. I need a hot meal and a soft mattress."

"I agree. We'll find something to eat before we go, and we'll turn in the minute we return."

Theo's hands, busy squeezing water out of his curls, stilled. "Return from where? I'm plenty tired, Pearson. I had no plans to go anywhere."

Pearson averted his gaze. "I thought we'd ride out to Whitfield Manor. You know. . .check on our new friends and see how they've fared."

Theo flashed his crooked grin. "By 'friend' you mean Mrs. McRae's daughter."

Pearson lifted one shoulder. "They're both very nice ladies." He wouldn't admit it to his merciless comrade, but in the four days since he'd met her, Miss Addie's big eyes and dainty chin hadn't left his mind.

Theo smirked. "Indeed. I thought you weren't ready for the bridle, stallion."

Tossing the towel, Pearson nodded toward the bathhouse. "Go wash the mire from your body. . .and rinse the sass from your big mouth while you're at it."

Laughing, Theo lobbed the wet cloth back at him and ducked inside the door.

With a hopeless shake of his head, Pearson ambled to their room.

Theo appeared a few minutes later, just as ornery, but looking more like himself. Pausing in the doorway, he gave Pearson a long look. "Are you spit and polished enough to go see this girl? I won't have you embarrass me."

Pearson tilted his head. "For a man who didn't want to go, you seem mighty eager."

He grinned. "Once I cleared the mud from the seat of my trousers, I felt better. Must've been weighing me down."

The buggy ride to Whitfield Manor was short but pleasant. The well-traveled road out of town soon turned into a winding uphill lane beneath spreading oaks.

In the circular drive, Pearson gave instructions to the driver to wait and then climbed to the ground.

Bailing out the other side, Theo passed behind the rig and came to join him. "What will you say to her?"

Heading up the stone walkway, Pearson shrugged. "I'll figure that out when I see her." At the stately front entrance, he took a deep breath and rapped with the gleaming brass knocker. Immediately the door swung open with such force, it startled him.

Theo gripped his shoulder and pulled him back a couple of steps.

A small boy, so wraithlike and spry he put Pearson in mind of a fairy, gazed with hollow eyes past them to the yard.

With a wry smile at his jumpy friend, Pearson stooped to eye level with the child. "Hello there. I'm Pearson, and my friend here is Theo." He offered his hand. "What do they call you?"

Ignoring Pearson's hand, the boy grunted and angled his body to see around him.

The intensity of his stare raised the hair on Pearson's neck. Instinctively he twisted to see behind him.

"What's he looking at?" Theo whispered.

"I was wondering the same."

A woman in a starched white apron and cap appeared from the shadows and latched onto the boy's shoulders. "Sorry, suh. He ain't supposed to answer the door, but he do it anyway. Can I help you?"

Pearson stood. "We're here to pay a call on Mrs. McRae."

She blinked up at him. "Did you say *Mrs.* McRae?"

He lifted a brow. "Mrs. Mariah McRae? I understand she's a guest here."

The boy began to moan and sway, so she nudged him gently down the hall. "Oh, yessuh. She was a guest, but she lef' on the train two days ago."

Regret sank like a stone to the pit of Pearson's stomach. He'd tried to wait a respectable amount of time to come calling, but now it appeared he'd waited too long. "May I ask where she went?"

"Gone back to Mississippi, I think." She pointed behind her. "I can go ask—"

"No, don't bother. We won't intrude." No sense disturbing the old lady.

"All right then," she said. "You gentlemens have yo'selves a nice day."

She stepped inside to close the door, but Pearson raised his hand. "Miss?"

The crack in the door widened. "Yessuh?"

"If I leave a note, will you see that Mrs. McRae gets it?"

"I'll do my best."

He fumbled at his pockets. "Let's see. . .I need something to write on."

"I'll bring you something, suh."

"And an envelope, if you don't mind."

"Yessuh. Wait right here."

The woman returned quickly and passed him a sheet of frilly stationery and a pen. The paper had bluebonnets around the border like a watercolor painting and smelled of flowers.

Pearson held it up and wrinkled his nose.

Smiling slightly, she shrugged. "That's all I could find."

Using Theo's bony back for a desk, Pearson jotted a few lines and signed it, then sealed it in the envelope. "Will you ask Miss Whitfield to send this?"

She nodded. "I'll ask."

"Much obliged."

Tipping his hat, he yanked at Theo's sleeve. "I guess that's all we can do. Let's go."

His heart a pulsing lump in his chest, he trudged down the steps. Mississippi seemed worlds away from Texas, which meant it might take a miracle to see Addie McRae again. On the way to the rig, he decided there were drawbacks to being on the outs with the One who specialized in miracles.

Ceddy sailed toward Addie in the upstairs corridor then whisked past her in a blur. Whirling, she called his name, but he ignored her. Wheeling around the corner, he burst into his bedroom and slammed the door shut behind him.

Two days ago she might've followed, but she'd grown accustomed to some of his behavior. Most anything could set him off, and seldom was it anything she'd done.

"Very well. I'll bring your afternoon snack," she announced to the empty hallway and then smiled. "Might get one for myself as well. Delilah's been baking again."

Smoothing her crisp linen skirt, she preened before the mirror as she passed. She'd worked for many families around Canton, caring for their children, but Miss Whitfield was the first employer who supplied a smart uniform.

Adjusting her white cap, she stepped closer to the upstairs window, her gaze drawn to someone milling in the yard. Pressing her nose to the glass, she gasped. Incredibly, Pearson Foster, the man who'd haunted her thoughts for days, and his Italian friend had come to call.

It took a second glance for her to realize they were at the end of the walkway climbing aboard one of the hired buggies from town.

"Great heavenly days!" she shrieked, hurling herself for the stairs. She reached the bottom landing and bolted for the front door. "Wait, don't leave!" she cried as she ran across the porch. Teetering at the top step, she slapped her hand over her mouth, shocked at her shameless lack of decorum.

No matter, they hadn't heard. The wagon turned at the grove of trees and disappeared down the lane.

Part of her flooded with relief that no one had witnessed her bellowing like a weaning calf. The other part shriveled inside with disappointment.

"Missy McRae? What is you doing?"

Spinning, she stared dumbly at Delilah.

Delilah hitched her shoulder toward the drive. "You know them boys?"

"Yes. Well, not exactly. What did they want? What did they say? Why on earth did they leave so soon?"

Delilah placed one hand on her hip. "Which of them questions you want me to answer?"

"All of them, please."

Biting her lip, she nodded. "Well, they wanted your mama. That's about all they said. And they left on account of she ain't here."

Addie stared. "They asked for my mother? Are you certain?"

"Yes'm. Called her by name."

"Did they say anything about me?" The second the words tripped off her tongue, heat crawled up her neck and flaming fire lit her cheeks. "I mean. . ."

"Sorry, Miss Addie. Your name ain't come up." Grinning, Delilah gathered her skirts and turned from the door. "Now, if you be done with questions, I got to take this letter to Miss Whitfield like I promised."

Seconds later, the import of her words pierced the troubled fog in Addie's mind. Racing inside, she caught up with Delilah, knocking at the door of the study.

"Come in," Miss Whitfield's muffled voice called.

Addie tugged on Delilah's sleeve. "Wait, please," she whispered. "Do you mean to say those two"—she pointed toward the front of the house—"the men who were just here. . .left a letter for Miss Whitfield?"

"No, ma'am."

"Oh." The breath left Addie in a rush. "Well, all right then." She waved with her fingers. "Carry on."

Delilah turned the knob. "They left a letter for your mama." Pulling an envelope from her pocket, she stepped inside the study and closed the door.

Pearson watched a robin flit by the buggy and perch on the edge of its nest. Tracked a cat squirrel up a tall pine. Considered the bald spot on the back of the driver's head. Anything but meeting Theo's mournful gaze.

"Sorry, old man," he finally said.

Embarrassed, Pearson shrugged. "For what?"

Theo widened his eyes. "Don't try pretending with me. I know you too well." The tip of his tongue appeared in his cheek. "You're pretty disappointed, aren't you?"

"Don't get sentimental, Theo. She's just a girl like all the rest."

"Is that so?" He dug his elbow in Pearson's side. "Then why do you look like you're about to cry?"

Growling, Pearson returned the favor, except with more force. "You don't know what you're talking about."

Theo wagged a finger in his face. "I've seen that expression before. Many times, in fact. You look this way after every bum lead on Jean Lafitte's gold."

"What?" Angry with himself for the girlie shrill in his voice, Pearson crossed his arms and turned his back on his friend. Much more lip and he'd be tossing him over the side.

"What is it about this one, Pearce?" Theo continued, oblivious to the danger he was in. "You didn't take on this way when you left Pearl behind at Rosie's."

"Do yourself a favor, pal. Change the subject."

His gruff tone sounded so ominous, the driver glanced nervously behind him.

Laughing, Theo held up his hands. "All right, just tell me one thing." He pressed his face dangerously close and raised his brow. "What did you write in that letter?"

"Let it go, Theo. I'm warning you."

He chuckled. "Very well. I'll leave you to mourn in peace." His voice lowered dramatically. "Just remember. . .I'm here for you."

"That's supposed to cheer me?"

After a last hearty laugh, the maddening Italian settled against the seat humming an off-key tune, his big eyes taking in their surroundings.

Left to his thoughts, Pearson questioned his reaction to the news that the woman he'd known so briefly had departed Texas.

Miss Adelina Viola McRae had affected him more than he cared to admit. . .to Theo or anyone else.

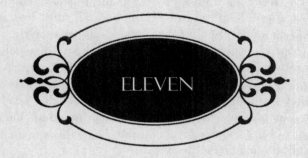

ELEVEN

Her mind consumed by thoughts of Pearson's visit, her curiosity piqued by the mysterious letter, Addie found it hard to concentrate on her job. Balancing a tray with Ceddy's afternoon snack and a generous serving of milk, she bumped open the door of his room with her hip and stepped inside.

Her first day as Ceddy's governess, she'd knocked before entering his inner sanctum. Flustered when he never answered, she'd gone to Delilah for advice.

Finding more humor in her display of common courtesy than Addie felt was warranted, Delilah took pleasure in demonstrating the futility of the gesture. She stationed Addie inside the room so she could see for herself that when a knock sounded on Ceddy's door, he pressed his ear to the other side and listened.

Addie wondered if he failed to recognize the sound as a request to enter or if he didn't bother to care. The accepted customs of polite society seemed wasted on his simplistic view of life.

Delilah may have said it best once she'd opened the door and peered inside, laughing. "He don't know no better!"

Mr. Uncomplicated sat on the floor behind the bed when she entered, the back of his blond head the only thing visible.

"Good afternoon, young sir. I've brought your goodies."

Not a whisper of response. No hint of notice.

731

"Look here. Lilah used her last jar of dewberries to make you a cobbler."

The little shoulders rounded over his task.

"Ceddy?" Addie placed the tray on a table and walked around the bed. He played quietly in front of a humpbacked trunk, legs splayed to the sides and a mound of colorful rocks stacked between them. One at a time, he took stones from the pile and lined them up by color.

She observed him for a spell, burning with curiosity about what might be going on inside his pixie head. Over the last two days, she'd come to enjoy watching him immensely. He was such a beautiful boy, looking at him brought her pleasure. More than that, his behavior fascinated her. Quiet and docile one minute, he could explode in motion or erupt in frightened cries the next.

Picking up the tray, Addie placed it next to him. With the hem of her skirt, she waved the aroma of the fresh-baked treat in his direction, smiling when he dropped the rock clutched in his hand and made a grab for the cobbler.

She'd rather he'd reached for the fork. Still, it was progress.

Squatting to his level, she held out the milk. "Don't you want to wash it down?"

He raised both shoulders and leaned away from her.

"All right," she said, sliding the tray closer. "I'll put it where you can reach it when you're ready."

Reaching blindly behind him, he felt for the glass and shoved it over.

"Why did you do that?" she cried, whipping off her apron to use for a mop. "Look at this mess."

The door squealed open and Delilah blinked at her from the hall. "Miss Priscilla be looking for you."

Startled, Addie shot to her feet, wiping her wet hands on her skirt. "Oh gracious. Tell her I'll be right along."

Delilah shook her head. "No, Miss Addie, she right out here in the hall."

Addie whirled as Miss Whitfield squeezed past Delilah. "Not looking anymore. I see I've found her."

"Ceddy's having his afternoon snack," Addie announced stiffly. The silly words echoed in the room.

Thankfully, Miss Whitfield smiled. "With his usual flair, I see." She shook her head at Ceddy's sticky hands and face, the berry stains like terrible bruises. "Wipe up this milk, please, Delilah, and bring a wet rag to clean him up." She grimaced at Addie. "He doesn't like to take his milk, but I suppose you've figured that out."

Addie released a breathy laugh. "He managed to communicate his wishes fairly well."

"We should've warned you, I suppose. We have to beg and bribe him. But it's quite good for his health I understand."

"Yes, ma'am. So it is."

Miss Whitfield's demeanor changed. "I suppose you're wondering why I'm disrupting your workday." Deep creases appeared between her eyes. "I wanted to discuss your mother's recent visitors."

Addie's stomached tightened. Before she could think how to respond, Ceddy howled, the sound so piercing she cowered and covered her ears. "What on earth?"

He had finished the rows of stones, laid out in front of him in a patchwork of color. The square they formed lacked a corner, one empty slot marring the perfect symmetry. Screaming as if in pain, he tapped the space with his gooey pointer finger.

"What is it, dear?" Miss Whitfield asked, her voice taut and anxious. "Merciful heavens, what does he want?"

Delilah returned at a run, and Miss Whitfield spun toward her. "Bring another dish of cobbler. Quickly!"

"Yes'm," she cried and dashed away.

"Wait, don't you see?" Addie said. "He doesn't want to eat. He wants—"

With a frustrated grunt, Ceddy bent over his design and forcefully swept it away with his forearm. The rocks scattered in all directions, one striking the windowpane so hard it cracked.

"Oh blast! Look what he's done. Addie, can't you do something?"

She'd been asking herself the same question. On instinct, she dropped to the floor in front of Ceddy and rattled her mother's beads.

Their effect was immediate. The shrieking died on his lips, and his head whipped around to face her. A sweet smile softened the lines of his face, and he swiped at a lingering tear.

Clutching her hands together, Miss Whitfield plopped onto the bed. "For pity's sake. Have you ever seen the like?"

Delilah burst in waving a mottled scoop of cobbler on a saucer. "I come as quick as I could."

Addie's hand shot up. "Wait, please. Not yet."

Ignoring the treat and everything else in the room, Ceddy scooted closer to smooth his fingertip over the polished jasper.

Addie crowded her finger beside his to stroke the stone along with him. "It's very pretty, isn't it?"

Disappointment filled her heart as he abruptly pulled away. In rash impatience, she'd stumbled over one of his boundaries.

Dismay turned to wonder as he tugged a big book from under the bed and set to frantically flipping the pages. Stopping on a dog-eared sheet, he crab-crawled into her lap, dragging the book behind him. "Uh," he grunted, jabbing one of the small photos on the page. Catching the necklace in his curled fingers, he jangled the pendant.

"Is he—" Miss Whitfield started.

"I believe he is," Addie said. "He's showing me they're the same." She touched the little square; the stone in the picture was medium green with flecks of red scattered throughout. "Jasper. Also known as bloodstone. You're exactly right. Very good, Ceddy." She beamed at Miss Whitfield. "Very good indeed."

Just as fast as he'd come to her, Ceddy scooted from Addie's lap and gathered his stones, this time aligning them in the order they appeared on the page.

Delilah advanced with the saucer, but Miss Whitfield shook her head. "Take it back to the kitchen. He doesn't want it."

She crooked her finger at Addie and strode to the door. "Stay with him for a spell, Delilah. Should you need us, we'll be in the study."

A lump in her throat, Addie followed Miss Whitfield down the hall. Just inside the door, the woman abruptly turned and embraced her. "I knew it," she whispered against Addie's ear. "I knew my instincts about you were good." Pushing her to arm's length, she smiled. "You're going to be wonderful for Ceddy."

"But I didn't do anything."

"Oh, my dear, but you did. And I'm grateful." She pointed at the straight-backed chair. "Now on to less inspiring topics. Take a seat, please."

Sitting across from her stern-faced employer, Addie fought the urge to loosen her collar.

Slipping on her spectacles, Miss Whitfield leaned across the desk, one brow drawn to a peak. She placed a sealed envelope between them. "As I said before, I have a few questions about the young men who came to call earlier today."

Addie nodded. "Yes ma'am?" The woman's silence pressed her to continue. "To be honest, I don't really know much about them." Bending closer to the letter, she frowned at the faint outline of bluebonnets. "I don't understand. Isn't that your stationery?"

Miss Whitfield nodded. "Delilah provided it for them."

She turned the envelope over, and Addie stared at her mother's name scrawled in large, neat letters. Surely Pearson Foster had written the letter. The forward act was just the sort of thing she could imagine him doing. But why?

"Does your mother know these men?" Miss Whitfield asked, interrupting her thoughts.

Addie swallowed. "Not exactly. We met them at the station when we arrived."

She gaped at Addie over the top of her wire frames. "Did you say *met* them?"

"I mean, they just suddenly appeared and offered to help with our luggage."

The poor woman's eyes bulged. "Why would your lovely mother give those two ruffians the time of day? They looked so"—she wrinkled her nose—"unkempt."

"You saw them?"

Miss Whitfield waved toward the front window. "A glimpse is all, but it was enough." She stared thoughtfully. "I had the oddest sensation that I'd seen them somewhere before. . ." She shook her head. "But that's not likely."

Shriveling under Miss Whitfield's air of disapproval, Addie didn't dare jog her memory. If she knew they were the same men on horseback in town, she'd bust a stitch.

She wrung her hands in her lap. "They were really quite nice."

"Nice? Well, they certainly don't look it. What are they doing in Marshall?"

"They're here to raise a shipwrecked steamboat or something of that nature. I believe he—Mr. Foster, the tall one—said they were wreckers."

A glint of understanding flashed in Miss Whitfield's narrowed eyes. "Wreckers indeed. I know just the steamboat they hope to raise, and I know why." She snorted scornfully. "Those two aren't wreckers, dear. That at least is an honorable profession in most circles. They're treasure seekers, Addie. A vulgar pursuit at best, not to mention a reckless waste of time."

Addie sat forward in her chair. "Treasure hunters?"

"They're after the gold that went down with the *Mittie Stephens*."

Now that Addie thought about it, Pearson Foster had sounded vaguely mysterious about their intentions. "Ma'am, is the steamboat you mentioned in a nearby lake?"

Miss Whitfield lifted her head. "Lake Caddo." She nodded. "I'm right, then, aren't I? They're after the *Mittie*." She absently worried the corner of the letter with one tapered nail. "Oh Addie. What do you think they want with your mother?"

Addie shrugged. "I can't imagine. We spent a very short time with them. After lunch they escorted us to hire a rig, and that was the end of it."

"You took lunch with total strangers?" Miss Whitfield snatched a small crocheted doily from the corner of her desk to fan herself. "Oh my, I hope no one saw you. What was Mariah thinking?"

Addie's spine stiffened, and she drew up her chin. "My mother may be a bit unconventional at times, but she's ever the lady. There was nothing improper about our behavior."

Biting her bottom lip, Miss Whitfield lowered her makeshift fan and leaned to touch Addie's hand. "Forgive me, dear. I never meant to imply otherwise. I'm a bit concerned, that's all."

Her eyes drawn to the letter again, Addie cleared her throat. "This mystery is easily solved. I have errands in Marshall this afternoon." She reached across the desk. "I'd be happy to forward this on to Mother. I'm sure she'll send a timely explanation."

Snatching the envelope before Addie's fingers reached it, Miss Whitfield shook her graying head. "Don't trouble yourself." Her stern voice left no room for argument. "I'll take care of it."

As she stared at Mr. Foster's bold handwriting, her brows knitted above her glasses. "I need to give the matter more thought. To be honest, I haven't decided if I should mail it at all."

"But ma'am, is that—" Shocked by her own boldness, Addie tucked her chin and stilled.

Miss Whitfield shook herself from her thoughts and drew a breath.

"My place to decide? I'm convinced it is. If not for me, you and your mother would never have come to Marshall. Consequently, you'd never have met those two peculiar men." She opened a drawer and slid the letter inside. "That's all for now, dear. You may go."

Firmly dismissed, Addie rose from her chair and turned toward the door.

"Adelina?"

She slowed to look over her shoulder. "Yes, ma'am?"

"Take some time while Delilah's with the boy." She motioned with her hand. "Change into a fresh uniform. I'm afraid you're wearing a good portion of Ceddy's milk." A smile warmed her eyes. "Get in a nice nap if you'd like. I imagine Delilah's urging your charge to do the same. You'll find our pace slows down considerably this time of day."

Touched by her thoughtfulness, Addie ducked her head. "Thank you, Miss Whitfield."

Passing Ceddy's door to her own, she glimpsed Delilah tucking the covers under his chin, heard her deep, rumbling voice humming a quiet lullaby.

Inside her room, Addie quickly shucked to her dainties and pulled on a dressing gown. Wrapping it around her, she sank into the comfortable chair beside the bed and breathed a relieved sigh.

She was tired lately, as the bags under her eyes bore witness. She always found the early days of a new assignment tedious, what with getting a firm grasp on things and learning her employer's expectations. This job made the rest seem paltry.

As her tense muscles eased, her thoughts swirled in a drowsy fog, centered on Mr. Foster and his troublesome letter. Three points of interest tickled her scattered mind, roiling from the mists and taking an ugly shape: One, Mr. Foster seemed quite taken with her beautiful mother the day they met. Two, he'd made a special trip from town to call on her. And three, the most scandalous act of all, the blackguard had written a note to her mother on Miss Whitfield's lavender-scented stationery with the bluebonnet border.

Addie sat up gripping the arm of her chair, all possibility of a nap driven away by outrage. These truths led to one inescapable conclusion. Pearson Foster wasn't drawn to Addie. The unscrupulous rogue had designs on her mother!

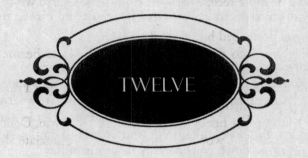

TWELVE

After a restless night pondering the shocking revelation about Mr. Foster's indecent intentions, and a stressful morning coaxing Ceddy to eat his porridge, Addie had little patience with his refusal to drink his afternoon glass of milk. Why Miss Whitfield seemed so adamant for him to have it, she couldn't fathom. Surely they could remove from his diet a beverage he so fiercely detested.

They sat together at the breakfast nook in the kitchen. The sun, muted by the magnolia tree near the window, shone patches of mottled light across his face.

"Please, honey," Addie pleaded. "Have a few sips, and then you can leave the table."

He swung, but she snatched the glass away in time.

"Mercy! It's not that bad, is it?" She wrinkled her nose and stole a taste of the frothy drink. The creamy liquid slid over her tongue, cool and refreshing. "My goodness. It's actually very tasty." Her stomach growled, but she resisted the urge to drain the glass. Shrugging, she placed it out of his reach as Delilah entered the room.

Leaping up, Ceddy ran to bury his face in her apron.

Delilah smiled. "I'm glad he don't drink it no better for you, Miss Addie. I's startin' to think he jus' be spiteful."

"I can't imagine why he doesn't want it." Addie swiped away the white mustache clinging to her top lip. "It's delicious."

Ceddy moaned and tugged on Delilah's skirt.

"Poor mite. He hungry, too."

"I know," Addie agreed. "Miss Priscilla thought with an empty stomach he'd be more receptive to the milk." She smiled wryly. "It didn't work."

"Why you don't feed him?"

"We're going into town for lunch today." Addie beamed. "We're having the Ginocchio Salad. Have you ever tried one?"

Turning to the sink, she snorted derisively. "No, and I don't care to. Whoever heard of putting pecan meats in lettuce?"

Addie spun on her heel. "Why, I'm surprised at you, Delilah. You're such a creative cook, I would've thought you'd appreciate diversity in food preparation."

Delilah blushed. "Thank you, Miss Addie. I don't understand them big words you always spoutin', but thank you jus' the same." She took the milk from Addie and poured it in the dishpan. "When Miss Priscilla asks if he took it, you let me answer. I'd sooner have a lie on my conscience than see Little Man pestered anymore."

Addie grinned and patted her arm.

Miss Whitfield swept in wearing a wide-brimmed hat and a lavender dress with velveteen trim. Delilah had laced her corset so tightly, the contraption forced her torso forward on top and her hips backward, creating the silhouette of a stuffed pheasant.

She glanced at the empty glass in Delilah's hand, and her mouth flew wide. "He drank it? How wonderful." She smoothed the back of Ceddy's head. "There's Auntie's good fellow. I knew you could do it."

Ceddy pulled away and slid behind Delilah.

Addie cast her co-conspirator a secretive look and hurried to change the subject. "My, don't you look lovely, ma'am."

Miss Whitfield's lips pushed outward in a pout. "I simply hate to be called 'ma'am,' Addie. Makes me feel like a crone. And 'Miss Priscilla' just reminds me that I'm an old maid. Can't we dispense with formality? I'd like you to call me Priscilla, if you don't mind."

"Yes, ma'am." Addie grinned and brought her hand to her mouth. "I'll try to remember."

Priscilla patted her arm. "Good. Shall we go then? That salad of yours is sounding better by the minute."

Pearson stabbed at his plate and brought up a forkful of pecans and lettuce covered in thick mayonnaise. "This was a good idea, Theo." He shoved in the bite and proceeded to talk with his mouth full. "It's the first time since we left the lake that I can't taste mud."

Theo nodded. "Enjoy it while you can. You'll get another mouthful once we hire a couple of hands and head back out there." Closely studying his plate, he avoided Pearson's eyes. "You're not going to turn this into another search for Lafitte's gold, are you, Pearce?"

Pearson wiped his mouth. "Now, what did I say? We'll give it a good effort, but if we don't have any luck, we'll call it a wash. Didn't I promise?"

Chasing a sliver of pecan around his plate, Theo nodded. "You did, but I know you. You're like a blind bulldog. Once your teeth are buried in something, you don't know when to turn loose."

Dropping his fork with a clatter, Pearson sat forward and stared. "I don't know about blind, but I am seeing things." He pointed. "Isn't that the lovely Miss McRae?"

Theo spun around. "Oh yeah, that's her. I'm not sure about the mourning dress, but there's no mistaking that heart-shaped face and those big eyes."

Accompanied by an elderly woman, Addie stood with one hand on the shoulder of the odd little boy they'd briefly seen at the mansion. The stiff, black uniform she wore tried hard to hide her charms but couldn't succeed. She stared around the room, most likely watching for the maître d' to seat them.

"Looks like we were lied to," Theo said.

"Yes, it does." Pearson stood. "Let's find out why."

"Wait!" Theo called, reaching a hand toward him.

Ignoring his friend's caution, Pearson strode across the room and bowed to each of the women in turn. "Good afternoon, Miss McRae. What an unexpected pleasure."

The color drained from Addie's complexion, and the big eyes in question rounded in surprise. "Mr. Foster, I didn't expect to see you again so soon."

He smiled. "I didn't expect to see you at all. You're supposed to be in Mississippi, aren't you?"

The older woman stiffened and stared down her nose. "I beg your pardon." Her tone, more than her words, invited Pearson to return to his table and to his lowly station.

He shot her his most charming smile. "Forgive me, ma'am. I'm acquainted with Miss McRae here, but you and I haven't been introduced. I'm Pearson Foster, of the Galveston Fosters."

She relaxed slightly and nodded, good breeding getting the best of her. "Priscilla Whitfield."

He caught her hand and lightly kissed it. "Dear lady, you're a legend in Marshall, and I'm honored to meet you."

"Yes." The single word wavered with doubt.

"My friend and I rode out to your lovely home the other day." He studied her face for recognition. "We spoke with your maid. I assume she told you?"

She sniffed. "I'm well aware of your visit."

He turned a shaky smile on Addie. "We came to call on you, to be exact."

"On me?" She lifted her chin, ice in her voice. "Or my mother?"

Thrown off by their chilly reception, Pearson searched his mind for something to say.

Miss Whitfield beat him to the draw. "If you'll excuse us, we'd like to be seated now."

Jumping at the chance, he spun and pointed behind him. "Won't you join us? The hungry-looking fellow in the corner is my business partner. We'd be happy to share our table."

Theo, leaning over the back of his chair, grinned and raised two fingers in a jaunty wave.

"Well, I. . ." As flighty as a snared grouse, Miss Whitfield searched about the room for an avenue of escape. "We appreciate the offer. Perhaps another time."

Pearson opened his mouth to protest, but the boy, standing docile and quiet until then, let out a shrill cry and darted behind the old girl.

Turning one way then the other like a dog chasing its tail, Miss Whitfield tried to pull him in front of her. "What is it, Ceddy? Come here, child."

The piercing howl grew louder, and tears flooded his eyes.

Catching his arm, she bent to look at him. "Heavens! His face is deathly pale. What happened?"

"I can't imagine," Addie said. "He seems frightened, doesn't he?" Concern clouded her face as she knelt in front of him. "Ceddy? What is it, darling?"

Forgetting herself, Miss Whitfield spoke her mind. "Could it be Mr. Foster's hair? I'm sure he's never seen the like."

Flustered and embarrassed, Pearson gathered the strands off his shoulders.

"I told you this wouldn't work, Addie." Miss Whitfield stood, glancing around at the staring diners. "Whatever has him bothered, it's obvious we can't stay now." She guided the boy toward the exit. "Come, let's get him home. Your salad will have to wait for another day."

Desperate, Pearson caught Addie's sleeve. "If not lunch today, maybe a picnic tomorrow? The hotel will provide a nice basket, if you know of a sunny spot."

She tugged her arm free. "No, thank you. Now, if you'll excuse us. . ."

Pausing on the threshold, she turned. "By the by, Miss Whitfield decided to mail your letter. In fact, we've just left the post office." Tilting her head, she gave him a knowing smile. "You'll be happy to hear that your missive is probably on its way to my mother as we speak. I'm certain my father will find it most entertaining." Nose to the sky, she flounced out the door.

When the stunned haze cleared, Pearson slunk to rejoin Theo at the table.

Glee in his eyes, Theo cleared his throat. "A picnic?"

Pearson released a ragged sigh. "Don't start. It was all I could think of at the moment."

"Sorry, old man," Theo murmured.

"Stop saying you're sorry for me, will you? You said the same the day we left Whitfield Manor."

"I couldn't help it. You looked so dejected when you thought she'd gone." He pointed. "Pretty much the way you do now."

Balling his napkin, he tossed it at Theo's face. "Forget about her. I plan to." Shoving away the salad that seemed so appetizing just moments before, he sat back in his chair. "Let's get out of here. It's time we focused on hiring a couple of hands. The sooner we're done and out of Marshall, the better."

Theo pointed over Pearson's shoulder. "What about those two? They have an out-of-work look to them."

In the far corner, a couple of men sat hunched over their plates, one short and gaunt, the other portly and balding. Both stared out the window with bulging eyes.

Following the direction they gazed, Pearson saw Addie and Miss Whitfield outside the glass, still trying to calm the sobbing child.

"Will you look? They're gawking at Addie."

Theo shrugged. "They're men, Pearson. They're going to watch a pretty woman."

"I don't like how closely they're watching."

"Is that so? I thought we were going to forget about her." Theo nudged his shoulder and stood. "Come on, they're leaving. Let's see if they're interested in work. Or if they know someone who is."

The bony man with the hollow eyes glanced up fast when they neared his table. Tensing, he lowered the money he'd been counting out for his bill into his lap.

Theo ducked his head. "Afternoon, sir. My name is Theodoro Bernardi. We don't mean to intrude, but my friend and I are looking for a couple of locals with idle hands and strong backs."

The men looked ready to bolt for the door.

Pearson edged Theo aside and held out his hand. "Pearson Foster, gentlemen. Forgive my blundering associate. He's trying to ask if you might be seeking gainful employment. We're hoping to hire a pair of laborers."

The meatier of the two waved them off. "Barkin' up the wrong oak, mate. We ain't lookin' for work."

His companion's hand shot up. "Not so fast, Charlie." Grinning up at Pearson with tobacco-stained teeth, he shrugged. "We ain't locals, guvnah. If that don't worry you none, we might 'ave a go. What sort of job are you peddlin'?"

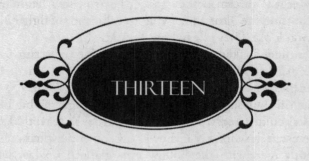

THIRTEEN

Denny gnawed his bottom lip as Mr. Foster and his clownish friend strolled away from the table. Once they passed through the archway and left by the double doors, Charlie clutched his sleeve. "What in blazes are you doing? Why'd you take the job?"

Denny shoved his hand aside. "Think, mate. Those two were talking to the old girl, which means they likely know where she lives. And Charlie, me boy, where she lives is where we'll catch up with that snivelin' brat."

Charlie nodded, a light in his eyes. "And where the brat is. . ."

"I'll find me blessed diamond."

Charlie cocked his head and scowled. "Yours, Denny? We're in this together, you and me."

Denny glanced away. "Sure, that's what I meant."

"Why don't we just follow them home?"

"Well, that was me plan before that strapping big bloke loomed over the table."

"I see your point." Charlie rubbed his bristled chin. "You think the woman recognized us?"

"How could she? She ain't the same one as before."

"You sure about that?"

"Yeah, mate. This girl is younger. . .prettier. Did you notice the uniform? She's a governess to the lad, or some such."

Charlie blew a breath. "The boy knew us right off. Nearly choked on me nosh when he set to squawking."

"Yeah? Well, he's mute. Who's he going to tell?"

Pretending a sudden interest in his food, Charlie swirled cold potatoes with his fork. "You promised not to hurt him, right? No matter what?"

Denny's hand snaked out and caught him by the scruff. "You leave the planning to me. If it was down to you, we'd be on that sinking washtub still, swabbing the deck to pay our passage home."

Drawing his hulking body into a shrunken knot, the big oaf looked like a scolded child. "Sorry, Den. I don't want him hurt, that's all. He's just a wee tyke, after all." He glanced up. "And an orphan, remember? Like you."

Denny shoved him against the back of the chair. "Like me?" He snorted. "Did you see his frilly white shirt with the ruffled collar and cuffs? Those leather shoes with the perky bows? Just one of those shoes cost a month's wage for the likes of us, Charlie Pickering." He pointed a trembling finger, his voice shaking. "That boy's life is nothing like mine."

Reclining against the seat, he crossed his legs and stared out the front window. "We'll take that job all right." He absently stroked his chin. "We'll bide our time, get close to those two blokes. Maybe they'll lead us right inside the house." A slow smile crept over his face. "Who knows? We could be sipping tea and nibblin' biscuits at Ceddy Whitfield's table."

Charlie leaned closer. "You reckon?" He beamed stupidly. "I'd like that."

"Meanwhile, we'll follow them wherever they go. The first chance I get to lay me hands on that boy, I'm takin' it."

Pearson strolled onto the porch ahead of Theo, searching the street for signs of Addie McRae. Spotting the back of her carriage turning toward the hill, he let go a deep sigh. Why did that little girl persist in running away from him? Even more distressing, why did he care?

"Why'd you go and hire those men?" Theo demanded behind him. "They know less about the *Mittie* than we do."

"You're the one who marched us to their table."

"It's a little hard to tell a man's foreign from across the room."

"We need help," Pearson said over his shoulder. "They looked able to haul a dragline. Right now, I'd hire old women."

"Old women might be more helpful. We don't know what we're doing, Pearson. Or where to start. We need locals."

Pearson turned and swept his hand up the street. "Find me a local, and I'll hire him."

Theo stood in front of a bulletin board nailed against the wall, his fists on his hips. "I hope you mean that." Motioning to Pearson, he moved aside to make room. Planting his finger against a handwritten notice tacked to the board, he nodded. "Here's where we'll find all the laborers we need."

Pearson read the first few lines then scowled. "A church social?"

Theo nodded. "Of course. It's perfect."

Feeling smothered, Pearson stalked away. "I don't think it's perfect."

"Sure it is, Pearce. The whole town turns out for these things."

Waving his hand behind him, he drew a deep breath. "If you want to, go ahead. But count me out."

"It's just a church service, buddy. I remember a time when you wouldn't miss one."

"That was a long time ago."

Theo stood quietly for too long. It didn't bode well. "Come on, paisan. What happened to you?"

First Addie's stinging rebuke, and now this? Could the day get any worse? "I know you mean well, Theo, but change the subject."

Theo shook his head. "Not this time. Look, friend. . .you've kept this feud with the Almighty going for five years. Don't you think it's time you made peace?"

Anguish washed over Pearson, as fresh as the day his family died. Gripping the arm of a nearby bench, he lowered his body before his trembling legs gave out. "Mind your own business."

Theo spun closer, surprising Pearson with tear-filled eyes. "It is my business. I spent more time in your house than my own, more time at your mama's table than mine." A wobbly grin slipped through his grief. "We both know it wasn't because of her cooking."

"So?"

"So I know the thing that made them proudest of you was your faith. I also know that if Mama Foster was here, she'd be sad to see you've shut God out."

Pearson's throat threatened to close on his pain. When he could speak, his protest came out a croak. "But she's not here, is she? Neither is Pa, my brother, or my sister." He swiped at his eyes. "That little girl was three years old. She never had a chance at life."

"Thousands perished that night, Pearson. God didn't single out your family to die."

"I never said He did."

Theo splayed his hands. "Then what? What do you blame Him for?"

Leaning over, Pearson gripped his head in his hands. "For singling me out to live."

Scalding tears dripped onto his boot and slid over the side, washing the dust away in little rivulets.

Theo crossed the porch and gripped his shoulder. "I'm going to that service tomorrow. I really hope you'll join me. It's time you forgave yourself for being alive."

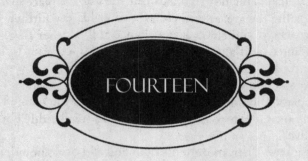

FOURTEEN

Addie hurried downstairs and lit out for the dining room, late for breakfast again. She hadn't quite settled into life at Whitfield Manor, and her duties to Ceddy kept her jumping. There seemed never enough time in the harried mornings to wash up, air out her uniform, arrange her curls, and find her place at the table before Delilah appeared with the food.

Dreading her employer's disapproving glance, Addie slid to a stop outside the door to check her hair and smooth her apron.

"Addie, is that you? You're not dawdling behind the doorpost again."

Addie's shoulders drooped in defeat. "Yes, ma'am." She sighed. "I mean, yes, it's me."

"Stop lurking, dear, and come inside."

Drawing a quick breath, she charged into the fray. "Morning, Priscilla. So sorry I'm late."

The woman's forehead drew to a troubled knot. "What are you wearing, Adelina?"

Addie paused with one hand on the back of her chair and gazed down at her skirt. "I'm sorry. I tried to press out the wrinkles, but my time grew short."

"I don't mean the state of your clothing, child. I'm referring to what you have on. Are you going to church in your uniform?"

Addie gave her a vacant stare. "Oh my. Today's the Sabbath? I completely lost track of the days."

Priscilla picked up her knife and spread a thin layer of butter over a slice of toast. "Get back on track, if you please. I'd like you to accompany me this morning." Her head tipped toward a vacant place at the table. "Sit down before the grease on your eggs congeals any further, and then you can go upstairs and change. I promised your mother I'd see to your spiritual welfare, and I always keep a promise."

"What about Ceddy?"

"He's going with us. Delilah won't be here to watch him. She worships with her family on Sunday mornings."

Addie fingered the folds of her uniform. "As Ceddy's governess, shouldn't I leave this on if we're going to town?"

Priscilla wiped her mouth. "In one of those pompous homes up north, perhaps. We're far less formal around here. I won't require you to wear that dour old thing to God's house."

"Well. . .if you're sure."

"Yes." Priscilla nodded firmly. "I am. I should think you'd relish the chance to show off those pretty spring dresses in your wardrobe. I must say your parents provided well for you." She flashed a sweet smile. "Besides, Addie. . .you're not just Ceddy's governess. I consider you a friend."

Heat rose to Addie's cheeks. She slid into her seat, unfolding her napkin in the same motion and laying it across her lap. "I'm honored. I want you to know I feel the same."

"Then it's settled. I'm going to show off my new friend to my church fellowship."

Addie beamed. "That sounds lovely."

Delilah bustled in, snatching up serving trays and wiping away scattered crumbs. She startled, one hand on the coffee decanter, when Priscilla abruptly cleared her throat. "What are you doing, Delilah? Leave those, please. We're not done eating."

Delilah licked her bottom lip and glanced over her shoulder at the grandfather clock. "You ain't?"

"As you can clearly see, we've hardly touched our plates. I know you're in a rush to be on your way, but allow us to finish our breakfast, please, before you clear the table. In the meanwhile, lay out warm clothing for Ceddy. It actually resembles a winter morn outside, though I doubt the chill will linger past noon."

Addie swallowed a bite of toast and nodded. "The weather has been quite mild and pleasant. I hate to see it end."

Delilah still hovered, thoughtfully gnawing her bottom lip.

"Didn't you hear me, Delilah?" Priscilla swirled her index finger, motioning her out of the room. "Go on with you now and allow us to eat."

"Yes'm." Settling the platter of bacon with a wobble and replacing the silver urn, Delilah backed toward the kitchen door, a troubled frown on her face.

Priscilla sat back in her chair with a sigh. "Oh, for pity's sake. Fry a fresh egg for Addie then go on and leave. This mess can wait until you return. I won't be held accountable to God if the St. Paul Baptist choir lacks a contralto."

"Yes, ma'am," Delilah said, stressing both words with equal fervor and a bright smile. "I'll bring that egg right away." She left in a rush, leaving Addie and Priscilla chuckling after her.

They ate quietly, accompanied by the clink of silverware on china and the steady tick of the tall clock. Growing increasingly aware of Priscilla's watchful eyes, Addie glanced up. "Do you need something, ma'am?" *Priscilla, Priscilla, Priscilla,* she chided herself. Why was it so hard to remember the woman's preference?

Studying the delicate face, etched with concern, Addie realized the reason why. Miss Whitfield reminded her very much of Miss Vee, her childhood governess and family friend. She held such respect and reverence for the old dear, she couldn't call her Viola if she tried. Not only that, but Addie's parents had distilled in her a proper respect for the elderly. Priscilla Whitfield's request was in opposition to years of parental training.

Thankfully, whatever was on her mind seemed to take precedence over how she should be addressed. "I've been thinking all night about Ceddy's. . .episode. . .in the hotel restaurant." She crinkled her brow. "What do you suppose got into him?"

Addie cleared her throat. "His behavior was that much out of character?"

Priscilla nodded. "Indeed, even for Ceddy."

Addie laid down her fork and rested her elbows on the table, her hands folded under her chin. "He seemed afraid of something."

"Yes, I agree. Terrified, in fact." Pain flashed over Priscilla's face. It twists my heart in knots when that boy has a need he can't communicate and I can't cipher. I feel as though I've failed him."

Addie leaned to touch her hand. "You mustn't think that way."

"It's hard not to. I'm responsible for a boy who's a riddle, and I lack intuitive skills." She glanced up. "Unlike you, Addie. Just a few days with Ceddy, and already you sense when his cries are because of a stomachache or when his fits are due to frustration. It's quite a gift, dear."

Flattered, Addie lowered her lashes. "More experience than a gift, I think. I've worked with children from an early age, and my house is filled to the rafters with younger siblings."

"Call it what you will. I consider it an answer to prayer." She turned her hand over and squeezed Addie's fingers. "Thank you for staying."

Their eyes held until Delilah burst in, sliding a golden-topped egg onto Addie's plate. With one quick motion, she scooped the ruined egg onto the same dish and scurried for the door, untying her apron. "Thank you kindly, Miss Priscilla," she called over her shoulder. "I'll be back as quick as I can."

Priscilla sat up and stared. "Mercy! I've seen lightning move slower. Yet when I ask her to hurry, she creeps about moaning and clutching her back."

Addie grinned. "Is she like this every Sunday morning?"

Priscilla reached for a triangle of toast and dipped her spoon in the jam. "Yes, she is. I've often wondered what they've got going in their house of worship that we're missing in ours. Personally, I've never been in such a rush to get to church." She winked. "Maybe we should abandon our plans and join Delilah?"

The grandfather clock let out a series of no-nonsense gongs, drawing Priscilla's eyes to its ornate face. "I suppose you'd best get that egg down and go dress. Our service starts in one hour."

Suddenly starved, Addie obediently tucked into her food, finishing with a last bite of buttered biscuit and the dregs of her glass of milk.

In her room, she laid out her favorite dress, the pale blue taffeta with lace collar and sleeves, so striking against her dark hair. It was her father's favorite, too, and she smiled fondly remembering his proud grin when she wore it.

The thought of his dear, trusting face pained her stomach and made her furious with Mr. Foster all over again. The thought that anyone would seek to dishonor her parents' marriage boiled the blood in her veins. How dare the pompous dandy? Did he presume to think his attention would flatter her mother? That she would for a single moment think to hide the note from Father?

Before, Pearson's arresting good looks drew her wistful thoughts to him. Now he seemed dark and ugly despite his sun-washed hair and the golden glow of his skin. What mischief had he been about in the restaurant with his ridiculous invitation to a picnic? Wasn't the clandestine note to a married woman bad enough? Did he think to use Addie to get to her mother?

Priscilla had been shocked that they'd shared a lunch with two strange men. If she ever realized what Addie knew about the letter she'd mailed, she'd be scandalized.

"Addie?" Her tinny voice echoed from the stairs, jerking Addie's head toward the door.

One thing was certain. . .Addie wouldn't tell her. The thought of such behavior burned her cheeks with shame. She couldn't imagine voicing her suspicions aloud. Stopping briefly at the mirror to pin on her hat and straighten her sash, she grabbed her parasol and hurried down the hall.

Priscilla peered up from the bottom landing and smiled. "Are we ready?"

Addie gave a jaunty nod. "We're ready. I've dressed Cedric in long pants. Just let me get him from his room."

Downstairs, Priscilla led the procession onto the wide porch and down the steps where the carriage waited.

Despite the predicted chill in the air, warm sun rays on Addie's shoulders promised it wouldn't last. She drew her light shawl around herself and smiled. They were in for a beautiful day.

The ride seemed over before it started as the driver pulled up to a handsome brick building overlooked by a tall steeple. Leaping down, he helped first Priscilla then Addie and the boy to the ground.

The sidewalk leading to the steps was empty. Except for a cluster of men hovering over a smoking pit out back, the grounds were deserted. Tables with bright, checkered cloths dotted the grassy yard on both sides of the building. Beneath the trees, colorful quilts were spread.

An usher opened the door, nodding a welcome. Strains of music and voices raised in song floated to them from inside the foyer.

"Gracious, I suppose we're later than I thought. I'd hoped to introduce you before the service started, but it looks like that will have to wait." Priscilla winked and took Ceddy's hand. "Might be more fun this way. We get to make an entrance and set them to whispering."

Addie grimaced. The last thing she wanted was to cause a stir in church. Gulping, she followed Priscilla to a vacant spot on a pew near the front, squirming as their passage down the aisle provoked upturned faces and curious stares.

At the end of the hymn, the minister raised his head, a big smile on his face. "So glad you could join us, Priscilla. As you can see, we saved your place."

Unfazed by his banter, Priscilla nodded and settled regally on the pew. "Morning, Reverend."

Friendly chuckles followed.

Much to Addie's discomfort, he swept his arm her way. "I see you've brought a guest. Who might this lovely young lady be?"

Catching Addie's hand, Priscilla stood, dragging her to her feet. "This is my friend Adelina McRae, formerly of Mississippi. She's going to be living in my house and helping me with Ceddy."

"Fine," the minister boomed. "We're so glad to have you. Congregation, please welcome Adelina McRae to our midst."

The room erupted in a round of hearty nods and friendly voices. Beside her, Ceddy moaned softly and clapped his hands over his ears.

"The Lord has richly blessed us with guests today, hasn't He?" He turned his smiling eyes on the front row. "I see we have two other newcomers right here. Stand up, please, gentlemen, and introduce yourselves."

Addie's intake of air sounded so loud in her ears she thought those around her were bound to hear. There was no mistaking the tops of their heads, one dark and curly, the other twisted coils.

They stood, Pearson's shoulders so wide they blocked sight of the organist. His delighted eyes were fixed on Addie, and likely had been since he'd first heard Miss Priscilla call her name. "My friend here is Theo Bernardi, and I'm Pearson." His simpering smile mocked her across the sea of curious people. "Pearson Foster from Galveston."

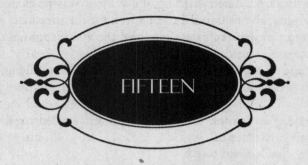

FIFTEEN

I don't believe it!" Priscilla leaned to whisper. "Can you imagine the gall?"

"No." Addie scowled and pulled her gaze from Pearson's searching eyes. "I certainly can't."

They sat in a rush of satin and crinkle of petticoats.

"What are they doing here?" Addie murmured as the preacher went on with the service. "Do you suppose they followed us?"

Her friend shot her a look. "Highly unlikely, dear, considering they were inside when we arrived."

Flustered, Addie busied herself with soothing Ceddy while her troubled thoughts swirled among the rafters.

Pearson Foster in church? She feared for those sitting in close proximity to him, for they were surely in danger of lightning bolts. Remembering the day they met and his annoyed reaction to blessing the food, Addie nibbled her bottom lip.

Unable to contain herself, she inclined her head for a peek past the person in front of her. Sure enough, Pearson sat twisted in his seat, boldly staring her way. She drew in her chin and inched closer to Ceddy on the pew, out of his line of sight. In all her experience with the opposite gender—albeit limited, thanks to overprotective parents—she'd never met a more vexing man.

Between Ceddy's bored wiggling, her own troubling thoughts, and Pearson's furtive over-the-shoulder glances, Addie hadn't a clue what the minister's message contained. She thought it may have been a cautionary discourse on the perils of judging your fellow man, but she couldn't say for sure.

Distracted by her musings, she failed to stand for the closing prayer until Priscilla tapped her shoulder. Humiliated by Pearson's quick glance and knowing smile, even more embarrassed that he'd caught her looking again, her cheeks glowed with heat. Dismissed with a hearty invitation to stay for the social, they stood and waited their turn to file outside.

The pastor had approached Pearson and Theo, engaging them in a lively discussion as they passed. Addie couldn't resist watching Pearson go by. The trouble was, he stood out wherever he went. His unusual good looks drew the eye of everyone around him. With his golden skin and hair, the man seemed to glow.

Priscilla stepped into the aisle. Catching Ceddy's reluctant hand, Addie slipped in behind her and followed her out. In the yard, a flurry of Priscilla's cronies descended in a cackling rush. Eager to introduce her to each of them in turn, Priscilla tugged her this way and that until Addie's arm grew sore from the press of her fingers.

Throughout the session of greetings and the endless string of polite questions, Addie remained acutely aware of Pearson, still in quiet conversation with the minister and several other men who had joined them. She told herself his soaring height was the reason she couldn't keep her eyes from wandering his way.

The tone of the men's conversation had somehow turned. Instead of lighthearted banter, two of the men seemed to be teasing Pearson and his friend unmercifully.

A dark cloud of resentment had settled over Theo's face. Smiling and nodding good-naturedly, Pearson seemed to take it in stride.

Noticing Addie gazing past her shoulder, the young woman across from her turned to see what held her attention. "Very handsome men, wouldn't you say, Adelina? Especially the tall one."

Her older companion wrinkled her brow. "Mind your tongue, Dora. You're on church grounds."

"Sorry, Mother. Just stating the obvious."

Pretty is as pretty does goes for men, as well, Addie thought, but she wouldn't say so.

After another round of boisterous laughter, the men dispersed. Theo and Pearson were immediately swept up by a second group of curious folks, but the minister strolled Addie's way. "Miss McRae, wasn't it?"

Addie smiled and nodded. "Yes, sir, but you may call me Addie."

"My pleasure, considering we'll be spending every Sunday afternoon together. I have a standing invitation to lunch at Whitfield Manor." He raised his brows. "Although today it appears you're my guests. I'm Reverend Abner Stroud, in case our dear Priscilla failed to mention." A good-natured grin lit his face. "Part-time barber, full-time preacher. I can trim a man's hair and save his soul all from the same chair." He leaned closer and winked. "Of course, it's not me doing the saving, you know. I'm just an instrument in the Master's hands, much like a straight razor's a tool in mine."

Narrowing one eye, he tilted his head. "Which brings to mind a scripture, if you'll indulge me. 'For the word of God is quick, and powerful, and sharper than any two-edged sword'"—his sudden swipe through the air with an imaginary weapon made Addie jump— "'piercing even to the dividing asunder of soul and spirit, and of the joints and marrow, and is a discerner of the thoughts and intents of the heart.'" He offered a wide grin. "Pretty much says it all, doesn't it?"

Glancing at Pearson, Addie squirmed. Should the sword of the Spirit happen to pierce her anxious heart, dark rage and deep distrust would spill out.

Priscilla nudged the reverend with her elbow. "Speaking of discerning a person's thoughts and intents"—she nodded toward the lively circle surrounding Pearson and Theo—"I see you've met Marshall's latest opportunists."

Reverend Stroud checked over his shoulder. "Yes. Yes, I have. *Wonderful* fellows, in fact. Pure-hearted, honest men."

Addie and Priscilla blinked at each other.

"Th–they are?" Addie stammered.

Lacking an ounce of decorum, Priscilla extended her arm and wiggled a bold finger. "I'm referring to those two ruffians. The newcomers with the odd hair."

"Yes, indeed," the reverend said. "Fine Christian men, the both of them."

Priscilla gaped. "Are you quite sure?"

He nodded firmly. "I have a sense about such things. Knew it from the moment I looked into their eyes." He twisted around to gesture with his nod. "Especially the tall fellow. Very sensitive to godly matters." He frowned. "Something holds him captive though. I'm not sure what."

Priscilla smoothed her gloved fingers over her mouth. "Well, I'll be. . . I took him for a cheap, money-grasping treasure seeker."

Reverend Stroud laughed aloud. "Priscilla Whitfield. Didn't one word of my sermon penetrate?"

"I'm not judging, Reverend. For a fact, they're in town hoping to make a fast dollar."

"My dear lady. . .you can't possibly know their motives for wanting to raise the *Mittie*."

Disappointment furrowed her brow. She'd lost her edge in the debate. "They told you what they're up to?"

"Seemed to have nothing to hide." He smiled. "A good thing, since Sam Donley from the department store and a few of the others were giving them quite a hard time just now." He studied her pursed lips then rested his hands on his hips. "I'll admit to knowing less about women than most crusty old bachelors, but why should their interest in a downed steamboat so offend you ladies?"

Addie nibbled her bottom lip, unable to answer. She dared not mention her reason for disliking Pearson.

She needn't have worried. Priscilla had no such qualms. "Plundering shipwrecked vessels and digging for lost treasure isn't exactly an honorable profession," she said. "I would think they could find better use of their time."

"It's a dangerous pursuit, Priscilla. One that takes a tremendous amount of courage and faith. Given half their fortitude, I'd trade in my shears for an eye patch and blade." He winked at Addie. "Instead of a preaching barber"—his invisible sword slashed the air between them— "I'd be a swashbuckling minister."

"You, Reverend?"

"Yes, indeed. The lure of lost gold drives many men. In most cases, it's due to a heightened sense of adventure rather than greed. Whatever the cause, the trait can work in their favor in the end. Such men have a great appreciation for the abundant reward promised to the believer."

His dancing gaze jerked past them. "Here come our fortune hunters now. I admonish you two to make them feel welcome."

Confusion glued Addie's tongue to the roof of her mouth while Pearson and Theo descended. The reverend's words clashed against recent events with the force of sparring horns. How could the man who sought to woo her mother's affections be the one Reverend Stroud described?

Rocking on his heels behind Pearson, Theo grinned foolishly. "Afternoon, ladies."

Pearson stood straight-backed and tall and nodded her way. "Miss McRae, it's nice to see you again so soon." A winsome smile warmed his face. "It's interesting how we continue to cross paths in a town of this size." He gave her a penetrating look, his bronzed forehead creased. "Do you believe in destiny?"

Before Addie could gather her wits to speak, her companion swept closer and held out her hand. "Mr. Foster, isn't it?"

Still watching Addie, Pearson dutifully took hold of Priscilla's fingers. "Miss Whitfield." He withdrew his gaze. "We had no idea this was your place of worship."

Addie studied him through lowered lashes. *He's telling the truth.*

"Oh yes," Priscilla said. "For many years. We're pleased you decided to join us this morning."

We are? The warmth of her voice and genteel manner were entirely too friendly.

Priscilla patted Pearson's hand. "Reverend Stroud was just telling us what fine Christian soldiers you are."

He arched expressive brows. "He was?"

She raised her chin and drew a deep breath—as if she'd made up her mind on an important matter. "Gentlemen," she said brightly, "I'd be honored if you'd accompany our party to Whitfield Manor after the social for coffee and conversation. I'd like to get to know you better."

Pearson's startled gaze darted to Addie, likely to gauge her reaction. Unfortunately, she didn't disappoint.

Ceddy squatted in the cover of the hedge surrounding the churchyard. Too cool in the shade, but at least he was out of the sun. He didn't care for sunshine on the top of his head. Did not like it one bit.

He dug with the ragged edge of an oyster shell, searching for colorful stones and scratching his name in the dark earth between his knees. Drawn by the musty smell, he tossed the shell aside and buried his fingers in the soft, black dirt.

The evergreen branches behind him stirred, teasing his back. The faint crack of a broken branch reached his ears.

Ceddy stilled. Waited. Then sniffed and went on digging.

The stir became a rustle, and fear slid up his spine. Ever so slowly he turned. Afraid to look, he lowered his eyelids and peeked through shiny lashes.

Sunken eyes. Skeleton teeth. A twisted face leered through the bushes. "Boo!" its gravelly voice barked.

Ceddy opened wide to shriek, but a row of dirty fingers clamped over his face. Cruel hands dragged him through the hedges to the other side and rolled him to his stomach. His nose, so close to the ground, sucked dust that tickled his nostrils as he struggled to breathe.

"Hold him tight, Denny. Don't let him wail."

"I've got him a'right. You do like I said and search his pockets. Pat him down good, now."

"Don't fret, mate. If it's on him, old Charlie will find it." Rough hands slapped at Ceddy's clothing and fumbled with his pockets. Heavy breathing. A labored sigh. "Nothing this side. Help me flip the little beggar."

Ceddy's body lifted as though weightless and spun, landing him on his back. The creepy eyes of Mr. Currie bore down on him. "Search every nook and cranny, Charlie," he snarled, still watching Ceddy. "Leave no stone unturned." He smiled, his dark teeth and crinkled skin a horrid sight. "You catch that? I made a funny. No stone. You get it?"

Ignoring him, Charlie sat back on his heels. "It's not here. Must be stashed somewhere."

Mr. Currie muttered a vile curse, words Aunt Priss never allowed uttered, his hurtful grip tightening on Ceddy. "Blast the luck!" He sighed. "Well, no matter. We'll get our hands on it yet."

"How you reckon to do that?"

"You leave that to me." Holding the oyster shell against Ceddy's neck, Mr. Currie jerked it in one quick motion.

Ceddy gave a muffled cry of fear and pain.

"You see that, boy? If you tell, that's what will happen to you, only for real. I'll come in the night and slit your throat. Bleed you like a butchering hog."

Charlie spun on him. "Aw, Denny, don't hurt him. And stop spewing such awful things. The boy can't understand a word."

"Don't be so sure. Look at the fear in his eyes. His aunt said he was smarter than most."

"Remember, the poor lad's mute, so who's he going to tell?"

"I'm making sure he don't find a way."

The scary man leaned close, his smelly breath hot on Ceddy's face. "Listen real careful-like, little pollywog. I'm going to turn you loose now. You're to stand up and stroll across the yard like you 'aven't a care in the world, yeah? Hands in your pockets, whistle a tune if you like. No trouble now, right?"

Staring past the grimy calloused hand over his mouth, Ceddy tried to nod but couldn't summon the strength.

Mr. Currie shook him so hard his bones ached. "Right?"

"Leave off him, Denny! You know he can't answer."

"All right then. You just do like I say, or I'll slice up your old auntie before I cut out your gizzard. The governess, too, and I'll make you watch." Jerking Ceddy to his feet, Mr. Currie shot him a final warning glare then slowly withdrew his hands.

Ceddy stared at the ground while the evil man roughly brushed dirt off his clothes.

"Off with you now," he whispered, shoving him through the hedge. "And not a word."

Longing to dash away to Aunt Priss's skirt, Ceddy drew his shoulders to his ears and walked stiffly to the carriage, resisting with every ounce of his strength the urge to run.

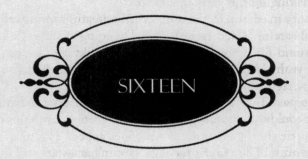

SIXTEEN

Pearson drove his hired rig up the hill behind Miss Whitfield's fancy carriage. Lilting voices drifted to his ears, those of their hostess and Reverend Stroud. As near as he could tell, Miss McRae hadn't spoken a single word since they'd left the churchyard.

Theo nudged his side. "You sure you're not Irish? You're the luckiest man in Texas."

Lifting his brows, Pearson grinned. "Why's that?"

"In the span of a church service, the old lady went from despising you to loving you." He splayed his hands. "And you didn't have to do a thing."

Pearson laughed. "I used to think of it as God's favor. Unmerited grace. Nowadays, I'm not so sure. Whatever it is, I don't deserve it, but I won't turn it down." His gaze drifted to the back of the carriage, and warmth spread through his chest. "Especially in this case." He grinned. "Besides, I knew my charm and good looks would eventually sway her."

"Don't get cocky. You still haven't won the trust of her pretty governess."

His elated mood dampened at Theo's words. Addie had carefully avoided him at the social, an impressive skill considering he sat right across from her while they ate. She'd picked at her food, not in the dainty way of a self-conscious woman but as if she'd lost her appetite and he was the cause.

He frowned and glanced at Theo. "Why do you suppose she finds me so disagreeable?"

Theo's booming laughter echoed off the trunks of a passing grove, drawing looks from the party up ahead.

Pearson jabbed him in the arm. "Will you stop braying and pretend you have an ounce of decorum?"

"I'm sorry," Theo howled then covered his mouth. "It's just funny to hear those words coming from you. That's usually my line."

"Well, keep it down."

Theo sobered and his eyes softened. "Doesn't feel good, does it?"

It didn't feel a bit good, in fact. Especially coming from this particular female.

"Take heart," Theo said, grinning. "Your charms are still in working order. You've got the old lady's devotion, and every unattached girl at the social is at your beck and call."

Pearson flashed a wry smile. "I wish I'd had as much luck befriending the men. As soon as they heard we were seeking the *Mittie*, they lost all interest in taking a job. Most backed away as if we'd uttered a curse."

"Maybe we did." Theo raised a brow. "Maybe the *Mittie* herself is cursed."

Pearson jerked his head to scowl at him. "That's absurd."

"Is it? It would explain why she's still out there."

The buggy up ahead rattled over the uneven ground and pulled to a stop in the circular drive. Pearson pulled in behind them, set his brake, and climbed down.

"Welcome, welcome," Miss Whitfield called, waving them up the stone path. "Please come inside."

The boy pulled free of Addie and bolted, taking the steps so fast he tripped. Scrambling onto the porch, he pounded the door with clenched fists. When it opened, he scurried past the maid and disappeared inside the house.

"What pulled his tail?" she asked, hands on her hips.

"Oh good, Delilah, you're home," Miss Whitfield said. "Put the kettle on, will you? And slice up some pie. We have guests."

"Right away, ma'am," Delilah said, taking their burdensome coats.

Pearson had shed his hours ago as the weather grew warmer and felt relieved to be free of it.

Theo leaned close to Pearson. "Look at the size of this foyer. Pull in a table and bed, and I could live in here."

He'd meant the comment for Pearson's ears only, but his voice carried in the vast room.

Miss Whitfield smiled over her shoulder. "It's far too much room for one crotchety old lady, and a shameful waste of space." Her gaze shifted to Addie climbing the spiral stairs, likely following the child. "Having dear Addie move in and my great-nephew underfoot helps ease my conscience at the vulgar pretentiousness of such a dwelling."

Pearson nudged Theo.

He shrugged and made a face.

"Let's retire to the parlor, shall we? Delilah will be right in with our refreshments."

Filing into the splendid room, Pearson rubbed his stomach. After the lavish spread on the church grounds, he wondered where he could cram another bite. By the uncomfortable look on Reverend Stroud's face, he guessed he felt the same. The man looked due for a tonic.

The afternoon passed in pleasant conversation. Confirming Pearson's suspicions, the reverend requested a ginger tea instead of coffee and pie. After his second cup, and several discreet belches, a livelier glow appeared on his cheeks.

Propping his arm on the back of the velvet couch, he beamed at Pearson. "So you're after the *Mittie*. As I told Priscilla here, I'm quite envious. What I wouldn't give to go along on the search."

"Really?" Pearson placed his coffee on the low table between them. "You're the only man in Marshall who feels that way."

He waved his hand. "Oh, don't mind them. They're bound by fear and superstition." He chuckled. "A fact that works in your favor, I suppose. Otherwise, she wouldn't still be out there somewhere."

His face aglow with interest, Theo sat forward. "What are they afraid of?"

The reverend sobered. "No one knows unless they're from the area. Those who do aren't saying. It's like they're afraid to talk."

Theo nudged Pearson. "I told you it was cursed."

Reverend Stroud's attention jumped to him. "Cursed, eh? That's what the Caddo Indians believed. They'd walk a mile out of their way to avoid the site."

Excitement firing in his chest, Pearson scooted to the edge of his seat. "Which means they knew the exact location?"

"Yes, I suppose they did."

"Where could I find a Caddo Indian?"

He smiled and shook his head. "If you found one, Pearson, it would do you little good. Those remaining few along the lake feel the same as their ancestors did. Bad medicine, they call it. I doubt they'd help you." His eyes sparked with remembrance. "However, there is one person. The fellow's not an Indian, mind you, but he may as well be." He paused. "But I'm afraid he might be just as hard to find. They call him—"

"Catfish John," Pearson and Theo finished for him.

Laughing, Reverend Stroud sat back and crossed his legs. "I see you're already acquainted with Marshall's own Daniel Boone."

"Not yet, sir," Pearson said, "but I hope to be."

Settling into the cushions, the reverend turned the warmth of his smile on their hostess. "Priscilla? I believe I'll take a slice of that rhubarb pie now, if there's any left."

"Of course," she said, laying aside her plate and standing. "Boys, would you care for more?"

Theo held out his saucer. "I could go for another piece. Best pie I've had in years."

Pearson stood, handing the dish to Miss Whitfield. "None for me, thanks. But I could use some fresh air."

"Help yourself to the back porch swing. I want you all to make yourselves right at home. I simply won't have it any other way."

Rounding her chair, she motioned for him to join her. "Come, I'll walk you into the hall and point the way. I adore lazy Sunday afternoons, don't you, Mr. Foster?" Pausing, she gripped his arm. "Oh pooh. I'm going to call you Pearson, if that's all right?"

He smiled. "Of course."

Following her instructions, Pearson navigated the hallways until he reached the double doors at the back of the house. Pushing past the screen, he stepped onto a wide, covered veranda overlooking a whitewashed gazebo and a lush garden that sloped downhill and out of sight. From this vantage, atop the rise, the whole town of Marshall lay at his feet. His soul at ease, he drew a deep breath and braced his hands on the high back of the swing.

Too late, he noticed the small black pair of sensible shoes placed neatly beneath the contraption. It swung sharply forward then rocked dizzily back.

"Oh!" Addie cried. Struggling to sit against the motion of the seat, she clutched her book with one hand and grasped the cushion under her head with the other, dragging it to the ground.

Horrified, Pearson rushed to her aid, trying to steady the swing while he helped her up.

"Mr. Foster!" she shrilled. "What are you doing?"

"I'm so sorry," he croaked. "I didn't see you."

Her eyes had the sleepy glaze of one just awakened from a nap. "How could you not see me? I'm right here. If I didn't know better, I'd think you were trying to launch me into the daffodils."

Leaning to pick up the cushion, he used the time to wipe the smile off his face. "I assure you I had no designs in that direction." Unable to resist, he added, "Though you would be a charming addition to the garden."

Addie huffed and crossed her arms. "Flattery will not earn my forgiveness."

Pearson handed her the pillow. "Tell me what will, and I'll get right on it."

She shot him a sullen pout and tucked a curl behind her ear.

He motioned to the empty spot beside her. "Do you mind if I sit while you think it over?"

She gathered her book and shawl. "You may take my place. I really should—"

He lifted a staying hand. "Please don't go."

Her mouth set in a firm line, she turned up her fetching face and studied him.

"Unless you have to, of course." He smiled. "Otherwise, I'd really appreciate your company."

Settling against the cushion, she gave a curt nod. "I suppose I can stay until Ceddy wakes from his nap."

They sat quietly, Pearson gently rocking the swing with one foot. He stared across the misty miles stretching toward town, trying to regain the sense of peace he'd felt before. The woman sitting beside him stirred him to anguish instead. He'd never desired the acceptance of a person so strongly. Never craved a woman's interest so dearly. His stomach pitched when she shifted toward him on the seat.

"So. . .um. . .do you like Marshall so far?"

An effort at small talk. It was a start. "I do. The townsfolk seem to be goodhearted people, and the weather's nice."

A smile twitched her lips. "And which hour's weather would you be referring to?"

Pearson laughed, a little too loudly. "You make a good point. I'm used to the fickle nature of the climate though. It behaves the same in Galveston." He raised one brow. "Is Mississippi a little more predictable?"

This time she nearly grinned. "Not in the least, although we don't boast of the fact as often as you Texans do."

He'd already taken note of her eyes, of course. They were her best feature. Wide most of the time, as if soaking in her surroundings. Intelligent and strikingly brown. But he hadn't noticed the dark rings circling her pupils, lending a depth to her gaze that pierced right down to his soul.

"You don't much favor your mother, Miss McRae," he blurted. "Except for the color of your hair. I suppose you take after your father?" Leaning, he lifted his finger toward her face. "Did you know that your eyes—"

She stiffened and drew back. "What do you mean I don't favor her?"

He lowered his hand. "Well, nothing, really."

"What were you implying?"

He squirmed at her angry tone, the motion jostling them. "It's just that, with your fair complexion"—he smiled and pointed at her nose—"and that little smattering of freckles, well, you're—"

"Not nearly as pretty?"

Pearson's gut twisted. "That's not what I'm suggesting at all." His unpracticed foray into the art of flirtation wasn't going well. "Your mother's a beautiful woman, but—"

Addie stood, cutting him off midsentence. "You've said quite enough."

Struggling against the ridiculous, pitching swing, Pearson pushed to his feet. "I'm only trying to say that I find you quite attractive."

"Oh stop! Honestly, Mr. Foster, I won't have you use me this way. Secondhand flattery is a low-class, despicable ploy to get to my mother. You should be ashamed." Gathering her skirts, she marched to the door. Pausing on the threshold, she turned. Her pretty features were twisted with rage, but the glint of a tear shone from the corner of her eye. "And just when I'd started to doubt my suspicions. . ." Jerking the screen nearly off its hinges, she swept inside.

Pearson gaped after her, speechless. She couldn't really believe what she'd just said. He didn't know much about Mississippi women, but if they went to these lengths to discourage a suitor, he'd stick with Texas girls.

Angry with herself for her threatening tears, Addie charged up the stairs.

Only moments before, when her drowsy lids closed on the pages of *Villette*, her mind had replayed the events of the day. She'd finally concluded that if her employer and Reverend Stroud vouched for Mr. Foster, then she must be mistaken about him. She would defer to their good instincts and put all her suspicions aside. How foolish Addie felt now to consider trusting him. All the man could find to talk about was her beautiful mother.

Outside Ceddy's room, Addie paused to compose herself. As sensitive as he was to change, he would notice her distress right away. She didn't want to upset him. Wiping her eyes and smoothing her skirt, she put a smile on her face and opened the door.

On the threshold, she frowned. Ceddy wasn't sitting in the window seat, his favorite spot, or sprawled on the floor surrounded by rocks. His bed, where she'd left him huddled under the quilt, was empty. His shoes and stockings, always the first things off when he entered his room, were no longer scattered across the rug.

Spinning, she rushed along the hall calling his name and checking every room and closet. Finding nothing, she hurtled down the stairs and bolted for the kitchen, praying she'd discover him tracing planks on the kitchen floor.

She recruited Delilah, and together they searched the bottom floor. Addie peeked discreetly inside the parlor, smiled and backed out again when Priscilla glanced up.

Hurrying upstairs in a panic, she went over the top floor again while Delilah scoured the yard. Her heart pulsing in her throat, she met Delilah on the bottom landing and questioned her with frantic eyes.

Trembling, Delilah shook her head and pulled Addie into her arms. "It's time, honey," she whispered, her voice breaking. "You can't put it off no mo'."

Cringing, she nodded. Breaking free of Delilah's comforting arms, Addie marched woodenly toward the parlor, praying for the strength to tell Priscilla that Ceddy was gone.

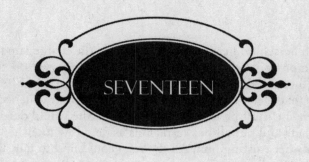

SEVENTEEN

His head whirling, Pearson pushed out of the swing and opened the door. Spotting Theo striding toward him, he pointed over his shoulder. "You won't believe what just happened."

He bit back the rest when Reverend Stroud rounded the corner, white-faced and shaken.

Theo clutched his shoulder. "Pearson, the little boy is missing."

Pearson looked past Theo into the hall, half expecting to see Ceddy crouched at the foot of the stairs. "Are you sure?"

"The women have searched every inch of the house," the reverend said, "and called until they're hoarse."

Spinning, Pearson stared toward the garden. "I saw the maid running over the grounds, but I never imagined. . ." He firmed his jaw. "The boy's got to be here somewhere. He couldn't get far on foot."

A tearful Miss Whitfield pushed past the reverend and Theo, wringing her hands. "Ceddy's simply gone. We've looked everywhere. In the pantries, closets, and storerooms. The bedrooms, sitting rooms, and his late grandfather's den." She shuddered. "Even the abandoned servants' quarters. There's no sign of him."

"Has he ever done this before?"

She shook her head emphatically. "Never. He's a slave to routine and seldom varies his actions. This time of day he's always in his room napping then playing with his rock collection." Her hand twistin intensified. "Poor Addie. She's distraught. Blames herself for leaving him alone for so long."

Guilt twisted Pearson's stomach. She'd tried to go to the boy, but he'd held her. "Don't fret, ma'am. We'll find him." Spurred into action, Pearson directed the reverend to search the front of the estate and Theo to scour the thick woods to the right of the property. "I'll take the garden slope and the stand of trees to the left."

"I suggest double duty, gentlemen," the reverend said.

"How's that?" Theo asked.

He set his mouth in a grim line. "Pray while you look."

Pearson nodded then vaulted past Addie's daffodil beds into the grassy yard. With the onset of dusk, the serenity of the well-laid garden became a shadowy, ominous maze. Meticulous in his method, he crisscrossed the yard, checking the limbs of every tree and the base of every hedge. Topping the slope, he trudged downhill to the property line then cut along the picket fence and ducked into the trees, calling Ceddy's name. Theo's voice, and the reverend's, echoed back to him in the distance.

For the second time that day, he said a prayer. *God, please watch over Ceddy. Help us find him.*

The first stole into his mind that morning in church, the sermon washing over him in waves of healing oil, the scriptures in his ears like soothing balm. Taken by surprise at how he'd missed God's house and the fellowship with believers, tears had threatened and a plea rose unbidden. *Help me to forgive You.* It seemed a forward, sinful prayer, but it came from the depths of his wounded soul.

Show me the way back to Your side. Would God honor such a prayer? Pearson hoped so, because without help he'd never find his way through all the pain.

Exhaustion and thirst, more than the closing darkness, drove him toward the house. They'd wasted enough time. They'd have to go for help.

Theo and Reverend Stroud stood in the foyer speaking in low tones as he walked in. They spun with questioning eyes.

Pearson shook his head, and they slumped in disappointment. "Sir, can you round up a search party from your congregation?"

He nodded. "We're of like minds. I was just telling young Theo the same."

"Then we'd best go get them. It's getting dark and cold out there. We may be running out of time."

Delilah appeared, running halfway down the stairs, her heels loud on the steps. "Miss Priscilla," she shrieked, "you best come quick."

The woman burst from the parlor with a startled glance then ran up the staircase faster than Pearson thought possible for a woman her age.

Tight on her heels, they spun into the boy's room.

"Thank you, merciful God!" she shouted.

Addie sat on the floor, holding the sobbing boy close to her breast, rocking him gently. He appeared drained, his head drooping, his arms hanging limp.

"Is he hurt?" Priscilla asked.

Tears shining in her eyes, Addie released a breath. "I don't think so. He was under his bed the whole time, cowering in fear."

"How could that be?" Miss Whitfield asked, as if she couldn't make sense of the words.

"On impulse, I lifted the quilt and found him rolled into a shivering ball. Something has frightened him half out of his wits."

Pearson knelt beside her. "Do you want us to go for a doctor?"

"That might be a good idea."

Miss Whitfield shook her head. "There's no need, Pearson. I'll send my carriage."

Ceddy's hand fell open, and a large white rock slipped from his fingers, rattling across the floor. He whimpered and stirred.

Glancing up, Addie sought Pearson's eyes. "Will you get it for him, please?"

Pearson picked up the milky white stone, surprised by its weight, and offered it to the boy.

His small fingers closed around it possessively, his breath catching on a sob.

Miss Whitfield motioned toward the door. "Leave us alone with him, gentlemen, if you please? I'd like for Addie to dress him for bed."

"Of course," Pearson said, pushing off the floor. Realizing Addie couldn't rise with the boy in her arms, he bent to gather the frail, still body to his chest. Cradling Ceddy's head, he gently carried him to the bed and laid him down. On impulse, he smoothed the hair off his forehead then patted his cheek. "Rest well, little fellow."

"Oh my," Miss Whitfield whispered, her fingers working the lace collar at her throat. "He won't usually allow strangers to touch him. You must be very good with children."

He gave her a tight smile. "I had a brother his age."

She touched his arm. "Had?"

"I lost him five years ago. In the Galveston storm."

Miss Whitfield tightened her hand. "I'm so very sorry, dear."

Ceddy stirred, almost asleep, winding his arms above his pillow and lolling his head to the side.

Addie gasped and rushed to the bed. "What on earth is this?"

"What is it, dear?" Miss Whitfield scurried to join her.

When she gasped, too, Pearson and the others crowded close to see. From ear to ear, an angry red line marred the skin of his neck. Droplets of blood had oozed and dried in tiny pearls along the ugly scratch.

Grabbing the lantern off the table, Miss Whitfield held it over him then groaned as if in pain. Ugly bruises covered his cheeks like black and blue fingers stretched over his mouth. She lifted his shirt, revealing more bruising on his stomach and along his sides.

Addie gently probed the wound on Ceddy's neck, and he moaned in his sleep. "What could have done this?" she demanded.

"You mean who," Reverend Stroud said. "Was he playing with anyone at the social? A ruffian or bully perhaps?"

Miss Whitfield glanced over her shoulder. "Oh Reverend, another child couldn't have done this."

He shrugged. "You'd be surprised."

"It wasn't here before we got home," Addie insisted. "I would've seen it."

"Not necessarily," Theo said. "Not with the cut tucked under his chin like that. And it takes awhile for bruises to show."

"That's why he 'fraid," Delilah announced from the doorway. "Some fool been hurtin' him."

The circle of people gazed around at each other.

Straightening, Miss Whitfield clenched her fists at her sides. "I don't know who did it, but when I find out—and I will get to the bottom of this—there will be swift reckoning." The rage burning in her eyes left no doubt of her sincerity.

"I'm relieved we found him, at least," the reverend said. "Poor little mite."

"Do you really think this happened at the church?" Pearson asked.

The man shrugged. "Anything is possible these days, and if you don't mind my saying, it would be preferable to the alternative."

"Which is?"

Reverend Stroud's throat worked furiously before he spoke. "That someone in our midst is the culprit."

Addie opened Ceddy's door and stole another look. By the light of the lamp she'd left burning, she watched him sleep. His long lashes fluttered occasionally, and his rosy mouth puckered. A beautiful boy awake, he seemed angelic at rest.

Backing from the room, she pulled the door closed and leaned her head against it. What had happened to him that day? How could she have allowed it? She should have watched him more closely instead of Mr. Foster. "If only I could go back and change it," she whispered.

"Wishing won't make it so, dear."

Startled by the voice behind her, Addie jumped.

"Forgive me," Priscilla said, drawing her dressing gown tight. "I couldn't rest either. Is he all right?"

"He seems to be."

"Good." She stretched, twisting her head back and forth, as if working out the kinks. "It's not your fault, Addie. I don't want you thinking so."

"Of course it is. He's my charge."

"A lot took place today, most of it out of his normal routine. You can't be prepared all the time. I neglected to watch him, too." She frowned and nibbled the corner of her lip. "The thing I can't put out of my mind is this: we were with trusted friends the whole time. It just doesn't make sense, unless. . ."

"Go on."

She glanced up. "Follow me, if you please. I want to talk to you in private."

A deserted hallway in the dead of night seemed private enough, but Addie wouldn't say so. She followed Priscilla to the end of the hall and into her large, ornate bedroom. The scent of lavender met her at the door, and soft rugs cushioned her feet. Uneasy to be in her employer's private space, she paused just inside and waited.

"Come along," Priscilla said, patting a striped divan. "Have a seat right here."

Addie trudged obediently to the sofa and perched on the edge.

Priscilla climbed into an overstuffed chair and tucked her bare feet beneath her. "The matter I want to discuss will require strict confidence, Addie. I wouldn't dare broach the subject unless I felt you were mature enough to keep a secret."

She nodded. "Yes, of course."

With a sharp inhale, Priscilla leaned forward and began. "What if I told you I suspect Mr. Foster of harming Ceddy?"

Addie's heart lurched. "Why would you think such a thing?"

"I don't like having these thoughts, believe me." Priscilla fell against her chair. "But you heard Reverend Stroud. 'Someone in our midst,' he said. Addie, you've been around Mr. Foster more than I have. Do you think it's possible?"

"To be honest, I can't imagine it." Addie's first instincts were to shout down her accusations. Yet she suspected Pearson of something nearly as vile.

"How well do we really know him?"

How well indeed? Addie raised her head. "Wait, he was with me on the swing, so how could he be guilty? He didn't have the opportunity."

"I'm afraid he did. That's what haunts my thoughts. I directed him to the back door and then went out to the kitchen. He was standing at the foot of the stairs when I left him. Who's to say he went directly to the porch?"

Weakness swept over Addie's limbs, leaving her feeling helpless. Why did the urge to defend Pearson surge so strongly through her veins? "It seems preposterous. Why would he hurt a little boy?"

"You heard him say he lost his brother in the storm. Perhaps it twisted his mind."

Staring thoughtfully, Addie confessed the truth. "Actually, he lost his entire family that night. Pearson alone was spared."

Priscilla's eyes widened to deep, troubled pools. "There. . .you see? I've heard of these kinds of cases—the most charming and agreeable men living double lives, eventually found culpable of murder and mayhem. Like those two in London, Dr. Jekyll and Mr. Hyde."

"But Priscilla. . .they're a work of fiction."

She blinked. "They are?"

"Of course."

She waved dismissively. "Still. . .think about it, Addie. Both times when Ceddy grew so frightened, at the restaurant and again today, Mr. Foster was present. The boy has never acted in such a distraught manner before. It's the only conclusion I can make."

Addie held out one last shred of hope. "But you saw for yourself, Ceddy was totally relaxed with him. Even allowed the man to carry him to bed."

Priscilla touched her bottom lip. "Yes, there is that. But he was drifting in and out. Perhaps he didn't realize who held him." She sat forward and folded her hands. "I know it's a lot to take in. Believe me, I've struggled with the idea for half the night, and I hardly believe it myself." Her lips tightened. "However, my first responsibility is to Ceddy. I won't expose him to a dangerous man." She sighed. "But now that I've befriended Mr. Foster, it does present a perplexing set of circumstances."

Addie nodded. "To say the least."

Priscilla curled her fingers at her temples. "It's a dreadful failing of mine, Addie. I tend to become familiar with people entirely too soon. It's my trusting nature, I suppose."

Addie knew another impetuous lady with the same weakness. If her mother hadn't allowed the two men into their lives, they wouldn't be having this strange conversation. And Addie wouldn't be battling an attraction that made her uncomfortable. "How can we prove that Pearson is innocent?" Addie asked, certain that he was.

Priscilla gripped her knees and stared at the darkened window. "I don't know at present. But I assure you, I won't let the matter rest until I uncover the truth."

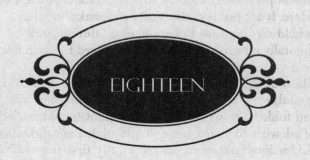

EIGHTEEN

A week had passed since Pearson last saw Addie. His reason for wanting to had drastically changed. After the accusation she made, of his improper interest in her mother, he wanted a chance to deny her charge.

The previous Sunday, Reverend Stroud accepted their offer of a ride home from the mansion, and on the way they'd waged a lively debate on the treasure of Jean Lafitte. The man seemed drawn to the legend and was quite knowledgeable of the details, a fact that forged a bond between them.

Since that day, Pearson spent hours at the bachelor's table, breaking bread and sharing ideas on where the pirate's bounty and the *Mittie* might be found.

As Pearson left the parsonage the day before, the reverend milked a promise from him that he would be in church, a promise he meant to keep. "Almost ready, Theo? We're about to be late."

Theo pulled on his boot and stood, shaking his pant leg until the cuff slid down. "Have you counted our money lately?" he asked, clearly distracted.

Pearson glanced at the bright sun outside the window and laid aside his coat. "Why should I? You're the bookkeeper for this operation."

Theo winced then met his eyes. "Not such a good one, I'm afraid. Somehow we've gone over our budget."

"Meaning?"

"We won't be able to stay in this hotel much longer and still afford to eat."

One hand on the door, Pearson stilled. "Let me see, die of exposure or die of starvation. Those are the options you're giving me?"

He nodded. "If you want to keep paying our help, it is."

Drawing a deep breath, Pearson shook his head. "There are a couple more alternatives, neither one very pleasant."

"Let's hear them."

"We could get part-time jobs."

Theo frowned. "I'm so tired after dragging the bottom of the lake every day, I couldn't do justice to an employer. What's the other idea?"

"We find somewhere else to stay."

"Such as?"

"I don't know yet. Reverend Stroud would take us in, but there's barely enough room for him in that little cabin."

Theo's eyes narrowed. "The light's beginning to dawn, brother. I know what's brewing in that reckless head. You're hoping to wheedle an invitation from Priscilla to stay at the mansion."

Pushing him into the hall, Pearson laughed. "That wouldn't be proper, would it? Not with two unmarried ladies inside." He winked. "But there's always the servants' quarters."

"Those gloomy shacks haven't been lived in for twenty years. Braving the elements might be better."

Pearson laughed and patted his back. "I'm surprised at you. You've slept in worse places, like the cot in Rosie's storeroom, sharing a bed with rats as long as your arm."

"I was younger then. And foolish. I'm a man now and partial to comfort."

"Like lumpy sofas and musty quilts?"

Theo nudged him. "You've slept in worse places, too."

They entered the Ginocchio's bustling lobby, Theo beaming and raising his hat to an attractive woman at the desk. She blushed prettily, but her companion glared and moved closer, sliding his arm around her waist.

"Uh-oh," he whispered, hurrying his steps to the door. He strolled along the boardwalk beside Pearson, quiet for a change. Just as Pearson had begun to enjoy the silence, he cleared his throat and glanced up.

"Don't get me wrong, paisan, I'm happy we're attending church again, but. . ."

"Why am I going?"

He nodded. "I'm not your judge or anything, but I'm fairly certain a desire to see a woman isn't a scriptural reason to go."

After the trouble with Ceddy at the Whitfield place, Pearson thought better of mentioning his skirmish with the vexing Addie McRae, who could teach a thing or two about the art of judging people.

"Though I do mean to have a word with Miss Addie at my first opportunity, I assure you I'm not going to church to see her. I promised the reverend I'd be there, and I'm bound to keep my word."

Guilt burdened his soul as they walked from the hotel to the church. The truth was he hadn't told Theo the whole story. His decision to attend the service had nothing to do with Addie, but there was a lot more to it than keeping a promise to Reverend Stroud.

Since the church social, Pearson couldn't shake the desire to return. The need to feel the serenity he'd experienced consumed him, both in the service and afterward, while standing on Miss Whitfield's back porch.

Too many years had passed since he last felt calm inside. Having stumbled onto a taste, he craved it more than food and drink. If God's house was the source of that peace, it's where Pearson wanted to be.

The towering walls of the Kimberley Mine threatened to close in on Denny, and the soaring blue sky above the big hole spun his head. Sweat beaded on his top lip, tickling his nose. To wipe it off would attract attention. The blighters watched always, suspected everything.

He tried not to look at Tebogo, the big black wandering a half morgen away on a patch of weathering blue ground. The Cameroon cigars Denny used to bribe him had cost him dearly, but if the duck-footed bloke pulled off his trick, Denny could buy a passel of stogies.

Tebogo had done it before and succeeded, risking his hide to make another man rich, and for paltry recompense. Whatever drove such shortsighted behavior, Denny was glad the foolish man was willing to take the risk.

Without breaking his stride, Tebogo strolled into the unsorted field where Denny had spotted a brilliant flash. With the barest wrinkling of his toes, he snatched the kimberlite rock with his foot then meandered past Denny.

In a convincing show of clumsiness, Denny dropped his spade. Bending at the waist, he snatched the stone and promptly swallowed it.

Excitement swelled his chest, and he bit the inside of his lip to hold back a smile. At last! Boundless treasure had lain in wait for luckier blokes than he, far less deserving men growing rich and powerful in droves. Now his turn had come.

Casual as could be, he shouldered the spade and made for the huddle of shacks serving as an office. He'd turn in his tools and collect his wage, then—

A firm grip on his neck halted him in midstep. Cruel fingers dug in and spun him around.

The guard's leering grin shot fear to his chest, and he lost the power to breathe. . . .

Denny's eyes flew open. His heart pounded so hard, he feared for his life. Working to slow his breathing, he gazed around at the tattered rug and torn wallpaper of the rooming house.

When would he stop dreaming of that terrible day?

The attempted theft earned him a stay in the compound, bound in handcuffs, force-fed castor oil and stewed fruit until his traitorous body returned the stolen property.

His ill-fated assistant fared worse. He paid for his folly with the loss of his foot.

Denny rolled out of bed and sat on the side, holding his aching head. The bottle he'd drained the night before mocked him from the floor. Drawing back his foot, he gave it a swift kick then howled as pain shot from his toe to his throbbing temples.

Charlie reeled over and fixed him with a bleary stare. "Have you gone spare, mate? What's the good of all that racket?"

"Shut it and go back to sleep."

Growling, Charlie sat up instead. "Too late. Me heart's pounding out of me chest. What's eatin' you?"

Denny cast a surly glance around the room. "I'm sick of this rotted slum of a flat. We should be living like kings by now. Riding a luxury liner to an island in the Pacific."

Charlie's mouth grew slack, and he stared dreamily. "Yeah? That sounds nice, Den. So why ain't we?"

"'Sounds nice, Den. Why ain't we?'" Denny mocked, throwing a pillow at his head. "Why do you think? We ain't got that blooming rock yet, now, have we?"

Charlie ducked and shook his head.

"We've been working our fingers to nubs for those two blokes, braving snakes and gators and dragging all manner of rubbish up from the deep." He spat on the floor. "Not a thing to show for it but short fingers and aching backs."

Charlie shot him a sullen glare. "You said we'd follow them so's we could find out where the boy lives, but we ain't done it."

Tapping his forehead, Denny grinned. "I don't tell you everything, now, do I? We don't need to follow them because I already know where the boy lives. It don't take long in this town to find out who Miss Priscilla Whitfield is or where her big mansion sits."

Confusion flashed on Charlie's face. "Then why ain't we gone after the diamond?"

Denny vaulted from the bed and slapped a hand over his mouth. "Pipe down, will ya? These walls are like onion peels. You want to compete with half the blokes in this seedy dive?"

Staring with frightened eyes, Charlie shook his head.

Settling to Charlie's lumpy mattress, Denny heaved a sigh. "I got a wee bit distracted, I suppose." Staring thoughtfully, he slipped his arm around Charlie's shoulders. "You see, I can't help wonderin' why those two are dragging the bottom of a lake." He gave Charlie a shake. "They take us for a couple of mugs. Think our accents make us stupid." He gave a harsh laugh. "We ain't stupid, are we, Charlie?"

The idiot shook his head. "We ain't stupid."

"That's right. And as long as nobody knows what the boy has, we've got time to help our friends find what they're looking for, maybe see what other trinkets there are in that big house. If my hunch is right, we'll be leaving town with more than a big white rock."

Charlie's shoulders slumped. "What if the boy don't have the stone no more? He could've lost it. Or chunked it away."

Denny shoved him against the wall, bumping his head so hard the window rattled. "Don't you say that, Charlie. You hear? He's still got it, all right." Squinting his eyes, he stared toward Whitfield Manor. "But he won't keep it, you can bet on that. If I have to kill somebody to get it."

The week since Addie last saw Pearson passed in a dizzying blur. It took days to settle poor Ceddy into his comforting routine.

As happy as she felt to see the Sabbath roll around again, she dreaded it with equal measure. What challenges might the day hold? How would Ceddy react to returning to church, the most likely place where he'd been harmed? Or to seeing Pearson, who Priscilla believed to be the culprit?

As for Addie, she didn't think for one minute that Pearson had hurt Ceddy. He might be a cad in matters of the heart, but his gentleness with the boy was genuine. Whoever the vile person was who cut and bruised Ceddy, nothing could convince her that it was Pearson.

She heard the boy whimpering before she turned the corner into his room.

Delilah stood over his bed, holding a warm cloth to his bare stomach while Ceddy rolled back and forth.

"What's wrong with him?"

"He got a touch of misery in his belly, that's all. It happens on occasion."

"Like this? How frequently?"

"Oh, 'bout twice a month, I s'pose."

Addie frowned. "Come to think of it, the same thing happened last Wednesday. The poor dear lost his lunch. What do you suppose is causing it?"

"I cain't say, Miss Addie. I ain't no doctor."

"Have you called one?"

"Oh yes'm. Lots of times. He say nothing wrong, near as he could tell."

"Well, it's happening too often to ignore." Addie crossed to the bed and smoothed his forehead. "What did you give him for breakfast?"

"He wouldn't eat this mornin'. Miss Priscilla got mos' his milk down, but that's all he had."

Addie jerked her gaze to Delilah. "He drank milk?" She returned to watching Ceddy. "And this was the outcome?"

"Yes'm, I s'pose."

Priscilla swept in, tugging on her gloves. "Are we about ready?" Pausing at the door, her eyes flashed to Ceddy. "Oh my. What ails him?"

"His stomach again, Miss Priscilla," Delilah said.

Hands on her hips, Addie faced her. "Did Ceddy drink his milk last Wednesday?"

"I don't recall," she said, her brows furrowed. "Wait. Yes, I do." She beamed proudly. "I coaxed him to finish every drop."

Bracing for battle, Addie stamped her foot. "You're not to give him any more milk. And no sugary sweets."

Both women gaped at her.

Delilah straightened. "But he love his treats, Miss Addie."

"No more, I say."

Worrying her bottom lip, Priscilla approached the bed. "Oh Addie. Are you certain? Sometimes Delilah's cookies are all that will settle him."

"Do you trust me, Priscilla?"

She thrust her shoulders back. "Implicitly."

"Then let me try this, please. It's my theory that a constant diet of sugared foods may be contributing to Ceddy's bad behavior. He's always much worse after he's eaten a treat."

"But the milk? It's good for him."

Addie shook her head. "I don't think so. He holds his stomach and moans for hours after ingesting milk. It's why you have to force him to drink it." Moving to the bed, she patted his flushed cheek. "Poor dear. He's smarter than all of us."

Priscilla stared at Ceddy, her eyes dazed. "If it's true, then it's very astute of you to make the connection, dear."

Crossing the room, she stood over Ceddy's bed. "He does look miserable." She sighed. "Very well, Addie. You'll have a chance to test your theory." She turned, a determined set to her jaw. "Delilah, no more desserts. And no milk."

"But Miss Priscilla. . .what do I do when he come pulling on my skirt and moaning like he do?"

"Give him dried apples instead," Addie said. "Or a spoon coated with honey." Bolstering her courage, she voiced her next concern. "And we should stop treating him like an invalid. He can do many things for himself, but we've allowed him to become lazy. He's perfectly capable of combing his hair and dressing, yet he stands like a limp doll and lets Delilah do it for him."

"Are you sure, Addie?"

"Quite sure. And another thing. . .everyone talks over him, past him, about him. Hardly ever directly to him. We must start addressing him as though we expect a response. He understands very well, whether he appears to or not."

Delilah huffed. "I talks to him all the time, but he don't say nothin' back. How you gon' converse to a body who don't answer?"

Addie briskly nodded. "Yes, he does. Granted, not vocally. You have to watch him closely, but in his own way, he answers."

Priscilla slid her arm around Addie and leaned to kiss her forehead. "I can't tell you how grateful I am for your keen insight and concern for Ceddy."

A blush warmed Addie's cheeks. "I'm very fond of him."

"And it shows." Priscilla patted her shoulder. "Go dress for church. You could use a day out of the house. I'll sit with him this morning."

Addie shook her head. "I couldn't allow you to miss church for me."

Priscilla stole a glance at Delilah. "Perhaps we could both go, then, if only. . ."

Delilah's big brown eyes rounded.

Smiling, Addie walked to the door and held it wide. "I won't have either of you missing your service. Ceddy is my responsibility, and I'll sit with him today."

Truthfully, she felt immensely relieved. While she hated for Ceddy to suffer, staying home with him solved both of her problems. She wouldn't have to deal with his reaction to being at church, and she wouldn't have to deal with her own scattered emotions about seeing Pearson.

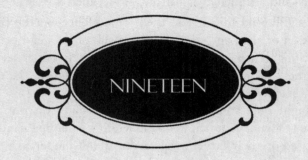

NINETEEN

Standing with Reverend Stroud on the steps of the church, Pearson's heart pitched at the sight of the Whitfield carriage. His disappointment when the lady of the manor climbed down without Addie stung more sharply than he cared to admit. Happy to see his new friend nonetheless, he smiled broadly as Miss Whitfield approached. "Morning, ma'am. Good to see you again."

"Good morning, gentlemen." Her wary eyes slid to his and then away so fast, Pearson's stomach clenched. Something was obviously wrong.

"Priscilla, I hope you intend to remove your hat for the sake of those seated behind you," Reverend Stroud teased. "Mercy is a virtue, you know."

Her trembling hand reached for the sky blue contraption sprouting assorted feathers and bows. "Do you really think I should?"

He chuckled. "Why break with tradition? Besides"—he nudged her—"haven't you noticed? No one ever sits behind you."

Instead of laughing with him or offering a barbed retort, she edged toward the door. "I'd best go inside. The service will be starting soon."

The reverend's brows rose. "I hope not, dear lady, since I'm an integral part."

With a tight smile, she slipped inside and disappeared.

Pearson and the reverend exchanged looks.

"What was that about?" Pearson asked.

The man shook his head. "I've never seen her like this." He chuckled. "Perhaps I can figure her out by the close of service. My sermon is rather lengthy, I'm afraid. I'll have plenty of time to observe."

Pearson followed him inside then joined Theo on the front pew. The sensation of someone staring at the back of his head persisted so strongly throughout the singing and the message that followed, he gave in a few times and stole a glance behind him. Each time, he met Miss Whitfield's startled gaze.

He caught only snippets of Reverend Stroud's discourse on the importance of loving your neighbor and lending a helping hand to those in need. Based on their earlier conversation about the servants' quarters, he suspected the reverend had directed his sermon, at least in part, to Miss Whitfield. Too bad she didn't seem to hear a word.

Her odd behavior so distracted Pearson, it robbed him of the peace he sought. After the closing prayer, unlike the week before, he didn't feel as if he'd even been to church.

Outside, a welcoming committee—self-appointed no doubt—of Marshall's unmarried daughters and their mothers descended on Pearson and Theo. To Theo's delight, they brought baskets of baked goods and pretty smiles. Beaming like a cat in a birdcage, he bowed as they filed past, whispering promises to each of them that he'd taste their gift first.

Grinning and shaking his head, Reverend Stroud strolled to where Priscilla stood anxiously wringing her hands. After a hushed conversation that didn't appear to end in her favor, he waved them over.

Pearson pried Theo from the circle of tittering girls and urged him toward the carriage.

"Gentlemen, we're graciously invited to the manor for lunch, if you have no prior plans."

Pearson ducked his head, trying to read the lady's face. "Are you sure, ma'am? We don't want to intrude."

She drew herself up and took a deep breath. "Of course, Mr. Foster. I wouldn't have it any other way."

Seven days ago, she'd insisted on calling him Pearson. Something was definitely wrong.

The milk Priscilla forced on Ceddy that morning would trouble him no more. Most of it now splattered the front of Addie's uniform; the rest puddled on the floor.

With one hand she held a damp cloth to the poor child's forehead; with the other she tried to work his arm free of his nightshirt. "It was a wise move to abide by my suggestion, Ceddy," she told the drowsy-eyed boy. "Otherwise we'd face a skirmish to rival First Manassas the next time you're offered milk."

He groaned and rolled to one side.

She hadn't the heart to jostle him further, so she tucked the covers around his thin shoulders and left him be.

The sound of footsteps on the stairwell, too slow and heavy for Delilah's yet too quick for Priscilla's, stirred her heart to pounding. Before she could react to her fear, Priscilla hurried into the room.

Addie's hand went to her heart. "It is you! Heavens, you frightened me silly."

"Addie, you won't believe this," Priscilla whispered. "He's downstairs."

"Who?" she asked, but she already knew. "Not Mr. Foster?" Snatching the rag from Ceddy's head, she swiped self-consciously at the sour mess on her skirt.

Closing the door quietly, Priscilla whirled, a frantic look in her eyes. "The very same. Only it's even worse than that."

Addie didn't see how it could get any worse, but she didn't bother making the point. "What happened?"

"He's going to be living here."

Her hand stilled, clutching the cloth. Pointing at the floor, she frowned. "Here? In this house?"

"Nearly as bad. In the servants' quarters out back."

Addie knew the place she meant. The row of crumbling buildings along the back corner of the property.

Many questions raced through her mind. Only one made its way to her lips. "Why?"

"Are you asking why they want to or why I let them?"

She waved the back of her hand. "Yes, both of those."

"If I understood right, they're trying to conserve money so they might continue their search for the *Mittie*."

"And?"

Priscilla's face flushed, and she paced the room. "Reverend Stroud pressed me to allow it. The man is simply thick when it comes to social graces. He asked me right in front of those two. I had no choice but to agree."

Addie bundled the rag with Ceddy's soiled clothing. "What are we going to do?"

"That's what I asked myself the entire ride home."

She stopped walking and faced Addie. "It's all so perplexing. When I spend any length of time with that young man, the idea of his hurting anyone seems outlandish."

Addie nodded. "I know just what you mean." Except for his fixation on a married woman, Pearson seemed a most agreeable man. She didn't hold it against him for finding her mother attractive. He wasn't the first to fall under the spell of Mariah McRae. The unforgivable part was his seeming determination to follow his wayward heart.

"And I trust Reverend Stroud's instincts completely, or I would never have agreed. Yet we can't lose sight of the fact that *someone* hurt our boy. To answer your question, dear, here's all we can do— we'll welcome Mr. Foster and his friend to the estate. After all, some hold with the notion of keeping one's enemies near enough to watch." She offered a tight smile. "You can't get much closer than your own backyard, now, can you?"

Dazed, Addie shook her head.

"There's more bad news." Priscilla grimaced. "Until repairs are made, they'll be taking their meals with us and—"

"Excuse me?"

"Freshening up inside, too."

"Oh my, that seems too close."

"Don't fret, dear. Between you, me, and Delilah, we won't let Ceddy out of sight for a moment."

If Priscilla knew the true reason Addie felt uncomfortable around Pearson, she'd be stunned.

"I don't want you to worry, honey. Together we'll see this through." Drawing away, she wrinkled her nose. "Oh my. What's that horrid smell?"

Addie held out her skirt. "I fear it's me, courtesy of Ceddy."

Priscilla waved her toward the door. "Go on and freshen up for lunch. I'll stay with him until you return. Delilah is laying the table, but I'll send her up the minute she's finished."

"Where are the men?"

"In typical male fashion, they couldn't wait until after the meal. They're tramping through the cottages out back, deciding which one is fit to occupy."

"Can't Delilah bring a tray upstairs for Ceddy and me? Surely you don't need me at the table."

A shocked look crossed her face. "Of course I do. I'll need you to spend as much time as possible with Mr. Foster, Addie. How else will you help me decide if he's to be trusted?"

Pearson patted the beam in the center of the room, flinching when plaster rained down on his head. "She warned us they were in disrepair. I'm afraid she wasn't kidding."

Theo, far handier with a hammer and nails, scurried around the room like the only ant at a picnic. "They're not so bad. Nothing that can't be fixed."

"So this is the one, boys?" Reverend Stroud asked.

"Yes, sir," Theo said. "It's the most structurally sound of the three."

Pearson dared to look up again. "Can you do something about this ceiling? I don't relish paint chips as a complement to my meals."

The reverend laughed. "Oh, but you heard Priscilla, son. You won't be taking your meals out here."

Pearson studied his face. "I think the lady said a lot of things she didn't want to say. Are you sure we're welcome to stay?"

The reverend patted his shoulder. "Don't mind her quirky ways, son. I've known Priscilla for many years, and her heart is good. If I had to guess, she's worried about how others will view your presence on the estate. I'm sure she's intent on protecting the reputation of that pretty little governess."

Pearson nodded. "That's high on my list of priorities, too, sir. If you think there's any chance of talk in town, we'll make other arrangements."

"It's not like you're sleeping under the same roof." He shook his head. "Leave the gossips to me. Once I place my seal of approval, no one will dare speak a word against them." He motioned toward the door. "I think we've seen enough. Now that you've picked your cabin, I suspect I can commandeer a work force from the congregation."

Theo grinned. "That would be a big help, sir. I won't get much out of Pearson."

"I'm sure they'll be happy to lend a hand." He patted his stomach. "Fellows, by now the table is groaning with platters. Delilah's the second-best cook in Harrison County. Let's go sample her wares, shall we?"

"Second?" Pearson asked. "Who's the best?"

He waved his index finger. "Never mind, for now. I may let you in on the secret someday. For now, let's keep that comment between us."

Miss Whitfield met them in the hall and ushered them to the dining room.

Addie, already seated, glanced up as they entered, offering a smile to Reverend Stroud and Theo, a curt nod for Pearson.

True to his word, the reverend seemed eager to try every steaming dish as soon as the 'Amens' were said.

Not to be outdone, Theo took a healthy serving from every bowl passed to him.

His conscience raw from feeling he'd forced himself on the gracious lady seated at the head of the table, Pearson had no appetite.

"Is everything all right?" she asked, her troubled gaze on his hands, lying still next to his plate.

He ducked his head and picked up his fork. "Oh yes, ma'am. It looks delicious."

She watched him for several minutes, her mouth fidgeting as if she couldn't find the words she wanted to say. "If there's anything else you need, please say so, and I'll get it for you. Delilah is busy with Ceddy today. He's ill, I'm afraid, and confined to his room." She studied his face, as if waiting for his reaction. "The poor child isn't the same after his frightening ordeal. Of course, we won't be leaving him alone anymore." She cleared her throat. "That is, there will be someone with him at all times."

Pearson felt the need to squirm under her attentive gaze. "I think that's a wise idea."

She took a bite of sweet potato and nodded thoughtfully. "Can you imagine the sort of man who would deliberately injure a child?"

He met her eyes. "No, ma'am, I can't."

"It's a deplorable act, don't you agree?"

"I do indeed."

"You mentioned a little brother. . . ."

Pearson laid down his fork.

"If anyone had ever harmed him, how would it make you feel?"

The room stilled. The others stopped eating to watch the exchange.

"I can answer that question from experience."

Her brows peaked. "Oh?"

"You see, someone did harm him. In fact, he lost his life."

"I don't understand," she said. "I thought your family died in a storm. No one is responsible for that."

He shrugged. "Maybe not. Then again, they might not have died if I'd been there to help."

"Oh, Mr. Foster," Addie said from across the table, "you mustn't think that."

Her unexpected sympathy surprised him. He longed to look at her, but shame kept his eyes on his plate.

Theo leaned past him to see Miss Whitfield. "No one could've saved them. Not a soul from the neighborhood survived. If he'd been there, instead of on holiday with my family, he wouldn't be sitting here today."

Reverend Stroud reached across the table and gripped Pearson's hand. "I'm sure Pearson knows that in his head. Sometimes the heart is slow to follow."

Embarrassed and angry with himself for displaying his emotions so openly, Pearson cleared his throat. "I'd love a piece of that cake now, if nobody minds."

Her cheeks damp with tears, Miss Whitfield stood. "Coming right up, dear. Along with a nice hot cup of coffee to wash it down."

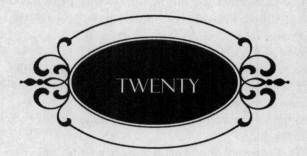

TWENTY

Addie sat quietly in the parlor, the first peaceful moment she'd had all day. Muted sunlight, peeking around the edges of the drapes, a single lantern, the wick turned down low, and a waning fire in the fireplace provided meager light in the heavily shaded room.

After the meal, the others retired to the coolness of the garden. Addie hurried upstairs to relieve Delilah. Finding her napping on the floor by Ceddy's bed, she'd covered her with a blanket then tiptoed out and shut the door.

Addie tried hard to match the mood of the house, but her restless heart was anything but quiet. She didn't want to ache for Pearson Foster's plight, didn't want her mind consumed by thoughts of a man attracted to a married woman.

The parlor door swung open. Pearson stood on the threshold, blinking against the dimness. His squinted eyes came to rest on her then widened. "I'm sorry. I didn't realize anyone was in here."

He began to back out the way he came, but she held up her hand. "It's all right. Can I get you anything?"

He smiled, the sight of it stirring her heart. How could a man with such an appealing face be capable of any wrongdoing?

"They're asleep." He pointed toward the garden. "The reverend nodding in a chair, Miss Whitfield in the swing, and Theo sprawled on the ground in the sun. I didn't want to wake them, so I thought I'd wait inside."

She motioned. "Won't you come in?"

He cocked his head. "You don't mind?"

"It's a little too quiet in the house. I could use the company."

The shock on his face pained her, but why wouldn't he be surprised? She'd been anything but cordial. "Besides, there's a matter I'd like to discuss with you."

He propped the door open with the stop and crossed the room. "Fancy that. There's a matter I'd like to discuss with you, too."

"I suppose the only question now is who shall go first. Have a seat, please."

Settling into Priscilla's overstuffed chair, he stretched out his long legs and crossed his ankles. "No question there." He waved in invitation. "Ladies first."

Not nearly so confident with him sitting so close, she folded her hands in her lap. "This is awkward. I'm not sure where to begin."

"If you start by apologizing for last Sunday's outburst, it will save us a lot of time. Then we could dispense with both of our topics at once."

She gaped at him. "You're joking."

He shook his head, not a hint of teasing on his somber face. "That's my first rule. When it comes to my reputation, I never jest."

Scowling, Addie crossed her arms and sank against the sofa, at a loss for words.

He suffered no such impediment. "What is it with you, Miss Mc-Rae? How have I so thoroughly offended you?"

Her chin jerked up. "I should think it would be apparent."

"Well, it's not in the least."

The passion in his tone startled her. She pressed deeper into the cushion.

"If I knew what I'd done"—suddenly smiling, he drew in his feet and sat forward—"I would shower you with apologies until you forgave me."

Surprised, she glanced away.

"A word of warning, Miss McRae. The more you withdraw, the more determined I become to win your friendship."

She raised flashing eyes. "I can see how some women find your flattery appealing, but I assure you, it won't work with me." The burning in her chest intensified. "Or with my mother."

He cocked his head. "Your mother again? What does she have to do with anything?"

As absurd as it seemed, his offhanded attitude toward Mother made Addie madder than ever. "Have you so quickly forgotten her charms? What do they say? Out of sight, out of mind?"

"Mrs. McRae is a delightful woman. A kind and gentle soul. I haven't forgotten her at all."

Addie pushed off the couch and stormed to the hearth. "I suppose you penned all those compliments in the letter you sent her?" She hugged her waist. "Mr. Foster, sir, what were you thinking?" In the silence that followed, tiny hairs stood up on her neck.

Pearson angled his head. "So that's what this is about?

Insufferable blatant arrogance! She spun. "Do you presume to suggest I'm jealous of my own mother?"

Pearson's eyes flew wide. "Jealous?" He scooted to the edge of the chair, his wide stare closing to slits. "I think I'm beginning to understand now. When was the last time you heard from her?"

"Not since she left, if it's any of your business."

He nodded slowly then stood. "I expect you'll be hearing from her soon. At that time you may regard me in a different light, but I fear this conversation will be the source of stinging embarrassment." He drew a shallow breath. "For both of us." With a curt nod, he strode for the door.

"You're just going to walk away?" Addie called. "Without bothering to explain your deplorable behavior?"

"That's my second rule, Miss McRae. On the matter of my honor, I never stoop to defending myself. I let my actions do the talking."

Ceddy shot up in bed and stared. His chest burned from holding in a scream, and his stomach hurt. Eyes darting, he took in every corner of the room, terrified of what he might see.

Lilah lay beside him on the floor, breathing loud in her sleep. Scary Mr. Currie and big, ugly Charlie were gone. He clawed around his neck, but the sharp white shell cutting his skin was gone, too.

He slumped against his pillow, panting hard. Safe. In Aunt Priss's house.

The fog began to clear, and his heart slowed. Were the men only there in his dream?

Cold without his nightshirt, he drew up his knees and cuddled deeper into the mattress. Feeling for the quilt he'd kicked off in his sleep, he jerked it over his shoulders. The white stone flew up, crashed to the floor, and then rolled into Lilah.

She sat up rubbing her head. "Who done walloped me?"

Ceddy spun out of bed and slid on his knees to where Lilah sat. Shoving on her shoulder, he felt around the blanket and in the folds of her dress. "Mmm-muh."

"Now, jus' hold on, lil' mista. Don't go meddling about with me. I got nothin' of yours." She chuckled and held her hand over his head. " 'Less you hankerin' after this old thing."

Feeling up her arm, Ceddy's eager fingers closed over the rock. Fumbling it away from her, he sat back on his heels. "Muh."

"Yes, yours, and that be jus' fine with me. I got no use for that shapeless old paperweight."

Ceddy's middle rolled and growled. Clutching his stomach, he tapped his mouth with his knuckles.

She laughed. "I reckon you is hungry." She stroked the back of his head. "Trouble is I don't think what you want is what you bound to get."

He pushed her again.

Struggling to her feet, she groaned. "Wait jus' a minute. Old Lilah don't move so quick no mo'." Patting his hand, she picked up the blanket, folded it, and tossed it on his bed. "Let's get you dressed so we can go down to the kitchen." Her growly voice lowered to where he barely heard the rest. "See if we can't stir up some old, dried-out fruit. Maybe dip you out some honey or some fool thing. Never in all my days have I heard of giving a poor child—"

She twisted around. "Well, looky. Here's Miss Addie now with your snack. You shouldn't've troubled yourself, miss. I was on my way downstairs."

"It was no trouble," Miss Addie said. She swished past Ceddy with a tray and set it on the table. "I needed something to busy my hands."

Something besides strangling the life out of one Pearson Foster, Addie thought.

"I have a new treat to try today. One of my mother's old recipes, and I think Ceddy will like it." She lifted the dishcloth off the saucer of hasty pudding.

Delilah eyed the sticky-topped dish. "I thought you said no more sweets."

"There's no sugar in the batter and only a touch of honey on top. We'll see how he does."

"I can tell you how he gon' do," Delilah mumbled, "before he ever lay eyes on it."

Ignoring her nay-saying tone, Addie crossed to the wardrobe. Nodding at the pitcher and bowl atop the washstand, she pulled out his clothes. "Wipe him down so I can dress him, please."

With Ceddy scrubbed and combed, Addie sat beside him on the floor, his favorite place. Pretending far more confidence than she felt, she placed the dish in front of him. As an afterthought, she turned the saucer so he could reach the spoon, an addition to his mealtime routine he had finally accepted.

Ceddy wrinkled his nose and nudged it away with his knuckles.

Delilah's low hum said, "I told you so."

"Ceddy, please try some," Addie pleaded. "I truly feel it's for your own good."

"He missing his treats, Miss Addie. Powerful bad. He cry and moan and hang on my skirts till he wearies me fit to be tied."

"He'll get used to the change." She eased the pudding toward him again. "We have to give him time."

Delilah sucked a breath through her nose, the cords in her neck protruding. "I don't mean no disrespect, miss. I swear I don't. Only I never heard such an outlandish notion. How could a little cane sugar hurt a body? Children grow up on they mama's cakes and pies. I cain't see how—"

Addie lifted one hand to shush her. Smiling, she tilted her head at Ceddy.

One small finger hooked the edge of the dish, teasing it closer. Gouging a hole in the pudding, he carefully tasted it. Swaying side to side, intent on spinning the white stone, he picked up another gooey scoop and crammed it in his mouth.

"Oh my, his spoon," Addie said. Grinning at Delilah, she shook her head. "I don't even care. We'll work on etiquette the next time."

Priscilla appeared at the door suppressing a yawn. "Here you all are. Where is Mr. Foster? The reverend is ready to leave, and I've summoned the carriage."

Pushing to her feet, Addie crossed to the basin and dipped the corner of a towel. "I don't know where Mr. Foster might've gone. I saw him briefly in the parlor, but he left before I did." She dropped to her knees and wiped Ceddy's hands. "Maybe he returned to looking at the servants' quarters."

Delilah picked up the empty saucer from the floor. "I'll look in the kitchen, Miss Priscilla. If he in there, I'll send him out front."

"Thank you," Priscilla said as she slipped past.

Taking a backward step, Priscilla gazed down the hall until Delilah's footsteps echoed from the stairs. Then she entered and closed the door.

"Addie, I've made a decision about Mr. Foster. I don't see him capable of evil in any form." Her brows rose in a hesitant question. "Don't you agree?"

Choosing her words carefully, Addie shook her head. "I don't think he hurt Ceddy, if that's what you mean."

Priscilla clutched her hands. "I'm so happy you concur. He's such an agreeable young man." She smiled. "Actually, both he and Theo are a pleasure to be around. I do enjoy their company." She chuckled, staring over Addie's head. "They tell the most amusing stories about growing up together on the seashore. I laughed at their antics until I grew hoarse." Sobering, she glanced at Ceddy. "Of course, I'll continue to watch his interaction with my nephew. . .just in case." She placed a hand on Addie's shoulder. "But my heart tells me we should look elsewhere for our culprit."

Addie nodded and tossed the soiled towel toward the hamper. "I think that's a wise decision, Priscilla."

TWENTY-ONE

Reverend Stroud went straight to work the next morning and convinced a few members of his congregation to lend their idle hands to something other than the devil's workshop—evidenced by a six-man crew descending on Pearson and Theo as they were beginning to tear out the rotted interior walls of the chosen servants' cottage.

Glancing up as the reverend appeared on the threshold, Pearson offered a warm smile. "The cavalry?"

"I'm a man of my word, son." He flashed a crooked grin. "Come to think of it, I'm a man of God's Word. Either way, I have to keep my promises." Shaking Theo's shoulder playfully, he picked up a jellied biscuit from the platter provided by Delilah. "Ever notice how similar the word *cavalry* is to *Calvary*? Both are instruments of rescue, and in your case"—he pointed at the members of his flock—"both terms are appropriate."

"And I'm grateful to God for both," Pearson said, ducking his head when Theo shot him a startled glance.

The reverend rolled his shoulders and flexed his hands. "Now then, gentlemen. . .what can I say to help?"

Grinning, Pearson braced his knuckles on his hips. "You can start with a prayer, sir. Nothing else will get this place livable."

The unflappable man nudged him. "Oh ye of little faith. These fine men can raise a barn in an afternoon. They'll have this done quick as a wink."

Patting his back, Pearson laughed. "They have considerably more time than a wink. We're paid up at the Ginocchio through the next two weeks."

The reverend drew back and stared. "Two weeks? They can restore the whole wing in that amount of time. You'll each have a place of your own when we're done."

Caught off guard, Pearson gazed around at the crowd of men. "You'd do that for us?"

"We would, though Priscilla will benefit as well. She's been worried about the state of these old houses for too long."

Pearson offered his hand. "I'm humbled by your kindness." Nodding at the circle of beaming faces, his chest swelled. "And by your sacrifice."

The men filed past, smiling and shaking his hand, then set to work.

Last in line, Reverend Stroud caught Pearson's fingers in a firm grip. "It's what we do. And speaking of one's vocation, how will you two raise a lost steamboat while you're swinging hammers and sawing boards?"

Pearson handed him another biscuit then took one for himself. "We planned to get a start here and then head on out to the lake. Our hired hands should be on their feet and ready to go by then." He grimaced. "Those two have a hard time finding the floor in the mornings."

"Late sleepers?"

Pearson nodded. "Something like that."

The reverend nodded thoughtfully. "In this case, you have to take on whoever's willing, I suppose."

Through the hammering and ripping of old lumber, a knock sounded at the open door. A timid Delilah peeked around the jamb, searching the dim room. "Reverend? You be in there?"

He strode toward her. "I'm here, Delilah."

"Miss Priscilla saw all those rigs pull around back and knowed you had a hand in it somehow. She sent me out to fetch you up to the house for breakfast." Her eyes cut over to Pearson. "She say to bring all of you." A worried frown creased her brow. "You'd best throw down those trifling biscuits and don't tell Miss Priscilla I brung 'em out here. She say to come hungry."

Addie stood before the gilded mirror and stared at her ashen face. Since the moment she'd spotted Pearson from her window, her heart had fluttered near her throat. The sight of him likely marked the first of many mornings she'd need to battle her rage.

Calling on a lifetime of breeding, she took a deep breath and steeled her spine. At Priscilla's request, she'd go to breakfast and treat him civilly at the table. Civil, in this case, had little to do with warmth, and Pearson would understand the difference very soon.

He said the more she withdrew, the more determined he'd become to befriend her. "Humph! Prepare to become most determined, sir," she told her scowling reflection.

She turned at a knock on the door. "Yes, come in."

Delilah poked her head inside. "Miss Priscilla say hurry down those stairs. You have guests to entertain."

"Where's Ceddy?"

"Fed, clean, and spinning wooden soldiers in his room. Never saw a child play in such a peculiar way with his toys."

"Thank you, Delilah. Will you be able to sit with him while I'm at breakfast?"

"That's where I be headed now." She grinned. "Reckon I'll sit and spin right along with him."

Addie laughed and gave her hair a final pat before starting for the door. "Well, mind you don't get dizzy."

Mingled voices greeted her as she descended to the hall. Swallowing hard, she opened the door on the long dining table and Priscilla's boisterous laughter.

"Here she is now. Take a seat, please, Addie, so these fellows can start." She unfolded her napkin onto her lap. "They've waited so long for you they're bound to be starved."

Two men leaped up at once to pull out her chair. Though seated right next to her, Pearson wasn't one of them.

Gritting her teeth, Addie pasted on a broad smile. "My apologies, gentlemen. I didn't mean to take so long."

"Quite all right, young lady," the reverend said. "You're a vision this morning and worth the wait."

Nods and mumbles of agreement circled the table, Pearson conspicuous in his silence.

Addie flashed a smile. "Why, thank you. Now who can pass me the jelly?"

Reverend Stroud held up his hand. "May we ask God's blessing first?"

Cheeks flaming, Addie folded her hands in her lap. The reverend would think her an infidel, and it was Pearson's fault. He kept her in a constant state of distraction. Her humiliation wasn't fair, considering the true heretic seated at breakfast was Pearson, given his aversion to prayer—a fact witnessed the day they met.

"Pearson?" Reverend Stroud glanced his way. "Would you mind offering our thanks?"

Addie's stomach sank. Despite Pearson's insufferable arrogance, she didn't want him to be embarrassed. A man like him likely didn't know how to pray.

His cheeks colored a bit, but he promptly bowed his head.

Addie followed suit, waiting breathlessly to see what he could possibly scramble to offer.

"Great and gracious heavenly Father—"

Startled, she jerked her head up. Feeling like the word *infidel* might be an appropriate description for her, she hurriedly lowered it and closed her eyes.

"—we thank You for Your bounty and ask Your blessing on this food and those who partake of it. We humbly ask for guidance and protection as we start another day."

He said more, closing by invoking the Savior's name, but Addie's fevered mind had strayed. How was it possible? The person who squirmed uncomfortably through a prayer the day they met had offered an eloquent, heartfelt blessing.

She glanced at the reverend, his cheeks bulging with food. Had the man of God wrought a miracle in such a short time?

Priscilla passed the scrambled eggs to Reverend Stroud. "What's the state of our repairs, then? Are the buildings worth saving?"

"Ah, dear lady, you ask this of a minister? Everything and everyone is worth saving." Smiling, he handed off the bowl to his right. "I can tell you this much, our project supervisor is worthy of his hire." He winked at Theo. "With this young man at the helm, we'll build a structure you can be proud of."

The tips of Theo's ears turned bright red. "Thank you, Reverend."

Until that second, Addie hadn't taken Theo very seriously. Seated across the table from her, he squirmed beneath the attention, chewing on his bottom lip to keep from smiling. The humble gesture touched her heart.

Upon closer inspection, he was actually a nice-looking fellow. Some would even say handsome. His dark clownish curls and peculiar manner of speech drew attention from the delicate arch of his brows and the pleasing shape of his mouth. His wheat-colored skin and brown eyes. His—

A heaping platter jutted in front of her face. "Pork?"

Pearson, anger etched on his face, held the tray of ham. Something besides rage flashed in his eyes. He'd caught her staring at Theo and didn't like it. Did he find her unworthy of his best friend?

She shook her head. "I don't partake of unclean beasts, Mr. Foster." She tucked her chin and lowered her voice. "Or pork."

Deliberately crowding her, he leaned to offer the meat to the man at her left.

She lightly shoved him.

He jabbed her with his elbow.

Furious, she twisted in the chair, offering him her back. "Priscilla, tell your guests the story of the grandfather clock."

Giving encouragement, the clock struck the ninth hour.

Priscilla smiled and launched into the charming tale, complete with the song at the end.

While she spoke, Pearson gradually inched closer until she could feel his warm breath on her neck.

Flustered, she swatted the swirling, tickly hairs.

He laughed, low and throaty.

She imagined the satisfaction of dumping her plate in his lap.

"Miss Priscilla?" Delilah whispered from the threshold.

Priscilla glanced up from buttering her flapjacks. "What is it, Lilah? You're interrupting breakfast."

Her eyes were wide. "Little Man need Miss Addie."

Priscilla glanced at Addie and back. "Something you can't handle?"

She shook her head. "Not this I cain't."

Addie pushed back her chair, the harsh bump it gave Pearson's leg bringing warm satisfaction. Served the gangly rogue right for scooting improperly close. "I don't mind, Priscilla. I'll go see what he needs."

She followed Delilah up the stairs, curious questions pressing at her lips. Before she had time to voice them, Delilah pushed open the door and stood aside.

Ceddy sat in his usual place, his favorite box of rocks on his lap.

Nothing seemed out of the ordinary.

Addie shot Delilah a puzzled frown. "What's the urgent problem? He seems fine."

"Oh, he fine enough." Her brows rose, wrinkling her forehead. "Only your special necklace ain't."

At Addie's openmouthed stare, she nodded. "Go on. See for yourself."

Dread crowding her throat, Addie hurried over and dropped to her knees beside the boy. Her darting gaze scanned the box in Ceddy's lap, and her heart pitched to her throat. "Oh Ceddy," she breathed, tears blurring the terrible sight, "what have you done?"

The small jasper stone he once kept in the box was gone. Grandmother's polished pendant jutted from its place. The clasp and beads were gone.

TWENTY-TWO

Pearson rubbed his throbbing shin beneath the table. Blast that infernal female! He'd never met a more vexing woman. Each time he gained the upper hand in their curious game, she played a marked card.

Blistering under the heat of another's stare, he looked up.

Theo watched him, a teasing grin on his face.

In no mood for his taunting, Pearson challenged him with a raised brow.

Still smiling, Theo shook his head and tucked into his scrambled eggs.

"So, Pearson," the reverend said, "tell me more about your drowsy hired hands."

Pearson folded his napkin and laid it beside his plate. "There's not much to tell. They're an odd pair, I know that much. Aimless drifters, I think. Full of questions, but fairly closemouthed about themselves."

The reverend bit off a corner of his biscuit. "Most drifters are."

"They're foreigners," Theo said. "Fresh off the boat from South Africa." He held up his spoon. "With accents as thick as these grits."

Knives and forks stilled their clinking, followed by shared laughter.

A wrinkle creased Theo's forehead. "What's the joke?"

Pearson chuckled again. "That's a funny observation, coming from you."

"What are you saying? I speak plain enough."

Pointing at the white mound in Theo's spoon, Pearson grinned. "Not that bad, but close."

Theo thumped his chest. "Now you hurt my feelings."

"Mercy sakes, we're out of syrup." Miss Whitfield added the last thick drops to her skillet cakes. Peering into the hall, she heaved a sigh. "I suppose Delilah's still upstairs." Pushing back her chair, she plunked her napkin on the table and stood. "Excuse me, gentlemen. I'm a little shorthanded this morning. I'll have to run out and fetch it myself." She waved at their plates. "Carry on. I won't be a minute."

As though anyone would have waited.

She slipped into the hallway leading to the kitchen.

The reverend turned to Pearson. "I didn't want to say anything in front of Priscilla. She's so easily flustered."

Dread settled in Pearson's stomach. By the look on the man's face, his next words weren't good news. "Go on, sir."

"It's probably nothing to worry about, but there's a lot of talk around the church about a series of petty crimes taking place in town. Folks are getting nervous and starting to point the finger." His gaze flitted to the window then returned, his stare direct. "You and Theo are the only strangers living in town. People have noticed, and they talk."

Theo's fist came down on the table. "What?"

Incensed, Pearson half rose in his chair, but the reverend waved him down. "A conclusion I promptly squashed." He forked another flapjack and idly spread it with jam. "Your workmen never crossed my mind until just now. They're recent additions to our fair town as well."

Theo sat forward in his chair. "It's true, they are. They must be the ones who—"

Reverend Stroud held up his hand. "Careful, son. You didn't appreciate the finger pointed in your direction without cause. You don't want to be guilty of the same." He shrugged. "I'm only suggesting you keep a watchful eye on them." A small frown creased his brow. "Unless you have reason to trust them, of course."

Pearson shook his head. "There's nothing about their conduct so far to encourage trust."

He gripped Pearson's shoulder. "Then I repeat my caution. Be careful."

Addie sat on the floor with her hands clenched in her lap, tears coursing unchecked down her cheeks. Mother had entrusted her with a precious possession. Two weeks in her care, and it existed only in scattered pieces. Finding those pieces had become the most important task in Addie's life.

A frantic search of her jewelry case, the floor in her room, Ceddy's room, and the hallway in between had revealed nothing. With Delilah's help, they looked in every likely place inside the house—with no luck.

She turned to her young charge and dropped to his level. "Ceddy?" she whispered. "Please show Addie where you left the beads."

Moaning softly, he spread his fingers over the collection box and shrank away.

Delilah slumped on the side of the bed. "He feel your anger. You won't get nothin' out of him while he do."

Addie swiveled to look at her. "Anger?" Spinning to Ceddy, she held out her hands. "Oh honey, I'm not angry with you." But was she?

He offered her his shoulder.

"I only want to make it right again." She nodded at the top of his unresponsive head. "To fix the pretty necklace." She sniffled. "It doesn't belong to me, you see. It's my mother's, and it's very, very dear to her." Her voice broke, and she turned away, unable to fight the sobs shaking her.

Delilah drew in sharply. "Don't you cry, Miss Addie. We gon' find it somehow."

Addie covered her face and let the bitter tears fall.

A timid little hand ventured into her lap and closed around her finger. Ceddy tugged, grunted, and tugged again, trying to pull her to her feet.

Amazement penetrated Addie's heartbreak. Gathering her legs beneath her, she pushed off the floor and followed him from the room.

They descended the stairs. Addie shot a questioning look over her shoulder at Delilah.

Eyes wide, Delilah shrugged.

At the base of the staircase, Ceddy veered right instead of left toward the main rooms of the house. A hallway Addie only vaguely knew existed led to a single door.

Ceddy opened it and pushed into the room, hauling her with him.

A large, inviting space drew her in, filled with high shelves and wall-to-wall cases lined with books in various bindings and muted colors. A massive desk, framed by floor-to-ceiling windows, dominated the room. The heavy brocade drapes were open, and beams of dusty sunlight slanted to the floor.

Addie raised her brows at Delilah.

"This be Masta Whitfield's den before he passed," she whispered. "Miss Priscilla's brother. Nobody come in here no more except me, for to dust, and Little Man on occasion." She nodded at the walls. "He like to study inside these books."

Ceddy pulled a tall, rolling ladder from the corner and climbed to a shelf over Addie's head. Panting from the strain, he pulled out a large book and struggled to tuck it snugly against his chest.

Addie crowded close to the ladder, her arms lifted to catch Ceddy if he fell. When he struggled down the last rung to the floor, she stepped back and sighed with relief. "Oh my, Delilah. Should he be allowed to do that? It seems dangerous."

Delilah wagged her head. "Ain't no stopping him. We done tried."

Running across the room, he heaved the book on the desk, opened the cover, and thumbed through the pages.

Addie peered over his shoulder. "Oh look. It's a Bible."

Delilah grunted. "Yes'm, the family Bible. He love the old pictures. 'Specially David and Goliath."

Ceddy stopped flipping and stepped aside, scrambling into the high-backed leather chair.

Addie's heart leapt. Mother's beads lay tucked inside the worn pages. She picked them up with trembling fingers, cupping them in her palm. The clasp that held the pendant was undone but thankfully still attached.

Delilah nudged her. Smiling, she opened her hand and gave Addie a peek at the pendant, evidently plucked from the collection box before leaving Ceddy's room.

With all the parts in one place again, the burden lifted from Addie's shoulders. She hugged Delilah, this time fighting happy tears.

Ceddy bounced several times in the chair then sprang to the floor. Closing the Bible, he lifted it and scurried for the door.

"No, Little Man. You ain't supposed to be carrying books out from here."

Paying Delilah no mind, he rounded the corner and disappeared.

Her shoulders slumped. "He determined to keep us busy today." She patted Addie's arm. "I'm glad you found your necklace, Miss Addie."

Addie gave her a trembling smile. "So am I. I prayed so hard."

At the top of the stairs, Delilah followed Ceddy while Addie rushed to her room. Pulling a chair around, she climbed onto the seat and took her canvas bag from the top of the tall wardrobe. Slipping the button free from the loop, she opened the bag and shoved the beads and pendant to the bottom. There they would stay until she saw her mother again. It wouldn't do to let Ceddy see them anymore. Her heart several pounds lighter, she returned to his room.

He lay on his stomach on the floor, his raised feet crossed behind him and the family Bible propped open in front. Taking stones from his collection box, he carefully placed them, one at a time, on the page.

Intrigued, Addie knelt beside him. "What's he doing?"

Delilah turned from emptying Ceddy's basin into her mop bucket. "He do that all the time." She pointed with her chin. "Matches up his rocks with the picture there."

On one side of the book, the page header read EXODUS CHAPTER 28 over twin columns of text. On the facing page, the picture Delilah indicated was a muted lithograph of the high priest's chest adorned in his breastplate. *Aaron*, Addie's memory supplied.

A wiggly tongue tucked in the corner of his mouth, Ceddy worked diligently, lining up colorful stones to match those in the Bible.

"Come and see, Delilah. They're all here. Topaz, sapphire, emerald, amethyst. . ." She gazed up in wonder. "Surely these stones aren't actual gems?"

Delilah tilted her head. "Cain't say, Miss Addie. I reckon most of them are. For years, folks been helping Little Man collect rocks for that old picture. Old Masta Whitfield took uncommon pleasure in it."

Pointing, she laughed. "I see the old one is back in its place 'stead of your pretty pendant, and he ain't even squawked. Seem like he don't care to see you cry no mo'."

Awed by the display, Addie ran her fingers down the page. "They're a perfect match." She paused. "Except for this one." She pointed at the rough white stone at the end of the second row and laughed. "You could never mistake this old thing for a diamond."

Leaning to peer where Addie pointed, Delilah snorted. "Lordy, I s'pose not. Looks like it come off a crick bottom."

Ceddy sat up and swiped his arm across the picture, raking his handiwork into a jumbled pile. Patiently, one by one, he picked them up and started over making the rows.

"What on earth?" Addie said.

Delilah glanced at her. "Don't that beat all? Left to it, he gon' do that over and over all day long."

As she watched him, sadness nearly brought Addie to tears. "Why do you suppose he does it?"

"Why Little Man do anything he do, Miss Addie? In six years working for the Whitfields, I never saw no rhyme or reason to the boy." She lifted the handle of the bucket and crossed to the door. "I finally decided to accept him like he be."

Once she'd gone, Addie returned her attention to Ceddy, still drawn into his obsessive game. Wasn't acceptance what all living souls craved?

In her initial interview, Priscilla said Ceddy's mother made the decision to stop chasing miracles and accept her son as he was. She shared how the boy relaxed and flourished in an atmosphere of love and approval.

Chewing her thumbnail, Addie pondered this truth in comparison to the ways in which she felt led to help him through mental stimulation and dietary changes. In doing so, was she going against the express wishes of his mother?

Ceddy took a long, lazy glance from the Bible to his pile of stones, his lowered lashes and the dreamy look in his eyes signaling the onset of a morning nap. Giving in, he folded his arm beneath his head and released a sleepy sigh.

His innocence and beauty stirred powerful emotions in Addie's heart. Couldn't she be a source of unconditional love *and* a teacher and guide devoted to a better life for him?

With gentle fingers, she smoothed the silky hair off his forehead and prayed for wisdom. More than anything else in the world, she longed to see him soar.

TWENTY-THREE

After two irksome weeks of hammering, loud men's voices, wagons rumbling past the windows, and a hectic breakfast table, the servants' quarters rose from the rubble and ascended to their former glory—at least according to Priscilla.

Amid the chaos of construction, Addie and Pearson waged a war of sorts, he bent on childish taunting and she pretending to pay him no mind, but ignoring him became harder every day.

In the years since she'd first noticed an attraction to the opposite gender, Pearson Foster—an impossible candidate for suitor—attracted her the most. It seemed a terrible injustice.

Avoiding him had been the only help for Addie's frustrating affliction. Once he moved his belongings into the little house outside her bedroom window, an event scheduled to happen any minute, she'd have to scramble for another solution.

As if on cue, a rig rolled around the side of the house and pulled up to the refurbished dwellings. Addie tried to look away, struggled to move from the window. Instead, she stepped aside and peeked from behind the curtain.

Pearson lowered his long-legged body to the ground, stretched like a bear emerging from its winter lair, and yawned indelicately.

Theo spoke from the driver's seat, drawing his attention.

Lit by the morning sun, Pearson's upraised face was, without question, the most glorious sight she'd ever seen.

She imagined her mother's voice, the way it sounded when she scolded. *"Adelina Viola McRae! What are you thinking?"*

She stiffened her spine. "Mother, I do not know!" Clenching her fists, she whirled and stalked from the room.

Priscilla met her on the stairs. "There you are. Don't fret about being late. Ceddy's already washed and fed. Delilah's with him in his grandfather's den." She smiled. "He has her scaling that monstrous ladder bringing down books." Her smile became a chuckle. "Last I saw of her was the ruffled hem of her bloomers."

Sidling past, Addie laughed, too. "I'll go and rescue her."

Priscilla caught her sleeve. "They're fine for now. Breakfast is waiting."

Blast, Addie thought. She'd nearly made good her escape.

"Pearson and Theo are here," Priscilla continued. "They're unloading their belongings out back, and then they'll be joining us."

Addie shuffled her feet. "Um. . .I'm really not hungry this morning."

As if she found the concept astounding, Priscilla drew back and stared. "Of course you're hungry. Breakfast is very important, dear. How do you expect to chase after Ceddy all morning on an empty stomach?" Taking her by the shoulders, Priscilla nudged her gently into motion. "March into the dining room, young lady. We'll have no more such talk."

They reached the bottom of the stairs as the screen squealed open and footsteps sounded in the back hall. Addie's stomach churned.

Rounding the corner, Theo smiled a greeting. "We came right in without knocking, just like you said, ma'am."

Priscilla nodded. "You did exactly right. Come along; the table is spread."

Pearson smirked at Addie over Priscilla's head. "Good morning, Miss McRae. I trust you slept well."

Addie held his mocking gaze. "A clear conscience brings peaceful rest, Mr. Foster." She flounced in front of him and fell in behind Priscilla and Theo.

"What kind of rest does a judgmental spirit bring?" Pearson whispered, trailing close on her heels.

Gritting her teeth, she took her usual place at the table, praying he would sit anywhere but at her side.

Answering her prayer, Theo slid into the next chair, and Pearson sat across from her. She immediately regretted her rash request. Seated in a position where he could watch her every move was infinitely worse.

Priscilla asked the blessing then shook out her napkin. "How are you finding your accommodations, gentlemen? I trust you'll be comfortable."

Pearson shifted his intrusive gaze from Addie to her, his expression softening. "You've provided us all the comforts of home, ma'am. I'm not sure how we'll ever thank you." He lifted his brows, sincerity shining from his eyes. "I insist you allow us to pay something for room and board."

She smiled. "Nonsense. The hard work you put into the reconstruction more than pays for your stay."

Pearson opened his hands to take in the bountiful breakfast. "But all this. . ."

"It's my pleasure, dear." She handed him a platter of crispy bacon. "You can thank me by eating hearty. Since my brother passed, I've missed having a hungry man to feed."

Theo leaned across the table and took the tray from Pearson. "Look no further for a big appetite, ma'am. I'll be happy to oblige."

Amused by his enthusiasm, Addie shot him a bright smile.

Grinning around stuffed cheeks, Theo winked. A muffled ruckus stirred under the table, and Theo's eyes widened. He gulped his bite of food and frowned at Pearson. "Easy, paisan. Take care with those big clumsy feet."

The picture of innocence, Pearson ducked his head. "My apologies, friend."

Watching the scene unfold, Addie frowned. Unlike the last time Pearson reacted to her interest in Theo, it didn't appear he disapproved of her as a possible match for his friend. If she didn't know better, if it wasn't an impossible conclusion, it would seem like Pearson was jealous of Theo. She shook her head to clear the unsettling thought.

"Are you all right, Addie?" Priscilla asked. "You've gone a bit pale."

Addie blushed and dropped her gaze to her plate. "Yes, ma'am. I'm fine." She stole a peek at Pearson.

He watched her with guarded eyes.

The rest of breakfast passed without incident. Pearson's and Theo's appetites didn't disappoint. Between them, they ate enough for four men.

Priscilla and Theo launched into a discussion about the wallpaper pattern she had planned for his room. Before Addie could catch her breath, the two excused themselves and left the dining room, still chattering about the appropriateness of flowers for a gentleman's boudoir.

Dabbing honey on a biscuit for which she had no appetite, Addie carefully avoided looking at Pearson—until the toe of his boot tapped her ankle. She tucked her legs beneath her chair then glanced up. "First Theo, now me? His comment on the size of your feet may be justified."

Crossing his arms, he settled against the chair and shrugged. "It does take a lot of leather to cover them, I suppose."

She squirmed to the side. "Since you're aware of their considerable range, kindly confine them to your side of the table."

"I'll confine my feet if you'll contain your icy disposition. I'm getting a chill over here."

Addie sat upright. "You are without question the most insufferable man I've ever known."

"Oh really?" He cocked his head. "Then why do you find my company so pleasurable?"

She suppressed a shriek. "I don't find your company pleasurable in the least."

A smile twitched his lips. "Yes, you do."

Addie shot to her feet. "How dare you?"

"What? Tell the truth? I'm an honest man, Miss McRae, with myself and others. It might be time you do the same."

She gaped.

"I'm also a busy man. I don't have time for deception."

She gripped her napkin so tightly her knuckles ached. "You're confusing our roles, Mr. Foster. I haven't deceived anyone."

Leaning forward in his chair, Pearson pinned her with solemn eyes. "If you believe that, you deceive yourself most of all. If you don't enjoy my company, you'd have left the table the minute Miss Priscilla left the room." He waved his arm. "Do you see anyone left to impress with your painstaking show of false manners?"

Chest heaving, she couldn't speak.

His gaze intensified. "Tell me. . .if you dislike me so much, why are you still sitting here with me, playing with food you don't intend to eat?"

Sick with fury, Addie stalked around the table, unsure until the last second whether she was going for his eyes with her nails or heading for the door.

He caught her in the hall, his big hand closing on her wrist. "Addie, wait. . . ."

"Let go of me."

"Not until you listen."

"To more insults?" She struggled, but his grip held her fast. "You have nothing more I want to hear."

"I'm sorry. Truly sorry. I didn't intend to go that far." He released a labored breath. "Your silence has driven me crazy for weeks. I only tapped you with my boot to get you talking."

Fighting tears, Addie refused to look at him. "Only you did most of the talking, didn't you?"

He shook his head. "That wasn't me. No more than the proud show you put on is the real you. Addie, you like me. I know you do."

She seared him with a glance. "Now who's deceiving themselves? Nothing could be further from the truth." Jerking free, she ran for the stairs.

Pearson's stomach twisted into knots. He'd set out to tease Addie, draw her out, but the game got out of hand.

He watched her climb to the second floor, her face averted, white knuckles gripping the rail, and a lump swelled in his throat. He longed to run after her, make her hear him out, but it was improper to go upstairs uninvited, and morally questionable to follow a lady to her bedroom.

Concerned about morals, sonny boy? After what you've just done?

Clenching his fists, he spun away from the stairwell and stalked to the back door.

The best he could do for Addie McRae was to steer clear of her. Given his strong feelings for the lady, it would prove a daunting challenge—even if he didn't live in her backyard.

TWENTY-FOUR

Somehow Addie survived the twenty-four hours since Pearson's humiliating display. She'd managed by avoiding him like an infectious plague the day before. He made it easier by staying gone all afternoon and then declining Priscilla's invitation to dinner.

Arising early, she wasted hours of dread and a well-practiced speech intended for Priscilla should she try to force her to breakfast again. She'd gladly brave hunger, thirst, and whatever else was required to avoid Pearson Foster for the rest of her days.

Luckily, Pearson had a speech of his own prepared and left for the lake without crossing the yard to eat. Remembering Theo's dejected scowl and slumped shoulders as the wagon rumbled from the yard, Addie felt a twinge of guilt and wondered where they were taking their meals.

"Adelina!" Priscilla's shrill, panicked voice echoed through the house from behind the study door.

Addie swiveled on the kitchen stool and gaped at Delilah. "Oh my, she sounds distraught."

Delilah's eyes bulged with dread. Hurrying over, she yanked the fork from Addie's hand. "You'd best run on. Last time she squealed like a butchering hog, the smokehouse be on fire."

Ceddy, who'd been squirming through lessons on dining etiquette, moaned and flapped his hands.

"Calm him, please," Addie called as she rushed from the room. Crossing the hall, she burst inside the study.

Priscilla sat behind her desk, her eyes wide, peering through her reading glasses at a sheet of paper. The off-white stationery with the pretty scalloped edges was Addie's mother's.

Addie's knees wobbled and heat flooded her face. "What's wrong, Priscilla? Has something happened to my family?"

Priscilla's vacant gaze shifted to her. "They're fine. Sit down, please."

Hurrying across the room before her weakened knees caved, Addie settled in her seat and tried to still her pounding heart. "Is that a letter from my mother?"

Her white-rimmed lips drew to a firm line. "It is." Shuffling the papers on her desk, she pulled out a sealed envelope, a match to the one in her hand. "There's one for you, too," she said, handing it across to Addie.

Addie caught hold of the precious missive, but Priscilla held on to the corner.

"Kindly wait to open it. I think you'll want to hear what she wrote to me first."

Addie swallowed her protest, the letter a hot coal in her hand.

Priscilla glanced over the top of her rims. "Shall I proceed?"

Addie nodded.

Clearing her throat, she started to read.

Dear Priscilla, my gracious new friend,

I pray the weather in Texas is still fickle, as I find the notion simply charming. I want to thank you for having me as a guest in your home. I can't remember ever feeling so welcome and look forward to the chance to reciprocate someday soon.

I'm most grateful to you for forwarding Mr. Foster's letter. I can't tell you how pleased I was to learn of his intentions. From the day we met, I developed a fondness for him and sensed he felt the same.

Addie sat forward, clenching her fists.

Priscilla glanced up. "Do you want me to continue?"

"Yes," Addie croaked in a voice she didn't recognize.

Adjusting her glasses, Priscilla lifted the paper with shaking fingers.

You may find this difficult to understand, but I learned from a trusted old friend how to listen for the voice of God. I experienced what some might call an inkling about Pearson, but I prefer to think of it as a divine nudge. That said, I won't make a hasty decision about something so precious without more information.

I feel, dear lady, that you and I made a similar connection. Would you be willing to meet Mr. Foster, spend some time with him, and report back to me on what manner of suitor you feel he would make?

Addie held up her hand. "Please don't read any more." She sat quietly for several minutes, fighting tears. "I don't know what sort of trick is being played here, but that. . .that brazen request did *not* come from my mother."

Priscilla turned the page over and held it close to her face. "Well, her name is signed at the bottom." She held it up for Addie to see. "Is it her handwriting, dear?"

Addie leaned to stare at the familiar script until the letters blurred. "It certainly looks like hers, but it can't be." Her wounded heart shouted a firm denial. "Priscilla, I'm horribly embarrassed. What must you be thinking at this moment? Of me, my mother, my entire family?"

Priscilla's mouth quirked to the side. "I'll admit it's a little unorthodox, and a touch scandalous for my taste, but you shouldn't become so distraught, Addie."

The conversation had taken a dreamlike turn. Common sense told Addie there was a terrible mistake. The notion that Priscilla Whitfield would agree to weigh Pearson as a possible suitor for her mother was preposterous.

Priscilla leaned over the desk. "I'm sorry. You're upset. I suppose I should've asked you from the start how you feel on the subject."

"To tell you the truth, ma'am," she said—forgetting in her angst how Priscilla detested the formal address, "I don't really know what's happening."

Propping her elbows, Priscilla stared blankly at the single sheet of stationery. "Well, there's more, but if you don't understand by now, I doubt it would serve to clarify." She nodded at the envelope clutched in Addie's hands. "Perhaps you should read yours now. Maybe it will help."

Addie accepted the letter opener from Priscilla and cut a slit in the top of the envelope. Unfolding the note with trembling fingers, she read silently to herself.

> *Dearest Addie,*
> *How pleased I was to receive a letter from Pearson. Pleased, but not necessarily surprised. I told you to allow God to orchestrate your destiny. Isn't He a gifted maestro?*
> *I had a feeling about young Pearson from the start. I sense a kind and sensitive heart beats in his chest, and I saw you as a woman for the first time, my lovely daughter, through his admiring glances.*
> *At last, a worthy suitor for you! I pray our Pearson passes Miss Whitfield's scrutiny. I can think of nothing I'd like better than agreeing to his request to spend time with you.*

Addie's hands shook so hard, the paper rattled. "Pearson asked permission to spend time with me?"

Priscilla's slender eyebrows lifted. "Well, of course. Whom did you think? I'm decades too old for him."

Quivering inside, she read the last line.

> *Proceed with caution, Adelina, but trust your instincts. They're a gift from your ancestors.*
>
> > *Much love, darling,*
> > *Mother*

Drained, Addie slumped against the chair. Trust her instincts? Hardly. It seemed the wisdom of her ancestors had skipped a generation.

When she'd confronted Pearson, he said she'd see him in a different light once she heard from her mother. How right he'd been. He also said their heated conversation would be the source of embarrassment. Touching her flaming cheek, she wondered how she'd ever face him again.

"Still with me, Addie?"

Glancing up, she met Priscilla's worried gaze and tried to smile. "Just barely."

"Did she clear things up for you?"

Addie sighed. "As clear as a hog wallow."

The lady smiled. "I know it's difficult. Whether you're expecting it or not, the first approach of an interested suitor can set a girl's head aflutter. As hard as it may be to believe, I had my share of inquiring young men in my day. None who I ever warmed up to, unfortunately."

A thoughtful look stole over her face. "Do you suppose we have only one opportunity for love, Addie? Only one other soul destined just for us?"

"I surely hope so."

Her lips drooped into a frown. "If that's the case, life becomes quite difficult should one of the parties take a misstep."

Remembering the poor dear's fondness for Dr. Moony, Addie's heart panged.

Priscilla folded the letter in her hand in half and then in quarters. "At any rate, Addie, I should think you'd be pleased with Pearson's interest."

"Oh? Why is that?"

She colored slightly. "Forgive me for making the observation, honey, but you do watch him rather closely. And you sort of"—she waved her hand in front of Addie's face—"light up when he comes into the room."

Addie stood, her fists clenched at her sides. "I most certainly do not *light up*!"

Priscilla puckered her lips and shifted her weight. "Of course, dear. Whatever you say." She pushed to her feet with a grunt. "If it helps, I feel I've observed Pearson well enough to sanction your courtship, if you're agreeable."

Suppressing hysterical laughter, Addie held up her hand. "I don't think—"

"I'll write to your mother right away. Meanwhile, your duties await you. Where is Ceddy?"

Addie pointed behind her. "In the kitchen. Delilah took over his lesson on holding a fork."

Priscilla smiled. "Then you'd best run along. He'll have her pinned to the wall with it by now. Table manners have never been his strong suit."

Addie eased toward the door, her mind struggling for the words to protest. How could she explain why a courtship was impossible without telling Priscilla how she'd misjudged Pearson?

More importantly, why did a part of her pray it wasn't too late to make amends?

TWENTY-FIVE

The sunshine reflecting off the rippling water bored through Pearson's eyes and bounced to the back of his head. Now it hunkered inside, throbbing to get out.

Their dragline had proved very effective at snagging almost everything off the bottom, including stumps, logs, anchors, and bottomed-out dinghies. Exhaustion and frustration combined had driven Pearson and Theo to take a break.

Long ago, Denny and Charlie had tied up their boat and left for the day, complaining as always about the long hours and low pay.

Pearson sat in the bow of the boat.

Theo reclined astern, idly flicking the surface of the water.

Addled by pain, Pearson decided to confide in him. After several false starts, he gathered his nerve and looked up. "Have you ever loved someone who didn't love you back?"

"But of course." Theo gripped his heart. "Every pretty girl I see."

"Stop. I'm serious."

Theo shrugged. "I don't think I've really fallen for a girl yet. Not the way you feel for Addie. Like my papa always said, *amore* is a fickle beast."

Pearson nodded. "I loved my family, of course, and they returned my affection. Then your parents, after the storm. They drew me in and made me one of their own. It's only natural to open your heart in a case like that."

Theo nodded. "True."

Pearson stared at the crisscrossed branches of a red oak tree bending close to the water. "I've been thinking about Pearl lately."

Theo's head came up. "Rosie's Pearl? One girl at a time, Pearce. Unlike me, that's all you can handle."

"I'm talking about the way I disrespected her. If you think about it, I'm facing a similar situation. I can't help how I feel about Addie the same as Pearl couldn't with me. She didn't even try to hide how she felt."

"Tshh! She couldn't. The girl was well smitten."

"And I didn't bother to care." Pulling leaves from the oak, he tore off pieces and scattered them over the water. "It grieves me now how lightly I treated her feelings." Shame burning in his heart, he stared out over the lake. "Do you remember what I said the last night I saw her? That I had no interest in the likes of her?"

Theo inhaled. "You meant no harm."

"I meant nothing, because I was too cocky and full of myself to realize I was hurting another human being." He sighed. "I suppose I'm reaping what I've sown."

"You can't help who you love, pal. Or who you don't."

"True." He jutted his chin. "But you can help how you conduct yourself. Instead of flirting and leading her on, I could've treated her with respect." He stared across the top of the trees. "This time, I care completely about a person who doesn't feel the same about me." He flung the bare stem at the water. "I need to walk away, forget about her, but for the first time in my life, I'm not in control of my emotions."

Theo whistled, low and ominous. "Not a safe place for a man to be."

"I might've agreed with you before." He shook his head. "Not now. The truth is, you realize deep down that you'll love this person, need to protect them, and long to be with them whether they return your devotion or not." He fixed on Theo's searching gaze. "Learning this, I know the reason it happened to me."

"There's a reason?"

The truth burned on Pearson's lips, but it was holy fire. He nodded. "There is, because once you love a person without conditions attached, you get a glimpse of how God feels about us."

Twilight etched the trees on the darkening sky like drawings in black ink as Pearson and Theo rode their rented mounts up the hill toward Whitfield Manor. They'd worked at the lake until hunger hollowed their bellies and thick mud seeped from their pores.

Pearson scowled at the thought of missing another meal at Priscilla's well-laid table. If she issued another invitation to dine, he intended to accept, the troublesome Miss McRae be hanged.

Feeling Theo watching him, Pearson turned and raised his brows. "What are you trying not to say?"

Theo shrugged. "Just wondering how much longer you're planning to drag the lake. I'm pretty sure we've struck bottom by now."

Pearson chewed his lip. "It doesn't make sense. We're dragging the spot where the locals claim she went down. I felt sure we'd hit her by now." He sighed. "It's like Lafitte's treasure all over again."

"You don't think. . . ?"

Pearson smirked. "That I'm bad luck?"

"No!"

"Then what?"

"I hesitate to say." Theo glanced to the side of the lane. "The last time I accused them, the reverend shamed me." He sat up straighter. "Blast it all, I'll say it anyway. You don't suppose those two fellows we hired have already found something?"

Pearson frowned. "We'd know if they had."

Theo shook his head. "How easy would it be for them to cross off one section of the grid, tell us they found nothing, then return later and claim their findings for themselves? We'd never be the wiser."

"They're not even sure exactly what we're searching for."

Theo snorted. "You're fooling yourself. They know something. That's why they won't ask. All their pretend stupidity is getting mighty suspicious."

He made a good point. Pearson lifted one shoulder. "I wouldn't put anything past those two. All we can do is keep a watchful eye."

"No, paisan. There's something else we can do. We could get rid of them, continue searching on our own, even with double the work on our shoulders."

They pulled into the Whitfield driveway and slid off their horses. Pearson gathered his reins and handed them to Theo. "I'm not ready to send them on their way just yet."

Theo wrinkled his brow. "Why? Those slackers are deadweight."

"They're more valuable than that, buddy. They're men who've led a hard life." A little embarrassed, he stared over Theo's shoulder. "I'm planning to ask them to church. Introduce them to Reverend Stroud."

"What for?"

"Have you ever seen a couple of fellows who could use a fresh start any worse than Den and Charlie?"

Properly chastened, Theo hung his head. "Yes. You and me—before we received one." He patted Pearson's shoulder. "You're a good man."

Pearson chuckled. "I'm a starving man. Go tend these animals. I'll find our hostess and plead for food."

Theo struck out for the barn.

Pearson made his way around to the back of the house. Stamping his feet in the yard to rid his cuffs of lumpy clods, he tiptoed onto the porch and knocked at the screen door.

Delilah appeared, her mouth dropping wide at the sight of him. Humming low in her throat, she studied his muck-covered feet, filthy clothes, and mud-plastered hair. "Land sakes, Mr. Foster. What you done fell off into?" She shook her head. "And where is it, so's I don't fall in, too."

Pearson grinned. "Don't worry. Our mud hole is hours from here. You'd have to ride out there and fall in on purpose." He nodded behind her. "If we promise to bathe first, do you suppose we could have a bite to eat?"

"Of course you can," a singsong voice announced behind her. "We'll fix you a late supper. I won't have it any other way." Delilah moved aside, and Priscilla took her place at the door. She raised the glasses hanging from a chain around her neck, and her startled gaze raked him head to toe. "Oh, but you'll have to clean up real nice, Pearson."

He held his arms out to the sides and laughed. "Are you saying I'm welcome as long as I leave the bottom of Caddo Lake outside?"

A prim smile puckered her lips. "That is exactly what I'm saying, young man."

"Then I'd better get started. It could take awhile."

He moved to bound off the porch, but she held up her hand. "Wait, son. I have a matter of utmost importance to discuss with you."

He frowned. "With me?" Dread pricked his heart. Had Addie said something? "Shouldn't I wash up first, ma'am?"

She peered behind her into the darkened hallway. "I'd rather speak my piece while we're out here alone." Reaching into a pocket on her skirt, she pulled out an envelope and tapped it with her finger. "I suppose you know what this is?"

He gulped. "I–I'm afraid not." He gave her a furtive glance. "Should I?"

Whether he should or not, she didn't bother to say. "This is the answer to the inquiry you made to Addie's mother." Turning her head to the side, she narrowed her eyes. "You know. . .the *special* request."

A dragline snagged Pearson's heart and plunged. He'd waited weeks for the answer. Now, when it didn't matter anymore, Priscilla held it in her hand. He stared at the letter, speechless.

"I want you to know," she whispered, "the decision about you has been left in my hands."

"The decision?"

"About whether you're a fit suitor for Addie."

After what he'd done to her, Pearson felt the most qualified to decide, and the answer was no.

"Given the unusual circumstances, Mrs. McRae asked me to get to know you better and report back with my opinion."

Two days ago, such an arrangement would've been the best possible outcome. Despite her quirks, Priscilla Whitfield seemed to genuinely like and respect Pearson. He felt confident she'd deliver a positive report to Addie's mother.

Now, it wouldn't matter. The girl wanted nothing to do with him, and he couldn't blame her.

Priscilla tucked away the letter and clasped her hands. "So. . .I wasted no time in penning a prompt response, telling the McRaes that I've come to know you quite well and wholeheartedly offer my endorsement." Beaming, she watched his face, clearly waiting for his response.

"Have you already mailed the letter, ma'am?"

Her bright smile lit up the back porch. "I have indeed. I sent my driver to town this afternoon. By now it's on a northbound train, wheeling its way to Mississippi."

The dragline dipped lower, hauling his busted heart deeper than Caddo Lake. Now, not only would Addie despise him, but her kind-hearted mother would know him for the cad he was.

Pearson backed off the porch. "Theo will have water heating by now. I'd best get a start on all this dirt."

Flustered, she reached a faltering hand. "But. . .aren't you going to say something?"

He nodded. "Thank you, Miss Whitfield. I appreciate your faith in me." *However misplaced.*

Brightening, she waved. "Think nothing of it. I wish you and Addie the best possible outcome." She turned to go inside then paused. "Hurry, if you can. I'm sure Delilah's already setting the table."

His big feet hauled him to a stop. Gripping his forehead, he drew a ragged breath. "Um, on second thought, I'm not feeling so well. I'll just send Theo over, if you don't mind."

The screen squeaked shut, and she hustled to the edge of the porch. "Are you all right, dear? Shall I call a doctor?"

"I'll be fine."

She clucked through thin lips. "Are you certain? Just minutes ago you were anxious to eat."

"Too much sun, I suppose. Please don't fret."

She sighed. "Very well, if you're sure. I'll send something out with Theo, in case you change your mind."

"Thank you."

"If I don't see you again, have a nice night." She touched the back of her hand to her chin, and her blush seemed to glow in the dim light. "Considering the good news about courting Addie, I trust you'll have pleasant dreams."

Pearson scowled in the approaching darkness. By rights, his dreams should be agreeable, since his waking hours had turned to a nightmare.

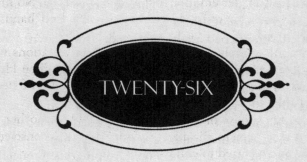

TWENTY-SIX

In the three days following the arrival of Mother's letter, Addie, Pearson, and Priscilla tiptoed about one another in a dance to rival Anna Pavlova's dying swan, though not nearly as graceful. Addie and Pearson took great care to avoid being alone. Priscilla, blushing and smiling, seemed determined not to miss anything should the courting commence.

Shared meals in the dining room were intolerable. Addie abandoned the back porch swing, her favorite spot, in favor of a private haven on the opposite side of the house—a wicker chair tucked into a corner of the front porch. Seated there in the late morning hours, she watched the antics of a pair of mating squirrels racing along limbs and bounding off knobby pine trunks.

Addie could learn a few tips on the art of wooing a man from the feisty little female. The moment her pursuer's interest in the chase seemed to wane, she'd rise high on her haunches and swish her bushy tail until she caught his eye again. Then off they'd go in their frantic chase, madly chattering.

Addie sighed. Why were matters of the heart so less complicated in the animal kingdom?

Dark-bellied clouds rolled in overhead, and lightning struck in the distance. Perhaps the approaching storm would postpone Pearson's workday at the lake and bring him home. Questioning why she cared, she decided the time had come to find the answer.

The very first day she'd met Pearson, when his hand closed over hers on the handle of her luggage, a fierce attraction fired in her heart. From that point on, her emotions raced out of control. No matter how diligently she tried to resist, his rumbling voice and handsome face invaded her thoughts.

She'd heard of such things in whispered conversations with other girls, her closest friend, Hope Moony, for instance. When Hope's beau began to court her, she burned Addie's ears with tales of stolen kisses and tender glances.

Remembering how hard Pearson had tried to woo her, and how determined she'd been to misjudge his efforts, Addie's conscience ached. No wonder he'd resorted to childish and rude behavior.

Far less experienced than the little female squirrel, Addie had bungled any chance of a beautiful romance. Instead of displaying her feminine wiles, she'd thrown acorns.

Sliding forward in her chair, she gripped the arms. Was it too late? Surely, despite the aloofness he displayed toward her lately, he had to feel a spark of his original interest. If Addie swished fast enough, could she fan the spark to a flame?

The steady clop of hooves drew her gaze. Just as she guessed, Theo and Pearson rode up the front drive and disappeared around the side of the house.

Addie stood, determination surging up her spine. The little squirrel had stretched high on her haunches until her mate found her. Addie didn't know if Pearson could forgive her, but part of standing tall so he might see her again would start by offering an apology.

Theo rubbed his shoulder. "I told you rain was coming. If you'd listened to my stiff joints, we could've slept longer."

Laughing, Pearson braced his foot in the stirrup and slid to the ground. "I thought only old men predicted the weather with aches and pains."

Theo dismounted. "Old bones or old injuries, they work the same." His head jerked up, his eyes wide as he stared over Pearson's saddle.

Pearson's fingers, loosening the strap on his saddlebag, stilled. "Is someone standing behind me?"

Theo nodded. "She will be in five, four, three, two. . .hello, Addie."

The last person Pearson expected. He swiveled on his heel.

Addie stood with her hands behind her back, her pale features carved in flint. "May I speak with you for one minute, Pearson?"

Anger he thought had cooled flared in his belly. "One? I suppose I can spare that."

Her slight wince shamed him.

"I mean, of course I can," he said in a softer voice. "Just let me stable the horse."

"I'll take him," Theo offered, reaching for the reins.

Pearson bowed to Addie and gestured toward the house. "In that case. . ."

Addie took the lead. Lifting her ruffled hem past her tiny shoes and stocking-covered ankles, she gracefully navigated the stone path to the porch.

Pearson followed her up the steps, surprised when she perched delicately on the swing and patted the seat beside her. He dutifully sat, trying hard in his confusion not to gawk at her.

She took a deep breath and faced him. "I'll get right to it." Her breath quickened, and her hands twisted in her lap. Despite her declaration, she couldn't seem to get right to anything.

"Pearson. . ."

He shifted in the seat, bracing the dizzying motion of the swing with his feet. "Yes?"

Gently rocking, she nibbled on her bottom lip and stared with frightened eyes. "I owe you an apology. I misjudged you, insulted you, and accused you of unspeakable behavior, all without just cause. I based my suspicions on how things appeared, not how they really were. I made decisions about you without thinking them through." Her pretty chin trembled. "From the second we met, I cast moral judgment based solely on your appearance instead of what was in your heart." She shook her head. "I've behaved like a spoiled, willful child."

Doubting his ears, Pearson stared.

Addie puckered her lips, working her mouth nervously. "Aren't you going to say anything?"

He sniffed. "What's wrong with my appearance?"

Amusement shone from her eyes. She covered her mouth but

couldn't hide her smile. "After what I've done, that offends you the most?"

He cocked his head. "I suppose that seems vain."

She chuckled. "Perhaps a touch."

Pearson braced his arms on his knees and laced his fingers. "It's just that"—he shot her a crooked grin—"my looks have never bothered a lady before." He left off the part that, of all the ladies he'd ever known, her opinion mattered most. He couldn't look at her pretty lips still twitching, glee tucking deep dimples in her cheeks, without laughing. "Addie, it's easy to defend my honor, because I've never acted dishonorably with a married woman." He lifted a strand of his hair. "Not so easy to defend this."

Drawing in her shoulders, she shrank against the seat. "I never said I found your appearance unpleasant." Her shy smile surprised him. "Quite the contrary."

His spirits soared. "Really?"

She nodded.

They sat together, both blushing, both fighting silly grins.

Pearson broke the silence. "You heard from your mother, then."

Her pink-tinged cheeks flamed red. "Yes." She stared at her fingers, twisting in her lap. "And you were right." She buried her face in her hands. "I'm very embarrassed."

He longed to pat her shoulder. "Don't be. I say we put the whole thing behind us. Forget it ever happened."

She made fists in the folds of her skirt again and looked away. "Because we both live on the grounds, and we're forced to take our meals together?" She nodded. "I suppose a truce would make life easier."

Pearson gently touched Addie's arm, and she lifted her chin. Uncertainty danced in her eyes. "No, Adelina Viola McRae. I want to forget because I still want to court you, and if you say yes, life won't just be easier. It may never be the same."

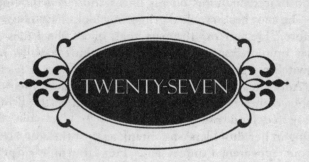

TWENTY-SEVEN

A ddie said yes.

    Bursting into her room, she ran breathlessly to her wardrobe to thumb through her frocks. What did a girl wear to a picnic?

High wind had whisked the plump black clouds away to the south, taking the threat of rain with them. The sun, as bright as the promise of the future, had peeked out to take their place. Pearson decided it was high time they went on the picnic he'd once invited her on, and what better place than the beautiful gardens of Whitfield Manor?

Tittering like a girl, Priscilla gave her permission for Addie to go unchaperoned—not much of an indulgence on her part, since she could see them on the lawn from any room in the house.

Addie chose a high-collared white tea dress with lace inserts and contrasting linen panels at the front, sleeves, and hem. Tea dresses, according to an article in the *Ladies' Home Journal*, were designed to "display a woman's femininity, charm, and grace." Twirling in front of the mirror, she hoped Pearson would see in her any one of those attributes.

While she slipped upstairs to dress and arrange her hair, Priscilla and Delilah scurried to the kitchen to prepare a basket filled with food. They met her at the foot of the stairs, wide-eyed and beaming.

"You look lovely, dear," Priscilla gushed.

Delilah added a brisk nod. "Jus' as fresh as a flower, Miss Addie."

Addie felt her cheeks warm. "Thank you both." How odd, and somewhat sad, to be stepping out for the first time with a gentleman caller without her mother present to share the occasion.

As if she'd read Addie's thoughts, Priscilla wrapped her arm around Addie's shoulders and squeezed. "I shall write a letter to your mother tonight describing how wonderful you look. She'll be so proud."

Addie turned into her embrace. "Bless you, Priscilla. That would mean so much."

A knock rumbled from the rear of the house. Priscilla spun toward the sound, clutching her collar. "Oh my, that must be Pearson. Lilah, answer the door." Delilah hurried to comply as Priscilla straightened the sky blue sash at Addie's waist. "Normally it would be scandalous for a man to come calling at the back door." She grinned. "But under the circumstances. . ."

Fighting a sudden impulse to hide behind the woman's skirt, Addie swallowed hard and stood up straight like Mother had taught her. Unsure of what to do with her hands, she clasped them behind her then brought them around to steady her fluttering stomach.

Pearson ducked around the corner looking a little unsure of himself, too, his tall, sturdy build dwarfing the wide archway. Blushing, he produced a small bouquet of yellow roses and presented it to Addie. "I hope you don't mind, Priscilla. I saw them on the way across the yard and thought of her."

Priscilla laughed. "I don't know, Pearson. . .magnolias might be more fitting for this Mississippi girl than a Texas yellow rose, but they are lovely." She patted his arm. "And I don't mind a bit."

Addie accepted the flowers, the stems bundled in a man's handkerchief. "Thank you, Pearson. They're beautiful."

A smile lit up his handsome face. "Are you ready to go?"

She nodded.

Delilah hefted the covered basket. "Hope you folks is hungry, Mr. Pearson. Miss Priscilla had me pack enough for Jesus to feed the five thousand."

Priscilla swatted at her. "Hush, Delilah. Don't you go blaspheming the Savior." She winked at Pearson. "Your lunch won't feed the masses, but I expect you two will eat your fill."

Raising the basket to his nose for a sniff, Pearson grinned. "Do I smell fried chicken?"

"You sho' do, Mista Pearson, with all the trimmin's. There's a hearty slice of chocolate loaf cake for each of you, too."

He offered Addie his arm. "Shall we go?"

Her breath caught. Smiling into his eyes, she placed her hand on the crook of his elbow and let him lead her through the hall and out the back door.

"You children have fun!" Priscilla's voice echoed from inside the house.

Stopping to pick up a folded quilt he'd left hanging over the gazebo railing, Pearson draped it over his arm and shepherded her over the grounds. Past the waist-high maze of hedges, wisteria bushes, and Texas sage, they ducked between a pecan tree and a tall stand of honeysuckle vine.

Pearson spread the quilt on a patch of bright green grass and placed the basket in the center. Turning to her, he held out his hand. "May I help you sit?"

Addie accepted his aid and perched demurely on the ground. She marveled at the myriad sensations she felt, all new and every one distressing. Her stomach quaked, her fingers trembled, her head felt light, as if the slightest breeze might send it bouncing over the lawn like a bubble.

She had no idea that nurturing a budding relationship was so stressful. How did generations of people before her survive the perils of courtship?

"Are you all right?"

As she glanced up, her heart lurched. She wasn't the least bit all right, and his voice, as rich as clotted cream, didn't help. She crossed her fingers. "Yes, of course."

He gazed over the slope of the grounds. "This is a real nice view, isn't it?"

She nodded. "Peaceful."

His head whipped around. "That's it, peaceful. I noticed it the first time I stepped out the back door." Leaning close to her, he pointed in the distance. "See the way the horizon stretches on forever? It sort of draws you in. . .makes you forget about everything else."

Addie smiled. "So that's why you didn't notice me in the swing the other day."

He grinned. "Not until you squawked."

She straightened her back. "Sir, I never squawk."

Laughing, he reached for the basket. "Are you hungry? Let's see what those two put in here."

He unloaded dishes and silver wrapped in napkins first, carefully arranging them as if he were setting the table for a Thanksgiving feast. Next came a platter of fried chicken. Lifting the tea-towel covering, he wiggled his brows.

Giggling, Addie took it from him and served both their plates.

Carefully inspecting each offering, he placed Delilah's "trimmin's" in a circle around them then rubbed his hands together. "Let's give thanks for what the Lord provided."

The irony of his words, considering Delilah's comparison, turned Addie's giggle to a belly laugh.

Pearson caught it, too, and joined in. "No loaves and fishes, but I'm just as grateful, aren't you?"

Her heart surging, she nodded. She happened to be grateful for much more than fried chicken, but of course she wouldn't say so.

The meal passed in a pleasant haze of delicious food and delightful companionship. Pearson charmed her with stories of the Gulf Coast and his exploits there, of Rosie's Café and Jean Lafitte's gold. He told how deeply he loved Galveston Island before grief drove him to the mainland.

Addie told him about her home state since he'd never been to Mississippi. She described small-town life in Canton and how much she missed her family and friends.

Laughing like children, they sat face-to-face on the quilt and played rock-paper-scissors.

The afternoon passed too quickly, though Addie wished it would never end. Eventually, her responsibility to Priscilla and sense of duty toward Ceddy lured her thoughts to the house. Gathering the remains of the picnic into the basket, she stood. "I really should go inside now, Pearson. It's getting late."

Drowsy-eyed and leaning on the trunk of the pecan tree, he roused himself and stretched.

Addie held up her hand. "Please, don't trouble yourself. Sit and stay awhile. Enjoy the view."

Pushing off the ground, he reached for the basket. "Don't be silly. I'll help you into the house."

She held the handle away from him and shook her head. "I'll be fine. I promise." The warmth of his chest against her shoulder quickened her breath. Glancing past him to the row of second-floor windows, she stepped back, imagining Priscilla's watchful eyes at every one. "There's no reason to cut short your relaxing afternoon. Besides"—she smiled—"I believe I can find my way home."

He inclined his head. "Are you sure?"

She nodded. "Quite."

He gave her a lazy smile. "I'll see you at supper then."

Ducking to hide her delighted grin, she nodded. "I enjoyed myself very much, Pearson."

"Mm-hmm." He tipped her chin with his knuckle, spine-tingling warmth in his dancing eyes. "I enjoyed myself, too. You're very pleasant company."

Breathless, her cheeks flaming, she pointed over her shoulder. "I really should be. . ."

He caressed the skin of her throat with his finger while his gaze seemed to drink her in. "You'd better run along now, sweet Adelina."

With a jaunty wave, she slipped past the honeysuckle vine and tripped lightly up the stepping-stones to the house. Her feet barely touched the ground.

Hunger drove Ceddy from Grandfather's den. Tracing his finger along the slender strip of wood on the wall, he turned right at the end of the hall where the strip ended instead of left toward the kitchen as he usually did. Drifting toward a square pattern of light on the floor, he reached the screen door and pushed his way onto the porch. Walking the narrow crack between two broad planks, he reached the top step and teetered on the edge.

Mama's voice echoed in his head. *"Dangerous on your own, Ceddy. Hold my hand, darling. My hand or Daddy's."*

Only. . .where had those hands gone?

Covering his ears, he bailed off the porch and burst into the bright sunlight, running with all of his might until his side hurt too much to go on. Hugging himself, he glanced over his shoulder at the house, troubled by how far away it seemed.

Without reassuring skirts nearby, the unfamiliar garden and the great blue sky overhead scared him. He ducked between the hedges, staring at the comforting ground and waiting for the pounding in his chest to stop.

A row of tiny ants marched between his feet, stretching into the distance in front and disappearing behind him. Crouching, Ceddy followed alongside the line with his finger until he could no longer reach then took two clumsy, squatting steps forward to trace it again.

A long shadow fell across the ground, and terror gripped his stomach.

"Ceddy?"

Lurching away from the tall figure blocking the sun, he scrambled to find his feet but fell flat on his stomach instead. His mouth went dry, and the pounding in his chest sped up. Try as he might, he couldn't gather the strength to run. Helpless tears blurred Ceddy's eyes, dropping to the ground in a silent spatter.

Big hands gripped his shoulders and set him upright.

His breath caught on a sob, and his body tensed, but he couldn't move to struggle free.

Strong arms scooped him high, carried him to a nearby bench, and set him down. "Don't be afraid, little fellow. I won't hurt you."

He knew the gentle voice. He'd heard the same one drifting up the stairwell in Aunt Priss's house.

The man with peculiar hair sat beside him. "Are you supposed to be out here by yourself? Does Miss Addie know?" His long fingers ruffled Ceddy's hair. "I expect she doesn't. You're trying to cause a stir again, aren't you, young man? If those three women find you gone, you'll have the devil to pay."

The rise and fall of Ceddy's chest began to slow. Pressing his ear to the man's warm side, he stilled to listen to the hollow thumping sound. Burying his face in the soft shirt, Ceddy took a deep breath. He smelled like Daddy.

"Tell you what. . .how about we hurry you back inside before you're missed. If you promise not to do this again, there's no need to tell them, is there?" The man stood, easing Ceddy to his feet. Taking his hand in a firm grip, he led him through the garden, up the steps, and across the porch. At the door, he crouched and dusted the dirt off Ceddy's hands and knees.

"There you are. Now get inside before they catch us." He patted Ceddy's cheek then stood, opened the screen, and nudged him inside. "Good-bye, buddy," the man whispered as Ceddy meandered toward the kitchen to find Lilah.

TWENTY-EIGHT

Denny slipped up behind Charlie and jabbed him hard in the side. Charlie's satisfying jump and shriek sent Denny into gales of laughter.

Charlie scowled. "Why would you do that to a mate, Denny? I reckoned you for a gator."

Denny hitched himself up on the back of the wagon and elbowed Charlie in the ribs. "I did it for a lark. And who says we're mates?"

"Aw, you're not still cross with me?"

"Except I am, ain't I?" He pulled at the legs of his trousers. "Look at me, will ya?"

Charlie lowered his chin to his chest. "Come on, Den. I never meant to land us in the drink. I lost me balance is all."

"Why in blazes were you standing in the first place? A boat is no place to pitty-pat around, Charlie. Suppose I'd landed on one o' them viper's nests?"

Charlie snickered. "I like what they call 'em." He stared over Denny's head and smiled. "Cottonmouth. Sounds nice, don' it?"

"Well, they're not," a gruff voice behind them warned. With a clatter that shook the wagon, Pearson Foster tossed a shovel and chain into the bed. "You'll not find a nastier snake."

Denny grimaced and shot him a furtive glance. It wouldn't do that he'd caught them slacking again. He smiled, pretending interest. "Worse than the coral snakes we heard about?"

"The coral's venom is worse, but he's less likely to bite you. A cottonmouth is more aggressive."

"And there are really nests of them in the water?"

"Not nests exactly, but large groups will ball up during mating. You don't want to fall into one of those."

Charlie shuddered.

"Sounds bloomin' awful," Denny said.

"And you don't have to fall on one to be bitten," Pearson continued. "They'll chase you down."

Charlie gaped, his mouth slack.

Denny tilted his head. "Are you having us on, mate?"

Pearson gave him a blank stare. "Come again?"

Charlie smiled. "He's asking if you're having a laugh."

Staring toward the lake, Pearson shook his head. "There's nothing funny about a cottonmouth."

The other fellow, the bloke called Theo, strolled toward them. "I'd sooner face a snake than another giant fish." His eyes widened. "I think the one we saw this morning swallowed Jonah."

Pearson laughed. "He was as big as a baby whale, but that's not likely in these parts."

His eyes widening, Charlie whistled. "That large, was he?"

"Stretched as long as two grown men," Theo said. "When he surfaced alongside the boat, I almost bailed out the other side."

Denny cleared his throat. "I can't make out why you fellows are risking your hides out here. Must be something special hid down in that mud, eh?"

Pearson's mouth tightened. "What one man considers special wouldn't carry the same weight with another."

Denny shrugged. "Still. . ." Leaning closer, he narrowed his eyes. "How weighty is this prize you seek?"

Dodging the question, the blighter tossed Denny's words back at him. "You two are risking your hides just the same, aren't you? And for as little as a day's pay."

Not willing to push too hard, Denny laughed and slapped his leg. "You're a tough one to crack, you are. Well, you can't blame a chap for trying, can you?"

Gripping the end of a rope, Pearson wound it around his arm. "We'll call it a day, gentlemen. It's been a long week. I'd like to be home in time for supper."

Theo smiled. "Now there's an idea. Besides, we're getting nowhere."

Hopping to the ground, Denny swatted Pearson's back. "Whatever you say. You're the boss, ain't you? Besides, there's always tomorrow."

Pearson shook his head. "Not tomorrow. It's the Sabbath."

Since the start of the job, the man's silly observance of a holy day had cheated Denny and Charlie out of a day's fair wages. Struggling to hide his impatience, he nodded. "Right. My mistake."

Laying aside the rope, Pearson gripped his arm. "Say, Denny, I've been meaning to invite you to join Theo and me for church. If you'd like to come tomorrow, you'll be properly welcomed to the community, and Reverend Stroud prepares a soul-stirring message."

He smiled over Denny's shoulder. "You, too, Charlie."

Fighting a sly grin, Denny thoughtfully nodded. "You know, that sounds right nice, Pearson. Charlie and me, we'll be there."

Charlie frowned. "But Den—"

Slapping him hard on the back, Denny laughed. "The walls may cave when we walk through the door, but you can look for us, all right." He shook Charlie's shoulders. "We'll be there, won't we, Charlie?"

The old fool scowled but managed a nod.

"Good," Pearson said. "That's good." Tipping his hat, he pulled his horse around and climbed into the saddle. "When you get to town, unload the equipment behind your boardinghouse and turn in the wagon. There's no sense paying the extra day's rent. We'll hire it again on Monday."

Denny saluted. "Sure thing, boss."

Returning the salute, Pearson rode away beside Theo.

Charlie jabbed his arm. "Why'd you go and tell him we'd be in church? I don't want to go."

"Oh yeah? Well, you're going, so get used to the idea."

"But why?"

"Why do you think, Charlie? Use your noggin, will ya?" He ticked off the reasons. "We show up at church. Meet the Lady Whitfield, all proper-like." Grinning, he wiggled the last digit. "Next stop, the old girl's mansion for tea." He pretended to hold up a cup, his little finger extended. "I can see meself hobnobbing with Marshall's finest, can't you?"

Finally catching on, Charlie beamed. "I reckon you're the smartest chap I know, Den."

Hitching his thumbs in his collar, Denny struck a noble pose. "Charlie, old boy, I just might be."

Twisting in the saddle, Theo stared behind them, his face set in an ugly frown.

Pearson whistled for his attention. "What's so interesting back there?"

He lifted the side of his cap and scratched his head. "I don't trust those two."

"Save your eyesight, friend. I doubt they'll do anything crooked while you're watching."

Theo sniffed then settled to the front. "You really think they'll be in church?"

"I hope so. I really do."

The reins slid in and out through Theo's fingers. "Pearce, you may not like what I'm about to say."

Pearson slumped in good-natured defeat. He hadn't liked it the first three times Theo said it, but it didn't sway him. "Let me guess. You're certain we're hunting in the wrong place for the *Mittie*. That, or else Denny and Charlie have already found her."

Theo winced. "We've wallowed in mud for so long, I'm starting to snort and squeal." He spread his hands. "With nothing to show for it."

Staring off into the tangled brush and low-hanging trees, Pearson nibbled inside his cheek. "I admit it's getting harder to believe she's down there. But everyone we talked to pointed us to Tow Head."

Theo shook his head. "That's pretty vague. It's a big area."

"It's a big lake. I'm starting to fear we jumped in the water too soon."

They shared a wry grin.

Pearson sighed. "We need more information."

Theo cut him a doleful glance. "We need Catfish John."

"I'm beginning to think Catfish John has a lot in common with Santa Claus."

Theo chuckled. "I'm beginning to think the *Mittie Stephens* has a lot in common with both of them."

They rode in silence for a few yards before Theo looked his way. "There's something else I've been meaning to say. You want to guess this one, too?"

Thinking the quiet was too good to last, Pearson smiled to himself. "I've run out of guesses. Just say it."

"I don't know." Theo winked. "You get all grumpy when I sweet-talk you."

Wishing he'd been less accommodating, Pearson groaned. The twinkle in Theo's eyes scared him. "Do I want to hear this?"

"No, but listen anyway." The teasing gone from his voice, he leaned forward in the saddle. "I just want to say that I'm proud of you."

"Me? What for?"

"For working through your anger with God."

Running his thumb along a seam in the pommel, Pearson smiled. "I don't have all the answers about that night, buddy. I probably never will. But I'm ready to trust God without answers."

Theo wiped his eyes with his sleeve. "I'm glad, Pearce. And happy for you. Do you mind if I ask what changed your mind?"

Pearson released a cleansing breath. "Reverend Stroud helped me realize something I'd been missing." He met Theo's earnest gaze. "My family died tragically, and I lived. Most folks would say I'm the lucky one. Only I didn't get the better outcome. They've tasted heaven and wouldn't trade places with me now. I'm the one left to slog through life until it's my time to enter glory." He laughed. "I used to feel guilty because I thought God took my family in death and spared me. Now I'm tempted to be angry because He left me behind."

Theo smirked. "He left you here for my sake. He knows how much trouble I get into without you."

"If I thought that was true," Pearson said, feigning a threatening glare, "you'd be in so much trouble."

TWENTY-NINE

Addie barely noticed her supper, though the heaping plate sat right in front of her. She took a bite or two of pork roast, a swallow of sweet potato, and nibbled the corner of her muffin, but it all tasted the same.

Eating, along with other mundane activities, had taken a trifling place in her life. Only breathing and being with Pearson held any importance now, and not necessarily in that order. Thoughts of him consumed her waking hours, visited her at night in pleasant dreams.

How glorious the act of falling in love! How soul consuming! She couldn't fathom how she'd lived thus far without knowing such bliss. Surely she was the first since the dawn of time to love so deeply. Otherwise she'd have heard the virtues of love extolled, the aching beauty of sheer emotion shouted from lofty places.

Pearson's dining-room behavior hadn't changed. He still jabbed her with his elbow, pulled his chair too close, and whispered playful taunts, his breath warm in her ear. The difference was in how it made her feel.

Priscilla cleared her throat, pulling Addie from her fog.

The sound lacked the same effect on Pearson, who seemed engrossed in tracing the crocheted pattern on Addie's sleeve.

Embarrassed, she pulled her arm into her lap and nudged him.

Glancing up with glazed eyes, he nodded at Priscilla. "Yes, ma'am. I agree."

She covered her mouth and tittered. "I appreciate your agreeable spirit, dear, but I haven't said anything yet."

Addie sucked in her bottom lip, biting hard to keep from laughing.

Theo, showing less restraint, nearly spewed a forkful of meat.

Squaring his shoulders, Pearson pressed his napkin to his mouth—more likely to wipe off a guilty grin than food. He seemed less interested in eating than Addie did.

Priscilla pushed aside her plate and smiled. "There's a wonderful baked custard on the sideboard, Theo." She glanced at Addie and Pearson. "I doubt these two are interested, but I'll cut us a slice, if you'd like."

"Oh yes, ma'am," he said. "I'd like."

Addie sat back and idly propped her elbow on the chair arm.

Drawn to her crocheted pattern again, Pearson ran his finger along her sleeve.

"As for you two," Priscilla said, swiveling their direction, "I suggest you step into the parlor and wait for us."

Pearson stood, perhaps a little too fast, and pulled out Addie's chair.

Narrowing her eyes, Priscilla shot Addie a pointed look. "Sit on opposite sides, please."

"Yes, ma'am," Pearson said, ushering Addie across the room.

"And leave the door open," Priscilla called as they ducked into the hall.

Laughing uncontrollably, they burst into the parlor, Pearson holding his side. Offering his arm, he strutted to the sofa and eased her down. With a lively bow, he marched to the chair across from her and sat. He angled his head, a pleasing grin stretching his full lips. "You look nice tonight."

Satisfaction warmed her heart. The extra time she took while choosing a dress had paid off. "Why, thank you."

"What about me?"

She glanced up. "Pardon?"

"Don't I look nice?"

She giggled. "Oh, Pearson!" He looked much better than nice, but Addie dared not say so.

Pearson laughed at his own joke then sobered, staring at something over her head. He sat quietly for so long, the click of the parlor clock began to wear on her nerves.

She strained to see where he looked. "Um. . .is something wrong?"

He scooted to the edge of his seat. "How do you feel about the ocean?"

The question caught her off guard. "I've never given it much thought."

He raised his brow. "Will you?"

She tried to swallow, but her throat was dry. "Will I. . . ?"

"Give it some thought. I'd be interested to know if you'd consider living on an island someday."

The vague nature of his question, confusing yet fraught with insinuation, left her at a loss. He'd told her he never intended to return to Galveston, so why should her opinion of the ocean matter? "I'll think about it." She tucked her chin. "But I'd like to know why you're asking."

He grew silent again, but this time it felt different—like the hush after the last chord of a beautiful song.

"Addie, look at me."

Cheeks warming, she tilted her face.

Pearson smiled, mostly with his eyes. "That's better. I don't want to say this to the top of your head."

Her insides quivered until she feared he'd notice her shaking. "Yes, Pearson?" Her voice came out barely a whisper.

"Addie, I—"

A scream echoed through the house. Footsteps thundered down the hall from the dining room.

Addie and Pearson bolted from their seats and dashed for the door. They met Theo and Priscilla near the stairs.

"Merciful heavens!" Priscilla shouted. "That was Delilah."

"Where did it come from?" Pearson asked.

They didn't have to wait long for the answer. She screamed again, and the door behind the stairwell flew open, striking the wall with a bang.

Addie ran around the banister with the others on her heels.

Delilah met them running down the hall. She shook violently, and her eyes were wide and staring. "There's somebody out there," she shrieked.

Priscilla gripped her shoulders. "Calm down. Where?"

She pointed a shaky finger at the wall. "Right outside. They peered through the glass at me."

Pearson and Theo needed no further information. They spun as one and rushed down the back hall.

As they turned the corner, Theo's voice carried to Addie. "Did you know there was a room back there?"

Their voices faded out of reach, and Addie prayed for their protection.

Priscilla's eyes grew wide. "For heaven's sake, Delilah, where is Ceddy?"

She lifted her gaze to the top of the stairs. "He up there in bed."

"What were you doing in the den? You should be with him."

"He mighty restless tonight. I come to fetch him a book."

"Well, go to him. I'm sure he heard you bellowing. Poor child is probably frightened out of his mind."

Delilah hustled to obey, tripping over the bottom step in her haste.

"I'll be up soon," Addie called as Delilah reached the top landing and sprinted out of sight.

The screen door opened and closed. She and Priscilla gawked at each other then clung together in fear while they waited to see who would appear.

Addie breathed a sigh of relief when Pearson's dear face rounded the doorpost.

"Whoever it was, they're gone now."

Theo chuckled. "I'd have cut and run, too. Delilah has a healthy set of lungs."

"Do you mind if we take a look inside?" Pearson said. "I'd like to see the window they were looking through."

"Of course," Priscilla said. "Right this way."

Their footsteps echoed in the narrow passage. In a hushed voice, Theo repeated his earlier observation. "I didn't know there was a room back here."

Addie smiled, "Neither did I. Not for the first two weeks I worked here."

"It's my brother's den," Priscilla provided. "He designed it this way on purpose. The man coveted his privacy."

Inside, the spaciousness of the room struck Addie afresh, especially given the fact that it was so well hidden.

Evidently thinking the same, Theo softly whistled.

Priscilla nodded at the large window behind the desk. The drapes were drawn aside with ornate ties. "Had to be that one. The others are on the slope. Too high off the ground."

Pearson strode to the desk and peered out into the darkness. Turning, he studied the room as if from the intruder's eyes. "Do you keep any valuables in here, ma'am?"

Priscilla crossed her arms. "I honestly don't know what my brother kept in here. I don't enter often." She winced. "Too painful." She gazed around her. "I suppose that's why I haven't changed anything. This way it seems he'll amble through the door any minute and light a cigar."

Addie squeezed her arm.

Pearson pushed off the edge of the desk and joined them. "I'm afraid there's nothing more we can do tonight. At first light, we'll search for prints and see if we can track them."

Her eyes bulging, Priscilla looked over his shoulder at the window. "Do you think they'll come back?"

Pearson shrugged but offered an encouraging smile. "Theo and I will take turns watching the house. Will that make you feel better?"

She clenched her hands at her midriff. "Oh, much. Thank you, boys. I'm ever so glad you're living on the grounds. I feel protected knowing you're right outside the door."

Her heart thudding, Addie scurried behind the desk and lowered the blind. As an added measure, she undid the ties.

"Thank you, Addie," Priscilla said. "We'd best say good night now and go see to our boy." Wringing her hands, she started for the door. "I do hope he wasn't frightened by all the commotion."

Pearson tugged on Addie's sleeve as they left the room. She peeked over her shoulder, and he mouthed the words "*Good night.*"

"*Good night,*" she mouthed back, her heart aching to hear what he'd planned to say in the parlor.

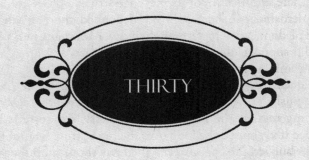

THIRTY

Sunday dawned bright but a little cool for late May. Addie leaned, bottoms-up, over her canvas bag, searching for a shawl to wear with her dress. She'd taken great pains to pack the perfect one, the style a little dated, but it would wear well with her linen gown and matching bolero jacket. Not that it mattered. She wouldn't need it past ten in the morning.

"Not a very ladylike pose, Addie."

She spun toward the door. "Priscilla! You startled me."

"I knocked, dear. I was beginning to get concerned."

Addie laughed. "I'm sorry. I didn't hear you. I was rummaging inside this bag."

"Are you nearly ready? It's time to go."

"Yes, and I'm sorry it's taking me so long. I'll be right there, I promise."

"We'll wait for you downstairs. By the by, you did a lovely job dressing Ceddy. He looks so dapper."

She beamed. "Thank you."

The door closed on Priscilla's smiling face.

Addie bent over her luggage again and snatched the folded shawl from the bottom, tugging it free. Spotting the jasper pendant, she took the time to wrap it along with the beads in a white lace handkerchief and then tucked the bundle into a corner. Before closing the top, a peculiar sight caught her eye.

Disbelief flooded her heart as she lifted Ceddy's ugly white rock, the rough edges snagging her favorite blue blouse. Balancing the stone in her hand, the significance of its presence struck a blow.

Ceddy had been in her room. He'd opened the bag where she'd hidden the pendant yet left it untouched. Even stranger, he'd placed his own prized possession alongside hers.

But why? To keep it safe?

Inhaling sharply, she stared dumbly at the wall. *Dear Lord, what could it mean?*

Hearing voices in the hall below the stairs, she tossed the stone inside the bag and slipped the loop over the big button. Scrambling onto the chair, she shoved the bag into the shadowy recess atop the wardrobe and climbed down.

Draping the shawl over her shoulders, she hustled from the room.

Priscilla stood downstairs, her hands on Ceddy's shoulders. Addie smiled at the sight of him. Standing tall and straight beside his great aunt, he looked the fine young gentleman in a suit jacket, ruffled blouse, short pants, and stockings.

Delilah hurried over with a silk scarf, knotting it around his neck with practiced hands. "There you be, Little Man. Now you won't take a chill."

"I invited Theo and Pearson to ride with us this morning." Priscilla bumped Addie's arm with her shoulder. "I thought you might be pleased."

Addie tried to hide just how pleased she was, but the twitching corners of her mouth gave her away. "Oh Priscilla! Don't you tease."

Her shoulders shook with laughter. "I don't mean to, honey, but you two are the cutest things." She picked up her pretty lace parasol and gloves from the entry hall table. "Unfortunately, they had to decline. It seems Pearson invited guests to church this morning. He and Theo rode out early to meet them and walk them over."

Disappointment weighed Addie's heart, but she pushed it aside and replaced it with pride. Pearson cared deeply for others. It was a trait to be admired.

Delilah excused herself and hurried out, late for choir practice again.

Priscilla herded Ceddy toward the door, waging and losing a brief skirmish over a handful of colorful rocks peeking between his fingers. "Very well, young man," she said when he started to cry. "But you'll keep them in your pocket inside the sanctuary."

Addie wanted to pull Priscilla aside and tell her what she'd found in her room but decided not to spoil the mood of the day. There would be plenty of time after church to ask her opinion on the bewildering find.

The morning was lovely, despite the cold lingering beneath the fringed cover of the carriage. Riding down the gently sloping hill, Addie remembered the first day she'd arrived, excited and frightened, with Mother at her side. It seemed like a scene from another lifetime.

Seated between them, Ceddy nodded drowsily until Priscilla eased him against her side. Gazing down at him, she took advantage of his grogginess and lovingly caressed his pink-tinged cheek. The gesture pained Addie's heart.

"We'll have to watch him carefully," Priscilla whispered. "Don't take your eyes off him for a minute."

Addie smoothed a stray wisp of his hair. "Not even for a second."

Ceddy slept the whole way, his chubby mouth slightly parted, his lashes grazing his cheeks. Moved by his innocence and beauty in sleep, Addie shared teary-eyed smiles with Priscilla for the rest of the ride.

Pearson and Theo stood on the steps of the church with Reverend Stroud and several others. As the carriage rumbled up, Pearson turned his head, his searching gaze finding Addie. Pausing in midsentence, he flashed a dashing smile.

Addie's stomach tumbled.

Beside her, Priscilla cooed like a mourning dove.

"Priscilla, please!" Addie hissed.

Pearson seemed to have eyes only for her. Excusing himself, he strolled to meet them at the end of the walk. Offering his arm, he handed her down. "Good morning."

"Yes, it is," she said.

As if remembering his manners, he turned to greet Priscilla. "And how are you, kind lady?"

She gave him a bright smile. "Very well, thank you."

Nodding at Ceddy, he lowered his voice. "Looks like somebody didn't sleep well last night."

"After all the ruckus, I'm amazed he slept at all." Priscilla cuddled him closer. "Poor lamb. I almost hate to wake him."

"May I carry him inside for you?" Pearson offered.

She waved her hand. "Oh no. You two run along. I'll let him rest for a few more minutes, and then we'll join you."

"Are you sure?" Addie asked. "I could wait with you."

"Go ahead with Pearson, dear. No sense in both of us being late."

Beaming, Pearson offered Addie his elbow. He escorted her inside, up the aisle, and to her usual seat in Priscilla's pew. Leaning, he dropped his voice to a whisper. "There are a couple of fellows I'd like you to meet after the service."

Aware of several sets of envious female eyes, Addie nodded and lowered her head.

She longed to sit up front next to Pearson, but such behavior wouldn't be proper, especially with Priscilla absent. She comforted herself by studying the pleasing width of his shoulders, the ripple of cloth against his broad back, and his valiant attempt at combing his hair.

Of course, she made her observations with furtive glances, timed when the women surrounding her directed their meddling curiosity elsewhere.

Priscilla appeared at her side with a rumpled Ceddy in tow.

Scooting aside to make room, Addie eased the dazed boy between them and urged him to sit. She winked over his head at a grim-faced Priscilla.

Ceddy clung tightly to the rocks she'd warned him wouldn't leave his pocket. Knowing her stubborn little charge, Priscilla must have decided giving in was the only way she could coax him inside. In the end, indulging him worked in their favor. Instead of the usual fidgeting and whining during the song service, Ceddy passed the time lining up the stones on each side of his legs.

At the close of the final hymn, Reverend Stroud took to the podium with a broad smile. "Good morning, congregation."

He waited for the answering rumble of pleasant voices.

"We have guests among us today." Gazing down at Pearson, he nodded. "Pearson, if you'll do the honors."

Addie breathed a prayer, confessing pride as her tall, handsome suitor stood. Was there a more striking man in all of Texas?

"Good morning," Pearson said to the worshippers. "I'd like to introduce Mr. Denny Currie and Mr. Charlie Pickering, my special guests this morning."

Beaming, Addie nodded along with the others at the two men standing with him.

Beside her, someone drew a frantic rush of air, the gasping sound after holding one's breath too long.

Glancing down at Ceddy, Addie felt her own breath catch.

His eyes were wild and impossibly round. Heartrending terror masked his pale face. Before Addie could call Priscilla's name, he leaped to his feet and shrieked with all his might.

THIRTY-ONE

*B*edlam.

Familiar with the word, Addie had never witnessed it in action until now. Stunned silence had reigned a moment, until the last echo of Ceddy's guttural cry faded to the rafters. Wasting no time with the steps, Reverend Stroud bounded from the platform, fast on Pearson's heels.

Concerned people filed into the aisle behind them as they passed, their heads bobbing as they tried to peer past each other's shoulders.

Ceddy screamed louder as Pearson and his friends approached. A mindless, feral creature, he launched his body over the back of the pew, clawing to escape.

Addie caught him midair, the strain on her arms pulling her off her feet. As she teetered across the back of the pew, panic chilled her limbs.

Pearson's arms wound about her waist, saving her from toppling into the lap of the wide-eyed woman behind her. He set her on her feet while she fought to cradle Ceddy's rigid body.

"Is he hurt?" the reverend shouted over the noise.

"I don't know," Priscilla cried. Tears streaming, she took Addie's arm and herded her and Ceddy toward the exit, carelessly shoving the crush of curious people aside.

Pearson, Theo, and their friends followed them into the midmorning sunlight. Hurrying to the carriage, Priscilla opened the door while

Pearson lifted Addie—Ceddy and all—into the seat.

Burying his face in Addie's neck, Ceddy sobbed uncontrollably. After a moment, he spread his fingers to peek out from behind them, his frightened blue eyes lighting on Pearson and his friends. "N–nuh!" he screeched, squirming against Addie. "Nuh, nuh, nuh!"

"Gentlemen, please!" Priscilla shouted over the din. "Leave us so we might calm him."

"Of course, ma'am," Pearson said. His anxious gaze studied Addie's face. "Are you all right?"

She nodded, and he backed away.

"Driver, take us home," Priscilla called, kneading Ceddy's tense back.

The man shouted at the horses, and the carriage circled in the lane and rumbled away from the church.

They were nearly home before Ceddy's frenzied sobs quieted to whimpers. Smoothing his hair with trembling hands, Priscilla lifted haunted eyes to Addie. "In all these days since Ceddy's attack, has he once been exposed to Pearson?"

The question caught Addie unprepared. "What do you mean? Of course he has." Grasping Priscilla's train of thought, she shuddered. "Well, he must have been. Pearson's been in the house as much as we have."

Priscilla shook her head. "I've given it careful thought, and I don't think so. Ceddy was always upstairs or in the den with Lilah."

"Are you sure?"

"I believe I am."

Addie racked her mind. "Is that possible? I don't. . .I honestly can't remember."

Falling against the padded seat, Priscilla heaved a ragged sigh. "Have we done the unthinkable, Addie? Have we offered Pearson our approval without allowing Ceddy a voice?"

Addie's hand came up. "Stop it now. Pearson's not capable of hurting Ceddy, and you know it."

"I thought I did." She gestured at Ceddy. "But look at him. You saw how he reacted to the man."

Desperately shaking her head, Addie cringed at the terrible thought. "No." She held up both hands. "I'll never believe what you're suggesting. Please don't leap to judgment without proof. I've made that mistake, and it's not fair."

Priscilla caught Addie's fingers and held them to her cheeks. "I'm sorry, but we must think of Ceddy. I know how fond you are of Pearson, but it's time we faced the bitter truth."

Pulling free of Priscilla's grasp, Addie shifted in the seat. She needed time to think things through, time to find a way to exonerate Pearson. Because no matter what the "bitter truth" turned out to be, Addie wasn't fond of him—she was completely, hopelessly in love with him.

Ceddy shuddered against her, and she drew him close, her feverish mind replaying the terrible scene at church.

One troubling memory niggled away at her mind. In the midst of the fracas, while Ceddy had been so distraught, one of the men with Pearson watched with an odd smirk on his face. It seemed a cruel reaction to a child's pain. Whatever else happened, she didn't relish seeing the horrible man ever again.

Pearson sat on the back row of pews, his heart thudding painfully in his chest. He'd never witnessed a child so frightened, and it shook him to the core. The awful sight also stirred the recurring nightmare of what his precious siblings had endured before the rush of water closed over their heads. Running his hands through his hair, he struggled with the jarring comparison.

Theo slid in beside him, his normally olive complexion bleached white with shock. "What happened to him?"

Pearson shook his head. "I'm still trying to figure it out."

Reverend Stroud paused on his way up the aisle. "Fellows, there's no sense going ahead with the service. No one's able to pay attention. Let me close with a prayer for young Ceddy; then we'll retire to the parsonage for lunch."

Nudging Theo, he smiled. "Yes, I can cook. I'm a bachelor. I had to learn or starve."

With the service officially closed, no one seemed in a hurry to leave. Groups of people stood around in clusters, whispering and shaking their heads.

His lips drawn in a firm line, the reverend took to the podium again. "I'm comforted by knowing none gathered here today will yield to gossip and malicious speculation, neither here nor outside this building. Let's show our sister a bit of Christian charity."

Passing sheepish glances, the congregation broke from their cliques and ambled quietly to the door.

A grim smile on his face, the reverend crossed the room to join Pearson and Theo. Gripping Pearson's shoulder, he gave him a little shake. "Are you all right, son?"

Pearson sighed. "I'm worried about Ceddy." He bit his lower lip. "Addie and Priscilla, too. Did you see their faces? I feared Priscilla might faint."

"No one likes to see a child in distress, and it's even harder in Ceddy's case. Since he can't express himself, you're left trying to guess what ails him." He patted Pearson's back and glanced around the building. "What happened to your guests?"

Pearson shrugged. "They saw no reason to stay. I think they felt out of place and a little rattled, besides."

The reverend nodded. "I'm sure they did." He stared over his shoulder at the podium. "It's a shame really. I prepared a nice message on forgiveness of sins. They looked the sort who might need to hear it." He exhaled. "Maybe another time, huh?"

"I hope so."

Theo, his mind forever stuck on food or pretty women, tugged the reverend's sleeve. "Let's hear more about this hidden talent of yours."

Reverend Stroud chuckled. "My cooking?" Motioning at Pearson, he wound his arm around Theo's neck and walked them to the door. "Why waste time talking when I'm prepared to prove my claim?"

Inside the parsonage, the man wasted no time showing off his skill. He whistled while he built a roaring fire. Then, excusing himself, he left the cabin with an ax and returned with a freshly plucked chicken. Singeing off the pinfeathers on the open flames, he took a cleaver and split the bird like the parting of the red sea. He wasted no time cutting it into pieces, handling the knife like an expert. Afterward, he floured, spiced, and fried them to a golden-crusted delight.

Delegating tasks to Pearson and Theo, they spread a well-rounded meal over the table and settled down to enjoy the fruits of their labor.

"You didn't lie, sir," Theo bragged. "You can cook."

Reverend Stroud forked another leg onto Theo's plate. "Flattery has its rewards, young man." He peaked his brows. "And I'm not allowed to lie, remember?"

Groaning, Pearson pushed back his plate. "That was as good as anything I've eaten at Priscilla's. In fact, I tasted Delilah's fried chicken on Friday. It didn't hold a candle to yours."

The reverend touched his finger to his lips. "*Shhh*. Don't let her hear you utter such sacrilege. Delilah's known as the best cook in the county and takes pride in her reputation. If she knew she was only second place, it would crush her fragile spirit."

Light dawning on his face, Theo pointed. "It's you! You're the best cook in Harrison County."

The reverend's laughter rumbled. "Keep that fact close to your chest, please. If the truth gets out, my congregation will stop inviting me to meals."

Pearson took a big mouthful of creamed potatoes. "Given your talent with an iron skillet, I don't know why you'd care."

The reverend winked. "Because I can doesn't mean I like to." Leaning back in his chair, he patted his rounded belly. "I'm a little lazy, you see, a vice that's gone a long way toward nurturing and cultivating this shameful paunch."

They laughed together, Pearson enjoying the comfortable absence of decorum shared only with other men.

He and Theo insisted on helping to clear the table and wash dishes. Theo noticed the dwindling wood box and went outside to split logs.

Hanging the dried and oiled skillet on a hook by the stove, Pearson glanced at Reverend Stroud, busy drying and stacking plates. "Sir, what do you think happened to Ceddy?"

He raised his eyes. "Are you reading my mind now?" Sobering, he reached to place the clean dishes on a shelf. "I was just pondering the same. It came on so suddenly and seemingly out of nowhere."

"Forgive me for asking, but was his outbreak so unusual? He's a sweet boy, but he does have a nervous disposition."

"Ceddy gets in a lather quite often, but never without cause. He's set in his ways and doesn't cotton much to change." He shook his head. "But in all the years I've known him, I've never seen him like he was today."

Pearson shrugged. "So we're back to my original question. What could've happened?"

Reverend Stroud folded the dish towel and leaned against the washstand. He seemed to be weighing his words before he spoke. "I've chewed on whether to mention this or not, but. . ."

Pushing the crock of melted grease to the back of the larder, Pearson turned to give the reverend his full attention. "Go on."

"Perhaps by divine inspiration, I happened to be looking directly at Ceddy when he cried out. I watched him go from serenity to shock and then to terrible fear in the space of an upward glance."

His grim expression shot prickles of dread up Pearson's spine. "A glance at what?"

Compassion in his eyes, the reverend placed a hand on Pearson's shoulder. "You, son. When you stood up with your guests, Ceddy was staring straight at you."

Denny plopped on the thin mattress and pulled off his boots. "For the love of—" Scowling, he tossed one of them at the wall. It hit with a dull thud and slid to the floor. "Up before the sun to wash our merry faces and slick back our hair." He cocked his arm and threw the other boot. "And all for naught." He twisted to see Charlie better and frowned. "Didn't even get an invite to the mansion."

Charlie gaped at him. "What did you expect? The whole muddle was our fault." His jaw slack with dread, he glanced at the ceiling. "We shut down a church service, Denny. What's the penalty for that?"

"They'll never pin it on us, you dolt."

"I don't mean them." Charlie pointed toward the ceiling. "I'm talking about Him."

Laughing, Denny grabbed a pillow from behind him and hurled it across the room. "You're a right ignoramus, Charlie Pickering."

Charlie dodged, a sheepish grin on his face. "I sure was scared. Suppose all those people find out why the lad was squealing?"

"Well, they won't, will they?" He swung his legs over the bed, a thrill surging inside. "Do you know why they won't find out?"

Charlie shook his head.

Leering, Denny drummed his fingertips on his forehead. "Because we're too smart for 'em."

Standing, he walked to the window and leaned on the sill. "I'll tell you another thing. We weren't invited to tea at the mansion today, but we're going anyway. I won't be cheated out of it by that sniveling boy."

Charlie's jaw dropped. "Again?"

"That's right, old boy."

"But they almost caught us the last time."

"We'll have to be more careful, won't we?" He pivoted on his heel. "It's time to make our move, Charlie. I'm done wading through muck to see what those blokes mean to pull from that accursed lake. We're going to Whitfield Manor, invited or not. Only this time we're going inside." He clenched his fists. "It's high time we got a look at our bauble."

THIRTY-TWO

Addie sat with Priscilla at Ceddy's bedside. The poor child sobbed piteously and would not be consoled.

Delilah, wringing her hands in the corner, wiped her eyes on her apron and slipped toward the door. "I–I'll be back, Miss Priscilla."

Priscilla looked over her shoulder. "Where are you going?"

"To the den for jus' a second. I got an idea."

She returned quickly as promised, lugging the family Bible, and shoved it into Addie's hands. "Try this, Miss Addie. His mama used to read aloud to him all the parts where it talk about stones. It soothe him somehow."

Priscilla nodded. "That's right, Lilah, she did. How clever of you to think of it."

Ceddy wailed again, and Addie arched her brows. "I'll try anything at this point." Taking the book from Delilah, she spread it open on the bed. "Does anyone remember a passage right offhand?"

Priscilla leaned across and flipped the pages, coming to a stop in the book of Revelation. Sliding her finger along the margin, she came to rest on the twenty-first chapter and tapped the page. "Read this."

Addie held the Bible up to the light. " 'And he carried me away in the spirit to a great and high mountain, and shewed me that great city, the holy Jerusalem, descending out of heaven from God, Having the glory of God: and her light was like unto a stone most precious, even like a jasper stone, clear as crystal.'"

Priscilla tapped again. "Now this."

"'And the building of the wall of it was of jasper: and the city was pure gold, like unto clear glass. And the foundations of the wall of the city were garnished with all manner of precious stones. The first foundation was jasper; the second, sapphire; the third, a chalcedony; the fourth, an emerald; The fifth, sardonyx; the sixth, sardius; the seventh, chrysolite; the eighth, beryl; the ninth, a topaz; the tenth, a chrysoprasus; the eleventh, a jacinth; the twelfth, an amethyst. And the twelve gates were twelve pearls; every several gate was of one pearl: and the street of the city was pure gold, as it were transparent glass.'"

Ceddy, his clenched fists buried in his eyes, grew still. His heartbreaking sobs quieted to shuddering hiccups.

"More," Priscilla whispered.

"Where?" Addie said, her mind scrambling for pertinent scriptures.

Delilah's nimble fingers swiftly turned back to chapter four. "Right here."

Addie inhaled deeply and began. "'And immediately I was in the spirit: and, behold, a throne was set in heaven, and one sat on the throne. And he that sat was to look upon like a jasper and a sardine stone: and there was a rainbow round about the throne, in sight like unto an emerald.'"

His eyes still hidden, Ceddy's lips, red and swollen from crying, tilted at the corners. The beginning of a smile.

Addie inhaled sharply. "It's a miracle."

"He like this one, too," Delilah said, swiftly turning the thin sheets of paper.

Leaning closer, Addie read in a breathless voice. "'Behold, I lay in Sion a chief corner stone, elect, precious: and he that believeth on him shall not be confounded. Unto you therefore which believe he is precious: but unto them which be disobedient, the stone which the builders disallowed, the same is made the head of the corner, and a stone of stumbling, and a rock of offence, even to them which stumble at the word, being disobedient: whereunto also they were appointed. But ye are a chosen generation, a royal priesthood, an holy nation, a peculiar people; that ye should shew forth the praises of him who hath called you out of darkness into his marvelous light.'"

Ceddy lay quietly asleep at last, the hint of a smile still gracing his face.

Addie closed the big book, her hands folded on the cover. "Who would've thought just hearing these words would bring such comfort?"

Delilah touched her shoulder. "Forgive me, Miss Addie, but them ain't jus' any words. They been comfortin' folk for many an age."

Smiling through her tears, Addie nodded. In a rush, the stress of the day overwhelmed her. Compassion for a scared little boy, mixed with fear and sorrow for the man she loved, brought her to tears. Needing the same comfort for her wounded heart, she folded her arms on the Bible and wept.

Priscilla pushed off Ceddy's mattress and hurried around the foot of the bed. Gathering Addie close, she helped her to her feet. "Delilah, stay with Ceddy until I return."

"Yes'm." Uncertainty thick in her voice, she added, "Don't cry, Miss Addie. He gon' be all right now."

Priscilla led Addie down the hall and opened a door. Even blinded by tears, she knew by the scent of lavender that they'd entered the lady's boudoir. Guiding her over soft rugs to the striped divan, Priscilla eased her down.

Addie hadn't been inside the big room since the first time they'd discussed Ceddy's attack and the possibility of Pearson as the culprit. It seemed ironic to be revisiting the bedroom and the horrible topic at the same time.

"Dear, sweet Addie. . . ," Priscilla began.

Addie held up a hand to stop her. "I'm sorry, but whatever you say, whatever circumstance is causing you to think the worst of Pearson, I can't possibly agree. Please don't ask me to."

Priscilla reared back, her shoulders stiff and her hands folded primly. "Adelina, I care for him, too," she said quietly. "Has it occurred to you that I want to see him exonerated as much as you do?"

Addie frowned. "You do?"

"Of course! Pearson has come to mean a lot to me." She studied the fingernails on one hand. "But you see, if he's not who we think he is, I've not only failed Ceddy; I've failed your mother's trust. And most especially, I've failed you."

Addie slid to the floor at Priscilla's feet, resting her cheek on her knee. "If Pearson is not who we think he is, then your Dr. Jekyll and Mr. Hyde story has come to life in our midst, because the loving, gentle man I've been spending time with could never, ever hurt a child."

Reverend Stroud pulled out a chair, nodding at Pearson to take the one opposite. "Is there anything you'd like to tell me, son?" He took a deep breath. "I'm a good listener, and I've seen a lot in my years behind the pulpit. It's very hard to shock me. Perhaps I can help you."

Ignoring the offered chair, Pearson scowled. "It sounds like you're inviting me to confess something."

The reverend rolled his tongue inside his cheek. "That option's available, but I'm merely offering you a chance to talk things through."

"What *things*?"

He shook his head. "I can't break a confidence, but there are still a few people in Marshall who question your integrity."

"I thought you'd put those rumors to rest."

"I did." He paused. "Those concerning thievery and malicious mischief." He drew in his lips as if chewing on the rest. "It's the new allegation I'm concerned with, made by a trusted source." He waved his hand. "I took the charge lightly when I first heard." He gazed into Pearson's eyes. "Maybe too lightly."

A chair to hold him up became a good idea. Pearson pulled it out and dropped into the seat. "Since you obviously believe I've done something, I think I deserve to know what it is."

Reverend Stroud placed a gentle hand over his. "That's the peculiar part and the hardest part for me. I haven't really known you long, but I'm having a difficult time believing it, despite compelling evidence of your guilt."

"Guilt?" Angry now, Pearson pounded his fist on the table. "Don't you think you need to tell me what I've done before pronouncing guilt?"

"Did you lift a hand to harm Cedric Whitfield?"

Pearson's head roared. He gripped the sides of the table to still the spinning room. "Why would you think me capable of such a thing?"

"Because the night we found that poor boy, tormented and bruised, there was no one in the house with us but you and Theo, and Theo was with me all evening. Now today. . .in church. . .the moment Ceddy's eyes lit on you, he screamed like he feared for his life."

Shaking his head slowly from side to side, Pearson fought to breathe.

"If Priscilla thought I could hurt that little boy, she'd never have let me stay on her property."

Pain flashed on the reverend's face. "She would. . .if a trusted friend and pastor vouched for you, swayed her to trust you."

"You mean Priscilla thought—"

The reverend looked away.

A wealth of hurt clogged Pearson's throat. "And Addie?"

Before he could answer, Theo pushed the door open, his arms loaded with split wood. Rolling the logs into the wood box with a bump and clatter, he turned with a proud smile. "I filled the box outside, too. Is there anything else you'd like for me to do?"

Pearson bolted from the chair and breezed past Theo so fast he spun him around. Outside on the porch, he stared with wild eyes, a wounded animal unsure where to run. He'd once told Addie, in a show of bravado, that he never stooped to defending himself. The truth was he'd never had to until now. His ethics and moral character were part of who he was, and no one had ever questioned them.

Since he'd come to Marshall, he'd been accused of one unspeakable deed after the other, and the accusations cut deep. For Addie to think him a wife-stealing lothario was bad enough, but for good people like Reverend Stroud, Priscilla Whitfield, and his darling Addie to suspect he could harm a child was too much to bear.

Behind him, Theo cautiously placed a hand on his shoulder. "Pearson? What's wrong, buddy?"

Shame coursed through him for running out like a coward instead of standing his ground. Wheeling, he marched to the door and burst into the reverend's home.

Reverend Stroud raised his head, sadness etched on his face.

"Sir," Pearson said, his chest heaving, "I don't know how, but I'll prove my innocence to you and the others. I'll win your confidence again or die trying."

The reverend nodded. "I pray you can, son."

Pearson turned to leave, but the man of God called his name.

He paused with his hand on the knob. "Yes, sir?"

"Where are you going?"

Pearson hadn't considered it until he asked. "We'll be camping out at the lake. I need hard work to occupy my hands and a quiet place to think. After today, I doubt we're welcome at the mansion."

"I'll be praying, Pearson. If this turns out to be a mistake, I hope you'll be able to forgive me."

Pearson's shoulders slumped. "I already have."

Motioning to Theo, he walked out and closed the door.

THIRTY-THREE

Denny sat in the back of the hired wagon and stared up at the grand old house. A thrill surged through him as he considered the mansion up close and in the daylight. He nudged Charlie. "Look at her, mate. To think that I'll have a house like this one day soon. . .only bigger and finer."

"You mean we will, right, Den?"

He frowned. "Yeah, yeah, that's what I mean." As he gazed at the tall white columns, impatience squeezed his chest, and he found it hard to breathe. "The only thing standing in our way lies somewhere behind those walls, just waiting to be found." He elbowed Charlie again. "Pay the driver and ask him to wait."

Charlie leaned to offer the man his fee then followed Denny off the rig. "Are you sure we should be hanging around here in broad daylight? I don't think it's such a good idea."

Denny straightened his collar and tugged on the hem of his new coat. "Good on you that no one needs your ideas. Shut it, and let's go." Approaching the imposing entrance, Denny pulled back his shoulders and puffed his chest like a pigeon. "Yes, sir. I could get used to the high life, old boy. I surely could."

Charlie chuckled. "I reckon we'll have to before long, won't we?"

"You've got a point there," Den said, reaching for the brass door-knocker. "I mean, besides the one on your head."

Charlie started to grouse, but Den punched his arm hard as the door cracked open.

A stern-faced maid in a ruffled white cap stood on the stoop. "May I help you gentlemens?"

Denny yanked off his hat. "We're here to see the lady of the house." At her slight frown, he pasted on a bright smile. "It's a business matter."

"On a Sunday? She expectin' you?"

He tilted his head. "Not exactly, but it's very important."

Doubt soured her face. "Who should I say is calling?"

"Mr. Currie."

"And Mr. Pickering," Charlie added then lowered his eyes at Denny's scowl.

"Tell her we're friends of Mr. Foster," Denny said.

She jutted her bottom lip as if trying to make up her mind. "Wait here," she said and closed the door.

By the time she returned, Denny had started to doubt she ever would. "Right this way," she ordered, shuffling aside to let them in.

Denny's breath quickened. Stepping over the threshold, he drew in sharply, filled with a sense of wonder. He never imagined that money would smell of lavender.

The maid led them down the hall to a set of double doors. Thrusting them open, she motioned for them to enter. "Jus' have a seat on the sofa. Miss Whitfield be right in."

Denny raised his brows at Charlie.

With a gap-toothed grin, Charlie winked.

Strutting across the room, they sank together into the plush upholstery.

Denny ran his hand over the satin-covered arm with a whistle. "You ever feel anything like this?"

Charlie shook his head, beaming like a mug.

The clatter of footsteps in the hall stiffened Denny's spine. Sidling to the edge of the couch, he summoned his false smile and practiced what to say under his breath.

The white-haired lady stepped into sight under the arched entryway, the picture of class and old money. She crossed the room and offered her hand. "Good afternoon. I'm Priscilla Whitfield. I understand you have business with me?"

Denny stood to shake her hand, and Charlie followed suit. "Yes, ma'am. My friend and me, we've come to inquire about a room to let."

A tiny frown creased her brow. She backed into a big chair near the window and lowered herself down. "A room? I'm afraid you've been misinformed, sir. This isn't a boardinghouse."

Denny shook his head. "Oh no, missus. I never meant to imply that it was." He gave a shaky laugh. "I reckon I'd best explain meself. You see, we're associates of Mr. Foster, Charlie and me."

Unless Denny had lost his touch, the lady winced at the mention of Pearson's name. "Of course." She peered at them sideways. "Now I remember. You were his guests at church today."

"Yes, missus." Thrown off a bit, Denny swallowed hard and continued. "Therefore, we're privy to the fact that you've recently restored a set of houses out back."

Understanding sparked in her eyes. "I see." She ran her birdlike hands over the neck of her blouse, fiddling with the pleated fabric. "Well, regretfully, you've still been misled. I have no intention of offering those houses for lease." She stood. "I'm sorry you wasted your time coming all the way out here. In the future, Mr. Foster should be careful not to misrepresent the facts." Standing over them, watching expectantly with crossed arms, she left them nothing to do but take their leave.

Denny squirmed with irritation. His plan to use Pearson's name to gain favor had gone bust. He pushed off the sofa, dragging Charlie up with him. "Well, despite this unlucky turn of events, I'm ever so glad to have met you."

Her smile seemed more forced than his. "Likewise."

The maid appeared, as if she'd been standing outside all along.

Miss Whitfield nodded at her. "Delilah, show these gentlemen to the door, please. We've finished our visit."

Dejected, Denny followed the maid's starched white bow and swishing black skirt down the hall. Remembering his real reason for being inside the house, his gaze darted to the staircase and the three doors past the entrance to the back hall, making mental notes of the layout. Odd that he didn't see the boy or any sign that a child even lived there. "Nice place," he said casually.

"Yessuh," she said, her hand on the knob.

"I suppose there are plenty of rooms, yeah? How many all told?"

"Ain't never counted 'em, suh."

He laughed. "The bedrooms, then? Surely you know how many bedrooms there are."

"Six, I reckon. Four upstairs and two down."

"Six bedrooms!" Charlie cried. "Can you feature that?"

"And you have people to fill all those rooms?" Denny pressed.

"N—no suh." Biting her bottom lip, she shifted to the other foot.

"So how many are actually used?" He smiled innocently. "I suppose those downstairs for sure, right?"

She stiffened and jerked open the door.

He'd gone too far. Blundered where he shouldn't. Smoothing the brim of his cap, he dropped it lightly on his head. "I reckon we'll be on our way. Much obliged to you, miss."

She nodded curtly. "Yessuh."

On the way to the rig, Charlie glanced over at him. "I didn't know we wanted to let a room from the old girl."

Seeking the heavens, Denny sighed. "Just come with me, and try not to ask stupid questions."

"Where we going?"

"Back to the boardinghouse to scrounge a bite to eat, since Whitfield hospitality don't exactly measure up to what we've heard." He scowled. "She didn't exactly invite us to tea, now, did she?"

"And after that?"

"We'll pack our gear and sneak out on the tab." He lowered his voice as they neared the rig. "Then we'll make our way back here, find out for ourselves who sleeps where." He tugged on Charlie's sleeve. "One thing's for certain. . .I won't leave this house again without my blasted diamond."

Ceddy shoved against the cold glass pane. Toppling backward out of the window seat, he fell on the floor and bumped his head. Clawing his way under the bed, white spots swam with his tears.

In the house.

He gasped.

In Aunt Priss's house.

His breath came so fast his head began to swirl. Scrubbing his eyes with his fists, he tried to erase the terrible sight.

Gone now. Gone. The wagon took them away.

Hadn't it?

The window drew him. The need to be sure. He stole a peek over his shoulder but couldn't get his arms or legs to move.

The dark space beneath the bed didn't feel safe anymore. He wanted Daddy. Daddy's voice, his hugs, his smell.

Ceddy stilled, and his head came up. He could find Daddy's smell if he looked hard enough. But first he had to stop shaking.

THIRTY-FOUR

After picking up a buckboard from the livery, Pearson dropped Theo at Weisman's Department Store with orders to buy enough supplies to last a few days out at the lake. Turning in the middle of the road, he headed up the lane toward the hill.

Dread weighed his heart at the thought of going to the mansion, but he needed to pick up a few changes of clothes for him and Theo. He wouldn't run from a confrontation with Priscilla or Addie, but he didn't think he had the nerve to initiate one.

Not that he was scared. Only guilty people feared the finger of blame pointed in their direction. But until he had proof of his innocence, he knew he'd regret the things he'd find to say, especially to Addie.

The first time he forgave her for thinking the worst of him—they didn't know each other then. Now, only days later, she believed him capable of another terrible deed, this one much worse than before. Well, this time, he couldn't let it go. Not after she'd made him think she loved him.

He turned in at the drive and slowed the horse. If he could slip in and out without being seen, it would suit him just fine.

Driving up to the old servants' quarters, he set the brake and climbed down. Glancing toward the house, his heart settled to the pit of his stomach. He'd spent many happy hours inside the walls of Whitfield Manor. He didn't like thinking he might never be welcome again.

A pang of homesickness weakened his knees. For the first time in years, he longed for Galveston, where he'd known only love and acceptance, no questions asked. He missed Rosie, Pearl, and Cookie more than he could say. The sooner they settled their business with the *Mittie Stephens* and pulled anchor, the better he'd feel.

Turning from the house, Pearson went inside to pack. Moments later he returned to the rig, an overstuffed bag slung over his shoulder. He tossed it into the bed. Reaching for the post to climb aboard, he paused at the sound of his name.

Addie hurried toward him, dressed in his favorite white dress, loose curls framing her pixie face.

She looked so beautiful his stomach ached. Gritting his teeth, he wondered why she'd gussied up to accuse him.

She gave him a bright smile. "I'm so glad you're home." Glancing at the bag, she frowned. "Are you going somewhere?"

He gripped the wagon rail until his fingers hurt. "Yes, for a few days."

She studied his face. "Weren't you going to say good-bye?"

He lifted one shoulder. "I didn't think it was necessary."

She blinked, a crease growing between her brows. "Forgive me, but I don't understand."

He averted his eyes. "Spare the false manners, Addie. We're past that, remember?"

Her throat rose up and down. "What?"

"Reverend Stroud told me what you think of me. You and Priscilla."

Eyes rounded, she opened her mouth to speak, but Pearson held up his hand. "Don't say anything, please. I just want you to know that I came back to life after meeting you." He ran a trembling hand through his hair. "After you melted my heart, I even came back to God. For that, I'll always be grateful I came to Marshall."

He braced his foot and pulled up on the seat. "I told you once that I let my actions defend my honor. For the first time in my life that's not enough." He untied the reins from the post. "As soon as I figure out how, I'll prove my innocence. Once I do, I'll be leaving this town for good."

He clucked at the horse, and the buckboard started to move.

Addie ran alongside, grasping for a hold on the rig. "Pearson, please stop. I never believed it for a second. I promise."

"Go inside, Addie," he called. "I need time to think. We'll talk more when I return." With the sound of her sobs ripping the walls of his heart, Pearson turned onto the lane and rattled downhill.

THIRTY-FIVE

Addie stumbled through the back door, blinded by tears.

Delilah caught her just inside the screen and gathered her into comforting arms. "Hush now, sugar. You jus' hush. Ain't no man worth all this."

Priscilla rushed into the hall. "Delilah, what happened?"

"I seen the whole thing, Miss Priscilla. Mr. Pearson rode off with this lil' ol' thing scramblin' after the wagon, crying and pleading for him to stop."

Priscilla rounded her eyes. "Heavens, Addie. Why would you do that?"

Addie stiffened, anger easing some of the pain. "Because I love him, that's why. And because he's innocent. I know he is."

A hush fell in the hall. "How do you know?" Priscilla asked at last.

Addie tapped her chest. "I feel it in my heart."

Priscilla shook her head. "A heart in love can't be trusted. You're viewing him through gilded lenses." She crossed her arms and walked to peer outside. "I take it you confronted him. What did he have to say for himself?"

Addie glared. "I didn't mention a word. As a matter of fact, he broached the subject." Remembering her upbringing, she softened her gaze. "Priscilla, how could you tell Reverend Stroud such an awful thing without proof?"

Priscilla spun. "How did you—" She touched her trembling fingers to her mouth. "Oh my. That's who told Pearson." A thoughtful look crossed her face. "I never asked the reverend not to tell, but I'm quite surprised he broke my confidence. I suppose he had his reasons."

"What reason could he have for bringing me into it?" Pacing, she wrung her hands. "Pearson is so angry with me. I don't think he'll ever forgive me."

"Adelina, may I remind you that man more than likely hurt my nephew? Why should you care if he's angry?"

"Until I have undeniable proof of any wrongdoing, I can't help but care. Pearson insists he didn't hurt Ceddy, and I believe him."

Priscilla glanced at Delilah. "Speaking of Ceddy, where is he?"

Delilah inched toward the stairs. "I looked in on him awhile ago. He still asleep."

"Go see to him again. He must be starved. He slept straight through lunchtime."

Delilah raised her brows. "You want me to wake him?"

"Yes, and then go fix him something to eat."

"Yes'm," Delilah said.

Addie glanced up in time to see the back of her skirt disappear around the corner.

Priscilla slid her arm around Addie's shoulders. "I know how hard this must be for you, dear. You had no reason to mistrust Pearson, and now you've set your affection on him." She tightened her hug. "For your sake, I pray we discover the whole thing is a terrible mistake." She pressed her cheek to Addie's. "Let me take you into the parlor. We'll have Delilah bring in a nice cup of tea."

Passing the staircase, Delilah's moans jerked them to a standstill. She stood on the top landing, twisting her apron into knots. "Miss Priscilla. . .Ceddy, he ain't in his room." She looked behind her as if hoping to see him there. "I even peeked under the bed."

"He's probably just in the den."

"No, ma'am. I was in there dustin' before I heard Miss Addie squawking outside."

Mildly alarmed, Addie pointed up the stairs. "Go and check my room. I recently discovered he likes to go in there."

She whirled and slipped from sight.

They waited for what seemed an eternity, passing worried glances between them and staring at the place where Delilah had stood.

When it seemed she'd never return, she popped into view. "He ain't in there." Twisting her apron even harder, she shook her head. "I scoured all four bedrooms. Closets, too."

Priscilla waved her handkerchief. "Go look again. You know how well he can hide."

"Nowhere left for him to hide. 'Less he done crawl up under a rug, he not up here."

Her face pale, beads of sweat popping out on her lip, Priscilla clutched Addie's arm. "I'll see if he's in the kitchen."

Addie's heart raced. Lifting her chin, she waved for Delilah. "Come help Priscilla search the house. I'll go look in the garden. He may have slipped past while I was talking to Pearson."

Frantic, she raced out the door and sailed off the end of the porch, taking no time for the steps. Gathering the hem of her dress, she ran through the hedges calling Ceddy's name.

By the time she'd covered every inch of the backyard, Priscilla stood on the porch wringing her hands. "Delilah's looking out front, but nothing so far. I can't believe he's gone missing again, Addie. Where could he be?"

"Don't worry, we'll find him just like the last time, in the last place we'd expect." Her brave words were for Priscilla's sake. Inside, her stomach trembled.

Delilah bustled around the side of the house. "Did you find him?"

Gnawing her bottom lip, Addie shook her head.

"What's that?" Priscilla called.

Addie's gaze followed the direction she pointed. A cloth lay on the ground, its bright white hue in sharp contrast with the rutted drive. "I don't know."

Veering away from the bottom step, she hurried over. "It must be something Pearson dropped."

Standing over the bit of cloth, partly driven into the dirt by a wagon wheel, Addie covered her mouth to hold back a scream. She whirled, and her panicked gaze found Priscilla through a blur of tears.

"What is it?" Priscilla repeated, this time in a frightened voice. Nearly toppling over the edge of the porch, she staggered to the ground and hurried toward Addie with Delilah on her heels.

"It's my white lace hankie," Addie said. In a flash she realized she'd never told Priscilla about finding Ceddy's stone.

Priscilla slowed. "Is that all? For heaven's sake, you scared me."

Addie bent to pull the handkerchief free. "You don't understand." Holding it aloft, she gaped at the muddy track. "The last time I saw this, it was wrapped around my jasper pendant inside my canvas bag—alongside Ceddy's treasured white rock. He slipped into my room and hid it there to keep it safe."

Priscilla blanched. "Then. . ." She stared down the drive, making the very presumption Addie prayed she wouldn't, the same deduction Addie struggled against. Terror darkened Priscilla's eyes. "Ceddy was out here." She swallowed hard. "With Pearson."

Addie held up her hand. "Now, Priscilla. . ."

"Where was he going?"

"He didn't say."

Wild-eyed, she gripped Addie's arms, mostly to hold herself up considering how hard she trembled. "We have to call the sheriff immediately."

"The sheriff? No!"

"We must. He could be taking him anywhere." She gasped. "You don't think he's headed for Galveston, do you?"

"Pearson left here alone. I watched him go."

"Did you search the wagon?"

Pushing the large cloth bag out of her mind, Addie shook her head. "For heaven's sake! Listen to yourself. Don't you see it doesn't make any sense? There's no reason Pearson would take him."

Her lips pursed. "I'll look for Ceddy first and try to make sense of it later."

She began to stalk away, but Addie snatched her arm. "Please don't call the sheriff. Not yet. Ceddy could still be here somewhere. We haven't finished searching the grounds or the woods."

Priscilla didn't look convinced.

Addie waved her hand to take in their surroundings. "Wouldn't you hate knowing you went chasing a wild goose and left Ceddy out there somewhere, alone and frightened?"

Her frantic gaze darting around the perimeter, Priscilla sighed. "You're right. Either way, we need help." She started for the house again, talking over her shoulder. "Delilah, have the driver swing the carriage around. I'm going to see Reverend Stroud."

Still displeased with the reverend, Addie cringed. "Why him?"

"He'll call out the congregation to form a search party." She gave Addie a pointed look. "And he's the last person, besides you, to talk to Pearson. Hopefully the reverend knows where he's going."

"And if he does?"

Her mouth set in a determined line. "I'm going after him."

"Wait for me," Addie cried, hurrying her steps to catch up to her. Priscilla frowned, and Addie raised her brows. "I want to be there when you find out you were wrong."

THIRTY-SIX

Ceddy lay still under the wagon seat, counting the big brown stitches running the length of the tan-colored bag. Reaching the last thread, he ran his finger to the other side and started over again.

The cloth bag smelled funny. Partly of the sea—like the great rolling ship he rode with Auntie Jane—and partly of Daddy. Only it wasn't really Daddy's smell. Just the man with the odd hair.

He drew farther into the shadows as the wagon came to a creaking stop.

The springs above his head moaned as the man climbed down.

Laughing voices. The squeal of the tailgate. A thud shook him, then another, as crates came sliding toward him. Holding his breath, he waited for the noise to stop.

The seat groaned.

One, two, three, four boots in front, a wall of boxes in back. The man who hugged like Daddy, close enough to touch.

Ceddy tightened his grip on the crystallized carbon gemstone and held Miss Addie's jasper next to his cheek.

Safe.

Pearson drove northeast out of town and took the road to Caddo Lake. The sun overhead felt wrong, the gentle breeze out of place. The day seemed like any other pleasant Sunday afternoon, instead of the second worst day of his life.

Shouldn't the sky be overcast? Lightning striking? A foul wind whipping the trees?

Seated next to him, Theo talked until his voice grew hoarse, chattered until he made no sense, blabbered until his life hung in the balance.

Pearson nudged him hard with his elbow. "Take a breath, would you? It's not working."

Theo grimaced and clutched his arm. "What was that for?"

"I didn't meet you yesterday, paisan. You've done the same since we were kids." He laughed. "Come to think on it, it never worked then either."

Propping his boot, Theo reclined in the seat and folded his arms. "I hope you know you're talking in riddles."

"I hope you know I'm onto you. You're trying to distract me from my thoughts, but you're wasting your breath. That, and robbing me of the will to live."

Theo cast him a worried glance.

Pearson forced a smile. "Don't fret. Things will never get that bad again."

Theo nodded. "So. . .do you want to talk about it?"

Pearson blew a shuddering breath. "If you can explain to me what happened, I might." He shook his head. "How could I have gotten it so wrong? Addie had me convinced she cared about me."

"She does, and you won't persuade me otherwise."

Scowling, Pearson quirked his mouth. "If you're right, I don't understand her brand of caring. There's no loyalty in it."

Theo pursed his lips. "Wait a second. . . . How did Addie come into this? I thought we were talking about you and the reverend."

Pearson snorted. "The reverend brought it out in the open, but she's in on the whole thing."

Theo propped his arms on his knees and stared at his laced fingers. "You do realize I have no inkling of what you're talking about. One minute we're enjoying the reverend's company; the next you're tearing out of the house and spouting something about your innocence." He glanced up. "And now you're mad at Addie?"

"That's right—you didn't hear." Pearson sighed. He didn't relish airing the details of his humiliation, but his best friend had a right to know. "I'll tell you, but hold on to your hat." He sucked in a deep breath. "They think I'm the one who did it, Theo. They think I hurt Ceddy." The vile words soured his mouth.

"What?" Shock gripped Theo's features. "That's plain crazy. Who came up with that drivel?"

"Evidently Addie, Priscilla, and the reverend."

"Reverend Stroud?" This fact seemed to bother Theo the most. "I thought he was our friend."

"That's the worst part. He was trying hard to be a friend when he brought his suspicions to light. To tell the truth, when I consider all the strikes he had against me, I start to believe it myself."

Theo gave a disgusted grunt. "So how do you plan to do it?"

"Do what?"

"Prove your innocence."

Pearson sighed. "I don't know. I'll start by sitting lakeside and clearing my head. Maybe if I run the facts past, one by one, they'll start to make sense."

He stared at the blue sky through the pine trees filing by. "Ceddy Whitfield's a great kid, but the most important thing for me to do is steer well clear of him."

The carriage pulled to a stop in front of Reverend Stroud's humble little house. Climbing down behind Priscilla, Addie followed her past the rickety gate and through the front yard.

Absent of grass, the dark, moist dirt was a crisscrossed pattern of chicken scratches. Stiff-legged hens darted out of the way. Red-combed roosters sat on fence rails, flapping their wings in a brave display. Dodging a brood of chicks, Priscilla mounted the steps and rapped on the door.

Reverend Stroud opened to them wearing old trousers, one suspender fastened over a plaid shirt, and a surprised expression. He looked nothing like the man who smiled down from the pulpit each Sunday. He stepped aside with downcast eyes. "Come in, ladies. I believe I know why you're here."

"I'm afraid you don't, Reverend."The tears Priscilla held in check for so long found an outlet in the presence of her pastor. "It's Ceddy!" she wailed. "He's gone, and this time he's not hiding under a bed. This time he may be in dire peril."

He glanced at Addie, and she gave a curt nod.

The scriptural admonition to give pastors double honor and high esteem for their labors pricked Addie's conscience. Swallowing her anger, she resolved to address her sense of betrayal later, in prayer to the Lord. "It's true, sir. He may be in the woods or somewhere past the garden fence, but he's nowhere on the grounds."

He motioned them inside then hurried to a kitchen chair, snagging his boots and dingy socks on the way. Struggling into them, he fired breathless questions. "How long has he been missing?"

"We thought he was sleeping," Priscilla said. "It could've been hours."

"Did you look in the servants' quarters?"

Addie gasped. "No! I don't know why, but we didn't. He could very likely be there."

"What sort of dire peril do you fear, Priscilla?"

"I believe he may have been taken." Her mouth hardened. "By Pearson."

His hands gripping the top of one boot, the reverend paused and glanced up. "Pearson was there?"

"Yes. And when he left, Ceddy was missing."

He lowered his head, rubbing his eyes with finger and thumb. "I just spoke to Pearson awhile ago."

"We know," Addie said, unable to keep the bitterness from her voice. "He told us."

The man's earnest gaze searched her face. "I hope you'll forgive me, Addie. I didn't tell him outright that you suspected him, but I didn't deny it."

She sank into a chair across from him. "That's just it, Reverend. I don't suspect him. I never did. I could never believe Pearson capable of harming a child."

Reverend Stroud heaved a heavy sigh. "I'm beginning to share your instincts, Addie." He shot a cautious look at Priscilla. "Forgive me, dear, but after listening to the man, watching his eyes, I think we've unjustly accused him."

"His eyes?" she spat.

The reverend nodded. "The window to a man's soul, remember? There's not a hint of darkness to be found in Pearson's."

Priscilla marched to the table. "Then how do you explain the fact that they've both gone missing?"

He held up his hand. "No one said Pearson's missing. He's merely gone to the lake for a few days, to nurse hurt feelings and devise a way to prove his innocence."

Her chin jerked up. "He's headed for Lake Caddo?"

"He and Theo both."

Whirling, Priscilla beat a path to the door. "Come, Addie. If he's bound for the lake, then so are we."

"Not so fast, dear lady," the reverend called. "Before you run off half-cocked, I'd suggest you slow down and allow us to look for Ceddy." His gaze jumped to Addie. "Starting with the servants' quarters."

THIRTY-SEVEN

Denny's turn had come at last. He may have opened his eyes that morning in a shabby boardinghouse flat he couldn't afford, with musty bedding and grime in the corners, but those days were over. Soon he too would fall asleep each night in a house with six bedrooms and satin-covered sofas in the parlor.

"We're still going up to the mansion, Den?"

The question pulled Denny from his pleasant daydream. "How else will we look for the rock, old boy?" In his present joyful mood, he couldn't summon an ugly name to spout.

Charlie twisted on the seat and pointed over his shoulder. "But we passed the carriage in town."

They had tiptoed past the landlord's room and slipped out the back door without paying their bill. Hustling over to the livery, they'd tossed their luggage in the rented buggy and headed out of town. Bouncing along Washington Street, they rode right by Miss Whitfield and the governess, going somewhere in a frightful hurry.

Denny beamed. "Most accommodating of them to leave, don't you think?"

Charlie studied his fleshy hands. "I'm trying to follow, Den, really I am, but it's paining me 'ead."

"You didn't see the boy with them, did you?"

Charlie shook his head.

"If he's there in the house, then our diamond is, too. Now the only thing standing in our way is that skinny maid."

Turning off the lane, Denny dashed past the circular drive and pulled in close to the back porch. As he approached the door, excitement simmered in his chest. He smiled at Charlie, touched his finger to his lips, and stepped inside the cool, shaded hall.

The house was quiet, the only sound the purring of a ceiling fan somewhere up ahead. Their backs to the wall, they slid along the railing until Denny could get a peek at the staircase and the areas beyond.

Nothing stirred. He'd never known a house where a boy lived to be so quiet. It seemed abnormal. But then, Ceddy was hardly a normal boy.

Motioning for Charlie to follow, he reached the landing in a few quick paces. Leaning, he peered upstairs, fully expecting to see scurrying shadows or hear some sort of movement. Raising his brows at Charlie, he placed his hand on the banister and took one cautious step.

A low growl shot fire through Denny's chest. He spun, nearly falling over Charlie in his haste.

Charlie, panic in his eyes, sat down hard on the bottom stair, as if he'd decided to take a rest.

The maid loomed behind them, an upraised knife in her hand. "Don't you all go up there, you hear? Turn around, now, and skedaddle."

On closer inspection—and Denny happened to be looking close— the knife turned out to be a letter opener. Not that it mattered. No doubt her twitching fingers, tightly clutching the handle, would gladly wield it to the same disastrous end.

"Calm yourself, little gal. There's no need to get fidgety."

"Uh-huh. I'm 'bout to show you fidgety." She tilted her head. "Go on, do like I say and leave."

Easing past Charlie, Denny raised his hand. "Dreadful sorry, but I can't go just yet."

She licked her bottom lip. "What you mean?"

"Listen, we're not looking to hurt anybody."

Her gaze drifted to the letter opener. "You ain't lookin' to hurt nobody? Is that what you jus' said?" Glaring, she lifted the makeshift weapon higher.

He took another sliding step. "There's something here that belongs to me, and I mean to have it. The sooner you help me find it, the quicker you'll be shed of us."

She blinked her confusion. "If you left a hat or cane or some-such here, why you don't knock at the front door and ask?"

"No hat or cane, darlin'. The item in question is far more valuable." He eased off the bottom step and moved to the side of the banister, giving her a clear shot at Charlie. "My friend here is about to go upstairs and have a look around, and there's nothing you can do to stop him."

Charlie's eyes widened.

Denny gave him a firm nod.

Gripping the railing with white-knuckled hands, Charlie started to climb.

Falling into Denny's trap, the maid lunged, aiming the crude knife at Charlie's back.

Denny's hand shot out and cruelly gripped her wrist.

She screamed, and the opener clattered to the floor.

Bending at the waist, he picked it up and held it to her throat. "Where's the boy?"

Her body heaved against him. "M—Masta Ceddy? What you want with him?"

He gave her a shake. "Answer the question."

"He ain't here."

"Sure he is."

"No, suh. I swear it."

"You want me to tell you how I know you're lying? Charlie and me just saw his old auntie and the hired girl in town. The brat wasn't with 'em."

Her chest rose and fell in a sob. "Don't you go callin' Little Man no brat."

Losing patience, Denny pushed the point a little harder against her skin. "Tell me."

She gasped. "Masta Ceddy gone missin' again, and we cain't find him."

Releasing her, he spun her around. "What do you mean 'missing'?"

"He runs off on occasion." A sudden thought sparked in her eyes. "Miss Priscilla gone for help. Half the county gon' show up here any minute. Search parties and such." Her throat bobbed. "It won't do for you two to be caught inside when they come."

Denny cursed and gripped her shoulder. "If you value your life, take me to his room." He shook her hard. "Go on! Which way?"

Stumbling over her feet, she struggled to the stairs, slid past Charlie, and clawed her way up the banister.

They fell in behind her and followed her to the first door on the right. Swinging it wide, she hurried inside and huddled in the corner.

Denny's gaze darted to the cheery quilt on the bed, the bright rugs, and the scattered toys. Confident she'd brought them to the right place, he took an anxious breath. "He had a rock when he came here."

She frowned. "A rock?"

"That's right." He made a circle with his finger and thumb. "About this big."

"Yessuh?"

His heart thudded in his chest. "White it was."

She nodded. "Yessuh?"

"Do you know where he kept it?"

She shook her head.

Bile rising in his throat, Denny held the letter opener over her head. "You'd best start figuring it out."

Leaping like a gazelle, she shot across the room to a large upright chest. Opening the lid, she tilted the contents onto the floor. Reaching for a shelf behind her, she swept several crates over the edge with her arm. They fell with a crash that emptied their contents. Dashing to the bed, she scrambled beneath it and pulled out several square display boxes. Crying now, she dumped them onto the mountain of stones in the middle of the room. "There be more in the closet," she panted. "You want me to fetch them?"

Denny stared in disbelief. Rocks of every imaginable color, shape, and size lay in a heap at his feet. "What the devil is this?"

"Little Man's collection, suh."

"This ain't a blessed collection. It's a quarry!"

Backing away from his shouting, she cowered next to the bed.

Denny hooked his thumb at Charlie. "Get started, mate. This lot could take all night."

"Right, Den," Charlie said, dropping to his knees.

Casting the maid a warning glare, Denny knelt to join him. "Best hurry, too. If what she said is true, we ain't got much time."

Delilah met the carriage before it rolled to a stop, waving her arms overhead and screaming.

Priscilla gasped and turned a sickly shade.

Addie bailed out the side without waiting for the driver's assistance and ran to grip Delilah's arms. "What's wrong? Have you found him?"

She wailed an answer Addie couldn't understand and fell sobbing onto her shoulder.

Fearing the worst, Addie turned flooded eyes to Priscilla. "I can't understand what she's saying."

Climbing down, Priscilla rushed to her maid and spun her around. "Delilah, get hold of yourself. Tell us what happened."

"They come in the house," she shrilled. "I took your letter opener and tried to make 'em leave, but they wouldn't go."

"Who?" Priscilla shook her. "Who came in?"

"Those two men. The same ones who come earlier today askin' for to let a room."

Priscilla flinched. "They came back?"

"Yes'm."

"Whatever did they want?"

Delilah stamped her foot. "Aren't you listenin'? They ain't made no social call. They broke in at the back door. Went up to Little Man's room. Threatened to kill me 'less I helped them find one of Ceddy's rocks."

A chill crept up Addie's spine. She suspected which stone they wanted. But why?

"One?" Priscilla's mouth lifted in a smirk. "Out of all he has? How curious. Did they find it?"

Addie knew the answer before Delilah spoke. Unless they had Ceddy, they hadn't located the white rock. She shuddered. Or her pendant.

"They ain't found it, but not for lack of trying. They tore up most every room in the house."

Her eyes wide, Priscilla stared over her shoulder at the mansion. "They ransacked my home? Where are they now?"

"They left once I told them Mr. Pearson mos' likely took Little Man."

Addie's stomach lurched. "Why did you tell them that?"

"I had to, Miss Addie." Her bottom lip trembled. "In all my days, I never been so scared. I jus' wanted them to leave."

Addie smoothed her back. "Don't fret now. In your place, I might've done the same."

Pressing her temples, Priscilla stared at the ground. "None of this makes a lick of sense. I can't keep up anymore. Ceddy's missing. Pearson's gone. Strange men are rummaging through my house. . ." Her frightened eyes begged Addie for answers. "What on earth is happening?"

"Calm yourself, dear lady," Addie said, taking her elbow. "Come inside, and I'll brew you a cup of tea."

Priscilla tensed. "I'm a little afraid."

"It's all right now," Delilah said. "They gone."

"I don't mean them." She sighed. "I'm scared to see the damage they've done."

Addie's fingers tightened on her waist. "We have to go in, Priscilla. Suppose they left behind a clue to finding Ceddy."

She inhaled sharply. "Do you think it's possible?"

"I don't know, but let's go see." Tugging gently, Addie coaxed her into motion.

Breathing harder as they approached the door, Priscilla allowed them to lead her inside.

Along the downstairs hall, drawers were pulled out, curio cabinets emptied. The parlor fared no better. Cushions from the sofa and chairs littered the floor, and a music box from the mantel lay in pieces.

Back in the hall, Priscilla's shoulders relaxed from around her ears. "It's awful, but nothing we can't put to rights."

Her eyes bulging, Delilah shook her head. "You ain't seen Masta Whitfield's den yet. They busted it up pretty bad and stole all his guns."

Priscilla gasped. "They took my brother's weapons?"

"Sho' did. Broke the glass and reached right in. Left nothin' behind but an empty case."

Priscilla moaned, and tears slid down her cheeks.

Delilah waved her hand. "That's nothing. Wait till you see up them stairs."

"Oh Delilah, don't tell me."

She shook her head. "I won't, 'cause I cain't describe it."

Clutching Addie's sleeve, Priscilla stared through the rails of the banister. "I can't bear this, Addie. Go with me, dear."

Addie squeezed her hand. "Reverend Stroud and his search party should be here soon. If he's able to round up men to look for Ceddy, surely he can enlist the women to help us clean up." She rubbed Priscilla's arm. "Just remember. . .the only things irreplaceable are our loved ones."

Priscilla nodded, a wistful glint in her eyes. "You're right, of course. And wise beyond your years."

Addie didn't feel wise. She just felt terrified for Pearson and Ceddy.

Upstairs, she crept over the threshold of Ceddy's room and groaned. Behind her, Priscilla cried aloud.

Ceddy's entire collection lay scattered over the floor in a rainbow jumble of rocks and stones. His bed had been stripped, the mattress slit open and the stuffing pulled out. They had dumped his clothing out of his drawers, smashed and broken his toys to bits. No books remained in the bookcases. They'd been pulled out and tossed aside, their spines cut open and covers ripped off. Ceddy's beloved collection boxes lay splintered and empty.

"Merciful heaven," Priscilla said. "What could be so important in a child's room?"

Her hands at her hips, Addie turned full circle. "It would have to be something quite valuable, wouldn't it?" Her gaze jumping to the broken boxes, she pointed. "Ceddy had a few precious stones in his collection, didn't he? A sapphire, an emerald, and a few others?"

Priscilla nodded. "Yes, but they were very small stones. Surely not worth much." She sighed. "Definitely not worth all this destruction."

Bending to pick up one shattered container, she blinked back tears. "These were far more costly in terms of sentimental value. Ceddy's father made them with his own hands."

Addie squeezed her shoulders. "I'm so sorry."

She lifted her chin. "We'd best go see the damage to the rest of the house."

Addie nodded. "Are you sure you're ready?"

She shook her head. "No, but I suppose we must. It can't be any worse than this."

Still hovering near the door, Delilah grunted. "I wouldn't place no wagers, Miss Priscilla. Them vicious dogs turned desperate by the time they reached your rooms."

Moaning, Priscilla let Addie lead her down the hall.

THIRTY-EIGHT

Pearson pulled the wagon to a stop. Puffing his cheeks, he blew a frustrated breath. "I don't want to push her any more, Theo. She's limping pretty bad."

They sat staring at the horse's twitching ears, as if waiting for her opinion on the matter.

Theo twisted his mouth to gnaw on the side. "The lake is only a mile or so farther. You don't think she'll make it?"

Giving it a few seconds' thought, Pearson shrugged. "We're talking about a horse, partner. If you want to know if the patch in the bottom of a dinghy will hold, I'm your man. But an animal. . ." He gave Theo a sideways glance. "You should know what to do. You have a horse."

Theo's finger shot up. "Papa has a horse. I just borrow him. He gets a limp, I take him home."

Pearson leaned forward to think. "She's been hobbled for a while now. If the extra mile will cripple her, I won't risk it. The liveryman will put her down. You want her death on your conscience?"

Theo held up his hands. "Then what are we supposed to do? If you haven't noticed, we're out in the middle of nowhere."

"I can see that."

"It'll be dark in a couple more hours."

Pearson squinted at the low-riding sun. "I see that, too."

"We need time to set up camp, build a fire, heat some food."

"I agree. Do you have a suggestion?"

"Yes, I say we press on," Theo bellowed, banging his fists on his knees.

Pearson caught his wrist. "Did you hear that?"

Theo's head swung around. "Hear what?"

"A voice."

Theo smiled. "Yes, mine. Echoing off the trees."

Pearson shook his head. "This was close by. Like the moan of a woman or child." Shifting his weight, he gazed behind him, a chill going up his back. "I'm almost positive I—"

Theo nudged him in the side with his elbow.

Irritated, he turned. "What?"

Struck dumb, Theo pointed.

It took Pearson a few seconds to see him.

A man had stepped out of the woods, so wild in appearance he blended with the surroundings. His hair, mostly dark but streaked with strands of gray, curled behind his ears and from under his hat. The beard and mustache he sported appeared dark at the roots but frosted with white. A pair of baggy denim pants covered his legs, and a shirt stitched together from hides draped his torso. He balanced a muzzle-loading shotgun over his shoulder.

It crossed Pearson's mind, a bit late, that they carried no weapons at all. He raised a hand in greeting, boasting a confidence he didn't feel. "Afternoon, sir."

The stranger stood ten feet away, as still as the tree he leaned against, watching them with a lazy smile. His eyes, older than his years, brimmed with wisdom. The warmth in their depths, clearly visible from across the way, eased Pearson's mind. The man glanced toward the west. "I reckon it still qualifies as afternoon. Won't be for long though." He pulled his hat lower and peered at the wall of trees. "You're a fair piece from civilization. If I were you boys, I'd get where you're going. This road will soon be thick with critters you wouldn't want to run into."

Theo cleared his throat. "Such as?"

"Bobcats. Coyotes. Black bear. You might stumble across a red wolf, though I doubt it. Nearly all of them have been killed out." He sniffed. "Sadly, your fellow man might prove the nastiest. It's not unusual to stumble across a no-account up to no good out here."

Pearson's pulse quickened. "You know a lot about the area, then?"

He pursed his lips. "More than most, I'd say."

Staring, Theo lowered his voice. "Um, that couldn't be—"

"Old Saint Nick himself?"

"Or the next best thing," he muttered, chuckling under his breath. "Like I said before, you're the luckiest man in Texas."

Pearson grinned. "And like I said before, I don't deserve it." Climbing down from the rig, he made his way through the underbrush with his hand extended. "Sir, would I happen to be in the company of the infamous Catfish John?"

The man clasped Pearson's hand, a slow smile lifting the corners of his mouth. "I won't bother to ask how you know my name. Sorry I can't offer you the same compliment, mister."

"That's understandable. I'm not legendary."

At this he laughed aloud. "It's a sad day if staying out of the way and minding your own business makes a man a legend." He turned to greet Theo, high-stepping over the tall grass. "Mind my asking where you fellows are from?"

"Galveston, originally," Theo said, "but right now we're staying in Marshall. We were headed up the way to Tow Head, but our horse fell lame."

Interest sparked in his eyes. "Up to Tow Head, huh?"

"Yes, sir."

He cut his eyes to Pearson. "Doing a little fishing, are you?"

Unable to hold his gaze, Pearson looked past his shoulder. "Well, not exactly."

Deep-throated laughter rumbled in John's chest. "As it happens, boys, I have heard of you. You're the two who've been asking about me and the *Mittie Stephens* from here to Marshall and back."

Feeling the warmth of a blush, Pearson nodded. "I was getting to that." He grinned. "We were hoping to ask you some questions."

Shaking his head, he brushed past them. "First let's have a look at your horse. I wasn't joking when I said you need to be on your way before nightfall." Catfish John lifted the horse's foot and placed his palm on the side of the hoof. Three seconds later, he lowered the leg and stood. "You're in luck. You've got a hot nail here, but I don't think it's a direct hit."

Theo shrugged. "What's that mean?"

"When the smithy shod this animal, he drove the nail too close to the quick. If I'm right, this one's not too bad. It's tender, but not likely to get infected."

Pearson braced his hands on his knees and leaned to stare at the hoof. "If you're wrong?"

"Then he's pricked the horse's flesh. This can go bad quick. She'll wind up with an abscess."

"What do we do then?"

"You shoot her—what else?"

At Pearson's stricken look, he chuckled. "You'll have to pull off her shoe. Allow the infection to drain. This kind of injury takes a long time to heal." He patted the horse's rear end, and she gave an answering shiver. "But I don't think it's that bad."

"So she can safely pull us as far as the lake?"

John nodded. "I'd say so."

Standing, Pearson breathed a relieved sigh.

Glancing toward the orange-tinted sky, Catfish John dusted his hands and shifted his gun strap. "I'll let you be on your way. The sooner you're camped in front of a fire, the safer you'll be."

Pearson tried to think fast. "Can we give you a ride somewhere?"

He smiled and pointed at the mare. "You're hardly in a position to ask. Besides, I have a mount tethered a few yards into the woods."

Determined not to let him get away, Pearson cast aside his pride. "Sir, we've been slogging through mud and swamp for weeks now and getting nowhere. I'm pretty certain if we'd found you sooner, you could've saved us a lot of sweat." He grimaced. "I know a man like you must be busy, but—"

Catfish John laughed. "I steer well clear of busywork, son, unless it's something I like to do."

Thinking fast, Pearson smiled. "That makes your time even more valuable, doesn't it? So I hate to ask, but could you spare us a few minutes? We'd sure like to ask some questions."

Chewing the ends of his mustache, Catfish John seemed to stall. "I suppose I should. Maybe once you hear me out, it'll save you more trouble than you think."

Pearson's heart surged. "That's our hope."

"Mine, too, but not for the same reason." He pushed his hat off his forehead. "First, let's get to your campsite and build a fire." Stalking toward the trees, he called over his shoulder, "Going after my horse. Be back directly."

Pearson spun toward Theo, rubbing his palms together. "You hear that, paisan? He'll be back directly." He clapped his cupped hands. "We found Catfish John!"

Theo grinned. "No, he found us. You think he'll really come back?"

"Sure he will. Don't even suggest otherwise." He pointed toward the rig. "Shuffle those boxes around and make yourself a place to sit. We can't ask the famous Catfish John to ride in the wagon bed."

Laughing, Theo hurried to lower the tailgate. Climbing into the bed, he shoved the parcels aside as he worked his way toward the front.

His hands stilled on a crate, and stunned surprise hit his face like a blow. "Whoa! What the. . . ?" Reeling, he fell on his behind, and his head whipped around. "Pearson? You need to see this."

Alarm chilled Pearson's blood. Running for the rig, he held his breath as he peeked over the side.

Ceddy Whitfield lay asleep beneath the seat with both hands curled under his chin. His rounded cheeks were flushed bright pink, and his hair was damp with sweat. He snored quietly, a string of drool from his mouth puddling on the wooden boards.

Tightening his grip until the rail creaked, Pearson gaped at Theo. "I guess you know what this means, paisan. I'm in a world of trouble."

THIRTY-NINE

The horrible men had pulled Addie's canvas bag off the top of her wardrobe and upended it on the floor. Grandmother's beads were there, kicked across the room like discarded trash, but the jasper pendant was gone. With all her heart, she prayed Ceddy would have it when they found him. If not, her chances of seeing the treasured pendant again were slim.

With greater fervor, she prayed they'd find him.

Reverend Stroud had come, bringing men to comb the woods. One look at the mess in the house, and he'd left again, returning with two wagonloads of chattering women. They were scattered throughout the mansion—with Priscilla running herself ragged trying to supervise all their activities at once.

Each time she found herself between tasks, she begged the reverend to take her to find Pearson, so she could see for herself if Ceddy was with him. The reverend talked her out of it by reminding her he was only one person. He couldn't stay and conduct a proper search and, at the same time, leave to take her somewhere else. He'd finally appeased her by promising to take her at first light.

Addie knelt beside Ceddy's bed, painstakingly matching shards of wood together like puzzle pieces. The boxes were far from perfect, and the glue would have to dry before he could replace the stones, but at least he wouldn't have to see them broken to bits. Remembering how the slightest change upset him, Addie fought the desire to smash the culprits the way they'd smashed Ceddy's things.

Delilah had helped her sort the rocks the way he kept them, as closely as she remembered at least. Staring at the mounds, Addie wondered how stressful it would be for him, seeing his collection in disarray. Especially when he realized the precious gems were gone. Her shoulders sagged. What sort of man stole from a child? Was any amount of monetary gain worth a single one of his tears?

She considered the missing white stone, Ceddy's favorite. Delilah confirmed that the intruders were looking for one suspiciously similar. Rummaging through the pile, she picked up a white rock, turning it over in her hand. It didn't look to be any different from the one Ceddy favored, the one the men tore Priscilla's house apart trying to find.

It may not look different, but the facts say it most certainly is.

Realization teased the dark corners of her mind. Ceddy placed his gemstones in perfect order on Aaron's breastplate on the Bible page. The only one he hadn't accurately matched was the diamond.

She gasped. Or had he?

Waltzing with the thought, she shook her head. Where would a little boy get a rough diamond of that size?

Struggling to her feet, she stared dumbstruck at the map of South Africa on Ceddy's wall. "Dear heavenly days," she said breathlessly. Clutching her skirt, she streaked from the room and barreled down the stairs, nearly tripping in her haste.

Standing beneath the ceiling fan, both hands filled with salvaged possessions, Priscilla turned at the sound of Addie's footsteps. "Oh my, slow down. It's very dangerous to run on the steps."

Reverend Stroud came toward them from the kitchen as Addie reached her. Panting for breath, Addie gripped Priscilla's shoulders. "I know what those men want—what they tore the house up trying to find."

"Yes, dear. Delilah told us. They were looking for stones from Ceddy's collection."

"Not just any stones. They're after the diamond."

Priscilla gave her an indulgent smile. "What are you saying, Addie? Ceddy didn't have a diamond. Just a few tiny gemstones, gifts from his grandfather. Hardly more than chips, really." She shook her head. "No diamonds."

Addie gripped her shoulders tighter. "What if I told you the large white rock he carried about was an uncut jewel?"

Her eyes flashed with disbelief. "I'd say you have a vivid imagination. You saw the size of it, dear. A gemstone that large would be worth a fortune."

Addie nodded. "Exactly."

The reverend studied Addie's face. "How would Ceddy get his hands on such a thing?" He tilted his head at Priscilla. "Could it have been your brother's?"

"No, Reverend. My brother wasn't the type to let an object of value go to waste."

Believing more in her theory by the second, Addie felt excitement rise in her chest. "I'd like to put forth the possibility that Ceddy brought it with him." She nodded firmly at Reverend Stroud. "When he came from South Africa."

"Nonsense," Priscilla said, though doubt muddied her tone. "If he had, his aunt Jane would've mentioned it."

Swiveling to face her, Addie raised her brows. "Not if she didn't know."

Priscilla opened her mouth to speak, but it froze into a gape. Her troubled gaze darted from Addie to Reverend Stroud. "It all makes perfect sense," she finally said. "That's why Pearson has tormented poor Ceddy. He's after the diamond, too."

Addie's jaw dropped.

Priscilla nodded firmly. "That's why he hurt my boy. . .trying to force information from him."

"Heavens, no. Pearson knew Ceddy kept the rock clutched in his hand most of the time. He even retrieved it that night it rolled across the floor and gave it back. Don't you remember?"

Priscilla's brows dipped in an ugly scowl. "He would in front of us, now, wouldn't he?"

Her heart an anvil in her chest, Addie clutched Priscilla's hands. "You've come to the wrong conclusion again. We're talking about the men who broke into the house today. Whoever they are, they somehow know what Ceddy has."

Addie pointed behind her. "I think the poor dear's out there now, hiding from those ghastly men." She bit her trembling lip. "We're going to find him, and when we do, you'll see that Pearson had nothing to do with his disappearance."

Priscilla fixed her with a cold stare. "Addie, I know how you feel about him. I was rather fond of Pearson myself, but—"

"Oh please," Addie interrupted, "don't speak in the past tense. You must still care about him."

Priscilla's mouth narrowed. "I don't know what those strangers were looking for, but they don't have Ceddy, and he's all that matters. I know in my heart he's with Pearson." Fisting her hands at her waist, she struck a stubborn pose. "Reverend, I need you to take me out there. I won't rest until I see for myself."

Matching her determination, he set his jaw. "Then you'll spend a restless night. I won't take a woman to such rough country after dark. If we haven't found Ceddy before morning, we'll strike out at first light."

Rolling from under the seat, the boy sat up and yawned.

Speechless, Pearson watched in disbelief. One peculiar little fellow had single-handedly ruined the possibility of proving himself to Addie.

Sleepy-eyed, Ceddy wrinkled his nose like he smelled something foul and smacked his lips as if he tasted something worse.

Pearson shook Theo's shoulder. "He's thirsty. Get him some water."

Theo snagged the canteen and shook it. It gave an answering slosh, so he scrambled over and held it out to Ceddy.

The boy stared blankly.

"Here"—Pearson crawled up beside them—"let me try."

He took the flask from Theo and opened the lid. Pulling Ceddy toward him, he cupped his hand under his chin and offered a drink.

Ceddy got a taste and drank heartily.

Wiping the boy's mouth with his shirt, he glanced back at Theo. "He has to be hungry, too. What do we have?"

Theo fumbled inside the crates but came up empty-handed. "All of this needs to be cooked."

Panic crowding his throat, Pearson rummaged in the box closest to him. "There has to be something he can eat. Didn't you get any bread? Or crackers?"

"I have a slab of venison jerky," Catfish John said, startling Pearson half out of his boots. He stood peering over the rail, watching Ceddy. "I didn't know you had a child with you."

"Neither did we," Pearson said grimly. "The little guy's a stowaway."

Humor flashed in John's eyes. "Your plight gets more exciting by the minute."

Pearson groaned. "I can't take much more excitement."

Sliding his shoulder pouch around, the man dug inside and handed a bundle to Theo. "There's enough jerky for all of you. Help yourselves."

Regret weighing his heart, Pearson heaved a sigh. "I'm afraid we'll have to cancel our little inquiry. I have no choice but to get this boy home straightaway."

Catfish John nibbled inside his cheek. "Aren't you forgetting something?" He jerked his thumb at the horse. "She won't make it, and it's a long walk to Marshall."

Pearson sagged against the wagon seat, pulling Ceddy with him. "In the flurry of finding the child, that little detail slipped my mind." He pleaded for good news with his eyes. "How long before she can make the trip?"

He shrugged. "Not more than a couple of days. A week if she's got an abscess."

Pearson's heart plunged. "Sir, the stakes of our plight just rose. I'm afraid my life is about to get very complicated."

John pointed at Ceddy with a grimy finger. "I take it there's a feisty woman somewhere who might be irked at you for this?"

"No, sir," Pearson said with a shudder. "Two feisty women."

"Even more deadly." Doing a poor job of hiding a grin, he climbed into the passenger seat. "I'm starting to be glad I accepted your invitation. I don't want to miss how this turns out."

Ruffling Ceddy's hair, Pearson climbed over the seat and took the reins. "You'd best rethink your position before it's too late."

A mischievous glint in his eye, Catfish John crossed his arms. "Not a chance."

Pearson urged the poor little mare onto the road at a slow, careful pace. Peering behind him, he couldn't resist a smile.

Theo and Ceddy sat like braves at a powwow, their peace pipes long strips of dried venison.

As they rode, Catfish John volunteered a lesson on the origins of Caddo Lake. "Legend has it she was fashioned by the New Madrid Earthquake of 1812. I reckon it could be true, since Reelfoot Lake in

Tennessee was formed the same way. Some folks disagree, but either way, the Great Raft caused an influx of water that filled the existing basin."

"The Great Raft?"

"A log jam creating a natural dam on the Red River, at least a hundred miles long before they busted it up in 1873."

Theo piped up from the rear. "Excuse me, sir. Do I call you Catfish, John, or Mr. John?"

Catfish John chuckled. "Plain old John will do."

"Well John, we've found plants out here that we've never seen before. I'd bet you can tell us the name of those bothersome weeds covering the lake bottom."

"Sounds like you've run into some coontail moss."

Theo grunted. "You could say so. Over time, we've hauled up enough with our drag to cover Texas."

John laughed. "I expect you've snagged your share of yonqupin, too. They're the lilies."

Theo rolled his eyes. "Oh yes, sir."

"What are the tiny, floating plants?" Pearson asked. "Like bright green lentils with stems?"

"Sounds like duckweed," John said.

"Duckweed," Pearson repeated. "Sticks to a fellow. I've come up wearing it like a shroud."

John nodded. "Gators do as well. They lurk in duckweed to get a jump on their prey."

Pearson grimaced. "We found that out the hard way."

Slapping his leg, John hooted with laughter. "So you've come up close and personal with Caddo's nastiest citizen?" Leaning away from Pearson, he seemed to take inventory. "I'm impressed with you fellows. It's been weeks since you started sniffing around for information. I figured you'd be long gone like the rest." He patted Pearson's back. "You have grit, I can say that much."

Pearson angled his head. "So you knew we were looking for you?"

John lowered his chin, mischief glinting in his eyes. "Let's say I had an inkling."

Theo leaned between them. "But we left word all over the docks stating exactly where we'd be." By the end of the sentence, his voice had risen to a soprano.

Pearson shoved him back with his elbow. "You'll have to excuse my friend. He gets as wound up as an old woman sometimes."

Looking ashamed, John twisted on the seat. "Sorry, fellas. If I got excited about every greenhorn treasure seeker who came asking about the *Mittie*, I'd spend all my time holding their hands. The truth is, you ain't the first to come looking for her, and I doubt you'll be the last."

Staring directly into his eyes, Pearson shrugged. "That may not be true since we're the most determined."

John seemed to weigh his words. "Well, son. . .that's good news and bad, considering."

"How is it bad?"

He held up his hand. "We'll save that conversation for later. The thing is, I trust you mean what you said." Shifting his pack around, he pulled out a drawstring pouch. "I think folks around here might've taken you boys too lightly. I'm starting to believe you would've found the *Mittie* by now"—tapping tobacco into a square of paper, he lifted twinkling eyes—"if you'd been looking in the right place."

FORTY

Addie hardly slept. Her disquieted spirit magnified every sound in the creaky old house tenfold, and she spent the better part of the night praying for Ceddy's safe return.

The few minutes she dozed were fraught with restless dreams. Only once, in the pitch darkness of the wee hours, did traitorous musings of Pearson's guilt invade her loyalty. With a thudding heart and quickening breath, she'd shoved them away.

She almost preferred the thought of Pearson having Ceddy. It seemed far less frightening than the boy wandering somewhere lost and alone. Yet that would make Priscilla's hunch right, and the repercussions were unthinkable.

A single memory of Pearson's russet eyes awash with grief was all it took to renew her faith. A man couldn't suffer such pain and then inflict it on another. Unlike Priscilla, Addie had gained entry into Pearson's beautiful soul. She bore personal testimony of his goodness, only no one cared to listen.

Her mind returned to Ceddy. For just a moment, she imagined him in his bed, curled beneath his special quilt, as bright and colorful as his rocks. Remembering the mattress tossed aside, its innards exposed, the quilt ripped into jagged pieces, Addie's heart broke.

Ugliness lurked behind such evil acts, something more sinister than thievery, as if the person responsible bore malice against the objects themselves. Or jealousy of Ceddy for having them.

A light rapping on the door startled her from her thoughts. Sitting upright, she pulled the covers up to her chin. "Who's there?"

"Jus' me, Miss Addie."

"It's all right, Delilah. Come in."

She peeked in, the lantern in her hand unable to light the deep shadows under her eyes.

Addie sighed. "I see you slept no better than me."

"Yes'm." Tiptoeing across the threshold, Delilah hurried to the window and pulled back the curtains. With only darkness outside, it did little good. "I mean, no, ma'am. I ain't slept worth spit for worrying about Little Man."

Addie let the covers slide and stretched her fingertips toward the ceiling. "Is it time to get up already? It feels like the middle of the night."

She nodded. "Miss Priscilla say if you insist on going, you best be dressed and downstairs lickety-split. She ain't gon' wait on you." She opened Addie's wardrobe and pulled out her plainest dress. "I believe her, too. She say she ready to go, and she ain't even hungry." Turning from shaking out the frock, she stared with bulging eyes. "Can you believe it?"

Addie couldn't, but it wouldn't be nice to say so.

When she imagined the pain driving the poor woman, her stomach lurched. "Oh Delilah. I'd pay dearly to go back in time to a few days ago. We were all so happy then."

Delilah shook her finger. "No, Miss Addie. Don't wish away time, not forward or back. God got every second planned, and we shouldn't go to meddling."

Tilting her head, Addie watched her face. "Every second? You really think so?"

She nodded firmly. "I know so."

Addie longed for such childlike faith. Unfortunately, her personality tended toward the meddling side. She swung her legs off the bed and felt for her slippers. "So you don't think He needs our help occasionally? To make things turn out all right?"

Delilah's eyes grew wide. "Go ask Abraham and Sarah. I s'pose if they had a do-over, they'd leave the 'turnin' out right' up to God."

Addie considered the story of Abraham, the biblical patriarch, and

Sarah, his wife. Instead of waiting for God to send them a promised son, they took matters into their own hands and arranged for another woman to bear a child with Abraham. Their efforts brought about disastrous results.

Probing with her toes for her house shoes again, Addie heard Mother's voice in her head. *The ways of God are wonderful. . . . His generous heart unsearchable. . . . Keep watch at all times, and allow Him to orchestrate your destiny.*

It seemed simple. Trust in His goodness, watch for His hand in the affairs of her life, and then get out of His way.

Delilah swept Addie's slippers aside with her foot. "You don't need those. I'll fetch your stockings then help you with your frock and your outside shoes. Miss Priscilla gon' be stomping up them stairs any second hollering for you to hurry."

Delilah's prediction came true. Before she could help Addie fasten her dress, Priscilla blew through the door barking orders and clucking her tongue. "Not a dress, for pity's sake. Wear riding breeches at least."

"But we're traveling by wagon," Addie protested.

She pointed at her own split skirt. "We must be nimble and unfettered. No telling what we'll encounter out there."

By the time Addie selected and put on the appropriate attire, Priscilla was outside in Reverend Stroud's wagon. Delilah had just enough time to hand her a basket as she spun out the door. Carrying the food to the rig in the same basket from which she'd shared a picnic with Pearson, Addie felt her heart squeeze. She missed him desperately.

What would happen once they found him? Addie would be ever so glad to see him, but how would Priscilla react to finding her theory was wrong? Addie felt certain she clung to the notion out of desperation. After all, if Pearson didn't have Ceddy, who did?

"It's about time," Priscilla called as Addie hurried down the front steps.

Handing up the basket, she climbed into the backseat with a grimace. "I came as fast as I could, considering I dressed myself twice."

"Good morning, Addie," the reverend said.

"Morning, sir."

Priscilla patted his arm. "There's no time for social graces, Abner Stroud."

He cast a startled glance. "It's not like you to address me by my first name, Priscilla."

"Forgive me, but I'm a little distraught. You've kept me waiting hours too long to go to Ceddy's rescue, and there are still hours ahead of us." Her hand fluttered in the air. "Now please. . .carry on."

The reverend flicked the reins and started the horse in motion. Unable to contain the question, Addie leaned to tug her sleeve. "What will we do if Pearson doesn't have him?"

With a frantic shake of her head, Priscilla stared off into the woods. "That won't happen. It mustn't," she continued, her voice breaking.

Reverend Stroud slid his hand down her forearm and squeezed her white-knuckled fist. "We'll find him, dear lady."

She twisted to face him, her eyes pleading.

"The men are tirelessly searching. They've vowed to continue until young Ceddy is safely back in your arms."

Addie raised her hankie to muffle a sob as silent tears slid down Priscilla's delicate cheeks.

Pearson's eyes flew wide. As he stared at the cloudless morning sky, his mind scrambled for the answer to what had startled him awake. A gentle, sighing breath against his ear jerked his head around to the heart-jarring answer.

Ceddy lay asleep on Pearson's shoulder, one skinny arm across his chest. Smiling, Pearson cradled the boy's head with his palm, the thin blond hair the softest thing he'd ever touched.

The little fellow had definitely taken a shine to Pearson. Highly inconvenient in their present circumstances, but the fact surprised and pleased him.

Easing the boy to the blanketed wagon bed, he glanced at Theo gently snoring next to them, one gangly arm thrown over his eyes.

They'd offered to make room for John, but he'd pulled a bedroll out of his pack and spread it on a high spot, carefully winding a coil of rope around the edges.

"Why the rope?" Pearson had asked.

"Snake won't cross it," John explained.

The bedding still lay on the ground, but the man was gone. Pushing to his feet, Pearson scanned the horizon but saw no sign of him.

Theo sat up squinting. "Heard him rustling around before daybreak.

Figured he was leaving."

Climbing down from the buckboard, Pearson shook his head. "Not unless he left everything behind." Staring toward the water, he shrugged. "Maybe he's gone fishing."

"Good guess," Theo said, pointing with his chin. "Considering one of the boats is gone."

Pearson propped his hands on his hips. "Go find wood to stoke this fire. I'll get started on breakfast." He blew a frustrated breath. "John likely figures us for greenhorns. We've slept half the day away."

Ceddy slumbered right through the brewing of coffee and the sizzle of bacon and eggs—surprising since he'd napped so long the day before while tucked under the buckboard seat. The minute he awoke, he came to sit at Pearson's feet, scratching in the dirt for rocks and pebbles. Stretching his fingers, he wiggled them toward Pearson's coffee cup.

Drawing it away, Pearson shook his head. "Sorry, old man. None of this for you."

"I know just the thing." Theo pushed to his feet and hurried over to rummage in their supplies. Returning with a pot filled with sloshing liquid, he set it over the fire and stirred it with a metal spoon.

"What's that?" Pearson asked.

"Powdered milk, sugar, and chocolate mixed in water." Theo smiled into the swirling cup. "This way, he can have his own brand of coffee."

Testing the warmth with his finger, he poured out a cup for Ceddy. "There you go, big fella. See how you like it."

Ceddy took the cup and lowered his face, smelling first. Smiling with pleasure, he took a taste then several big gulps.

"I think your concoction is a hit, paisan," Pearson said.

Theo beamed. "Who doesn't like sugar and chocolate?"

Resting his back against a log, Pearson reflected on his conversation with John the night before. The man so skillfully avoided explaining his disturbing comment, Pearson might've thought he misunderstood. Except he knew he didn't.

Lucky for John, the outrageous remark went right over Theo's head. Had he heard John say they weren't dragging the right spot for the *Mittie*, the man would've gotten no rest from the relentless Italian.

If John really thought they were searching the wrong place, he didn't care to repeat it. He steered the conversation to their surroundings instead, seeming to relish the role of schoolmaster.

"The allure to Caddo is its mystery and beauty," he'd said, his eyes glowing with pride. He pointed out the trees as they neared the lake, some Pearson knew and some he didn't, calling their names like beloved children. "Those right there are water oak. The ones next to them are red oak, and the tall pine there is loblolly. We have pin oak, sweet gum, and river birch. Those on the water with sprawling trunks are red cypress."

Pearson learned the names of the fish they'd become acquainted with over the weeks—flathead catfish, blue catfish, channel cat, spotted bass, white perch, bream, and paddlefish.

John explained that the eggs of the paddlefish were sold up north for caviar. He said the massive creature that surfaced close to the boat, frightening Theo out of his wits, was likely an alligator gar, a type of fish that grew in excess of six feet.

Ceddy moaned, pulling Pearson from his thoughts.

He patted the boy's shoulder. "What's wrong, partner?"

Wincing, he groaned and clutched his stomach.

Concerned, Pearson pushed to his knees and bent over him, pressing his palm to his forehead. "Are you sick? You don't feel feverish." He met Theo's eyes across the campfire. "What's ailing him?"

Theo shot to his knees, shaking his head.

Writhing now, the distraught boy wailed as if in pain.

Comforting Ceddy the best he could, Pearson struggled to hold him still lest he hurt himself.

From out of nowhere, a wagon rattled into the clearing.

Pearson glanced up to see Priscilla Whitfield barreling toward them, a jagged stick in her hand. "Get away from him," she screeched, swinging with all her might.

Pearson sprawled backward, pulling Ceddy with him to protect him from the flailing stick. Twisting around, he shot to his feet, clutching the screaming boy.

Addie hunkered ten feet away, her pretty features limp with shock.

FORTY-ONE

Addie squatted on the ground, her legs too weak to hold her. Her eyes met Pearson's across the distance, his filled with deep regret. The unthinkable had happened, despite her faith in him. Her glimpse into his soul had been a lie.

Priscilla saw Pearson for what he was. He'd used Addie's lack of experience to reel her in. Despite Delilah's admonishment against meddling in matters of time, she wished with all her heart to roll the clock back to the day she'd lost her heart to him. How had she been so blind?

"Addie?"

His mellow voice sought to work its magic, but Addie shot to her feet, shaking her head to escape his spell. "Give Ceddy to Priscilla this instant."

"Addie, please. . ."

"Let him go so his aunt can comfort him."

Pearson glanced at the sobbing boy as if he'd forgotten he held him. Placing him on the ground, he patted his back. "Go to your aunt Priscilla, Ceddy." He nudged him forward. "Go on, now."

Clutching his middle, Ceddy stumbled into Priscilla's skirts. Dropping to her knees, she gathered him close. "Oh darling, are you all right? Auntie was sick with worry."

Reverend Stroud came to stand behind Priscilla, one hand at her back.

Pearson's tortured gaze leaped to him. "Reverend, I know how this looks, but if you'll just listen, I can explain."

The reverend nodded at Ceddy. "The child being out here with you is all the explanation we need." His shoulders slumped. "I wanted to believe in you, son. I tried my best."

Holding his hands out to his sides, Pearson pleaded with his eyes. "I give you my word. I wouldn't lay a harsh hand on that boy."

Struggling to her feet, Priscilla guided Ceddy behind her. "You're lying," she shrieked. "Look at him—he's crying. What sort of evil man would harm a boy like my Ceddy?"

"Miss Whitfield, he didn't—"

She whirled. "Hush, Theo Bernardi. You're no better."

Howling, Ceddy rocked back and forth, his hands over his ears.

"You are a worthless, conniving weasel, Pearson Foster," she spat, her tone even louder. "Worming your way into decent people's lives, simply for gain. Your unbridled greed sickens me."

Ceddy stamped both feet and cried harder.

Taking his shoulder, Priscilla urged him toward Addie. "Take him, please, while I deal with these scoundrels."

Jerking away, Ceddy shot around Priscilla and rushed to Pearson, wrapping his arms around his waist.

Forced off balance, Pearson backed into the log and dropped to his rear. As if by instinct, he cradled Ceddy, drawing him under his arm. "It's all right, buddy," he cooed. "Don't cry. Everything will be fine. You'll see."

Snuggling closer, Ceddy pressed his cheek to Pearson's side.

The clearing froze to a haunting lithograph, the silver edges shimmering through Addie's tears.

Pricilla spun to stare at her, trembling hands clutching her mouth. Her eyes, visible above her fingertips, were wide with shock.

Pearson pulled his tender gaze from Ceddy and searched Addie's face.

She turned aside, unable to look at him. In his darkest hour, her fiercest trial, she'd failed them both.

"And there he was," Pearson said, squeezing Ceddy's thin shoulders. "Curled under the seat fast asleep without a care in the world." He raised his brows. "And he never made a sound the whole time."

Pearson sat around the fire with the others, brewing a fresh pot of coffee and relaying the story.

Priscilla, her eyes red from crying, stared in a daze at the flames. "Yes, he does that," she said vaguely. "He can lie for hours counting cracks in the floor."

"Anyway. . ." Pearson grinned. "I aged ten years when I saw him."

Reverend Stroud shook his head repeatedly and mumbled under his breath, reaching often to give his back a gentle pat.

Addie had perched on the log beside Theo, looking everywhere but at Pearson.

Ceddy played quietly in the dirt, making soft grunting sounds occasionally as if in pain.

Knowing Addie didn't drink coffee, Theo warmed a cup of his chocolate drink and placed it in her hands.

She glanced up. "What's this?"

He smiled. "Just taste."

She took a sip and gave an appreciative nod, but then a startled look crossed her face. "Is there milk in here?"

He nodded. "Made from powder."

Her long lashes fluttered, and her gaze snapped to Ceddy. "Did he have any?"

"I made it special for him."

She and Priscilla shared a meaningful look.

"He can't tolerate milk," Addie said. "It gives him a terrible stomachache."

Understanding flashed across Theo's face, and he blushed. "I'm sorry. I didn't know."

Pearson nodded. "That explains why he was crying."

Priscilla leaned toward Pearson and stretched out her hand. "Oh Pearson, please say you forgive me. I won't rest until I have your pardon."

Clutching her fingers, he gazed into her eyes. "I don't blame you, ma'am." Smoothing Ceddy's blond head, he smiled. "I'd react the same if my child was threatened."

Tears tracked down her cheeks. "I promise never to doubt you again."

"I hope you mean it." Pearson sighed, the pain of betrayal still fresh. "I'd do anything to keep your trust." He flicked his gaze to Addie, but she ducked her head.

Reverend Stroud placed his big hand over Pearson's and gave a firm shake. "I wish you could see into my repentant heart, son. I'm racked with grief over misjudging you."

"I won't say it didn't hurt, sir. Especially coming from you. But all I want now is a fresh start for everyone."

The reverend nodded. "It's far more than we deserve."

Watching Addie, Pearson felt a deep ache in his heart. Obviously suffering, she wouldn't forgive herself long enough to seek his forgiveness. He bore her silence for as long as he could. Proper or not, he was going to take her out of the others' hearing and settle things between them.

Gripping the log, he poised to stand. "Addie. . ."

She jumped like she'd been jabbed then raised her head. Before he could invite her on a walk, her attention shifted to something over his shoulder, alarm written all over her face.

Pearson turned.

The missing rowboat skimmed across the water, breezing toward shore. John, a stringer of fish in his hand, leaped to the bank and idly wrapped the towrope around a bush.

"It's all right," Pearson said, his hand going up. "It's only Catfish John."

Reverend Stroud whipped around. "Catfish John? You don't say!"

John glanced toward the newcomers and slowed his pace. Scanning the gathering, a big smile broke out on his face. "The feisty women you dreaded, I take it?"

Pearson grinned. "None other."

"I see they let you live. Have you been granted a pardon?"

"Yes, thankfully." He motioned toward the women. "Allow me to present Miss Priscilla Whitfield, Miss Addie McRae, and Reverend Abner Stroud."

John nodded. "Forgive me for not offering my hand." He glanced at the fish. "You wouldn't thank me."

Theo swung around the log and took the stringer from him. "I'll clean these for you."

John handed them over. "Thank you, young man. I hoped somebody would offer. I like catching fish. I just don't like cleaning them."

Pearson motioned for him to take a seat. "Let me pour you a cup of coffee. I know you must be hungry, too. We saved you bacon, eggs, and biscuits."

He accepted Pearson's offering with a hearty nod then squatted in front of the fire to eat.

Lifting her chin, Priscilla stared longingly at the skillet of leftovers. "I wouldn't mind having a plate, if there's enough."

"Of course, ma'am. Forgive my bad manners." He filled three plates and passed them to Priscilla, the reverend, and Addie.

She took one but didn't seem to find the food very appetizing.

"How did you find him, son?" the awestruck reverend asked, pointing at John.

Pearson blushed. "With my matchless tracking skills and bloodhound nose."

John grunted, and the reverend angled his head.

"All right then. He found us about a mile up the road, floundering like fish out of water. We had a lame horse and not a lick of common sense between us to decide what to do. John showed up and rescued us."

"Happens a lot out here," John said around a big bite. "More than you'd think."

Unable to contain his excitement, the reverend scooted to the edge of his seat. "Well, have you asked him all your questions? Is he going to help you find the *Mittie*?"

Pearson shifted his gaze to John, who seemed suddenly quite engrossed in his dish. "I've asked him a few things, but he's not been especially obliging. I suspect he's determined to avoid helping as much as possible."

Silence fell over the gathering.

Regret danced with irritation on John's face. "I'll only say this much because I've taken a shine to you, son. You haven't found her because you're searching miles from the actual site."

"What?" Theo rose from the water's edge and stormed toward them. "This is where the locals told us to look."

John sighed and set down his plate. "The fact is the history of Caddo wasn't chronicled very well, and most of the facts have been overblown for years. Some of the old-timers were masters at spinning a yarn, and now we're never sure what's completely true. That's why most tales and legends begin with 'It was once said,' 'The story I was told,' or 'As far as I know,' and so forth."

"So nobody really knows where she is?"

John puckered his mouth. "I wouldn't say that. But with limited information, it would be hard to nail down her location. And those who know aren't willing to tell."

"Why not?" several voices asked at once.

He smiled. "Unspoken agreement around the Caddo. To protect the site."

Reverend Stroud frowned and nibbled his bottom lip. "Why's that, John?"

Priscilla set down her cup. "Well, it's obvious, isn't it? Why should he reveal his leads to a possible fortune?"

John's head shot up. "Not so, dear lady. I'm afraid you've missed the mark."

Pearson offered to refill his cup. "Do you mind telling us why, then?"

Theo's ears turned bright red. "No matter the reason, it's not right. If they're not interested in raising her, they shouldn't stand in the way of those who are."

"Shouldn't they?" John asked, his voice hushed. "Sixty-one people died that night. When the fire aboard couldn't be put out, the captain gave the order to head for shore, but she grounded in shallow water. The forward part of the *Mittie* was in flames, the stern over deep water. Desperate, the pilot and engineer continued pushing for land. Unfortunately, this action dragged those who dove to safety into the turning wheels, crushing and drowning them."

Not a sniff, sigh, or shuffle of feet broke the silence that settled over the campfire.

Priscilla's cheeks held an unswallowed bite, and her fork stilled over her plate. "How utterly grim," she finally said, breaking the stillness. "And tragic. I never heard that account before."

"For most of them," John continued, "that site is their final resting place. People here feel that raising the *Mittie* is akin to robbing a grave."

An unexpected dagger of pain laced Pearson's heart. The storm that claimed his family's lives had also stolen his chance to stand over their grave sites and grieve their passing.

Before he accepted their terrible fate, he'd combed the island for weeks with other mourners, searching frantically for them. The rush of water that collapsed the wall of his house had carried their bodies out to sea. The most precious treasure he'd ever sought had slipped through his fingers forever. How would he feel if treasure seekers were to comb through their belongings in search of gold? He took a ragged breath and vowed to search for the *Mittie Stephens* no more.

Laying aside his dish, John stood. "I've enjoyed your company for too long now. I'd best be on my way."

Pearson stood with him. "Finish cleaning his fish, Theo, while I saddle his horse."

With a creel of skinned catfish and a bundle of bacon and biscuits tucked into his saddlebag, John prepared to take his leave.

Pearson offered his hand. "I can't thank you enough."

"Wasn't much. Just a little advice on a horse."

"Not that," Pearson said. "Thank you for setting me straight about the *Mittie*."

John grinned. "I hated to in a way. You seemed so determined."

Pearson hung his head. "Men who seek treasure can be a mulish lot." He shrugged. "I suppose we have to be. If not for you, I might've gone on dragging this spot forever."

John raised one brow. "Will you keep looking?"

Shaking his head, Pearson crossed his heart. "After the story you told? No, sir." He raised his right hand. "I give you my solemn word."

John gave his back a hearty pounding. "I'm glad to hear it. You just might've been the one to succeed." Swinging into the saddle, he took up the reins.

Pearson caught the horse's bridle. "You said we were looking miles away from the actual site. That means you know where she is."

He gazed fiercely into Pearson's eyes. "I have your word, then?"

"I said it, didn't I?"

John nodded. "The *Mittie* went down in Buzzard Bay on the southeast side, about two and a half miles from Swanson's Landing."

The name dashed cold water down Pearson's back. What had the old sailor in Rosie's Café said?

At the midnight hour, just below Swanson's Landing, a steersman alerted the pilot that he'd caught a whiff of smoke.

Blast! He'd had the answer all along, but he'd barreled ahead of himself, too cocky and headstrong to slow down and remember. Some treasure hunter he was! Smiling at himself, he released John's horse and stepped back. "I suppose some things aren't meant to be."

Pushing back his cap, Catfish John saluted and rode away.

Swiveling on the ball of his foot, Pearson started toward camp. "But then, some things are." He strode purposefully to Addie and hauled her to her feet. "Come with me. We need to talk."

She took a quick breath but didn't resist.

Pearson glanced at Priscilla. "I trust you'll allow me to speak with Addie alone for a few minutes?"

"Of course. If Addie doesn't mind, that is."

"She doesn't," he said, pulling her away from the clearing.

They walked several yards down the road that led to Marshall.

Addie plodded in silence, her arms crossed at her chest.

Out of earshot of the rest, Pearson caught her shoulders and eased her around. "We're not walking to the gallows, you know."

She ducked her head and lifted one shoulder.

"Aren't you going to talk to me?"

"There are many things I want to tell you, Pearson. I just can't find the words."

He touched her rosy cheek. "Then don't say anything. It's not necessary."

She wagged her head. "I've utterly failed you. As a confidant, a friend—"

"Don't say that, honey."

"It's true. You're the one who shouldn't speak to me. I made you prove yourself over and over, yet it was never enough." She covered her face. "I'm so ashamed."

Shifting his weight, Pearson watched her and waited.

"I won't blame you if you never talk to me again," she continued. "In fact, I can't imagine why you've bothered now. I'm not worth your time."

He crossed his arms and rocked on his heels.

"If it makes you feel better, I had perfect faith in you all along." She sighed and buried her face deeper into her hands. "Until the moment I saw you with Ceddy."

Pearson stood quietly for so long, Addie peeked between her fingers. "Well? Aren't you going to respond?"

"When you're finished."

She blinked at him and lowered her hands. "With what?"

He waved. "Your apology. You see, men just blurt it out. Two little words and we're done. Females take the long way around." He chuckled. "We wind up at the same place; it just takes you women longer." Catching her hands, he pulled her to his chest and kissed the tip of her nose. "Let me know when you're through, so I can get on with forgiving."

Addie leaned into him, the smell of her hair intoxicating. "Oh Pearson, don't tease. This is serious."

He leaned to peer closely at her. "I'm completely serious. I need all the bad feelings between us gone, so we can finish our unfinished conversation."

Her breath caught. "Which one would that be?"

She knew exactly, but he wouldn't call her on it. He chucked her under the chin and grinned. "The one in the parlor. About living on an island."

"Oh yes." She sounded out of breath. "I remember now."

Pulling her hands to his mouth, he kissed her fingers. "I'd like to have your answer now, if you don't have anything else to do."

She pouted her lips. "First, kindly answer the question I asked you."

"Which was?"

"Why do you want to know?"

He released her hands and cupped her face. "Because I think it's time I went home." He trailed kisses along her chin. "And I want you to come with me."

Her eyelids drifted closed as she surrendered to his searching lips. "Is this an improper advance, sir?"

He shook his head. "There you go, falsely accusing me again." Her eyes flashed open, and he grinned. "This is a very proper advance, Miss McRae. I'm asking you to retire your last name and become Adelina Viola Foster of Galveston, Texas."

Her arms circled his neck and she pulled him close. "And my answer is yes."

FORTY-TWO

Ceddy rose from his place by the fire and wandered toward the wagon, drawn by the pattern of the wheels.

"Where are you going, darling?" Aunt Priss called. "Stay close, you hear?"

Ignoring her, he crawled into the shadowy space underneath, running his hands along the loop of wood. He counted the spokes as he went—one, two, three, four, all the way around until he reached fourteen.

Finished, Ceddy scooted to the next and then the next, tracing the circles as he went.

With all four wheels accounted for, he sprawled on his side under the wagon. In a daze, he stared toward the flickering campfire, spellbound by the pie-shaped pictures created by the spokes.

The drone of voices in the background soothed him. His eyelids fluttered, but he struggled hard against sleep.

"Here they are now," Priscilla said as Addie and Pearson rejoined them at the fire.

Addie's cheeks warmed, certain the others would take one look at her and guess she'd just received her first kiss, her first and only proposal.

They'd decided to keep the news a secret until they returned home.

Then they'd tell Priscilla and ask her to place a call to Addie's parents so Pearson could ask permission.

Pearson sat on the fallen log and patted the spot next to him. Blushing deeper, Addie sank down beside him.

"We were just about to tell Theo the news," Reverend Stroud said. "Now you can hear, too." He launched into the story of the break-in, how two men behaving like savages had threatened Delilah and tore the house apart. "I hate to tell you, son, but they were your friends, Denny and Charlie."

Pearson glanced at Theo. "They're no friends of ours, Reverend. Just hired hands. If you remember, we didn't trust them from the start."

"Yes." He nodded. "And Theo's premise that the criminal activity in town can be blamed on them is most likely correct."

"Thank you!" Theo said, slapping his leg.

"I'm sorry, Miss Whitfield," Pearson said. "If I hadn't hired them, maybe they'd be long gone by now. I hope they didn't take anything you treasure."

"It's not your fault, dear boy." She beamed over her shoulder at Ceddy. "In fact, God placed my greatest treasure in your hands for safekeeping." She winced. "I only wish He had advised me of the plan."

Addie gripped Pearson's arm. "They wouldn't have left if you hadn't hired them. Not without the one thing that brought them to Marshall."

Pearson frowned.

"The rogues stole a few tiny stones from Ceddy's collection. Oh, and some weapons—"

Pearson grimaced. "I hate to think of them with weapons in their hands."

"However, I think I know what they were after, what they chased Ceddy across the ocean for." Her face flushed red with excitement. "Only they came up empty because Ceddy has it with him."

Pearson peered across the clearing at the boy. "He doesn't have anything that I know of."

"If you check his pockets, I believe you'll find two very interesting stones. One is a jasper pendant that belongs to me. The other is a very large diamond."

Theo coughed, choking on his chocolate drink. "How could Ceddy have something that valuable that we've never seen?"

"We have." She gave Pearson a teasing look. "In fact, our treasure hunter held the diamond in his hands."

Staring blankly, Pearson scratched his head. "I'm sure that's something I'd remember."

She nudged him with her elbow. "It's that unsightly white rock he favors. Unless I'm mistaken, it's an uncut diamond."

Pearson looked skeptical. "If it's true, where did it come from?"

"Allow me to answer," Reverend Stroud said. "Before he came to live with Priscilla, Ceddy was a resident of South Africa. His parents were missionaries in a village near Pretoria." He lowered one brow. "Are you familiar with the diamond mines of South Africa, son?"

Interest sparking his eyes, Pearson nodded. "I know the Cullinan region. The largest rough diamond ever found was discovered there."

The reverend nodded. "Exactly."

Pearson searched out Ceddy under the buckboard and stared. "So you think he. . ."

"Would you recognize it for a gemstone, now that you know what you're looking for?" Priscilla asked.

"Yes, ma'am," Pearson said. "I'd like to think so."

"Let's find out." She twisted around to the wagon. "Oh Ceddy! Come here, please. Come to Auntie, darling."

Ceddy batted his heavy lids, fighting to keep them open. His name echoed in his ears, and he wanted it to stop. Moaning, he raised his head and searched through the slices of pie for the source of the noise.

Gasping, he snapped his eyes open. Sleepy no more, he felt fear churning in his tummy. Blinking fast, he looked through a different slice, hoping the picture would change. Panting, whining, choking, he scooted out the back of the wagon and crawled like a crab to the bank.

Hide! Need to hide!

His legs tangled with a length of rope on the ground. Clenching his mouth against a scream, he kicked his way free. Reaching the rowboat, he scrambled inside and ducked behind the seat.

His skin tingled. His chest ached. The hairs on his head prickled. He longed to peek, to see if they were coming, but didn't dare. Turning on his back, he lay very still in the rocking boat and watched an osprey soar.

"That's right, mum," Denny said, striding out of the woods. "Call the wormy little blighter out of hiding and save us the trouble."

The old lady's head whipped around so fast she nearly lost her teeth. Crying out, she latched onto the reverend.

Pearson leaped from the log and turned, easing the pretty little governess behind his back.

Theo, Pearson's mop-headed puppet, pushed himself off the ground. Both gents' eyes followed the pistol in Denny's hand.

Denny beamed. It felt good to have one up on them for a change. "Sorry we're late to the party. We'd have been 'ere sooner, but we ran into a little trouble in town. Seems our landlord don't appreciate the way we settle our accounts." He nodded at Miss Whitfield. "But he bartered for some of the items you so generously donated, missus, and was pleased to call off the sheriff once we offered them in trade."

She glared. "You devil. How dare you steal from me!"

Denny pointed at his chest. "How dare I?" He nodded at Charlie and laughed. "It was easy, weren't it, Charlie?"

Laughing, Charlie wobbled his direction, his shotgun waving wildly.

"Be careful, will ya?" Denny shouted, shoving the barrel aside. "Watch what you're doing."

"Sorry, Den. I ain't used to it yet."

Denny scowled. "Don't expect to be. I'm taking that thing away as soon as we sort this out." He faced his captive audience. "Speaking of which, I'd like to get the ball rolling, if you don't mind. Now where's the boy?"

"He's not here," Pearson said.

"Go on, don't take me for a mug. I heard the old cow calling him."

Miss Whitfield stood, defiance in her eyes. "You're going to leave my nephew alone. Do you hear me?"

Denny laughed. "Feisty, ain't she?" He pointed past her with the nose of his gun. "She was facing the wagon when she called for the brat, Charlie. Go take a gander."

The old girl balled her fists, her eyes wild. "Don't you go over there!"

Denny hooted. "I think we're onto something." He shoved Charlie's shoulder. "Don't listen to her. Just do like I say. Now go on."

Watching her carefully, Charlie lumbered past.

The little governess paled.

The old woman started to cry.

Pearson held up his hand. "Can't we talk about this, Denny? You seem to be a decent person at heart."

"No, he's not," the governess spat. "He's a no-account thief who's envious of Ceddy." She challenged Denny with her eyes. "Isn't that so, Mr. Currie? You're petty and small-minded enough to be jealous of a lovely little boy?"

He aimed the pistol. "Shut it, missy."

Pearson tucked her behind him again. "Hold on there, Denny. You don't want to add murder to your sins. Why not put that thing away before there's an accident?"

"Please don't hurt my Ceddy," Miss Whitfield called to Charlie.

Charlie looked inside the wagon bed, under the seat, and beneath the rig. He circled it once then came back scratching his head. "He ain't 'ere, Den."

Panic shot up Denny's throat. "Sure he is. He 'as to be." His fingers tightened around the pistol. That barmy nipper wouldn't do him over again or he'd wind up a nutter himself.

The four standing in the clearing passed worried glances.

Furious, Denny squared around to Charlie. "I ain't 'ardly in the mood for this, mate. We rode all night, and I've missed me kip. Don't make me come look for meself."

Charlie pointed behind him. "Look all you want. He ain't there."

Miss Whitfield skirted the log and took a few staggering steps toward the buckboard. "Then where. . . ?" Clutching her throat, she screamed, her howls echoing off the trees.

Risking Denny's pistol, Pearson ran to her. "Priscilla, what's wrong?"

She pointed a trembling finger at the bobbing rowboat, floating forty yards out on the lake.

He gripped her arm. "Ceddy?"

A gulping sob escaped, and she nodded.

"Can he swim?"

She shook her head.

The governess moaned and covered her mouth.

Charlie spun and stared at Denny.

"Don't stand about like an 'eadless chicken," Denny shouted, breaking into a run. "Go after 'im, you witless dolt."

Charlie held out his hands. "How?"

He waved his arm toward the bank. "The second boat."

Pearson and the other men poised to lunge, but Denny trained his pistol on them. "Get back before I drop you where you stand."

They raced for the other vessel and jumped aboard, Denny pushing off with a mighty shove before he wobbled his way to the seat. "Don't just sit there, Charlie. Row!"

Charlie snatched up the oars and leaned into them, skimming the boat easily across the water. Shouts and screams reached them from the bank, but Denny focused on only one thing.

A brilliant future awaited him less than ten yards ahead. At last, Denny Currie would have exactly what he deserved.

Ceddy lay very still in the bottom of the boat. His hair, swirling in a shallow pool of water, tickled the back of his neck, but he didn't feel like laughing.

Holding his breath, he squeezed his eyes shut against the voices in the distance—far away but scary—and tried to think of Mummy. He smoothed his cheek with the back of his hand the way she used to, but it didn't feel the same.

The middle of his chest swelled like a puffer fish, and he nearly cried out.

Must be quiet, Little Man. Must be careful to be quiet.

Mummy! I'll be good, if only you'll come and get me.

The words were muddled sobs in his ears.

His eyes flashed open. Water lapped against the side right next to his ear.

Not safe.

He shook his head.

Not safe. It's not safe.

A hard bump, and the boat rocked under him.

Ceddy's heart squeezed, and a scream rose in his throat as Charlie's fat fingers latched onto his arm.

His leering face appeared overhead, close enough to touch. "We got 'im now, Den." His head turned, long hairs growing from inside his droopy ears. "He's ours now."

Ceddy's trembling fingers slid down to his pocket and cupped the two big stones. Drawing them out, he slammed the side of Charlie's face as hard as he could swing.

Charlie's eyes rolled back. Wobbling briefly over Ceddy's head, he slumped.

Straightening both arms, Ceddy blocked him, shifting his weight to the side.

Charlie slid between the two boats with a terrible splash and disappeared.

"Charlie?" Mr. Currie bawled. "Where are you, mate?" He stood up in the other boat, towering over Ceddy. "What happened? Where'd he go?"

Moaning, Ceddy scrambled over the seat to the other end and perched on the side.

"Where's Charlie?" Denny screamed. "Where is he?"

In a rush of splashing water, Charlie shot up between them, both hands madly grasping for the boats.

Cursing, Mr. Currie did a curious dance before he toppled.

Ceddy bounced high off the end and hit the water on his back.

FORTY-THREE

Pearson raced to the bank and dove. Cold water closed around his head as Addie's frightened screams echoed in his ears. Rising to the surface, he swam, demanding more from his body than he ever had in his life. With every stroke, he pushed harder, his mind consumed by thoughts of Ceddy sinking beneath the murky lake.

Charlie flailed near the rowboats, the whites of his eyes shining. There was no sign of Denny.

"Help us," Charlie whimpered, reaching out his arm. "Please help Den. He can't swim."

Three feet away, Pearson drew a breath and flipped, diving toward the bottom with hearty kicks. His heart sank as he realized Charlie's thrashing had stirred the muddy bottom. Mushrooming silt billowed toward him, impossible to see through.

His chest ached and his head pounded. Frustration swelled inside him in crushing waves.

He hadn't been there for his family, but he was present this time. He kicked harder, driving toward the bottom.

Please God. . .help me save him.

Ceddy drifted down. He kept his mouth shut and held his breath the way Daddy taught him, but he longed to cry for help. Little fish darted past, and he reached for them, but then he fell into a black cloud and had to close his eyes.

The stones in his other hand shifted, and one began to slip. He swiped his thumb across it and felt the pointy end of Miss Addie's jasper.

Bloodstone. Heliotrope. Banded quartz.

He saw her sad face, wet with tears. Latching onto the escaping jasper with both hands, he let the diamond slide away.

Pearson broke the surface of the water and drew a gasping breath. He sighted off the stern of the boat Ceddy fell from and dove toward the deep again. Charlie's pleas to save Denny followed him down, but his only thought was of Ceddy.

His eyes useless within the foggy churn, Pearson relied on touch, spreading his arms and groping in all directions. One second before he shot to the top for more air, the barest tip of his finger connected with soft, swirling hair. With a strong thrust, he lunged. Scooping Ceddy's limp body from the lakebed, Pearson pushed off, kicking furiously.

Arms reached for them as they rose. A dripping wet Theo and Reverend Stroud leaned over the side of the boat ready to pull Ceddy aboard.

"Is he all right?" Priscilla shrieked from the shore.

Praying he'd be able to tell her yes, Pearson lifted Ceddy toward the men.

Gripping his wrists, Theo jerked him up and laid him on his side in the boat bottom. His little body heaved and water rushed from his mouth.

Pearson pulled himself into the boat and crowded close, briskly rubbing Ceddy's back. A final trickle poured from his lips, and he started to cough.

Cheers rose from Theo and the reverend, echoed by Addie and Priscilla.

Racking sobs spun Pearson toward Charlie.

He slumped in the other boat, one hand over his eyes. "Don't you even care about poor Denny?"

Pearson shared an ominous look with Theo. "Get Ceddy to the women."

Theo nodded.

Pearson stood on the seat and brought his arms overhead. Launching himself overboard, he plunged for the third time into the muddy Caddo Lake. Using the same method as before, he skimmed the bottom, feeling his way with his hands. Coming up empty, the need to breathe forced him up top.

Charlie's crying had become hysterical. "Where is 'e, Mr. Pearson? Where's me best mate?"

"I'll find him, Charlie," he called and then plummeted again.

Halfway down, in a spot where the mud had settled, something solid bumped his back. Spinning, he came face-to-face with Denny, tangled in coontail moss. The long, twisting weeds held him like a bug in a web. His tortured eyes stared, and his mouth gaped in a soundless scream.

Swimming around behind him, Pearson pulled hard on the collar of his shirt, ripping him free. With very little hope of reviving him, he hauled him toward the light.

Addie rushed into the shallow water and helped haul the rowboat to shore.

Priscilla danced on alternating feet as the men lifted Ceddy and hurried to place him in her arms. She sank to the ground under his weight, cradling him on her lap. "Don't cry, darling. Hush now, Auntie's here."

Kneeling beside them, Addie murmured comforting words while wrapping Ceddy in her shawl and picking bits of debris from his hair.

"We almost lost him," Priscilla said, meeting Addie's eyes. "But for Pearson, he'd be down there still." Visibly shaken, she rocked Ceddy. "And after the way I treated that young man, I'm so ashamed."

"We have to forgive ourselves," Addie said, patting her back. "It's what Pearson wants. All we can do now is try to make it up to him."

Ceddy lifted his arm toward Addie, something clenched in his fist.

Firing a questioning glance at Priscilla, she opened her hand. The jasper pendant fell into her palm, the stone cool against her skin. Gripping it tightly, she shed tears of gratitude. "Thank you, honey," she whispered. "Thank you for keeping it safe."

Struggling away from Priscilla, he staggered over and fell against Addie, sinking to his knees in her lap. He stroked her cheek with the back of his hand and shook his head. "Nuh. N—nuh."

Priscilla covered her mouth with her hand. "Oh Addie. . .I don't believe it. He's comforting you. His mama used to soothe him the same way." She shook her head. "It's the first time in his life he's done such a thing."

The first boat reached the bank in a jubilant celebration. Pearson rowed the second to shore in a tragic shroud of grief.

Denny's body lay in the bottom of the boat, his head cradled in Charlie's lap. The big man cried softly, sniffling and running his sleeve under his nose.

Pearson had sacrificed Denny for Ceddy, but there'd been no other choice. Still, it grieved him to the depths of his soul.

Rowing in ten yards down from the others, he leaped to the bank where Theo and the reverend met them and tied up the boat.

Charlie gathered Denny's body and prepared to stand, but Reverend Stroud held up his hand. "Leave him here for now, son. We don't want the boy to see him."

Stretching out his arm to brace Charlie, the reverend helped him to dry land. Charlie winced and probed a gash beneath his left eye, the skin around it swollen and bruised.

"That's a nasty cut," Pearson said. "Did it happen when you fell from the boat?"

Charlie shook his head. "The little nipper smashed me in the face." He pouted a bit. "With Denny's diamond."

Pearson's head came up. "A diamond? Are you sure?"

"I'm sure, all right. Saw it coming from the corner of me eye." He held up his fingers in a circle. "Great white stone about this big around."

So Addie was right.

Pearson patted him on the back. "We'll find a doctor in town to look at you," he said, then ran to join Addie and Ceddy.

Ceddy lay cuddled in her lap, his arms wrapped around her waist. Longing to offer comfort, Pearson massaged his shoulder. "Is he all right?"

Tears in her eyes, she nodded. "He's quite shaken, but I think he'll be fine."

"That was a close call."

"Entirely too close," Pricilla whispered, her voice choked. "Thank you, son." A startled look crossed her face. "Heavens, that sounds so inadequate to express what my heart feels."

Pearson smiled. "It's plenty." He reached for Addie's hand and frowned. "What's this?" he asked, his fingers fumbling with the large stone.

"My jasper pendant. It's very precious to me. It belonged to my grandmother." She smiled down at the boy's wet head. "Ceddy kept it safe for me."

Pearson turned it over in his palm. "It's very nice. I'm glad you got it back." Remembering, he lifted his head. "Where's the diamond?"

"He doesn't have it."

"Sure he does. He bashed Charlie with it."

Her brow creased. "Priscilla searched his clothing. It's not on him."

"Do you suppose he hid it?" Theo asked.

She shook her head. "He would've hidden them together."

"Then where?"

She shrugged. "I can't imagine." She stared at the lake. "You don't suppose he dropped it?"

They shared a look before Pearson stood.

Combing the ground, he retraced their steps to the bank, searched inside the boat and in the shallows beneath it. Finding nothing, he and Theo rowed out to the spot where Ceddy went down.

Steeling himself to return to the cold water, Pearson dove repeatedly and groped along the bottom. He searched until exhaustion forced him to quit.

Back onshore they held a meeting to decide what to do. Reverend Stroud agreed to stay behind with Charlie and the body while they used his wagon to take Ceddy and the women home. Pearson promised to send Theo back with the sheriff, a fresh horse, and the liveryman to tend his wounded animal.

"Are you sure you can handle things here, Reverend?"

He made a face. "Of course."

"I don't think Charlie's dangerous without Denny's influence, but be careful just the same."

The reverend tossed a look over his shoulder. Charlie sat on the log by the fire, staring into the flames. "He's a broken man, son. I think he's harmless." He nodded at the shotgun he held and patted the pistol at his waist. "But just in case, I think I'll be fine."

Pearson gave him a wry smile. "No swashbuckling involved, but you're finally getting your adventure."

He nodded at Charlie. "Yes, but I regret that it's under such tragic circumstances."

Seeking the heavens for guidance, Pearson approached Charlie and sat beside him on the log. "I can't tell you how sorry I am about your friend. I wish things had turned out better."

Charlie sniffed. "It ain't your fault. You 'ad to bring up the lad." He turned with tormented eyes. "It's on me, what 'appened to Denny. I upset the boat and 'e fell." He wiped his nose on the back of his hand. "Denny fell and 'e couldn't swim a stroke."

Pearson tightened his hand on his shoulder. "It's not that simple, Charlie. Denny fell because he was standing up."

Charlie blinked at the fire. "Yeah? Den always told me not to stand up in the boat."

"That's right. And he drowned because he got tangled in the weeds. If not for that, he would've bobbed to the surface and held on to the boat until we pulled him in."

Charlie faced him, his eyes pleading. "So it ain't my fault?"

Pearson shook his head. "It's not your fault."

His plump bottom lip trembled. "Denny was me best mate."

"I know, buddy. I know." Standing, Pearson gave him a gentle shake. "Will you be all right?"

He stared up at Pearson. "I'm going to jail, ain't I?"

"I don't know. I suppose that's for the sheriff to decide. But if I can do anything to help you, just send for me."

Charlie's eyes narrowed. "You'd do that for me? After what we done?"

"Sure I will." He lifted his chin at Reverend Stroud. "So will the reverend. Just remember that, all right?"

Tears flowing freely, he nodded.

Addie touched Pearson's arm. "We're ready to go."

Over her shoulder, he saw Priscilla in the wagon, cradling Ceddy and trying to keep him warm. Theo sat in the driver's seat holding the reins.

Behind Pearson, most likely buried in lake-bottom mud, lay the biggest treasure he'd ever sought. In front of him stood the most valuable.

Glancing at the boat that held the body of poor Denny Currie, Pearson suppressed a shudder. Just like he'd said to Catfish John—some things weren't meant to be.

FORTY-FOUR

Addie stood at her bedroom window, watching Pearson and Ceddy in the garden. Pearson chased him through the hedges, deliberately allowing him to escape. Catching up to him occasionally, he'd lift him high and swing him in the air. Ceddy's delighted squeals echoed across the yard.

"Isn't that a wonderful sound?"

Addie turned to smile at Priscilla, standing on the threshold. "Yes, it is. A glorious sound."

She crossed the room and joined Addie at the window.

Outside, Pearson strode back and forth with Ceddy chasing at his heels like a clumsy, flop-eared puppy.

Priscilla placed a hand at Addie's back. "I want to thank you for sharing your good news with me. It's an honor, especially knowing you told me before you telephoned your mama."

Addie leaned into her. "We wanted you to know. Besides, since we're having the wedding in Marshall, I'll need your help to make plans. Mother can't come until the day before the wedding."

"And your daddy?"

She beamed as brightly as the light in her heart. "He's coming with her. They're bringing my sisters as well."

Priscilla nodded. "Well, your news was a fresh breath after the ugliness of the other day. We needed something happy to focus on." She patted Addie's waist. "I can't tell you how proud Reverend Stroud is that Pearson asked him to officiate."

"He's a good friend and a wonderful pastor."

"That he is."

Addie sobered. "As happy as I am, I'm very burdened at the same time."

Priscilla's mouth dipped into a frown. "Goodness! Why? A bride shouldn't be burdened."

"I'm going to miss you all so fiercely when Pearson and I leave for Galveston." She choked back her tears. "Especially Ceddy."

Priscilla tugged her arm, drawing her to the bed. "Sit down, dear. I have something I've needed to discuss with you, but I couldn't find the right time. I suppose you just gave me the perfect opening."

Addie watched expectantly while Priscilla settled onto the bed next to her and clasped her hands in her lap.

"Adelina McRae, the changes you've wrought in my great-nephew are nothing short of miraculous. He's alert, receptive to touch. He's making eye contact more and more, and the biggest blessing of all, he's becoming affectionate. This morning he looked me full in the face and smiled." She beamed. "It came and went so fast, I thought I'd imagined it, but my heart says I didn't. It's as if you reached inside him and turned a switch."

Addie squirmed with pleasure. "I feel sure the change in his diet was the key."

"I wholeheartedly agree, but how did you know that simply removing dairy and sweet foods would bring about such a change?"

"Well, I—"

"It's a gift, Addie, the incredible instincts you have."

Addie's cheeks warmed from the undeserved praise. "Yes, it's exactly that. . .a gift. So I can't really take the credit. I pray over all my charges, and I truly feel God gives me special insight into each child." A sweet smile stole over her face. "However, it's different with Ceddy. God has also given me a special love for him."

Priscilla sat quietly for a minute then adjusted her skirt and swiveled toward her. "I was going to wait to bring this up when both you and Pearson were present, but if you're going to provide me with such an ideal opportunity, how can I delay?"

She gripped Addie's hands. "What would you say if I asked you to take Ceddy with you?"

Addie studied her face. "You mean to Galveston?"

"Yes."

Confusion crept over her. "Well, of course. We'd love to take him for a visit."

Gnawing the side of her mouth, Priscilla squeezed Addie's fingers. "I don't mean for a visit, dear. I mean permanently."

Addie felt doused with cold water. "You're not serious."

Priscilla stared at their hands. "Ordinarily, I'd never ask, never intrude upon your new life." Her dewy lashes fluttered, and she looked up. "But we both know Ceddy is no ordinary child. He needs special attention. You and Pearson are so good with him, dear. So good *for* him. He's blossoming under your nurturing care." Her bottom lip trembled. "I love him desperately. And I'll miss him terribly. But I want the best for him." She tightened her grip. "Naturally that would've been his parents, but Ceddy was cheated out of a life with them. The next best thing is you and Pearson."

Addie took a moment to probe her heart. She wouldn't accept without knowing her true feelings about taking on such a responsibility. What she found within her soul was pure joy.

"I can't think of anything I'd want more, but I'll have to speak to Pearson before I give my answer."

Priscilla's eyes lit up. "I understand."

Addie angled her head. "What about the rest of your family? Won't they object?"

She waved her hand. "Let me handle the wolf pack. I've learned how to manage them over the years." She shrugged. "Besides, I have legal guardianship, left to me by both parents. With that comes the right to make important decisions on Ceddy's behalf."

Patting Addie's knee, she stood and walked to the window. "If I decide to assign his custody to a trusted teacher to further his education, who can argue the point?"

Addie followed her to the window seat and gripped her frail shoulders. "I'm honored, most of all because I know what a sacrifice you're making. You're going to be lost without him."

A sob shook her. "More than you know." She caught Addie's hand. "But we must face reality. I'm not getting any younger." She laughed through her tears. "And that little scamp is more than I can handle alone."

Pointing down at the yard, she chuckled. "And here he comes. You'd better ask Delilah to draw his bath."

Addie sighed. "I'm surprised he'll go near water after his close call."

"So am I, dear. So am I."

Pearson chased Ceddy onto the porch, swatting him just before he jerked open the screen and barreled inside.

Delilah met them with a smile. "Whoa there, Little Man. Where you be to go?"

Giggling, Ceddy slipped behind her skirts to hide from Pearson.

She twisted around, tried to pull him away, but then gave up with an indulgent smile. "How you this afternoon, Mista Pearson?"

He grinned and stretched out his arms. "Couldn't be better, Delilah. It's a beautiful day."

"Yessuh. That old sun be shining bright."

Peering behind him, he frowned. "It is? I hadn't noticed. I'm so happy, this day would be beautiful in a downpour."

Her laughter echoed in the foyer. "I reckon it would, what with you and Miss Addie planning your nuptials and such."

He ducked his head to peer down the hall. "Where is my bride? I've come to call on her."

Herding Ceddy, Delilah led Pearson into the downstairs foyer. "Go on and sit in the parlor. I'll fetch her."

Pearson took a seat on the sofa and ran his hand along the padded arm. The last time he'd been in the room, he'd almost told Addie he loved her. Stunned, he realized that though they were engaged to wed, he'd still never told her. Chuckling to himself, he determined to correct the grave oversight the minute he saw her.

"There you are, Delilah," Addie said from somewhere in the hall. "Priscilla wants you to draw Ceddy a bath."

"I'm two hops and a jump ahead," Delilah said. "Me and Little Man on our way right now."

"Good. Mr. Pearson didn't leave, did he?"

Pearson's insides warmed at her anxious tone.

"No missy. He waitin' for you right there in the parlor."

With no further ado, the door burst open and his breath caught.

Addie stood on the threshold, as fresh and radiant as the day she stepped off the train in Marshall. A wide ribbon in a dark coffee shade cinched her middle, setting off her tiny waist against the beige dress. The neckline plunged lower than he'd ever seen on her, a large bow in the center adding a touch of respectability. Dangling strands of pearls crisscrossed the top of her bodice, swinging each time she moved. Gracing him with a broad smile, she crossed the room with a pleasing swish of layered skirts. A fragrant cloud of magnolias reached him before she did.

He rose to meet her. "Honey, you're beautiful."

She paused then stretched out her hands. "I give you permission to greet me that way from now on."

"I'm certain I will. I won't be able to help myself."

She giggled like a girl. "Can I expect this sort of flattery when I'm old and gray?"

"I promise."

Gazing into her bottomless brown eyes, he remembered the vow he'd just made. "I love you, Addie. Did you know that?"

She stirred in his arms. "I should hope so, since you asked me to be your wife."

He kissed her nose. "I didn't want there to be any misunderstanding on that score."

She beamed. "I love you, too. I have for weeks and weeks."

He nodded. "I knew it all along."

She swatted his arm, and he jumped back, laughing. Recalling the main reason he'd come to see her, he reached into his vest pocket. "I almost forgot. I took the sheriff with me to the rooming house where Denny and Charlie stayed. The sheriff informed the landlord they'd paid him in stolen goods, a fact I'm sure he already knew. It wasn't hard to convince him to surrender Priscilla's things."

He held out his hand. In his palm lay Ceddy's stolen gems. "Can you see that these get where they belong? I know how upset he's been at their loss."

Addie ran her finger over the dazzling stones, a topaz, a sapphire, an emerald, an amethyst, and. . .a small but brilliant diamond sparkled in their midst. "Oh Pearson, he'll be so pleased."

He grinned. "It's not as big as his last specimen, but it'll fit better in his collection box."

She picked up the gem. "Where did you get it?"

Lowering his eyes, he toyed with the buttons on her puffy sleeves. "The landlord of the rooming house has a collection of his own. I saw the diamond and offered to trade him."

Catching his eye, she lifted her brow.

He shrugged. "I had no more use for a couple of rowboats, oars, and a sturdy lift rig—a Yale & Towne hoist and pulley to be exact."

She melted against him and pressed her cheek to his chest. "You're the dearest man in the world."

He smiled against her hair. "Not really. I just care a lot about that little guy."

They swayed in silence for a blissful bit, and then Addie raised her head. "Do you, Pearson?"

"Do I. . . ?"

"Care about Ceddy."

His brows dipped in the middle. "Very much."

"Enough to raise him as our own?"

He held her at arm's length, dread dampening the excitement he felt. "Oh honey. . .get that notion right out of your mind. Priscilla would never allow it."

"It was her idea."

He gave his head a little shake. "I don't understand."

"She's decided we're the best thing for him. She wants us to take him to Galveston."

He gripped her arms. "Really? Oh Addie, it's a wonderful idea. Galveston is a great place to raise a boy. I'll take him fishing, teach him to sail a dinghy, we'll search for treasure together." He finally inhaled. "He'll love it there."

Addie laughed. "May I take that as a yes?"

He hugged her to his chest. "Absolutely yes! Tell her we accept."

Grasping his hand, she squeezed. "I'm so glad you feel that way. I was afraid you might say no."

He pulled back enough to peer into her face. "Why would I even consider saying no?"

A spark of humor lit her eyes. "Well, he *can* get into trouble on occasion."

"That's all right. So can I. Just ask Theo."

Addie turned. "Maybe I'd better. Where is he?"

He sobered. "He's taking Charlie to Reverend Stroud's house. The reverend's taking him in."

"Oh, I'm glad." She took his hand and pulled him toward the sofa. "Come sit down and tell me all about it."

Seated next to her, Pearson found it hard to concentrate, but he gathered his thoughts and continued. "Since Priscilla decided not to press charges—"

"Once you persuaded her not to, you mean," she interrupted, smiling proudly.

"Charlie's not a bad person at heart. He's a follower. With the reverend agreeable to mentoring him, it seemed the perfect plan. Let him follow a good man for a change."

"It's a wonderful idea." She picked up a pad and pen from the low table. "Speaking of ideas, I need some from you on the wedding preparations. There are a thousand little details to attend to."

He placed his hand over hers. "I've been meaning to tell you. You'll have to plan without me for a few days. I have preparations of my own to make."

She blinked her confusion.

"I need to prepare you a place to live. To do that, I have to leave for a few weeks."

She leaned back and stared. "You're leaving Marshall?"

"Yes, honey. You see, my parents' house"—he swallowed hard—"my house now, I suppose, was repaired and remodeled after the storm, but it hasn't been lived in since. I have no idea what condition it's in. I'm sure it needs to be cleaned and aired out at least."

She pouted her lips. "I don't want you to go."

He squeezed her hand. "I'll be back before you can miss me."

"Impossible. I miss you already."

Laughing, he drew her close. "Keep yourself busy planning our wedding. I'll just show up and say 'I do.'" He took the pad she'd scratched in and flipped to a clean page. "Right now I need a list of everything you want laid in stock in your new home. I want everything perfect for my new wife."

FORTY-FIVE

Pearson slid off his boots and socks and walked to the edge of the rolling surf. The pull of the ancient tide stirred the sand between his toes, drawing it away in a rush. With the same force, Galveston Island had drawn him to return to his childhood home, a lure he could no longer resist.

Turning his face to the wind, he breathed deeply. The pungent salty air smelled like home.

More than anything, he longed to have Addie standing by his side. There were many things to show her, things to teach her about life on the coast, and he felt anxious to start.

He had two challenges yet to face before he could relax and enjoy the promise of a new beginning. First, he had to tell Pearl he'd be bringing a wife to the island. Second, he had to overcome the pain of walking into his house for the first time since the disaster. The thought of either confrontation had kept him lingering too long on the shore.

Theo, hungry and eager to see their friends, had gone ahead of him into the café. Brushing the hair from his eyes, Pearson picked up his boots, squared his shoulders, and walked up the beach. Time to brave the first hurdle.

Drawing a steadying breath, he pushed open the door and stepped inside.

Rosie squealed from across the room and rushed at him. Throwing her fleshy arms around his neck, she peppered kisses on his cheek. "If you're not a pleasant sight! I told Theo if you didn't come through that door soon, he'd have to leave my soup alone and go find you."

Pearson gave her a crushing hug. "I missed you, Rosie."

Pulling away, she propped her hands on her hips in mock indignation. "You did not, or you would've come home before now."

He leaned close to whisper. "I wouldn't have left in the first place, but somebody sent me on a treasure hunt."

She winced. "Theo told me the outcome. Sounds like a bigger dead end than Lafitte's gold."

He slung his arm around her neck. "Don't worry. I don't regret going." She didn't know it yet, but it was the best decision he'd ever made.

Theo sat at a table across the way, dipping thick-sliced bread in a steaming bowl.

Pearl flitted around him, filling his glass, passing the salt, laughing and talking the way she always did. When she glanced toward Pearson, her dimples flashed briefly in a quick smile.

He waved, but she didn't respond, intent on serving another bowl of soup to Theo. He must've been mistaken. She hadn't seen him yet.

Dread was layered like ice around Pearson's heart. He had to hurt Pearl, break her heart, and he'd rather sever an arm. "Listen, Rosie. . . there's something I need to tell you."

"You can tell me anything, darlin'," she bellowed in her usual boisterous tone.

He shushed her. "I'd rather say this to you first. I may need your help breaking it to Pearl."

Interest flashed in her eyes. "That serious, is it?"

"Just the happiest news of my life." He glanced toward Pearl. "But not everyone in this room will think so."

"Oh," she whispered. "You mean Addie."

"Theo told you?"

She nodded. "He told us both."

Pearson cringed. "Pearl knows?" It explained why she hadn't returned his wave.

Pearl swept past, and he ducked behind Rosie. "I despise the thought of hurting her. Was she very upset?"

Rosie snickered behind her chubby hand. "She's trying to be strong, honey."

Returning to Theo's table with a saucer of bread, Pearl giggled with delight at something he said.

Pearson took another peek. "Well, she's putting on a brave face, that's for sure."

Rosie patted his arm. "I hate to disappoint you, sweetheart, but Pearl's fickle heart has moved on."

"What?" Pearson gaped at her. "In just a matter of weeks, she's already tossed me aside for someone else?" He grinned. "My ego is getting a lashing lately."

Rosie chuckled and slapped his arm. "I thought you knew. Pearl falls for a different fella every week." Leaning in, she fought a smile. "It gets worse."

He shook his head. "How could it?"

"Her new interest happens to be a friend of yours."

Pearson touched his chest. "Of mine? Rosie, I don't have that many friends around here, except for—" He spun to stare at Theo, sopping up Pearl's attention along with the soup. "Theo?" His voice grew shrill at the end. "It can't be."

Rosie nodded, her eyes twinkling. "Not a week after you left, she realized it wasn't your absence she grieved. Pearl couldn't get Theo out of her mind. She missed his constant smile and teasing ways." She made a face. "His full lips and dreamy eyes. . . Her observations, not mine."

"Not a word about me?"

"Um, yes, there was the one thing. It seems Theo has much nicer hair."

Pearson's head reeled. "Well, I'll be. I suffered terrible pangs of guilt for nothing?"

Rosie patted his back. "Sorry, honey. I suppose you did."

Sobering, she lowered her voice and tilted her chin at the flirting couple. "I sure hope Theo feels the same. Just between you and me, this time, I think it's serious."

Hours later, Pearson stood on Broadway Street outside the big house where he'd been born. His heart pounded and his mouth felt dry, but memories of the good times he'd shared with his family swirled in his head, dulling the pain he'd dreaded.

Staring down the sidewalk, he saw his brother, shouting with laughter over learning to pedal a bicycle. His dapper father strolling home with his walking stick. His smiling mother pushing his sister in a pram.

He saw a Christmas tree in the window, a wreath on the front door. Busy Saturday mornings raking leaves and painting fences. Lazy Sunday afternoons sipping lemonade together on the portico.

These things he could look forward to again, only this time shared with Addie and his own rowdy brood, beginning with Ceddy. The promise of such a future filled him with hope and a great sense of expectation.

Pearson had an odd sense of his family drawing near, surrounding him with loving arms to celebrate new beginnings. Such thoughts might be fanciful, but God's presence, urging him toward a life filled with blessings, was achingly real. The time for crushing grief and the burden of guilt had passed. At last he could move on.

Drawing a deep, refreshing breath, he began by taking the wide front steps two at a time and striding confidently across the broad front porch.

At the door, he smiled and patted his front pocket. If the extensive list inside was what it took to make Addie happy, he'd make sure to furnish her new home with every item. He only hoped it wouldn't take long. His heart yearned for Marshall and his wedding day. The day he would finally make Addie his bride.

FORTY-SIX

The minute Tiller McRae's boot heels touched the station platform in Marshall, Texas, he wanted to snatch up his eldest daughter and book passage home to Canton.

As if she'd read his mind, Mariah gripped his arm and held on tight. Was she anxious to see Addie, or were her thoughts running similar to his?

"Do you see her?" Mariah shouted over the huffs of the steam engine and the other shouting voices.

Tiller shook his head. "Hard to see anything in this churning mob." He glanced at the smallest of their wide-eyed traveling companions. "Hold tightly to the girls, Mariah."

Gathering them under her shawl, she shaded her eyes and peered in the distance. "She said she'd be here."

"Then she will," Tiller said.

Thomas and Hope Moony appeared in the passenger door behind them. Holding tightly to the rail, Dr. Moony stepped to the ground then turned to help his granddaughter.

Tiller offered his hand as well then scowled at Dr. Moony. "This is your fault, you know."

The doctor shot him a good-natured smile. "I should by now. You've reminded me often enough."

"Credit where credit is due, sir. If not for you passing Miss Whitfield's letter to my Addie, I'd be home in the garden, not waiting to meet the stranger who's marrying my daughter tomorrow."

Hope gave a merry laugh. "I'm the one who should be angry, Mr. McRae. With my wedding planned for months, I'm appalled that Addie will beat me down the aisle."

Tiller snorted. "She wouldn't be if I had my say-so."

Carrie tugged on his coattail. "Father, where's Addie?"

He leaned close to her ear. "She'll be along, ladybug. You just stay close to Mother. And hold your sisters' hands."

Drawing his friends and family away from the noisy train, Tiller allowed his gaze to sweep the crowd. His heart stilled when he saw her, disbelieving what his traitor eyes were telling him. "I sent my baby to Marshall and got back a woman."

Mariah clutched his sleeve. "Where?"

Struggling against the lump rising in his throat, he pointed. "There."

Addie hurried across the platform, reminding him very much of her mother at that age. Mariah once had the same youthful spirit, the same happy smile—he cringed—the same glow of a woman in love.

The man trailing behind her didn't seem quite as happy.

Tiller grunted. "He's much too old for her, Mariah."

She nudged him.

"What happened to his hair?"

"Tiller McRae! Lower your voice."

Squealing, Addie rushed to him, his little girl again for just a moment. "Father, it's so good to see you."

"You, too, honey."

Too quickly, her arms slipped from around his neck and she moved on. "Mother, I missed you so."

Mariah held her for as long as Addie stayed still but stepped back and smiled while she leaped in circles with her sisters and then Hope.

"How could you, Addie?" Hope said, beaming. "It's ill mannered to steal my thunder."

"I'm ever so sorry! I never planned it, I assure you."

Dr. Moony touched her arm. "Let me have a look at you, child."

She turned into his embrace. "Hello, Dr. Moony. I'm so glad you could come."

"My, but you're lovely, Addie. You'll be a beautiful bride. I'm so grateful Priscilla invited me to share your happy day."

A cloud passed over her face. "She didn't exactly invite you, sir. You're meant to be a surprise."

His bushy brows shot to the sky. "Come again?"

Easing free of him and the topic, Addie returned to the tall stranger standing awkwardly off to the side. Hooking her arm through his, she walked him over and presented him proudly. "Dear ones, this is my Pearson."

Looking a little surer of himself after Addie's enthusiastic endorsement, he offered Tiller his hand. "Mr. McRae, it's nice to meet you."

It took all of Tiller's grit to be cordial. "Likewise, young man. I've been eager to get a look at the man who's about to run off with my daughter."

Mariah cleared her throat. "Pay no attention to him, Pearson. He still sees her in pigtails."

The line of his shoulders relaxed, and his tight smile became a hearty grin. "Mrs. McRae, how nice to see you again."

"Likewise, dear." She caught his hand. "If I told you I knew from the start that you were the one for my Addie, I don't suppose you'd believe me."

He gave her a little wink. "I certainly would. I suspected the same myself."

Tiller suppressed a groan. "If you two are done with the reunion, I'd like to get the girls away from this throng."

"Of course," Pearson said. "Come right this way. Miss Whitfield sent her carriage."

Herding the little ones, Tiller and Mariah fell into line behind Hope and the doctor. Tiller leaned to whisper in Mariah's ear. "I'm not sure I like him. Too swaggering for my taste."

Her mouth twitched. "I seem to remember a cocky young rogue who didn't pass muster with my family at first."

Tiller sniffed. She'd struck below the belt, as usual. "All right. I'll give him a chance."

Dr. Moony touched Addie's elbow. "Do you mean to say Priscilla doesn't even know that I'm coming?"

She gave him a reassuring smile. "Don't worry. I promise you'll be fine. She'll be positively thrilled at the news."

Addie tucked her lips and took a calming breath through her nose. It would be fine, wouldn't it? Truthfully, she'd had misgivings all morning about meddling. A great many years had passed since the two were close friends. Dr. Moony had enjoyed a successful marriage. Seen the birth of his children and grandchildren. Lost a wife. Suppose the things they shared in common so many years ago they'd long since outgrown? Glancing at the fretful man in the backseat of the carriage, she reminded herself it was too late for second thoughts.

At the mansion, she and Pearson led their guests through the great hall and into the parlor. While they took their seats, Addie stood at the threshold, watching for their hostess.

Delilah pushed out of the kitchen with a tray of coffee and her special scones, and Addie hurried to meet her. "Where's Miss Priscilla?"

"She still upstairs. Told me to fetch these refreshments."

"And Ceddy?"

"He's napping."

Dashing by Pearson at the parlor door, she pointed inside. "Entertain them," she whispered, "while I go for Priscilla."

"What?" he said hoarsely. "Addie, no."

Ignoring his frantic expression, she waved him inside. "You'll do fine. I'll be right back."

Feeling she'd left him alone to face the gallows, she hurried upstairs to a reckoning of her own. She knocked at Priscilla's door and waited for her soft-spoken invitation to enter.

Priscilla turned from straightening her sash in the mirror. "Your parents are here. I saw them from the window." She smiled. "You must be so happy to see them."

"Oh yes, I am. Aren't you coming down to meet them?"

"Of course, dear. I'm on my way now." She took Addie's arm. "From the window, your sisters looked like precious little ladies stepping down from my carriage. And that red-haired father of yours cuts a handsome figure." A tiny crease gathered between her brows. "But I'm curious. . .who was the older gentleman and the pretty young girl?"

A chill coursed the length of Addie's back. "Priscilla, um, that was Dr. Moony and Hope."

Her steps faltered and she froze, one hand on the doorknob. "No, it's not, Addie. Don't tease."

Addie swallowed. "I'm afraid it's true."

She shook her head. "Impossible."

"I hope you don't mind. I invited them as a surprise."

The truth dawned on her in waves, slowly eroding the doubt in her eyes. "That stoop-shouldered old geezer downstairs is Thomas Moony?" She touched her forehead. "The man with thinning hair?"

Addie nodded.

Spinning, she hurried across the room to her mirror and gaped at the pale image staring back. Trembling fingers lifted a lock of her white hair. "My heavens, it's true. We really are that old."

Addie gulped. "Are you upset with me?"

Her likeness glanced at Addie. "Only for forcing me to accept my own mortality, dear. You see, my Thomas is ageless and handsome, forever a dapper twenty-year-old boy." Tears glistened in her eyes. "When I'm with him in my memories, I'm forever young, too."

Addie cringed. Mother's meddling ways were nothing compared to this. "Please don't cry, Priscilla. I'm a horrible toad, and I can't believe what I've done to you."

Turning, she caught Addie's shoulders. "No, dear. Don't be silly. It caught me off guard, that's all." She wiped her eyes. "You've given me a wonderful surprise, and I'm very, very grateful. It will be wonderful to be with Thomas again after all these years." She smiled. "Under all the bags and wrinkles, we're still the same people, aren't we?" She patted Addie's back. "Let's you and I go greet our guests."

Downstairs, Addie opened the parlor door, afraid of what she'd find. She needn't have worried.

Her parents sat together on the sofa, holding hands and chatting quietly with Dr. Moony. Hope and Pearson sat across from each other in the matching chairs, attempting to talk with three little magpies sitting at their feet.

By the gleam in her eyes, Carrie had fallen under Pearson's spell. She sat with her arms propped on his knees, drinking in every word.

Dr. Moony rose as if pulled from the top with a string. His appreciative gaze fixed on Priscilla, growing more admiring with every step he took in her direction. Evidently, he held no memories carved in stone. "Priscilla, I don't believe these old eyes."

She held out her hands. "Thomas, what a nice surprise. Welcome to my home."

He caught her fingers and held on for several long minutes, studying her glowing face. "My, my. Forgive me for saying so, but you're as pretty as ever."

She lowered her lashes, her cheeks flushing bright pink. "Go on with you, Thomas Moony. I see you haven't changed a bit."

Addie smiled at Pearson. He grinned up at her and winked. Perhaps she'd inherited Mother's flair for successful meddling after all.

FORTY-SEVEN

Addie stared at herself in the looking glass, magically transformed into a bride. Unlike most girls, she hadn't given much thought to her wedding day. She'd focused too strictly on breaking free of her overprotective parents and forging her own destiny, never dreaming how important it would one day seem. Whispering a prayer of gratitude, she thanked God for looking past her stiff-necked independence and intervening in the affairs of her life.

Mother stood behind her, fastening Grandmother's beads around her neck. Today, as promised, they would become hers. "There's so much history bound up in this ancestral necklace," she said. "Someday we'll sit together, and I'll tell you all about it."

Addie smoothed her fingertips over the jasper pendant. "Since you saw them last, there's a lot of excitement bound up here, too." She grinned. "Some of it I may never tell."

Mother's brows rose. "Such as?"

"Suffice it to say, if not for Ceddy, our tradition would've ended with you."

"Speaking of traditions. . ." Holding up one finger, Mother spun to the bed. Returning with a small rawhide bag, she reached inside and held up a pair of shoes. "These are your grandmother's wedding slippers. She got married in them, and so did I. Unless you object, I'd like you to keep with this custom as well."

Addie touched the butter-soft leather and sighed. "They're exquisite."

Mother helped her slip them on. Then they both stared at Addie's reflection in the mirror.

"You're a vision, honey." Sudden tears flashed in her eyes. "I got married in black, did you know that?"

Tearing up herself, Addie shook her head.

"We were still in mourning for your grandfather." She smiled. "It sounds scandalous, I know, but at the time, it wasn't. And it turned out to be the most wonderful day of my life."

Addie swiped at an escaping tear.

"I remember gazing in a mirror much like this one—without the gilded edges, of course—wishing my parents were alive to see me wed." Mother wrapped her arms around Addie's neck. "I'm grateful to God you have a large loving family to witness your day."

"So am I," Addie said. "More than I can say. But I wish Miss Vee had come."

"So does she, but she's far too frail to travel. I promised to persuade you and Pearson to visit Canton soon."

Addie turned to rest her head on her mother's shoulder. "You were right, you know. About everything."

Laughter rumbled in Mother's chest. "Wait and say that again in your father's hearing."

"Oh, but it's true. You saw Pearson's character right from the start, despite his unusual appearance. And you said God had amazing gifts in store for me." She smoothed her mother's back. "I can't imagine a more precious gift than a life shared with Pearson."

A knock came at the door. Mother opened it to Father's stunned face.

He scratched his temple then shook his head at Addie in wonder. "Look at you, little missy. You're a bride."

Addie ran into his embrace. "I love you, Daddy."

His arms around her tightened. "You haven't called me that since you were three." He lifted her chin. "Are you ready? They're waiting for us downstairs. I think your young man is getting anxious."

"Has Reverend Stroud arrived?"

He gave her a wry grin. "I'm afraid so. And I can't find another reason to put things off."

Addie nudged him from one side, her mother from the other.

"Whoa there, soldiers. Hold your fire. I can tell when I'm defeated." He held out an arm for each of them. "Shall we?"

Priscilla met them at the foot of the stairs, her eyes aglow. "Addie, you're a lovely bride."

Addie smiled. "All thanks to you."

Mother wrapped her arm around Priscilla's waist. "Addie's right. You've done a wonderful job with her wedding dress and trousseau. And the garden is prepared beautifully. I owe you for my daughter's happiness today. Thank you for stepping in when I couldn't be present."

Priscilla hugged her back. "It was a joy. Addie's become the daughter I never had."

Delilah appeared in the background, her eyes red and swollen from crying. "Excuse me, Miss Priscilla. I done pack all Little Man's bags, like you said. And I tucked in the family Bible like you say to." She sniffed, her dark eyes jumping to Addie. "Miss Addie, you gon' take good care of him for me, ain't you?" Her bottom lip trembling, she wiped her eyes on her sleeve. "Missin' that chil' gon' be the death of me."

Addie pulled her into a hug. "Don't cry, Delilah. You'll see him again soon."

Laughing, Priscilla patted her arm. "Heavens, Delilah, you're taking on worse than me. I told you I'd take you along when I visit with Addie this fall."

Touching Addie's shoulder, she smiled. "We're sending his collection boxes along in his trunks, but the rest of his rocks will be shipped to you later." She rolled her eyes. "I hope you have ample room."

Fidgeting beside her, Father caught her eye. "Are you ready, honey?"

She grinned at him. "That's the second time you've asked. Are you hoping for a different answer?"

He shrugged and took her hand. "You can't blame a man for trying." He ushered her outside the back door into a wonderland of muted light.

Priscilla and Delilah had fashioned hundreds of luminaries and placed them throughout the garden. Chairs lined the yard, overlooking the gazebo where they would take their vows.

Priscilla pointed across the lawn. "How do you like his hair?"

Pearson, so handsome in his suit he took her breath away, leaned against the gazebo rail talking to Reverend Stroud.

Addie gasped. "I've never seen it so. . .controlled."

Priscilla nodded. "Delilah helped him comb it." She patted Addie's shoulder. "Enjoy it while you can. With all the carrying-on he did while she smoothed it out, I doubt he'll ever submit to it again."

Theo, who had arrived that morning from Galveston, stood in the company of a rather loud woman Addie didn't recognize and a pretty young woman who clung to his arm.

Ceddy sat in a circle of little girls, all trying to talk to him at once.

Raising his head, Pearson spotted her. Excusing himself, he loped across the yard.

The burnt-sugar eyes she loved, as clear as a handblown demijohn, latched onto her, and she couldn't pull away.

"You're beautiful."

"Thank you." She giggled. "So is your hair."

Bowing slightly, he offered his arm. "Are you ready to marry me?"

Addie winked over her shoulder at her father. "Yes, I am."

Near tears, she leaned for a last hug from her mother and father as their little girl. The next time they embraced, she would be Mrs. Pearson Foster.

Winding her arm through his, she let him lead her off the porch. Through a heady haze of bliss, Addie saw joyful friends and family, bright blue Texas skies, and an endless horizon.

Reverend Stroud smiled brightly as they approached. Stepping into the gazebo ahead of them, he turned wearing his minister face. "Shall we begin?"

Standing stiffly beside her, Pearson nodded.

A bundle of happy nerves, Addie barely heard the reverend's opening words. He awoke her from her daze by calling her name.

"Adelina Viola McRae, do you take Pearson to be your wedded husband, to have and to hold from this day forward, for better, for worse, for richer, for poorer, in sickness and in health, to love, cherish, and to obey, till death do you part, according to God's holy ordinance?"

Addie bit back a mischievous smile. The truth was, she'd take Pearson any way she could get him. This time, of course, in order to make it official, she would say so.

SCONES

Sift one quart of flour; add half a teaspoon of salt, a teaspoon of sugar, a tablespoon of lard, one beaten egg, two teaspoons of cream tartar, one of soda, and a pint of sweet milk. Mix to a thick batter, drop in squares on a very hot, greased griddle, and bake brown on both sides. Serve with butter and honey.

The Good Housekeeping Woman's Home Cook Book
Arranged by Isabel Gordon Curtis (Chicago: Reilly & Britton, c. 1909)

COBBLER

Make from any sort of fruit in season—peaches, apples, cherries, plums, or berries. Green gooseberries are inadvisable, through being too tart and too tedious. Stone cherries, pare peaches or apples and slice thin, halve plums if big enough, and remove stones—if not, wash, drain well, and use whole. Line a skillet or deep pie pan—it must be three inches deep at least, liberally with a short crust, filled rather more than a quarter-inch thick. Fit well, then prick all over with a blunt fork. Fill with the prepared fruit, put on an upper crust a quarter-inch thick and plenty big enough, barely press the crust edges together, prick well with a fork all over the top, and cook in a hot oven half to three-quarters of an hour, according to size. Take up, remove top crust, lay it inverted upon another plate, sweeten the fruit, then dip out enough of it to make a thick layer over the top crust. Grate nutmeg over apple pies, or strew on a little powdered cinnamon. A few blades of mace baked with the fruit accent the apple flavor beautifully. Cherries take kindly to brandy, but require less butter than either peaches or apples. Give plums plenty of sugar with something over for the stones. Cook a few stones with them for flavor, even if you take away the bulk. Do the same with cherries, using say, a dozen pits to the pie. Serve cobbler hot or cold.

Dishes and Beverages of the Old South
By Martha McCulloch-Williams; decorations by Russel Crofoot (New York: McBride, Nast & Company, 1913)

EASY FRUIT COBBLER

1 stick butter
1½ cups sugar
1 cup flour
1½ teaspoons baking powder
⅔ cup (or a little less) evaporated milk
Blackberries, dewberries, or peaches
Cinnamon

Melt butter in a 9x13-inch baking dish. Mix ¾ cup of sugar, flour, and baking powder together. Stir in milk. Pour over butter. Add berries (I usually smash mine with a fork first), pouring evenly over batter. Sprinkle with rest of sugar and a little cinnamon. Bake at 350 degrees for 30 minutes or until browned. Delicious with vanilla ice cream.

Courtesy of Cooks.com

MARCIA GRUVER'S southern roots lend touches of humor and threads of faith to her writing. Look for both in her Texas Fortunes and Backwoods Brides series. When she's not perched behind a keyboard, you'll find her clutching a game system controller or riding shotgun on long drives in the Texas Hill Country. Lifelong Texans, Marcia and her husband, Lee, have five children. Collectively, this motley crew has graced them with a dozen grandchildren and one great-granddaughter—so far.